Stand to Resist!

In loving memory of Robert and Pauline Akroyd:
Grandparents worth writing for.

I love you Granny and Grandpa

Stand to Resist!

"*O*n the first day, the Great Star bathed the endless skies in glorious inception. Darkness vanished, and the light came through. Within their sacred illuminations, deities resided, housed by a single glimmer in which they lived in harmony. One light. One body. One ominous melting pot.

Life had not yet been conceived by concept. The Gods sat in their single star and remained in comfortable silence. The Great Star had been the unifying construct where all was virtuous and flawless. Imperfection was yet to be conceived. These deities laughed and loved each other for the first day, living in relaxed coordination. Nothing went wrong. Light had consumed everything. One God ended the day by exclaiming: *"Such brightness, it exceeds me!"*

On the second day, seeds were planted. A ball of rock was placed in the centre of the empty universe and watched over constantly. They petted the ball and protected it from something that did not exist. Instead, they had not considered keeping it safe from its creators. The ball began to be argued over. Bickers of who *owned* the ball ended when the Great Star finally agreed it was no ones. They were Gods and Creators, but they were not parents. Many hated this decision. Five Gods ended the day by announcing: *"Such dullness, it congests us!"*

On the third day, well…there was everything. A clap of the hand unveiled life. Water came to the ball of rock. Grass grew and oceans spread around it. One God asked for a name, and the rest decided: *Farhawl.*

What was Farhawl? A paradise, one might say, and that it was best left untouched. To them, perfection was the keeper to impurity's cage. Evil sustained its ruthless vanquish and an imbalance persisted. Only happiness. Nothing else.

Boredom turned to rampant detest. The Gods turned their bickering into brawls. Clashes began to spark solar flares across the entire universe. The third day became one of fire. Those tired of its empty perfection called it an atrocity and committed the unholiest of acts: creating life. Plankton roamed the depths, fish looked to the coasts, reptiles sprawled the fields and eventually the land was conquered by the ultimate being. Mankind was born. Some of the Gods left the Great Star. In the distance, the first constellation was made. Twelve Gods ended the day by discussing: *"What means will it take to preserve this new life in pure glory?"*

On the fourth day, the war began. The Gods invented the devil inside an infantile concept – the conflict of will and freedom. This devil was not of omnipotent origins, nor of omniscience or benevolence, he was a mortal. In their desire to give perfection, the God *Sunar* granted mankind its greatest weapon upon creation: it was not fire nor the spears they used to hunt. They were given the liberty of will.

An eruption scorched the universe. The deities ripped the Great Star apart, taking portions of the light with them. Each one announced that they would bring perfection to their own pocket, to promise lands across the distant voids. The sky was littered with white dots, barely reminiscent of the lost wonder in the sky. Many lights dimmed out over the millennia as the gods murdered one another.

Sunar was left alone. The last act of order came from Sunar's punishment. For making the Devil, the free will of the mortals on Farhawl, he was to stay by the planet's side, unable to move until the day he withered out and died. One God remained there and ended the day by weeping: *"Perfection is dead!"*

Persecution came about on the fifth day. The stars separated permanently. Unity was dead. Sunar thought all day and concluded that would forever satisfy him; he smiled to himself and let his light shine brighter than before. From God, to spectator, he let out one final flash of grace before going silent forever.

"You will be devils as much as you will be gods. I watch over you, but I leave fate to your own imperfections."

And so, God was dead. Sunar became the sun and he let himself watch the world's meddling with its own vile agency. For he had realised the greatest reality that the other Gods had forgotten: life – a stain built on its horrors, its persecutions and its crimes. It was too complex to be perfect. Where good prevailed, evil lay in the cracks. And where evil stood predominant, mankind would rather kill itself than live with its wounds."

- Book of Pedigrees: Farhawl

Act One

The Great War

Chapter 1

The Hunt for the Shy Fox

There was something in his eye: an autonomous speck of dust hellbent on using its liberty to annoy the ever-loving shit out of him. Its inconvenience was trivial at worst, yet it had interrupted the most peculiar of daydreams.

It had been butterflies and wasps again – the strange juxtapositions between pure bliss and the sudden usurp of horrific colours. Stains of red and white, black and blue, all flashing at a thousand miles per hour, appeared as a disconnected wander of his imagination. Typical, if anything. He enjoyed walking around those weird spaces in his head for it was a quiet place. And it was refreshing, more importantly; it was just something that broke the status quo of waking up every morning to plough a field or to shoot the mole that had made a burrow at the end of their garden.

Yet he had always been told that the nation rested on his back, that he – the sole warden, keeper of the plenty – was there to ensure that Kelan never crumbled. Though that begged a question to him every morning: why was he the only one working on the farm if it was that important? Well, of course the Crown would say it was because abled bodies were spread across all other sectors of Kelan's society, but it was so astounding that such a critical role, as hailed by the gold-valley monarchs in the capital, was situated to a few figures per farm. He dwelled on it a lot, denouncing question after question. Maybe he searched for reasons to neglect his social standing, but he did relish in the thought of an outward-adventure. Every farmhand did, as if part and parcel to the role. There was always a sunnier hill to sit on, his mother would say, but they were always colder on the peaks.

His mind had raced through the prospects of irrelevant social-emancipation for so long that he'd forgotten there was ever even a speck of dust bothering him.

"Oi, you loungin'?" And there, the throat of all his bane barraged him with the usual accusations. A clip of the fingers around the back of his head dragged him out of his thoughts and back to the farm.

"Sorry."

"Don't sound it."

"Just thinking, that's all."

"Don't care. I saw the bugger north-north-east a second ago."

His father was a whimsical man. He carried all the prowess of a withering flower, yet spoke as if his life was fifteen years backward to the past. Old habits did die hard, after all.

Following the sun's positioning, he let his eyes fall onto his father's callout. He shook his shoulders, creating a leathery friction on the right side of his neck. He'd held the shotgun for so long he'd almost forgotten it was in his hands, as the weight simply became a natural burden on his arms.

"There. 'Bout forty metres. You see it?" He couldn't. Across the khaki pastures, a slender beast with a ginger coat stalked cautiously between clusters of maturing wheat. As far as camouflage went, it had gotten lucky.

"Where?"

"There. Right there." His father's desert-like dry hands found their way to his gun's body. A steady guidance pointed it to where he saw, hyper-focusing their attention to the exact location. Looking a little closer, he could see it. The fool's gold dirtiness of the covert creature: a fox disadvantaged by the day, creating its own business in a place unfit for its presence.

Breathe in. Breathe out. Same lessons he had as a child. Handle the weapon with care. It's not a toy, he would say, but a means of defence. Why kill a fox? *'Cos it's not to defend yourself, kid, but to defend your land.'* The same moral of the story, over and over. In. Out. In. Out. He'd shot many before. That time was no different.

But in came the slow crescendo of an engineer's melody; the raw arrival of dominance, at the helm of a thousand crewmen. The dust and grains settled on the farm's soil shook first, then came the thunderous climb of high-powered turbines. The fox made a dash into the wheat, and Rhys pulled the trigger, firing at nothing in the end.

He cursed to himself, as the roar of the machine overwhelmed the land. The churn of its engines assaulted the midday stillness with the voice of a manmade deity. And when it chose to, it soared the farm, casting an eclipse upon the valley. They covered their ears the moment it was on top of them.

There, dominating the heavens, was the gliding mass of technology. A cylindrical monolith pieced together with aluminium and fire, in came the demigod in the field of war. Their eyes deadlocked onto its gargantuan scale with as much awe as there was confusion. Any sight of its tremendous armament, its vicious twin-barrelled orchestra of aeronautical cannons – littering its head and tail – presented astronomical concern for the purposes of its arrival. And the way such an absurd machine of war housed an arsenal greater than some armies perplexed them both. Though, in time, the disturbance continued toward the horizon, over the hills, until only a gentle whisp of its engines lay on the wind.

When the world was still again, he looked over to confirm the fox's departure.

"Off it went." He nudged the elder with his elbow and clicked the safety catch in place. A quick yank at the gun's barrel broke it forward, and he withdrew the single buckshot round.

"Saved a bullet, but y'wasted an hour. Guess we'll be here again tomorrow."

"And what if it doesn't come back?"

"Fucker's will, kid. These mutts make the same piss-ups we do in foreign territory." He walked back into the porch, sluggishly, with the clatter of a slightly undersized walking stick taking point ahead of him. Each step was made with the usual beaten limp. "They get scared and they make mistakes, go lookin' in places they shouldn't, over and over, to make things better. And then, bang! Dead. Things the ranks taught me, son, and you'll be damned if I hadn't seen plenty of foxes out there."

He never contested the disjointed wisdom of his father. There were things he never spoke about, especially the years that held his most uncherished days – of active voluntary servitude to the Crown. And what had he gained from it? A shitty farm stuck between privately owned land kept unploughed, for the local countryside lord's aesthetical pleasing, and a slice of terror to haunt his dream forevermore, or so he put.

To think that every day, in his mind, linked back to those fateful days, the ones that he gave only hints about. His mother had hammered in to never pester the man of the house when he came back covered in blood, and though the medal they put on his heart was glimmering, the rags he returned in were far from clean.

Unsure on how to respond to his father, he just nodded politely. A second passed and he cleared his throat, settling the single-barrel shotgun to one side against the porch wall.

"What was that about?"

"The ship?"

"Yeah, the ship." Its growl had decayed, and order was restored. The world returned to its silent self. With a tap of the walking aid, he began pointing to the skies.

"Patrol, maybe." He wished that he knew. Talking out the arse at least made it sound like he did. "Bah, I don't know. They don't tell me nothing anyway."

"Would be a bit weird to disclose information with us, though."

"Aye, for you maybe, but the lads ne'er forgot about me. They'll tell me all what there is to know, 'slong it concerns me and the ranks."

It would've taken such little effort to tell him that he wasn't a serving man anymore, but it went nowhere. A rift between them had been opened the day he returned from Redus with mud on his shoes and blood on his brow. Neither quite understood each other's needs. One wanted an active father who was there to open the possibilities of life, whilst the other one sought the help of his bottled beverages to wipe clean the slate of memories.

They constantly heard the boys and girls of nearby towns wander past them on daytime grocery visits across the hills. Empty phrases like *"Oh, dear, I heard he's been through so much."* They all barely scraped the barrel, and the late summer nights of its anniversary acted as the little spying glass into those days.

Yet, it was worth holding his tongue on talking of those days. Things were different then. Fifteen years had passed, and such disasters were a thing of the ages. Contempt with changing his thought, he reclaimed the rifle and nodded to his father, quietly muttering to him that he was going to put it back inside.

13

Though the summer's end was on approach, the grace of the sun was at an all-time peak. A million rays of sunshine cleared the clouds each morning, and basked the world in a glorious warmth unlike any other. He was no religious man, but the ways in which his father kindly whisked away the daily troubles for daylight praising did bring a positive vibrance amongst the farm, filling the void left from his mother's business ventures.

Inside, however, it was quite the contrary. A dim and exhaustingly tidy abode, fit with just enough windows to satisfy a recluse. It took a good minute to readjust to the light. When his eyes favoured the darkness, he walked across to the end of the sitting room, where the gun rack sat above the soot-covered fireplace.

Moving the weapon to its mount, he wacked its stock against the mantlepiece of trinkets, knocking something to the ground. Quickly, he planted the firearm in its resting place and took a knee beside the fallen decoration.

A band wrapped around his lungs as he realised what he had defiled. He whipped around his gaze through the scrambled masculine furniture haphazardly placed in unfurnished corners, then to the darkness of the closed door to the front porch. A quiet relief, or rather the tension of silence. He looked back down to the floor and scooped the little oak frame in his hands. Turning it over, the clatter of gold and iron confirmed his little worries.

The plaque at the frame's base read as such: '*For indescribable acts of courage,* --- [there was a claw-like scrubbing of the middle word, seemingly done so with a knife] *and deliverance from another's hell – Corporal D. Hendricks.*'

He knew that if seen, his father would've just brushed it off with the usual negligence towards his pride. Just a piece of metal, he'd say, or that it was meaningless. Still, his wife knew better. It was more than a trinket, even if one the owner hated. She called it a lesson, but never found the time in her infrequent visits to explain what that lesson was.

Carefully, he placed it back on the shelf with the utmost precision, and let out a calmed sigh as it fit perfectly where it belonged. He ensured that he had aligned it with the dust outline its rectangular base had sat within.

Time drifted for a second as he rested on the floor. He wasn't exhausted, but the ample opportunity to break the daily string of events was always enticing. He looked at the other little monuments on the mantlepiece, even if he had seen them all a thousand times before: a potted plant, ever so slightly degrading in colour on its left side, an empty jewellery box with brass mimicking the gold standards of its shell, two photographs placed in the same frame, with the top being of a blurred wedding whilst the bottom showcased a familiar faced infant, and on the very right sat a certificate with his name on it. The fact he had it framed and never once brought it to a recruitment office or employer had hammered in the wasting hours of his stagnant days.

And off to the side, facing the wrong way inward, the forever unhung backside of an old painting. He'd once tried to hang it up somewhere, but for whatever reason his father insisted on keeping it where it was, where the contents of its canvas remained untouched. It wasn't like the man wanted to get rid of it. It would've been far too easy to just burn it in a firepit outside, or sell it to some nearby market.

Then, just as his eyes were getting lost again in old reminiscences, the much more tactful voice of wheels on the granite road could be heard. Its engines purred, unlike the airship's growl, and it slowly crept closer to his homestead. No road passed their house, only a single lane leading up to the farm's edge near the house.

He flashed a quick look to a faded calendar on the leftmost wall. Middle of the week. No scheduled deliveries, as he'd imagined, so the gentle approach of the road-creeping vehicle left his mind wandering again.

"Lad, come out 'ere. Someone's coming." His father pried the door open with his free hand but his stare never left the oncoming truck. As wished, he got back to his feet and jogged to the door, stepping back into the blinding light to witness the untimely arrival of unwanted guests.

To the door he strode, with a nervous hand held onto his forearm, and he surveyed the two-truck convoy pulling into the driveway. In an instant he knew that something was up the moment it stopped twenty metres in front of their home.

A colourful coat of arms had been painted onto the doors of the leading vehicle: a little hawk sat upon an iron gate with the wreath of rosemary leaves arching over its head. At the bottom, on a golden ribbon, was the group's identity – Her Majesty's Royal Military Police.

The main cabin swung open, and he caught the initial glimpse of a shin-high leather boot firmly planting against the steps off the vehicle. A much-too old shine was cast from its body, clearly smeared with an hour's scrubbing of polish the day before. Its owner descended to the soil, and stepped out from behind the truck door.

He wore a sharp, sapphire officer's cap given the same glimmering treatment as his boots. Brass adornments, cradling the nation's yellow and blue flag at its centre, sat where his forehead was. A yellow lanyard – hooked around two buttons on either temple – gave what he must've thought was additional flair to an otherwise plain piece of attire. Down the body were the iron-pressed pristine creases of his parade uniform, decorated with a few medals across the left breast. Two more men jumped from the vehicle; however, they were outfitted with a far less performative aesthetic. Helmets with the inscriptions of MP, chest rigs, combat fatigues and even their own rifles. He noticed his father's face trickle down.

"Damien! A wonderful surprise, I'm sure." The boom of his voice obliterated the peace – a presence so commanding and smug that his brash tone immediately rubbed the family the wrong way. When he addressed the father, he smiled with his teeth. They could tell it wasn't out of courtesy. "How are you, old lad?"

Upon arrival at the porch's bottom step, he extended his hand with a sort of "shit-eating grin", as aptly were the smug described by his father.

The air hung for a short three seconds. His father refused to meet hands with the officer and kept his distance.

"Well, can't be too friendly now, can we?" The eloquence of his voice sounded plasticky, as if built up just for the daylight encounter. The armed military policemen had finally followed suit and arrived at either shoulder. He watched as the officer waved his hand like he was swatting insects, and the soldiers stepped back. "Anyway, may I come inside?"

"What for?" The hostilities of Damien's first response pried a quick smirk from the officer. He shook his head and let out a little giddily-made chuckle.

The greying brown hair of the man gave the officer an ounce of an outgrown youth that Damien had lost. Just barely younger than his father, the farmhand studied the man with caution towards his wry tidings of pleasure.

"Crown business."

"Y'can't take me back."

"It's not always about you, Damien," he pointed to the sky and flicked his fingers forward, "and I'd say it's telling on how quick you are to assume."

At the twirl of his wrist, the two military policemen walked forward and pushed their way through the front door. Damien, held up by his walking stick, did little to protest. If the state walked over him, then so it would. He grumbled and followed slowly behind the officer, who made headway for the living room.

It was as he passed the farmhand that the young man noticed one of the few medals on his heart – a similar silver and gold colourings of a commendation equal to that of his father's framed possession.

Back inside the hovel, the officer paced between the crooked shelves and picture frames. His eyes were plastered to one corner of the room where he'd taken notice of the tilted painting faced away from him. The dimensions, scale and even the backboard rear were all too identical to that of his recollection.

"Could we do with a drink? Brandy, perhaps? Been a long shift."

"You shouldn't drink on the job."

"Well then it's a good thing you're my last stop." The officer looked around. His guards stood without an emotion on their face, with cold-steel stares eyeing up the farmhand in particular. "So, how about it? A host should provide for his gentlemen."

"You won't be stayin' long." Damien nodded to his son, propping his place in the corner of the room whilst he took his time getting to his usual wicker chair. "Now out with it, I don't have time for this."

The officer looked back to his escorts and held out a flat palm toward them. From within their fatigues, one unfolded an envelope crammed into their inner breast pocket. Once claimed by their superior, the smartly dressed man briefly held it up to show Damien and his son the rich, albeit creased, purple ribbon stamped at the centre by a crumbled wax coat of arms. They recognised the colour, yet its royal presence gave little confidence.

"New directorate. Bureaucrats of the region thought it'd be good to have individual letters per case. Waste of paper." He pried his finger beneath the top folds of the envelope. Realising he'd forgotten the ribbon, he held out his hand again as one of the soldiers planted a knife firmly in his palm. He sliced through it quickly, and the message was for his taking.

He approached a nearby desk, a sofa-side table used to keep beverages nearby, and moved the coasters to one side whilst he ironed out the creases with his bare hand. Damien looked at his son who looked back at him. The father frowned with the greatest of frowns. He'd seen his parent miserable most days, yet the difference was that it had been fastened with worry rather than the typical brood of morning fatigue.

With the paper in a more presentable state, the officer mockingly cleared his throat and held it out before his eyes with all the exaggerated pride of a stenographer in a courthouse.

"Registration: 051342050 – a Mister Rhys Hendricks." He looked to the farmhand with an amused grin. The son refused to entertain his scornful wit under the pretences of his sudden intrusion. "Just over six foot. Occupation is that of familial employment. Farmer. No owned property. Twenty-three years of age, three months added on yesterday. Educated, maxed out with a qualification in agricultural studies. This all sound correct?"

The way he watched Rhys' anxious unsettlement gave the farmhand all the indication that the officer had practiced the letter. That tensed-up cheek muscle smile broke his confidence down in an instant. The superiority in his influential presence merely stormed his quiet little world and let the unknown winds of a greater issue flow in.

Quietly, Rhys nodded. It wasn't enough to satisfy the officer, who nodded back with his eyes telling him to confirm it audibly.

"Yes…it is."

"Has there been any change in circumstance since you last had it all noted down?"

"No, there hasn't-" The sudden jolt of the man's hands, pressing the page down into the table for all to read, interrupted Rhys' repressed timidity.

18

"Lucky you. Always good to have a mother in the office, right?"

With the letter mostly unread, and unattended, Damien leant over from his chair and plucked it with two fingers. He leant back into his chair and read it quietly to himself whilst the officer extended a hand toward Rhys.

"1st Lieutenant Galbraith." He gave the whole chipper-and-cheerio mask a tight fit around his skull. The way in which he composed himself was enough to nauseate the man. And as he moved, the clatter of his medals chimed like the bells atop of a jester's cap.

"Why are you all dressed up?" Damien pressed forward, his eyes still indulging the contents of the letter.

"Oh, well. Getting a transfer. It's my last chance to wear them and, well, it's always good to impress an old friend."

"Fuck off."

"The cheek, honestly…" He gave Rhys a glare with open, beady eyes, the sort that was drowned by liquor and hate, with a slice of smugness on the glass tip. "You been reading up on the news, lad?"

Furthering his interrogation, Rhys nervously shook his head. That time, Galbraith thankfully didn't pressure an audible response, but the stoic tone of a revelling judge made him feel almost compelled to. Almost.

"Well, then you're in for a shock." Without warning, he beelined straight for the hidden canvas and grabbed onto its frame, turning it around. Damien looked up from the letter and physically recoiled a little at the sight of it.

And there it was. The painting of the crimson flower, thorned at the neck down to its roots and sat in a field of apocalyptic calamity. Fire raged around the bud until it formed a ring a fury, and it slowly closed in on the place. From the top edge, two fingers retracted from the stem with gaping pricks across the skin, bleeding a vibrant river onto the rose. Rhys had seen it but only a few times, as Damien's zealous intent to keep it hidden had limited the few opportunities he had to admire it.

Cracking a great smile, Galbraith held it up and admired it. A world long gone projected into his eyes.

"No credit, as per usual." He pointed to the bottom left corner, where Damien's signature sat beside the ever-so-tiny detail of an additional layer of paint. "Bastard even scrubbed me out. By the stars, you really are a lunatic, Damien. You bloody well are."

"I think we've had enough of your presence," Damien quickly interrupted, "and I'd be very grateful if you could do me one last favour and get the fuck out of my house!"

A pause stood between them. Rhys' eyes frantically darted between Galbraith and his father. The makings of such anger came as he finished the letter. A tightly-clenched fist crumbled the paper into a ball as he seethed at the mouth with greater fury. Damien forced himself through the pain of standing on his own crippled legs. There, he hobbled over, walking stick in hand, to meet Galbraith face to face. It didn't matter if he was a little shorter than the officer – two goliaths of past wars had met in the centre of the room.

"Why are y'here?"

"The Queen's orders."

"What-?"

"It's the Reds. They've done it."

"Done what?"

"Declared war."

Still became the sticky summer air that humidified the Hendricks' sanctum. A thousand thoughts crossed Rhys' mind as he felt powerless to interject their debate. Buzzwords of monarchs, syndicalists and conflict brokered an uneasy enigma. To where the day was going was unknown, and he was scared to pursue the answers.

"And you want him? Why him?"

"The Crown requires all who are, by law, required to serve to do so. She's building the People's Militia of Kelan, so to speak. A defacto army to stand ready should the need arise." Galbraith did little to back away from the defensive stance of the father. Whether he tried to stop him or not, he was as powerful as he was a hard-working man: nil.

His eyes rolled around in their sockets toward Rhys, to which he nodded at him carefully.

"You've got a new assignment, lad. Me and the boys have been tasked with rounding up the lucky winners. Congratulations, son, you're going to be a *hero*."

"This-…this is madness! Fuckin' madness! You get your bleedin' hands off of my property, my home, and my son, before I-"

"Give it a rest, will you? It's bad enough having to deal with codgers like you a hundred times today." The self-satisfied smirk on his mug spoke otherwise. Though unsure of how and why, Rhys knew there was at least an ounce of pleasure taken from Galbraith's personal investment. A cold dish of injustice; that was how the two veterans reunited. "Rhys. Outside, you're heading off."

"But-"

"Not. A. Word!" He made a quick retreat from Damien upon cutting off Rhys' leftover thought. The young man had his hands in shackles with the chain firmly in Galbraith's hands. On the final steps outside, Galbraith gave the helpless father a grimace of staunch intensity. "You deserve this – old fuck."

And not a word of true help was said. Damien persisted his outcry all the way to the truck, yelling expletives and crying bloody murder to the men with guns. The light outside had never felt so dark until that day, where the dark cloud of political happenings had swept the unknowing from their doorsteps to no avail. And Rhys disliked the smile Galbraith struggled to suppress as he turned his back on the father.

When he looked back, he witnessed the rare sighting of two teardrops flowing from the elder's eyes. It pained him like the impalement of bayonets unending, and the fingers of the devil wrapped around his skin so violently. He was dragged to the back of the truck, where a small dogpile of dirtied bodies were crammed in, all sharing the same fate.

Chapter 2

The Declaration

"War is upon us."

As the words left her mouth, the courtroom fell into chaos. The panicked breakdowns of ministers and executives, nobles and advisors, set the once grandiose hall of serenity in feral motion. Where a small gramophone had played the sweet sounds of summer divertimentos had been crushed by the uproar of disordered politicians. Shouts back and forth, denials and unending gasps – a wild asphyxiation of the truth to their woes – and the realities of ideological madness shifted at that very hour.

"The blame is on you, and the Crown!"

"Only the syndicalists would pull such a move!"

"Oh, suck it before I sock it!"

Collars were trapped in harshened coils of clenched fingers. Noses pressed against one another and the spits of aggressive tones painted the cheeks of their opponents. In an instant, the apes had been set loose in the cabinets, whilst the tigers toyed at the far end of the court in wait for the lioness' announcement.

Down came the gavel. Eight strikes against the podium tried to clamp down on the turmoil surrounding them. The lords locked arms with the ministers, and each dared one another to strike first with feigned reasons. But on the nineth cry of the gavel, the Queen's voice boomed throughout the halls of the capital palace.

"Order, people, order!" Though gradual, the begrudged scorns crawled to the fringes of the room and festered behind attentive ears.

All heads swung to the executive throne of the nation, where the old glimmer of jewels and gold shined down on them. The rubies and peridots decorated the brow of a woman, cabbed with age, who stared with hyper-fixated eyes upon her cabinet. The hall fell silent under her command. She leaned forward and the ancient creak of her throne echoed between the marble pillars neatly scattered around the ministers.

Her stoic expression was enough to empower her sense of superiority. Dissenters and opposition leaders remained as such, for her position was absolute in the name of her flag and country.

"These are serious matters, and I should hope the better – from all of you – as we avoid infantile deliberations and derailments." Leaving her throne behind, she approached the walls of her elevated podium and fixed her posture. To her left, two ranks of armed guards glad in golden ceremonial armour scanned the hall attentively. And to her right sat a far younger, yet less composed woman. The monarch nodded to her and smiled as she always did. "Now, may you please pay tribute with your attention, my people, as I continue the proceedings."

She dared not to look her own ministers in the eyes. Giving them such power would do little to benefit her place in the courthouse, where great velvet curtains danced between marble statues and monuments to past Kings.

"As expected, the Ferusian Syndicalist Union have done their best to undermine Kelan's autonomy through political espionage and ideological crusades through our public sectors. Yet despite their meddlesome antics, their attempts break before our unshaken resolve. In their defeat, we received a letter from the exiled ambassador of Ferusia stating that under their skewered pretences, we are now in a state of international conflict."

Outside the royal courthouse, the clouds drifted overhead and blocked out the sun, snuffing the rays of light breaking through the stained-glass high up on the walls. The room dimmed with the mood, and their silence maintained. Some listened, others held private vigils over the fate of their homes, families and futures.

23

The younger woman to her right felt a tight uneasiness in her chest. Her heart pounded at the state of affairs, and she tapped her fingers on her lap in a measured rhythm. Ways of war dishonoured the goodhearted, and she wished for her mother to not stray down the same path as her father.

She adjusted the circlet on her head and rubbed a free thumb across its golden frame. What little credence the heiress held was enough to demand her attention, presentation and education from the most extreme political gathering to date. Such responsibilities were all but terrifying, provided they saw through the crisis well.

The Queen continued, with a soft-wrinkled hand on her heart and a graceful raising of her voice.

"It is in my duty to ensure that our nation survives, fellow ministers, and I shall do so with extreme effectiveness, as direct descendant of Sunar's line!" A slight cheer flowed from the hundred mouths of avid loyalists, and she tempered their confidence with the wave of a hand. "Five hours ago, the Ferusian military launched an attack on our integrity, striking at Hayana Atoll with unprecedented discrimination. After a three-hour struggle, we received our final message from our garrison forces, who – to the brave end – reported all they could until overwhelmed."

"An outrage!"

"Curse the Reds, for they slaughter our people!"

The eldest ministers cried out in shock and rallied the bewilderment of the cabinet to express their discontent. Their fists struck the sky as they demanded justice, for the past no longer mattered – the present-day blues trumped all need for context. The attack was on their sovereignty.

"And under the grace of the stars, our nation needs to find its time to unite all withering factions to one goal: survival." All ministers and aristocrats waved their powerless papers in the air in agreement. "Our armed forces are strong, well-trained and to the standards of the modern times, but our military is to be overwhelmed by numbers immeasurable at this rate. So, taking liberty of my authority, I have worked with my advisors; here, I make the executive decision to put into effect Article 5 of the Emergency War's Act."

Her daughter's attention perked up as her mother double-crossed her false promise. She'd risen to her feet and looked around in disbelief at all the nearby advisors, guards and ministers who seemed unfazed by her call to arms. A belligerent cry bellowed throughout the halls, as the words that solidified a dark future left the Queen's lips.

"We shall enact the universal draft. We will show them that they shan't win this war and that – by our duties as people, politicians and leaders – we shall lead this nation to victory!"

A roar and applause set the world ablaze as her blistering tongue lit the bonfire. Soon, her daughter reached out and grabbed the wrist of the supreme ruler over all, a privilege she had that most were forbidden from.

Under the bellowing cheers and fiery debates occupying the courthouse, she raised her voice to her mother's ear.

"You said you wouldn't do this!"

"Stand down, Lylith, for I said I would do no such thing unless necessary."

"But what you're doing is-" Lylith's protest was cut short.

"-is what I must do to ensure survival. We'll talk about this later."

She turned away from Lylith – she had been stunned by the weight of a thousand worlds unloaded onto her back. In just a day, millions of fates were drawn up by legislation, the cause and effect of deaths unprecedented. Such pessimistic naivety had soured her mood, and Lylith obediently returned to her shrunken throne, left to hear the inelegant jeers and promises of victory.

"On the blood of our brothers and sisters, the dead and innocent in Hayana, we will not let this aggression surpass us. We will crush their armies in the seas, in the skies and, if they so dare, on our own soil!"

~~~

The enflamed sunlit hours were over. The motionlessness of the night – the darkness soaked in twilight glimmers best experienced in seclusion. For Lylith, her private screening of moonlit beams against her window failed to quell the sickness in her mind.

Usually, the bold and rich colours of her bedroom promoted a calm mindset, with the velvet sheets of her duvet and mahogany warmth of the cabinets in every corner. And the great mirror, two metres wide and hide, that returned her beautiful face was there to remind herself of her fortunes in life. Yet such privileges were not of her concern, for the hours had put together a civil crisis that she saw as unjust and unfathomable.

Earlier that night she had cried on her window sill as the moon had risen over the horizon. The waning gibbous state of the otherworldly satellite lost the grace of its full exposure. And after a while, the clouds came overhead to reduce its silver bloom. The greyish glimmers faded and the spectacular shine of her silverware, circlets, golden picture frames and perfectly hung dresses disappeared with it.

All the little trinkets and details that the architects had planted for her comfort made her feel ill. There she was, sat with luscious possessions that existed simply to reflect her status. And in her emotional state, they taunted her placement, her exclusion from the dawning age of warfare. Such unfairness, she thought, had doused the common man.

She unbuckled her dress and changed into a night gown, before she collapsed back onto her silk purple pillows at the head of her bed. But before she had a chance to clean her mind of her worries, a gentle knock came at her door.

Quickly, she sat back up and pressed the little creases in her gown out with her thumb. With a clear and soft voice, she called out to the visitor.

"Come in."

The slow creak of the door emphasised how empty the grand halls were. Each centimetre of the hinge's movement reverberated and echoed its call like a voice lost in a private mountain range. A faint light peered through the door's cracks but was soon extinguished by the flick of a switch. There in the doorway was her mother, Queen Tala Redgrine, accompanied by two faceless guards.

Lylith's face drooped at the sight of her future self – the very person she was expected to become – and her lack of a smile sold the notion.

"Oh, hello." The Princess unenthusiastically muttered. Her mother raised her hand, ushering the two guards back into the corridor, and closed the door behind her.

"Are you well?" She pondered aloud. Lylith didn't answer straight away. "Philip brought your condition to my attention."

"What of it?"

"I just wanted to make sure my daughter was okay. Is that not fair?" A stern remark pushed back. She shook her head in response, lazily turning toward the window. The cloud coverage was gone and the midnight glow had returned. Tala walked into the light, highlighting her aged features with a monochrome filter. "A mother should be allowed to worry for her children, regardless if they're twenty or five."

"Yeah, well…" Lylith sighed, breaking her calmer façade. "I just don't get it."

"I know you don't-"

"Why did you enforce that policy, earlier in the court today? That is what I don't understand. Just…why?"

"Great leaders make difficult decisions, my lovely." There wasn't a hint of smugness or pleasure from Tala's mug. She held a steadfast ease about her words, believing every detail she said without a lick of irony.

She paced carefully around the room, her arms locked behind her back, with the fabrics of an elongated florid dress dragging behind her. Her grandiose stature came as no surprise. Every little thing, from the open call to war to the pressing of a pronged fork into a juicy steak, was done with such proprietorship that Lylith had once believed her mother owned the globe.

Such levels of power trumped any notion of victory she had in her beliefs; confidence on immeasurable levels were convincing enough to the frail 'revolutionary', not that Lylith was much of one herself.

"Mum, I-" A stern gaze landed on her. She was forced to recompose her words with additional care. "Mother, I apologise, but I just can't see this as anything other than immoral."

"And why do you see it that way?"

"Because it's war, mother, and there's nothing more cruel than political bickering slaughtering thousands."

Tala politely acknowledged her words with a slight nod. Something about her wordless remark provoked a furious reaction within her daughter. Impulses ran through her body, flaring up a storm of dissatisfaction. Lylith shot up onto her heels and swivelled to face the ruler of all things she'd known.

"It's immoral, I say! The liberties of our subjects aren't games in which we can play. They are rights in which we should safeguard."

"Lylith, understand that under the grace of Sunar, the worship of absolute liberty becomes the crutch of amoral practices." Unshifted by Lylith's raised tone and offensive stance, Tala maintained a resolute composure in both body and voice. "I don't know how many times I have to say it, but are many occasions in which those who share your virtues do not know what they want."

"But mother-"

"And what? Do you think the idled and unfulfilled will step up and withstand the red wave, or would they gladly let it consume them, only to wish later on that things would go back to how they were now?" A cold look returned the monarch's persistence.

"Don't make the same mistakes my father did."

"That was different, as was he." Lylith felt perplexed by her persistence to undermine her point, yet that was how things always had been – a struggle to rise above her senior's sense of righteousness. "Your father was a kind and considerate man, and those are your best qualities, my dear. But Oscar, he…well, he was on the offensive, he was involving himself in the happenings of a nation we saw little benefit from. A hundred thousand casualties is no easy medal to wear, but it was preventable; by staying out of all the trouble, we could have avoided the suffering. Here, my lovely, we are under attack. We cannot sow pretty seeds on the situation. Men and women of the Syndicalist Union are on their way to destroy us, to annex and puppet our way of life."

Long-winded arguments created a compulsive withdrawal from Lylith's full attention. Her repulsive sense of disagreement fundamentally challenged her school of liberated thought, and she hated it. The little things she did to contest her mother's supreme rulership over the situation. What minute emotional baggage she pressed against her gave Tala the cold realisation of leadership through stoicism.

Who was she to question what had raised her? The question on every nobleman's lips was clear-cut – what honour must she have given up to embolden her sensibilities? Tala had no answer for them, and her daughter did all the more challenging with little action taken.

"I feel like you're taking great pleasure out of this decision." For once, bafflement struck the Queen's nerve. "Maybe this will secure you some popularity if we win – they'll call you a hero-"

The second Tala's palm collided with Lylith's cheek a grey cloud eclipsed the midnight radiance; a shadow cast itself upon the bedroom, letting in the night.

An aching sting sat on the Princess' cheek. The abolition of her jeering tune had gagged her voice and silenced her thoughts. Her focus went toward the sharpness of the nail that had clipped her temple or the ground zero of her mother's skin and bone missile. She withstood the desire to cry, yet the invisible taping on her lips gave Tala the time to rebuttal her insolence.

"If for one more second you truly believed that, I would have you relieved of your place as heiress and would seek your cousins as replacements. How, in the Star's hour, dare you peddle such claims on your own mother! Shame!" She barked in a loud whisper, measured precisely to not worry her escort outside. "I take no such pleasure from this. I make decisions I must, not decisions I want to. Learn this or you should see yourself hanged at the gallows by your own people."

With repulsion, she wiped her hand against her dress and made haste for the door. Before leaving, she turned and glared at her daughter as the offense she took boiled over.

"Take your own ignorant naivety with a pinch of salt, Miss Lylith Redgrine. Your adulthood has only just begun – don't squander it for pettiness in the face of evil."

Tala left as she came, quietly. Just before she made her departure, she had taken a second to recompose herself for the guards outside with a long pause. Then, she was gone, leaving Lylith to her own thoughts and hours.

Into the night, she laid awake as if expecting something to happen. She wanted the door to be swung open, a parade of bugles and walking drums beating the woes away, and a banner that would read: *"Victory!"* or *"Crisis Averted!"* A light-hearted thought, but such promises didn't come around.

Lylith ladled her defeated mood with a stare to the beige photograph sat on her bedside desk. Gentle hands plucked it out of its frame and laid the paper-thin memory between her fingers.

It was a scaled down, privately requested printout of the only photo she remembered being taken by her father's side. There, in a pyramid triage of heights, she was at the bottom of the picture – her smile brought the only shard of colour to its monotonous singularity.

She conjured an array of options in a single night's worth of creative confidentiality. Her recent traversal into adulthood had left her bitter about all of that day's occurrences. The discrepancies of the court's moral justice – and to what she sought to evolve someday – had dug a blade into her sense of hope. To which, she gathered her thoughts to the stories of which her father had told her. His face looked back at hers, friendly yet emotionless, and she envisioned his voice re-reading the tales of a thousand heroics.

When the dawn broke, and from the flames of the sun itself came the fanned ferociousness of war, martyrs came and went from the humblest of commoner to the greatest of national leaders. Old Kings of turbulent times, with blades in one hand and beacons in the other, braved night and day to do as they were destined for. Enticed by their almost mythological presence in Kelan's history, the rising of the sun saw a determined woman with a hunger for virtue – to lead by example, she thought, was to be there with the people.

Her post was of no importance to her anymore. The happenings of politics were faint, and the waves of a self-titled fate swept her off her feet. Caution was of little debate, and she went into the following morning with an atypical leaning toward solidarity.

The crimson god awoke from his rotary slumber, and Lylith bathed her skin in its benevolence. In open, flat palms she held her prayer:

"Gracious be thee,
To come and guide me,
On the land where thy eye first lands.
Bless our deeds."

Chapter 3

Tinker, Tailor. Soldier, Postman.

The older optimists twiddled their thumbs as they assured small promises to the rest of the conscripts. A roughly 40-year-old man cracked a wonderful smile that was only seen by blind eyes; the day had ended hours ago, and the never-ending truck ride to somewhere kept on moving.

"Give it a few months; politicians will put it off 'cause they don't have the bollocks." The man jabbed the nearest go-lucky pals of his with a wrinkled elbow and jeered at the grey fate given to him.

The others made an attempt to laugh, provided they could call a shrunken titter anything more than a little chinwag. Ultimately, much of the would-be confidence of confused men and women placed in military-marked vehicles had been squandered. Many made mutters of stolen liberty and clashed with those who justified their government's decision as duty, survival and obligation. Some bickered but the impatience of their drivers, plus the two soldiers sat in the back with them, made it abundantly clear that their job wasn't to quell those strangers' woes.

Rhys watched the older man tell stories with those he'd faintly remembered: a neighbour from the nearest town, a market-stall owner who'd once sold him fresh fruit, a boy just a year short of adulthood who'd used his truant years to play tricks on nearby towns and the woman who always ran past his house on every Wednesday and Friday. The physically fit, non-essential workers filled out the new boots in the back of the truck, whilst the childless women were tapped into as a source for additional manpower. And what had it created? A slow, raggedy cargo hold for a diesel-fuming truck, made from workers and marketeers, farmers and students – anything the sector had to offer.

In the end, Rhys lost interest when two individuals debated whether the large pool of initial conscripts would spiral into an economic crisis during or post conflict, but the silent like himself tried very hard to make sense of their situation. The day of normalcy, broken by the new order: better to lose the farmer than the farmland.

If what the officers had said were true, when the sun started to set at the back of convoy, the militia's purpose was to be a garrison force above all else. Plentiful but short of a professional standing army, one that already existed in dwarfed numbers. Training would be given, bedding and food, as the economy shifted its focus towards a swift defence of the homeland. At least, so as the news went around the mouths of the optimists.

Galbraith's two-vehicle column had joined up with a larger body of transports, ranging from military trucks to the odd civilian-commandeered milk float. Save for the unusual warmth of the summer's night, no one considered the journey to be anything other than unpleasant.

Across the valleys, Rhys saw the lamplit villages and towns pass by. Some roads took them directly through them, others kept them afar. The cobblestone pavements were bereft, emptied to allow for uninterrupted military movement, but the windows were open and the towns' civil spectators watched the convoys saunter past. Yellow streetlights made only the hands of waving children visible. Heads of the house looked on with pride or concern, and for good reason; none of the living generations had witnessed a mass mobilisation of such tremendous magnitude. Throughout the day and night, truck loads of men and women poured through and left just as quickly as they had arrived. Faces were captured in split-second moonlit spotlights – for the first and possible last time, many of these men and women were seen as defiant heroes set to extinguish the upcoming flashpoint.

Rhys saw the little five-year-old hands wave at him from a thatch-roofed cottage bedroom window. He wasn't sure if it was a true send off for him or a generalised gesture towards those headed off. Worse still, he was just as clueless as the child was for where they were headed or what fate laid in store for them.

Later on, when the villages became sparce and off their path, the trucks approached a gloom on the night-sky horizon. Fluorescent beacons beckoned for their attention, and those bundled in the backseats of the truck gradually became more attentive. A mechanical whistle screamed into the night. Those who were still in deep slumbers were dragged back into the conscious turmoil. The trucks slowed themselves one by one and formed a disorderly queue to an obscured building complex to their front.

Curiosity struck the man; Rhys tapped his neighbour on the shoulder to garner their attention.

"Hey, where are we?" He said with a tempered volume. A sickly scent filled the back of the truck.

"Train station, I think? Taking us to someplace important I imagine."

It was the best answer he was going to get out of a conscript like himself, and so he sat back with mild complacency. The truck started and stopped a few times before his viewport came in line with the target building.

"Alright, out you hop! Don't loiter. Stand on the side of the pavement and get in line with the entrance." Orders came through rapidly and the drop-door at the truck's rear swung down. Immediately, the first few men and women clambered out the back one after another and dashed to the spotlighted pavement as instructed. Rhys followed suit. Best to not cause any trouble, he thought.

By the time thirty seconds had passed, the truck had been abandoned by all except the driver, who steadily drove on for the next vehicle in the convoy to unload its many passengers. To the very letter of their orders, Rhys fell into line with the countless other bodies. All of them were men and women of varying ages, from as young as a quiet sixteen-year-old lad to the wrinkled face of a middle-aged wanderer.

Again, the blare of the whistle caught his attention. The lingering taste of exhausted fuel maintained a heavy presence on his tongue. Looking down the line, he saw the mishmash of uniforms processing those placed into service. Train conductors barely bantered with the military policemen. A young man and an older woman fell out of one another's favour and started bickering over something small.

"Keep orderly! Or-de-rly!" An officer made his way over and forcibly separated the two like children in a school queue. The disorder at hand only instigated anxiety across the line. Every few seconds, they'd be two steps closer to the station's entrance, where about ten tables sat with smartly dressed officers behind them.

In due time, Rhys found himself at the cold iron gates of his future. It was built on a rotary system for one way passage. Once in, the exit was out on the far side of the station.

A quick exchange of yes and noes later and a palm on his back guided him through the gate. And there, in clear sightline, were the three-floor carriages of their final chariot. Inscribed with fancy typography were the words: 'Spirit Star'. First impressions were everything, and the only connection Rhys could draw between the train and its flamboyant title was the exhaustion of fumes and heat from its mechanical engine core. It held all the prowess of a horse carriage and all the mettle of a light breeze. No armour. No specialised military adornment. Just a commercial diesel locomotive filled with the next generation of garrisons and coastal guardsmen.

There wasn't a moment to stop and take in the sheer size of the train. The flow of bodies against his back, barking orders from conductors and officers, and the desire to get out of the heavy crowds left him in constant motion. Soon after arriving, he was straight at the train's outer stairwell – a man clutched his arm and pulled him towards one of them. Before he could process what was going on, he was halfway up the steps to the top floor.

He passed by the windows to half-empty cabins, where he saw a group laughing in one room, and on the floor above there was a woman crying in a friend's arms. An obstinate voice ordered for him to press on and, as the conscript was told, he did it without question. The number of eyes painting their shattered gazes upon his spine made his skin crawl and shudder. The engines began to whir as around half of its passengers had already made their way aboard. He heard conductor's whistles clash with those of the officers, who threw orders around like sacks of potatoes. *Go. This way. That way. Up. Down. That door. No, that one.* The wonders of ill-prepared disorganisation had done so much to stress out Rhys, to which a sharp pain clung to his skull. All the noise, the scents of sweat and fumes, and the waves of scared, afraid, confident, determined and confused bodies did everything it could to create an internalised panic.

Once the open doorway, suspended three floors high, swallowed him, the transition between the unintelligible reverberance to a condensed silence was striking. It was as if he'd crossed into another day. People spoke in whispers which, when layered in a total mass, only mimicked that of a single person's shout.

Funnelled by the noise, he walked aimlessly between the cabins, peering in with slight discomfort at some of the large gatherings. He yearned for the freedom of space after the hours of shoulders pressed tightly against him in a six wheeled tin can.

And – to his surprise – there were several cabins without occupants. Though the line of conscripts went on for a while, he suspected that the size and number of carriages available at least permitted pockets of solitude. He seized the space for himself and collapsed on the cushioned seating. It wasn't much to appreciate, but compared to the hard-wood benches of the trucks it was like laying on Sunar's hair.

There, he almost fell asleep. There were still many discomforts laid beside his musings. War. Duty – all socio-political concepts foreign to the private life of the independent man. The day had shown him little ease or compassion, and with that he cursed it with a pathetic sigh.

His eyes swayed in their sockets and took in the soundless cabin. Wooden walls hid the metallic structure of the train and gave it an augmented impression that only the nouveau riche held. The reinforcement struts were made from silver spoons and the glass was tinted to slightly obscure the underwhelming decorations from the outside world.

Every so often the train's siren would make itself known just as his attention went elsewhere. The pounding sensation in his head merely soured an already bitter night. An ill-tuned, unmelodious creak came through the bustle of the train. He lay dormant. That was until the voice caught his attention.

"Oi, can a beggar take his throne?" Rhys leapt out of his skin at first contact. He pulled himself up and blinked up a storm. "Ah, sorry mate. Didn't realise you'd nodded off."

When his sight cleared, Rhys saw a figure leant against the wood-coated iron door frame, arms folded. A warm smile sprawled across the arrival's face. Two rotund glass lenses – precisely cut to sit inside its monel frame – were propped high-up

35

on the bridge of his nose, as if they'd ought to pay just as much attention. And that cleverly enlarged smirk tried to compensate for his smaller scale; he was a tad bit of everything more for where his height fell short.

He, rather exaggeratively, rubbed a muddied hand through his hickory hair. Rhys leant back against the walls of his seat and shook his head.

"Cheers, mate." He strode in as if he belonged there, closing the door behind him. His nonchalant slide into the chair was smooth and carefree, and the casualness of his motion confused Rhys as much as it tried to put him at ease.

Soon after he had made himself comfortable, the final alert of the train's approached departure called to the station. Rhys peered through the window to see the last remaining bodies tumbled into the carriages whilst the conductors and officers rallied themselves for a due send-off. A personal whistle screamed outside their door as a commanding voice told them to get to any available seats immediately. No one else shuffled into their cabin, leaving the two young men to themselves.

Then, the inertia pulled him forward like a finger had tugged at his collar. The blood rushed to one side of his body but soon settled in its natural flow. A metallic grinding of gears and powered valves vibrated the confines of their cabin. The noise was tremendous at first, but as the train made headway for the station's exit the sound died down. That initial force had, however, made a number on his stomach. If he had eaten anything in the past hours, it'd have been on the floor by then.

"Steady on, mate. You don't look too good." Back again to break the silence, the other man's chipper-and-cheery tone spiked as the train's engine tempered. He dawdled at beady stare at the sickly farmhand. He reached into his jacket, a denim summer overcoat, and pulled out a small packet of an unlabelled meal. "Want some?"

Rhys groaned. One of those exhausted ones, in particular. He was fed up with the day. So much for such little time. A thousand new faces for a man used to only one. To say it was overwhelming was quite the understatement.

"Suit yourse-"

"What is it?" Rhys asked through a drawn-out yawn.

"Dunno, don't care. Swiped it from the pocket of an officer sat next to me." He gave it a sniff as he opened it. "Can't smell anything from it."

He reached into the beige paper packaging and tore out a crumbling, parched biscuit. For a few seconds, he scrutinised it with immense thoroughness, flipping it to analyse each angle. Then, he took his first bite, contemplated the flavour and nodded with another smirk.

"Want some?" He asked with a full-mouth.

"Is it…good?"

"Great – if you enjoy horse shit."

"Can't say I've tried it." The man cracked a little chuckle from behind his smile as he took Rhys' word. Even if the guest's description sold it short, he held out a hand to receive the rest of the biscuit collection.

Several bites in, he understood what the man meant. The flavouring was all wrong. He couldn't discern if someone had put far too much salt or sugar, or both, into the biscuit, whether intentional or not. His left eye watered as he squinted a little too hard, but downed the meal regardless. Food was food and he couldn't safely bet that the military had packed en-route meals for conscripts.

"Quality, isn't it?"

"Sure." His brow buried his eyes as he tightly shut them for the final gulp. At that rate, he'd had preferred a shot of poison instead.

"So, what's the name?" Rhys gazed back at the man, hesitant for a second. Triumphantly, the man gave him an upbeat reassurance. "Name's Mateo."

"Rhys."

"Well met, mate." He extended a hand, and Rhys took it in his, accepted the hand-shake out of courtesy. He hadn't quite put his finger on whether he found the man annoyingly optimistic or as a welcome change from the monotone chaos of his newfound fate. "You from far away?"

"Hendrick's Farm." Mateo gave him an urging stare. "It's…near the town of Shrinley."

"Not a clue."

Both leaned back in their seats and gave a second of their time to listen to the clattering of steel wheels marching across the tracks. Outside, the animated scene of the station had been exchanged for a panoramic landscape of the nightly hills. A silver beam was made clear in the sky, but the interior lights of the train made it difficult to make out the details of the countryside. Just the tips of hills and gatherings of far-away forests.

Rhys spotted the distant lights of more towns and villages. They weren't much of a show, and the nearest cities were numerous hours apart from one another. A few laughs could be heard throughout the train, and the calm tone of the journey could've been blissful to Rhys had it not been birthed from unholy circumstances.

"So, what are you, a gardener?" Another sudden enquiry. He looked at Mateo and shook his head.

"Farmhand. For my father."

"Ah, fair enough." Mateo reached for his jacket again. He fumbled around with the inner pockets for a bit before drawing out nothing. He cursed beneath his breath. "Fuck, forgot it."

"Forgot what?"

"My patch." Rhys returned the similar expectant gaze he'd been shown. "Oh, it's the little patch I wear back at work. You see, I'm like…actually the most important person in Kelan."

"Is that so?" Easing into the conversation, Rhys smiled a little at his weighted claim.

"Mate, you doubting me? Alright, here's a little game." Mateo adjusted himself in his seat and leaned forward to face him. "The nobleman wants to set out a new decree, so he goes to the radio line. It's kaput. So, he needs the technician, but how can he call him without the radio? In that case, he wants to go and tell everyone in person, but he can't do that one by one – takes too long and he's a busy man, doing all that royal shit or something. So, what does he do, mate?"

"Write a let-"

"He prints a letter! And that's where I come in. Chief Postman Aviadro, man of the hour. When the tech fails, you bet your arse I'll be the messenger to keep the key to society turning: communication!"

He held up a jokingly triumphant pose, using the faint bulbed lighting in the ceiling to capture his features just right.

"You're full of shit." Rhys came out with a laugh. "Is this your sales pitch to me?"

"Hey, respect the foundation before you admire the building. I'm keeping my community afloat with proficient postage."

It was almost a wonderful engagement and Rhys pondered over how at ease he felt. The grandiose carriage of fool's riches clattered a crowd of a thousand toward a life sentence, and yet the back-and-forth chatter with a stranger put his mind to rest, if only for a few minutes.

Mateo went on for a while, listing off the highs and lows of being the self-proclaimed hero of the social hierarchy. As fascinating as it was to have met someone capable of talking with bottomless lungs, Rhys did drift off a little. The tiredness had dragged each minute by painfully. Slowly, his eyes naturally floated toward the window, only to be met with a surprising differentiation.

Outside, there was a nocturnal abyss laid out in full. He hadn't quite noticed it before, but the distant silhouettes of the terrain and towns were no more. It was just a void; no stars, no lights. Even the moon itself had vanished. And the poor man was in his carriage, drawn by an iron stallion, being carried through the far reaches of darkened space.

He was losing himself to the sight. The sound of Mateo's voice dissolved as the darkness saturated his attention. He was caught in its unfamiliarity. Something unseen had clipped a leash to his sleeve. He endured it for a minute. It dared him to continue. Until a voice cracked through the void.

"So, what do you make of all this then?" Mateo asked, dragging Rhys out of his little trance. He turned back to face him. He was still smiling, but the room had gotten noticeably darker along with the mood.

"Of what?"

"Of *this*, mate. Conscription and all that. What do you think about it?"

Rhys let the question settle in at first, taking a little bit of time to process it. He hadn't thought too much of it, in truth. It sat on his tongue for a while longer.

"Rhys?" Mateo repeated himself.

"Oh, uh-...yeah;" he gathered his thoughts and adjusted himself in his seat, "I'm not – I mean I don't really know. It's all come at me so fast that..."

He placed his forehead onto his fingers, gently massaging away the lump of woes on his brow. It was all coming back to him; the face of his father, the absence of his mother, the men who led him away. It was immediate. There was no chance to protest. Law dictates this, duty requires that. There was a fragment of optimism in the back of his mind, holding dear the initial purpose of the militia: to garrison and reserve. A buffer should things go wrong.

If he had been told a day prior, he'd have expected the grandiloquence of a parade, the men and women in uniforms with great smiles on their faces; a cheery march toward victory. What he had gotten was despair, locked with a grey mood between the officers who'd cuffed his liberty.

"You still with us, air cadet?" Mateo snapped his fingers in front of his eyes, forcing Rhys back into reality.

"Yeah – yeah, sorry."

"You were saying that it all came at you too fast and…?"

"Well," Rhys said with little articulacy, "it just all frightens me a little. I mean, I'm no soldier. I had no intention of being one."

"I get you."

"And, well, this just all came out of nowhere. I've lived a quiet life. Don't have much variety, then suddenly the extremes-"

"-come out and bite you. Yeah. Couldn't say I planned this." They were left in silence whilst Rhys fumbled with his thumbs. And the night began to settle. The hypnotic rhythm of train tracks passing, vibrating the cabin gently, was soon lost and unidentifiable. Mateo broke the silence one last time. "Ey, but we can't be going about it with frowns and scowls. I'll catch you when I wake up, mate."

And just like that, he sprawled across his seat and was fast asleep in a matter of minutes. Rhys, on the other hand, was left stranded in conscious thought. That trepid blackness in the night sky consumed everything outside. He placed a hand against the glass and was greeted by a peculiar frosted touch. He withdrew from the seasonal dissonance and tucked his hands into his clothing. One last glance at Mateo tempted him into giving in.

As the queen had severed his freedoms, the dead of night fed on his skull, and he fell fast asleep on the train to a new, uncompassionate life.

Chapter 4

Fresh Boots

Rise at the crack of dawn – called the train whistle – and behold a new home. Rhys was awoken by countless voices and mechanisms layered interminably. Thousands of words gathered in the hallway. His vision was blurred. In twenty seconds, he'd blinked enough to wipe away the clouded lens, and he was met with a half-expectant Mateo observing the bustling corridor. By the time Rhys stretched, he caught the postman's attention.

"Oi, there's a bit of a stir." He stepped away from the door and pressed his face against the window. Outside, a new industrial complex had submerged the scenic view. "Looks like we're here."

"Where?"

"Guess we'll find out in a second."

The disaster of his tumbled slumber was worsened by the lack of impunity he felt. When making his way to his feet, he felt as compelled to do so as a prisoner in shackles, and the militia held the end of the chain.

Sure enough, it was a crowded mess outside the cabin. A queue had formed down its narrow twists and turns but it made no headway. Rhys caught wind of an officer's information dump, to which he gathered the detail of a 'carriage-by-carriage disembark'. No matter, he thought, it gave a few more minutes to adjust to the end-of-summer light.

Outside sat a dwindled wonderland made from industrial sparks and dirtied bodies. Swarms of the constricted walked toward the main entrance with their liberties packed in lockers back home. Pillars of steel rose from the concrete floor like erect tendrils beneath the sea and held up an aluminium phonetic typeface, one that spoke with a stainless shimmer. It was the cleanest thing in the station. Rhys peered to the left of the window to just make out the full word.

"Mullackaye…?" He read to himself. Didn't strike a bell with him, so he turned to more informed source on hand. "Hey, Mateo. What's Mullackaye?"

"Rings a bell, why?" Rhys ushered him over with a waving hand, and he joined him at the viewing glass. He didn't need to follow the farmer's finger. The letters were as loud as they could be. "Ah, shit."

"What is it?"

"It's *Fort Mullackaye.*"

Rhys was a little intimidated by its rugged alias. Nothing about it sounded – or from the front station appeared – homely for a place he was expected to live in. Mateo's uneasy tone hadn't helped either.

"Wait, what's wrong? Is it-"

"I wanted to go to Fort Charlottesville." The quip wouldn't have caught him off guard if he didn't sound genuinely bothered. He rolled his eyes and refocused on the manic state of the conscripted masses.

Many were funnelled down iron-fenced strips in lines of two, all leading toward a second processing station. Above them, a draconic catwalk housed sixteen military police officers and a two-man nest. None of them aimed at the conscripts, yet the unease of their swivelled guns having a near perfect field of view over them did little to calm him. It was from the window that he also got a good look at the crowd itself. Maybe a few hundred were already off the train, waiting in the usual disorderly fashion. He saw mostly Kelan's own. Sprinkled among them were foreigners from faraway lands. The potential Osakan and Redus hid between unmatched crowds taken from the villages and towns. It was a plainly toned collective, with varying degrees of clean clothing and greased hair.

"Queue's thinning, get up!" The sting of a morning whistle ricocheted down the hallway behind him. A piercing squeal, like a hoglet's cry, irritated the pair. They cursed underneath their startled breaths. "Come on. No dilly-dallying! Get to the line, get registered and head to your assorted barracks when told!"

Mateo flashed a grin and bumped him with a greased-up elbow.

"You better walk with me, mate. You'll be wondering senseless otherwise." The smile was all too welcoming. And Rhys, a little determined not to lose sight of the brightened addition to his day, took up the offer with a half-smile.

"Only if you don't get me lost."

"That'a man!" He chuckled, giving Rhys a pat on the shoulder. Mateo adjusted his glasses to better fit onto his nose and dove headfirst into the bundled line.

It took a bit of shifting, but soon they'd hit the queue ahead of a few grumbling souls. Their backs were immediately met with the driven force of fifty tightly crammed bodies pushing on ahead. The corridor reeked of sweat and bile, and the faint stench of vomit tarnished the ostentatious absurdity of the middle-class train.

Further down, Rhys stumbled across a pair of voices amidst the rough. He peered over the heads and spied one of the cabins, then occupied and transformed into some sort of friendly interrogation room.

"-to the point where he just...did it?"

"How'd he break it?" The first voice questioned the second, referencing the hard-to-miss shattered window to the cabin.

"With his arms and legs, I think? Just kept kicking at it until it eventually broke. And then-"

"He leapt out?" The man with the 'MP' armband asked. The second voice was a woman with frizzled hair and a cigarette in her hand, like something straight out of a detective flick. She nodded. The line gradually pushed on, but Rhys heard just a little bit more. "Do you know of any places of interest he may go? Any significant place he'd disappear off to?"

"No. He just rambled about the state of the crown and-" Up ahead came the gritted-teeth shout of the commanding officer.

"Stop dawdling around. Check the rooms to make sure no one's left on board!"

When he looked back, Rhys had lost sight and sound of the interluding investigation. Another story lost to the wind, where he could just spectate and walk by for just a passing second. Hell, it was more exciting than what he was used to back home.

Mateo snorted to himself and made a quiet chuckle about something that had popped into his head. He nudged Rhys again and dug out a remark with a full smile.

"Bit of an extreme reaction to the on-train service." Regrettably, Rhys did find himself smiling a small amount and failed to hide it.

"Out of taste, don't you think?"

"Ah, well…" Mateo drifted off back into his mind, only to quickly change the subject. "Fuck, man. Hard to believe this is actually happening. But you know what, fuck it. We're here now."

A greeting party of smoke and the stench of exhaust fumes welcomed their arrival. Rhys felt a little less contained once he'd exited the cramped halls of the Spirit Star express train, though he wouldn't have called it liberating. Above them was a concrete roof, almost as thick as the walls holding it up. Everything was built to stand. He'd never seen something so monolithic ever before. All that tension he'd eased returned as he was dwarfed by the enormous station. Every wall was freshly caked in steel struts. What little natural light pushed through dusted roof-top windows marked out rectangular paths toward the door.

At last, they had made touchdown. The descent down the rickety metal stairs had been an uncomfortable one. His shoes made first contact with Mullackaye's cobbled ground and the moistened sound of water – poorly blended with disinfectant – made itself known through the court of voices.

Mateo took the lead in navigating the slow drive through iron-barred fence track. It was a single-lane pathway, railroaded to the next part of their lives as determined by their masters. Reluctant minds pressed on as the simple sights of gun-toting officers made sure they didn't try anything. Not that there was a lot to try, Rhys affirmed the finalisation of their new careers. Once again, he told himself to remain calm. Things would remain nominal. It had to be a token of a short-lived age, where war is tested and then retracted in the face of annihilation. He knew not of the greed humanity was capable of, or how capable of men were at holding Death's hand.

When they reached the desk, it was a simple procedure: name, age, region of birth, sex and so forth. Then, a few seconds of sleep-deprived eyes scanning through sheets of paper. Once they'd found their name in the alphabetical list of 'expected conscripts' taken from a pre-boarding list, the bureaucracy could move on to the next man. Mateo went first without much hassle.

He plucked out a few details about his newfound acquaintance. 23 years old. Hailed from the Thorne region. Nice place, he thought, at least from what he'd heard.

For Rhys it was much the same. The bare minimum of individualism used to defer him from the countless faces before and after. He was a name on a register picked out by a dirty fingernail. To feel like less of a unique face, he'd arrived at the right fort.

The processing was complete. The officer at the desk scribbled something down on a small slip and handed it to him. Before he could a chance to read it, a hand was placed on his back and he was gently guided toward the station's exit. Mateo waited for him, and they were caught in a less claustrophobic environment, thinned out by the slow process of pencil-pushing.

"What's yours say?" He asked the farmer with a taste of intrigue on his tongue. Rhys hesitated. He noticed a similar slip of paper in the postman's hand.

"Oh, right," he looked to his and read it aloud, "so – 54th Defensive Regiment. Bravo Company. 4th Platoon. Squad 2. Report to Warehouse 15J?"

"You're shitting me?" Mateo broke out a wide grin.

"What?"

"That's mine as well. Down to the squad." The little laugh he gave was infectious, and even Rhys let out a small chuckle. "The luck of the draw! At least I know a guy, huh?"

Tiny miracles like those went a long way for men like Rhys. He smiled with genuine relief, knowing that his brief episode of amity wasn't to end in that hallway. He thought about how insane the chances were but kept the words to himself. Mateo swung a hand onto his back and made jest at the luck that the stars had given him. A life of endowed excellence, or something like that. He lost his attention span and retreated to his own mind as they went on their way toward their next stop.

Mateo harassed a nearby officer for directions whilst Rhys, still caught in his thought, looked around him as their emerged from the building entirely and arrived at the inner-sanctum for the regional military force.

The morning had a virulent chill about it. The past day's summer breeze had been body-snatched by browbeaten cold gale. Fragments of the sun's light poked through a heavy cloud coverage and a light mist covered the distant ends of the base. What lay beyond the Fort was obscured by towering battlements. Steel-reinforced concrete encircled the perimeter of the fortification, far greater than his sight could comprehend. The typical medieval concept of a castle was but one piece of the complex. Its scale matched that of an independent large town, with its civil amenities having been replaced by industrial and militarised districts. From where he stood, he could clearly make out the ends of a runway adjacent to five grey bunkers.

They stood somewhere on the outer rim of Mullackaye's interior. The titan walls glared down at them as a ray of sunlight angled from the top. A grand shadow had casted across the negative space – areas in which neither building nor roads crossed. Occasionally, a little sandbag nest would be found sat in the open with an 89_{mm} anti-aircraft emplacement buried inside. There were many of these, all crudely constructed for means of training to be easily dismantled at any given moment.

Then, the sound of the atlas' boots thundered into the zone. Tremors through the split tarmac travelled through his shoes and into Rhys' spine. The thud – a hundred and ten tonnes of hydraulic pressure – rippled the air with every step. He turned to face it, and from around the corner came a two-vehicle column of the most tremendous machines he'd ever witnessed.

A quadrupedal, mechanised walker. Its engine bellowed out through steel teeth. At its helm, a figure sat within an enclosed cockpit, and peered through a small viewport. The legs were padded with steel plating across any conceivable spot that didn't hinder the hinges. A thin black smog spewed from its rear exhausts as its iron lungs exhaled its cooked fuel. It stared straight ahead with its prime feature – the 94_{mm} gun affixed to its head. The leading walker's skin was a nightly shade of black, decorated with insignias and labels, whilst its following brother was coated in an olive-drab tone, similar to that of the common soldier's attire.

A man's voice called from the other side of the path, hailing the small cluster of men and women Rhys had found himself falling into.

"Clear the way!" They pushed themselves back as the vehicles confidently strode past. Rhys watched where its feet landed; the unattended cracks in the tarmac began to make sense to him.

And, though slow, the machines eventually faded around another corner, disappearing behind a building. The crowd of conscripts dispersed. Mateo and Rhys were left to their own procrastinations.

"Fuckin' hell, that was a bit-" Mateo paused and recomposed himself. "-I mean, I'm glad those are on our side, right?"

Rhys only gave a silent nod in response. He looked at the fresh imprints of its steel toes and shivered a little. Of course he was glad they were on his side. Just the thought of facing off a behemoth, like those walkers, terrified him. All the things he'd read about Kelan's modern armament sprang a new leak in his confidence. Ever the more worried, he struggled to keep his brooding fears from surfacing.

The pair advanced in the right direction. It was quite a length walk, darting between alleys and half-empty streets of barracks and armouries. Supposedly, they were just the first wave of conscripts to have arrived at the base. And with the masses he saw, Rhys' heart sank at the thought of a thousand – no, a hundred thousand – more non-combatants having guns put into their hands. But they were just a garrison force, weren't they? What did he have to worry about?

The deeper they went into the fort, the more brutalist the buildings became. So many were purpose-built to withstand the apocalypse. Rhys had never seen a hospital or commanding officer's lounge appear so threatening. Instead of flowers, window-sills had mounts for machine guns and boxes for rations, medical supplies and ammunition – all emptied due to a lack of local emergency. The pair also spied groups of the Royal Armed Forces, the standing army, engaging in firing drills at ranges, or practicing weapons maintenance. None of them poked at the conscripts with friendly stares, and their begrudged mutters did little to temper the foul mood.

Eventually, the pair had hit their destination. A great warehouse, fit with a large iron door, left slightly open for individual bodies to pass through. Some of the shrills and cries of the active outside were inaudible from the inside, something he discovered as he disappeared into the dark interior of the warehouse.

The place was lit by a multitude of eye-sores – lights strung up by iron tubes – which burned far too bright to feel natural. Other than that, there were the usual windows bridging the walls to the roof, angled to allow the minimum of sunlight into the mechanic's hiding place. Rhys was surprised to see a display of prowess waiting for them. On either flank, spaced out rows of quadrupedal walkers sat, dormant, presenting the armada of the company. Most of the machines were of the same model, with small variations. Some had muzzle breaks at the end of their guns whilst others had additional coaxial machine guns soldered into their bodies. One stood out, only having two legs, and a box-shaped cockpit atop of its legs locked in hyperextension.

Yet the workshop too was as dormant as the machines inside. A table sat in the dead-centre of the warehouse. Another pen-pusher, he noticed, sat with her legs crossed beneath a folding table covered in brown tea stains.

A small gathering preceded their turn, and so the pair latched on to the back of the group.

"Stars be damned-" Stunned, he ushered out his disbelief. Just in front of them was a man, built with a deity's muscle set, with his back facing them. However, he looked to his arm, and froze.

Like the softest shackle ever built, a small hand cuffed the wrist of the goliath. The six-foot six wall of pure strength stood before a small and timid eye, held within the sockets of a youthful face. She had all the features of her adolescence, robbed from its homely crib and placed in a warrior's shoe set. Her hair still had traces of gold buried within chestnut filaments, draped over her eyes; with irises as erratic as the infant's confusion upon birth. She chewed on a peppermint – Rhys could tell by the lingering scent – and tightened her grip on the burly figure's arm. The father and the daughter had been brought to war, and the sight itself sickened him to the core.

The girl's eyes met his for a brief minute. Had it been that obvious how discomforted he was? Her responding gaze wasn't one of reassurance, or of passive acceptance, but of similar disbelief. She couldn't have been any older than sixteen, he guessed.

Catching her glimpse, the giant followed it to Rhys and Mateo. Whatever imposing impression given by his stature was wiped clean as he gave the friendliest of smiles from beneath a fleece of facial hair. His skin was moderately tanned – mixed between that of a Redus native and common Kelan man – whilst his greeting stood as the brightest thing in the warehouse.

"You alright?" He gifted them a little nod, but whether it was out of respect or mutual acceptance was unclear to Rhys.

"Yeah, we're as good as it gets today." Mateo stepped in, thrusting a hand towards the man. His attempt at an iron grip was juxtaposed by the man's diamond clutch. Firm, yet gentle: the type of interaction that told a man everything he needed to know about his acquaintance. "You part of the company then?"

"Bravo?" He gave a little look around, eyeing up the walkers and small queue ahead of them. A little sigh left his lips, and he went back into thought for a quick second. "Guess so if I'm here. You lads the same?"

"We are."

All three of them scrambled about their minds and thoughts to find something to say. Small talk seemed to have left them, and the air was strung-up with awkwardness. They twisted their boots on their heels. A summer whistle, a semitone off key, came from Mateo's mouth. Then, he broke the silence.

"Oh, right. What platoon?"

"Oh. 4th. Second Squad."

"Bullshit? So are we." The postman took great pride in his little digging, scavenging up his members before the official induction had come through. He gave a courteous nod toward the giant. "Name's Mateo."

"Oslo." He looked down at the girl and, visibly, his throat tightened. A finger pulled at his collar whilst he came to terms with his own circumstances. "And – this is Evelyn."

"You out on a father and daughter day trip to the army then?" The little joke came with no laugh from the audience. A grim stare from Oslo held the silence a little while longer. He looked at the young child and shook his head.

"It's complicated."

Just as he drifted off to nowhere in particular, the line ahead of them thinned. A commanding tone brought them to attention, and they shuffled toward the desk. Rhys assumed it was going to be the exact same process. Name. Age. Whatever, do-dah. Instead, they arrived to be greeted by uniforms of approximate sizing. Green combat fatigues: a button shirt, trouser with belt, boots and cold-weather smock. One by one, they collected them, alongside an assortment of small patches and identification slips. Nothing formal, of course, or longstanding. It'd take time for things like dog tags and official service numbers to be properly registered.

Rhys' turn however was slightly different. Those before, Oslo, Evelyn and Mateo, all went up, got their gear and were pointed toward the right direction. In the farmhand's case, he was stopped in his tracks. The woman at the desk eyed through her papers thoroughly and plucked out an additional envelope, held together by a little blue ribbon.

"Hendricks, right?" She pressed him with a cigarette-tormented tongue. The aroma leaked from her lips like the flames of the oldest wyvern. Tobacco, amongst other things.

"Yes, ma'am." He whipped up his formalities.

"I got a letter here. Special input from up the chain. Says you're the new SNCO by proxy." He didn't blink. A blast of pure shock ripped through him. The stun, like a policeman's baton, had struck him so hard his nerves had frozen up. "Take your stuff. Captain Laskey will do a full brief either tonight or tomorrow."

"Hey – uh…" He paused as a single eye rolled up towards him. Hesitantly, he corrected himself. "– Ma'am. Why have I been-"

"Input from up the chain, do you listen?"

"Yes, ma'am, but-"

"What am I, your therapist? Fuck if I know. Now head over to that door there. There's a little office for your group in the platoon quarters. And hurry up, the line's getting long."

He peered behind him. They'd materialised out of thin air. One minute, gone, the next: present. Feeling the pressure lay into his heart, Rhys made no attempt to slow himself down. He gathered all the little trinkets and clothes given to him and scurried off to the side, where Mateo and the two allies waited in silence.

"Aye, the fuck was that about, mate? You starting a spat already?" Mateo said in a loud whisper, pulling him toward the wall and out of earshot. Where an officer would've cut him down with vicious language, the postman mocked the issue with his eternalised cheek.

"They said," he took a second to clear his mind, "that they've put me into an SNCO role?"

"Mate, I have no idea what that means."

"Senior non-commissioned officer. Like a…like a Sergeant, or something?" All those ramblings from his father had paid the fee to peer inside the military structure. A small stroke of luck – enough to give him an insignificant amount of preparation for what was asked of him. "It's all beyond me as to why."

"Are you a manager in your off time or something?" Oslo chimed in.

"No…nothing of the sort."

He took the minute to adjust to his senses. A spin of the mind and expectation had displaced the diminutive cohesion that lay in his hands; in fractured pieces, he made a jigsaw from his confusion with several of its pieces missing. He had been snared in an early morning web of the personal politics that ran rampant in the infancy of the militia.

The coupling of newlyweds, soldier and citizen, played a heavy hand on the incoherence for Rhys. Either someone saw hidden potential within a man without so much of a sprinkle of experience or there simply weren't enough professional NCOs on hand. Not that he blamed the Royal Armed Forces. To stomach seeing the wives and husbands they vowed to protect be carted up to the firefight wasn't exactly a popular attitude, from what he imagined.

Yet why did it matter? As far as they all knew, the militia weren't a combat effective force, at least by conventional means. They were a stopgap in case things went drastically wrong, but with morale mostly on the upturn there wasn't much chance of military disaster striking Kelan's turf.

Oslo, with Evelyn still fastened onto his arm like a starving leech, led the way down toward their assigned door. A spruce plaque sat above the entryway. It had already been choked with the dust that had settled on its lettering. *4th Platoon,* it said in an obnoxious brass font. All nice and proper but lacking the crude personality of the conscripts themselves. How many plaques simply highlighting the platoon did the military have? Enough to gather cobwebs. Without much fanfare, he entered the platoon's subsection.

He peered to his left and right, eyeing the narrow corridor. He hadn't gotten half-sick of cramped spaces and yet they were all that the militia had to offer. A series of established officers lurked in a nearby office enjoying a joust of banterous insults at one another. He heard the distinguished clink of glasses followed by the fragrant whiskey set to dress their tongues.

Down the hall, to the right, sat the door leading to the second squad's gathering room. The group opened the door and revealed a gloomy descent down a splintered stairwell. They peered around Oslo's shoulders and eyed the depths. A pathetic glimmer sourced from a single light bulb at the basement's end. A faint voice was heard from within.

Eager make the first move, Mateo gave a great smack of the palm on Rhys' shoulder.

"Homely. Let's have a gander, shall we?" With a convivial little rub of the hands, he took the plunge one step at a time. The voices cut themselves off as the creak gave away his unprecedented arrival. Soon after, Oslo took Evelyn down with him, and Rhys was left to follow through to the underground.

At the bottom, there was a weird smell about the air. Rhys linked it to the kind of scent found in a run-down barn, or a house that had been left to fall apart, brick by brick, for several decades. The thick layer of sour-smelling paste made crude work of covering up the cracks in the walls. And the steps – how they creaked. Even then, he wondered if they were going to collapse; the elaborate ruse to further trap him in the military's basement. However, they held themselves together, and he arrived at the final step.

The animals sat in their cages and their eyes peeled upon their unbeknownst pack leader, call surrounding a largely misshapen table. Rhys landed lastly and caught sight of several eyes, carefully analysing him after they'd made the rounds on the preceding triage. And in the quickest manner, he too flicked an observation their way.

Six of them; quite a lot to take in for the short space of time allotted to him. He made the first stride to the corner, where a paper-thin sense of camaraderie had been set in stone. First to catch his glimpse were two men, one foreign and one far too fitting for the soldiery. He knew at first glance that the first man was from Redus – down to the little cultural chequered pattern on a tool belt he wore – whilst the other fit the bill as a pure Kelan native, or at least as close as they got, with his strikingly rich moustache.

On their left stood the scrap heap of the group. An unkempt sprog decorated in the grime he'd been found in. He gave a yellow-tooth grin toward Mateo as they approached one another.

"No shit, you're the one from the West Avenue factory?" The first sign of life amidst the conscripts.

"How'd you know?"

"I'm the post officer in the area."

"You're pullin' my leg!" And like mothers, they met in the middle to talk up their storm, centred entirely around the mishaps of the local area they'd hailed from. Rhys passed his attention down the line.

Among the thorns, Rhys picked out the roses at the head of the table. Two women closely locked in a whispered conversation – lookalikes at first glance, but with discernible differences upon closer inspection. Chestnut gold, strings of glorious tidiness and a clashing aura of confidence to discomfort split between the two. Siblings, he guessed, and he would be right.

And holding on to the wing of the group was a plain and rather unremarkable young man, likely of similar age to Rhys himself. In that shortened scrutiny, Rhys saw nothing that 'stood out'. A conventionally attractive man, straightened jawline and a dress-code that made it clear he'd held himself to an elevated regard.

A few of them got talking, more to themselves than to Rhys, but all the conversations seemed to stray away from the important subjects at hand. He listening out for the keywords: war, military, army, Ferusia. The fact neither were brought up in the first five minutes made him wonder if it was all on purpose, that swiping the dirt beneath the rug was just a better way to comfort themselves in the foxhole they'd been buried in.

An inanimate object took his intrigue. A slip of paper attached to a clipboard, off-centre on the central table. The clip looked a little rusted but the paper was as crystal-white as the harshest of winters. He looked around at first, just to confirm that none of the others planned to go for it. Maybe they'd already read it, or perhaps they avoided it intentionally. A few seconds of dallying on the side-lines let him have the floor and Rhys made his move.

He swiped up the clipboard and retreated to the fringes of the fluorescent lightbulb's shine, enough to keep the contents visible.

He scanned through the first few lines and made out the general gist of it. A registration built in Squad 2's name. He went through the list in its appropriate order, plucking out only the important details to him.

2nd Squad – 4th Platoon – Bravo Company
Designation – Infantry (Militia Formation)

Acting SNCO:
- Staff Sergeant Rhys Hendrix

Acting ICs:
- Sergeant Christopher Normans [Pathfinder]
- Corporal Mateo Aviadro   [AT]

Main Body:
- Lance Corporal Johan Kaelo   [Rifleman]
- Specialist Tyran Rhodecca   [Walker – Pilot]
- Private Ryan Richards   [Rifleman]
- Private Oslo Verdana   [Gunner]
- Private Gwendolyn Carlyle   [Combat Medic]
- Private Sabrina Mistral   [Rifleman]
- Private Tamara Welks   [Submachine Gunner]
- Private Stephan Kaelo   [Rifleman]
- Private Dynis Riley   [Marksman]
- Private Evelyn Verdana   [Rifleman]
- Private Ella Mistral   [Combat Engineer]

The minor and trivial details of the page rubbed him the wrong way, like how the soldier role designation wasn't quite perfectly aligned. More importantly, there were more names than there were bodies in the basement. He scanned the small gatherings and made his best attempt to label them according to their registration.

To the best of his ability, he was able to place names to the present faces. He knew Oslo, Evelyn and Mateo, and so they were easy to cross off. The moustached native was his sergeant, and the lance corporal was the young man on the wing, Johan. He brought to his attention the whereabouts of his brother, Stephan, as well as his already acquainted allies: Dynis and Tamara. Tyran was quite clearly the specialist by Christopher's side. Finally, the Mistral sisters. And that was all he had on hand. A large handful of the group, with the others having left to either explore or catch a whiff of fresh air.

Rhys introduced himself with a clear yet quiet voice. The voices welcomed him but the eyes were most definitely sceptical. He could feel it: the burn in his forehead from around seven seared stares. Judgement came as clear as dawn. And he didn't blame them, not then.

For what reasons were the responsibilities placed upon his shoulders? Nepotism? A little lust by fate, or perhaps it had made a clear path to becoming the best person he could – a trial made in a volcanic event. It would be his catalyst for self-improvement. That's how it had always been advertised. Then again, hollow shells like his father did little to peddle those beliefs.

So much for the meritocracy. While it was alive and well in the regulars, down in the infant militia it was all but dead and desecrated upon.

"So, what comes next?" Mateo flipped the silence and made an attempt to bring them all to the centre. Since discovering his own role, he'd tightened the laces on his boots and buckled up his belt. An all-natural display of confidence, regardless of his situation.

"Oh…?" Rhys looked through the papers, scanning through each little detail. "Well, I've got a meeting with a Captain…Laskey, I think?"

"She's the company commanding officer." Christopher raised a hand from the back of the room. "It'll be an induction briefing. Then straight into training. Same with most branches"

"Oh, thanks."

Rhys eyed up the printing, more so out of a need for an excuse to not face them all head on. Part of him pled for training that'd deconstruct him, maybe tear him down from his anxious roots and sprout out a new flower of confidence – a rose, perhaps.

Chapter 5

Regicide

The creak of parched hinges called to Lylith, pulling her eyes toward the doorway. As it slowly opened, echoing gently through the confinement of her dormitory, a head poked through with gleeful eyes and a paternal smile of jubilation. Relief had arrived.

Lylith's waking hours were flooded with incessant courtly orders, focusing on – what were to her – insignificant economics set aside for the war effort. In that time, she'd used her prestigious position to tug unseen strings; she plotted under her mother's noses and had organised a concoction unexpected of the crown. Her mind eased upon seeing the figure's elderly smile greet her.

"Miss Redgrine, just so we are parallel on this, are you sure this is what you want?" The servant cautiously let the door close behind him, knowing full well that the untrusted walls had eyes and ears planted within them.

"I am. Might I say again, I cannot thank you anymore than time will let me. There aren't enough words to-"

"I'm just doing my duty, Miss Redgrine." The kindness that was her servant mentor. Philip: A wrinkled figure with a story to tell for every scratch and bruising on his skin. He was to be her alibi, her falsified herald to spread inconsistent truths to the court. "I trust that your heart will engage in profitable endeavours for our greater good."

Soothing to the touch, his voice slithered between her attention. A serpent's sting was left unnoticed by her royal excellency. With thinning hair reaching near transparency, Philip finally came into the full view of the candlelit twilight.

"When my mother questions you tomorrow morning, or if the

guards become violent, are you sure you're willing to go through all of that simply for my moral pursuit?" She spoke with delicate apprehension. Her concern tempted a withdrawal from the operation – truly, however, Lylith only wanted the affirmation from Philip, that her pursuit was worth all the risks to their stoic hopefulness.

"My interests remain in Kelan's court, Miss Redgrine. I'll do whatever I need to align with my principles." He quietly murmured, uttering a few grumbles before returning his focus back to his superior. "I can't follow the path you have been given. My life is within these walls, doing what I can for the people, not the Queen. For that, you should do what our brothers and sisters desire."

A sparkled tear trickled out from beneath her butterfly-wing eyelashes. She lost control over her emotional diversion, sifting a conflict within her soul; to throw all her privilege away for a guidance only she saw as righteous. For a second, he took her in his arms and surrounded her with sweet embrace. It would be the last time the two would ever have the chance to.

She'd emptied her bread basket so that she could fill it with fruit; Lylith had prepared herself to, as she put it, valiantly join the frontline with those who'd had their freedoms stripped from them. If those who'd served her well required a protector, an angel with a loaded rifle, then she would damn well become it. Leaders were made to inspire, not to disown nor abandon their subjects.

She leant into his embrace for a moment longer. Overwhelmed by their familial warmth, falsified confidence and a naivety for the weight of one's actions quickly flooded her mind. Without second thought, she convinced herself she was ready.

"Now, let us discuss the order of the plan one final time. No point ignoring all this planning to scuffle your chances now, is there?" A silent shake of the head retorted his gentle guidance. Lylith's nerves were at an all-time-high, perfection in the execution of their plan was necessary.

"So, we begin here." She started, holding the dance floor for him to take the lead.

"It'll be the harshest hill – no, mountain – that you must clamber over. Outside, our hired loyalists are in the shadows. Our timing should be perfect to avoid the light patrols outside."

"And the hallways?" Lylith asked.

"There'll be as clear as I have made them, sweetheart." It was all a little exciting – the espionage of a future hero, she thought very fondly about it. "Then, you'll make it to the garden door. You meet the men at your disposal and scurry away. Don't look back."

"For all that you've done, I should only peer in your direction-"

"Don't." He sternly repeated. "I don't want to see you leave, and you shouldn't see me stay. It'll be better that way."

A wave of dejected sorrow washed over her and scattered her diamond memories like pebbles. The harsh tone sold her on the reality at hand. It was to be her final moment in the castle, so long as she would continue to serve. But all was needed in order to elevate herself as a mistress of justice, a populist's road of redemption.

The journey to Fort Mullackaye would last for months, considering the stoppages, changes in transport and exchanges of incognito cooperation. If there was one shard of advice she'd taken from her mother, it was of her notoriety. Lylith couldn't enter the militia as Lylith, but instead as a new person, a new identity and as an easily forgotten individual. Any information on her whereabouts would only go back to the Queen's ears. Philip had construed a few arrangements to provide basic necessities along her travels. Though not much, it was enough to introduce her to marksmanship, survival and simply being the lowest woman on the hierarchal pyramid.

Lylith drew a chilled hand to her eyes, wiping away what credulous tears she'd spilt. Each droplet was ice cold. This would be it. Everything she had been taught, shown and told had led up to the day where she would become her own master.

"Let the stars bring you luck, prosperity and fortune, Philip. You've served me well these years, and if I am to return, I will bring you opportunities to make best of your waning years." She smiled tastefully towards her assistant and prodded his wearied state. Philip struggled to force a reciprocated grin, though he managed the tail end of a jovial beam.

"I don't need luck, Miss Redgrine. All I need is for you to see to the end of the war. Your fate will only save the nation the day it comes." He heaved a heavy sigh.

"You and your candour, Philip, is going to be the death of corruption someday." She saw no hidden quills scribbling behind their backs. They were safe, both she and him, and they cared little for if their differing optimism blinded them. The royal world mattered little to her in the moment – her future would be held for those days. And so, with a silent shifting of her steadfast lips, she kissed his withered cheek and daringly marched into the blackened corridors of the palace. Before she vanished like the spectral queen of a better tomorrow, she turned to Philip and spoke with tenacity. "Goodbye, we shall meet when the sun is at its brightest."

Outside her room was the reddened marble road bannered with coats of arms, notorious family crests, ceremonial weaponry and the age-old paintings that eyed her final tour of her home. Every second spent lurking was filled with hushed breathing, only hoping she'd remain covert and to never be enquired that late into the moonlit hour.

With the Royal Guardsmen's' patrol shifts being rescheduled the following morning, Lylith exploited their tiredness and anticipation for relief to move gently through their shadows. Her journey wasn't lonesome. She spotted familiarly-attired sentinels talking to one another. For once, their carless and lax behaviour served to her delight.

She stood in the shadows and eyed their golden chest plates with a melancholic disdain. Those enriched vests had once symbolised greatness. Hell – the days of which Oscar reigned, without so much as a lick of interest in foreign affairs until his hand was forced by those inside. The guard that spoke of prosperity and peace. She reminded herself of how they were once personal protectors. Highly skilled individuals, recruited for their passion to preserve a blooming monarchy. She even remembered the one who'd taken interest in her childhood. Emelia, or something. But those days were gone, and the ostentatiously militarised nature of her protectorates gave little reason to go follow them into the breach.

In that moment, she had disengaged herself from the present day, wanderlust kicked in while she faintly staggered through the shadows of the palace. Eventually, a sudden clatter took her peaceful sentimentality from her and forced her to creep behind the low-hanging banners nearby. The princess was concealed only by the darkness of her shadowy retreat. Her gaze silently drew upon the nightly crescendo.

Metallic clatters of boots, medals and armoured plating echoed through the hallways. As luck stroked her hair, she clasped her mouth shut and watched the chattering guardsmen saunter by. She waited until they had left the corridor before she exhaled, dragging her delicate feet from under the banner and back into the shadowy flanks of the hallway.

Her bedroom wasn't as close as she'd hoped to the main garden. The final stretch of her silent escape would lay in the flowery pathways outside, arguably the most open of them all. In all the twenty or so years she'd spent alive, never before had she felt nerves like she did then.

Her heart-racing momentum was brought to a close, finally seeing the great chamber doorway she yearned to go through. It was open, much to her delight.

As she placed her soft and gentle touch against the handle, Lylith pushed herself through the tightly ajar gateway. Her eyes darted behind her. She scanned for any unwarranted presences eager to halt her escape.

Still clothed in her darkest daywear, she made for the twilight escape.

Two individuals, dressed in ragged clad, lurked within the shading just behind a nearby pillar. On edge, their eyes darted from side to side, where they stood quickly to attention upon seeing Lylith arrive. One reached for his jacket's inner pockets, unsure of who had found them. To their liking, it was only the faint emergence of their target. Lylith stepped forward and nodded at them politely.

"You must be my transporters?" Lylith coughed, shivering in the chilling shadows of her own home. One of them linked his arms through hers and shackled them together. Stepping out into the full view of the moonlit garden, they made their hurried dash towards the distant front gate, where a black truck waited for them.

"Just keep walking, your highness, we've not got the time to stand around and chat about-"

"Oi!" Cast with flames and fury, in came the boom of a lone guardsman's command. "Who the fuck are you, ey? State your busin-" He never finished. The second transporter reached into his pockets and drawing a silver handgun. He fired twice, straight into the guardsman's chest. Lylith's eyes widened, and she jumped back in a wild spring of fear. Once the second shot made its mark, the guardsman dropped onto the floor. He had crumbled a pool of his own flowing blood.

She stood motionless – as she felt the shooter's hand grab onto her arm and tugging her down the pathway, her breath became unsteady.

"What the – you fucking idiot, what the hell are you thinking?" The first escort was quick to the verbal draw. The gunman didn't say much and only made a dash for the truck. She tripped once or twice.

Her thoughts were swarmed on the fresh and alive playback of the crumbled corpse. Her breath was short, panicked and confused. The unfortunate witness, and the compromise of her deadly escape. A rush of blood went to taint her fair cheeks.

Soon after they'd started running, the shouts and sudden crescendo of a quick-reaction force could be heard. Lights sprang to life on the exterior walls of the palace, blinding the once silent garden with havoc. The three escapees didn't stop, despite the additional effort to drag a stunned Lylith.

"Focus, your highness!" One shouted, continuously looking behind him as several uniformed individuals scrambled out of the darkness. Some rushed to the side of their fallen comrade and hopelessly checked on his condition, whereas the others looked across the straight pavement, and loaded their rifles quickly.

From their point of view, all they could see was the prettily dressed Lylith being dragged away by two anonymous felons. They hesitated at first. Astonishment only clouded their judgement for a second until they took pursuit, firearms then unslung and raised to their eyes.

"Stop! Halt or we fire!" A second later came the bolt action rifle's blast in their direction.

 The first shot screamed far louder than her rescuers pistol had done, shattering what little tranquillity was left in the night. The bullet slammed into the pavement beside their boots mere metres from them, chiselling the stone with a harsh ping.

"Keep going! We're nearly there – look!" The hired escorts called out in a gruff panic. No longer was it a simple job gone wrong – they'd entered a political game of life and death, where their lives sat on the sharp end of the stick. Lylith felt their grasps tighten as they forced her to begin sprinting alongside them.

Birds were shaken from their nests as a second gunshot broke through. The man to Lylith's right began to decelerate. Her eyes met his as blood spewed from his chest and onto his shirt. He had been struck.

"Concentrate your aim! Do not hit Miss Redgrine!" Their pursuers commands grew louder as they gained momentum. Some of their pursuers would stop, line up a shot and pull the trigger, just to miss out of a fear of hitting the wrong target.

The first transporter had fallen. His brown, short buzzcut collided with the cobbles as he collapsed under his own agony. There was little to do. The image of spilt blood trickling between the cracks and gapes of brick burrowed into Lylith's head. She had witnessed death again.

In her silent mental suffering, the skirmish broke out further, with her surviving escort drawing his pistol and firing ferally back at the aggressive Guardsmen hot on their heels. The roar of an engine broke through the criminal ambience, and ahead of them a third and final man leant from the window of the now-clear truck.

Lylith didn't know how to react. She let out another squeal as the shots rained upon them.

Their bolt action weapons continued to spew rightful decadence towards her arranged crewman. Occasionally, a shot would come closer to her than it did her violent accomplice. Each time, she crossed her heart and hoped to never die.

Closer…it was so much closer. She could smell the fumes of the roaring engine ahead of them. Only a few more metres were left. Another shot sprang past them and punched a hole into the rear compartment of the truck. A clean circular reminder was left in its impact, telling Lylith's escort of the pure power he'd made a challenge to.

With a stroke of impure luck, they reached the vehicle. Another bullet soared past their heads. The escort wasn't hesitant to start lifting her inside the rear compartment, swiftly swinging its door open and almost tossing her inside with the strength of a lion. The change in urgency pained her knees as she fell, legs first, into the cabin's wooden floor. The escort didn't clamber in and instead focused on shutting her door and turning, letting off a few more shots from his handgun.

Across the door's viewport, a body slammed back against it, with blood trailing against it, and the bullet could be heard, failing to pierce the door. A dent came in its place, with his body having absorbed most of its impetus. Lylith screamed. She could hear the dead man crumble against the bumper, falling limb when a second following gunshot put him down, permanently. The life in his body was gone, leaving only Lylith and the driver left.

Hesitation be damned, and aware of his comrade's death, the driver kicked the vehicle into motion. Lylith shrieked at the sudden inertia that dragged her along the carriage's floor, hitting the very same door drenched in her ally's remains. The collision broke her spirit, and she coiled into a foetal curl to beg silently for the nightmare to end.

No more shots were heard, though. Only the squealing of wheels tearing down open roads, blasting through the streets and tearing down decrepit alleyways. The Capital's hospitality, was no more. They were left unobstructed with mostly empty streets ahead of them. In due time, they squealed onto the highway and sped off into the night.

Lylith remained in her infant posture, whispering to herself over and over.

"Please Stars, let this end. Let this end." She begged with clasped hands. Finally, she permitted herself to shed her pure misery and torment through streams on her cheeks. The driver didn't say a word. Neither had much else to say.

~~~

A precipitous flash and surge of heat burst above his head. Rhys could feel the mud flickering up onto his face. Stains tainted the skin on his ached arms, blending with the hog's blood beneath their slithering push forward. The heaving rain heavily weighed them down, burdening the militiamen with additional baggage. A succession of explosive clatter spewed lead just above their dangerous coating. Layers upon layers and lining upon lining of barbed wire narrowly rested atop of their pit, crowning their helmets with spiked metal thorns. It pushed each participant's head into the soil and pig's blood. The course intertwined with that of the firing range, where lifelike simulations of suppression narrowly soared over each militia squad's advance. Rhys kept his eyes focused onto the ground, using only the corners of his eyes to see ahead. He dared not to hesitate, knowing that his body would be open to scrutiny by his superiors, as if to make a sick example out of his audacity to expose weariness.

An officer's eyes began to burn into his back as he led the way. And just behind him, something new had caught the officer's attention.

Latched onto her sister like a doll, Ella cried out whilst Sabrina made sure to pull them both through. The past week of training had already broken her minimal confidence, bringing many disconcerting judgements upon Rhys' crumbling squad. Her pitiful yelps of anxiety were drowned out by the constant gunfire. Rhys turned his head over his shoulders, stopping for just a second to encourage his subordinate the best he could.

"Come on, just keep moving forward!" He tried to call, spitting out the flickers of earth still resting upon his lip. It tasted foul, like the sweet tongue of death had tempted his withering tongue.

"Here, El'. You aren't making it easy for me…" Sabrina, eyes locked onto the course ahead, dared not to look back and maintained her heading. And as her worries came true, the interception of an officer's articulation suppressed their chances of continuing free of trouble.

"Private Mistral, get a fucking move on! Move before I make you move." The officer leant close over the barbed wire. "Come on! Go! Let go of her you fucking child!"

The dictatorship of his iron-coated fist ensured they'd train, only out of the fear that they'd anger the beast inside the command chain. But it was for their betterment, they said, to experience the worst in training so that hell didn't seem so bad when they arrived. Breaking them was only the first step into making killers out of them.

Rhys wanted to tell Ella to just ignore him, to subside his remarks that were made to garner a reaction out of her, but the adrenaline of training pushed him onward. Instead, he kept quiet and made sure not to kick Sabrina in the jaw as she struggled closely behind.

He was among the first few to reach the end of the course. Drenched from head to toe in substances most filthy, the stench of the exercise set him aside, and he vomited into the nearest corner. One by one, the remainder of his squad began to emerge from the hellish pit.

Staring at his arms, Rhys eyed his newly stitched rank insignia. He again wondered how – under the world's torment – he'd landed a superior position over the likes of Christopher or Oslo.

Then he coughed up the last bits of his previous meal. And while he had been dumping his food into the soil, a tight fist approached Ella as she made it out alive. It grasped her by the arm and collar.

"What the fuck was that, Private?" The two sisters were separated by the brute that held her.

Both stood relatively attentive but for opposing reasons. Ella held her breath out of fear.

"This isn't a game; this is the process that decides whether you live or die. Learn to hold your own or you'll be catching blighters the moment you wake up! Are you as good as dead, Private Mistral?"

"N-no, Sir." She stammered out. Fear melted her gaze into a frantic panic. She looked everywhere but into the blazing irises of her superior.

"Say it louder! Scream it!"

"No, Sir!"

The fist unclenched from her collar and she staggered rearwards. Her natural retreat didn't save her from the next order.

"Twelve laps, both of you. I'll beat that shit-filled dependence out of you if it's the last thing I do. Go! Get out of my sight!"

Sabrina and Ella left upon his orders, with a dirty silence encompassing both of them. Within the blink of an eye, their drenched, stained bodies were lost in the sea of unfamiliar militiamen, charging out to compliment the disappointment on her. Rhys followed them with his eyes, sighing as they disappeared into the rainfall.

He stood back up straight with a bleeding heart. He wiped the vomit from his lips, only covered it in mud and grime.

He was pale faced and astounded by the absurdity they'd been through in a matter of days and weeks. Some seemed to take it better than others, with Oslo and Christopher sailing through the exercises rather excellently. Dynis and Tyran were neck and neck in their performance, whilst the rest of the squad gently lagged behind. It was almost as if transforming citizens into warriors was nigh impossible.

"Fucking hell, she'll be chewed up by the end of the week." Mateo's voice encroached the ambience of training recruits, rainfall and complaints from fatigued soldiers

With fogged glasses, he stared up towards Rhys and gave his back a pat down. Right after that, he wiped the muddied and bloody hand on his own cleaner backside.

"You think they'll actually discharge her?"

"Doubt it, Sabrina seems to be doing well, mate. Don't know about the other lady." Rhys sighed and collapsed onto a patch of grass to his right.

Five hours ago, the day's worth of training had started, and already they'd been pushed to their limits.

"Shit, I don't want to be *that guy*, but they're fucked. What if one of them caps it? Devastating, wouldn't it be?"

"Shut up…" Rhys panted and vomited off to the side. There, he sat in silence, watching with vested interest as the two souls struggled in their laps.

Chapter 6

The Mess Hall

An orchestral ensemble of struggled respiration, battered muscles and the groans of the aching flooded the mess hall. The room reeked of mud, sweat and blood. On one side, Rhys laid in his catatonic perdition, kept awake by the prickly sounds of darts piercing the target board nearby. Every sticky brow and coffee-tone soil – that coated the unclean uniforms – discharged the scent of discomfort and fatigue. Stenches like those were of commonplace. It was quite nostalgic; it wore the familiar whiff of his agricultural homestead in one dirtied aroma. Next to the troubled SNCO sat an unsurprisingly quietened Evelyn. Oslo was out – somewhere unknown – leaving him and a small pack with the duty of caretaking.

He hadn't truly been able to secure that sweet slumber he'd hoped for. Their trials and tribulations over the past weeks had blistered his feet and bludgeoned his will, making even the commodity of sleep a laborious task.

He eventually was rubbed on his arm as a shift grazed his right side. His sullied irises turned to Evelyn. She was already looking up at him with an unsettled insecurity.

"Are…you okay?" She stammered out her query to the half-awake SNCO beside her.

"Yeah, I'm fine." Rhys assured her as he rubbed his eyes. It was the first time they'd properly spoken. "Are you?"

"You looked a bit annoyed earlier today; are you angry at us?"

"What?"

"Are we disappointing you?"

Her woe came as a surprise. Any indication of irritancy had been absent for as far as he knew. He reassured her with a very faint smile – a bronze portico made to appear golden.

"Why would I be annoyed at you? You've all been showing me up." Though he tried, she immediately deflected his comforting words with but another harrowing question.

"Do we have to do this? I don't even want to be here. Do you?"

Blank and blunt – straight to the point – and she had the adult running amok his muse to gather his own stance.

A still infection of unpeaceful thoughts deluged his mind. Rhys remained mute. He still hadn't appropriately dwelled upon what he thought of his duty or the cruel bestowment of military conscription that dampened his ideals. Or had he? No, he knew his stance. It was all pointless; a coat over political incompetence. A need to do things caused by other people. Yet had he a choice? He never thought about what would've happened had the Ferusians came to his doorstep and if he had resumed sitting it out. Would they have shown the same sensibility?

Evelyn could've easily justified why she shouldn't have been anywhere near the military complex. Even by the laws of the nation, her conscription should never have been agreed upon. Vindictiveness of the state hadn't been fair nor kind to her. Yet, Rhys found it difficult to justify his malcontent in that moment.

"I..." Pause. Nothing came out of his mouth as he stared ahead, dumbfounded by his inability to find reason. "Well, I guess I don't *want* to be here, but maybe I have to. I don't know. Sometimes you don't have a choice. Guess it's best for me to do something for the country than to do everything for myself, right?"

Uncertain by his response, Evelyn looked away and nodded silently. She seemed unsatisfied, or just indifferent, to his answer. Instead, she hummed quietly to herself, leaving only the sounds of darts hitting the dartboard to levy the stillness.

Rhys was equally as uncertain. Barely anyone had questioned why a child like herself was there, sat amongst a group of men and women armed with rifles and grenades, as if she belonged there or was one of them. Fifteen years old. He'd learned how old she was through Oslo. Just shy of sixteen, and she'd been asked to participate in what adults protected her from.

But the sudden intrusion of another woman broke apart his thought-process.

"Budge up."

On his left, Gwendolyn – the squad medic – waltzed over to the seated pair and squeezed into Rhys' side. She was among the older three of the squad – a slave to her doctoring practice. She'd been occupied with the darts game, and her triumphant grin over her own miniature victory left an approaching Mateo scowling.

"What are you two talking about?" She asked. Rhys actually welcomed the questioning – it made a mess of the silence he'd created.

"She asked me if – well – I wanted to be here?"

"And?" Gwen smiled to herself, pressing onto his queasiness until he coughed up more of his empty words.

"Well, I'm not. I'm just unsure if that's irrelevant if, y'know…I have to be here?"

"I guess I can relate to that. It'd be a bit weird to say *I like war*, but mind you I'm a bit more fluent in duty than you might be."

The subtle brag irritated him but he let it slide. Nearby, in his own little corner, Mateo shifted his glasses across his sweat-stained nose, and wallowed in the spoils of defeat. To no surprise he'd lifted Rhys' spirits by showing a little inconsequential misfortune. Finally, he meandered over with his head hung low.

"*Fluent in duty*? Come off it, love, the bosses aren't here to give you a pay rise." He provoked her with a tenderised jab and stood beside their table. Before she could respond, he took attention to Rhys instead. "How's things been in the highchair?"

"I feel as if I've been shot and stitched back together." They shared a small titter between two lads, whilst Gwen kept her eyes fixated on the Corporal.

Evelyn started to hum. When Rhys looked over, he noticed her swirling, piddling patterns into a notepad, one he hadn't noticed before.

"Hey, what have you got there?"

At first, she didn't respond, continuing her tune to herself and gently swaying her head to the beat of her scribbles. Rhys peered over the top of her head as covertly as he could, taking a long moment to stare in awe at her artistic piece. Etched into the paper, her graphite scene was nearly complete. Two lines of standing bodies, carefully shaded to mimic a decadent night, stood in their rows and ranks. It took Rhys a few seconds to realise she'd been drawing a recent memory: rifle training. In the dead of night, the screams of gagged flashes and chambered cartridges still left a violent sting in their virgin ears. Some nights were met with indirect interruption, where other training militiamen would parade their gunfire all through until morn.

Rhys didn't sleep in the same quarters as his squadmates, instead being granted a slightly ostentatious homestead lavished in rich wood and thick concrete walls, and yet the sounds of the gunfire still found their way into the hallway. Worst still were the nearby tank training grounds, with marching mechs rumbling the core of the earth as they strode by his window.

He snapped back to the present. A little smile grew on him as he found himself locked on to the sketch.

"That's a very pretty drawing. Do you sketch often?" Rhys enquired.

A quiet nod gave him his answer, to which she looked back down onto her project. He was stranded in the ambience of the mess hall again. No words. At least he had something to watch.

Taking notice of the silence, Gwen poked him on the arm and struck yet another conversation up.

"I know you've probably been told this a lot but I didn't realise you were a farmer's boy. You don't exactly strike me as one, with that whole clean look you have going about you?"

"Clean...look?" He stared down at his clothing. Patches of dried-up mud and the withering state of his greased-up hair juxtaposed her...compliment? Wait, was that a compliment, he asked himself? Her snide lark, the curl of her aged lips, didn't quite land the confidence-booster he'd hoped for. "Uh, yeah. I am a farmer's son-"

"I'm from a farming bunch."

"Any siblings?" Her intrigue only grew the more he spoke about, his responses short and less flaunted than Mateo's personal soliloquys.

"Don't have any."

"None at all?"

"None."

There, the topic died for a few seconds, once again letting the familiar accomplice of silence sneak its way back between them.

Gwen twirled her hair. Rhys twiddled his thumbs. Evelyn turned her pencil. Mateo didn't do anything but gawk at nearby soldiers. Eventually, finding his inability to pass the time quickly, he forced a conversation out into the open.

"So, you were a Doctor, Gwen?" Mateo kept the life going.

"*Were*?" She raised an eyebrow.

"Well, you're not a practising professional anymore, are you?"

"You don't lose the title of 'Doctor' just because someone gives you a gun."

Rhys, intrigued to see where it would go, sat on the side-line and listened, partially reluctant to influence or expand its destructive influence.

"Why not? He isn't a farmer anymore. You aren't really a doctor anymore."

"That's-" He sniped her with a jovial prod.

"Doesn't matter, we're militiamen now. No need to flaunt a doctorate around."

"I'm not flaunting; I worked hard for my position and am continuing to do so. Everything that happens in my line of work will benefit my future, and hopefully other peoples', patients especially!"

Her plight was all too comedic for Rhys. He leaned back in his seat and gladly watched it like the stage plays of the capital. An all too entertaining distraction, if anything.

"Unless you get shot and killed. I mean that won't benefit your patients if you're dead." The shit-eating grin plastered on his face just kept growing and growing, and he was savouring every moment of it. "Live in the present, not the future."

The pettiness levels were beyond safe-measures. Each jab was met with his own little remark. He was on the attack, and he had no intention of easing off the trigger.

"Primarily, I'm a doctor, Mr Aviadro, and-"

"Corporal Aviadro, thank you."

"Shut up and let me talk!" Gwen caressed the bridge of her nose, sighing and muttering obscenities to herself. "*Corporal* Aviadro, I'm a doctor because I've devoted my life to it and earned the title, it's a weighty concordat that'll-"

"So, what, are you gonna show the Ferusians your little certificate? Tell 'em: *'You can't shoot me, I'm a doctor, not a soldier!'* Don't think they'll care, mate." Gwen opened her mouth, as if to say something. A single index finger pointed to the ceiling, waiting to wag it upon Mateo's condescending belittlement, yet no words left her gaping jaw.

"Are you two done?"

Rhys placed his voice between theirs and rubbed his eyes with a dry palm, all the while still clinging on to that faint smile. They were a disaster waiting to happen, but as long as it happened in those walls and not on the field, he felt no need to go too far in to stop it.

Most definitely, Mateo was aware of the pettiness at hand. He thrived in it.

"I'm done, boss man." He said.

"Whatever." She spoke.

An hour or so drifted by. Conversations were flat, slow or barely fuelled by drama. Rhys spent most of the time replaying previous training activities in his head, thinking about where the squad was headed in their transition into shields of Kelan's sovereignty.

In reality, only a few of its members stood any sort of fighting chance at that moment. There was a crack-set of shooting from Dynis, Oslo was a behemoth of a gunner, Christopher had some formalised training from elsewhere, Tyran sat within a mechanical harbinger of death and the rest fell short of soldiers.

Luckily, the war had only been seen on the high seas between both sparring nations, combing the watery graves they fought over. Small islandic atolls, archipelagos and nearby naval outposts had become playing fields for marine divisions to get at one another's throats. Control for the surrounding settlements and tiny landmasses continuously fell into the hands of the Ferusians, only to be contested once more by the Kelan navy. He'd heard in passing of the savage landings on those islands and how they'd claimed the lives in the hundreds, thousands even.

There was still talk of Hayana Atoll – a largely unrelated island mass far off the northern coastline. He'd seen the pictures of it, a somewhat tropical paradise compared to the grogginess left in Kelan's fields. To him, it had never mattered. But those days it became everyone's matter – vigils and prayers were said for those who lived there. It came up in strategic conversation almost daily. For a place he'd never see the light of, it was all so strange to have a location martyred.

They had said it was a courageous battle for the heavens. Pilots were shipped in and out of the area, taking off in aircraft Rhys had only read about. Skycarriers and occasional dreadnoughts rocketed above Fort Mullackaye, shuddering the world beneath them. All information regarding the war's progression was kept behind a lock and key. Lieutenant Galbraith was especially tight-lipped about the entire situation.

The dithered conspiracy of a premature end to the war left many militiamen to slack in their training and effectiveness. To them, the war wasn't going to land beside them. It'd remain far, out of sight and out of mind. No word on the naval situation had led many to believe the war was far smaller than initially predicted. A scrap, nonetheless.

Rhys eventually withdrew from his thoughts when he noticed Mateo frowning upon himself. He squeezed next to the seat his accomplices sat upon.

"Have any of you seen Stephan or Johan recently? They've kind of been distant from the group most days."

"Half of the squad is distant." Gwen muttered, folding her arms and tilting her head toward the floor. She closed both her eyes and tiredly mumbled. "Have any of you seen Captain Laskey? We're led to believe our Commanding Officer is our go-to director but I've never actually seen them."

"During our briefing, she was quite self-contained. Didn't say anything more than she needed to." He shrugged, compelled to at least provide some relevance to the discussion. "When I went to meet her, she spoke quite softly."

"So?"

"Well, I expected someone of her status to be a little more intense, I guess."

Conversations turned to whispering as the sound of rain-drenched boots crossed the void between the soldiers' tables. Rhys was caught into the rhythmic heartbeat of the shoes, and looked over to see familiar husks wandering idly through the vapid hall. Leading the pack was one Lieutenant Galbraith, followed only by a drowned-out Ella.

Intrigue piqued up Rhys' general interest, spying the pair as they passed their proximity. Donned in a leathery coat, drooping just below the knees, Galbraith kept one iron grip on his belt, whilst the other hand freely clenched, moving tables and chairs out of his way, regardless if they blocked Ella's path behind him. His hair had been kept dry by the sharply polished tip of his cap, accompanied by the glossiness of its brass badge at the helm of it all. And looped beneath his left arm, into the epilate and back onto itself, was another orange lanyard.

Ella was beyond colourful. Her enriched brightness had faded for a pale diminish, fading into the greys and whites of the concrete palette. A freshly extinguished flame emaciated in her distant stance; she'd melted and spilt into the floor. Her feet dragged beneath the weight of her clothing, submerged by the downpour outside. Eventually, the two separated. Galbraith pointed and mouthed something at her. Rhys imagined it was some sort of insult, or order, as she complied immediately, disappearing through the furthest doorway and back out into the open season of rainfall.

The soldiers' eyes met that of the lieutenant, who brutishly sauntered over with fumes leaving his nostrils. Rhys slowly moved aside and with one hand he grasped the rim of the table. Evelyn didn't look up from her drawing, whereas Gwen and Mateo quietened down.

When the devil finally arrived upon his doorstep, Rhys saluted the officer. The fear of error forced his sharp welcoming. Their eyes met somewhere in the middle of the vacuum left between them.

"Staff Sergeant, do you commonly check up on your subordinates?" Each word was carefully enunciated.

"W-well…"

"It's a simple question, Hendricks, do you regularly check up on your squad?"

"Yes, Sir." Rhys submitted to his interrogation.

The lieutenant took another step closer, bridging the gap left between them. Feeling his throat tighten, Rhys kept his mind on focusing his breathing and maintained a steady beat to the sound of his nerves.

"Well, you're making a shit job out of it, aren't you?" He spat. "Private Mistral can work wonders with a wrench but can barely keep up with the rest of you. See to it. Immediately."

The order sent a rugged chill down the staff sergeant's spine.

The lieutenant stormed off to go deal with something far ahead of Rhys. Sabrina was nowhere in sight. He looked to the triage at his rear and was returned a silent shrug.

There wasn't much choice in the matter. Rhys grabbed his things and said his temporary goodbyes to the three. All of them were in low mumbles.

He hurriedly strode to the hallways, circumnavigating the mess hall several times before finally settling at the exit. Through the glass he saw nothing but rain, fog and the passing bodies of drowned-out figures. The unfamiliar soldiers, all from similar backgrounds, towns, careers and imprisonment had faded into one silhouette. Uniforms and masks, glasses and goggles. Rifles and slings, training grenades and webbings. The fatigues and the coats, the drabs and the camouflage.

Duty called. He gently opened the door and stepped into the swampy concrete marsh. Showers of an unending swarm laboured his dance through the rain. His woollen fatigues were encumbered as they soaked up every little drop. He trudged through Mullackaye's open fields of stone, glass and metal. There wasn't so much a sense of direction – but he laid his bets on one place she'd have ended up at. A safe guess, at least.

Purgatory housed his weary body. Only the sound of the wind occupied the blackened space. He walked; his webbing was slung around his body. *Click-clack.* The sound of a soldier's bolt. Not his. A hydraulic wheeze came from his right, far into the summer showers.

By then, he was just killing time and delaying the inevitable responsibility of talking with Ella. He knew as much about her as he did the others. She was a fair woman, beautiful even – for lack of a poetic description. But she was an enigma locked behind Sabrina.

At last, he crossed paths with the regimental warehouse. The sound of sparks and mechanics inside was all but hopeful. Quickly, he darted inside.

Straying inside the metallic lion's den barraged Rhys with the clattering of hammers to nails and welders to steel. At the far end of the warehouse, a customary behemoth awaited him.

Four gargantuan limbs stretched from its armoured base. Flattened surfaces, in a brutalist, angular design, littered the surface of the walker. Its coat was a little scratched but all-in-all it was quite spotless. He saw spots of drying paint, freshly dressed on its colder areas.

Sat atop of its artificial body was the finishing touch, bringing it all together. 94_{mm} of raw, cylindrical power. Nine centimetres of harrowing steel, tungsten and aggression. It was as close to the doctrine of strength as he'd ever come. And it was impressive, albeit a little daunting. Besides its main cannon were a pair of coaxial $7.62x51_{mm}$ medium machineguns. He only knew this because of the handcrafted inscription painted onto the side of each gun's receiver.

By one of the iron feet, a frail engineer worked busily on an open panel she'd made. Rhys looked at her from afar, cautiously making his way over to her. At first it was hard to really tell if it *was* Ella. There was an aura of confidence as she knew what she was doing with full control.

He soon found himself stood only two metres behind her. She chipped away at a small handle, humming silently to herself in a watered-down state of comfort. The world around her had been blanked out. He peered over her grime-stained shoulder and noticed her soldering a gap between two metallic components.

If asked, Rhys wouldn't have been able to explain what she was doing. Everything that wasn't a tractor was beyond his expertise, and even then, he wasn't much of a mechanic to begin with. The soaked woman worked through the crevices, curling her petite fingers between the piping and wires.

Delicacy ran through her touch whilst she patted its iron shell. She wiped her eyes with her sleeve, and dyed her left cheek with another layer of grime, besides what she had already washed off in the rain.

Ella manoeuvred her way out of the open compartment, exposing herself to the chilling atmosphere of the warehouse. In her short break, she let her breath tremble whilst her fingers sank into the fabrics of her shirt. Crossed legs and an arched back gave her a low profile, and she embraced herself.

In his silent saunter, Rhys staggered in place, sending a signal to Ella with the wave of a hand. She caught sight of the shadow, turned around and jumped in place. She spun and staggered back onto her weakened feet.

"Sorry, I...I didn't see you there." Her words ran dry of vigour. A drought of energy was still stripped from her ownership. The days had taken their toll on her.

When she faced him, Rhys got a clear glimpse of the fatigue in her eyes, the redness of their bloodshot state. Black rings trod around her eyelids and an inability to properly stretch her fingers as she, rather awkwardly, chose to reach out and shake his hand. He took it with hesitance, and she retracted it soon after.

"Can I sit?" She huffed, and he immediately granted her the need.

"Holy shit, what did they do to you?"

Genuine surprise had him at a loss of formality. He took a knee off to her side, and tilted his head to peer at her battered face.

"It's...fine." She stammered.

"No, like – fuck, you're not okay."

"No, it's...just tiredness." Her insistence left him at a bit of an impasse. Had he known her better, he would've dug into her state with compassion. However, the strangerhood he felt held his tongue back.

The pain lingering across her body was unimaginable. He could assuredly say he had handled awful days of harvest, but never had he been pushed to such limits out of punishment. The voice of his thoughts sank. If one thing was clear, he pitied her state.

Neither said a word, not for a short while. He simply listened to the sound of her struggle. He offered her his canteen and she immediately emptied it into her system.

He didn't know if it was willpower, stupidity or the anxiety of disappointing her peers that had kept her working, even after all she'd been through that day. When he saw her eyes go back to the vehicle, time and time again, he spoke up.

"What are you working on?"

"Just..." Ella began her sentence before lifting her head back up to meet his. "-making sure its not falling apart, I guess."

"You can tell when it is?"

"You get used to the smaller details when you sit with them a long time." Half-heartedly, she turned back to the machine, and nodded at its cleanliness. She took another deep breath, and cleared her words. "This one is ours – or Tyran's."

"And you keep it all in shape?"

"The guy drives it and I repair it." She pulled herself closer towards it. "I really…like it, I guess, compared to the things they let me practice with."

Suddenly, the passionate endorsement of the vehicle gave her that little burst of energy. She was compelled to talk. It eased her and completed the confidence she so heavily distanced from.

The depths of her thoughts were brought into the spotlight. The energy she'd garnered was spent on breaking herself back down, ransacking that confidence she'd detracted. Her breath was unsteady and the colour of her eyes greyed in favour of the egregious place she was in. She looked at Rhys. He looked back at her. And from her lips trailed a soft voice.

"Am I going to die here?"

A ghastly clutch compressed his heart. The agony of her words, trembled by her fears, tore his confidence. He couldn't answer at first and his mind raced through a hundred thoughts.

What brought upon her existential dread was unprecedented. They hadn't seen combat, yet the news of death and of violence on the horizon did little to settle her nerves. How many had died so far? There were battles across the sea. And to her, and lingering on Rhys' mind, what would happen once the seas had been conquered? Kelan sounded as if it had no intention of rolling over. The crown played for keeps. And by lord, by saviour and by king, there would be blood.

Her eyes had been kissed by defeat weeks into her new life. Agonising mornings progressed into oppressive evenings. Someday, it felt as if the Ferusian military would make its daring attempt spearhead into Kelan. Their hopes to tear the monarchy apart and to brutalise any soldier that stood between them perpetuated the fear of the people.

Ella was never going to survive that. Neither would he. They were faceless pawns on the tips of the player's pinch. He'd told himself, like the words of his battered father, that he was at the will of the hierarchs. His life was a millimetre in a mile. Everything he amounted to was nothing. And as a soldier, he'd live and die as one, short-lived and sanctioned without the grace of the stars. He would be buried as an unnamed victim in a graveyard for demons. And angels like Ella weren't spared. She was a gunsight waiting to be acted upon. Begging to the sky,

Rhys whispered a hoarse prayer to himself. They would die. They would die horribly, or quickly, or suddenly without even realising it. No one would know. And those who did would eventually die too. She asked if she was going to die, and he knew that deep down they stood no chance. So, he opened his mouth and uttered the best he could.

"You'll make it through."

A lie.

Chapter 7

Heaven's Platoon

Orders were rare, scarce and infrequent. Days had dragged on without any assignments, leaving laboured soldiers alone in the dirt to gather dust. Regular exercising was maintained at an irregular pace. Momentary bliss had trailed off, sparsely disintegrating into distant memories, and the days moved on with a distinct lack of meaning. Upon the completion of their training, the militiamen received no ceremonious satisfaction. There was no fanfare or parade. There was equally no deterrence from hard labour. Warehouses needed to be kept in check. Walkers needed to be maintained. Routines of intense physical exercise were forced upon Squad 2. The 54th Defensive Regiment continued their days as if they'd never graduated.

And then, on a rather fetching morning, the sun had decided to expose itself from behind the infinite tide of rainclouds and sadness. To celebrate, an order finally came through.

It wasn't anything special. Previous weeks had seen them leave the base only for the means of walker test-driving and formation training in the nearby hills. That time, however, things were to be a little different.

Farhawl lit up, shining its tentative beacon to the heavens above. Those cast underneath it were glad to have left the walls for a while, even if for a few hours.

And when the sun came out that morning, the spirits of Squad 2 were lifted along the horizon's shift. A collective sigh spread like wildfire, and it was one of relief. Captain Laskey's words were clear: move across the designated pathway, ensure things were as they always had been and to then report the lack of activity as every other patrol would have.

Some members had overslept, whilst others laid fatigued and restless, unable to defeat the adrenaline-high caused by relentless training. Mateo was out cold when Rhys first rounded up his subordinates. He was curled in his thin bedsheets, his body tangled around the rusted springs of his mattress. Not too far from him, Christopher sat slathering his boots in polish, Stephan coated his helmet with a thin net-veil and Johan smoked a cigarette just outside. A sense of undefeatable normalcy. Ever the static hour, Rhys thought, and ever the static day.

Despite their grogginess, the morning itself was dazzling, decorated with a shining example of Kelan's natural beauty. The fatigue of a few men dared not to blister its glorious atmosphere. Meadows of roses, daisies and dandelions stretched further than the horizon. Hills concealed hamlets, rural communities and humble towns that were scattered far and wide. Windmills perched themselves atop of the highest grass-peaks. Across the highways of wind, gliding over the overbearing whiff of flora, the birds soared in synchronisation.

A genuine smile arrived on Rhys' face. For just a day, he thought it was going to be a wonderful highlight of their lifeless occupation.

His gaze was plastered onto the clouds above. Whilst the remainder of the squad worked on moving the walker to their starting point, Rhys took in the views and filled his lungs with a homely freshness.

Home had never felt so close as it did that day. The sky moulded and shaped itself, mimicking the reaches above the abode he'd hailed from. Like everyone else, he missed home. Warm beds, wood-fuelled fireplaces and wardrobes containing years of memories within, all far away. Squealing kettles, shutters opening and closing in the autumn wind and the final wavering of grass frolicking in the gales weren't easily replicated anywhere else. Throughout the entire Kingdom, no place would ever be a suitable replacement for home.

Then again, the separation from his parents did bear some of its own fruits; there was a bittersweet relief knowing he didn't have to witness his father's common breakdowns. Cruel, maybe, but ultimately something he couldn't stay exposed to. The alcohol itself was already enough.

Pebbles strewn across the cobbled pavement began to shudder as a behemoth approached with a violent tremble. He turned around and eyed the steel stallion that ambled towards him. Around it, his squad were in escort, though Evelyn and Stephan were perched atop of the tank.

Cracks in the concrete floor were widened by each step. The artificial toes carved into the soil with ease.

He stood aside and let Tyran pilot the beast past him. His smile faded once the squad passed him. Some went off to the side to finish the last remaining drags of tobacco.

Nearby, a synchronised stomp of boots and raising hands caught his Rhys' attention. The sea of soldiers parted to present a golden pathway for the central figure.

A certain Captain Laskey moved through towards Rhys with a parade staff tucked beneath her left armpit. He attentively fixed his posture and gave her the appropriate salute.

"At ease, Staff Sergeant." She sort of grumbled out her words: half-awake, half-asleep.

She took off one of her pearly-white parade gloves. Her eyes were shielded by an olive peaked cap, circled with golden stitching and crimson lacing. The tip was drowned in such a slather of polish that it shone a reflective ray straight back into Rhys' eyes. The second glove was harshly torn from her other hand, before both garments were tucked into an in-jacket breast pocket.

Rhys paused, lowered his stance and eased his shoulders back as she wordlessly tweaked her dressing. Seconds ticked by. Laskey took her own time focusing on the nitty details of her jacket, the rotation of a brass button or the excess thread that had come loose. His patience wore thin and he politely prompted a return to conversation.

"Ma'am?"

"Came to see your lot off." She immediately sprang back to life and honed onto his eyes. "Well, and to inform you of a small development to not overlook."

"Ma'am?"

"You might have heard this already from looser lips: last night two Ferusian reconnaissance aircraft were reported to have passed over Mullackaye's local area."

"I hadn't heard."

"Well, we scrambled someone to intercept it." The Captain mimicked the whirling path of a fighter as she pointed upward. Her tone was as close to formality as it could be. Informative, concise and commanding. Each word left her mouth with every even syllable enunciated greatly. "We don't know what they were doing, or if it was looking for targets of significant value. Not much of a direct threat, but all patrols from here onward are going to be looking for anything suspicious. We fear that maybe our Kingdom's back-lands could house Syndicalist instruments."

"Anything specific to keep an eye out for, Ma'am?"

"Drops, mainly. Anything out of the ordinary. Find it and bag it. We'll take the situation as it comes."

"Yes, Ma'am." The two saluted one another and closed the conversation. Laskey returned to her sawdust-scented office. The squad were left to fulfil their orders at once.

Seconds after the Captain disappeared back into the walls, Rhys gave the order to move forward with a moderate yell. The ravenous churning of inner hydraulics, the sparks of wires and the excess exhaust filled the air as their walker was brought back to life. And under the heat, they set off.

Twenty minutes passed without a titch. Evelyn hummed her usual tune to herself as she struggled to maintain her grip on the metal giant. Rhys remained at the rear at first to make headcounts over and over again – a passive entertainment for the first two miles.

Tamara, the blonde lass from Johan's hometown, begrudgingly carried the squad's radio-pack. She silently complained about its unwieldy ergonomics and how it reduced her ability to function. But someone needed to haul it around, and she'd drawn the short straw.

Eventually, Rhys marched his way up to the front, standing near an unfazed Christopher, weathering the heat as if it were just an aesthetic difference to the day. Rather interestingly, Rhys noticed that his eyes would lock onto the trees, roadsides, ditches, hilltops and buildings they passed on their journey – every one of them, in fact. No detail went unnoticed, and he silently mouthed off the scenery to himself.

Mateo opened up conversation as he always did. The usual small talk came to light and, for what felt like the first time ever, they were all talking to one another.

"You were a police cadet? Got any stories from the academy?"

"Medical degree? I mean, at least you're certified."

"Y'think she lied about her age?"

"Wish they gave me a lighter gun."

"By the stars, Galbraith is a real bastard, isn't he?"

"As far as things are going, I'm sure it can't last that much longer."

The last phrase was brought forward by Sabrina. The optimist confidently smiled, both to herself and her sister. She was almost sure of it. Maybe. For once, Rhys made the attempt to challenge it with a friendly intrusion.

"How can you be so sure?"

"Call it a hunch." As he looked back at her, she winked at him. Wait, did she? He was sure of it. A little sprouting of embarrassment went to his head, and he looked away as Sabrina chuckled to herself.

All around them were the breathtaking, sun-kissed valleys of green and beige. Wheat fields scattered across the bases of hills, small huts watched over them from afar and the broken fences and stone walls narrowed down their path. Every metre they travelled was accompanied by the thunderous trudge the walker made.

Every so often, civilians – who'd so far avoided conscription – wandered on the same trail they did, passed by and said the traditional greetings: the "good mornings" and the occasional praise for the serviceman. Some felt their appraisal lift their spirits. It was a good reminder to them that they had the whole country's weight resting on their shoulders. Though, Rhys still struggled to take their compliments in any other way than a kick in the teeth.

Their admirations for the soldiers were more akin to a 'thank the stars that's not me'. The queen's brush had left them largely ignored that early into the war. They had their way, and they could proudly stay in the purple-veil that they saw their nation through. Complete loyalty, only until its troubles landed on them.

His mind raced back to the start – the day where he was conscripted. The crying father and confused son. He was in no position to love what surrounded him. To him, it was destructive to the wellbeing of the citizens, for if he left the military with a clean slate, the emotional pain he went through was enough to create a pound of bitterness.

There wasn't an inch of him that didn't doubt the legitimacy of his cause. To protect Kelan – that was what the badge of honour said, in plain text. The weak, the troubled, the helpless and the innocent. They all fell under the shielded umbrella held above their heads. Yet there was a child among their ranks, and barely anyone batted an eye.

But as all things lay, there was no room to think all about that stuff. It hesitated him. They'd hammered on for hours in training how the good soldier didn't hesitate to do the right thing. Problem was, he was so caught up in what was right that he couldn't focused one bit.

At the sun's peak, the blistering heat showered down on them in full effect. Johan stripped most of his gear off and lugged it onto the back of the walker, next to Evelyn. Oslo removed his jacket and laced it around his bag. Dynis and Tamara waltzed in the shade whenever it became available, no matter how little it was. Sun-drenched buttercups illuminated the adjacent moors, highlighting beauties of the world beside them. In the distance, a hilltop windmill sat in isolation, rundown and abandoned from what looked like years of industrialisation on the horizon. Fort Mullackaye was just visible through the trees. It was a quiet place to face the trial.

On the side of the dirty road, they stopped to rest. Most of the squad sat beneath the tank and basked in the shade. They'd started their patrol several hours before and it was the first chance they had at a rest.

"Fuck me, it's hot…" Johan groaned out the obvious. He removed his helmet and wiped a waterfall of sweat from his brow. Rhys remained up and about. He'd circle the tank and stand on a small knoll beside them, overlooking the uncut grass beyond. The landscape had likely been left untouched for years. A stench of nearby manure was made only more potent by the blend of shit and sun.

Rhys largely ignored the happenings of the squad behind him, their fumbling around with the walker and attempts to beg Tyran into letting them use the tanks interior fan. None of it concerned him. The monotonous continuation of the day had brought nothing but unwell thoughts and speculation on the future that laid before them. He looked down to his firearm, eyeing its wooden and metallic base, before instinctively checking that the safety catch was still on.

Muggy temperatures had begun to leave him mindless. He turned around at the sound of Mateo standing up to make his way over. On arrival, a quick pat on the back snapped Rhys' full attention back to the day.

"Mate, I'm going to take a piss. You need one?" Mateo's question took a short second to process, before a little grin crept up.

"Uh – no."

"Come anyway, rather not piss on my own."

He was dragged off by the sweaty palms. Together, they waded through the thick sea of greenery. Each glades' piercing top blades reached just above their stomachs. Both wavered further until they were at an acceptable distance to relieve their bladders.

Mateo unbuckled his belt and faced the other way, sinking into the taller grass far more than his taller Staff Sergeant. Nature was his natural censorship bar, blocking out what little Rhys wished not to see.

"You've been pretty quiet today, huh?" He stood – still waiting for that first golden stream to arrive – and yawned quietly to himself. "Something on your mind?"

"Nothing in particular." Mateo gave him the look of complete disbelief. "Tired, mainly. Missing home quite a bit."

"Nothing new then."

Then, the heavens let up, and out came Midas' Waterfall. He waited for an uncomfortably long time as the sound of soil being moistened dragged on. However, and rather peculiarly, something broke the regularity of one's release.

The stream made contact with something other than soil. Unbelievably to even himself, Rhys eagerly listened to Mateo's piss right as he pinpointed the sound of metal. The garden-hose paid no attention to it. And as he finished, he tightened back up his belt, giving Rhys the opportunity to cautiously make his move.

"Hold up."

He moved the smaller Corporal aside. He leaned down to take a look, but was barricaded by the piss-stained blades blocking his way.

"Aye, what the fuck are you doing?"

"Gloves?" Rhys snapped.

"What-"

"You got a pair of gloves I can quickly borrow?"

"What for?"

"Mateo."

"Fine! Fine." He patted himself down, fiddling with his pockets until he came across the garments. Rhys swiped it from his hand and put them on. "Mate, are you going mad?"

Rhys tore through the grass until he stumbled across something small. A box – with handles. He fiddled around its soaked edges carefully, latched onto one of the handles and gently raised it from the amber ocean it'd drowned in. Beneath the coating, a forest-tone aluminium shell protected, opaque and dull.

"I don't want those gloves back…" He nudged Rhys and stepped a little bit away from the stench of his own urine. Both continued to eye up the box, albeit with one a bit more distanced.

Three out of the cuboid's six rectangular faces were devoid of any markings. Dull, bland and featureless; only the occasional screw that they couldn't tear apart. On either of its sides, two long wires stemmed out of its body, and following it led to an identical box roughly two metres away. Rhys moved with the wires for a minute, noticing a small curve in their positioning, indicating a continuous circle of them neatly formed in the field. On the top face of each box sat a large glass bulb cased within little iron struts, not too dissimilar to alert beacons in the Fort. All of them appeared to be off.

He ditched the soaked box for one of the cleaner. After staring at it for another few seconds, he raised it to his ear and shook it. Nothing. There wasn't a rattle or a squeak from inside.

"You think it's just farming gear, or something?" Mateo asked.

"Out here?" He searched around him and saw nothing except the messy patches of tall grass and overgrown shrubberies off in the distance. The half-broken windmill off on the connected hill did little to bring life to the scene. "I have a hunch that this isn't farming land."

"And so, what are you thinking it is?"

"No clue. But Laskey mentioned something before coming out here about reporting anything out of the ordinary." He felt around the second box. Its shape wasn't quite the same. A few ridges were on the underside, as well as what looked like a panel. "You want to go radio it in?"

Mateo gave a slight nod and took off back to the knoll. Meanwhile, Rhys continued to analyse the box, taking more interest at the rear-end's panel.

There was no source of power, at least no clear sign of one. And after careful consideration, he took off the gloves, dumped them into the soil and pried at the hatch with a dirty fingernail. After a bit of fiddling, he hatched it open. A small indent into the body revealed a little tin switch with a factory new shine to it.

Rhys peered behind him. No one else was there. Curiosity started to get the better of him. He gave the box a few more look overs before he took the plunge for discovery. He flicked the switch.

For a few seconds, there was no change. He lifted it to his head again to listen inside when he felt it. A whirr. It was spooling up a shudder. Intermittent trembles spread to the other boxes and a low hum took to the sky. They gradually got louder and shook more aggressively. The hum became a whine, and then a bellow.

In a panic, Rhys staggered away and turned. The curse of surprise had him by the throat, where he anticipated the worst: for a fireball to engulf him on the spot. The rest of the squad emerged over the knoll, and witnessed him dash back in his retreat.

His heart raced as he clambered over the dirt mound and slid down the other end. Instinctively, they mimicked his sudden fright and pressed their backs to the soil hill. He could feel it. Imminent detonation. The warning call kept on crying, louder and louder until-

Nothing.

There was no explosion – no violent, thunderous clap tearing through the peaceful landscape. The earth didn't shudder. It retained its summertime slumber. A minute passed. The distant sound of the vibrating boxes faded and they all sat there, silently waiting for someone to make sense out of the fuss.

Confused, Rhys lifted his head from beneath his arms and rose over the peak to assess the situation.

A luminous light show had been set off. It scattered across the field, covering the grasslands in an overbearing smog of crimson flares. Each box flashed, and then sparked out the blood-tone circle. The drowsy sensation came over Rhys as he watched the signal flares bring the field to life. The smell hit them next – the scent of searing metal and grass being turned to ash.

He watched as the grass progressively fell victim to the heat of the flares. A solar torment from the sky and boxed signals lit up the beginning of a devastating spree. Mateo crawled up to the top of the mound and laid next to him.

"What the fuck did you do?" An unsure Mateo started with a chuckle, before breaking out into full-blown laughter.

A new form of panic settled into his chest. Acting fast, he slid down the mound and landed beside Tamara. He expected to grab the phone to the radiopack from her, but was surprised to see it absent from her back.

"Where's the fucking radio?"

"I gave it to Ryan."

"Without telling me? Stars' sake – Ryan!"

"Here!" He hailed Rhys with the wave of a hand. He stood atop of the tank. His attention was caught in the spectacle – the slow spread of flames scorched the tall grass patch by patch.

All the while, the guilt was settling in. Rhys scurried to his feet and ran for the walker. At the top, he was presented with a view of the flare's workings. Right in the centre sat a ring of twenty brightened signals – and they spoke with their cultist chant as they set the world ablaze. It still hadn't spread that far. There was good time left. He ran his eyes across the field and sought out a rough estimation of where the fire could rage onto.

"Here, take it."

Flat in his palm, Ryan held out the telephone connected to the radio. Rhys grabbed it – though in the stress he'd been intoxicated with, he dropped it at first – and, when firmly in his grip, he placed it to his ear and mouth. With the other hand, he twisted a few dials until the right channel was set.

"MC-11, this is DR-54-0402 – uh, message request, over?" Then came the short wait. A few seconds felt like a couple of hours. The radio spoke in static and left him to bear witness to the countryside's infernal rape. Rhys looked at Ryan, who had his gaze locked on toward the windmill. He paused, uncertain if something had caught his eye, and he spoke to Rhys.

"Hey, Rhys. I think I just-"

But he never finished his sentence. His voice was cut off by the surprising screech of a gunshot. All Rhys could hear after was the sound of his own scream.

Ryan's head had jolted backwards; a red mist exited the front and rear of his skull. The bullet had torn through both steel and bone and left its mark with a gaping hole in his temple. The anointed corpse was dumped into the dirt.

The radio fell back onto the top of the tank. Rhys stepped back, overwhelmed in shock, and tumbled off the edge of the walker.

Ruthlessly, Ryan's body smothered the grass below and a sudden shriek of fear responded to his fall. The clatter of rifles scrambling to their soldier's hands, conscripts pushing themselves away from the disgusting mess of the carcass and bellows of confusion encored the firearm's shot. Rhys' head slammed against the dirt path. His helmet soaked up most of the impact but rattled his skull. He'd hit the ground just after Ryan did, with the harsh impact having shoved the air out of his lungs. A hand reached out for his boots and it dragged him across the soil to cover.

As he was pulled beneath the walker, he caught another glimpse of the wounded earth, showered in a stream of Ryan's blood; and above them, the heavy smoke took to the winds. Ryan's eyes were permanently locked open and they stared straight into his squad leader's soul.

Seconds later, another shot rang out, that time slamming directly into the side of the tank. Soon, an entire orchestra of gunshots blasted in their direction. Bullets rattled against the tank's sides. The squad kicked themselves away from the metal beast and dug themselves into the side of the mound. Tyran disappeared into the cockpit, shielding himself from the wave of lead headed their way.

Someone quickly dragged Ryan's fresh cadaver to the pile of dirt and distanced it from the rest of the group. Gwen moved over to the body by impulse and promptly ran her hands across his body to check for some form of response. She knew he was dead.

Everyone knew he was dead, but the absurd abruptness of the kill had the immediate denial settle in first.

Tyran moved the tank. Its legs came back to life as it stepped away from the infantry. Several other members of the squad crowded around Ryan more so out of a need to confirm the horror was real.

Everyone's hearts were frozen. And those familiar in death made it their duty to make the first response.

Oslo hastily set Evelyn down in Ella's arms before he made a daring dash to the left. He didn't say a word; he just acted. His machine gun was tightly in his grasp. Time stood still for the rest as he rushed for a ditch some ten metres from the rest. In the motion, a few deliberate bullets came his way and narrowly missed his body and legs by mere centimetres. He dropped into the ditch and disappeared within. Christopher soon after gave the first order.

"Spread out, move across the mound. Don't bunch up!" A minute into the scourge, he'd found his own footing and micromanaged the squad across the tiny ridge, one by one. The walker shook the dirt path violently. It jolted, swivelling its turret in several directions, trying to find the origin of their aggressor. "Rhys, come on, where did the shooting come from?"

But Rhys' mind wasn't with the rest of the squad. Hell had snagged his eyes and placed them in front of a rancid display. His mind had been scratched up – the broken record replayed back the same scene over and over again. The splitting of Ryan's skull, the cutaway of his words and the shattering pierce of his helmet; each droplet of blood that sprinkled onto his face could be felt each over. And it was so sudden. Laughter had turned into screaming, a fear for the arrival of Death's little arrows.

He had been there, a figure that scarcely blended into the crowd of unworthy soldiers, then he wasn't. And yet there he lay in front of him, clearly still: broken and fallen, devastated and destroyed. His life had been stripped in an instant, a ripple had moved through the squad's morale. There was no more Ryan Richards – there was a dissected, inanimate thing that sank into the dry dirt beside a sea of flames. The smoke thickened, but Rhys still saw the body as clear as day.

Two tight fists wrapped around his webbing and shook him. Christopher had him by the shirt.

"Where are the shots coming from?" None of the squad dared to poke their heads from behind their cover. The suppression had them pinned.

"I think...the windmill...?" He stammered. "I think they're at the windmill!"

Christopher repeated the callout down the line, with each third person passing the message onward. Rhys kept his stance low and crawled across the floor. His left hand was soaked in someone else's blood.

Finally, the callout reached the walker. Sounds of gears churning from inside the machine spoke for the pilot; the turret angled itself to the crude structure. Distant muzzle flashes were made out from within the broken architecture, and several unclear bodies had moved out the door, to spread their effective fire. Part of the hill had been clouded by the grassfire that persisted.

Rhys faced Christopher, still short of breath, and tried to piece together his next directive.

"When..." A gasp left his mouth. Rhys struggled to level his breathing. It was taking more than a second to recuperate his mind. "When Tyran starts shooting, give it five seconds and then start shooting back."

He crawled across the dirt toward an on-edge Dynis. In his hands, he adjusted his optics with an unsteady grip, trembled by the moment's havoc.

"Dynis, when they start shooting, I want you to run to the other side of the road and find some sort of cover. Get a good line of sight and...just try to fire back."

The marksman doubtfully nodded, psyched himself up with heavy respiration and braced himself with a squat. It was to be a short rush across the road. The fire from the windmill persisted, crashing against Tyran's armour whilst the interior mechanisms loaded the first round.

Strained by the uneasiness of the situation, Rhys' lungs had been crushed by the weight of the fight. A life had been claimed and all he had to do was to make sure no one else died. It was simple. So simple. Treating it like a game, however, did little to comfort him. How he would do so was based on blind luck, making calls and recollections of old strategic training to piece together a crude plan of action. It wasn't a simulation, there was no Lieutenant Galbraith barking orders at them. The fate of their own future was upon their own shoulders, starting with Rhys' first official order.

And it all felt so unnatural. Ordering men and women to kill on command, never before had Rhys felt such inner contempt for the directionless circumstances he'd been forced into. He didn't choose that and he had never asked for it.

Everyone got into position but had the full-heart of an insect when it came to bravery. A highly concentrated level of fire barred squad from Oslo's ditch, Rhys waved his hands towards the tank, giving Tyran permission to reap what their attackers had sown.

Its interior ammunition belt was cocked by the charging bolt and – after a brief pause – he hammered his thumb down onto the trigger. Greater than any gunshot he'd heard before, the thump of its coaxial armament returned a vulgar package. Each shot sent a small shockwave through the air, rattling Rhys' chest and the stones on the floor.

Five.

Immediately, the pressure was taken away from the rest of the squad. Heads were pinned down and the exchange of gunfire had become a one-sided practice.

Four.

Whoever had opened fire on them had made a critical error. The tank was in view the whole time – strategically speaking, it was suicidal of their opponent. What were they hoping to have achieved?

Three.

But they had caught them by surprise and had executed a youthful member of the squad. Turmoil raged between the windmill and the grass mounds. Under a scorched sunlight, the fumes of the flares stripped the field of its greenery, and fogged the air with a taste of fire.

Two.

Rhys clenched onto his weapon tightly. Beneath his uneven breathing, he whispered words of praise to any deity watching over them. Teeth began to chatter. Life slowed down to a crawl. Every second in combat could've been his last. The firefight had delivered him to a place he could have never been trained for: The Inferno. Conflagration. Torment. Death.

One.

With one final inhale, instinct took over his moral plight. He raised his voice and shouted at the top of his voice.

"Return fire!"

Rhys was the first to poke over the hillock – with his stock planted firmly below his shoulder and sights aligned to his eyes. He aimed at the windmill and, in a state of deliriousness, he willingly pulled the trigger with the intent to kill a man.

He was grasped by a powerful drive – a sensation that had been passed through many soldiers, for generations on end and forever more. It stemmed from no emotional origin, nor was it of any good or evil. It was recoil, and it rattled his shoulder blade with each shot he let off.

Seconds after he began his volley, Dynis had cleared his dash across the road, and Christopher, Oslo and Sabrina immediately followed Rhys' attack. Ella covered her eyes with Evelyn's helmet, who had also tucked herself into her breast. She dared not to look upon her sister's wrath. The two remained crumbled on the floor, whilst the rest emerged one by one into the fray, exposing their heads for the chance at blasting an enemy's own open.

For twenty seconds, the pounding of gunshots upon the windmill refused to let up. Every now and then, a head they couldn't make out would try to stand up, shifting its retreat back into the windmill for additional safety, only to be cut down by the squad's sheet of fire. Three bodies dropped. A few more were left standing, cowered behind old stone brick walls and within shallow ditches. From the top window, a figure appeared, lining his own heavy machine gun. Another crack came from behind: Dynis' marksmanship pierced the chest of the man, pushing the body back into the darkness of the mill's interior.

The click came next. The rifles had dumped their first magazines and they each took it in turn to disappear back into the knoll, swap out the boxes and to return back to their position.

Oslo maintained his separated position and fired in strict bursts across a wide area. Anyone who poked their head over became the next target for his bout. Rhys turned over to the side. A fizzle, blended into the cackle of the field's fire, caught his attention, and he looked back at the walker.

Atop of the tank were the dangling wires from where Ryan had fallen – the radio. Drowned out and indiscernible telegraphic voices called out to him.

Rhys made no attempt to hide his fear and took a second to refill his lungs. Then, he dashed forward towards the radio.

A poorly timed run had opened the window of opportunity to his adversaries, who showered him with five pot-shots. His heart skipped thirty-nine beats as the whizzing of aerial killers zipped straight past his body, some slamming into the walker, some making their way into the bushes behind.

Rhys lugged it from the tank's body and scrambled back to the knoll, miraculously unscathed.

"-ay again, send message, over." He brought the microphone to his mouth with haste, meeting the operator mid-conversation.

"Mullackaye Command, we are under attack from an unknown contact. Message: we are under small arms fire and have taken a casualty. Request assistance, over."

There were another few seconds of silence from the radio, its crackling struggle to receive a clear signal only hindered by the stress of the skirmish. He questioned its reliability in the heat of the moment until, at last, a voice returned on the speaker.

"DR-54-0402, this is MC-11, say again: you are currently under fire? What is your location, over?"

"MC-11, we are along our patrol pathway, probably about a mile away from...the town of Stanezlok, I think. You won't miss it. There's a big fire. We are being shot at by numerous contacts and are engaging with both our walker and firearms. Please advise, over."

He coughed to the side away from the microphone as the ashy stain in the air entered his throat. The taste of hell had made its mark on his tongue. The water in his eyes fried under the pulverising heat.

"DR-54-0402, this is MC-11. Cannot confirm your situation but will scramble the nearest patrol unit to your location. Continue your assault until assistance arrives. Out."

Rhys threw the phone down by his side and gasped for air. Every disaster had unfolded. And he heeded the words of his commanders without hope for an alternative.

Continue the Assault? He had no choice in the matter, really. At some point, one of the two parties were going to run out of ammunition and he hoped it wouldn't be his own. He measured the options he had and landed on exploiting their biggest advantages – superior firepower.

Through a quick second of tuning, he mobilised his wicked mind and jumped to the side of the tank, waving to Tyran.

"Use the main cannon on the windmill!" Unsure of where he was going with his own order, he looked back at the rest and waved them over. "Tamara, Mateo, Christopher, Sabrina and I will move on the windmill, everyone else will continue to fire at it. Let's go!"

Rhys could barely hear his own voice, drowned out by the unearthly demolition. His ears were flooded with the drowsiness of the foul, rotting air. An odour of death followed his flared nostrils wherever he looked. Truly, he wanted to get away from the dirt mound and away from Ryan's acrimonious end.

Tyran ignited the fuse and launched a devastating high-explosive shell right on target, sending a tremor of brick, dust and destruction across the ridge. It drilled through the front wall and churned through stone walls, detonating upon impact. Smoke and fire engulfed the interior for a split second. The sound of crumbling stone acted as their whistle, and with the support of the squad's gunfire Rhys took to his feet and made first into the breach.

Whilst circling the mound, he saw where Ella was collapsed in fear. His heart sank, and the confidence he felt was replaced with manic action. Don't think, he told himself, or else he might've slipped up.

Soaring traced-out warheads showered the mill, assuaging the Staff Sergeant's advance. Rhys led the charge through the grass, narrowly avoiding the patches engulfed in the flare's fire, Mateo and Sabrina stuck closest to his flanks whilst the other two spaced out further. His heart raced. It begged him to stop and he wanted to appease it. He wanted to cower. He wanted to cry. But he was out there, in the middle of it all, and the only way to push through the underworld was to reach the other side.

His mask of confidence was but a shuttle that could've led to a shallow, unfinished grave.

Time deluded Rhys whilst he rapidly sped forward at every step. Voices speaking in unknown tongues became louder as he led them to the base of the compound. Unpleasant fragrances rotted the air. He could taste the death. Dust and clouds of chiselled brick still intoxicated the atmosphere. Tyran fired a second shell into the windmill.

Its impact was felt at the base of the ridge. Rhys' ribs rattled beneath his webbing. He waited another second, before he made a move on the final ascent to victory or death.

Each step came as a blessing and a query as to how he'd made it so far.

The fire from the knoll-hidden squad ceased as to not accidentally injure the allies that scaled the crumbling structure. Finally, with their weapons raised and fingers resting on their triggers, they peaked the climb. Rhys was the first to reach the first stone wall, where he urgently peered over, expecting to see hell's knights pointing their swords toward him.

On his left, Tamara and Christopher pushed far more aggressively. They moved beyond the stone wall and rushed through the ditches. Rhys couldn't see the ones they'd stumbled upon, but he did see the pathfinder raise his rifle, letting off three consecutive shots. Soon after, Tamara followed him into the ditch, whilst Sabrina and Mateo resumed their levelled climb. He poked over the wall again and cautiously moved with his eyes lined up to the iron-sight.

Before he knew it, he was nearly at the door to the windmill. In front of it, stones laid crumbled on the floor. Somehow, he'd pushed the sights of the dead around him out of the way. The ignorance was blissful. He made it his best attempt to block all indications of reality from his mind. To him, Ryan wasn't truly dead. Ella wasn't actually crying. The windmill hadn't been blown up. Mateo hadn't pissed on a metal box. All of it was a lie, an experience to show his skill, his mettle and his leadership. It was a façade; nothing was real. And the people he shot at were nothing but target practice.

Reality slapped him once more as he approached the door; an unfamiliar figure emerged from the darkness of the entryway. There was no decision made, for that would require the time to think, to weigh out the options and to act accordingly to comparison. Rhys simply noticed the weapon in the man's hand, raised his barrel to him and fired his own.

The instant he pulled the trigger on another man was the moment he lost the ability to bury the horror under fiction.

Ejected shells clattered against the rocks and cobbled pathways. The silent collapse of his adversary came without a sound. There was no cry of pain, no scream, no yelp of sorts. It was just like Ryan: instant and silent. The bullets hit their mark and swiftly drained the soldier. Plasma soiled the doorway and gave it a fresh streak of red.

His rifle's fire laid around six panicked rounds into the emergent soldier. The body dropped and tumbled like a torn bag of potatoes, where he finally rested against the frame of the broken door.

Unable to face what he'd done, Rhys dragged himself to the side wall of the windmill, where he eyed only the dry spots of brick that didn't indicate his work. A tap on his shoulder broke his fixation. He saw Christopher holding out an object for him to grab. His heart clenched at its sight. A fragmentation grenade, pin still intact. There was no timeline Rhys could imagine throwing that to kill.

There definitely were a few battered and bruised survivors left stood inside the building. Their calls were barely audible from the outside.

Rhys looked away from the grenade and willingly swapping places with Christopher. He watched with gut-wrenching anxiety as the pathfinder pulled the pin, ready to prime its detonation. The smoke and dust from the tank shells still obscured the occupants. And their voices were croaked like toads. Had one of them understood the Ferusian tongue, perhaps they would have held their assault.

And the worst had yet to come. Christopher tossed the grenade inside. The clunk of a metal ball hitting the rocks and tables was responded by a scream. A shout came from inside. The final breath of the Ferusian menace.

The explosion ruptured the walls they stacked against. Peppering fragmentation could be heard scattering inside, tearing through furniture, rubble, body and floor. The windmill coughed dust out of the doorway. Christopher was the first to go inside, followed by Mateo and Tamara. Rhys didn't follow, frozen in place whilst his lungs begged him to give up.

Sabrina was just about to follow the triage inside but stopped herself upon seeing her superior's hesitation. He didn't know why, nor did he really care, but she moved to his side and pulled him away from the doorway. Sounds of gunfire from inside put an edge to the trial on the hill.

And then…silence. There wasn't any shouting. The fields grew silent other than the dying flames that had no more patches to spread through. The red lights died down in the tall grass and the stench of death lingered everywhere. Gunfire halted. No one spoke. Rhys rested against the wall, sliding down it until he sat restless on the floor. He breathed. That's all he did – he made sure he was still alive.

Sabrina said something to him, but he didn't follow her words. His mind fell short of fatigue. The day had branded itself into his personal record, one that would never leave him for as long as he thought he'd live. It had been a day of sour intent. A day of delusion, fear and the ends. No longer could he hide behind a veil, one that told him the war would never reach their shores. Across the hilltop, around fifteen dead bodies lay in uneasy rest. It was clear. They were Ferusian. Their uniforms and tongues were undeniable. And again: their intent? Completely uncertain.

That day, Rhys had tasted death. He had seen it and, most importantly, he had delivered it.

Chapter 8

Bluecoat

Hysteria was the epidemic; it was the virus that broke apart the cells in Rhys' body. Will twisted into delusion; confidence contorted into insanity. The worst pain that he felt was the justification behind it all, for it was all too easy to convince himself he was in the right – and to most he was. Sometimes, however, that stubbornness was ripe with grief. For others, it lacked any emotion until it had hollowed out the executioners.

Later on, Squad 2 waited impatiently for relief. In sixteen minutes, four trucks had shown up, unloaded a platoon's worth of scrambled militiamen, and had reinforced the sector, directing any civilians away. Where they expected resistance instead had them meet with the ones who'd dragged themselves through the violence.

Those who refused to dwell on the circumstances paced around in large irregular perimeters, leading themselves away from the Ferusian corpses.

To some it felt as if it were a mistake. At the doorway sat a puddle of vomit besides a faceless body.

Mateo had emerged from the windmill with a pale face – struck cold by the sights inside. Tamara came out without a word to say. Christopher exited quietly, though not stifled. The look on his face terrified Rhys the most for he had lived with these pictures of death before. It was the ugliest look out of the three.

In his boredom, Stephan trudged through the aftermath and rubbed his hands across the bloody Ferusian bodies. A strong reluctance to show his disgust had infected his virtues, and to show disturbance or disbelief was unacceptable – so he turned to graverobbing. He took coins, photos or whatever memorabilia could find. Those mementos to him may have been treasured memories to others, but he didn't care. They were dead. He wasn't. That was their problem to deal with.

He eventually came across a folder, all laced and inscribed in the unfamiliar native idioms of Ferusia. He handed it to Christopher, who showed it to Rhys, getting silent permission to send it upwards to the authorities.

And the day seemed to end there. Rhys couldn't recollect what happened for the rest of those tiresome hours, nor did he care much for them. They went back to Fort Mullackaye. They were unable to finish their patrol, both mentally and physically, and were forced to hold a debrief. No one spoke about Ryan. Neither did anyone listen to the debrief properly. Rhys then isolated himself into an office and stayed there for the coming hours until he slipped into a nightmarish slumber.

Morning arrived on a dim horse. The previous day's sunshine had been replaced with a brooding rainfall. Across his dusty office window, raindrops trickled like clear crystallised bloodstreams. Beyond the mists of a hazed sunrise there was nothing but clatter. Sounds of mobilising machinery and the hundreds of armed boots marching into line spoke with the wind. News of identified Ferusian paratroopers – in the heart of Kelan's countryside no less – tore down the imaginary barricade the militia hid behind. Royal Army advisors paid visits in the morning and forced many to undergo another level of training. Tens of patrols were sent out each hour, spanning across the countryside in search of something to kill. He heard of the anger had taken control over the nation's armed warriors, heralding their vows to avenge the 'young fallen boy' – the martyr in the local, second page from a much more talked about story: the kidnapping of a princess.

Rhys laid on his desk, and his eyes watched the walls with the light turned off. It was a cramped office, barely lit through the window alone. He hadn't gone back to the SNCO's quarters the previous night, unsure if he'd have been able to sleep at all. When he woke up on the cold wooden desk, he didn't lift his head, and instead let his eyes focus on the cracks in the walls of his prison-like cell.

Something was still on his mind: how did they survive? They should've been dead. All of them should have been buried in the ashened plains. It just didn't make sense. Paratroopers: dead in an instant, attacking without cohesion and struggling until their last stand was squandered. Nothing added up, neither strategically or logically.

A knock came at the door. It was the first sound he'd properly focused on in the daylight hours. He lifted his head from the desk at a dying snail's pace.

Rhys rubbed his eyes, let out a coarse yawn and rose to his feet. When he held the door handle, he felt the chill on the brass, frozen by the void of his lifeless workspace. He turned it.

"Staff Sergeant Hendricks, may I come in?" Before the door was even half open, a somewhat recognisable voice clawed its way inside. Mutely, he opened it the rest of the way, seeing Laskey stood in the open. Rhys nodded and moved aside to let her in. A second figure followed behind her, dressed in dark coating, their face shrouded by a refined and elegant headdress. "Thank you, please take a seat."

He flickered the faint light on and obediently returned to his chair. It didn't cross his mind that he had given her no greeting. Laskey pulled up the rickety seat usually reserved for visitors, whilst the opposing figure stood by the door, clad in the shadow of the Captain.

She'd removed her cap, settled her usual parade staff down by her side and spoke with an unexpected litheness.

"How are you feeling, Hendricks? You've been holed up here for quite some time." He couldn't tell whether her concern was genuine or not. She spoke as if they'd known each other for years, or that they'd worked together through thick and thin as the legate and the centurion. Rhys didn't know her. She didn't know him. Her words would've meant nothing if he wasn't so desperate for a voice to comfort him.

"I'm…okay, I guess." Hesitation ruled his voice, slowing his words to a crawl. "Part of me is telling myself to not think about anything."

"You come from a military family, don't you?" She inquired, switching the tone to a more casual yet unnatural one.

"Not an extensive one. Just my father."

"What theatre?"

"Redus."

"I see." Her own voice trailed off, running dry of meaningless filler. "Allow me to send my condolences for Private Richards.

We've arranged for his burial later tonight if you so wish to attend."

No response. Deep down, an emotional torment from her grim reminder dressed his heart with incisions. The very mentioning returned him to the moment. The gunshot. The blood. The screams. He didn't want to speak up. Instead, he remained stiff-faced. It was obvious she wasn't there for anything other than business. He could see the folder at the back of the room.

The captain lifted her hand, and out from the shadowy backdrop came the figure who'd followed her inside. Rhys looked up to meet his eyes. He was another foreigner clad in Kelan's commendations – Osakan, the North-Eastern islands. Upon his nose, a pair of small, circular spectacles perched on the bridge. They were cleaner than Mateo's, but half-bent out of shape on the right ear-hook.

"Staff Sergeant, I'd like to introduce you to someone who's taken interest in your squad's recent findings: a particular Ferusian folder found on the body of one of their officers." Straight back to duty. Rhys was half-tempted to tune out their talk but their presence alone was enough to force his undivided attention. His eyes were still locked onto the Osakan officer, picking apart every little detail of his unrecognisable dark-blue uniform. From the eclipsed walls on the far end of the office, he stepped forward at Laskey's gesture and held out a hand of good intention.

"Pleasure to meet you, Staff Sergeant. I'm Officer Lee of the Royal Intelligence Office, I'm appreciative of the discovery your squad made yesterday." He spoke as fluent as any native. An immeasurable aura of value to the army came from the flick of his tongue. Immediately, Rhys was left a little discomforted by his nonchalant demeanour. Widespread uncertainty had settled into the morale of Fort Mullackaye. Frequent articles of air battles over harsh seas began to reach their walls, highlighting the increasing intensity of the war. And yet here he was, chirpier than yesterday's morning birds.

Rhys gently nodded. He took his hand out of compliance rather than kindness and shook it gently.

"Mr Lee, here, specialises in the decryption of Ferusian intelligence, amongst other things. He wanted to have a chat with you on the findings. You seem deserving of knowing at least.

Talk of the Fort, your squad is." Laskey's continuation rarely dragged Rhys' gaze from the other officer. Officer Lee withdrew his hand and laid out an assortment of papers upon Rhys' desk, pushing all pens and pencils out of his way. The Staff Sergeant didn't budge, only tuning his eyes to the words on the pages. As he leaned over the table, he saw a pinned stitching to his inner shirt: Thomas Lee, it said.

"Honestly, you've made a great discovery here. Spent all of last night translating. Easy work, surprisingly, just time consuming." He spoke without a second to breathe. A gloved index finger placed onto the highlighted key-phrases on the translation sheet. "We've struck gold. Look, here: *'The following day will see bombardments all across the shoreline before our amphibious landing will commence.'* Wonderful stuff."

Rhys scrubbed his eyes with his fingers again, leaned back into his chair and quietly went over the transcript. If anything, it served as a good distraction.

One question struck him soon after: why was he being told? He mattered little to anyone. The grand scheme was rested upon the men and women behind the scenes, like Thomas. They were the supposed table-turners of the war, the ones whose ties went all the way to Queen Tala's own box of yarn. And it wasn't like Rhys was a figurehead of the Royal Army and the forefront of all of Kelan's might. He was a militiaman. A conscript, a man of no value by both Kelan and Ferusia's standards, other than to block the opposition from his leaders. He wasn't a cog in the big machine, but the rust that settled upon it.

"We have written documentation now of where their ambitious move is to be, when it should happen and an idea behind what they expect to gain." From beneath the documents, he drew out the creased fold of a faded map. His finger ran to one specific plot on the northern coastline. "Point Duhoc, Hendricks. That's where we are expecting their invasion. All thanks to your interception of the paratroopers."

"Why are you telling me this?" He pressed on them a blunt question.

"Well, consider it a token of my gratitude. You were the ones who found the documentation, so I thought it'd only be fitting to tell you first. That and Laskey wanted to check up on you. Two birds, one rather large rock."

Rhys began to loathe his manner of speech – it seemed artificial, as if he were the ringleader of a circus. The pacing, the speed and its overall lacking a fitting emotion irked him.

When he chuckled to himself, it felt like Rhys was being laughed at, regardless if it was anywhere near the truth. Perhaps he'd kept himself in a negative space for too long, that happiness was no longer recognisable. The days had taken their toll on him. Vigorous training ramped up by the first real taste of battle – a man could only wonder what to do next.

"You should come have a drink with me. We can talk the day away!" Thomas suggested.

"I don't drink, sorry."

Rhys shifted from his seat, before gently adding on a stale '*Sir*' to the rejection. He tried to avoid a sour tone but couldn't escape it.

One salute cued his personal dismissal. He sauntered outside before they did, and he entered the concrete hallway to be blasted with the chilling temperature drop.

Where he once wouldn't leave his sanctuary, he'd stepped into the drowned light, exited the building entirely and sat down on the dampened steps outside. His arms tightly wrapped around his shoulders, trapping in as much heat as he could. Droplets of rain drooled through the seams of his hair. It soaked through his clothes and onto his skin. He shivered.

Ever since he'd been forced into arms, he hadn't shed a single tear. Every ache and pain in his muscles had been necessary before. They were part of a push towards embracing the trials of the future conflict. Figureheads who hid their emotions were looked up to for courage, bravery and level-headedness, he'd been told. Letting slip the tears of a thousand woes only muffled the morale of their soldiers and peers. Endless stabs in his heart pierced his sensitivity. He'd matured, as far as his officers were concerned. The feeble farmhand, son of a disabled veteran with a reputation of his own, was dead. A soldier had been born out of flame and the next step was to unveil the leader tucked away inside.

However, he didn't feel as if he had matured. Supressing his thoughts regularly fraught his mood. Impede growth, kill a Ferusian. Halt development, take a life. Stop thinking – kill who you once were.

Rhys was scared of the person who he'd have to become. He was blind to see any alternative between holding his own and suffering or giving up the ghost to be what they wanted him to be. He wanted out of the war, out of the line of sights of Ferusian cannons and out of the trenches his brothers and sisters in arms had dug. A skirmish had nearly broken the poor soul. How unkindly would have the rest of the war treated him? Kelan was no longer safe. It was proven that Ferusia had a way inside. How many more were already within their walls?

Paranoia brought his knees to his head. He rested his forearms on them and planted his eyes into his sleeves. He couldn't cry. Not now. Not ever. The time would be for when he knew it was all over. All he could do was wait in the misty rains until his next order came. Rinse and repeat, never to hang out and dry.

Just then the rain stopped. Or so he thought it had. Raindrops stopped trickling onto his scalp, but the infinite ambience of the heavy showers continued around him. He looked up and saw a daunting shadow lurk over him. A familiar face beamed down to him, using her own jacket as a shield above.

"Hey…" Sabrina said with a smile. Her face was one of uncertain positivity. Regardless of her curled lips, her eyes and brow told him about the immediate insecurity she too felt, like they'd been struck with two sides of the same blade. "How're-…why are you sat out here?"

Carefully chosen words tried to trek around the obvious. A young man was gone. They'd seen him die. They both knew that. Neither of them wanted to talk about it. Yet unlike Laskey's direct condolences, Rhys felt settled by Sabrina's personal approach. They only knew the man in death.

"I'm…" Rhys couldn't help but provide a meagre smile at her. "Showering." She joined his little titter, before offering a hand to her crumbled superior. Rhys hesitated but soon he lightly gripped it and lifted himself from the cold, wet stairs.

The sopped pair stood together for a second, unsure of what to say. Nearby audiences of marching troops passed by, thumping their boots against smoothened roads until they lingered off into the distance.

A new structural doctrine of professionalism had been pitched. The militia could slowly transition into an effective stopgap at the cost of its lax formality. The base had become a lot more crowded over the last few weeks. A near-endless stream of conscripts arrived in droves and he assumed that the skirmish would only fuel the trucks that collected the citizens.

"Terrible weather, am I right? All of Farhawl is coming down on us." Finally, Sabrina coughed through the silence. "You ever seen this much rain?"

"Not really." He responded, his hands cupping the droplets for measurement.

"I have."

"Really? Where?"

"One night, there was also a house fire then. I thought maybe the Stars were acting as firefighters for a night."

"Have they ever *'prodded into man's mishaps'*?" He derided her in light jest, alleviating the heavy mood with a mocking pastor's tone.

"Not a man of faith, then?"

"I don't think I have ever had a reason to. My father was but I guess I base little parts of my lifestyle on not being like him."

"If he's kind to you, then I don't think it's a good thing to aspire and love it." She slipped her jacket back on. Then, she tightened it up to encase what little heat she hadn't lost. For a second time she smiled at Rhys. She paused to let the sound of nearby walkers drift off into the mists around them. Their deafening steps faded, giving her the opportunity to speak again. "Hey, when the weather clears up, Ella and I are planning to go on a short walk together. Come with us, it'll be nice."

Her suggestion came out of a brightened veil, unmasked by the sweet smile she maintained. Blissful, soft and tender – her voice, when as lightly spoken as it was then, was a shared delicacy between her sister and herself, and it had Rhys reeled in.

"Why'd you want me to come?"

"Why not?" With the tilt of her head, she elegantly beamed. "Plus, with you around, we're less likely to be asked about why we're skiving."

Beyond the fog that had shrouded him, he saw the brightness in her proposition, and Rhys accepted her invitation with a gentle nod. The rapidity in which she had swooped in and lifted him from the emotional deluge had entranced him. A fabric of space and time tore open as he felt something in his chest: the fragments of a chiselled attraction.

~~~

A bump in the road; a collision of skull to glass pane. Lylith was discourteously awoken from her slumber with a knock to the head. She groaned in the backseat of the car, sinking back into the leathery throne she'd collapsed in. It was the fifth vehicle they'd swapped to since the escape, and weeks' worth of indirect travel had her exhausted, squandered into infinite fatigue. If there were ever a time to contemplate one's actions, it was during that trip.

House to house, campsite to campsite; Lylith had spent the gruelling days doing her best to avoid military police patrols and to stay underneath the radar. There were many loopholes to hurdle through, aiming for the more obscure regions of the nation. To head straight to their assigned hospice was to compromise the withering effort to search for her. Blockades and checkpoints across main roads had been set up in response to her 'kidnapping', recently bolstered by the news of growing tensions on Kelan's soil. Over time, however, they became less frequent as the public eye shifted back to the progression of the war, and her name came in passing as a grim reminder of Ferusia's indescribable acts of evil – so as the headlines put it.

Sluggishly, she lifted her head off of the seat's headrest, sat up and adjusted her new drabbed coveralls. Clad in nothing more than an olive button shirt and a miserly pair of grey trousers, she'd ditched the aristocratic clothing she'd left. If she were to join the ranks of the common man, she was determined to at least look the part. Living throughout affiliates housing and in forest-based campfires, she'd been slathered in dirt, grime and caked in dried mud, topped off with the weight of days' worth of rain.

How she'd made it so far relied on a single individual: her driver. The only one to survive the incursion at the palace, he'd been a silent guardian, watching over her not out of payment but a tightly-sealed duty she couldn't uncover. His loyalty was undying to something, beyond anything she'd seen before. Yet he didn't speak a word of it. Either the woes of his comrades' deaths had started to tear him apart or he felt silent disdain towards Lylith.

The scenery of great walls, lowland hills and skyscrapers had been replaced with mounds of rock, mountainous terrain and the dense forests of Eastern Kelan. They had covered majority of the trip, but yet she simply couldn't slip into the ranks of the militia as she was. It was a lengthy process, tedious and too cautious for its own good. However, Lylith knew it paid to be careful with such eyes pried for royal disappearances such as her own. Any sign of who she was could've railroaded to arrest, harming more people than she'd like. Those responsible for aiding her escape would be killed without trial. Capital punishment for the capital crime: achieving her self-honoured dreams.

Lylith looked out the window once more and watched the raindrops trickle across the glass. It was set to be the longest rainstorm in recent memory, and she'd ponder about when it would end or if it ever would.

"Are you awake?" The driver asked, the gruff and coarse voice barely alike her usual company.

"Yes…I am, thank you."

"Why are you thanking me?" Out of her courtesy, she looked back to the driver, unsure how to respond. His crude brick-wall of a response took her off side and had battered her kindness. Lylith truly owed the man her life, but even a 'thank you' was too much for him. She wondered if they'd ever see one another again when she returned from the frontline. If it were possible, a knighthood or any royal decoration was necessary, regardless if Tala disagreed.

Lylith sat in silence. There wasn't really any satisfactory answer she could give. There wasn't any reason to thank him for his question, and anything beyond that had cost him more than she'd ever given.

"We're going to stay here from now on." He pointed out to the left side of the car, where a small, ransacked house sat on the edge of an empty impasse. "Might be for a while. Your contact has organised the final preparation steps to take place here."

The contact: the unknown figure who worked alongside her loyal servant and the one who knew the ins and outs of Kelan's underbelly. She was yet to meet them but her trust in Philip transferred over to any shadow-colleague he worked with.

Squeals on the breaks lightly indicated their arrival. She sat upright. Lylith wiped her hand across the watery glass, smoothening out a full view of their home. Outside, a large allotment of fencing and wooden poles dotted around in an unorderly fashion, whilst the house itself sat in complete silence. Dull, faded bricks cried over their lost colour. At the door, a

109

figure emerged. Stood with her arms folded, the doorwoman waved to the car. The car came to a stop and she moved closer to its side, where she opened Lylith's door and poked her head inside with an elderly grin.

"Ahh, wonderful. Good t'see you alive and well, dear Princess." The partially-toothless smile left Lylith a little discomforted. Her voice was tipped with a thistle, with her tongue pushing between the gaps in her teeth. She pulled herself out and followed. She had to shimmy across the seat until she could step out into the rain. And she felt its weight – it was far greater than the previous night.

"Actually, it's just Lylith now." Kindly, she smiled to the elder, who trudged through the sea of mud leading to the front door. "Or, well…Miss Redgrine, if you want to be that formal."

Her chuckle fell short as the driver stepped out of the car, closely following behind her. Unlike him, the old woman made for a decent conversationalist.

"Oh, you're just such a dear, aren't you? I can already tell you'll be popular with the soldiers."

Inside, an assortment of sawdust and splinters littered the walls and ground, icing the wooden floor in soot. Several distant shouts and voices could be heard upstairs. A family, perhaps? Lylith couldn't tell in her initial scrutiny. Bristly paintings and handheld contraptions were left lying all around the house. A tinkerer's paradise – hundreds of bolts stripped from Kelan's arsenal of machinery, all repurposed for a comfortable life beneath the radar.

At the very back of the house, down the faint corridor and beyond the rusty doorknobs, a jaded dining room presented waited for her occupation. A long, dark oak table stretched from one end to the other, with two mirrors sitting parallel of one another. One of them was cracked, though only slightly.

Lylith was met with a thousand reflections of her own self, staring back at her or at her back. She couldn't recognise her own beauty – the drowned eyes of a solemn fugitive then stared into her own. Cold, pale and sodden skin pictured in a brass frame, the warm colour of her irises being the only temperance in the whole room.

"Excuse the noise upstairs, Miss, the family has been rowdy for the short while." Lylith chortled evenly at the elder's kindness, nodding wordlessly. "You've come a long way, 'aven't you, love?"

"Quite." Lylith looked away from the endless reflection and turned her eyes towards the chairs. The elder gestured for her to sit and so she did. "It's been uneventful, and a test of one's patience."

"A'ight, you've done great so far, love." Her senior moved across the hall, opening several draws and dusting off empty shelves along the way. As if the bite of the spring showers had frozen her in place, she stood motionlessly as she admired the hidden contents of one of the drawers.

"Well, may I have the privilege of knowing who my hosts are?"

"Just call me Sarah, dearie." Her sweetness was infinite, much unlike the men and women Lylith had to push past to get to where she was.

"I presume you know Philip, then?"

"Who?" The two paused. In her senile rumination, Lylith sat patiently, her hands folded neatly upon her dusty lap. Even in wolves' clothing, she maintained her sheepish mannerisms. "Sorry, dear, not a clue. Friend of a friend."

Lylith bowed her head in understanding. All that she could tell was that Sarah was nothing more than a forgotten soul, tossed aside by society to live in her own drabs, money be damned.

"Who is my contact?"

"Veils and grapevines, Miss Redgrine. You'll meet them someday when we finish up your prep here." Sarah finally walked over, a small folder in her hands. Circumnavigating its paper cover, a knot of string kept it all together. Lylith repositioned herself in her chair, acting more attentively than she had been before. "Y'know, you'll be doing our nation a great aid in your sacrifice."

"I don't intend on dying, Miss Sarah. What good is an inspirational figure if she's dead?"

Sarah looked as if she were about to rebuttal her claim, opening her mouth, but withdrawing her debate with an innocent smile.

"So she might not." Without delay, she moved to the document, and held it out in front of Lylith, placing it gently on the wooden surface before her. "In 'ere is a detailed dossier of things we will be doing whilst you're under our roof. Ev'rything from some shooting practice, physical training and changing y'look. Gives us time to wait for the search parties to drop down a bit, a'ight?

Lylith just nodded. She wasn't really in a position to refuse the help. They'd gone through so much for her ideals. Though it could take anywhere between a month to several, she was prepared to change who she was for the sake of the people, the nation and the soldiers she'd fight alongside. They just needed the armed forces to fend of the Ferusians long enough for her to make a safe arrival. To the exiled royal, there was nothing honourable in sitting behind closed doors making decisions that impacted extraordinarily little in the grand scheme.

Sarah's kindness was all-too familiar. She'd experienced particular mentors during her own royal childhood. Friends who'd taken the parental position where Queen Tala didn't and in the absence of the deceased King.

"You kind of remind…" She trailed off, catching Sarah's attention in her own stumble.

"I remind you of what, dearie?"

"An old friend. Emelia, her name was. Diamond in the rough where my parents did little for me. Perhaps a short-lived stepmother by heart." Her eyes turned to the blank spaces of the room. "She was Ferusian, by blood. Loyal to the crown. One day she just left, never came back. I do hope she is well in these awful times. The only thing I dread about coming to the front is having people like her against me."

"Don't worry, Miss." Sarah placed a feeble, wrinkled hand onto Lylith's own, bringing it up from her lap and onto the desk. "They chose their path – and you're on the one to the golden gates."

And in the moment, a chill went down Lylith's spine. Was it one of excitement or fear? Anxiety, perhaps. She didn't know. But she was so close, she could taste the victory of the battlefield on the tip of her tongue. It was near, an achievement soon to be grasped with clean hands. The people would chant a name of praise, the children of Kelan would be safe. To Lylith, she would put herself through the greatest discomfort she could think of just to give back to the people. She thought that her morals were absolute. Nothing could change her.

Chapter 9

Waltz

*W*here was the sunshine?

    The carnivorous display of Kelan's resolution to foreign invaders had created a thick veil in the sky and had blocked out the great star with ease; and in the aftermath came the encroaching rainstorm. Rivers flooded small valleys and distant fields became slogged with marshy panoramas. Bogs filled the moat-like trenches outside Fort Mullackaye whilst the concrete runways were drenched in the vast pools of the sky's tears. On any other normal day, the papers would run the headlines with talk of a watery disaster – an apocalyptic affliction to the Kingdom's lowlands. Yet, as it had done for the preceding months, the news only spoke of war, of its progress and listing off acts of valour unseen, or the sensationalised unease of one monarch's disappearance. The soldiers and militiamen barely spoke of the weather. Their minds had wandered into inescapable plains where war dominated their dreams and plagued their nightmares. Twenty-four-hour coverage from radio stations and the bold text on every company's '*page one*' story told them there was nothing else to talk or even think about.

    Rhys wasn't aware he'd been intoxicated by its rule. Forlornly, his wishes to write home to his father were constantly side-tracked by strenuous training exercises, weapon maintenance and paid vigils to fallen acquaintances, of many he had no connection to. He grew ignorant of the latter, and he pushed the death from his visions to force a new light to shine. He still had a promised invitation to uphold.

    And as the stars had given the day its blessing, one gloomy morning gave him the time. Sunshine had finally pulled through the clouds, and they had parted asunder. Heaven's gates shone upon the land. With that came a knock on the door.

Sabrina cheerfully gleamed up to the half-surprised Staff Sergeant in his officer. She'd dressed down from her usual military fatigues, rolled up her sleeves and had let her hair flow a little freer than usual.

"I hope you haven't forgotten." Giddily, she stepped inside and eagerly rummaged around to inspect his hovel. "By Sunar, you really do work in a foxhole."

"Did you just come here to berate where I work?"

"No, but maybe you'll tidy up a bit if I do." The smirk on her face was enough to convince him.

Quietly, she led the pair outside. Her hand wrapped around Rhys' wrist and, rather humiliatingly, dragged him where she wanted to go. Down the hallway, past the ever-rambling radio calls of sergeants, warrant officers, lieutenants and captains, and out into the light.

A pictographic landscape of dazzled puddles, escorted by the humid perfume of Kelan's late-summer aroma. Moisturised air extremified by the warmth of that sun-drenched morning gave way to a certain familiarity: springs that spanned across two decades; harvest, an exciting childhood event, materialised by the stench. A call to home. He could almost hear his father's voice telling him to take up the mechanical scythe and to hack away until the baskets were plentiful.

"Beautiful days do come by if we endure the shit ones. You just need to have more patience." Sabrina called out, though not to Rhys. At the bottom of the stairs stood a silent figure, hands crossed in front of her as the mirrored sunlight sprawled across her body.

"You already-" Ella stumbled and stammered, reconfiguring herself in the presence of her sister's guest. "Good morning, Staff Sergeant."

Rhys gave her a miniature wave with the small jostle of a dried-up palm. The pathetic attempt didn't go unnoticed. With what seemed like a great struggle, Ella tried to return a smile confidently. Quickly, she broke eye contact and went to the walls. Sabrina soon made it to her side and gestured for Rhys to join them.

"I invited him to come with us." The two muttered over some whispered talking points, leaving him in the dark. Ever the failed conversationalist, he hesitated before he treaded carefully to their side.

He tarried over what he should've said to ease in his presence. The air, whilst entwined with the fabric of a summer's splendour, was tight and awkward. A few more seconds and he'd have burst a vessel over what to say, and so he rushed to the first thing that had connected the two in the first place.

"Hey, how's the tank maintenance going?" Before Ella could respond, Sabrina propped herself between them.

"No, no. There's an embargo on military talk today, not whilst we're having our walkabout, alright?" Rhys and Ella looked at one another from across their host's blockade. Neither said a word, only shrugging and nodding in compliance.

Sabrina's confidence seemed to go beyond both of them. He hadn't really thought about it, but the way she had composed herself made it out as her being comfortable in the militia. During their skirmish, she hadn't curled up into a ball, neither did she shield her eyes and ears from the destructive soundtrack. No, Sabrina had leapt forward and had used her rifle as expected.

Truly, she was much alike Mateo, from Rhys' point of view. She just got on with it. No protest. All dramatics were put down. She did what she had to in order to get through the day: a commendable trait that he could do little to replicate.

At first, the two sisters mumbled between one another, continuing conversations they'd been having before he had joined the party. His gaze landed on the passing peace. The activity around the base had died down. An unaccustomed silence surrounded the majority of Fort Mullackaye. It was purely idyllic for an entire compound to be silenced in the beauty of the sunlit sky.

Then his eyes were magnetised to the sisters. First, it lay upon Sabrina. Something about her seemed to take his attention away from the recent woes. Whatever it was, it had transformed into an evanescent glee in his chest. Her voice naturally flowed between the thistles of their lives and clipped them on her merry way. In the face of his demons, she shone a foreign light on him and tickled his tastebuds with the sweetest flavour in a minor sample. The inexplicability of the sensation was insatiable. He tried not to dwell upon it. Yet the recent interactions they'd shared had taken him away from the rest of the squad. He found himself naturally gravitating towards her.

On the other end, there was Ella – a woman who clenched to his sister's arm at any given moment. The ravens of the conflict had already plucked at her chest. Her heart pulsed through fearful quakes. Things of the present and past placed her in still shock. In the sun-glazed morning, she was almost the spitting image of Sabrina – almost – though her affinity was mostly ruined by the patches of diesel stains and fluids on her outfit.

He didn't know what to say or why he was there with them. Perhaps, like a fly in the midsummer evening, he flew to their fluorescence to be willingly ensnared by their beyond-real beauty, or maybe it was the comfort Sabrina had pledged to sponsor that caught him good. Whilst he spectated them, he realised how it was how much the change in light was compared to the dimness of his office. He barely focused on their words for the first while.

"So, how's things with you?" Sabrina turned to Rhys, flashing her customary smile. Her mantra was blessed by the glistening smile that went with it.

"Tired, I think." He gave himself a dressing down with his eyes and placed a hand on his thigh. "I didn't realise my legs were this sore until just now."

"Mine too, but let's not let that ruin the hour!"

"So, where are we going?" Ella interrupted.

"To the walls! There's a spot just down the lane that's usually empty around this time. Looks right over the nearby valleys."

Neither of her guests had alternatives. She clenched onto Ella's hand and Rhys' wrist and brought them across the courtyards, through the seas of settled rainfall and up to the great stairs that lead to the top of the walls. Sabrina eagerly leapt up, two steps at a time, until they reached the peak. Across its fortifications, an entire plain laid before them, where distant forests topped the horizon and hid unseen villages under their protection.

Awe overflowed Ella and she wandered toward the edge. She held onto the stomach-high rim of the ledge with a petite grasp. The concrete was warm like a tropical cliff face, infused with the sunlight's kiss. She lost herself in her wonderous analysis of the waterlogged lands compressed into her picturesque paradise.

Sabrina and Rhys watched from the side. For the latter, there was a phantasmagorical plantation built with bricks of positive thoughts – the backbone concrete was formed with the rhinestone virtue of Ella's peace.

"It's wonderful, isn't it?"

"Hmm?" Rhys half-eyed Sabrina, whilst the other half kept itself planted on Ella's entranced dance across the rooftops.

"Seeing her happy. She's not built for this, not mentally. And I want her to remain as happy as she can, in case…" Her smile seemed to fade for a second, before she looked back to the Staff Sergeant. "You're doing a decent job, by the way."

"Oh – what brought that about?"

"Don't know." Sabrina flashed a quick wink. "I haven't seen anyone else in the squad say it, so I'll happily be the first."

"I…haven't really done anything though?"

"Who cares today?" She smirked to herself.

Ella moved along the parapet, smiling to herself. Initially, her childlike wonder prevailed. But then she replaced it with elegance, like that of a veteran artist in search for that perfect angle. A willowy stride carried her from one battlement to the other, peeping between the gaps as she basked in the rays of daylight. He couldn't quite recognise her, as there was always that one conversation they'd had that stuck with him.

"She's terrified, right?" Rhys broke the passionate connection with the sunlit day and replaced it with a darkened mist of reality. Sabrina didn't say anything at first, so he continued cautiously. "She asked me if she was going to die once. In the war-"

"What did you say?"

"I said she'd be okay."

Stillness. Sunlight. Silence. The two stood together, watching her distant meditation between the battlements.

"She just…she doesn't deserve this, Rhys." He stayed silent, listening to her fade away slightly. It was the first sign of anger he'd seen from her. "And I don't want her to die, the thought of it alone just…"

"Then let's promise that it'll never happen. All of us; we'll be okay, so long as we make sure of it." He lied between his teeth and made the smile with a deceitful and incredulous optimism.

"I'll hate you forever if you're wrong."

117

The two of them waited for a second, until Sabrina found her collected senses. She returned the smile, though far more believably, and jabbed him with another dampened question.

"Aren't you scared?"

"Yeah…I am." He trailed off, and the two were left on hold.

Though nothing else was said, he felt a hand discretely wrap around his forearm. The clutches of a passionate comfort, soft as a king's pillow, held him.

After a few seconds, she quietly let go and stepped away. He took the first steps forward and headed over to Ella, plastering another ersatz smile. All they had to do was look at the glistening sunlight and pretend everything was going to be okay. Ella needed it. Sabrina wanted Ella to have it. And Rhys? Well, he'd lost any semblance of it ever returning.

Chapter 10

The Storm

Their eyes were cast upon the obscured ocean with indifference. They'd all seen the graves before, and they were rarely shallow. From the bodies that washed up on the shore to the bottom of underwater caverns, there was no fear for man when the right wave was enough to end a ship's worth of sailors. Critters fed on their fallen and the apathy toward the merciless modern world ran rampant on the decks.

Nimble rudders corrected the headings – the dangers of shipwrecks and stones beneath the surface were narrowly avoided by ten to a hundred metres. Deeper waters were sought after, yet the roar of the coastal patrol's natural adversary kept them in a constant battle with their engines. In brisk motion, the scouting fleet spaced itself from the cliff faces of Kelan's coastline. Tidal turmoil crashed into the starboard face. Sprays of foamy, ice cold water tickled the sailors' faces. Hands turned blue in the nightly shroud of the hour. Frail voices called out to maintain the proper machinery of the craft, its floatation dependent on the coursing of its own journey. They were barraged from all sides by the coastal winds that came in from the south. On the bridge, however, the situation was a lot quieter.

Navigators and chief engineers wrapped themselves in puffy coats and crudely knitted scarfs that their husbands and wives had made for them. Some had tied themselves down to their chairs with rope, combating the inconsistent listing of the vessel. Half of the room had their attention funnelled through metal headphones, listening to the blips on dormant bulb-lit screens. Ping. Ping. Ping. No change. If any truth was shared among them all, it was that the inactivity was a sanctification to their disastrous setting.

Day after day, the fleet scouted ahead in search for the Ferusian Grand Navy. Only fragments of its outer shell were ever spotted, formations of freighters, destroyers and light cruisers drifting alone. And every ship that was spotted was immediately fired upon. There would be no discretion for any boat with a Ferusian flag on it.

For months, the war had raged in the sky and on the high seas North of Kelan. Each week that passed was another mile of lost maritime territory. The fleet was being pressed against Kelan's shore, choked and asphyxiated by their claustrophobic constriction against the cliffs. Their outer-rim archipelagos were lost by the hour. Small naval bases and radar sites on largely forgotten plots of sand held spats of bloody outcome. Marines faced off against hardened garrisons. Key facilities on small islands were burnt down, shelled by a hundred cannons before the squads moved in to clean up remaining Kelan's defences. And for many back homes, letters bearing grievances towards the dead were glorified through flamboyant prose – for who would feel pride in their sons dying on unknown spots in the sea?

At the helm of the capital ship stood a strictly uniformed figure who led the formation with a faded greyness to his skin. A pale beard coated his chin. On his brow, the brim of an officer's naval cap hung over his eyes, spreading a thin shadow on his colourless forehead. Only the light of the dim bulb overhead shone his position. The moon dared not reveal itself from behind the dark clouds.

The Vice-Admiral struck up a pipe, lit it with trembling gloved hands and he huffed as he battled the tilts. Streams of smoke flickered from the top of his lighter's flame. Another slope from the ship's side had made it difficult to light it, frustrating him and leaving him to abandon his comfort break.

He stared out into the abyss: the Eden of disjointed cruelty, where brave men settled on the seabed as ribcages and skulls. Beyond their reinforced glass barrier sat the greatest darkness ever known to man that stretched ahead and beneath them. Search lights were kept to a dim minimum. Only the silhouettes of his topside crew could be made out in the chasm of nightfall.

"Hatton, heard anything from Point Duhoc?" As he spoke, a drag of condensation spilled from his lips. He placed both hands on his arms and rubbed them madly for any sort of warmth.

"Nothing, Sir." The senior-radioman on the bridge shook his head. He leant back in his seat and removed his headset.

"Command said they'd prepared their defences there a week ago, but there's still no activity."

"Understand – maintain current headings."

The room returned to the whispering gossip of machinery and electronics. An odd metallic creak in pipes chimed off to the left side before it quietly settled.

Tiresome – that's what it was. All of their efforts were tedious, tiresome drags of extreme caution. Many had their hopes on lockdown, for there was great gamble in seeking and destroying the Ferusian presence on the sea. A single beast of their sky navy was enough to impose a great threat to the technologically inferior oceanic crawlers. Yet with even the odds stacked against them, each sailor seemed as begrudgingly committed as ever to take arms against their colossal adversary. They were a shield and a stopgap; they were the combination brass lock on the iron gate. For as long as they kept the war on the waters, the bloodbath could be washed away instead of staining the soil they so desperately defended.

The Vice-Admiral looked to the nailed portrait upon the bridge's wall. On it was the familiar portrayal of their monarch. Queen Tala's expression was one of diligence, a persistent vow to fend their menacing foe off until their guns ran dry of ammunition. By vision alone, he saw a tougher figure, a widow who would fix the woes of her blighted husband.

Her daughter's kidnapping had fractured her morale in a single night. She attended regular speeches and updated the people of the capital weekly. Her frowns upon the enemy grew less assiduous by the day. And like many in her ranks, she started to fall out of favour of duty and had joined the line of the bloodthirsty.

"By the shining grace of the Star's, you must have a contingency plan, prepared." He sighed to the painting. Then, he separated his gaze from Tala's portrait. A booming call to the bridge crew revived the activity. "Has anyone got a reading on the weather? I haven't scheduled a date with mother nature and it'd be awkward to run into her."

A small spectacle-wearing officer retorted his request.

"Just asked the coastal eyes, Sir. They say we'll get the edge of it if we're lucky."

121

Some relief that was. Rarely did good news pass by the ears of the fighters. If it weren't the fall of a naval base or the sinking of a colleague's ship, then it never came to their attention.

Aboard the KNV-*Rising Sun*, the Vice Admiral silently pled that its name would take literal charge of the storm.

Grizzled veterans sprawled across the decks. Those hardened by the turmoil of the nautical battlefield stood tall, braving the frozen winds and icy droplets thrown on them hourly. He pointed to the right corner with a crooked finger.

"None of the radiators working?" The Vice-Admiral coughed and watched the fog of his breath disappear in the pallid atmosphere. He was answered by shaking heads and returning expressions of a chilled nature. "Well, there's always a worse time."

Trailed by four smaller vessels, the *Rising Sun* moved through the night on minimal visibility. Reliant on its radars, the twilight sailing was met with the aforementioned forecast punishment. Whirling currents continuously called for the fleet's readjustment. And the smaller vessels struggled more than its parental leader.

"Foul seas are spells for bad happenings. I know you're tired, but keep those eyes peeled." The collective *'Aye Sir!'* that followed on brought the same egotistical joy to the Vice-Admiral as it always had. Seconds later, a buzz came through the headset of a nearby radar operator. He sat up straight, focusing his full attention with surprise. With the wave of an arm, he beckoned the Vice-Admiral over to his side.

"Sir, got an irregular blip on the scope. What do you think of it?" Both crowded before the waned amber monitor built into his station. He wiped the screen of condensation and saw the signal as his subordinate had: a significant beacon propped up by an insatiable rumble of the cabin.

"What the bloody hell was that?"

The Vice-Admiral took the headset from the operator and placed it upon his scalp. The sound...*BLIP*. It came at an increased volume. "Whatever it is, it's a big one. Hatton, tell the bow to load up four flare shots, contact the eastern strike fleet on hold, we'll hit them in the middle once we've got confirmation."

The luminous room became as shadowed as ever. All ships in his spot-and-scan fleet powered themselves to minimal functionalities and lay in silence. The sea crashed against their hulls in full might.

"Any chance that it's one of ours?"

"Command said it would contact us if there were allied movement across our sector. We can't tell if it's ships we're picking up or-"

"Where are we at the moment? Hatton make sure you're writing this down!" He moved his sleeve to his mouth, coughing violently into the cufflinks. A croak bellowed out of his stomach as he looked to the window with tired eyes.

"We're..." The subordinate paused. "About ninety-six miles from the coast of the Haria, west of the northmost point. At minimum, at least."

The Vice-Admiral's intrigue sharpened. Subdued interest in the matter piqued up and the crew snapped into order. All the while they pondered, the first officer braced to relay important intelligence to the coastal garrisons.

"Are the flare rounds loaded yet?"

"Not yet, Sir. Give it another minute."

"I want to see what it is before we lose its trace. Stand ready, prepare the squadron to full speed astern." Another officer off to his side barked out firing orders.

"Set the aim to the middle of where that blip is: two miles at a bearing of 331!"

The waiting game endured. They neared the deadline to their tranquillity. A continuous rocking of the boat became trivial to the compared matter. Chilled winds and water became but a discomfort and they clicked their jaws with anticipation.

Below the deck, crowds of sailors lunged each flare shell into their gun's breach, one after another. Down the narrow corridors, voices relayed the task's completion.

"Adjusting aim. Are there any changes to the reading, Sir?"

He tugged on his beard, settling his unlit pipe down on the counter, only for it to slide off and splash on the cold, moist floor. Across the darkened decks, the rumbling ambience of gears in motion reverberated the bridge. A banked turret shifted its direction. Its barrels rose upwards towards the sky and the *Rising Sun* finalised its preparations.

The Vice-Admiral checked the radar reading. The admitted to no change. He braced the order to fall their ships backward. In his vile curiosity, he moved towards the viewing panes at the front of the bridge and, across its misty, fatally cold sheet, he wiped a hand across the glass to spy their prize.

The crown asked for answers – he was going to provide them.

"Fire on my mark." His eyes drifted to the distant shade. The horizon had been embezzled by the twilight awning, present only in sound rather over sight. With their vessel saturated in stillness, tossed only by the violent approach of the storm's edge, he clenched onto the walls and raised his hand. "Fire."

A continuous ripple of fire bested the silence. Left to right – the quad-cannon waved its blasts one second after the previous. Four shells spiralled through the air and vanished into the night the second they left the barrels. Several officers joined the Vice-Admiral at the window.

Whistles tore through the nightfall. Seconds away from detonation, the Vice-Admiral held his tongue to the back of his throat and waited for the godly beams to unveil their target.

Gloomy waters were set alight as the flares burst in flight. A blazed performance of white magnesium and phosphorus showered the deprived sea in a glorious radiance as if the gates of Heaven had creaked open. The initial blast forced them to shield their eyes and to adjust to the sudden luminosity that scorned their peripherals. Fragmentations of burning substances split from the shell's collision and widened its branches. The Vice-Admiral blinked and cleared his vision to the ungodly flash he'd ignited.

With a curved palm over his eyes, resting on the greasy brow, he pressed himself closer to the window. And in the mists of their expedition, sat the demonic chariots that laid before his eyes.

A misstep in his heart caused him to choke. He spluttered with his eyes wide open. Momentary shock soon descended into intense scrutiny. On the flare's explosion, the hulls and brightened silhouettes of steel beasts rested in the distance. The water sea had been overwhelmed by an endless array of flags aboard armed ships, landing craft and carriers, all spread across a colossal horizon. The flares flickered and flashed their presence with a daring strobe. Where the light's reach faded, many more vessels laid in wait.

It was the greatest fleet known to man, sat right before the Vice-Admiral's sight. He staggered back to the helm, whilst the remainder of his crew were trapped in disbelieved shock.

"Set ourselves in haste! Emergency astern! Move into the shade before they can set their eyes upon-"

An unprecedented puff of smoke, layered with fire, spat from the front screen ship. An orange charge of heat rushed towards the *Rising Sun*, spiralling a tear in the atmosphere.

The eyesore of the explosion rattled the glass, the cabinets and crew. Flames ignited along the deck in ferocious execution. A concert of fire surrounded those stood on the bow, engulfing the open air in vanquish. Conquered souls flailed around in horrific desperation. The shot shattered the glass, tossing shards around and into the crew. Flickers of crystal daggers scraped across the Vice-Admiral's cheeks as he fell back.

Thunders of artificial chaos devastated the nightly silence. Every rattled pipe screeched after the gunshot. Smoke flushed into the bridge and overshadowed the room in seconds. Vapour, crisped wooden splinters and burning metal forged a foul scent – a stench of mortality.

The Vice-Admiral could feel the shockwave still violently shaking through his body. A muffled stung him. Perforated ears screamed for him to get up.

With weak hands, he placed a palm down onto the floor. A sharp stab came to his skin as the glass pierced his skin. In his desperation, he slid on both crystal and blood as the ship began to list. He dragged his body to the nearest wall to prop himself up. Wind had been taken from his sails, and he gasped for air. A croaked call went unnoticed. He wasn't aware that a second shot had been fired from the opposing dreadnought.

All he felt was the spout of flames that bled into the room. It narrowly avoided his head. His crew weren't so lucky, with some flung across the room. Screams and panicked cries sank into the obsolete. The Vice-Admiral was left to catch his breath, dazed by the succession and pacing of the engagement.

Several quickfire shots proceeded to take the tiny fleet's screen vessels out, each in single shots. A blink of an eye passed, and the fleet was ablaze.

There was nothing left – just the tilting mess of his own ship. Gravity began to grab onto his left shoulder and he slid gently down across the floor. Muted groans from bending metal begged for relief. Life had been relinquished from most of his allies on first contact. In the bridge, men and women crowded themselves in broken consciousness. Some yelled out for help, their arms or legs having snapped on a poor impact. He helplessly slid along the glass-stained deck and saw Hatton clenching onto his left eye, blood seeping between his fingers. He couldn't hear his pained screams.

His wits and attention only returned for the final minute of his fate.

As the KNV-*Rising Sun* began its horizontal descent to sea-bedding below, the Vice-Admiral clocked on to his final duty – to report his findings. There was no escape. He chose to die in completing his mission.

His broken body slid into the far-left wall of the bridge, near most of the shattered radio equipment. The second blast had ruptured their monitors and made shambles of the cables inside. Desperate to make amends to his clueless stumbling, he grabbed the first microphone he could find, just as the ship itself reached a forty-five-degree banking. He could hear the sound of the ocean rising up to his body.

"Call to…all stations…"

Panting for air, he begged in his mind for someone, anyone, to be listening to his cry. Thrice the firepower had annihilated the little fleet and the breach had been made.

"This is the…KNV-*Rising…Sun.* We're…going down. Encountered a large Ferusian fleet. Possibly the Grand Fleet." Through the microphone, the sounds of gushing water and bubbling abysses below crescendoed and the rich anxiety drew closer to his heart. "We're…at-"

A string of coughs blemished by the smoke and encroaching water filling his lungs suppressed his voice. And before the sun had risen the next morning, another had sunk to the base of sea.

Chapter 11

Mobilisation

Resound the alarm, for the ignition key had been turned and war had rocked into full-motion. There was an immediate cry of confusion that tore the tranquillity of the hour apart. The sleepers and tired had their bedsheets scrambled under red and orange flashing lights. The upheaval of the hour ran amok; unacquainted urgency threw many into misdirected panic.

A monophonic clear-tone announcer made her calls in drowsy professionalism – procedure treated the anomalous callout like dross. Outside, there were the thunderous engines that roared. In the air sat the tasteless plumes of truck-fumes and chimneys.

Thousands rushed to their assorted warehouses to have their moral shakedown by the call to arms. Never before had such an amassing been ordered in Mullackaye. To the fabled few, it was the beginning of a glorious step toward victory: the little park lane stroll through ice and fire that rewarded the brave. Yet the unknown truth that majority feared lurked within the words of their leaders, cooped up in the regimental bunkers. Among those who was called to action were the fighters of the 54th Defensive Regiment.

The sea of half-asleep soldiers stood clumped in a raggedy rank and file. The vast ocean of unknown faces stood out to Rhys, who latched himself on to the back of the collective. A hodgepodge of Kelan's lowest had all gathered in one place. Beneath pulsing lights, they were shuffled into place by their lieutenants until they loosely resembled a parade formation. At the far end of the warehouse was a makeshift stage made from an unused truck halfway through its repairs. Rhys shouldered his way forward a little, then pulled rank for long enough to skirt to his own company.

They'd been sprawled across a hundred or so bodies. Yet on the fringe stood one Mateo, busied by the task of defogging his glasses. He sank between two taller soldiers either side of him. On one end, Johan stumbled into formation with a weak posture brought upon by undeniable fatigue. He did his best to arrange himself accordingly to look the part.

A continuous chain of chatter clattered throughout the hall. Rhys soon joined the side of his identified squadmates, slipping in beside them without so much as a greeting.

"Mornin', Rhys." Mateo yawned, putting his glasses back onto his moistened nose. "Got any details?"

"I'm as lost as you are."

Wherever he looked, over the shoulders and smallest heads of the 54th, he noticed the disorderly status of the rabble. None of the officers chased up the informal outliers, for they were part of the board meeting, set hours before the end of the world.

"Think it's another drill?" Mateo asked as he began to bat the floor with his boots with an uneven rhythm.

"Could be."

"Guess we'll find out." Mateo's eyes fell on Rhys' fingers, which anxiously tapped his own sleeves in beat to his boots. "You see the others lurking about?"

"Nope. I just got here."

It was on his mind. Oh – the possibility, he thought, was ever the more prevalent. After having been force-fed the sight and sounds of a skirmish, he always feared the next step. There was always some way to escalate the problems at hand, and by the stars when a crowd of soldiers were awoken before the sun had risen, he held his breath at the thought of it all going to hell.

"Staff Sergeant, do you think we're finally getting sent out?" Johan slipped in and read the words on the wall. A stone cold stare had already troubled Rhys, but the obvious terror spelt out before him left so much as a shivered response.

"Not a clue."

Mateo gave a little glare at Johan and batted his arm with a flaccid fist. But before either could puzzle themselves over the virtues of reading the room, a call to attention. Like dogs on command, the regiment closed off all that they busied themselves with and paid heed to the highest authority in the warehouse.

Along the front, an indistinguishable figure scaled the truck and rose above them all. Rhys couldn't make out their face, hair, or anything of value; only the shimmering ribbons and medals across their chest gave any indication of identity. An officer that seethed with a sense of authority – and one of the many that Rhys didn't even know by name. The man didn't call them at ease.

"Thank you for assembling in due haste, though I wish it were under better pretences." The ceiling lights were dimmed after one bulb blew its fuse. A few whispered worriedly to themselves and the officer raised a hand, silencing them as any messiah would. "Two hours ago, the Armed Forces of Ferusia launched an offensive unlike anything we've ever seen before. For brevity's sake, a fleet of unimaginable scale was gathered to our north, where they have begun the first stages of securing the north-most peninsula of Haria."

A thousand hearts sank to the seabed. Faces smothered in fear sheepishly looked from one to another. A sense of denialism infected the many – heads shook and expressions stiffened at the matter at hand. And with a sour admission, the commanding officer spoke in the lowest of tones.

"I regret to inform you that Ferusia has squirmed its way onto the mainland."

The muffled cries of the shocked and bewildered were intercepted by lieutenants who struggled to settle the tension. A few choked on the news and let their tears take the fall.

"Under these circumstances," he continued, "High Command has commissioned three of Mullackaye's regiments to reinforce the newly established frontline. Among those three is us – the 54th. Other regiments will-"

Rhys eyed the floor. Of all the troubles, he felt as if he'd been dealt the worst hand. He didn't expect anything of the frontline except a pathed-out journey to the underworld.

Ferusia had made their mark on history. No longer was it a squad clashing another squad, but armies drawn up on maps to face each other down until one crumbled. Whether it was for annihilation, subjugation or assimilation, it didn't matter. Kelan was at the knife's edge and it dared to press its neck into the blade if it meant wrangling out of its adversary's grasp.

He thought of the man he had killed at the windmill. Of all the troubled musings he had, he chose the worst to dwell upon. How many times over was he expected to see that? The pale eyes of his defused nimbus stared straight at him. The dead – the pastel skin of the finished – flashed a sacramental smile. He envisioned the roaches that spilled from their mouths and the mites that burrowed from their chests. The smells and sights, sounds and strokes of a pathological evil. And it had placed its feet firmly on their doormat.

He hadn't been listening at all to the commander. Their words offered little comfort and only sought to spill objective circumstances. He failed to take it in, for what was expected to come next had haunted his sleepless nights for weeks.

"Oh shit…"

Slurred beneath his overwrought breath, a tempered anxiety shunted his mind into mediation with prospective disasters. In his distancing he'd not seen Evelyn for quite some time. And her name brought with it a staunch concern – for how many Evelyn's were in the crowd with him?

Their commanding officer kept talking. The gutters had claimed his attention beyond the feeble and useless attempts made at inspiring Rhys. Endless chain links bound his mouth to his mind. Questions had been left at their worst: unanswered.

At the blow of a whistle, the crowd dispersed at the speed of sound. The soldiers scrambled to find their squads both in and out of the warehouse. Shoulders barged through one another and several figures pinned their backs to walls in hope that an officer wouldn't notice them.

He was caught in a daze, looking from left to right as Mateo had seemingly vanished into thin air.

"Rhys, this way!" He called to him through the crowd. A tug against his collar pulled the confused SNCO in an unknown direction. He fluttered wherever the chariot that held him went.

In mere seconds, they were linked up with the squad. They were all loosely compacted in the corner beside the gates to the warehouse. Eagerly, they turned to him for a briefing, to which he stood there opposed by his own hesitation.

"I-"

"Bloody hell…" After a few seconds of inaction, Christopher muttered under his breath and marched to the front of the pack. "Alright, people, grab your gear asap. We don't have a lot of time to waste so make it quick, then run to the main station. If you can't find us when you get there, don't worry too much. Just make sure you're on the train and we'll go from there."

Riled up by the sudden clarity of Christopher, they nodded and followed through with the order. Rhys helplessly watched as they disappeared outside. The commanding subordinate then glared at him with shame.

"Stop fucking around and pull yourself together."

And then, he too had disappeared, leaving Rhys just a few seconds to himself. He cursed beneath his breath, more so at himself than anyone else, before he too picked up the pace and ran for the armoury.

Outside, a vicious rainstorm had caught up to Mullackaye. Winds bayed and the soil was drowned. A bog slowly formed in the patches of soil offside of the roads. Boots sank in the mess as many waited in line to gather their equipment.

Rhys lost his heading at first, but soon found himself on the right track. Along the way he stumbled across a familiar face, who too had found herself lost in the stress of the dispersal. Her face was worn down by inelegant nights of troubled panic. Where fate led her was to a stranding – a destitute grave laid upon the beaches.

He ran over to her first, but as tradition dictated, they didn't say much to each other. They gave each other a look of many words and phrases: *let's stick together / where are we going / we're done for.*

Desperation held her tightly. Something had changed for her in that moment. Ella wasn't on the verge of tears or hidden behind a fearful cloak. No, she looked defeated. Incarcerated, detained and imprisoned – there was no escaping it anymore. Their shores were littered with violence. The absolute getaway meant death or survival – to become a murderer in order to save herself. Her beaten momentum infected him too. Together they trudged onward toward the armoury.

But soon after, she had disappeared into the crowd again. She said something about helping Tyran with the walker that was being loaded up. And there and then, Rhys was alone again. No matter the queues and crowds of soldiers clutching magazines and rifles around him, he was as isolated as ever before.

The morning had descended into chaos in mere minutes. A single siren had blistered his early dawn. Haria wouldn't be his battlefield but instead his grave.

Juxtaposed to his stress came the mediocrity of gathering equipment, a trivial matter he'd done time and time again for training exercises. Some grumbling figure would hand him his firearm, his sidearm, smoke grenades, binoculars, mapping kits, ammunition, webbing, coat, scuffed helmet, and all things standard. The weight of it all pressed against his back and shoulders. Rucksacks filled with mess tins, field dressings, cleaning kits and incessant lists of operational tools only added to its burden.

All around him, unprepared knights stood in haphazard formation. He strapped on metal kneepads beside decomposed organisation of the militia. Men and women with torn morale joined the frontline as many things: cowards and heroes, nationalists and anarchists, volunteers and draftees, men and women, adults and teenagers, veterans and greenhorns. But of all things, they were one of the same; civilians with guns. Nothing more than freshen sacrifices yet to bathe in the baptism of battle.

And before he knew it, he was all dressed up to go play soldier. He left the armoury with a grim filter over the future.

Moving through the crowds led him toward the very same rails he'd come to Mullackaye by. He'd been nowhere near it since he'd arrived at on base and grown ever the more loathful of its brutalist metallics. The girders, iron struts, wooden boxes, the violent bursts of steam; it was all too disgusting to look at.

He tightened the chinstrap on his helmet and shielded his eyes from the rain with its small brim.

Every breath he took fuelled a thicker fog. The mist drew its brush and flooded the concrete wasteland with a dampened fleece. Nihilistic demons triumphed over the angelic choir that came with the soon-forgotten sunshine. An illusionary gloom blackened out the faces of the people around him, returning them to the figures of husks. A violent hysteria gnawed at his temple and he covered his eyes with bitter fingers. Unfamiliar strings guided his body towards the rendezvous point, where he was due to meet his squad in the last seconds of concord.

"Rhys...?"

The voice tried to break through the creation of dejection that had stolen his focus. Echoed and swirled a thousand times, the kaleidoscopic delusion of her words tugged at his sleeves. They dug their way through the mists until they were at his ear.

"Rhys!"

A rumble in his skull forced him to pull himself back into consciousness. The darkness vanished in the blink of an eye and revealed a troubled Ella stood in his path.

"Are you okay?" She delicately asked.

"Yeah. I'm just…" He stopped himself. Christopher's advice played over in his head on repeat. "Where are the others?"

"I don't know."

Her anxiety mirrored his with near perfection. Where her eyes darted, his imitated. Where her voice trembled, his latched on to hers. Rushed figures pushed between them from time to time, eventually reminding them of what they were there for.

"Stick close by, we'll board now and find the others later."

She hesitantly nodded. Her free hand grabbed tightly on to his webbing strap and she affirmed their heading with a point ahead. Together they weathered the crowd ahead.

As they fully entered the station, they spotted their chariot – the Spirit Star. Its all-too-familiar three storey carriages towered over their heads, all while exhaling fumes and spitting out repulsive scents into the station.

Along the rear carriages, walkers could be seen being marched one by one for transportation. Officers stood on wooden crates and tried to maintain stricter cohesion, with some having given up and ordering for them to board regardless of who they were with. The two lost souls moved in quiet unison. They finally reached the steps to their carriage. The ascent was their greatest obstacle, for every inch higher they went, it was ever the more unknown if they'd ever make it back. Soon, they reached the top, where they were funnelled into an empty cabin down dizzy clashes of luxury and filth found within the hallway's aesthetic.

The cabin floor had been stained with the dried mud of boots of travelling conscripts, and there was a tear in one of the couches. All style had been vanquished, and the single painting they had looked like it had melted into the walls. Brown and green palettes made it a soldier's haven – an uninspired mess of drabs and textiles that dashed all signs of comfort.

Ella was the first to collapse into a seat, falling beside the rip in cushioning. She curled herself into a tight mess in the corner and rested her head against the window. With sleepless eyes, she lost her gaze to the painting above the opposing seat. It was of a muddy field, yet the paintbrush work done on the canvas looked as if the artist had had a stroke midway through, leaving a messy stream of filth along the bottom edge.

Rhys closed the door behind them, and pressed his back against it, waving off any other soldiers who'd cramp up their desired space.

In the corridor, the condensed shouts of officers ordering soldiers to their seats continued for another twenty minutes. And beyond the pane of glass to the station, the crowds thinned. The wild air had been tamed with a moistened glitter, trickling down the window. Steam and fumes exhausted from within its funnels and clashed with the rain-trodden sky. The three-storey wonder machine squealed a few times. Its voice filled in for the empty silence between Rhys and Ella.

He stared at her blankly, trying to pick apart her thoughts from looks alone. A troubled gaze from her darted around the exterior crowd and monitored everyone who passed by the cabin door that Rhys had blocked. And as the sound of the train's occupants became settled, she opened her thoughts to him with saddened insecurity.

"Do you think Sabrina got on the train?"

Finally, she had shattered the stillness. Her fingers tapped against her lap or rubbed against her forearms, switching between the two in an impossibility to remain still and calm. "What…if she didn't get on? What if she's still waiting for me outside and gets separated?"

"She'll be on the train."

"But what if-"

"She's on the train. Don't worry."

"Okay…" Her shortened breath was wobbly beneath her dampened voice. She shivered as the cold rain that soaked her down plundered her body heat.

With feeble hands, she unstrapped her helmet and sat it aside her. Colourless, pallid and dead were her eyes, as was the hour.

An enchanted whistle blew outside. Several screeches of metallic gears kicked into overdrive. Their carriage was yanked forward suddenly. The inertia disturbed those who had found the time to settle in their seats.

Steel wheels to track, their chariot crawled down the exit line to Haria. Its payload was an assortment of battle-ready gravediggers and those who they'd be burying: soldiers, rifles, ammunition, walkers, trucks, explosives, horses, friends, foes, memories and secrets.

The train fixated itself on delivering the swift blow to the Ferusian invasion. It set itself ahead, twisting and turning between the directional tracks and it found its way to the next life on a one-way journey to hell.

Another twenty minutes went by without conversation. Ella had tucked her knees tightly into her chest and given away no sense of ease. Rhys was restless as he paced from door to window, window to door, before he eventually malformed into his own mess on the opposing seat.

The man of the shadows had spoken proudly of good news. Why had everything done the contrary to his confident claims? The documentation they'd gone through had no say of Haria. And to what costs had the garrisons of the peninsula paid, with greater preparation sent to the assumed landing zones at Duhoc? Now Rhys hadn't the mind of a strategist nor of a general, but he was bewildered by the ease in which they'd been trapped with. If anything, he wondered if it was his fault for handing over the document. Each fault that could've been his, he exasperated a thousand times over. To him, he needed a reason to push himself back down.

"So, we're headed to the frontline…" She watched the drowned countryside fly by her window as the Spirit Star reached higher speeds. "Is it…going to be like that time at the windmill?"

He hesitated. It was clear that, without a shadow of a doubt, it was slated to be worse than all that they'd been through thus far. Far, far worse – out of the frying pan…

"I don't know, sorry." He lied as he breathed.

The world between the two filled with a deathly growl of the droning engine. He hated it.

"I can't go back to that place." Her hands reached out to her face, softly wiping the few droplets left on her cheek. She inhaled and looked to the ceiling for answers. Her eyes bled for the hours ahead of her. "I'm so sorry. I'm just so scared, I...I have no control over this."

Her rye had fallen through loose fingers. Steel pocketed the congestion in her throat and she looked as if she were about to vomit.

Rhys fell into the watered glint in her eye. He made the first mistake of feeling her pain as if it were his own. The day in which she'd held Evelyn – at the windmill's brawl – she had pled the voices of a thousand beggars, asking for that return to normality. The housecat was stuck in the lion's den. Wrong place, wrong time. Did she deserve to be there? Maybe, who knew? Yet at that second, where he was lost at the glistening twinkle that watched the ceiling, he wanted her to be free at all costs.

The tears continued to trickle down her pastel cheeks. And then, the paraphernalia of harsh recollections came forth. Skirmish had been something he had tried to erase without mercy. Every night, a glimmer of its disaster slipped into his peaceful slumber. Images of Ryan's caved skull, and of the man he killed himself. And sometimes, the man in the doorway was someone he denounced his guilt for – going as far as to change the vision entirely so that someone else had pulled the trigger. It wasn't comforting. The haunting of a man's life loomed over him. And as he was on the train, it gave him the worst opening to dwell on his actions.

Rhys took a breath of the vulgar-tasting air and leaned back in the seat. He too stared at the ceiling quietly. With Ella sobbing on one end of the cabin, he struggled to withhold his own thoughts. He remembered the bullets piercing the chest, the Ferusian body slumped against the doorframe. Then there was the grenade in the mill and the aftermath had been painted on the shocked faces of his allies.

He wanted to believe that where they were headed as an extension of some brutal training exercise, for if the invasion was truthful, and Ferusian soldiers had taken a beachhead, then the windmill should have been a trivial matter.

Their window was obscured by the hammering rainfall. A precarious foresight flowed within its endless stream and made the world outside sway through its refracted delusion. Each stream on the glass was painted like angel's blood, clear yet copious. The beauty of the outdoors died with the summer and the autumn laid in a season of tremendous bog.

The further they drifted across the tracks brought them closer to the end of the world.

~~~

"He definitely made it onto the train, didn't he?"

"Of course, he did, he's not slow."

"*But* he is incompetent. Dumb and slow, thick and soft-hearted."

"And I don't blame him. A lot's been on his shoulders."

"A lot's been on all of ours. Clearly we've all been through the same shit because we were there."

"Johan, some people aren't meant to be leaders, and Rhys-"

"Exactly! And I don't want to be led by someone who shouldn't be a leader. Listen to the big guys, like Chris, more than anyone else."

The venom temporarily settled when Johan declared his standing. As were in the eyes of the Royal Army, a leader was someone with grit, determination and unrelenting fury that held no candle to fear. They, however, weren't in the Royal Army. They were but militiamen and conscripts. To him, honour came from the romantics of war.

"Look, Sabrina said he's been swarmed with paperwork after paperwork, officer after officer interviewing him about...*that* day." Gwendolyn opposed him with a moderate, half-hearted tone unbalancing her stance.

Beside her, Tyran scribbled down onto the rear face of a flyer he'd found under his seat, and sat opposite him was Stephan – gloating with a pretentious grin as he looked to his older brother.

"If he can't handle pieces of paper, how can he handle a squad of soldiers?" Johan's voice was remarkably clear-cut and proud, a tone in which he'd never dared to bring around anyone with a stripe or two higher than his own. "The man's a mess, has about the social abilities of a brick wall and probably couldn't tell which foot his boot is supposed to go on."

She gave up on him and scoffed aside with the cream-on-top roll of the eyes – and the fire in his eyes gave her all the reason to smile smugly to herself. The conversation had gone nowhere, all the meanwhile Tyran had observed the debate in his own corner, mostly keeping his attention to his struggled art piece. A half-spent graphite pencil sat between his fingers and he used one of Gwen's carbine magazines as a support for the paper.

He let out a little chuckle to himself as he tittered over their inconsequential chambered-debate.

"There's a great line of work in politics for you three. All problems, no real solutions."

"Oh, fuck off," Stephan pushed his way into the conversation, "don't just sit back and claim wisdom on Kelan matters, fuckin' twat."

"Woah," the aged Redussian smiled, "save your prejudice for the syndicalists, boy. You might actually do some damage."

"Can't do jack-shit if Hendricks is taking charge. Just how long would it be until we become the next Ryan?"

There was a high-tension silence left at the end of the boy's bloodied premonition. Even Johan stared at him with the brotherly intention to shut him up before he brought down his argument with tactless inconsideration.

"Take some initiative then. He'll ease into the role eventually. And if you expect quality-"

"Don't join the militia, right, I get it." Stephan rolled his eyes and looked away.

"You volunteered."

"Fuck you."

Stephan launched up and onto his feet, walked outside of the cabin and crossed over to another one several rooms down. Johan hesitated at first, unsure if he wanted to apologise or not, and awkwardly shuffled out without so much as a squeak.

Tyran grinned, turning back to his paper. Gwen hadn't been sure if it were wise add anything to where it'd been left. But the way she looked at the ground signalled enough for the Redussian to land on her point before she did.

"Ignore the kids, Doctor. Allies by chance, far-kept acquaintances by choice."

"I think they're just stuck in the wrong side of the military. You know, Stephan keeps a book in his kit marking down any heroics he's yet to do." She laughed to herself. When Tyran didn't join in, she faded back into a cold mutter. "I mean, like…they are desperate to be soldiers, but we're the militia. They'd be insane to expect only the best-."

"Didn't I just say to ignore them?"

She complied and snapped herself back into the order of silenced. Like many of the squad's personnel, she hadn't conversed too much with them outside of her usual triage – Evelyn, Mateo and occasionally Rhys. As the latter had distanced himself for a while, the days became somewhat lonelier without his humanly faults.

"Now, how does this look?"

Out of the blue, Tyran coaxed her back out of thought to shed light on his little handheld project.

He flipped over the page, revealing to Gwen a small sketch. Swirls, with what appeared to be roots and leaves, formed incoherent nature-based icons between the creases of the paper. She took it from his hand and rubbed her fingers across the strange balance of detail from one leaf and the simplicity of the others.

"I…don't know what I'm looking at, but it's nice." Gwen said, handing it back. "What's it for?"

He frowned a little at her weakened response but took it to heart as a useful piece of criticism.

"I saw Evelyn drawing and wanted to do it too. Self-teaching, just in my spare time. I think it'd make a good birthday present in the weeks or months' time." When he took back his art, he held it up to the ceiling light and studied his improvements with a self-loving smile. "I heard Oslo mention it at least."

Outside the doorway, several high-profile soldiers passed by, some decorated with sunlight-orange rope lanyards looped around their left arms and shoulders. A continuous stream of four, maybe five, of them eyed the occupants of each room. One peered in their chamber and moved along, only second glancing the Redussian once.

They were left to the silence. Gwen shifted in her seat, crossing and uncrossing her legs over and over again as she became ever the more restless.

"How long do you think this journey will take?"

"Not a clue, Doctor." Tyran said, his fingers going back to his scribbling art piece. "But I'll cherish the hours of silence we have here."

139

"Do you think the fighting will have settled when we get there?"

"I can only hope."

Tyran's mutterings came to a close. Gwen looked to her kit: the medical pouches and first aid tools at her disposal were all in her regular orderly layout, and she reorganised them for the sake of passing the time.

She thought about Ryan for a while, and about her duty to tend to the wounded; those poor men misfortunate enough to be claimed as a casualty. To her, he'd been swiped up on death's instant arrival. Every minute they spent nearing the frontline, she cursed herself beneath her breath. The smoke they were headed into hid away the fire that raged behind its mystical body. Insanity was on the horizon and prepared to strike at a moment's notice. She, like many others aboard the train, prayed that whatever happened on the frontline would be short, and that it would not break the soil they trod upon. For beneath their feet lay a dormant underworld – and its tombs were waiting to be occupied.

~~~

The knock on the door yanked Rhys back into the real world. He blinked to clear his vision and adjusted to the darkened cabin. A quick scan outside the window revealed a sullied, water-buried forest in the distance, the sun sat low on the horizon with barely an inch perched over. The exhaustion had him dazed. An unclear fade in his soul had forced him into the groggy consciousness. He looked across to the other seat, expecting to see Ella asleep or silently staring out into the free world. In her place, however, was a small note.

"Gone to find Sabrina. Sorry."

He reread it a few times, taking in the message with a sigh. He was alone again, as things tended to be for him.

A heavy fist battered the cabin door for a second time. He sharply turned to face the glass frame. There stood a figure impatiently waiting on the other side. Whatever sadness he'd felt before had been outcasted by the arrival of fear, a tense obstruction in his throat ruining his ability to speak. A hesitant hand reached out to the door and he opened it. He hoped for the glass to just be a trick of the eye, a refraction distorting the face that looked into the room. When he slid the entryway open, nothing changed.

"Staff Sergeant Hendricks, I'm coming in." Galbraith looked at him irritably. A stern glare forced its way through before he did himself. Rhys didn't get enough time to answer before he found his space invaded and occupied by his superior officer. "Is no one else here?"

"There was," through scourged anxiety, he cleared his throat. "Private Mistral, Sir. She's gone searching for someone else."

"I see." Galbraith said, his fingers tugging with his brass cufflinks before he took a seat where Ella had been. On his chest were liquid stains and a foul stench to go with them "Well, you seem to be okay with this lovely bit of isolation, don't you?"

Prodding the sensation of loneliness, the abandonment he'd had from the good in the world, Rhys felt an eye twitch in response. Feelings of desertion had him plucked by prying fingers. His squad were the only community he resonated with, even if barely toward a few.

"It's been a while since we've caught up, one to one, hasn't it?" Every word he uttered had a curled whip to it, a seared sharpness that silenced Rhys' responses before he'd even thought of them. Dread's injection was sent by a rusted needle and Galbraith, the tip of the prick, was the disease that slowly colonised his veins. "I must say, I was certainly surprised by the news of your previous skirmish, Hendricks. You know, maybe things have started to take a turn for the better, or just a stroke of luck."

From his hip, he unsheathed a flimsy flask and unscrewed the lid. He downed four long gulps. Its obscene reek hit Rhys' nostrils at full velocity. He felt sick.

"I...wouldn't say that, Sir." Anxiously, Rhys' hands sunk down to his own thighs and he dug his fingers into his trousers to keep them occupied.

"I dare to disagree. You see, there aren't many times a warrior gets to walk in the boots they've been moulding their feet for." His words were divided by infrequent drinks, and the vulgar tastes continued to hoarsen his voice. "You'll ignore the flavour if you plunge yourself in it first."

With a stiff grip, he pushed the flask toward Rhys, who was quick to move away from it.

"I don't drink, sorry." He was met with a frown. Reluctantly, he took it back.

There was silence for a small minute. Galbraith studied him, watching with a disdainful glare whilst anchoring his steel eyes to his face. A potent stench of alcohol frothed from his mouth and clothes. The same intolerant scowl tore at his confidence, piece by piece.

Covert musings hid beneath Galbraith's helmet. Rhys couldn't understand what the man wanted. His intricacies had been unveiled upon their first meeting: the violent conscription that tore a family in three. Since then, he'd seen nothing of the sort. A descent into a traditional drill sergeant, more or less, with the lurk of an unknown family connection.

"It's bizarre, isn't it?" Rhys hesitated at his inquiry, shifting in his seat and digging his fingers deeper into his trousers.

"Sir?"

"I mean, just fifteen years ago I was sat about this distance away, on this very train, looking at these same eyes, on an older face." He spoke coarsely, pausing to scan Rhys' growing anxiety. "He turned and he ran, far back home. Never did he consider coming back. And then, I grew up, or whatever…"

"I don't quite-"

"Just shut the fuck up, Damien." A harsh cut ran deep into his voice. He whispered his assaults, just barely withholding the temptation to explode into a violent scream. He called him by his father's name and regurgitated a decade's woes. "I see it. I see the same reflection in your eye. You – you're a fucking rat. An inexcusable, cowardly rat who breeds and shits out wastes into my rank and file."

Those quiet tones crescendoed to louder bellows. Galbraith's tongue became feral, and it curled into a sickled blade, sharpening his voice. His boots tapped on the floor, his primal urge to gain closure by bearing his fangs.

"I've been waiting for fucking fifteen years to tell you this, Damien, and I'm saying it! Incapable. You're a fuck-up – a cheap, no-good, sorry excuse of flesh filling the rank good men

142

deserve, and you'll amount to nothing until you're dead! You let me go and left me to rot, but I'm here aren't I? And I'll give you s-"

"Lieutenant!"

A booming call silenced Galbraith's zealous storm. From the entryway, a man emerged from around the frame, stood with a demanding posture.

"If I were to hear anymore nonsense from your drunken lips I'd have you admitted to the asylum. Now leave this SNCO alone and sort your blithering mind out."

Unlike ever before, the voice commanded the monster to move. Like a good soldier Galbraith did as he was told. He gave a final glance at the deceitful father's son and glared, before leaving the comforting seat behind and disappearing back into the corridor. His stagger could be heard throughout the hallway, melting away as the roar of the train's engines took over. A courteous smile of meagre embarrassment soon reflected the intervening officer's reaction.

A thick, black paintbrush of a moustache tight-roped across his upper lip and hung from the underside of his nose. Upon his scalp, an old olive cap, with polished brass engravings, covered his clean-cut, greyish-black hair. Despite the clash, his eyes and smile seemed spirited in every way. And upon his shoulder were the Captain's rank slides. A ray of sunshine fluctuated from his presence as he entered the room, and he took a quick seat opposite Rhys.

"Sorry, ol' chap. I think the stress of it all is getting to everyone's heads." In an affluent voice, he spoke with a chirpiness unseen by other officers. Rhys doubted he knew the context any better than he did himself. Either way, the Captain's soothing optimism was refreshing. "I hope he didn't cause much distress. You okay, lad?"

"I'm…" Rhys thought about it for a second. It was a general question, an analysis of the clash, yet he felt like it dug deeper than intended. He wasn't okay. There wasn't anything to be complacent with. The world was on a decline, and his personal understanding of the world had been replaced by a landscape of magma. His inner psyche wanted to unveil his exposed anxiety. He could feel it clawing its way through his throat. "I'm fine."

143

The lie seemed to do it for the Captain. Once sat down, he undressed himself of his cap and leaned into the barely cushioned seat. His relaxing aura transpired through the air between them. Emerging comfort rested in his eyes. It was as if there was nothing to worry about around him.

"It's officers like those that made me transfer. Can't trust them until your life depends on them." From his breast pocket, he drew a long cigar, wrapped in a finely tuned brown cover.

The little lighter in his fingers flicked open and set the tip afire in a crisp glow. A drag of smoke spilled from his nostrils and lips, and it flowed between the strands of his lavish facial hair. He held one out for Rhys, to which he kindly shook his head.

"Y'know, we never used to get this kind of tomfoolery back then. People respected each other, but things do tend to change, don't they? Maybe it's the weather." Heavy drag after heavy drag; he continued to ponder his thoughts at the staff sergeant. "What's your name, mate?"

"Staff Sergeant Hendricks...Sir."

"Well met, Hendricks."

In came the interval of chain-smoking cigars and sipping from what little fresh air remained in the room. The rotten smell of Galbraith's alcohol still stained the chair's fabrics, like that of a furnace's ashened leftover. Once blended with the rich, tongue-watering sore of the cigar, the room tasted like caviar and fine wine at a banquet.

"So, already an SNCO? Heavy boots, those are." The Captain tapped the glowing bud onto his sleeve. The black spot on his wrist darkened. "Don't worry, old chap, there's a lot to make up for in these times. Meet the right man and you'll go far, I promise."

Rhys felt a genuine smile on his face and he cleared his throat to level his tone with the empathetic Captain. He noticed Rhys' shift in temper and leaned forward with an open palm ready for the taking.

"Captain Alexander Arthurs Jr. Pleasure to meet the rabble, lad."

"Well met, Sir." Unsure of how to render himself, he stuck to the tone that Alexander had. He then took his hand and shook it, firmly.

"Take it the militia hasn't treated you lads well, then?" He gave no window of opportunity to respond. "Bah, don't worry. Things'll get better with time. Always have, always will. Just wait for the rainclouds to clear out a bit."

Rhys was infatuated with the confidence that he pioneered his introduction with. A hint of jealousy, mostly, but the demeanour of the unexpected officer had him joyful in minutes. His pride was concrete from the second he first spoke.

"What regiment are you from?"

"54th, Sir."

"Defensive boys? Decent, decent. You guys have Laskey don't you?"

"Yeah, she's interesting, I guess."

"You don't really think that, do you, Hendricks?"

"No, not really, but I'd be doing an on-foot tour of the nation if I said otherwise."

As they laughed, Rhys was locked in the thrill of his momentary bliss. It was exhilarating, much alike discovering a place of worship that separated the deathly hallows of the apocalyptic world from the place he yearned to be at.

"I've only had a few conversations with her, but she seems very by-the-book, if that makes sense?" Rhys said, fumbling through his thoughts as he recalled their meeting in his office.

"Indeed, ol' chap. She's good at what she does, don't get me wrong, but I just can't hold a conversation with the bird."

Arthurs took the last few puffs of his cigar, stood up and walked towards the window. At its peak, a small handle cranked open a tiny opening, where he discarded the ashy stick into the wind.

"Where's your squad, then?" He asked.

"Somewhere on the train. We mostly got separated when everyone scrambled aboard."

"And you were alone in this cabin all this time?" The Captain moved back to his seat and folded one leg over the other.

"No – I had a friend with me. Private Mistral. She – uh – left when I dozed off to go look for her sister."

"Good luck to her then, a game of chance finding anyone on this damn train."

The Captain stretched and sprawled across his chair in a slight second of informality before he readjusted himself; he peered over to the door and heard a muffled wheeze and whimper from the adjacent cabins. The day drew to its twilight hours, and the blast of chatter had subsided into inundated tension. Whilst those waited for the moment that they'd be set loose on leashes to the cavernous pits of the great war, they slept in cradles made from dirtied sticks and cloth – and their tears were as fresh as the rain.

"Poor buggers. I'll admit," Alexander huffed aloud to himself, "I'm a little shocked it had to come to this. Tough call to put out the militia just like that."

From outside of their window, the distant treetops disappeared behind great hills and plains, its lavish green life vanishing into the distance.

"Truth of the matter is that we don't get much of a choice."

Rhys' thumbs twirled around one another in circular motion as he reached back to his mind. Reflections of the societal devastation the war had so far caused fluttered visions before his mind.

In the plains of thought, he witnessed a bleak apparition spindled together by the weaves of his imagination; it stood clad in a long, grey coat and with its face blocked out by something unclear. There was an echo down the dream's vapid scape that sounded like the breath of a masked man. The Captain's voice drifted away when Rhys blanked out and plunged into the trance.

He saw city walls crumbling. The bricks had turned to dust. Windows were shattered, rooms ransacked and the bedrooms were left as incomplete chambers.

Through the sky-locked clouds, he noticed the fiery trails of artillery shells soaring beneath the bombers. Fireworks of shrapnel wrecked the clouds with unyielded brutality. A carpet of explosions submerged the cracked roads, one by one drawing closer to Rhys' dreamscape body. He cowered but felt no pain. Each sharpened metallic piece of shrapnel passed through his body and his ghostly manifestation remained unscathed.

When the dust settled, he saw the apparition again. Underneath its decrepit cowl was a faded abyss of emptiness, where its face should have been. It reached out with a hand of pure bone, moved closer to Rhys and taunted his helpless, immobile self.

"You drifting off too?"

The returning ease of the Captain's voice shook Rhys out of the daze. He blinked a few times and found himself back where he was before: in a quiet cabin with his guest.

"Oh…sorry. I just kind of… it wasn't due to the conversation, just-"

"It's alright, lad. We're all going to feel the pressure at some point." Alexander took his cap and put it back on, whistling a short second tune to himself gently. "Say, let's take a walk, ol' chap. We'll see if we can find your squad to pass the time. Must be pretty lonely without them."

After adjusting how far his cap-brim tilted forward, he smugly grinned and took to his feet, beckoning Rhys' pursuit with the wave of a hand.

Into the corridor, he saw the full scale of the Spirit Star's capacity. The endless corridors twisted and turned zigzag trenchlines. On either side there were rooms crammed with militiamen of several regiments. Men and women slept in semi-crowded groups and refused to split up their established groups of friends, lest it be the last time they sat together. Some comforted those who cried, others hyped themselves up with the maintenance of their weaponry. Large machine guns, rifles, carbines, submachine guns, bolt action rifles, handguns, revolvers, anti-tank rifles: the arsenal of an entire army lay dormant.

The walls of the train were empty. No framed paintings could honestly dazzle the discomforted gazes of its passengers. The chariot continued farther toward the breach of war. The hours ticked down. Several thousand trained draftees moved on eternal tracks. Some yearned for the future of the battle, others held onto their firearms and begged for them be saved by their own deliverance of death. There were many hours left to go. And though they were hardened by the growing tension, they were infinitely better than the ground zero of what was to come.

147

Chapter 12

The Grand-Star Collision

T ender were her hands; gentle were her fingers. Ella stretched and, with a great yawn, reached towards the fluorescent light planted in the ceiling. Her vision cleared and the world was a little bit lighter. Against her shoulder, Evelyn laid comfortably, intoxicated by the heavenly delicacy of Ella's motherly caress through her hair. The two shifted. The engineer beckoned for her childly squadmate to give her room to move.

Her eyes reduced the blurry aesthetic of the weathered day with a few blinks, revealing Sabrina, Oslo and Mateo all comfortably squeezed onto their own bench. She yawned again. Ella's body had locked up during her roughened slumber, stiffened and sore. The relaxation she'd indulged had been disturbed by the rudimentary conditions of their cabin. Seats with jagged springs beneath the cadaver felt skin gave nothing but sore backsides and ached spines.

"Rough sleep, El'?" Sabrina welcomed her back to the fold.

She softly leaned forward to take her sister's hand. Both of them smiled. After around two hours of aimless walking, checking cabin from cabin, met with the occasional bad mouth from those she disturbed, it had been a wonder to have collapsed in a room full of familiars – albeit at the cost of leaving Rhys alone.

Riddled with fatigue, she yawned a third time. A world still as grim as it had been for the last fifteen years met her next, subsiding Sabrina's careful touch for the roughened edges in the atmosphere. The sole tones of warmth and brightness stemmed from her squadmates, whilst the grey drab of the outside world painted a horrid picture of reality.

"Sorry, was I out for long?"

"For a while, like a log. You missed Eve's little art piece."

Before Ella could ask, she looked over to the smaller girl and saw her staring down at one of the many steel helmets. From where the temple would be, etched in by the tip of a blade, a floral outline had been carved into the steel shell.

"It's lovely, isn't it?" Sabrina added, appraising the craftwork.

Evelyn tried to hide her visible embarrassment whilst under friendly scrutiny yet she still mustered a weak smile in response. Oslo leaned forward, ruffled her hair and proudly smiled at her work.

"It was Sabrina's idea at first, to be fair. Eve's done some fantastic work though." He worked his way over and carefully plucked the helmet from her hands.

There was a paternal shine in his otherwise browbeaten stare; and the holy curl of each hand-carved petal entranced him for a little while longer.

Ella silently gestured for Oslo to hand it over, and after a second of registering what she wanted he delivered the prize. Up close, she began to eye it herself. She first made out the formations of an uncoloured flower. A faint smile slid across her lips as she recognised the rose, detailed by its folds and the circles in a strikingly professional visualisation.

"Well, I was thinking that Rhys could use something of a pick-me-up." Sabrina explained. "So, we took Oslo's helmet and let the magic happen."

Off to the side, Mateo treated the conversation with a little snide smirk off to the side, where he chimed in with a jovial mock.

"Oh, so romantic."

"Come off it, you." She shot back with the faintest grin on her face.

Ella paid little attention to their jest and found herself lost in the piece. She stroked her thumb across the etched marks. The dug-out trenches of the knife's tip were rough, hewn with flakes of metal on every line. A defined mark in the steel had assured its permanence at least.

Her internal glow exploded into a burst of indulgence at the artistic piece. There was something innately beautiful about it all. The way that a piercing dagger had been converted into a pencil, unleashing the vivid nature of her graphic serenity.

The rose – a flower of cardinal fascination. The folds of its distinctive petals housed tender perfumes. Oh, how she wished she could've been indulging in its rich, fruitful scent; how dearly it would wipe away the stenches of alcohol and sweat that lingered throughout the Spirit Star. And though the forces of dissent strode by, with tank treads cruising over the flowerbeds, the marriage of nature to war had such a small yet endearing brilliance to her. Such magnificent presentations of grandeur art kept Ella level-headed in an otherwise clouded mindset, such as nature always had done for her. Every sunrise over the horizon, snowy peak on distant mountains, every field of poppies and each glistened lake took her out of the moment.

Despite the transgressions at the windmill, she desperately refused to believe the world was to be as awful as it said it was. There had to still be light in every dark corner.

"It's beautiful." Ella handed the helmet back to the girl, who quietly beamed to herself. The clattering of tracks beneath them died down slightly. A gentle deceleration adjusted the train as it moved around a tight corner through a nightfall valley. "How far away are we now?"

"Not too far." Mateo pressed his face against the window. All there was to see were the silhouettes of the absolute darkness. "They say we might arrive at the forward operating base in – like – half an hour, maybe."

Evelyn started to look pale. Ever closer came the end to their mortal breather from battle. The final speckles of sand in the hourglass began to drop into the dusty cascade beneath. A distant battle raged on, only shrouded by the respiration of the train's diesel lung.

Like explorers of the stars, the journey to battle had been an alien experience fuelled by a surreal misunderstanding. Everyone had heard of wars off in the distant age, but never at any point had the soldiers truly been prepared for the modern age of gunfire and mechanisation. They had become perpetrators of tomorrow's history, sat in the single most important events of not only their lives but perhaps that of their children, and the generations that followed. The weight on each and every soldier's backs was insurmountable – yet many failed to realise this beneath the numbing mass of their kits.

The Battle for Haria had thundered on for over a day. And what a day it had been, for the foundations of a prehistoric bloodthirst lay in wait for their arrival.

Outside their cabin came the approaching voice that caught the interest of Ella. She leaned toward the door to the sound of two tongues, one of which was far more familiar than the first. Sabrina, however, took to the door eagerly, quickly snatching the helmet for delivery. She stepped out into the open and peered down the corridor with a hand waving toward the voices.

"Rhys! Over here!"

The others piqued their interest, and a chuffed Mateo sat himself up straight as he mumbled through a yawn.

"He's finally turned up?"

"Someone else is with him."

"Who?"

"Don't know. Haven't seen this one before." Sabrina then stepped out of the cabin and disappeared down the hallway. Ella peered out of the doorway. She gave one of those soft, queen-like waves at Rhys, who was at first distracted by the approaching sister. A smile quickly came across his face as he saw the radiant halo of Sabrina on approach.

An uncommon contrary to his ridiculed mind had been given a short day to show itself. The hours aboard the Spirit Star had granted him an unsteady path to the mute aspiration of peace. A near impossible task, virtually surrounded by reminders of the conflict, but Ella couldn't be anymore blessed as the fly on the wall to her squad leader's glistening ease when he met her sister halfway. Their voices were buried underneath the roaring engines of the locomotive. Eager eyes watched the exchange as Sabrina handed over the gift from behind her back.

His initial grin told Ella everything she needed to know. Things could have always been better than they were, and the little cherry-picked gifts of certain days made life a little bit more bearable in the shackles of the crown.

"So, does he like it?"

The whispered anticipation was barely contained within Evelyn as she excitedly sat on the edge of her seat.

"Looks like he loves it." Ella assured her with a smile.

Her encouragement left the teenager giddy, and she smiled uncontrollably. Euphoria took grasp of her chest as she sank back into her seat until she was deflated back into the corner. The angelic glint in her pure, crystalised eyes tugged at Oslo's strings. As temporary as their ecstasy was, the effects were amongst the best in the entire war.

Sabrina's returned with Rhys close by her side. The chippy tune to his attitude had shifted drastically since Ella had last left him alone. In a remarkable difference, he looked as if time had been kind to him. Their greetings were short and sweet; there was a genuine lift to the atmosphere. The conversation kicked off with his praise for Evelyn, who reddened in the corner over the excessiveness of his gratitude.

Rhys passed his clean helmet over to Oslo to complete their trade. The ceiling bulb flickered a few times before its luminosity excelled, brighter than ever. Drenched in the coated grace of their gathering, the laughter leisurely replaced the low-tone talks. Rhys began with a light and humorous chastise toward Ella's departure from their cabin, flowing as sweetly as water beneath broken bridges.

"Oh, this is Captain Arthurs, he helped me find you." He turned and presented the jolly Captain in the doorway.

From around the corner, the aged face stepped forth with a great grin. Oslo's expression changed upon the immediate inspection.

"No problem, I'll leave you to it, old chap." He then addressed the small crowd. "And I'll see all of you out there. We'll do those reds one to remember."

Just as quickly as he'd joined the party, he disappeared into the midnight corridor with a faint whistle left behind at their door. Oslo then looked at Rhys with a bewildered smirk across his face.

"You know who that is right?"

"Yeah, Captain Arthurs?" Rhys returned a blank stare.

"No, no, I mean…do you know *who* Captain Arthurs is? The officer who was there, in Redus?"

"What was he: a mythical being of sorts?"

"Nah, he's my mate from the pub." Mateo snorted. Then, he prodded Rhys' forehead with a long finger. "Never mind 'bout that, how've you been, mate?"

And time trod by at a painstaking pace. The conversation deviated from the helmet carving to complaining about the seats, to the horrendous weather outside and onto future procrastinations. Never once did anyone mention the war, let alone the battle they crawled toward. Its influence hung over their helmets and shamed them from above, yet they wielded paper umbrellas. Each hour, it'd spit its acidic rainfall upon them and would carve through their shields with ease. Lingering vapor of adulterated poison soured their air. Rhys' smile faded over time. The dragged-on minutes spoiled his glee. And in came the changing of his guard: giddiness to fear. He arrived at the beginning of his relapse, and when his uneasiness was largely ignored by the privilege of laughter before battle, Sabrina had taken notice.

She saw the slight discomfort in face – his mind had imprints of his sadness pressed into it, for he could not stand aside from the approaching horror. Her hand reached out to his and she grasped him with the softest squeeze. At ease, at peace, he breathed easy. And her touch unintentionally lured him into a sense of security, moments before it would all come crashing down, for above and beyond the Spirit Star's journey did a battle rage on.

Amongst the stars and clouds to the unseen night skies, wings clashed in violent haste. Speeds of unmatched potential were reached as aircraft darted between one another. Their guns blared and the smoke from the engines trailed behind them with every bullet that hit its mark. Streamlined hawks circled one another, each in desperate attempts to best their opposition. Two squadrons clashed. The birds of prey had taken the fight inland and loomed above the chaos of Haria's hills.

Aces dared to die in a make-all-ends skirmish to ward off the Ferusian interceptors. They lined their gunsights up and tailed their targets. A gavel of skill and chance dictated who stayed in a high-altitude rapture and who would tumble back down to Farhawl's bleeding soil. Between rattled explosions and cockpits that burst into fiery carcasses, a second wave of aircraft arrived onto the scene. On their undercarriages were heavy high-explosive cannons accompanied a multitude of mid-grade demolition ordinances. Dive bombers, with extreme prejudice on their pilots' minds. In their glass canopies were drabbed countrymen who scanned the area beneath their untouchable terror. They spied a stream of lights that quickly rushed across a

153

single trial. Their orders were clear – demolish the supply lines; and in their sights was a railway elephant ripe for targeting.

They prepared to bank their way into a menacing dive. What those pilots told themselves blended between formal orders or the hopes that they'd make the strike count. Many of them sat comfortably separated from the consequences of their fast-moving forays. Their dust trails were the problems of an enemy they were told to annihilate. Who among them cared if they cut the birth cord of their adversary?

Turning their noses toward the ground, the sirens on their undercarriage trumpets blared; the measured crescendo screamed its charge in the moonlit prelude, droning a dysfunctional symphony to those below.

From within the train carriage, they didn't hear much at first. Rhys had made his way to the corridor for space and Oslo replaced his seat to keep Evelyn close by. Mateo was occupied in attempting to locate the remainder of the squad.

The final hour, however, was then upon them. The inception was built on the foremost trickle of a whisper beyond the glass.

It started as a quiet mumble, a wail in the wind that could barely be distinguished from the rest of the mechanical stutters the locomotive made. The Spirit Star moved as intended, unable to see the flanking wasps armed with their stings. Out in the corridor he stood, and Rhys first heard the other cabins hush one another when a buzz in the sky came to light. His attention was drawn a second too late.

Just beyond the window came a burst of dirt, grass and stone kicked up in a violent tower of debris. Soldiers tumbled away from the windows, shocked by the sudden flash of light and flame before their eyes. Upstairs, sounds of pierced steel and shattered glass broke the deadened orchestration of temporary tenderness. Across the entire train came shouts and screams that pled down crowding halls. The walls shook as a pounding of explosive matter shelled their metallic chariot. Every connected shot rumbled the entire chassis; the interior cruelly screeched in request for relief. Begging souls jumped to the floor with hands covering their heads. Rhys still stood, staggered against the wall. Many poured into the hallways, distancing themselves against the faint pane shields that blocked out the elements, whilst the ratta-tat-tat of twin 15_{mm} guns showered the on-rail coffin. Its lighter, less explosive streams of bullets pierced through the walls and, before Rhys' eyes, he watched two men fall victim to a single bullet, dropping them dead to the floor in an instant with blood coating the carpet.

Amidst the vicious and ferocious engagement, the wails drew nearer. The night sky shrouded their approach. Only the glimpse of tracers headed their way showed their course.

Smoke blew from one of the nearby cabins, the disgruntled tune of steel, iron and wood churned up as a single explosive shot cracked through their window. Vicious HE rounds pelted their helpless position. An ashy plume tore through the hallway and a choking heat swept the hallway in an unrestrictive spread. Rhys' jacket was coated in a smog of black residue. He coughed and collapsed to the ground as the tension scolded his eyes. His ears rang as a second combustion tore down the other end of hallway. Everything blurred in the moment. Something of a furious hellscape slashed into the barrel they swam within. He heard the whistling of bombs, the very foundation of Farhawl shuddered under the payload's detonation. He didn't see the dead that sprawled across the floor anymore, nor did he smell the fire. All he felt was the listing sensation as the great Spirit Star began to capsize.

A dislodged carriage rippled its untimely suicide throughout the train. When one fell, the rest tilted and tipped, and the roar of steel scratching against the earth soon deafened Rhys. Ragdoll – back and forth, from wall to wall. The world went black the moment he conjured the wish for it to all end.

~~~

The day that the overworld and underworld collided was one of reckoning; for it was to be a day to dwell, to ponder upon what humanity had done to deserve such devastation. Leaves upon twisted branches would eternally combust, lighting up the darkness in a singular fiery blaze. The ground would shake, crack and split asunder. Chasms that led to the dark descent would open up, and civilisations tumbled into the deep where memories would be lost to the void.

Through the breach, mankind once again would beg to the gods, the stars above, and ask what they had done to warrant such punishment.

Millions, if not billions, of lives had been lost in the old world. Machinations of total annihilation had decimated all that there was. The globe refuted extinction, yet bathed in an eternal fire. The reprimand from the deities was a cleansing, a purging of the civilisation that hadn't realised its ways. So, the people of Farhawl asked: why had such fire and fury descended upon them?

All except Sunar laughed. An enthralled chuckle had spread between their collective taunt.

"Why do you laugh? You bring us famine, flooding, droughts and now war. To what ends have you created this final disaster?"

They continued to laugh. Pointing down at the mortals, they gleefully repeated their pleas in vicious mockery.

"You are misled. War is your own creation, and the torch that set ablaze your home is yours."

~~~

Burning fumes breached her lungs and she spluttered. A savage coat of smouldering ash choked her with nettled fingers. The first inhalation brought her out of her unconsciousness: a disturbing welcome to scorched carnage around her. Her eyes were dried the second they opened. Seeing the flicker of the flame before her, instinct told her to scream.

Her weakened arms dragged her towards the wall, and her hands were cut by the fragments of glass sprawled all across the floor. She winced at the blood trickling from the wounds on her palms. Her mind raced with a primitive desire to take flight. Yet she was frozen. Cowered in the corner, she attempted not to flee, but to stay put in a decree of helplessness. Her bearings were shrouded with smoke. A cackling of spouted flame tormented her memory. The roaring hiss forced her nightmares to manifest as they crawled to her mind; its ethereal fingernails stuck into her eyes and pressed in an appalled recollection. She forced her eyelids shut and reached out to nothing.

Finally, her sense of hearing was recovered and all she could hear was the tyranny manifested around her world. And the first thing to hit her was the echo of agony.

Countless screams, shouts and pleas for help fell short of the outside world. Fuel for the furnace, bodies for the boiler. The cabin's doorway hung above her head; the carriage had toppled onto its side. Out into the corridor, the fire spread intently. Screeches of men and women begging for safety, searching for their friends and loved ones, indiscriminately tore down her morale. She couldn't breathe. She didn't want to move. To leave the destroyed cabin was to face the flame. To stay and cower was to die. Even if she wanted to, she couldn't cry. Each tear dried up before it even left her eyes.

Not again, she thought. She didn't want to be consumed a second time. Unnerved blisters would form on her skin if she'd stayed put. Her body would turn to charcoal. Sabrina wouldn't be able to-

Sabrina. Ella felt a surge in her arms and legs as she tried to stand up. She urgently reached for the doorframe above her. There was no debate, she *had* to find her sister. She was convinced that had she been saved once before – and she luckily had – then it would happen again.

When she gripped onto the body of the door, she shrieked. Seared metal admonished her bloody palms upon contact. The thermic ache murdered her drive. Retracting her hands left her alone in the gathering plumes. Suffocation. Abandonment. Left in the tomb, her silent screams fell upon deaf ears. In a sea of shrieks, she was indistinguishable and forgotten.

Ever-glowing spite blackened what little wood was in her cabin. Fear took control over her body and dominated her will to pray. A second attempt at climbing out was met with vile repercussion. The fury of the burns boiled her outpouring blood, branding it into her skin as reddened chalk. Through the thick smog, Ella couldn't see what she was doing. Every attempt to open them brought a drought to her vision. Demonic chants of suffering tried to push her back into the chasm of the cabin yet she kept moving, withstanding the heat against her skin, and she hoisted herself up through the exit. Her arms pulsed bubbled blood throughout every battered muscle. Where her heart pounded, submitting itself to fatigue, her mind grew weary.

157

She stumbled out onto the corridor where she had arrived at hell's antechamber.

The cabins above and below had been completely choked out. On the walls, which acted as the sullied de facto floor, unlucky souls lay with seared skin. Some had clothing still alight. Faces of unrecognisable char stared back at her with lifeless eyes shrouded in sheets of soot. Apocalyptic devastation littered the train. She stumbled in one direction. Behind trapped doors, Ella saw a man engulfed in astonishing flames.

Her half-opened, brutalised eyes plastered onto his body, at the tearing of his clothing and the flailed desperation of his gargled call. His tongue spilt out the exhaustion of life and all things lost, where the demonic anguish that he announced overwhelmed her senses. Her ears rang when his screams pierced her eardrums and made disorder from her spirits. The ghastly transition from man to emptiness held her in place. Her escape was obstructed by her traumatic view. She couldn't move to help him. She didn't even try. Why didn't she try? Oh god, she thought, why wasn't she trying anything at all?

Dribbles of blood spilt from her hand to the floor. The droplets disappeared into the smoky abyss, as did the burning man. His mutilated face had been drowned in a sheet of smoke. Only the hand that reached out to her was left strung up, calcined until the limb appeared otherworldly. However, the destruction was terrestrial, homemade and cooked up in humanity's own melting pot – no ethereal being nor deity could've ever torrefied a man so ruthlessly.

A hand latched onto her shoulder. Ella kept her eyes tightly shut and screamed. The hand led her to the right. Their destination was left unseen. She wheezed; her lungs had been ignited by the roaring flames around her. Oxygen was sparse. Life had been rescued by the hook of her little finger. Her momentum had failed. Her energy was fleeting. Hope had departed well before the train had. Her legs continued to move as the hand took her through the chambers of the underworld. Wooden fragments dropped behind them; splinters of flaming aggression trickled against her skin. Her ankles brushed past bodies and fingers executed by Ferusia's hawks.

The sweat on her forehead had dried up. Lest she opened her eyes, her imagination painted a red picture of her surroundings.

Such mephistophelian imagery singed into her sinuses, before − with razored talons − her skin and muscle were torn off by the horror that humoured her hell.

The tug on her shoulder imposed an authoritative might and aggressively dragged her further down the hallway. A voice came with it: it told her to follow his trail with the utmost obedience.

"Watch your step." It called through the ash and steam. She looked down and saw open doorways to cabins beneath her feet, housing the dead and small firepits below.

Who the voice belonged to was irrelevant to her, for she felt a brush of cold, moistened air where she diligently followed to.

Parched tears dribbled down her cheeks. Between her hacked rasp, choked mumbles left her lips in deathly sorrow. Like a lost child, she moved her bloody hand forward and latched on to the arm that led her. And then-

The impetus propelled her into an old darkness. The bombardment of ferocious flares no longer boiled her eyes through the skin of her lids. The heat was left behind to irradiate her spine with a spiteful offence. Where she had arrived was instead a bitter and wet wasteland. First, the wind hit her. After that came the precipitation and the sharp drop in the temperature. A punitive wound forced her hands to clench together when the water mixed with her blood. Ella gagged until she could finally taste the oxygen around her.

Through bittersweet fortune, the figure had dragged her out into the real world. The shouts and cries of the cremated could still be heard from within, but by the turn of the minute they had melted away into the crackling of flames.

Ella collapsed back onto the burnt. Her eyes were tightly shut again and she dared to not open them, not again. Shock entangled her mind into agonising dread. Frail fingers trembled at the thought of what she'd seen, and what they had felt in their final moments. Taunting gales shuddered her core and her heart had been trounced beyond its bearings. As the pale droplets laid upon her skin, moulding with her rehydrated tears, Ella opened her eyes to a callous blaze.

Her eyes were stung, puffed and reddened by the smoke that had blinded her sightline. Those sat just before her eyes were indistinguishable, with murky expressions obstructed by a misty filter of her tears. She buried her knees into the bog. Her body fell loose and her knuckles pressed against the dead grass. Effortless flames danced behind her, incinerating the last few train cabins to torment its last few entombed victims, like a cage in the illicit netherworld.

"Move the injured away from it!"

Before her blurred sight was the figure who'd retrieved her yelling over her shoulders. She looked behind her and saw mystified figures dash back into the chaotic flames, returning with the smouldered, the injured, the long-gone or empty handed. Anxiety riddled her sense of direction and understanding. Where she was could've been anywhere: Haria, Mullackaye, the streets of Burno or hell itself.

A pounding sensation in her mind limited her demand for recollection.

"Private, are you okay? Can you hear me?"

She continued to gaze with watered eyes, still sniffling and gasping wildly. Her stare went through her saviour and she lost all control in her respiration. Her lungs were starved for air. She panted, over and over, faster and more aggressively – all whilst she pierced through his transparent body that had led her aside. Her soul was paralysed.

"It's okay, it's okay. You're safe now." Their voice faded back in. She felt a jacket drape over her shoulders as someone dressed her in a shoulder-poncho.

The fatal happenings had convinced her she was already dead. Her lips trembled in an attempt to mutter out any form of response. Slurred phrases were disjointed by her inability to breathe, troubled further with her flowing cry.

"Here, pass me your hands. I'm just going to wrap them up, okay?"

The crack in her skin threatened to shatter her completely, for she shivered like a machine with loose cogwheels. Her rescuer drew two field dressings and took her hand, binding the cloth to her skin and hiding away her burnt scar.

Their nimble hands then tightened the bandage and the final constriction of it caused a flinch in her expression. In her pain, she let slip a name.

"Sabrina…" She'd whimper; her pathetic sob distorted by the tremble of her lips. The spirit of her soul had left her. All there was to her was fright.

"Is…" they paused, before looking around at the nearby crowd with a yell, "is there a Sabrina here? Sabrina!"

Her rescuer took action. When sat on the soot-trimmed perimeter of a frenzied firepit, just a crumb of encouragement was enough to make the difference. They took their chances and hoped someone would heed their call, for Ella's sake.

But chance took concern and pity upon the woman's crumbled state. Amongst the crowds of frantic escapees and survivors, Sabrina pushed through at the call of her name. Reunification led to her embrace. Ella felt herself clasped in a gentle embrace, yet its comfort was numbed by the agony of the hour.

Boisterous flickers of flame left behind refused to die down. The screams were silent. Yet, she had no relief, as the worst had teased its arrival with the incendiary prelude.

Lifting her up, Sabrina rallied what little strength she had left to get Ella on her feet. Together, they remained locked in one another's arms, simply glad that they could see one another's face clearly. All the younger sibling did was cry. Even in her sister's haven, the asylum of familiarity, her emotions had been let loose in the drowned night. The rain soaked into their clothing, their skin and their bandages. Around them, figures moved quickly to scavenge what little was left. Rifles, ammunition pouches and the dead. Officers primed for chaos dragged out the salvageable fallen. Supplies had been damaged. The rear carriage had been completely decimated in the crash, and the remains of walkers and other armoured vehicles had been decimated.

"Come this way. That's right, just keep following. I'm here. I'm here again." Sabrina said as she tailed the edge of the crowd to find refuge with comfortable faces. Her sister's shrieks never ceased. She could see the child in Ella's painful cry. It tore at her heart.

The hour became incomprehensible. Stained minds couldn't escape the atrocity around them. Ten minutes into the fire, officers cared less for the dead. Their emotions took a pragmatic approach and they focused on rallying functional numbers to continue the march. In the flames were the desperately needed supplies to save the critically wounded. Some asked their superior officers to put one between their eyes, just to end the pain. Each gunshot flinched Ella and she wailed each time over unnamed men who'd given up entirely. Those who clenched to hope slowly bled in their brothers', sisters', lovers', fathers', daughters', friends' and foes' arms.

She collapsed back into the marshy grassland, about fifty metres away from the wreckage, and just waited with her face tucked into her knees. Sabrina came back and forth to her, bringing her own scavenged supplies. A spare rifle was placed in her hand. Its clips were fed into her blackened webbing. And one by one, faces she recognised showed up with charcoal smoke painting their faces.

First came Gwen. Her eyes were already dried out. She'd sobbed to her limit at the last four casualties she'd dealt with. Then, she'd stiffened her gaze and thrown herself to continue her work. She moved to Ella to call for relief. She dropped down beside her, and the two silently looked at the flames. Its dazzled fury instilled a potent layer of fear upon in the air.

Those who'd lost it all within the train were confused and unsure of what to do next. An old squad leader – who'd escaped by himself – had no trace of his team. With those who refused to wait around, he marched ahead into the darkness, toward their original destination. Ella wanted to walk away too, just not to the frontline.

In her spine sat an invisible gun that cattle-prodded her at any point she considered abandonment. It compelled her to appease it as to not ignite its trigger. Desertion was no option for her. When ruled by that unbreakable gun barrel, she'd willingly let the chains of her fate latch around her neck. Without it, she'd not move at all. Something needed to pull her along or push her forward. Someone had to explicitly give her an order and to force her to do so. Her free will had faded into the obscurity of faceless soldiers. She was owned by someone, be it a woman or the military. Her heartbeat restlessly pounded at her chest, almost as if it were trying to do what she couldn't do and to make its own way into the future, without a rifle in its clutches.

Gwen stood up upon spying a larger collective of Squad 2. She heralded them toward their position, absolutely relieved to see more of the same faces alive and as well as the day would let them. Evelyn had passed out in Oslo's arms, who was at the front of the pack. Rhys trailed on behind, with his eyes locked to the dirt below.

Ella's eyes finally separated from the void and scanned wildly at the collective.

Rhys.
Oslo.
Evelyn.
Poor girl.
Back to Rhys.
Dynis.
Johan.
Stephan.
All quiet.
Sabrina.
Rhys again.
Christopher was somewhere else.
Rhys, yet again.
Tyran.
Mateo too.
Gwen.

Rhys.

Time and time again, her eyes landed on *him*. Whilst the others hugged one another and thanked the stars of their survival, Rhys cursed the soil with an unfathomable, unreachable gaze. It had dropped so far into tartarus that she could barely see the faded colour in his eyes.

Dark abyssal clouds loomed over their heads, whilst the remnants of an aerial battle died down off over the horizon. Yet she was struck with the absentee: Ella noticed it in Dynis' eyes. He trembled. Something had been taken from him.

And it hit her, just like that. Tamara was missing. Fate had executed its cruel plan. Ella's eyes widened, easily opening the gates to her ducts. The dawdling silence spoke for her. What doubts she had on her judgement were proven wrong as Johan comforted his friend, mouthing her name off to the distance. An earth-shattering drop of her name sent him into a quiet frenzy as Dynis paced back and forth with fingertips held directly to his frozen lips.

As if Ryan hadn't been enough. The caveat to their string of luck came at the harvesting of an ally's life. Yet when her conscience told her to turn in her pain and move on, it came as no difference whether she knew Tamara well. A tragedy was a tragedy.

It then stuck to her like napalm. The liquid stain infused with her clothing and soiled her body with dust and dirt. Rotten stenches of foul death coated what little cleanliness she had left. Gwen and Sabrina hoisted her back up and made sure the mud didn't breach her bandaging. Another cuddle from Sabrina went unnoticed. The finer comforts of life had been brutalised by a sadistic portrayal of the war's wrath. The windmill skirmish and the derailment of the Spirit Star – destiny had placed a hit on her head, it felt like. Not for her to die, however, but for her to endure all the suffering of a thousand years' aftermaths.

Time itself wanted her alive to see it all. Bullets and flame, blood and bone, all expended to haunt her when she was alone. No time to sleep, no will to wake up. Ella couldn't christen herself in the fallen. She couldn't brandish her skin with the war's ravenous inferno. All she could do was cry until someone dragged her chains to the edge of a cliff, nailed it to the top and hanged her with an iron-link noose.

Rhys blankly stared at her. He didn't know what to say, or what to do. Oslo cradled Evelyn tightly in his hands, whispering to himself unspeakable vulgarities. Part of him wanted to say something for the people around him, like any good leader would do in an hour of downfall. Everyone, however, knew that he didn't have it in him to put together the words they needed.

Instead, he just haunted the spaces between them. Sabrina occupied herself with her sister and the group kept to themselves over what they'd been through, or they worryingly watched over Evelyn's frail breath with familial concern. For them, the purge was over. Another faceless warrior had been forgotten by history. No monument would ever utter Tamara's name, and neither would Rhys.

It pained him to tell himself that. A second person had fallen under his command. Both were out of his reach, out of his control, and yet he ridiculed himself with the guilt that the killers should have felt. A fizzled spark had started to flash from within his carcass: a desire to strike those who tortured them. It was a faint and distorted feeling, but he put it to rest with a numbed stare to the sky.

He heard the officers begin to funnel the surviving soldiers ahead. With a simple compass direction, the order came through: walk through the valley of shadows and make their way to the nearest forward operating base, the original destination for the train. Just because they were compromised, bruised, battered and gouged didn't mean they were going to stop. There was only one goal on their minds: cease the invasion. The costs had been too great already. Turning back was a vile betrayal to the crown, to the people and to the ones who'd already perished. It was there and then, or the endgame could be allowed to begin.

Inquiries stumped him and left him still-faced. Even in the fury of the fire, he'd first grabbed his rifle and had held onto it religiously. He hadn't grabbed any of the people around him as his confidence had been sheered by the horrors he'd witnessed. In the desperation of what could've been his final seconds, he had his firearm, his ammunition and his carved helmet. His hands relished in its blend of metal and wood to which they had acclimatised him for.

The stars looked down upon them, hidden away whilst the fire raged on, and the clouds shielded their jarring grace. Rhys stood in absolute dusk. His eyes moved from the gun to the wreckage. Larger groups of soldiers and fractured squads started the journey.

His hand tightly gripped the gun in his sling. What he was defending himself from wasn't quite so clear. It could've been the Ferusians or the officers around him, or whatever else the world had to throw at him. Distrust bred paranoia.

Any alleyway, field, farm, street, forest or hilltop was within combat's reach. Carnivorous fiends that shot upon them had awakened the looming panic. Murder had rekindled his unshaken fear. First-hand, he'd tasted Ferusian blood. With his eyes reflecting the flames of the wreckage, Rhys unexpectedly felt the forceful guilt of taking a life fade away. His memory of the one he killed no longer tormented him. It warped and moulded around an agitation, a desire to start taking things as seriously as they were. The flames whispered to tell him not to take the beatings he received anymore.

Be a man, they said, and get ready to fight back with steel.

165

His human nature beckoned for war. A call to arms was just the turning of a season for mankind. Summer to Autumn, the falling of leaves buried the dead. Terror chaotically toyed with Rhys' psyche. Conforming to the rules of the fighting pit could've been the only way out, at least that's how he saw it at the time. And as the light of the flames danced before him, showing him a path he still feared, he cleared his throat and turned to the group.

"Can you all walk?" He pointed the query at all his surviving allies. No one verbally responded. They all nodded at least. "Then wait here, I'll find Christopher, and then we'll leave."

He left them to wallow in the same sadness he'd been dragged down by. Of course, Rhys wanted to be by their sides; not to suffer alongside them, but to be a glistening beacon for them to hold on to. But his hope had been stretched far too thin. His discontent had begun to encircle him.

Through the dispersed crowd was his target. Christopher was stood near the back, treating the last soldier he'd managed to retrieve from inside. His face was caked in ash and blood, albeit not his. Near his side, Lieutenant Galbraith watched over his back, as if he were spectating.

"Christopher…we've been ordered to-"

"I know. Just give me a minute, I'll be over there soon." Even whilst calm and collected, Christopher's tone was still as uneasy as he'd ever heard it before.

Galbraith's eyes shifted to Rhys and the two took a piercing glare at one another.

"What're you lookin' at?" Rhys couldn't tell if he'd sobered up at all. Irritated, the Lieutenant placed a palm on his forehead, leaning over and picking someone else's helmet off of the ground.

"Nothing…Sir. Are you okay?"

"-the fuck do you think?" A brutish snide remark cut over his false concern for the officer. Both of them knew Rhys wasn't particularly worried about him. "It's fucking Redus all over again…"

He too looked solemnly at fervent, fanatical flames, and the pair of moral adversaries stared down the same firepit. It didn't die down. The heavy downpour did nothing to quell its dance. Circles of amber spiralled through cracked glass and the valley glowed in its basking rays.

Whilst Christopher hoisted up the injured survivor and moved him further towards the crowds, Galbraith was left beside Rhys with both of them left to dwell on the devastation. The latter shivered, the former did not. Aggressive pains ridiculed their foreheads. Seeing their own carriage on its side, ravaged by the dirt it'd been dragged through, neither could really appreciate the luck that had been bestowed upon their own.

At the helm of it all, the locomotive driving the convoy of carriages had taken the worst hit. Its funnel had been shattered and splintered into small iron pieces, whilst its walls had melted into the driver's cabin from where an incendiary bomb had directly hit. Hidden in the grass was a resting place for bodies then uncovered as the greenery burned away.

"So, are we just going to leave it all here," he angrily asked, his eyes fixated on the dark horizon, "and we just march ahead like nothing happened?"

"What else is there to do?"

"Well-…" He stammered, unsettled by the unending persistence of his life's pointless journey. "Call me hysterical but I can't just walk away from this."

"We've got orders, Staff Sergeant."

"People have just been killed, Sir."

"How unexpected."

"Sir, it's just-"

"In a war? You'd never imagine."

"Can you please stop taking the piss and-"

"-the fuck do you want me to do, raise the dead?" Galbraith's shouting cut through Rhys' delirious nonsense. A sharp tongue seethed a simmered anger from behind his teeth. "Stand around and getting nothing done isn't going to solve anything."

Under the cruel mask he'd brandished, his voice peppered Rhys in brutal truths that even he knew. Reflection upon the tyranny and apocalyptic discrepancies around them only served as a means to feel a little better. It cost time. Time fled onward, regardless of the situation. And Rhys had done his best to forget that the fate of Haria's invasion rested on every man, woman and child sent over with rifles in their hands. Lest they win, millions deeper into the heart of Kelan would bleed.

"You're a fucking joke!" The snarl pushed Rhys' outburst further into the mud. Ridiculed and hushed, he simply took the barrage as it came. "Now get moving. They're dead. The frontline ahead of us isn't. Be a good man and stop moping."

With a final swig, Galbraith set off before him. Only a few officers remained around the area, alongside medics who treated the final few injured who had a chance at survival. Rain splashed against Rhys' helmet and flowed off the rim. He watched as Gwen and Mateo helped attend an abandoned bearer's position for an occupied stretcher.

His eyes danced around in his sockets lifelessly, and he sought out the countless unrecognisable dead, the ones who didn't make it out alive. He couldn't part his sight from their crumbled states, transfixed to their resting places of ash and burns.

Logic battled with his emotional distress. Being left in the wake of the regiment's dire expedition would add his own body to the pile. He hadn't looked in the eyes of his comrades. His own pain hushed him and silenced all attempts to feel what they too felt. Bar a few, many of them weren't toughened to the core or nullified to the war's carnage.

Imperceptible strings tugged him toward the shrouded road that laid ahead. And without a goodbye or any sign of respect, he turned and walked away from the deceased, rifle close to his chest. In that minute, he'd decided he didn't want to choose. In a world bigger than his own personal understanding, what could've he possibly known about right and wrong? It was those who thought themselves larger than life that faced the greatest downfalls.

Chapter 13

Stillness

Patience; that's what they were calling it. Days stacked upon days, busied by prolonged waiting within tattered tents, all the while stood by in anticipation for a clash of two titans. Pavilions and canvas domes laid in bundled columns, rows and sections. One hundred and twenty-five of them littered the flooded land of Haria. More than half of those tents were specially allotted to treating the near-constant flow of wounded soldiers wheelbarrowed into the base. And the casualties were far more plentiful than the rations given to the healthy.

Limbless, exposed intestines, hollowed out chests, empty eye sockets and fingerless hands. The hours brought after wave and the mistreated. At every other hour a burial service was held around the back of the base. At first, they could afford to be entombed in pairs; then, as the battle continued, they were packed into triads. Four, five then eight. Twelve. Eighteen. The numbers kept amassing. Collective graves went from being a last resort to the standard procedure. Normalised pits sometimes housed hundreds at a time.

The Battle of Haria had lasted for an entire nine long, drawn-out days. Just about two-hundred and sixteen hours had been dedicated to carnage. A multitude of numbers circled around the loose lips. Two thousand. Five thousand. Twelve thousand. Still, no one was certain of how many had been killed on the northern peninsula, unaccounted for all the Ferusian deaths on top of that.

Initially, things had appeared bright for the cursed landscape. Despite the concentration of Kelan's coastal defence having been shifted to Point Duhoc, the remaining garrisons had taken each thrashing coming, standing with tooth and nail sharpened, with near-success. Three long hours was all it lasted – had it not been for the fierce support Ferusia had on hand, perhaps they could have held their ground. Bombardment after bombardment was followed by wave upon wave of infantrymen taken to the widened shores.

Droves of dove-winged warriors moved in flocks, taking each metre they got without surrender. When one was cut down, four more emerged from behind. Eventually, the coastal fortifications were overran by sappers and shocktroopers, and the lines were breached, exposing the flanks of half of the coastal bunkers. The brutal clash had then been brought from sand to dirt. By the end of the day, twenty thousand Ferusian troops had been landed across separate beachhead pockets.

And by that time, the Spirit Star had been derailed, and the Ferusian presence had tripled. The gaps in their holdings were filled in with fresh faces and steel beasts. On the verge of being pushed back into the sea, they advanced post-haste. Lives were then spent with great regret but they had gained a monumental profit. Each fort, trench and hamlet taken from the Kelan defenders was another asset under their control, for supply and logistical leverage. A scourge for the skies soon took the main stage. Close air support probed the earth in strict formation, rooting out the strongest pockets of the homeland guards. Fighters dared to dance in vile competition. And across the great horizon, two sky-dreadnoughts brought their arsenal to one another's flanks. The air was littered with a display of fireworks at the expense of people's lives.

Ferusia attempted several landings all across the peninsula, however their levels of success varied all across the board. Where small pockets of resistance opened up all along the coast of northern Kelan, it was in Haria where the invasion's triumph would be chanced.

The militia's march to the forward operating base had remarkably been the calm between twin storms. The firestorms that laid behind them were replaced with distant thunders ahead.

Not once did the rain give in. Three hours of walking drenched the wounded with the fatigued. Without working radio equipment, they were left to speculate on their destination's safety. By a stroke of luck, passing convoys soon rallied to their area and concluded the final leg of the journey with motorised transportation.

Rhys had witnessed five immobile soldiers take their final breaths in the discomfort of blood-soaked stretchers. Never once had Rhys' squad stop by to comfort them in their closing minutes. By the time they'd reached the trucks, that hope of victory had all but vanished. The night had taken enough from them. The offer of a tent-rooftop shielding them from the scarred skies came as a blessing, and they all slept uneasily, if at all.

Patience – they still called it that. Or anticipation. Dread, Rhys thought, and only that. Communication was limited and their orders were simply to hold and await further orders. Garrison duty, nonetheless, until it was their turn to be drawn from the roulette. Every few hours, four or five squads were sent off to the frontline to replenish the numbers lost. For days, Rhys had avoided being sent out there to die. So, he did all that he could and listened, in solitude, to the distant thunder.

Once a day, a new threat challenged the base's defences. Two aircraft circled overhead and made for a quick strike, only to be gunned down by its anti-air batteries inside. They weren't untouchable, but only for as long as the frontline persisted. Sometimes their bombs would connect to their targets, and the tents would be torn to shreds, occupants included.

Come the nineth day, Rhys had spent his time under the cover of his shared tent. Dynis, Gwen, Oslo and Evelyn were amongst the many faces piled inside. Members of the 102nd Fusiliers had been bunked with them, all who dipped in and out of tent like apparitions – some even left without a trace.

Nothing much happened. After hours of watching the perimeter and the skies, he'd been given the day to excuse himself and lay dormant in their tents. There weren't any recreational activities to partake in, except a few kick-abouts with a regimental football. Never had been Rhys' thing anyway. Fellow squadmates came in and out throughout the day, yet fairly few gave him so much as a nod.

Sat on the edge of her foldable bed, Evelyn occupied herself with the greatest therapy available: art. She used her blade and chiselled away at small pieces of wood she'd found littered around the base. Mostly unnoticed by the others, she was graced with the freedom of solitude to perfect her craft. Rhys, however, tried to force a smile as he approached her, long after his hours were spent watching rain drip through the ceiling of his scuffed tent.

She was lost in her work and appeared at peace with the world around her, only for as long as she could forget it.

But deep into the twilight hours came orchestrations of artillery, and the gunfire whispered in deliberate taunt – to remind them that death approached. Evelyn had pushed all of that out and aside. As long as she held her sharp paintbrush, there was no war.

His attention turned to the knife and he watched its glistened tip curl a beautiful swirl in the plank. From his distance, he couldn't figure out what her creation was. Something about embroidering on the flat face of the wood, visualising a smooth-edged creature he didn't recognise.

She set her project aside when Oslo finally returned from duty. He was trailed closely by a face neither had seen before. A young Osakan woman, holding her soaked helmet with shivering blue hands. When prompted by Oslo, she moved forward and stood the young soldier.

"Are you the girl who draws on helmets?" Evelyn's eyes lit up. The woman's question threw her into an embarrassed liveliness, and a strong sense of pride surpassed her. She shied back into her collar and awkwardly nodded. "Sorry if it's a bother to you, I was just wondering if – well, do you take requests?"

Her eyes moved to Oslo for approval. He shrugged back and left it up to her. And with the exchange of the helmet to her petite fingers, she went to work.

In any other circumstance, Rhys' heart would've melted at the interaction, yet that overbearing numbness to his chest did little to help. Beyond the fabric of the tent lay hundreds of injured men and women calling for nurses to cling on to their lives or to simply end it all. Through the material was the distant horizon of fire, seen beyond the hills and plains bogged down by seas of endless downpour. For once, though, the thumps of artillery shells and volleys of gunfire…were all drowned out by the girl who wanted to draw.

An hour dragged by. Rhys' eyes were transfixed on the helmet, the curl of the knife and the silent interactions between her and the client. They spoke softly to one another, as two innocents taken to the frontline by force. The visitor stood with angelic naïveté, even though, on a frayed sling, there was a mud-coated shotgun wrapped around her back.

By the time she'd finished, the sun had set behind the hills and the wolf-fur sky dimmed. Instead of crickets and owls were the cowls of combat and the hooded generals ordering another artillery strike.

From the dark corners of the tent Rhys eyed the finished piece. A tree, of sorts; he was unsure of the type. Her artistic visualisation had produced a sudden masterpiece that couldn't wait to be swept up in the havoc of the war.

The Osakan woman thanked Evelyn in ecstatic kindness before scurrying off to her own pack. Her eyes refusing to leave her gifted design. Rhys looked down at his own helmet to where the rose had been carved in. He grinned at first – he imagined all sorts of beautiful colours that could've filled in its precise linework. One day, he promised himself, he'd paint it himself. Crimson whirls of viscous paint would finalise the bright finish to the flower. And for once, it made him think of home.

His mind trailed off to the rose portrait in the corner of the dingy sitting room. His sweetened memories of home had once been overran by the court of discipline, and to reminisce of the past so longingly was daunting. His smile faded. For a short while, he looked at the helmet and yearned the homecoming he might've never gotten.

Then he thought of who he was. Tears would've welted up in his eyes if he'd been the same man he was before his draft. Had he seen who he became, maybe he'd hate himself more than he already did. It made him want to weep, but he couldn't. Who benefited from him crying?

Painful reminders of his rural abode were then set aside when the room snapped to attention. He lifted his head upon the call and rose to his feet, spying ahead to see who'd entered their hideaway.

"Staff Sergeant Hendricks?" Their eyes met. A familiar warmth rested in his elder irises. "Mind taking a walk with me?"

Without hesitation, he felt a surge of energy bless his soul. He saluted the Captain and strode forward, departing back out into the harsh world, with Arthurs' wisdom as a cordial shield against the strikes from the skies.

They trod across the boardwalks and wooden walkways, and the mud beneath them slogged like the depths of the far oceans. They moved through the base and he was shown surroundings he'd grown accustomed to. Medical tents, armouries and armoured vehicles that chanted in constant motion, and a flow of able bodies that departed where casualties came in from. Slender poles that bared coats of arms and the prestigious banner of Kelan's national pride aggressively waved in the strong gusts. Trucks stuck in the vile sludge had countless bodies stood behind, who tried their hardest to unbuckle the natural belt holding them down. Dressed in woollen and cotton military coats, hundreds of men and women marched from encampment to encampment. Some attempted to kick that small ball around, only for it to stick to the mud they trod around.

"Hard to have any pride when that very nation keeps throwing the elements against you." Rhys told the Captain. A hesitant chuckle was shared between their shared sleepless unease.

"Too right, my boy. Though at least what we're getting, so are the reds across the valley."

The pair sauntered away from jostled districts of tents and military activity and together arrived at a concrete gabion perimeter. Ascending a short flight of makeshift wooden stairs, they reached a watchman's post, unoccupied.

"Though as their progress indicates, they're not too fussed about it all."

Rhys looked out over the adjacent valley. Through a sentry's viewpoint, the scale of the defensive measures' development had caught him off guard. For something so temporary, the base had made it clear it would not budge for syndicalism. Previous perimeter patrols had seen an unfathomable number of soldiers digging into the very soil that threatened to drown them. Up in the watchman's post, he could see the completion of hundreds of lines in the dirt. Most, however, had been unfortunately overflooded by the horrific weather.

"We can't quite catch a rest. The stars are giving us a challenge. Bullies, the lot of them. Can't even rely on our trench system." As he analysed the battlefield, Rhys turned away from the drowned landscape and went back at Arthurs.

"You wanted to see me, Sir? Something specific?"

"Ah, right. Yes, there's always the bad news." He turned to Rhys, fixing his cap in the motion. "Two of your squadmates have been given permission to transfer units."

A jolt of confusion shot through Rhys. The quick delivery of the news took him off guard, taking jabs at his gut whilst he scrambled for answers. Two soldiers? Lest heaven had made its decision to shred all he held dear; he dreaded the names of the favoured.

"What...do you-"

"Private and Lance Corporal Kaelo." Johan and Stephan. Gods be damned, he had nearly broken into a fit of sorrow. The two seraphs he had grown fond of remained, but it didn't quite take away from the seriousness of two distrustful wanderers.

"They transferred?" Arthurs nodded in response. "How is that even possible? Why hadn't I heard about it?"

"Well, I'd assumed they'd spoken to you about it at first, but that's never the case is it, old chap? I do have their file regarding it, they have a copy for you." He tried to levy the bad news with a joyful tariff – and his joke fell flat judging by Rhys' pale-faced response: "Like a receipt, lad."

From within his inner coat pocket, he took out a small envelope pressed by an exclusive wax seal. With cold fingers, Rhys plucked it from the Captain and flipped it over.

A wax coating had been slathered rather excessively, as if the sealer had made several attempts to do their job correctly. A coat of arms, decorated with stoic lions and great beasts, was imprinted within the seal. Some of the letters had been so horrendously drowned that they appeared as incoherent lumps rather than any legitimate scripture. Part of him didn't want to open the letter. But that wouldn't have changed the situation at hand.

His finger dug beneath the seal and he caught a few layers of wax beneath his dirtied fingernail. He belittled its hold upon the contents inside. Under the dry cover of the watchman's post, he unfolded the letter and followed through the words:

After much discussion from the 54th Defensive Regiment's Commander-in-Chief, Field Marshal Van-Cielly has subsequently approved the soldiers' request to change unit.

Approval was granted under the notion that their leadership had been severely lacking.

The more he read, the less it made sense. The jargon of flamboyant formality complicated the situation. Lacking leadership? The insignificance of two unheard, lowly ranked militiamen seemed less than logical for a written report.

"Bureaucracy's a bitch, lad." Alexander coughed, pulling out another cigar to champion through. "Heard their father filled some big boots. Makes the dream work up in those platinum hills."

"Where have they gone? I saw them…a few days ago, I think?"

"Probably to wherever the document said they'd transferred to. I don't know anything about the lads, that's on you."

"I guess it is." Rhys muttered as he faced the ground.

On the first drag, Alexander gagged on his initial strong hit of the cigar, pounding his chest with a closed fist.

"Kaelo, right?"

"Yeah. They big?" Military documents he had access to rarely discussed the familial origins of his soldiers, only the information important to the leaders at hand. Alexander was far too busy in his coughing fit to answer. "I imagine so, then."

He read on with little more than a disheartened morale to compliment his failures as a leader.

Addendum: *Both Lance Corporal J. Kaelo and Private S. Kaelo let out several reports about the effectiveness of their squad's command chain. Claims cannot be confirmed. Investigation from local Officer is permitted.*

Mouthing the words as his eyes followed the text, he stumbled across the concluding mentions of investigation. When he looked up, the Captain gave a half-arsed grin and took the paper back from him.

"Lucky I volunteered and not someone else." Alexander pressed the remaining bud against the side of the post. "Don't really think there's much to talk about, but how're you feeling, as an SNCO, then?"

When he spoke, Rhys felt as if he could open up about things he'd have dared not told his other superiors. He wasn't quite sure how Alexander had the means to pry him, but it was a comforting thought to go by.

"As an SNCO?" He said, thinking to himself aloud. "I…don't think I'm good for the role."

"How so?" Bluntly, the Captain pressed through. Rhys was struck by its insistence, hesitant.

"Well…I panic on the inside a lot. Afraid, a lot. Spent too long in my mind talking to myself than I should've, instead of spending it with the people I'm supposed to lead." He found his words flowing out naturally. "I'm not supposed to be here, Sir. My own subordinates take over where I fall behind. I barely speak with most of them, spent days brooding over my mistakes and just…I'm terrified."

Alexander waited for a few seconds after he finished, gently nodding his head whilst he curled his thick moustache around his wrinkled finger. Following yet another chesty cough, he adjusted his sleeves.

"Look, son, it's not a bad thing to be afraid."

"Why, though?"

"Well, take it this way. If you're never even the slightest bit scared, when will you know when to reserve yourself? Being afraid can be a good thing – reminds the chaps you're human, after all. And you might be able to draw the line between bad and good if you are, lad."

Rhys looked away from him. On the cold, dampened floor they stood upon, his eyes lost themselves in the sediments below. The Captain continued to talk but was harshly blocked out by his own self-reflection. Rhys was scared. Petrified, even. But of what? Death? The loss of others? The nights had persisted to unleash horrific dreams and cursed nightmares. Retellings of the past and prophecies of the future. Blood. Iron. Will. Pain. Sadness. Rain. Separation. The complete collapse of Kelan's

177

welfare as an oligarchic Kingdom, right before his eyes. And unlike stories of the old, where one had to imagine the greatest shifts in continental civilisation, he was there on the frontlines being subjected to it by force.

Beneath his boots, the tiniest of stones flowed in droplet puddles, fading into the moisturised earth. Small, almost impossible to make out in the floor of lookalikes. Residue converged with the droplets seeping through tiny cracks in the roof. Regardless of how insignificant each one was, it'd been consumed by turning tides of the clouds above. Millions of its kind had been diluted. Its foundation had been replaced by a needle-sized sea.

"Captain, how can I better myself as a Squad Leader?" Interrupting his superior's unheard monologue, he left his eyes on the ground.

"Eh, well…it'd be hard not to admit you'd need some more coherence and a greater ability to improvise, to adapt into the chaos. Keeping your squad alive would be your priority, but sometimes you'd still have to risk it all for the greater image. All simple stuff on paper, mate." With a snap of the finger, he lifted Rhys' eyes from the floor to his face. "Chin up, lad. You'll get your opportunity to prove your courage. Just think about what you've got to hold on to and keep to it. You'll fear losing it, and that alone should be enough to make you do whatever you need to keep it around. Just know that sometimes, you can't save them all."

A thunderous clap rumbled the distant hilltops. A kilometre away, the rise and fall of stone, dirt and grass tore into the sky, collapsing and scattering across the land it'd originated from.

"How long are we going to sit here? Their shots get closer by the hour when their planes have gotten cautious." Rhys asked.

"You'll be out there within the next two days. Could be tonight, could be tomorrow. They'll send out the call soon." Alexander's voice shifted into one of dire understanding. He knew that beyond those hilltops and into the lands tainted by war there would be nothing but horror and agony. Rhys saw it in his eyes. A taste of the battle's foul palate preluded the poisonous approach of Haria's devastation. Both the Captain and he knew out there, humanity wasn't a concept, let alone an expectation. The difference between them was that, for Alexander, it was the

178

encore to his life of war. And for Rhys, it was the overture to his own private apocalypse.

"And our duties will be to hold the line? Would we ever get rest?"

"I don't doubt you'll get the room to breathe on occasion, Hendricks. Cop a blighter, you might, but that's a ticket home. At least it's not a constant stream of attacks. They'll bomb you out from across the horizon. And when you're at your weakest, they'll move in the infantrymen. We can't get our own tanks up to the frontline and I can sure-as-hell say they can't either."

Alexander drew out yet another cigar, himself stressed out by the thought of the battle. For what little time Rhys had known him, he saw more in his years of experience than he did in the facelessness of his squad. He *was* a soldier and a hero, to Rhys; the perfect model for the Queen's own personal warriors.

"Then why don't we redeploy to a position where we can safely rely on our armoured support?"

It wasn't much, but the doctrines taught in his infancy as a leader had always highlighted the superiority of the machine, the mechanical tool of war. To subside it seemed like an absurd irrationality prolonged by its creators.

"Command wants to deal as much damage to the unsupported landing forces at the cost of our own."

"And what if we don't, Sir?"

"Then we lose a sizeable portion of our experienced ground forces. It'll be open warfare from there onwards." Alexander pointed across the blotched lands toward the trails of smoke that had forged beyond the hilltops. "Smaller invasions are happening all across the North, but this region is where the bulk is headed. This is the main fighting ground and we'll deal our cards here in the hopes are driven for good."

Militarised players stepped up to the ring. The decks had been laid across the table, hands scurried for the stacks with weight to them. The stakes had never been so high before. Honour and pride were, for the first time, second to sovereignty, mortality and survival.

Solidarity had been vanquished and trounced upon by the declaration of battle. It was an all-or-nothing situation. One small mistake would write history for the following years. Powerless, Rhys felt as if he couldn't make do of anything worthwhile.

"Do you think our monarchs will regret this day?" Alexander spoke with bitter fidelity.

"I hope they do." Tired, drained from the week's hardships, Rhys let out a pathetic sigh. "Do you?"

"Powers conjure up wars for young ones to die in. They'll only regret it when the steps to their castles are soaked in blood." Gales slipped through the cracks of the watchman's post and froze his words in the air, hovering before Rhys. "People tend to regret things only when it doesn't go their way. If we win, we'll forget all about the horrors we leave behind. We don't like it, lad, but maybe the only good in victory is justifying the things we've got to do."

Chapter 14

The Contact

Deafened by the fifth shot, Lylith held on to her left ear with two calloused fingertips. Her discomfort outweighed her sense of pride and accomplishment, and she looked ahead to document her progress. There, she saw that she had only hit a single target. She collapsed to the floor and left her rifle to hang loosely from her shoulder as she rested in the sky-soaked debris. Her face was covered by a thin balaclava that hid away her face.

"Slacking. Try again in ten minutes." The driver called out, with hands buried in the pockets of his long coat. She excused her setbacks by eyeing up the clouded skies; torrential rainfall hampered her progress and have given her handler, the driver, the disappointment of watching her efforts fritter like snowflakes in a gale.

Around her, the run-down leftovers of homes and fields had been relatively silent. They sat along the edges of derelict tundra plains, where she had trained each day to physically prepare herself for the prosecution of war. These were the basic drills: marching, rifle maintenance and an assortment of small '*quality of service*' activities expected from her transition into the military.

The mould had started to fit her body. She'd seen herself, in the mirror, transform into someone new – remnants of Lylith latched on to her as they struggled to bypass her new mutations.

With her back against fallen bricks, her eyes circled around the deforested concrete jungle. What were once homes stood as hollow skeletons; they were the underpinnings and keystones to a fallen settlement scattered the wastes. Its purpose of sheltering the exiled, exonerated and vindicated movement was all too perfect for her needs.

Bricks laid in gravely piles. Fragments of shattered windows crunched beneath her boots as she marched up and down the ridge. Towering buildings – left abandoned – formed her own simulation of an urban battleground. It was her covert sheet of solitude that hid in the neglected hamlet. Governmental patrols never came by as they sat just out of the reach of each regional headquarters. Convoys generally took cleaner routes with easier terrain to cross.

Failed acclimatisation to Kelan's past, and rapid, industrialisation had turned a small and illustrious community into a breeding ground for conspiracy, and by all means did she revel in the opportunity it posed. Her metropolis home felt unworthy, undeserving of her judicious practice. And her thoughts materialised new strains of guilt built on the stigma of her lineage and origins, to which she accelerated her change to become the people's hero.

Sarah fed her with rusted spoons. She told her tales of misconduct, of pain and sacrifice, all linked back to the Monarchy. Tala, her mother, was painted as a forefront of modern suffering, and as a pathfinder to the end of the world. Her radicalisation was meagre, but at each turn, Sarah found herself disheartened whenever she embraced her feelings of love and familial affection towards that of which she opposed.

And there, Sarah's hospitality extended into a lead for her renovation. Lylith was no more. It was her arbitrary chain collar that bound her to the life she'd deliberately left behind forever. A new alias was born and she became her: *'Christa Lodvtz'*.

Her kindness had been borrowed from Lylith's blight and merged into the alter-ego. Both names cradled their own personas. Lylith was the princess, the caring figure who felt that she could only wait until they took the throne to make change. Christa, on the other hand, was an activist, a revolutionary, a soldier, a warrior, a future leader, a martyr in the right hands and a bridge built to carry her wishes across. She cut her hair and drowned it in coloured bleach. Her mannerisms shifted; her voice replaced her delicate tone as she conditioned herself into a new identity. She was enriched with a sense of liberty. She laughed and cried more. She spoke when unnecessary and blended in as the rabble she once overlooked.

Routines were in place to force her change. Early morning awakening, followed by light, dry meals. Training began soon after. Constant physical exercise, afternoon studies of her military theory. Everything accelerated faster and faster and she struggled to keep up with its pace. For a while, she had been angered by all inconveniences, by her failures and weaknesses. Where she couldn't perfect herself, she settled for second place.

Christa had once been a vessel, until she made a body out of the name. Restless hours of labour pushed her to the limits she had dreaded. And then, in her solitude, she'd spent the last days in her undisturbed schedule mobilising herself for war. She shot targets on the move whilst aggressively becoming her new self, the model soldier she dared to be.

In a moment of reflection, she sat still in the rain. The pebbles and the stones flowed down small streams by her feet. She lifted her firearm to her face, where she pressed its cold, metal receiver against her cheek. The bitter steel encased her skin in a nervous chill, but it gave her such a sensation to stay awake.

It was an old weapon, predating the modern standardisation that Kelan employed. An era-gone-by bolt-action rifle, not quite obsolete to the common soldier. She was grateful for having a firearm to begin with. With it, she could adjust to sensation of recoil and adapt to idea that someday she may kill a man with such tools.

She noticed a jammed case in the ejection port, trapped from her last exercise. Desensitised fingers wrapped around the bolt as she tugged at it with exhausted hands. Each pull audibly rattled through the scattered graveyard of civilisation. Beneath her breath, she cursed.

"Oh…for fuck's…" Clouded by her mutters, she barely heard the footsteps that came to her side.

"Here, let me do it."

She snapped to attention, scrambling at the sound of an unfamiliar voice. She half-heartedly rose her firearm and aimed towards a cloaked figure, clad in a long, dark coat. His forehead was shrouded by the perfectly clean cap.

Upon her instincts, she'd gotten ahead of herself. The rifle trailed his position as he sauntered over. His shoes crunched the broken bottles between them. A triumphant smile met her, conjoined to his condescending chuckle. A firm, gloved grip reached out and tightened around the gun's barrel and he tore it from her clutches.

"Look, I know it's empty, stop being so dramatic." His insouciant mannerisms subsided her initial impressions of him - a bias once given to the Osakan's high stance over her. He flipped the rifle onto its side, sought out the jam and drew a small blade. "See you were trying to push it back in, let me see if-"

Using the hilt of his blade, he pried the empty casing out of the firearm, then he closed the bolt. Brisk motion cycled the bolt again, three times, dropping out the succeeding bullet. He then pointed it away from them and pulled the trigger, leaving an empty click to discharge the primed catch.

"There, not so bad."

The man turned to face her and handed over her the weapon. In the process, she got a clearer gaze at his face. Definitely Osakan, she confirmed, and he was neatly decorated to fit the bill of any officer. Neatly kept circular glasses rested in front of his eyes, propped up by the bridge of his nose. He was clean shaven.

His movements were meticulous, steady and fluent in the body language of prestige. And, with a smile, he put his hands back into his coat pockets.

"How're you doing, Lylith?"

She had been left a little blindsided by the man's appearance. Her chest tightened as she felt the panic settle in. At first, she assumed he was an intruder, but no. His uniform was all too recognisable. She saw the patches, the medals her mother had given out on rare occasion. Stood before her was an intelligence officer.

Before she could rebuttal his arrival, a figure she did recognise lurched from behind the corner. The driver, her instructor throughout all of her training, moved into view and took a step just behind the officer.

"Christa, Mr Lee is here to talk to you." The officer's attention rose from his polite introduction.

"Oh, we've already moved on to that stage? Good progress!"

"I'm sorry, who is this man?" She turned to her instructor, holding a hand to the officer as if he were out of earshot.

"He's the Contact."

The ostensible figurehead to her operation, stood before her; it all took her by surprise. After a brief few seconds of silence, she braced herself with a stouter stance.

"I'll leave you two alone for a bit." On command, the instructor trudged away. Behind him, silence was left. Christa stared at him, her eyes searching for answers she dared to not ask for. Restraint held her down whilst he moved closer.

"Just call me Thomas. Let me rewind: how are you doing, *Chris-*"

"How's Philip doing? Is he okay? What's happening in Burno?" She bombarded him with questions strung together by short-paced pants. Of course, one deprived of all national news was left at balance with ignorance.

"One step at a time." Thomas scoffed. "Oh and – uh – you probably should take a seat, preferably indo-"

"Don't tell me he's been hurt!" She pled.

"Philip was detained by the Royal Guardsmen the day you went missing. Now-"

"What? Is…is he okay?"

"Look, right now that's not what's important, what is-"

"You can't just say that! Don't drop this… – this bombshell on me and just expect me to brush over it!"

She corkscrewed off her lid and let off a flare in her eye. Her display of relapse brought back Lylith in her entirety.

And Lylith didn't want to listen to the dichotomies of wartime business. When the newly met tongue came to her grounds, her shrine of rebirth, and gave her the surface of a long-sailed iceberg, she couldn't help but swim back after it to plunge to its underside.

"I've been in this place for weeks on end, deliberately putting everything behind me, and you just roll up and pretend that this is just something you can throw at me without premonition!"

"Put a fucking sock in it." His aggressive cut-off pushed her down. "When your officer talks to you, you listen, alright? Shut up and let me talk."

Thomas pronged his fingers on either side of his nose and exhaled – a cloud emerged from his throat in the low-temperature water world she trained in.

Backpaddling a little, he rose a hand out to calm himself whilst he took long, deep breaths to steady his frustration. Then, he rubbed his face dry of moisture and recomposed himself.

"Sorry – and I mean it, I really apologise – perhaps not the great introduction you need. And I'm sorry if Philip got hurt, but that was the risk he was willing to take. Besides, you should've known what you were getting yourself into. The resources and concessions we've poured into this project – just for you to be satisfied – has been immeasurable. Now please, humour me, and listen for a minute." He cleared his throat and adjusted his glasses, relieving the friction burns on the bridge of his nose. "I wouldn't originally be out here for another month, but we're cutting things short."

The man, holding a tight grasp on her destiny, came not to fill her with positive feedback but to alert her of dire straits. Obediently, she let the poison slip into her ears.

"Ferusia's made a move – a big one. We're stood face to face with a national invasion. In Haria, they're putting their cards all in."

There came the needle-drop; a wracked silence had her mind in flux and she eyed the stones she stood upon. Suddenly, the sky was snared by the brooding bellow of thunder, and the rainfall amassed its tremendous charge on the land.

Thomas cleared his throat and buried his hands into his pockets. His glasses were obtuse, fogged by the breath of the rainstorm.

"I'll give you two weeks to finish up what you're doing," he mumbled, "and then I'm taking you to the militia."

The dictatorial decider of Kelan's fate had dawned. She pictured the scramble for a sturdied defence, where thousands had been placed in the pockets of a cold, bogged down peninsula. On the cape sat the greatest clash in human history. Rifle against rifle and squadrons of bombardiers that rained havoc from above.

The narrative had shifted for her. The glorious push for victory had, in her mind, become a tale of resistance and a story about of a line held to the last man, woman and warrior – where she would stand atop of a hill of the people's enemy. Their decider was that of attrition, a challenge to see who broke first: the guard or the conqueror. And for Christa, the self-proclaimed protagonist to the future, she was ready for what she had to face.

"Two weeks, right?" She peeled the soggy cloth from her face, revealing her blue, chilled lips. A numbed expression of prowess shot back at Thomas. "War waits for no one, Sir. I'll do what I must."

The Officer gave a giddy smile as he took his glasses off and rubbed away the smog that coated its lens.

"Wonderful work, Private *Lodvtz*."

"Private?" Her expression immediately dropped.

"What? You thought you'd be a general or something?" At first, he chuckled, but when he saw her expression, he almost broke out into a bellied-laughter.

"Well…I requested to be in a state of leadership. I know that as the actual heir to the throne that-"

"No, no. Lylith Redgrine is the rightful heir. Christa Lodvtz isn't." She frowned at his condescending tone. "Look, what were you expecting? The Crown will hightail on your arse the moment they catch a hint. Hell, the main reason I'm allowed off my usual post to come here is to *conduct a search for you*. Just standing out in the open will get you killed, and we can't have that."

"And…why not?"

"With all due respect, I'm the one who calls the shots here. I've placed not only my own well-being on the line here, but yours *and* the nations." He puffed at the chilling tinge of the air. "Stop acting spoilt, you're an adult soldier."

"Then is it truly safe for me to join the militia?"

"Oh, of course. So long as you don't make a scene, you'll be as free as a carrier pigeon."

Left in silence, Christa made an effort to mask her disappointment. What should have been a turning point for her reality had been swept under a dust-covered mat by the same surrealist stories that drove her onward.

Her time spent as Christa had been fairly lonesome. No faces resided in her presence as friends. Strict professionalism, militarised daily practices and an abundance of muscle-aching tension had broken her personal connection to her assailants. The allies were nothing more than working figures preparing her for the next stage in motion. And yet she still treated them as if they were part of her journey, alongside her through thick and thin, until they too would bask in the glory of her ceremonious celebration at the end of it all, like honorary heroes.

"Should we go inside?" Thomas broke the tension that was left in her absent thought. "Always the part I miss of home –good weather."

Both moved on cue, taking their strides through the drowned emptiness of the forgotten settlement. As they trekked, Thomas' eyes wandered around the broken abodes and snuck into forgotten cracks left unnoticed. The eyesore was little more than a mock-up for Kelan's war-torn future.

Christa's mind slipped into a silent trance as she was escorted back to Sarah's house. She drowned out his voice with the pattering of rain against her hood. Bricks tumbled, dislodged by the bountiful monsoon, and resounded ancient cracks through the emptied land.

Her mind plucked at old memories, those harshly suppressed by her new alter-ego. Christa hadn't shared the same comforts as Lylith did. There were no rose-tinted windows that overlooked vast gardens. She hadn't felt the same touch of the velvety, aqua dresses she'd been naturally pampered with. Not a day of Christa's existence had been met with servants at her beckoning, guardsmen dedicated to her safety or the bequeathed excellence of twilight dinners. No, she'd spent her time grovelled in the dust of a former town, scratching at her bearings until she'd convinced herself to be a ruthless defender of the nation. Her own feet led herself across the shuddering rope bridge.

She realised she would be shipped to battle. Her worries could've been permanently left behind if she were to disappear amongst the crowds.

From beyond the heavens, the thunderous rumble shook the clouds. The rain grew even heavier, dampening the ground as both Christa and Thomas rushed back indoors, ushered in by the sweet old smile of Sarah.

Inside, the candles lit the dark corners of the dining room table. Sarah came in and out, carrying trays of stale, tasteless tea. There was no sweet, creamy milk to enhance the flavour, just the raw hot water and blend of ripped teabags melted into one mug. Christa drew it to her mouth and was greeted by its boiling temperature clashing against her frozen lips. Bitter. Vulgar. Distasteful. She ultimately missed the desired comforts of her old life, but she understood it was a necessary, meticulous sacrifice over such trivial materialisms. Besides, it wasn't as if the military themselves were known for their fine cuisines among the soldiery.

Thomas smoked a thin cigarette and muttered an old Osakan tune to himself. Something old, foreign to the trainee, whilst Sarah gave her an old, familiar look of any grandparent.

"So how do you two know one another?" As Sarah made a second passing into the room, Christa dug into the lore of her rulers.

"Work, good dear." Her elder said, placing down her tray with a strenuous, arthritis-ridden shake. She compensated for her frail vulnerability to the bite of the cold air with the thick pelt-coat of a black bear. "You meet a lot of faces in the field."

"Field work? What things did you do in the Intelligence Office, exactly?"

Christa was met with a whispered tut. Sarah coughed into her fur sleeves and wiped her chilled eyes with the opposite arm.

"Only the Crown gets to know, dear." Another dead end. Prying out their history proved futile as the sheet of secrecy draped over them. "Full of dirt and grime. Horror this and corruption that."

Christa turned her attention back to Thomas who still daydreamed alone in the corner. His cap had been placed aside his arm, resting upon the rickety, dusty table.

Truthfully, she was daunted by his presence. She uncomfortably shifted in her seat and looked away whenever his eyes ran to her direction. A hunch rested on her own thought: years spent in the cabinet of her mother's courtly orders had exposed her to the scheming connivers, the plotters and the sharp-tongued conspirators. She could smell their intent, the manipulative practices to further their riches, power and grasp over the nation. They came in many forms. The aristocrats, the republicans, the few syndicalists and the dictators, all placed in one large oligarchic chamber to debate hopelessly under the eye of the true monarch.

Thomas had a scent similar to theirs, yet there was a slight aroma of unfamiliarity in his intent. Every man had a goal and any in power had a plan to achieve it. She'd grown to distrust so many and still she'd grown complacent and unworried by his mysterious control. But what better option did she have? A close tie to Philip and a man who knew every crack in the powers that were; he was her best shot at fulfilling her activism.

"I've been scouting out squads for you to join, mainly." He finally spoke up. "To find the ones you'll be the safest within."

"But I'll be there, on the frontline, won't I?" Christa's words were met with a narrowed gaze before Thomas leaned forward in his seat.

"What is it you want out of this? I can't quite figure you out."

"Oh, well," she half-confidently announced, "I see myself out there, where the battle stands glorious. Helping the people, being one of them. In the thick of it, side by side with my-"

A strange glimpse came about his face. Judgement of the highest order, stared straight into her soul. She felt the discomfort wriggle forth and latch around her neck, where she coughed off to the side.

"I heard you were shot at when you escaped your palace. That the Royal Guardsmen tried to rescue you. There was an exchange of gunfire. Right?"

She remained silent for a second; her eyes were drawn to the dust-covered tabletop. A grey, distorted flash panned out before her in the darkness of the room. The flickers of blood and the fallen men silenced by ear-piercing beats of gunfire.

"There's not a night where it doesn't haunt me." She admitted, still in her gaze.

"Out there, you'll be dropped into hell, feet first. The people around you will die, perhaps in droves, and this time they won't shy away from aiming at you too." His voice thickened into a brooding grumble, harshened by the strict atmosphere. "You've felt the kick of a rifle's shot. The bullet feels much worse. Don't get ahead of yourself and think this is something you can head into unharmed."

"Of course not, Mr Lee."

Kicked down by the truth of her position, she complied with a bow of the head. She felt embarrassment for herself, getting ahead of the thrill she'd created. Like before, she'd realised it was a sacrifice of her honour, a legacy of her father's apparent courage in motion. She wanted to save the name of Kelan's people, to immortalise their struggle in her own memory and actions. Her drive had mutated into an adventure, a dangerous gloss-coating over the horrific practices she'd endure.

"I apologise." She piped down.

"Look, I may come off as harsh, but a lot has been lost already for *you*. So, from here onward, it's going to be clear that *I* have got the reigns of this chariot, and once you're ready, we'll head off together."

A silver-lining. Soon, she could abandon her isolation. Weeks on end cradled in the arms of a false destiny had left her numb. The bite of frost had agonised her patience. She wanted to do something for *someone*. In time, she'd taste war. Lylith would die, whereas Christa was to be baptised in an unholy act of martyrdom.

Chapter 15

The Beachhead

The blood-bathed sand had blended with the salted itch of the deep black and blue. Days prior, carnage had awoken. The beige-fawn canvas across the coast had been transformed into a lurid gateway to man's inferno. Spiked iron hedgehog crosses were left untouched by the passing stream of soldiers, mostly sunk into the drenched sand they resided in. Gaped bullet holes coated their plated sheets, where empty casings sat aside abandoned bodies. Ripped clothing, loose limbs and pierced helmets lay hidden between the countless lines drawn in the dunes.

For miles, the frontline stretched wide across the peninsula's tip. Every metre was sacred – each a step toward victory or crippling defeat. And at the rear of it all, the oceanside graveyard sat largely inactive.

Their walker had halted as soon as it had set foot on the beach rooted into the bog of rain-drenched sand. Worthlessly, they attempted to dislodge it and to regain traction, but it was to no avail. He clambered over the top wall of the troop-carrier and jumped, landing feet first onto Kelan's soil.

He cursed beneath his breath and pulled his feet out of the slog, before he trudged toward his mark. Accompanying officers and escort squads fanned out in scattered formation. They loosely trailed behind him, funnelled down narrow pathways of coastal defences and bodies. On each of their sides, small markers and signs laid out dangerous findings: ***WARNING – MINEFIELD.***

A few metres away from the first sign were the unrecovered bodies that laid disfigured, lost in the sea of unexploded ordinances. A logistics minesweeper rested along the perimeter, saluting them as they passed by. Most were left speechless, awestruck by the wreckage at every angle. Universally, they were glad they weren't among the first waves to have made landfall.

Eventually, they made it beyond the beach and walked through the valley of caved concrete bunkers. Thousands of chiselled markings painted their walls, bullet holes and explosive debris randomly assorted in amassed groups of concentrated fire.

"Major Schottenstein! Over this way!" Atop of a hollowed-out truck, half-sunk into the dirt, a roughened, young lieutenant raised his hand and beckoned for his attention. He asked, as they eventually met face to face: "Where's the colonel?"

"You were expecting one?"

"Richter was caught in an artillery barrage."

"My condolences." Schottenstein eyed the beach around him, and tucked his hands into his coat's pockets. "Colonel Tandler was caught in an aerial strike on his vessel – last night, that is."

"We're already that stretched thin?"

"Only until we secure more land."

Schottenstein sank his heels into the inundated muck whilst he eyed it with the flood of trepidation.

"Who's in command right now?" Stepping across the ridge, they ascended the final hill at the rim of the beach.

"A few lieutenant-colonels here and there: Schleswig, Kurtz and Heidemann, to name a few. This sector, though, is run by a Major."

"Just a Major? Who?"

"Westra, I believe, Sir."

Halting in his tracks, Schottenstein stared hopelessly across the valley. His accomplice paused, noticing his exhausted reaction.

"Sir?"

"Major Westra?"

"Yes, Sir."

"God help us." He cursed, dragging himself forward. The pair carried on moving across a vast network of wooden catwalks, all bridging over the horrendous quagmires the weather had casted.

Throughout the plains were the embodiments of absolute destruction which paved the way to the frontline. Bombed out trenches were flooded with rampant disease, rodents that scurried in rife struggle. Soldiers took turns to take aim at the vermin for fun. Reserve lines were parched, starved of entertainment. Within days, the sport of pest-control had become endemic.

Flooded lands hid away the trenches so many had fought and died over. Every few hours, the line would attempt to push forward, stealing the positions held by the steadfast defenders. Throughout their advance, an eerie silence haunted the world around them.

"Sir, what's wrong with Westra?" A dreary yet curious lieutenant returned to Schottenstein's previous mutterings. The taboo of distrust between the higher levels of the command chain made for great conversation, but did little to help with morale.

"Reputations are generally built on actions. I don't think she realises she leaves a path behind her that others must traverse through." Far off into the distance, he could make out the torn-up lands ravaged by days of fighting. Bombed out craters, shelled trenches and barbed wire littered the mud. Pools of thick, opaque mud hid the drowned beneath its oozing surface. "Worked with her back in the Greenfaire Unrest. If she understands her selfish ways, then she is already lost."

"I heard she's efficient, through and through. A real union wildcard."

"Yes, she was. *Brutally* efficient." He said, following his spite with a dismissive spit into the mud. Each word that left his mouth was iced in layers of gall. "Let's hope we get some decent commanders on field sooner rather than later. I can't count on her. Being favoured by the Union of Peace does not make her a good leader."

"Don't victories dictate a leader's credibility?"

"Not if they neglect and endanger the regiments beneath them. A pyrrhic victory is just as good as a defeat."

They marched through the sunken basins of Haria, narrowly traversing between the muddied pits and the crudely constructed catwalks. Logistics trucks lay in deep slumber as they had been ditched aside, trapped in pools of grime. Every metre was littered with broken rifles, abandoned empty logistics crates, ammunition tins, used artillery shells, used medical tents and the flow of reserve units taking the frontline with minimal confidence. Many lives had already been lost; many of the bodies that still laid around them were indistinguishable by allegiance. It didn't matter anyway. Suffering spoke all languages and followed all banners. It dressed differently, but never changed its birthday suit.

A squadron of interceptors flew close to the ground, using the low altitude to bypass the sky-high struggle for air supremacy. With their passing, a gush of wind nearly took off their helmets. The Major laughed gently at their passing, taken back by their daring flyby. And as soon as they'd arrived, they disappeared into the rain-drenched clouds.

"So, you've been to the front then?" Schottenstein raised his voice to talk over the increased upsurge of rain – the crescendo was amplified by its collision with metal boxes, puddles and wooden pathways.

"Oh yes, Sir. Looks awful."

"How bad?"

"We're mostly sat in the trenches we forced them out of – and we have to dig the gutters deeper, otherwise we're left stood in the faeces gifts left behind by our enemy. Last few miles we've taken have been particularly horrid. Couldn't get the artillery any closer than last time."

"It's safe to assume the tanks are just as bogged up?"

"You saw your walker, Sir," the lieutenant unenthusiastically chuckled, "simply getting them off the beach is just as hard as getting them inland."

"So, we're on our own until we can secure drier or hardened clay?" The Major looked around. Evidently, the bogged-out monsoon soil was too soft for any sort of armour. "Fuck."

"We made a push three hours ago that got repelled. Our forces have lost the initial drive."

Schottenstein sighed. He heard a distant rumble of bombs showering the horizon. A skyline of ashy plumes towered beyond the mist, reaching the skies above.

"We'll need the dreadnoughts, then." He concluded, then he looked at his pistol holster. "And I'm going to need a better weapon."

"You and me, both, Sir."

Dales and glens torn apart, the world shattered into pieces, havoc reigned around them. Echoes of battle grew stronger with every step forward. Soon, they could hear the rumble of gunshots spread all across the frontline. Within two miles of the front, they ducked down into used up trenches, where support lines of

195

soldiers, medics and sappers moved back and forth, drenched in mud. Silence lingered no more.

Hidden away in a dried-out bunker, Schottenstein found his station. Two feet of solid, battle tested concrete shielded its repurposed interior. A flow of warmth caressed his face when he walked inside. Life and comfort – a forgotten token lost in the translation of war. Inside, the conversion from pillbox to command centre hadn't been concealed. Detailed maps laid beside spent machine gun casings. A radio station sat upon a splintered oak table, where behind its receiver were fourteen bullet marks chipped into the wall. Cramped, dark and uncomfortable, its only invitation was the heater placed inside and the roof over their heads. Remarkably, it was rather quiet, if ignoring the occasional radio transmission and tempered ambience of conflict. At the far end of the bunker, she stood there with binoculars to her glassy eyes.

She was adorned with the harness of a combatant; a gladiator among footmen. Frigid wraparound goggles latched onto her steel helmet that rested just above its brim. Two utility belts crossed over her chest and back, clipping to the webbing belt on her waist. Gone was the traditional trench coat worn by syndicalist officers. Her distinctions lay in her epilates, the rank slides and pinned ribbons laid on the left breast of her shirt.

Her eyes laid upon the distant-yet-close battlefield. It seemed awfully calm, not a bomb in sight. He cleared his throat.

"Good to see you Coln-…oh." When she turned and saw his face, she frowned. "Major…?"

"Schottenstein. We've briefly worked together before."

"Is that so?" She folded her binoculars and tucked them into a pouch looped around her neck. She took a few slow steps closer, and her gaze was piercing. "And you're here for?"

"To take my companies and assist in this sector. Same reason as everyone else." To assert his position, he moved to her side and peered across the battlefield, overlooking her sense of presence. "Why did they put you in charge of a sector?"

"Does it matter?"

"It might."

"It shouldn't." A wire locked the two together, and their initial repellent from one another created a tension so tight they

196

could play a tune on it. "What's the logistical situation behind us?"

"There's a logistics plan? I hadn't noticed." Even in jest, his sarcasm infuriated her. "I'm surprised you haven't all starved to death. What assets do you even have on hand?"

From within her pocket, she drew out a crumbled letter and held it to his face.

"Five artillery batteries, two of which ran out of ammo about an hour ago. A fractured regiment or two. Fifteen companies are on the frontline. Apparently, we have air assets, but also apparently, we don't have them. Seven marksman teams. Nine mortar squads. No walkers. No APCs. A couple thousand grenades and a lot of spare left boots." She crumbled up the page. Westra angrily peered back into her binoculars. "If it's any comfort though, we've been ransacking this peninsula for every drop of blood its worth."

"We can't be too hasty in scorching the land beneath our boots."

"I don't care." Schottenstein turned and eyed her up. Her disregard for the welfare of their sector was anything but alluring – perhaps daunting was too soft of an adjective. "We'll be launching another attack in two hours, so long as they don't counterattack."

"Have they ever?"

"Not yet. We'll be advancing our sector with the others. I beg for you to not get in the way."

Outside, the rain maintained its course. A trillion droplets flickered against the treacherous marshlands of Haria. The hottest days had been tanked by weeks of downpour. And with the drowned land came the flooded bodies, drifting downstream towards the sea. In every puddle, it looked as if a concentrate of blood was always present. A hand could be seen loosely interred by nature, buried beneath the deteriorating soil.

Debris from devastated housing stood alone across the enormous battlegrounds. Fallen stallions and cattle caught in the initial bombardment had been scattered across, decomposed and decapitated. Charred wreckages of crashed fighters and bombers added to the final mix of crudely constructed barbed wire fences.

"Do you have any lead up to the assault?"

"A few artillery volleys are in place, it was all we could muster."

"Not going to be enough. You'll have hundreds of our own dead before you reach the trench."

"I realise that, but we've been ordered to keep moving."

"With that little regard for the soldiers you command?" He sneered. He turned to her with an enflamed distaste to her realist pessimism.

"Reality often isn't caring. A conflict of this scale is ought to shed blood, no matter what we do. Accept that, *Schottenstein* and you'll make gains."

Westra retrieved her nearby submachine gun that was leant against the wall to her right. She left the viewing port and glanced at the few maps around her.

"Then we'll call in an additional aerial bombardment." He suggested.

"Every commander under the sun has done that already, you'll have to wait a day for that." Her hands rummaged her chest rig, counting her magazines, before she made her way toward the door.

"And where are you going?"

"To the frontline, obviously. You can stay here; I'd rather not have you follow me with your persistent nagging." And as quickly as she'd readied herself, she disappeared back into the rain. Peeled eyes stalked her from afar wherever she walked. An unparalleled level of extremities, ranging from distrust to admiration, existed for her peers.

Schottenstein simmered down and sat himself down in a crooked wooden chair beside the map table. Left still were the radiomen and members of staff chipping away at their own duties. He let out a woozy groan and lamented his arrival with no grace.

The foul fragrance of carnage had been left out to dry. Its lifeless atmosphere lay still. Rugged cabins and bedrooms upon uncomfortable vessels felt like a luxury to his new placement. He missed the cold steel floor of the ship's interior or the near-constant noise keeping him awake at night. In all his years of service, he hadn't expected to have been greeted with the full extent of mankind's destructive ways.

A severe lack of their own machines worsened his taste and he saw the devolution to simple, brutalist strategies – trench warfare.

What was made clear beyond the bunker's viewport was indescribable to those back home. No one could claim they'd seen hell until they'd experienced total war. He dwelled on the matter and could only sigh in disgrace. He had to gather his morals, his stance and his people in order to hold any ounce of sanity.

If there were ever a reason to move forward with vile skirmishes ahead of him, it was to commit to an enduring duty to the people and the soldiers he led. For many, they hadn't entered a war driven by conquest. They had come for the bitter vengeance they'd been starved of. He soon cursed the people of Kelan with a violent condemnation. Until he would meet them, face to face in battle, there would be remorse. Mercilessness was the history of Kelan. Their foundation would have been their undoing.

Chapter 16

What machines do

The time had come. Wintry showers had ceased. Where the landscape lay flooded, the sky had granted the frontier a shortened window of relief. The land, however, remained as a great lake district that scoured the heights and valleys of Haria.

Squad 2 had also been selected. Days spent dawdled, fiddling with thumbs, carving out artwork, tossing rocks between one another and unkempt panic hadn't prepared them for the announcement. Alexander came by to Rhys' tent and disturbed his sleep with the shake of a shoulder. He told him that they were next, as was his own company. A long, dangerous march awaited them; they were set to traverse through several miles of a sunken vale, with the loom of death's threat ready to strike at any given chance.

Dreary, colourless skies looked down on them. No sun was in sight and a greyscale filter blotched the world like spilt ink. It was hard to remember what the sun even felt like. The storm had consumed everything for nearly two weeks. Nowhere seemed safe. And if the chilling rain, endless mud-filled craters or unsanitary conditions didn't kill them, then there'd have been plenty of opportunities for the Ferusians to do it themselves.

Twenty minutes: that's all the time they were given. Rhys dragged himself out of his crooked bed and rinsed his face at a nearby water tap. For all he knew, it could've been the last time he felt clean water against his parched skin.

For the last few days, he'd generally been quiet. There wasn't much to say. There never was. Evelyn continued to chisel away at helmets for the appeasement of her comrades whilst Oslo talked to her clients. Mateo took the responsibility of watching over Dynis, knowing full well that his personal loss was another nail on his crucifix. Sabrina and Ella rarely left their tent. Christopher occupied himself with on-base duties to pass the time. Tyran spent hours sat in an anti-air Walker, just waiting for an enemy squadron to fly over.

When Rhys collected him, he couldn't help but feel bewildered over how little those machines had participated in the conflict. Years of overhyping their capabilities, their reliability and yearning for trials by combat were downplayed by mother nature. To the corporations and manufacturing plants responsible for them, it was a kick in the teeth yet for the soldiers left unsupported across miles of savage trenchlines, it was a stamp to the throat with studded heels.

In came the terror and out went the will to march on. Upon leaving the base, behind the formation ahead, they lagged behind at a trudging pace. The Royal Armed Forces were quick to make their departure. That day was the one they'd been preparing for. Months, maybe even years, of trials, exercising, training and simulations all led to that one moment. To them, it was a day in which history would remember them. Even if they died, it would be for the betterment of the nation. Squad 2 did not feel such optimism.

Rhys stood at the front. He was spaced out from his squadmates by a few metres, as to reduce the collateral damage that could've been caused by a well-placed artillery shot. He knew that Alexander was somewhere along the cluster with his own unit.

The razing of iron stares sent them off with dread as they left the open gates of their base. They didn't fear for their lives, no. The eyes that laid upon them only feared that their death wouldn't be so painless.

Into the fog they trod. A trembling illumination flashed ahead of the group. The first hour was plagued by the mist, shrouding the horrors around them in translucent curtains. Corpses were rare that far back down the reservist lines, but those they did find were not from battle. The further they went into wonderland, the greater the madness that contained them. For Rhys, he wasn't looking into the spyglass from afar, staring at the unfolded pandemonium across the hills. He was there. The bedlam was beside him, beneath his boots and hung from leafless branches. Mud dribbled down a noxious stream. The support lines were scarce, left with reserve rifle brigades holding on with their faces to the ground and teeth brushed with soil. Within shallow dugouts and drained trenches, mute faces looked up at them, their eyes shrouded by the thin steel rim of their helmets. Some nodded to the passing squads as an act of encouragement, or simply as an understanding for where they were headed.

An ache toiled at the forefront of his muse. On approach to war, he dwelled upon *it* again. How many more times had he doomed himself to repeat? The blood on the doorframe and the soaked grass. The spent bullets on the dirt covered by the bodies that had fallen atop of them. In such a luscious, green spring day, total evisceration had been the only thing birthed. People were dead. Why couldn't he wrap his head around that fact? People had been killed, one of them by him or by his orders. He couldn't accept that as a part of war. There had to be another way.

And there he was, walking through the gorge of passing – there was no green, no grass or hot, bellowing sunshine. A defiled and brutalised world lay in a stagnant shade of russet, with unwelcoming auburn, coated by the flow of red that had sank into the brooding mud.

There was no silver lining to the disgrace. Every landmass they reached for was dead, rampaged and disfigured.

He spaced himself a couple more metres behind the squad in front. Rhys trod alone carefully, his eyes mostly to the floorboards. Dislocated planks caused many to trip along the way, with one imbalance causing the weighed down soldier to collapse under the load of their gear. The creaks beneath his boots unsettled his heart. He hadn't welcomed death, but he began to expect it.

Further through the valley, the floorboards widened, and he soon found Sabrina quickly move to his side. Her mouth was pursed shut; a quiet nervousness stood between them. The chatter of gunshots talked for them.

"Hey…"

Sabrina eventually said something as she nudged him with a metal-padded elbow. He looked at her, though she didn't return the gaze. Her face was concealed by a thin layer of cloth and her eyes were just visible under her helmet's brim. Whilst she had forged herself into an indistinguishable soldier clad high-shoulder to low-ankle in weaponry and gear, only the careful tenderness of her voice set her apart.

"How are you feeling?"

"Any guesses?" Even with painful visions freshly preserved, he gave way to ignorance in order to maintain his sensibility. He gifted her a smile, one aware of its misfortune.

"Shit? Depressed? Ready to run away and pretend like it'll go away?" A light, childish giggle came from behind her mask.

"Harsh. You know me so well." A feeble croak defined his internal anxiety for her. "And you?"

"I'm...approaching a similar stage too."

She shrugged off her woes and transitioned from her reservation to a cold and lifeless rant. He caught sight of her eyes turning into cracked glass.

"It's so impossible to even believe we're heading in now. Like we've – just that we've spent months doing everything for shit like this, and we don't feel the slightest bit ready. Hell, I don't think what we saw at the windmill was enough. And now I've got Ella being dragged to places she shouldn't be."

"But you're brave for sticking beside her, right?" He encouraged.

"Rhys," she turned to him, "do you think that being brave is no different than being stupid?" He didn't respond, alarmed by her shift to cynicism. "Like, everyone's pretending they're all up and ready for this. Their chins are so high-held that they can't see the hole in the ground beneath them. None of us are ready. I heard some guys back at base talk about how bravery is just stupidity weaponised."

"And do you believe that?"

She fell silent. A drag and a half passed as she carefully considered it. Then, she turned and looked at Ella from over her shoulder.

"No. Maybe... – maybe I'm just worrying. I've got to be brave so she can. If we're in this together, then we've got to make the best of it all, don't we?" As if he'd been kissed by an angel, Rhys felt his heart flutter just a little at her ever-optimistic conclusion. She'd stand decisively for her family. And in her, Rhys saw a person of whom he wanted to be – rich with confidence. Defeat came to those who gave up; Sabrina squared up to that possibility with a steel resolve.

203

Ahead of the pack, voices mumbled into the mist. At first, they were unintelligible. A breeze carried the individual verses until it came by their side. Harmonic gusts cradled their notes, and soon, an entrenched sea of men and women were heard singing a small, gentle tune. It came from the trenches and the clusters of sentries all packed like sardines in their rusty tins. Their faces greeted them as they sung in unity. Both Sabrina and Rhys stopped talking and looked into the pits, listening to the lyrics of the muddied and bloodied men.

> *"To home, you go.*
> *To home, you'll stay.*
> *To heaven,*
> *On ye merry way.*
>
> *I'll be here, with you;*
> *And you'll be here, with me.*
> *Together,*
> *We'll be free."*

A spiteful chill tipped their unpleasant libretto. The magnificence in their voices haunted him. He felt the disturbance of its showcase: for it was a performance that encored their way to hell. The last bastion of purity came from the echoes of a simple, two-versed tune on repeat as it fell behind them. Its homely presence numbed his fleeted heart. It was a choir of a hundred souls in wait for their turn to die.

Rhys' lips trembled. The ghostly ensemble faded as they carried on. Their paled faces, drained of colour, met the soil with a stare that travelled for miles.

"What sort of stuff are they expecting from us?" Mateo caught up to the pair and ripped them out of their place in the audience. As he came to their side, he staggered a little bit, crumbled beneath the weight of his anti-tank rifle.

"Holding the line, as simple as it goes." Rhys murmured, observing out ahead of them as the song faded into the mist in their wake. "The Captain told me the like to make pushes periodically. Usually they use artillery before, but another officer mentioned that the bombardments are getting weaker by the hour."

"Any reason why?"

"Lack of ammunition? Or maybe they can't move them with their own frontline. I mean, look at this land. I doubt you could get a car through here, let alone a howitzer."

"Can you just imagine though…" Mateo started.

"Imagine what?"

"The *Grand Army* of Syndicalism, the unions and workers, and all that jazz, were defeated by a bit of rain, mud and a few lads rejected from the actual army." He impersonated the voice of a high-profile radio presenter from Burno, proudly enhancing the bass of his vocal range. Sabrina let out a soddened yet genuine laugh, whilst Rhys only grinned at his lightened burden. "Addendum, our broadcast team has also discovered that the Royal Armed Forces of Kelan are utter wank!"

Lastly, Rhys was infected by the contagious joy. Everything had been fuelled by misery, from the lands to the war itself, and yet the small Corporal joyfully pranced around, cracking barely humorous jokes at the expense of self-pittance.

"I'm surprised you can even carry a tune today."

"When do I ever not?"

"Well," Rhys stumbled, "we're probably walking off to Farhawl's worst."

"Hey, it'll be bad – but what's the point of giving up the smile every now and then, right? Everything's going to be shit regardless of the day. Might as well chipper up, mate."

Soon, the silence crawled back in-between them. A few groups ahead of them sprawled out into trenches at their sides. The open fields soon mutated into narrow corridors fastened with corrugated iron and sandbags. Sabrina's padded shoulders were pressed to Rhys' as they filed into twos, then into a single file line. A ghastly aroma hovered in the air as they pushed through, navigating through the tightly packed groups of soldiers standing fast. Some lay asleep in caved hatches burrowed into the trench walls, whilst others sat on the firing steps and cleaned the grime from their rifles. The odd man would nod to them as they passed only to faintly warn them of their journey ahead.

The Reserve Line: two additional miles of intertwined trench systems hastily dug during the early hours of the Ferusian Invasion. Over the last few days, they had been reinforced and retrofitted to withstand a mildly long operation, but never for a permanent settlement. Constructed around old relic pillboxes, machinegun nests and coastal lookout posts, previously left as memorabilia to the country's founding, everything blended into one horrific bunker-land housing the murdered.

What ran rampant throughout was poor sanitation and the grievances of heaven's next lost sortie.

A couple miles of exiguous alleyways with badly painted signposts that told them where to go and scuffed, dirty soldiers obstructing their way made for the unkind approach to the last leg. Oslo carried Evelyn. He happily bore the weight of her equipment, so long as she didn't leave his sight.

Many eyes laid upon her. Fifteen years of age. She wasn't an infant, and yet Oslo carted her as if she were. She couldn't understand the soldiers around her. Despite the months she'd spent amongst the ranks, being compliant out of unfamiliarity, her naivety prevailed. It wasn't the same world she had envisioned. Her little, damp and forgettable village had nothing to prepare her for the brutality that waited. And in her dreams, she was still tucked into her spring bed, scribbling on the lamp-lit desk beside her.

The smell and the taste of the world was too much. She couldn't keep calm, her breath heavy and coarse. And though she didn't understand why Oslo's allegiances had changed to protect her, she let the fatherly embrace lock her in the brighter world she'd once imagined.

Overhead, the retreat of smoked fighter pilots left a trail of enflamed fuel smoking behind them. Voices of the depressed dampened the silence.

"Aye, is that one of ours?"

"Fuck, looks like it – don't it, Sergeant?"

"I ain't 'aving none of that. Flyboys 'ave been at it for days and come back empty 'anded. Pushovers, the lot of 'em."

"Watch your mouth, Crowley! My brother is a pilot!"

"Yeh well he ain't doing a good job, ain't he? Spending more time on the ciggy-smokes than the joystick by the looks of it!"

The sprawl of different accents, dragged from opposing ends of the Kingdom, harshened the widespread outcry that blistered the trench crowd. In another trench lane, hands were thrown and they narrowly missed the faces of their targets. A disturbing howl of soldiers attempting to deter and dissuade the infighting faded into the background as Squad 2 edged onward. It boded ill of the deliriousness of the frontline.

"Oi, Rogers. They started sending militiamen now…" One man would whisper to his other serviceman. "Things really that bad?"

"Saving actual manpower, maybe? Better them than me."

Jeering, colour-drained faces scorned at the passing crowd. Rhys wasn't beaten by their words, but more the reality that accompanied it. As much as his officers would say, he wasn't a soldier. He was a body for the count, a stopgap between the Ferusian gunsights and the Crown. Several militia brigades had been deployed in the days before them, instead filling the reserve lines and plugging the gaps in their defence. The batch he'd fallen into were a reinforcement troop, a gathering of misfits set to delay the onslaught.

He sighed, pushing through the crowd to make way for his own tribe. Their eyes trailed him like hawks to a dying breed. Every detail of his face, his anxiety and fear for what came next, was evident. Some felt no remorse for them and those who did remained mute. There was nothing they could say to fix their situation.

Labyrinthian twists and turns, corners and edges, scrambled his sense of direction. He found the nearest officer at the trench's intersection and hailed him with a raised hand and a courteous salute.

"What can I help you with, Staff Sergeant?" He bellowed, speaking in a constantly brutish temperament, as if he were under inspection.

"We're making our way to central sector frontline. Can you point us in the direction?" Rhys saw the man's eyes burn straight through him. Sutured by tradition, his demands were clear without words. And so, Rhys topped off his request with a quiet: "Sir?"

"Right, well a group just like you came by not long ago. Sent them over through open ground about seventeen minutes ago."

"Over the top, Sir?"

"That's right."

"But…why? Is there no direct route?" The brashness of Rhys' whispered weariness was most unwelcomed.

"Well, *Staff Sergeant*, the bloody trenches have collapsed flooded. Walls fell in on themselves. Lost two people about an hour ago." He spat. Rhys felt powerless to his impatience. He'd been too strident himself, simply determined to get to hell and back as quickly as possible.

"Is there no second route?"

"Do you need to be there right now?"

"Yes, Sir." Rhys couldn't face his eyes, feeling an inner discomfort from their mirror-like emptiness.

"Then you'll have to go out and up the same route. The nearest trench passage that heads directly there is about a thirty-minute walk back the way you came, and even then, it leads slightly to the left of where you want to go."

"Are you sure there's no other trench? Did you not dig more than one?"

Mistakably, he spoke out of line. He felt several other vicious eyes peel open. His gut twisted at his regrettably uncharacteristic abrasiveness.

"If you want to dig your own bloody trench, then be my guest. Quickest way is hopping over the top and walking straight over, we're barely connected anyway. You'll reach the frontline in about five or so minutes." Rhys looked behind him. The queue following his lead kept getting larger. A cluster of other squads all waited uneagerly. In the dreariness of the day, he'd lost sight of the group ahead of him, giving him control over the lantern. "Just don't dilly-dally and you'll be fine – just walk it and you'll get there. Now, there's a step over there. Get going so we can open up the pathway for people who actually need it."

Arguing was futile, a waste of the precious time they'd been allotted. Frustration pounded his mind and bruised it with agitation. They weren't treading on inconveniences but were on the thin tightrope lines he had to walk across. All roads led to that luscious release: the predetermined trail to the end.

He barged through the remainder crowd to the indicated step. At its side, an older man slept. Much alike his comrades, the stains of soil caked his uniform. Distinctions between a soldier and a peasant had been united under one battered individual. When he looked away from him, to the groups he led, he felt less of a man than he did a tool for harvest.

The trench's topside whispered in hysterical windstorms. The face of his final march forward permeated the supernatural clench on his throat. His body remained paralysed. A friendly trench sat on the other side, not an adversary's. Even if the guns didn't point their direction, something had chained him to the shadowy bottom of the gutter. Faced with fear, he internally screamed at himself to get a move along. His thoughts haunted his conscience with demeaning taunts. *'That was why the Kaelo brothers left.'* A viscous weight latched onto his shoulders. He didn't feel like a leader.

Close by, Sabrina cleared her own nerves and stepped forward, going through Rhys' ethereal halt. As if he were an astral manifestation, she passed through him without obstruction. Sturdy legs carried her up the steps, out into the open. Her head swivelled back to him, and she pulled down her balaclava for a split second.

"Might as well chipper up, huh?" Apathetic. Her smile felt devoid, indifferent to her usual grins. She'd lost a part of herself. Sheepishly, she clambered up the remaining steps and exposed herself to the anarchic landscape beyond.

A few followed in her footsteps straight away. The man asleep by the step's side snapped awake and grumbled with an offbeat croak. As he saw the men and women ascend the steps, he called out watchman's warning.

"Keep y'spacing! Don't stand too close, now!" He'd wrapped his hands tightly around his rifle and trembled in his cold, decrepit throne. Like a stuffed animal, he embraced it to his chest, the rattle of its loose parts chiming with his disturbed clasp. "Them barrages come and go, so keep your eyes high."

Rhys waited for the troop to ascend the stairway before he made his move. He stared at the watchman, not even hiding his wide-eyed glance. The vile leftovers of his sanity had been rocked by bombardments, gunshots and loose screws. The fists that held on dearly to the gun were threadbare. Fashioned with canvas gauntlets, Rhys saw the tears in both his mittens and skin. A grey and faded bandage sat beneath the glove on his left hand, covering up the missing fifth digit. Half-exposed cuts showed themselves through the torn material before disappearing under the frayed drab gloves.

Across his cheeks, tears from the sky gave him the emotion he couldn't bring up. It'd been rattled out of him, sieved out through small cracks in his body. Rhys kept his eyes trailed on his hesitant movement before he was noticed himself. The ran lightly began again.

"They won't let you get far. I'll bet my tongue on it, good Sir!" Disturbed by his crazed ramblings, the Staff Sergeant ultimately made his own way for the steps. Discomfort had forced him out into the open shooting range. Each step against the stairs creaked snidely. From the clouds, a gentle murmur of thunderous proportion sung from afar. "Hurry with you lads and lasses! Time doesn't wait for anyone."

His eyeline crawled over the trench's ridge. Unlike before, there was no clear path. All semblance of mankind had been eviscerated, ripped apart by explosives and abandonment. Wooden walkways were left unfinished, causing the trail to have been carved out by nature. Even mounds, built up knolls of dirt and fallen, leaf-stripped tree trunks created a foreign topography of a distant planet. Pits dug by shells and bombs dropped down as far as ten metres. At their bottom, little pools of mud and metal flooded the base. Wandering the wastes left the bitter air to catch onto their sleeves and jackets. Fanned out bodies spaced themselves as instructed. If one shell were to drop on them, then it would be left to the roulette of chance to see which individual stood in its blast zone. Some refused to break up their personal clutters, segmenting themselves into tight groups.

And all the while, the rumble of the distant dark clouds refused to fully disperse.

It didn't take long to catch a glimpse of another cluster. Only seven hundred metres out, hidden from sight by a crater of extreme diameter, Rhys saw the Captain stood by the edge of the mucky waters. He felt a short relief overcome him until he made his approach. The face of a man, one who knew how to navigate mayhem, gave a breath of fresh air.

From where he'd seen Alexander, a single shot, small calibre, rang out. On instinct, the pack ducked down, taking a knee into the mud. A voice out in the distance called to them.

"One of ours, don't worry!" The faint message got through to them, and with hesitation the militiamen gathered themselves to continue the journey. Rhys took to his own initiative and approached the Captain. His eyes were locked onto his own boots to ensure he didn't make a final misstep. On arrival, he saw Alexander stood at the bottom of the pit, eerily watching over a pool of mud.

He looked up and, instead of smiling, gave a gravely nod.

"Ah, you caught up. Good on you, chap." He waved, tucking his concealed holster back into his coat. "How's the walk been?"

Witticism couldn't hide his fallible tone. Held against their previous conversations, he talked as if he were down on his knees – forced by the heavy weight of the world. No tears streamed down his cheeks; only in his voice did he share the disappointment he truly felt.

"Are you okay down there? We heard a shot-" Rhys asked concernedly, leaning over to scan the pit's interior.

"It's fine, Hendricks." In low spirit, Alexander began to drag himself up the face of the crater. Rhys looked to his left, seeing a few of his own standing along the ridge, facing away from the centre. A stagnant sorrowful nature decorated the area. Their tongues were cut, and he gave no explanation.

"So, you weren't stuck?" He asked Alexander, drearily.

"Not physically, no." The Captain looked back into the pit for one last glance before he walked ahead. Rhys checked the fissure himself and saw nothing other than a loose ammunition clip floating in the dingy mud-water, the type that would be tucked into a soldier's webbing.

He caught up to the officer, trailing behind him a solemn mystery. His conscience told him to leave it in the pit as his superior had.

Alongside the howl of the daylight gusts, the rumbling distance lurked inside the dark skies above. The on-approach storm made itself methodically slow.

"Sir," Rhys asked, "sounds like another thunderstorm. Should we get going faster?"

"Where's your squad, Hendricks?" Ignoring his question, the Captain stopped in his tracks, eyeing the surrounding crowd.

"Uh – spread out, Sir. We were told to keep our spacing." Alexander nodded affirmatively, barely comforted by their conformity to military standards. He looked to the sky, whilst Rhys glanced around, taking a mental note of his squadmates' placements.

211

Fifty metres ahead of him, Sabrina walked close by Gwendolyn. The two had taken the lead early on, with Mateo lingering ten metres to the right of them. On Rhys' flank, Evelyn wandered behind Oslo, who's figure stood out distinctively, lugging around his machine gun. Tyran was amongst the crowd at the rear. A silent Christopher walked beside Ella, who'd pushed herself to the back. Dynis lurked *somewhere*, feebly. All accounted for, though as far apart as they could be. Between them were crowds of new faces from the same regiment as they were.

Sundered skies soon plucked up in chorus. Little beats of rhythmic machinery rose in unwavering crescendo. The climax was slow but steadfast. Ravaging the eerie imperfection of the world, ripples trembled the tops of mud-filled ponds. The air itself shuddered and the roar gloated its presence in pride. Rhys stood still and his eyes darted around the skies. Only the greyish belligerence of the clouds held their audible oppressor at bay. And the sound soon became unmistakable.

From fields to oceans, the very peak of human flight hung harshly overhead. Feral screams let out a vile warning call to the land around them. Alexander cursed beneath his breath; his words were quickly cut short by the manic bellow above. Out came the silver-coated brass whistle, loosely laced with tethered string. Without the slightest of dither, he pressed it against pursed lips and sounded his personal alarm. Eight times, he blew it. Heads swivelled from the sky to the Captain and panic weaved itself into their distress. Many sunk themselves into the ditches they had tried to avoid. The inhuman bludgeon in the sky sank downward and the vessel forced its way through the black clouds.

In the sky sat the horrors of war's workshops, all presented at first with a matte silhouette. Its hull dawned a dim shadow on the drowned land below. The chugging of propellers and minor rocketry abused the soldiers' ears. Rhys took several steps backwards. He slipped as fear ridiculed his sense of direction.

"Get to cover!" Alexander bolted for Rhys, forcing him onto his feet without restraint. "Spread out! Back to the reserve line!"

The dreadnought presented its arsenal with a chilling screech that tore through the air. Aluminium abraded against steel whilst it unveiled its cannonade through the outline of its ungodly grace. Its snarl goaded those helpless to its presence. The greatest machine in history spooled up its guns.

Breathless, Rhys made a run for where he had once come from. There was no space for rationality. He turned his back to the dreadnought and made headway for safety. Each step was a struggle, a timewaster playing with the tip of death's spear. He'd slip, frantically disturbing the balance between caution and the desire to return to the trenches.

Around him, the militiamen sprung into panic. Many committed to the rush back whilst others jumped into shelled out craters and buried themselves in dirt. Rhys refused to dig his own grave and took each metre as a blessing. Lawless lands took no mercy on the weak. And with the executioner descending upon them, there was only the heart-aching rush of the escape. The creaking of cannons lining up their barrels deafened him. He became numb. He couldn't hear its engines. He couldn't see his allies. His vision narrowed down a damp tunnel. Hushed. Unspoken. The world dimmed in volume until only his breath whispered to his ear. He saw the mouths move of the panicked soldiers. Their words were inaudible.

He didn't look behind him. Forward was the only way he could go. His feet trod carelessly around the giant lakes of mud he'd prudently avoided before. A firm, unyielding grip held his rifle by its rear handguard. The nomenclature of war had sent him on a frenzied dash. In the distance, his eyes spotted the waving arms of the trench-dwellers. The rear guard of the march descended into its depths, quite literally throwing themselves atop of one another. The animalism had been exposed. Fish in barrels – carcasses to vultures.

With a pounding heart, he prayed that he'd make the distance. But then the guns started to fire.

Rhys' eyes weren't drawn to the dreadnought's fire. He felt the shells hit the soil. Spaced out by three seconds, each blast rocked the land beneath his boots. Muffled extremities tore through the dirt and inched closer with every shot. Carpeting the surface of the land, astronomical volleys vanquished the world. He held his breath. The wind grew stronger. Artificed gusts brushed his back. Shockwaves hit harder. And soon, as his hairs stood on their ends, he let himself fall into the nearest foxhole.

His body descended into the shallow hole. He moved his hands over his head and pressed his helmet into his skull. If death were to land beside him, he didn't want to see it. Sleeves shielded his eyes. Quakes rattled the globe. There, he felt like it was on top of him.

Fear. When faced with destruction, powerless men hide in their shadows. Agony. The filaments of raw obliteration showered their skin. Abandonment. When alone in a ditch, there would be no god watching over them.

A final blast ripped the soil into a great plume. The smoke and flame of its sudden impact tossed grime across the land. Rhys felt the pattering of dirt against his hands, his helmet and body. It partially buried him with a sheet of tarnished clay. Submission took control. He lay still, quivering in the frozen moisture of the pit. As the final shell annihilated the ground, the world maintained its muted vigil. Twenty seconds passed and he lay still in the shadows of the pit. Someone latched onto his back and forced him back up. He was lifted, held with his own arm around their back. Alexander moved him in immediate haste, making the last two hundred metres of the journey. Through their escape, the ship behind them loomed ominously.

They descended down the steps and into the trench. His back was placed against the sandbag walls, and they waited. Rhys couldn't quite tell what happened after that. Things drifted by. Shells landed nearby a few more times. In the end, the ship drifted in place, watching and waiting.

Then, the land-based gunfire reignited. Across the horizon, far out into the distance, the battlefield lit up as the sun turned away. The moon illuminated the fiery brutality laid upon the frontline.

Equal amounts of firepower streaked through the sky. A scrambled squadron of fighters escorting Kelan's own dreadnought turned the heavens into a gladiatorial arena. Dexterity and military capability reigned as the battle for aerial supremacy continued, driving the Ferusian ship into a slow retreat to the clouds. The sounds never went away. The ringing in their ears – it persisted. Over. And over. And over.

The return to reality wasn't quite so easy. He rested against the wall, lopsided and effortless. His eyes went dry, blinking on rare occasion. All oxygen had been taken from his lungs and had been forced out by the disbelief of his survival. A new uprising of voices refused to head over the top. Whatever frontline was before them, it would have to face the enemy alone. No man, woman or child present in uniform dared to chance the ship's return. A few officers led brave souls over the top and never returned. A workforce of weary bodies was delivered, imposing labours of levels unseen. Engineers crudely constructed wooden struts, sheets of metal covering the ridgeline. Sappers hammered nails into dugouts and they hoped that they'd hold for the approaching storm.

All the while, Rhys was left silent. Ten minutes after his return, he was lifted from his position by friendly hands.

"Shit, man, you okay?" Oslo was the first to greet him. He took a hand and placing it upon his shoulder. Forced out of his trance, he nodded quickly, his mind still in overdrive.

"Is everyone okay? Where's the-"

"Take a breather, c'mon. Calm down. The others are this way."

Rhys noticed that as soon as it had started, the gunfire had stopped. No, the battle over the near horizon had concluded. They had become the new frontline.

Left to his thoughts, he followed Oslo, who barged through the waves of attentive soldiers taking post on the firing steps.

Time was fractured. Everything was in pieces. A slow rope had strung him up against torn up trees. He was left dangling, watching over the land in silent speculation. The rope dragged him through the streets of grime and blood. Nothing made sense. He'd lost himself for a minute.

Everything was lost.

Oslo's voice was the only thing he *felt*. The man looked troubled, worried to the glint of his own eye. Rampancy led his charge. He still clutched onto his machine gun. Eventually, they arrived at the junction of rest. Evelyn was the closest, waiting and crying to herself with asthmatic strife. At any glance, Rhys knew the unapologetic callousness they'd endured had taken its toll.

Toiled eyes stared at the walls. Mateo kicked his heels against the iron sheets he rested on. Dynis looked just as empty as before. Rhys walked through both of them, scanning either side of the walkway. Oslo hugged Evelyn, comforting her with hushes and embraces. Christopher was nowhere to be seen. Tyran expressed his exhaustion with a glance to the sky, an open mouth and a disbelieved chuckle as he was taken out of the moment. And then, there was Ella.

She was the last one, distanced by about thirty feet. A shallow corner, where empty mess tins and spent bullet casings rested, used and left aside, which gave her space to pace around. She spotted Rhys and rushed over to him as he approached her. Her hands, with unimagined tension, grabbed onto his webbing.

"Have you seen Sabrina?!" She wailed, her eyes bloodshot and ruined by internal discord. "Where's my sister? Was she near you? Was she-"

There was no response. Rhys' strenuous gaze of confusion and bewilderment presented her with a brutal answer. Her fingers unravelled from his straps as she melted backwards, falling against the thick, mud-made ramparts. A corrosion pushed her to the floor and tears returned to her eyes. Rhys moved to her side instinctively yet he couldn't find his words. She cried, her voice feeble and pathetic.

"Oh no...Please no, don't let it be like this. Not like this. Where is she?" Rhys placed a hand on her shoulder, though he retracted it soon after. The rain danced in her hair as she let herself be drowned by the skyward showers.

He'd seen tears before; streams of fear and anxiety weren't uncommon around the militia, but here they were of pain and misery: a heartbreak locked in the confinement of trench warfare. No machines drowned out her wails. No gunshots dampened the sound of her strained breath.

Unsure of what to do, he took a minute to stare at her, the crumbling maiden, in the vile fate she'd been left with. His body was weak and fatigued by the course of the day's unrest. He walked away yet faced her still. If anything, she couldn't have him turn his back on her.

Mateo moved to Rhys' side; his hands were placed firmly on his forehead. His eyes were wide open, strained and reddened by the heat he'd endured. A nervous wander of laughter stumbled from his loosened lips.

"Give us a fucking break, I swear." He cursed. "I can't go one metre without someone trying to kill me."

"Mateo, where is Sabrina?"

Rhys' deathly tone caught Mateo by surprise, zipping his flippant behaviour away. He wiped his smile away and hid his hands away into his pockets, speaking with a low and moderated tone.

216

"Uhm, well we haven't seen Sabrina yet. Or Gwendolyn...or Christopher, actually." No response. Mateo tried to fill in the silence himself. "Maybe they're just somewhere else in the trench." Still no response. "I'd suspect they're just having a rest, or looking for us...or-"

"Mate..." Both of their gazes sank into the soil, only to pull themselves out and to reach out to each other's. "How're the others doing?"

"See for yourself." A weary finger pointed behind him, back the way they came. The rest of the squad cowered together, huddled nearby to the section's entrance. "Dynis hasn't said a word. Tyran looks like he's in a spout of shock. Eve is terrified. Oslo's headstrong. I think that, physically, they're all okay."

"Right." The Staff Sergeant looked back down at Ella, still wallowing in her own disturbed – though very real – personal nightmare. Her face was buried into her knees.

"Do you think they're okay? The others, I mean-"

"I...hope so."

His mind was fuelled with recent memories of Sabrina. A tight collection of scenes, laughter, desirable stares and conversations all felt incomplete. All lacked the catalyst that brought them together: her.

"I'm sorry, Rhys. There's not much I can really say."

"Don't say it to me, she needs it more."

Nodding to the crying conscript, he made his way back over to Ella. She trembled and twitched in synchronisation to each foul breath she took. Asphyxiated by grief, her howls had been reduced to pathetic whimpers. Rhys could only be thankful she hadn't seen what had happened to her sister.

He gestured for Mateo to go back to the others and gave Ella the space she needed to suffer.

Alone. She would have truly felt deserted, abandoned by her one true kin. Cleaved from the cord of kin, her body waited in fragility. A summoning of pain had wrenched her flesh and blood from her side – a piece taken from the grand puzzle.

A crying wind blew over the trench top. Dead ends hid Ella away. Trapped with her guilt, she looked up to see if Rhys were still by her side. He was.

"Private Mistral, I-" He paused, shaking his head. "Ella, I'm so sorry."

217

He felt as if his words meant nothing. Empty highways of gusts delivered his estranged messages of comfort but disfigured them along the way. She looked at him with an uncomfortable glare. Her crimson eyes left an unsettling sickness in Rhys' chest. He couldn't cope with meeting the eyes of a victim. After all, there was no joy in eyeing mirrors.

A nameless wrath lay in her sculpted irises. She was shaped by the crippled blows to her composure. A string of prejudicial affairs had strewn their puppet strings. He could only describe her stare as one of furious intent.

"Am I going to die too?" She whispered, determined to get a solution for herself.

That time she wanted to believe it. There was nothing to take her mind from the pain. No tank, car or vehicle laid nearby, waiting for her attendance. In a battlefield where nature's course gave them hostile hospitality, she had no deflection.

He urged himself to answer but dared to not say a word. He felt guilty for something out of his control. Stories of legendary heroes preventing disaster seemed alien to the insufferable truth of the war. Rhys desperately wanted to give her an answer. However, the lies were no longer enough.

Chapter 17

Exodus

The anaesthesia denounced all states of material consciousness – and the soldiers, devalued by international subjugation, turned to husks and shells of men; their consciences had dispersed like the cigarette's vapour in a storm. The laughter fell away with him and her, elder and youth. The 'dear-old-blighty' banter lay as a carcass in the soil. Hundreds wrote down letters that were to never be delivered. Some passed the time with whistling or by singing in the morbid realisation of their numbered days. Others placed bets on the aircraft raging fire above. Two dreadnoughts flew by and exchanged shots between one another. No one saw the victor. Severe trauma ran rampant throughout the trench line.

Nature took its day job and buried the dead with ravens feasting upon their fresh carrion. The mist cleared as the sun had set.

The traumatised were left on the frontline with the few sane. Until replacements arrived, none of the lightly injured could leave for proper treatment. Sermons from regimental clergymen struggled to plaster back together the signs of the crumbled union against syndicalism.

Dated landmarks of bone, wood, iron and skin were used to name every corridor of trench, just so Private Doe could write home saying: "Mum, I died with the lads and lasses on Roger's Hand Avenue."

All livelihood had been murdered. The trees were dead. The grass was dead. The sun was dead. Only the half-alive mess of the central frontline let off a breath, and that was coaxed awake by eternal bombardment.

Several flanks of the frontline had been caved in by the dreadnought's salvo. Their position had become a pocket, a near-encircled, segmented graveyard for the next battle to come. A bulge, right across the tip of Kelan's defensive position. For the longest hour, it seemed as if there would be no hailing, and no miracle. There would be only destruction.

And he, Rhys – the tribulated patron, was surprised when the order came through. A unanimous cheer circulated throughout the dugouts, alleyways and graveyards. It came about first by word of mouth.

Two men, strapped in heavy in Royal Armed Forces munitions, stood at the quiet end of the trench, going through cigarette after cigarette. Rhys overhead them as they peppered their tongues back and forth.

"You 'ear that mate, proper evacuation and everything! We'll be out of 'ere by the third hour."

"Fuck, really? Thank the fucking stars, mate. Grace be upon us, tonight."

"Only took, what, eight- no, twelve odd thousand lives, weren't it?"

"Better late than never."

"Bah, the Queen can suck it. Bitch thinks she's being gracious 'n' shit. I can read between the lines, mate."

"You got something else in those smokes? Talking all crack-in-the-skull, you are."

"Fuck off. I think she sent all the bottom-class boys like us out 'ere to level 'er playing field. Get rid of serfdom, and what-not."

"But wasn't it the ol' field marshals and commanders keeping us here? I thought it was her intervention taking us out?"

"That's what they want you to believe! All this an' that, like she's some proper do-gooder. Fuck that, just a shitty version of her 'usband, ain't she?"

"Ah, mate I don't want to get into another squabble about that. I'm just glad we'll be leaving this shithole."

"Yeah, never even liked Haria. Place had shit ice-cream shops anyway."

The pair stubbed out their cigarettes and moved on with their night. Rhys trailed behind, simply out of curiosity, and found talks of an evacuation to be widespread. At first, he felt like he could smile, but then, the dust settled on his parade, and he realised what it meant: defeat.

For there was no honour in defeat, only shame. Contrarily, to triumph meant to slaughter and to indulge butchery. Had they pressed Ferusia off their shores, they could have given themselves the benefit of cutting short the slaughter. Their defeat, however, made one thing clear: the peace had been lost. War was foregone, and would be so long as the two nationalities stood on the same landmass.

Rhys lifted himself up and waltzed the route of dirt. Cluttered bodies stood packed up, brought together with dishonest celebration. Slacked lips repeated the words: evacuation, retreat and home. Some frowned whilst others grimaced. Costly days had given them every incentive to run, to hide away in the fields, forests, mountains and hills of Kelan's inland defences. No longer would they need to buy time with their lives as the currency.

A few remained peeved as they too understood the following trail from their tail-ended rush. An opening had been made. Ferusia could and would utilise their arsenal in its fully operational state. All out warfare was destined to begin.

Whilst treading ahead, a sentry on the firing post had his chest split open as a marksman's bullet pierced straight through him. Rhys only heard the body fall as he turned to see a crowd gathering around the murdered soul. A commotion raised, but the alarms were minimal. Poor luck, some said. For once, Rhys barely reacted, taking a few painful seconds to eye up the body before returning to his journey, gun tightly held in his hand.

At the end of The King's Head Street, just inside one of the emptied mortar pits, Mateo sat perched upon two crates of shells waiting to be fired by a cannon that didn't exist. Rhys gave him a little nod and a wave as he arrived. He noticed a cigarette perched between Mateo's lips.

"How's things?" He said, pulling out a quick and heavy drag before putting it out against the wall.

"In general, or…?"

"Well, yeah, but also out there." Tilting his head and carbine at the same time, he gestured toward where the man had been shot. Rhys hesitated to answer before he waved it off with a cold palm.

"Usual things." The bitter euphemisms poured from his soured lips.

"Ah, right," Mateo grinned, "you heard the good news, then?"

"The evacuation?"

"Absolute class, isn't it?"

"I guess." Rhys strode over to the boxes and gestured for Mateo to budge aside. He pulled himself atop of the wooden throne and, as he rested beside him, sighed. "Since when have you smoked?"

"For special occasions, mate."

They looked to the sky and spectated the grimacing night as it took full force. Hours spent waiting had disenchanted the stars. A greyed, monochrome piece of graphite had coloured in the clouds. The world appeared like a line of old-age police tape: a noir black and white strip above and beyond their heads. Rhys looked down to the bottom of the mortar pit and spoke with a jade mumble.

"You've kept yourself level-headed these last few days." He began. "I mean, how? Like, how many are we missing now? Ryan. Tamara…"

"Christopher, too."

"Johan and Stephan-"

"Fuck 'em. Those two aren't like us." Mateo reached into his thigh pocket and drew a second cigarette. Then, he ignited it with a lighter that very clearly wasn't his. "Just a bunch of rich kids attempting to get famous."

"But they had a point: I'm failing everyone as a leader."

Mateo snickered, inhaling the sweet fire, ash and tobacco between his fingers. In-between the coughs were the choked chuckles – amused toward his Staff Sergeant's struggled self-respect.

He placed a light hand on Rhys' back and gently shook it with an oddly firm grip.

"Mate, every ounce of shit we've been through was because of the Ferusians, not you." He deflected the blame with a tired grin. "You couldn't prevent some of them. A sniper, a train crash and a bombardment? Shit, just tell yourself you're part of the unlucky rabble and call it a day."

"It's…difficult to chalk up people's deaths to luck."

"Why, though? A poor fucker gets killed every day, now with the war around we've got it all coming out. Unavoidable, unless you're lucky. Dwell on your mistakes, but not your losses." As he continued, Rhys felt unsettled by the intervention he received. He returned his gaze to the ground. "If you wrap your head around it for too long, you'll do something stupid that'll get you killed. Sometimes you've just got to accept it. Like, I spent my whole life delivering fucking letters, right? I got curious, and y'know what?"

No response. Mateo's voice shifted in colour, going from the bright yellow chiptune whistle it always had been to a callous, grey and emotionless slab of slate. Dry-mouthed and with fire in his throat, he wandered his mind through the tacky viscosity of his thoughts, barely able to drag himself through.

"I read letters, loads of them, before I deliver them. You learn a lot about the world. Names from all sorts of people. *'Aunty Isara was murdered with an iron pipe.'* Or who could forget *'Mr Cremlin was swabbed over by a truck with his two kids.'* World's an endless-fucking-nightmare, but if I'd sat still and took it all in for just a minute, I'd off myself with a necktie-too-tight, mate."

"And," Rhys hesitated, "what is this supposed to be telling me?"

"Nothing – ignore it. Just talking, y'know?"

Quiet hushes sat between them. No noise, no whisper. The atmospheric ambience of cold wind, distant gunshots and planes high above the clouds left them with a gentle musical number, tuned not by audio but by the visualisations of tracers and casings.

"You seem like a good guy, Rhys." Mateo smiled again, placing his eyes into his palms to rub the layered bags from them. "A bit lost, but you're not a crook. Always in the heat, yet still always thinking innocently."

"Thanks, I guess." Mateo laughed to himself at his uncertainty. He nudged his superior once more with a closed fist.

"You never take compliments seriously, do you? Not unless it's from Sab-." He froze. A few seconds of tackled lungs soon left off with a sigh, and Mateo sighed. "Shit, I'd not really clocked on to the fact that…"

"Yeah, Gwen too." Drifting away into the night's cruelty, they remained perched atop of their stool of explosives. The innocent mind of Rhys felt incomplete, regardless of what Mateo had said. A brood of emotional distress would've gotten the better of him, it just needed the time to shed its skin.

"You been keeping an eye on Ella?" He asked Rhys, warming up to his cigarette's final budding.

"Spent two hours with her. Couldn't even look her in the eye or say anything."

"Maybe it's for the better you don't. Not while its still fresh. Like, fuck, man…it's been what, four hours? Six hours? Can't even keep track of the time." He left Rhys to his silence and they didn't say a word from then on.

Rhys' vision was left to the nightly grimness whilst it rested in the glint of his tired eyes. He felt as he looked: like he'd been dragged through the war-keeper's grounds by the legs. Rummaged hair sat tucked beneath his 2_{mm} steel skullcap and his skin was still caked by the dried mud left on his body.

Answered prayers still felt underwhelmed, though as to why was inexplicable. Rhys wanted to escape and to leave the violence, but he felt at that hour that it would follow him to the end of time. The evacuation wasn't something that granted a life free of shackles. It was a delay, a setup in a favourable position to challenge the inevitable storm. To prolong the war with manpower and steel was to slow down the great downfall.

Mateo's hopelessness had been hidden behind a smile. He had accepted everything wrong with the world. He chose to live by its standards with a fine line between losing himself and conquering the horrors with excellence.

Mateo smiled again. However, Rhys couldn't see it the same way as he had done before.

Sooner than they could've said anything else, voices arose from the other side of the trench wall. Shouts and splutters, coughs and calls for help. Both Rhys and Mateo sat up with piqued interest. The urgent demand for a medic debuted with a pained female voice asking for materials caught Rhys' immediate attention, and he leapt from his crypt and ran for the commotion.

Just around the corner, at the end of the corridor, he saw her. Dragged into the trench by her contemporaries, with a face tainted by mud, had arrived the Combat Medic.

"Gwen?" He whispered, lunging forward through the crowds as the familiar face collapsed into the dugout. She let out a gasp of relief as she panted at the thrill of her getaway. "Gwen, holy shit!"

Not a second had passed and he was at her crumbled side, where he saw the shredding and rips in her uniform. Indications of self-treatment did little to men her battered appearance, like the bloodstained bandages she'd wrapped around her forearms.

"Hey, Gwen? Can you hear me? Are you ok-"

"Shut up…"

She spluttered out coldly and wiped her mouth with a sullied sleeve. Blood covered the chest of her jacket, across the sleeves and onto her gloved hands.

"Alright, someone get a medic!" He called behind him as he turned back to her with a weary smile of anxiety. Mateo reached the rim of crowd, struggling to see over the shoulders of those blocking his way. "Holy shit, you've lost a lot-"

"It's not mine." Her eyes were restless as they darted around her sockets. "It's Sabrina's."

He felt an increasing pound beat against his chest – he assumed that it was just confirmation of her total annihilation, and he was pained again. The bleak reminder had forced an agonising stiffness that clogged up his throat.

"Well…let's get you some help. You made it just in time for a stretcher." Quickly, he changed the conversation just as fast as she'd arrived. Her face turned to one of frustration, shaking in denial.

"No, Rhys, she's still out there!"

"Who is?"

"Her!" Her lifeless voice was interrupted by a rasped cough.

"Sabrina?" His eyes tunnelled right through her. Blank stares were met with an uncontrollable drive as she nodded to confirm his deduction. "She's alive?"

The crowds dispersed as two stretcher bearers arrived at the scene.

"She still needs help; I came to get some." The medics hoisted her body onto the canvas cradle.

"Where is she?!" He frantically drilled in his investigation.

"About…" She clenched at her stomach, bruised by the furious and frantic circumstances that had led her there. With an aggressive point, she directed his attention back the very way she'd come. "Straight ahead there. Maybe five or six hundred-"

Her sentence faded into the mists of the moon-deprived night. The crib she lay within was carried away, and she disappeared out of sight in a matter of seconds.

Eyes drifted from the vanishing medics to Rhys. He sat against the floorboards with a boiled glance. A slight deviation from his calm and collected attitude moments before had shown up in place. A fragile stare moved to the top of the trench, the blood-soaked ladder in which Gwen had fallen from. Following his eyes, Mateo moved forward, shaking his head as he watched Rhys put a hand on the steps to no man's land.

"No, no, no. Come on, up you get." Assertively, he wrapped his own fingers under Rhys' arms and brought him to the side. "This way, we'll get you-"

"She's still out there…"

"Rhys, come with me, we'll-"

"Mateo, she's still out there. We need to go get her!"

He shook himself from Mateo's grasp and pushed through the trench, navigating the twists and turns throughout. A deafening machine had been ignited within his soul. The cogs of his internal drive pushed him through the crowds, with Mateo on his trail, calling out to him as he moved. That time, however, he hadn't made a straight line for the steps outside. And by the passing of two minutes, he'd reached the Officers' Dugout.

He entered without resistance, marching into the shadowy flicker of the candlelit room. Heavy steps alerted the council within, eyes turning and peeling to his intrusive barge. Rhys remained stiff-faced and saluted the group before him.

An array of officers faced him who were all equally confused by his arrival. Among them, Alexander waited at the back, sipping from a steaming cup of tasteless water. Only his equals and subordinates held the room's silence until one of them spoke up.

"Can we *help* you, Staff Sergeant?" A young, clean looking lieutenant piped up first, sticking his nose to the front of the group.

"Sir, I have received news that I have a live soldier out in the field who needs recovery." He lowered his quivering hand by his side and spoke as if he'd let a cork clog up his windpipe.

"Hold your horses!" Sceptical, the youthful officer pressed into the claim with a beady eye. "Where did you get this news from?"

"One of our own. Private Carlyle, combat medic to my squad. Said there's a Private Mistral still out waiting for help."

"And…?" His heart sank as the young lieutenant shrugged, looking between his contemporaries; all the while, Alexander sat at the back of the room, watching over with great interest.

"I would like to request an extraction group to-"

"Forget it." A second, older lieutenant spat as he stepped forward beside the youngster. The drive in Rhys' heart was grounded and jammed to a standstill by the officer's rational wrench. "The first wave will be pulling out soon, and I'd rather not complicate things."

"But-"

"Staff Sergeant, do you think there'll be a single man or woman in this trench who'd chance their opportunity to leave Haria to save a single Private, let alone to put more soldiers at risk to save one soldier?"

Quick to respond, Rhys sharpened his breath and stepped closer toward the candlelight, with uncertainty haunting his head.

"I'd chance it." A cloud of taciturnity filled the dugout. The moistened, dripping walls of mud and rotting wood lay still and Rhys' heart was left to skip several beats. He held his breath and his tongue, before uttering out a final: "Sir…"

The two lieutenants glanced at one another and turned back to see the others. Some shrugged, others shook their heads. From the shadows at the back, Alexander stepped forward and ducked underneath a low-hanging wooden strut.

"You'd like to go out there?" His tone was stern and his expression was of iron. A free hand scratched at his moustache, whilst the other lifted the boiled mug of water to his dried lips.

"No, Sir." Rhys mumbled, his confidence slipping away in seconds. "But…I feel like if there's no way of stepping around it, then I should at least do something – for my own group."

"Private Mistral's one of yours, aren't they?"

"She is." The owlish eyes of the other officers pierced right through him as they sensed his distress. They looked down upon him, and to many it was rightfully so.

227

"And what if you get yourself killed?" Said the young officer who jeered with a cunning fox-grin.

"Well then, lieutenant, he'd have made a very stupid decision – and it'd be his to deal with." Alexander spoke up. "But Gentlemen, it'd be a shame not to lead by example. Where's your spirit?"

"By all due respect, Sir, we aren't in Redus. We're not here to dance with theatrics, we're here to fight a war." Sharp tones rotted away the oak struts around them. As if he spoke only of despicable decomposition, Rhys felt his own heart rust. "What use is another SNCO with his face in the mud?"

"By the gods, it's no wonder your own men don't respect you. You'd let beasts fuck your wives because you could still fuck her tomorrow." For a minute, a burst of inspiration rejogged the machine in his chest. An idealist fantasy, a view of heroism and, more importantly, keeping a friend alive – the sense of honour in the dishonoured world. It was when men could use their words to incite dangerous feats that anyone knew a loved leader was present. "Come, Staff Sergeant, we'll get you kitted up."

Alexander strode outside first, splitting the cloth doorway asunder in his effortless gait. A warmth rekindled Rhys' cold sensation. He wasted no second to follow in his footsteps, leaving behind the clutter of protesting officers.

~~~

A raw disturbance crushed his windpipe with the indiscriminate pressures of his fear. All that sanctimonious talk had left him and the side of the devil's mare, and he had saddled his way onto his road to anguish. The inner turmoil was nothing short of inexplicable nonsense. Rhys' soul had been bruised and battered, with bloody fingernails that dug into his spirit. His chest had also been constricted by the restraining rig around his torso. An asthmatic uneasiness marinated his pleading unrest as he whispered to himself.

He watched as the departed made their way out of hell. In lines of thirty at a time, silent figures funnelled themselves down airless bloodstained furrows. Dehydrated faces under soaked clothing stared austerely at the road beyond. Some sang happy tunes of going home, whilst others kept their thoughts and prayers to silence. Half of The King's Head Street had been granted departure, with the remaining half standing on guard to cover their retreat. And as they did so, Rhys kitted himself up for his own objective.

Mateo shook his head whilst, off to the side, Oslo had tacked on to spectate the commotion that Rhys had stirred.

At one end, Rhys was mollycoddled with the imminent chance of death. Single bullets charged with enough gunpowder could change history – a lonesome farmer in the fields of battle was helpless to the powder keg of fate. And in Rhys facing that fear, however, was the lingering taunt of abandoning his ally, his friend and his chance at redemption. He could only retain his cowardice for so long – lest others would die at the hands of inaction. Fleeing would only bring him to the edge of the world, to a place where he'd have to fight the world in exhaustion. Death or dishonour, violence or retreat. The hour had offered two choices of pure disgust, both ugly coatings atop of the already unhappy world.

Finally, he lay down his rifle. The stand-in armourer presented him with a handgun, an easily accessible firearm in the heat of stress. It carried no burden other than the lives it could take.

Ready and set, he moved over to Oslo and Mateo with a worried look, taking a deep breath as he faced them.

"You'll do great." Oslo spoke softly, being the first to give him a pat on the back.

"Thanks. Have you told Ella yet?"

"She's with Evelyn. Thought it'd be best if they didn't know." He rubbed his callous fingers against his stubble, a light chortle in accompaniment. "So, you better not tank it today. Plus, you'll bring back a nice gift for her if you make it."

"If she's alive," Rhys nervously sighed, "then maybe we can start counting our blessings."

"I can count ours on one hand, mate." Mateo chuckled. He tapped him on the other shoulder, still dissatisfied by his call to action. "Don't take long. It won't be a while before we all have to leave."

"They won't leave us."

From the dingy undergrowth of wire and sandbags, Alexander stepped into the light with a courteous grin. He too was dressed in his battle garments, with a helmet that replaced his typical, pristine officer's cap. A rusty gaze lightened up the party as he took to Rhys' side. He flashed the SNCO with a brightened expression.

"Can't have you doing a two-man job on your own." His jovial and offhand attitude was just as infectious as it had been on the train. Rhys was brought a partial way out of his own decomposition.

"Sir?"

"They won't leave you if I'm with you, old chap. No one else has the balls to make an example, so...chip chop, let's get this underway, shall we?" The essence of Gabriel tightened his uniform and unsheathed his notorious bloom on the situation. Indecency would not stop his charmful attitude as he shot down an ounce of Rhys' anxiety. "Come along now."

The Captain waltzed carelessly between the crowds of grief-stricken soldiers and gave each of them the odd tap on the cheek and shoulder to lift their spirits up. He was their man of the people and a warrior of honour – so the heroics told. There wasn't any shame to him in acting improper. Fools stepping into fires were his specialty, and he seemed eager to showcase his assistance for the fellow man in battle.

Captain Arthurs wasn't any old rich man officer from top-league university in Burno, for he was a glimmering beacon. He was everyone's friend, even if they weren't his; where men fell in shadows, he willingly crawled into it with them, an infinite smile planted on his beard-coated mug.

"I'll be there to watch over you." Before he left, Oslo hauled his machine gun on his back and shivered, internally debating whether or not his duty was worth it.

"Think you'd be able to give us enough cover?" Rhys sincerely asked.

"Peace of mind."

The behemoth walked ahead of his superior. As they passed by the waiting soldiers, they gave them their grace with words from drunken, soddened lips.

"Good luck, mate."

"Be careful."

"Wish y'luck."

"Try not to catch a blighter."

The blessings fell short of encouraging. Many spoke with uncertainty, as if to say: *'better him than me'*. A brief shimmer of hope had soon faded once he heard the whispers of men and women, placing their bets on his chances of survival, let alone victory. Rhys' hand rested atop of his holstered pistol. His fingers caressed the tip of the bore and the grip.

He internally tuned himself to take another life, as it was part of the fear he felt. If a Ferusian crossed paths with his rescue attempt, he'd have to kill them. There was no debate. There was no chance to reason. He would, for Sabrina's sake, risk that shattered moral compass he'd tried to piece back together for her survival.

The firing steps stood before him; they were the very same skin-soaked stairs that Gwen had fallen from an hour prior. A straight line ahead, that's all they needed to do. Sabrina was nothing more than a frozen needle in a blazed haystack. Strategically, she'd have been a lost cause. Compassionately, a sliver of hope still tipped the great glacier of chance, and Rhys was determined to not let it drift away.

He whispered blessings upon himself and took a place next to the Captain. The incredulous night had laid its obstructions for him in the forms of bottomless mud pits, wire and midnight gunsights. He looked to Alexander.

"Right, you know the jig. Stay down, voices low and watch where you step, chap." He listed; his smile was still ever present. "I've got this little torch, see? So, tell me if you see something and we'll use it sparingly."

"Understood, Sir." Their voices faded into murmurs.

"And hey," the Captain prodded him, "we'll do fine, lad."

Oslo clambered up the left step and dug his bipod into the soil. Rhys passed him a pair of binoculars that was tucked into his webbing. He scrutinised the battlefield. Rhys couldn't help but feel as if it were in ineffectuality as another act done to comfort the idled professionalism that had plagued the militia's battering. For without the lamps, candles and glimmers of dugout fires, they could barely see ten feet in front of them.

Out in the field, instinct and presumptions alone defined who conquered its walkways and who drowned in soil with three holes in their back.

Oslo gave them the universal "go-when-ready" signal when he flipped his thumb to the sky. Dawn wasn't to arrive for another few hours. At least the cover of darkness benefitted them to a certain degree. And so, up the rickety stairs they crawled. Rhys unholstered his handgun, rested his finger on the trigger-guard and followed closely behind the Captain, taking his second stride out into the wastes.

His heart retched and heaved with a nervous tick. It implored him to survive, counterbalancing the dutiful desire to see his friend live.

The abyssal mud squelched beneath the soles of their boots. Held breaths and mutters of distress fell behind them, vanishing into the night as the world submerged back under a blanket of darkness. To their front, just before the horizon, a faint yet warm glow held the Ferusian banner's high in a trench once theirs. Their element of stealth grew weaker with every step further into limbo they traversed.

To seek Sabrina was to tempt the sentries of the frontline, but when they met themselves in the midst of no man's land, not a word was spoken among the dead that decomposed in the mud.

Wails and howls took to the sky. The wind scraped past their ears. A blistering chill seasoned each gust. Rhys tightened his jacket as he crossed his arms over his body, bringing his handgun close to his chest. His lungs were restocked with a frost-tipped reticence and the cold oxygen numbed his body.

A new light had been shed on the world, or rather a lack thereof. The same instruments that scattered the land – whether snipped barbed wire or leftover fragments of guns, shells and bodies – had been doused in a new palette. Revulsions of war had since been experienced by sunlight and mist alone. Day had been a time to fear, an era of terror that housed great impurities – where the dead were so easy to see. The night, however, was a place of reflection, where he saw the disastrous makings of the reaper in a gruesome dark tone. The heads that were split open, beneath the twilight hour, transformed into monsters and creatures of the night. He held his breath as he accidentally trod on a severed arm that was still dressed in its torn sleeve.

Fields of russet seas had transformed into oceans of black. Obscured incubi lay dormant, hidden from sight, until he'd stumble upon them. Just fifty metres from their frontline, he found a battered corpse.

He gulped, patted the body down and, after gesturing with a whisper for Alexander to flash the light in its face, he was relieved that it was only a man.

Rhys could see the fresh, mangled face of the man littered with shrapnel and yet he took an easier breath from it knowing they were an unknown soul to him. Guilt tackled his initial relief, but with one golden beauty on his mind he wrestled his way back to ignoring his muddied catacomb. An officious titter displaced his mind. As he was about to move on, he turned back to the body as he swore the body itself had laughed. It was an indication for him to turn back, but he didn't. An illusionary signpost had been nailed into place. It read: *'Here, men change.'*

"Alright, come on. He's already been toasted."

Alexander put it as grimly as reality itself was and tugged on Rhys' sleeve. He didn't need a reminder of the dogmatic ambience around them. Right then, looking at the bigger picture was to sacrifice one's individuality. To value little comforts created a happy and unique life. To take arms at reality would mean forever dispelling his chance to hold his good deeds to any regard.

And so, time ticked by. Feet slipped, hands dug into the dirt and glassy, emotionless eyes reflected the light from Alexander's torch. Coupled bodies, killed in pairs, became ever the more frequent as they went deeper into the heart of hell. All were unrecognisable. A lonely ligament here and a twisted lost torso there. The bombardment had been indiscriminate. Victims weren't killed; they were carved up and served on a muddied platter, mangled and torn apart like meat for mutts.

Rhys thought to himself in pessimistic fashion: *if Sabrina were even here, would she even be in one piece?*

He then pondered if her gentle beauty could be identified whatsoever. Had they strayed at the wrong angle, they could've missed her entirely. Mankind was vulnerable only to its own weapons as they rampaged through the splendours of Farhawl, be they ornaments or living pretties. No status of power, attractiveness, wealth or age could stop a bullet or a bomb.

New perceptions of their darkest playthings sat all around them. As his eyes adjusted to the dimness, he noticed the rust on

233

the wire, the blackened tears in the clothing and the unfathomable void of the flooded craters. Similar sights and landmarks stood out in the distance as haunted silhouettes. Apparitions taunted him with their lingering presence. He could hear their breath pass his right. It sounded cold, like that of a woman who'd lost it all. Born without brightness, given life through pain, each breath was met with a clenched whimper and whine. Sour teeth bit into its own tongue and he tried to centralise the pain elsewhere.

"Wait, Sir!" He whispered as something caught his eye just after he passed it.

A movement, coupled with the slosh of mud and silent breath. Alexander watched as he crawled across the open mound and into a ditch, where a shadowed-out body lay. It motioned in cold shakes; its quake was caused by the nightly chill.

"In here."

Drawing to the side of the cowered woman, Alexander drew the torch and flickered it to life, shining a bright yellow beam to her face. What followed was the discovery of a fallen figure, frayed from cloth to skin.

Her crystalline eyes were shielded and hidden behind tightly knitted lids. Curled fingers twirled into her palms with her cuffs dangled just below her nose. They twitched and coiled like a withering vine caught in a blizzard; her veneer of soil had made her one with the loam. Crimson stains topped her frail knuckles, frozen through time and space against her skin. Across her cheeks, scrapes and cuts ran through her temples. A rancorous blend of dirt and blood had danced across her face that ended in a dry encore.

Rhys lifted her hands carefully in his and she jolted. Her eyes remained shut and she flailed her arms weakly. A strained wrist slapped against the torch, tossing it across the ditch and leaving it face up to the sky. Its beam shone up and flashed rapidly. Alexander dashed for it. As he retrieved it, he swore under his breath.

"H-hey! It's me! it's me, Sabrina. Rhys. Rhys Hendricks." He spoke with a roughened, loud whisper. Then, it was as if his voice had caressed her brow with tenderness. Little, weak fingers unfurled, reaching out and they rested on his arm without any grip. Her eyes fluttered open and she saw nothing but the darkness around them. "It's okay, we're here for you. I'm here for you."

Not a word. Prolonged shock had left her mute. Her eyes barely glistened at all as the moon stayed tucked away above the clouds. And as her expression showed no life, no energy or familiarity to the once beaming, grinning, joyous woman he'd grown to appreciate, he struggled to decipher whether it was really Sabrina he'd found.

"Come on, people are waiting for us." He urged her to move, but she didn't.

"Hendricks, she won't be going anywhere like that." Alexander said worriedly. His fingers pointed to further down her body, where Rhys finally saw the extent of her condition.

Casualties in war had always had something from them. A bullet to the leg would take away their carelessness and a sight of a fallen friend would take away their spirit. Sabrina had more than her courage and infectious happiness stripped forcefully from her. Beneath her left knee, there was an absence of space. An empty region like a missing piece to the puzzle. She was left incomplete. In its place, a bundle of precisely layered bandages inserted underneath her trouser leg hid the damage. At the tip, a knot of her leftover clothing drenched in blood and soil.

Rhys couldn't draw his eyes from it. He was traumatically chained to its grim sight. Her pale hands called for him where her voice wouldn't, moving to his cheek. He felt the mud and parched bloodstains against his face and he finally looked back at her. A cold night had left beyond a nightmare for her. Her eyes, still caked in darkness, told him something – that she'd given up.

Her voice broke into a childish whimper as he shifted aside, where he took his gaze back to her broken stare. Without thought, he leaned over and brought her body forward, embracing her in a tight hug. Her cheek touched his, ice-cold and with a bite to it.

"What have they done to you?" He whispered to himself. Somehow, he refused to let a tear of his own take shape.

She was half-buried in dirt, leftover needles and packaging for medical supplies, all used and abused just to keep Sabrina alive and silent. Anaesthetics, used bandage wraps, a broken splint and rusting medical scissors. To call Gwen's persistence impressive would've been an understatement. Nearly two medical kit's worth of unrivalled craftwork had stopped the stream of blood from her

235

wound and delayed the cold death she awaited. Rhys had no idea how long it would've been until she'd died of hypothermia, or if she would've passed out and never have woken up again. Perhaps the pain he couldn't feel had forced her eyes into restless purgatory. No rest, no comfort. Only dreariness, blurred visions and fatal wounds. Her hours were numbered.

With imperfect care, Rhys placed his arms beneath her back and right leg, preparing to hoist her off the ground.

"Careful, lad." The Captain mouthed, softly peering to the edge of the ditch.

"Do we even have time to be careful, Sir? She barely looks alive."

"Hold your tongue, we'll get her out."

Slowly, Rhys lifted her from the floor. In his first attempt, she let out a shriek of agony. Her voice echoed through the air and rippled between the aftermath of hell's march. He stopped immediately and covered her mouth with his hand. The slather of her breath and tongue pushed against his palm whilst he, regrettably, muffled her down. The echo lingered for longer than it should have. He turned to Alexander with a troubled gaze.

"Fuck, Sir. How are we going to-"

"We can't do much else. Either we carry her and just go or we sit here until no one comes to get us." Alexander's tone sharpened. He could see the dominoes that toppled in the distance. "Look, this'll help."

He pushed ahead of Rhys, reaching into his open collar and unfolding a hidden olive scarf. He moved quickly, flawlessly. Hesitation didn't hold him back as he wrapped it around her mouth.

"Sorry lass, has to be done." Alexander apologised over her lowered tears. Her eyes widened and her breath seemed short. Confusion poorly mixed with her incurable shock left her in a panic. "There. Best I can do, now let's get a move on."

"Okay…okay…" Plight hampered his confidence. Reluctant to make a move, he loitered for a few seconds before he attempted to lift her back up. She sounded as if she were trying to say something, but the scarf gag soaked up all her agonised words.

236

"Here, give us a sec." Alexander assisted her off of the ground and into Rhys' firm grip. The decision was irrevocable. He had to commit to it. "You got her?"

"Yeah, I got her."

His eyes couldn't meet hers as tormented tears waterfalled down her cheeks. Whispered apologies from Rhys went unnoticed as her face clenched and twisted. She thrashed and contorted around in panic. Rhys pulled her in close with a tight restraint. With his hands occupied, he brought Sabrina and himself to his feet. The additional baggage sunk his boots into the ground, and he charged towards the journey home.

Alexander followed behind. He rested a hand on Rhys' shoulder for guidance. Within seconds, their dash had been met with complications. Unfamiliar terrain and small hills stood before them. Neither stopped to question it. They were headed away from the enemy frontline and toward their own. That was all that mattered.

Ten metres out, a sea of half-buried barbed wire posts laid at waist height. Rhys tested his strength by lifting Sabrina higher and he ignored the long trek around to cut time. He trod with care and was unable to see his own feet with the woman in his arms. Her cries became more frequent with every jog and stumble on the watered ground. Songs of teething wire that tugged at his trousers left him unfocused.

The wire shook and rattled during their trespass. By that point, the emptiness of the sky seemed to hold no space for secrecy. They crossed with care, until-

A crack in the air. The familiar, fearful sound of the gun being fired. It came from behind them, and the bullet scrapped through the wire, creating a small spark as iron clashed with lead. Instinctively, Rhys stopped and lowered himself into the wire, only to be pricked back up with a thousand cuts.

"Fuck it, go!" Alexander called. He gave him a light shove ahead. A second shot rang out and hit the mud to their side. Neither turned back to see the shooter and they kept their eyes faced on the ends. They dusted themselves down with the tiniest grain of optimism – they're nearly there, their minds yelled.

Third round. Alexander yelled out as they breached the end of the wire ocean. Rhys turned slightly, only to feel the Captain's hand push him forward.

237

"I caught one, I think!" He shouted through his adrenaline. "Keep going!"

Hastily, they ran through the offbeat world. They ascended yet another mound of dirt and ash and the bullet landed only a metre to Rhys' right, tunnelling into the hill and kicking up flickers of mud. Sabrina's muffled screams became jagged, forming a haunting white noise that begged for both the pain and tension to stop. Rhys held his breath again. Focus. No looking back. Only move forward. He told himself the fact that Sabrina would not die that day. No other determination would've driven him like that focus. He ran. Each slip through hell came as a blessing. The world cried out in fear. A thunderous bellow interluded the chaos from the tip of a rifle. Alexander let out a curdled scream.

With a second bullet lodged in his hip, the Captain said nothing that time. He kept running, grunting with gritted teeth biting into his tongue. Life was but a thin thread, waiting to snap.

From their front, a sudden burst of fire composed the night's exchange of bullets. Oslo's machine gun rattled at a paramount volume. Tracer rounds soared overhead, splitting the air into two as each zipped past. Two more gunshots rang out from behind. The skirmish was alive. A pair of bullet walls paralleled one another, with the retreating retrieval team stuck between them. Shouts were heard from their own trench. Only a hundred metres left.

Rhys called out ahead of them. Every gun could be clearly heard distinctive of the other.

The Captain's grip on his shoulder grew weaker, yet he still clenched on with perseverance.

"Just a little further, right?" He called. The chipper tone he spoke with had become coarse, as if he'd been sandpapered in his throat. Rhys was wordless. He simply held onto Sabrina and pressed forward.

He could see the lights of the allies that waited. The muzzle flashes of Oslo's firearm guided him to the same place he'd left. He counted the seconds, not the steps.

One.

Two.

Three.

Four.

"Come on!" He heard Mateo's voice through the salvo of sound.

Five.

Six.

Sabrina's cries curved to a breakdown to tears, her sobs attenuated in calamitous plea.

Seven.

"I need to reload!" A few more steps, the last leg left, all for survival.

Eight.

A lone, final gunshot was fired. Five hundred metres coming after, a piercing, twisted, spiralling projectile dug itself into skin and bone. Rhys tumbled forward, feeling a heavy weight push violently against his back. He tripped and collapsed into the dropdown of the trench. Both he and Sabrina hit the floorboards with a horrendous, heavy thud, and the planks creaked to their limit.

Sabrina's cries reached their peak. The scarf slipped from her mouth, crumbled and torn by her teeth. It fell to the floor and sank into the marshy undercarriage of the trench. Mouth exposed, she pled with broken, unrivalled bawls. All but she fell silent.

Tried as an adult, she'd reverted to an almost infant-like sorrow. Her yells begged to go home and called for a mother who wasn't there. She wished not to recover, or to take a rifle and enact violent justice, but to curl up beneath soft bedspreads and shiver. She'd been reduced to a show of bruises, blued skin, frozen fingertips and the lack of a limb.

And Rhys lay still. He placed his splintered hands against the wooden floor and pushed his body up. A tense stiffness had nearly paralysed his muscles. Tired disbelief kept him beat and weary. A loose swivel of the eyes and neck showed the emptiness of their return. Only the few on-hand soldiers waited for them, and were by their side with lacklustre coordination. They lifted Sabrina up, moved her away a few metres and called for a final stretcher. Rhys was simply lifted up to his feet and he pressed against the trench wall in his weakness. He couldn't focus. His breathing was unstoppable. Strenuous lungs hungered for air. Out of breath, he fell out of his own mind. Had he made it?

A human's touch gave him his answer. Mateo's arms wrapped around his back. He felt it. He felt *something*. Rare proof that perhaps he hadn't been killed. He smiled, unaware to his last conclusive realisation.

Absence in an empty trench could be as unnoticeable as a tank in a car show. Selective faces stood out, and unrecognisable contemporaries kept themselves clear. With a widened gaze, he turned, clambering up the steps in unforeseen rapidity. He felt Mateo's hand grab onto his heels, calling for him to stop. And as he scaled the middle step, he wished he'd listened.

Five metres from the trench lay a body. Face first in the mud. Across its jaw, the flanks of a glorious flock of facial hair softened in a pool of brain matter. A scalp lay exposed down to the bone. A gaped hole pierced one end of his helmet and concluded on the other side. A revolver remained locked in its unbreakable grip as it sank in the earth, though it was unable to fully bury itself. In isolated obscurity, it remained still. It would never move again.

"No…" He spoke irrepressibly, overpowered with the strong wave of hysteria. "No, no… that can't-"

Mateo pulled him back into the trench and towed his head away from both topside and the body. He opened his jaw to say something, nonetheless he fell silent. Arm around Rhys' shoulders, he escorted him anywhere else but there. He was transfixed on the dead, and the rush and adrenaline of an unrecognisable victory sedated him before dawn.

His stare went for miles beyond the gulley's walls. It travelled boundlessly and burrowed through all matter and obstruction in its path. He paid no regard to Sabrina's cries, nor her being pulled onto a stretcher, or the arrival of Ella to her side, overflown with her own emotional flash. No, he'd seen something devastating. The world hadn't cared if he were a hero, for his task had halted another life.

Later that day, dented bugles played a symphony of remembrance for one Captain Alexander Arthurs Jr.

Chapter 18

St. Quentin

Two painstaking days had rolled by and the cradled were sent unto a valley of sweet demise. By firing squad, the demons had been cut down and there was a terrifying silence. No gunshots nor bombs were heard. Along with their company, the squad had packed their issued belongings and joined the retreat among the final few waves to pull out of Haria. They were separated at first, with small pockets of troops that trod the cold footrail in cluttered groups, and they camped in opposing sectors – at the least, they were all on the path to the same holdout.

The autumn days had settled in, though there was barely any difference between the blood-trodden days of summer and the thunderous grievances of the year's equinox. Birds seemingly vanished into thin air as the morning shows of nature faded away and became a rarity. In just a few weeks, the North of Kelan had transformed into an atonement for sins. Amends were made not through happiness, but continued suffering. Nature itself had abandoned humanity's side and left it to wallow alone.

Cattle were slaughtered for meat when soldiers grew impatient of sickly rations that ran dry. Sometimes, a farmer would complain, but the highest authority of the masses quelled any sort of rebellious resistance.

For a while, it felt as if the only existence they'd known were two armies fighting in limbo. There was no civilisation, only remnants.

St. Quentin had become their place of residence for a short while. On the outskirts, a lofty stone brick wall trimmed the perimeter. Its glory had been stripped from its name and presentation as a dingy sky deafened its graceful voice.

A once powerful figure of strength in the age of sword and shield, its walls stood no chance against the modern teeth and claws. The elements had claimed half of the village, with vines that draped like thick curtains throughout. Then again, it was quite the site for appeased presentations, as those of the 54th had grown used to the brutalist bulwarks of Mullackaye.

Inside the settlement, a jarring stillness occupied the homes and the streets. Two men of aging stature gladly welcomed them upon arrival, with crude farming shotguns hung from their hips. They celebrated their return and gave the soldiers fresh vegetables, bread and alcohol. When asked where the rest of the town was, they simply answered that they had left for safer reaches. The men, however, claimed that they would protect their homes where the others wouldn't. Rhys wasn't around when they were told their homes weren't along the defensive line, indicating that they themselves were truly alone.

Before they'd even arrived, the squad had been split into pockets across the evacuation line. Their orders were clear, for once. Head to St. Quentin, await transportation back to Fort Mullackaye. Other regiments had dispersed across the edges of Haria as they hauled up their walkers and tanks to finally take the Ferusian expansion head-on. By a stroke of luck, the 54th Defensive Regiment hadn't been listed for frontline deployment, instead being reassigned to regarrison the Mullackaye region.

Rhys read the numbers along the roads. In the span of a week, the 54th had sustained substantial casualties from their arduous service. A single derailment alone had taken a hundred and seventy-two abled bodies from the regiment, excluding the fallen from other regiments. Then, the battle proved fatal for another two hundred militiamen, with a further five hundred injured and discharged from their posts.

This alone had seen disastrous effect across the entire regiment in which they had cut down, at least, 70% of their total worth. Rumours spread amongst the survivors that their regimental commander had been stripped of his rank, though sympathies for them laid in the eyes of a few – those voices dared to understand the position he was in, where his regiment were scattered and lost in a sea of hundreds of thousands crowding one peninsula. No one caught wind of the full story, but with so many dead and in need of replacement, it was no wonder that they were to return to their militarised home.

The numbers started to assail Rhys when he left himself alone in an abandoned corner shop, made mostly of empty shelves and forgotten work timetables that littered the counter. Eight-hundred men and women, gone or scarred – such an irreplaceable collective of lives and dreams, memories and endeavours, effortlessly wiped clean from all that they held dear. Many stated that the gods – that Sunar himself – had given cruel misguidance, but Rhys took a page from the religious texts he rejected:

"War is [our] own creation, and the torch that set ablaze your home is [ours]."

The weak perished and the frailer were left to bear the consequences of living. More than a small hamlets residency had been lost in the 54th. Far too many families had been left with an empty seat at dinner time.

He would've cried if he had the energy. Blackened contusions had made their mark on his skin. Apart from one visit from Mateo, Rhys had spent his time in St. Quentin in utter solitude. He wasn't sure if he preferred it that way, bearing in mind the habit he'd made of it.

Dust drifted through the scarcely lit aisles. Toppled shelves had sprawled empty tins on the withered oak floorboards. Remnants of another world still shone in elapsed corners. In one, furthest from the shop door, a large radio set sat dormant and alone. Afresh in a room of tradition, it stood out without issue, even in the darkness.

A bell rattled above the entryway as it were tentatively pushed open. He turned sharply; his hands were tucked into his pockets. A wave of grim morning light danced into the room first, easing the coffined wickedness of the isolated shop. And through the light, peering inside with caution and timidity, a timorous soldier made her way into the room.

"Oh…sorry to disturb you." Ella said in a soft and unkempt hum. A little stillness dawdled for a short while. "Can I come in?"

Rhys blinked twice and looked around the dark room. It always took another person for him to realise how truly alone and secluded he'd made himself in his hours of need.

"Uh, sure. Yeah." In an untimely manner, he answered her with a gentled tone.

She walked inside and closed the door behind her as carefully as she could. The bell chimed a second time. Neither said a word for a little while, both listening to the creaks of the floorboards and the faint mumble of conversations outside.

"How…are you okay?" He asked.

The dreaded question held more weight than he'd have liked it to have had. So much aggression, violence and trauma had pressed against them in such little time. Both of them knew the answer before he'd finished asking.

"Maybe." She trailed off. Her eyes and head delicately scanned the surrounding mess. "Was the journey hard at all for you?"

"Only a bit. You got here first though, didn't you?"

"Yeah, I came with the medical cart." They continued to edge around the obvious enquiry that sat so clearly between them. Ella drifted through the hall and made her way to Rhys without alacrity. "Have you seen the others?"

"Only Mateo. We walked with a small group." He let out a fake chuckle. "It's funny how we just all separated for two days."

"We had Oslo, Evelyn and Gwen all with us."

"And Tyran? Dynis?"

"Not sure." She glided her hands across one of the standing shelves, catching the dust on the tips of her fingers.

Rhys paced in a small circle. He had sat his rifle down against the wall with the safety catch firmly on. Then, he stopped and turned back to Ella, cautiously bringing the avoided concern to light.

"Is…there something in particular you need?"

"Pardon?" Her voice sounded troubled, prolonging her answer.

"It's not often you come to find me," he began, "and I just – assumed that maybe something was…wrong?"

A pained sigh cut loose her dread. Her eyes moved to the counter, not him, and she stared with weakness. Though she did smile. It looked excruciatingly familiar.

"She usually came to find you when you boarded yourself up in dark rooms." Trailing in whispers, her voice nearly silenced itself. "And I heard you were doing it again…so…"

244

"Well," he looked a little flustered toward the wall, "you could open the door so, nothing to worry about, right?"

When her voice finally faded away, Rhys couldn't move from his state of insecurity. Something struck him hard. He wasn't sure if it was guilt or his heart being touched by emotions previously forgotten. Paralyzed in place, he tried to pluck up the courage to thank her, yet he only stood with a faint flutter in his chest. And then, she walked right over his quip.

"She talked about some awful metaphor – and, like it was bad, but she liked it. Like…how you were some hedgehog, I think; that when anyone gets closer, they just get pricked away, unintentionally. And when they get hurt, you turn back to whatever burrow you have and hide." Despite the smile she put on for him, she began to verbally tremble. Her face lowered and her heart sank. "Sorry…I don't want to sound like I'm…telling you off. I'm in no position to-"

"You're fine." Rhys didn't really know what to say. Her emotional talk hit him with red-hot iron rods. Sabrina was still there, in the world with them, yet her words currently resided on her sister's tongue. Ella's flustered ramble made him believe that with an agonising ache to his chest.

"She hasn't spoken to me since. All she does is sleep, then wake up and cry, and then she sleeps yet again."

Rhys loosened his muscles and took two slow steps closer to her. Through the shadows of the derelict shop, he saw a faint streak of a single tear trickle down her cheek. As it always had, her agony only worsened his own.

"Are…I-" He stopped himself, again and again. The sensational rush of overreaching emotions had brought him to a standstill. His passive deviance to the promised path of blight had been set aside and he watched as Ella fell apart on the spot again.

"Why can't things just be normal?" She sobbed, placing her hands to her eyes. Her whispers turned to plighted wails of encumbrance. "Why can't we just live with nice things? Or have little worries, not whether my own sister will live to see tomorrow?"

"Hey, hey…" He walked forward and placed a quivering hand on her shoulder to try and draw her attention from the void he'd acclimatised for. She looked at him with watered eyes.

She respired with unhappy temperance. Abstained from her internal crisis, she'd entered her very own anarchic bombast whilst ignoring her own intentions of turning up.

"Sorry, I…I was supposed to be coming to help you but-" Her words were choked up by her self-deprecation. "Damnit, I can't even do that correctly."

"Don't say that." His words flowed naturally. Truth be told, he wanted to remain alone on that day, like she said he always had wanted, but a brightness and sorely missed sentiment kept him going. "Look, let's just have a quick sit down, maybe? Take a breather together?"

Eventually, she agreed to do so and followed him to the back of the shop near the boxed radio set. There was only a single chair, so he let himself slide down the wall onto the floor, leaving the seat for her. She looked hesitant to the offer, but still accepted it in silence, bar a few sniffles here and there.

Things progressed in an unusual manner. Both sat slumped in their seats as the shop's cold atmosphere seemed to silence the world outside. Their voices had dispersed like a fog, leaving a ghostly trail of mumbles as they left. Chilled winds tempered themselves and occasionally rattled the old windows to the building. To speak was to disturb the momentary bliss they had: peace, quiet and not a sound of war in earshot.

"I'm sorry for all the negativity." With her tremble, she uttered out her apology softly. Rhys sighed.

"It's fine. A lot has happened as of recent."

Silence again. To break the motions of stillness, he reached for his belt and drew out his canteen, unscrewing the lid. No smell left it. Just water, and sadly not the freshest. Clean, at least. He took a large swig, downing it in one go. Hydration felt like a godsend. Little daily activities from his civilian life had become comforts in the line of service. Stale meals were something to look forward to, knowing that a milestone had been reached. To eat was to be alive. Malnutrition was the chariot in which their hell came in on.

He thought back to Haria. It felt as if an aeon had long passed. Those fields of scorch, met with a drowning downpour that refused to stop, left the world in apocalyptic ruin. To forget such vivid sights was impossible. The blood, the corpses, the slaughtered horses and abandoned vehicles; the remnants of towns, villages, trenches and bunkers. And in full retreat, he felt tension knowing something that disturbed him: not that he'd escaped without a hole in his chest, but that he'd experienced it all and that it wasn't one devilish nightmare.

Oh, had the visions taken their tax on him. Hallucinations of freaked figures – clothed from head to toe in disfigured concealment – left him restless each night. The bags beneath his eyes told Ella all that she needed to know. He was tired not of the war, but of life in its entirety.

"No sleep?" She gently enquired.

"Not really. Only a little."

"Same."

"You hide it well." As he smiled, she did too. "Have we ever talked about our old lives?"

"Old lives?"

"Yeah, the lives we had before all of this?" Rhys eyed the rafters above them and smiled with the duality of nostalgia and melancholy. "It feels so long ago, it's unreal. But it was – what – months ago, maybe."

"You were a farmer, weren't you?" The chair creaked as she shifted her place.

"A farmer's son. That's what I was, but not who I was."

"Did you not enjoy it?"

"Oh, well, it had its moments. Harvest was always an exciting time in my youth and there were plenty of strange experiences around agricultural communities, but I didn't want to spend my whole life doing it."

She quietly took notes of the cobwebs, spiders and flakes in the wallpaper as her gaze followed his to the ceiling. She whispered the patterns of the faded skin to the walls: beige, unkept flower patterns, faded and turning grey.

His mind wandered for a bit whilst he relived many of the pure moments that he'd never quite crossed.

"What did you want to do?"

"I…don't really know." She turned back to him, giving him a look that instructed him to continue. "I never got the chance to do much. I just took care of my dad – see, because he was a veteran – and I had done all the errands asked of me when I was very little; and I rarely saw much of what my mum actually did."

"Oh…were they…?"

"Divorced? No, but it was…complicated." He chortled under the revelation of how trivial his issues had once been. "What I would give to have someone else's marriage be my number one issue in the world."

Very few positives stood out through Rhys' life. Most were dampened by mediocrity or how common they became throughout life. However, as the war housed his life and fate, he'd grown wise to the best moments of innocence. When Ella laughed, right there and then, it rammed through his chest and carried his heart with it. Even compared to Sabrina, a heavenly idyllic flutter in her voice felt so enthralling. No sunshine could outshine it. Any rainbow would seem colourless. A shock from lightning was nowhere near as sensual. Surreal, and angelic, her voice was. Maybe the fact it had been hidden beneath so much fear and anxiety that he'd forgotten what it was like to see someone forget the world they were in.

"So, what about you, then?" He shot back at her.

"Oh, I always wanted to do something mechanical. I started quite young, attended an academy and joined a local mechanics. Sabrina stopped by every day to wish us well, talk and to encourage me. Daily praise was just something special we had, I guess." Her shrug brought about a low hanging raincloud above her parade. The pause left Rhys silent, letting her find her words in her own time. "Well, my company was commissioned to work on transferring old parts – of outdated scout tanks – to those found in newer models and I just kind of fell in love with them. The complexity, the scale and…I don't know. I just like tinkering. It's therapeutic."

"Seemed like everything kind of fit into place with what you do now." His bruised knees were brought to his chest as he curled himself into a tight, yet warm, upright ball against the wall.

"It was a little encouraging. Not much-"

"You're doing great."

"-apart from the odd tinkering at Mullackaye, I haven't really had to repair many vehicles. Only a few walkers that fell into ditches on patrols and the odd officer demanding that his *Tactical Command Vehicle* should get a fresh coat of paint."

Again, her laugh broke through her shattered state. The tears on her cheeks had dried having evaporated against the warmth of her face.

Rhys stared at her with unusual admiration. As she spoke, the person she'd always been had been replaced by something more headstrong. Confidence ran through the woman when her mind was to it, not being tossed back and forth between terror and apprehension.

She noticed his gape and met it with another smile of her own. It was far too easy for Rhys to lose himself in the eye of genuine purity. Where his heart sat for his squad was inexplicable. Family could be bred from the far reaches of fury and in her did he see a collective that transcended blood and heritage.

Rhys and Ella both rose from their seats, and her eyes drifted over toward the oak floorboards. An anxious breath returned. Her heart and his were in stone whilst she quietly built up the courage, and there she edged over to him.

She let her arms encompass him, an act that immobilised him in place. His lungs held themselves and his face warmed to the humanly touch that surrounded him. Her head turned away from his and she buried it into his shoulder.

"Thank you for saving my sister." Her words, though cold and quiet, rode across a wave of delight. Sorrow transitioned into deserved relief. A time of hopelessness changed into something she could believe in. It was temporary, barely noticeable, but Rhys himself felt her sense of faith. Hope lived under all the cracks. Its truthfulness was indescribable, or unconceivable, but for once he didn't care. He drew his hands to her back and returned her embrace.

After an eternity, they parted from one another, and she looked away with an embarrassed smile plastered all across her glimmering face. Rhys didn't test her with provocation or jest and instead resorted to just silently beaming at her. He felt as if she'd deserved something of an uninterrupted bliss. Soon enough, she gave a noiseless wave, grabbed her rifle and hurriedly departed out of the building, back into the streets of St. Quentin.

Yet, he was left alone. He didn't brood. Instead, he pondered over something beautiful. Beyond the craziness that had engulfed his world, his life and his newfound allies, there was something of a dream still left in the air. To work wonders on others was to give him reasons to stay just the slightest bit happier. An undeniable amount of tragedy could never vanquish the tiny fragments of a good life. In some ways, they made them stronger.

And there he stood, lost in the same room as he had been before. However, he felt different that time. The hours in which he'd been riddled with guilt, from the devastation of Alexander to the casualty that was Sabrina, he'd finally taken a moment to peacefully contemplate things of little importance but great value. There was no doubt that in time, he would've had to face worse entanglements of conflict, but in the short minutes he had left alone it felt like he didn't need to worry about them.

Intrigue caught the best of him and he was taken over to the cubic radio. He looked at its boxed exterior and studied its bizarre blend of metallic sheeting with a chipped wooden finish from vertex to vertex. Its wiring burrowed into the wall behind it which led it up toward the rooftop, and likely to a small antenna. Antique, and expensive, he idolised it with the touch of recent ecstasies.

He rubbed his hands across its shell, caressing its dials and switches until he found the right one. A stroke of luck brought it to life. Its dying gulps of electricity gave it light and sound. The bulb-lit interface turned as he searched for any transmitting stations where he expected nothing else but military communication lines. Hitherto, chance held its surprises on prepared hands. It only came through faintly. And...

The calm piano rang out. It flooded the room with a progressive crescendo of chords and lullabies. Harmonic boons of outstanding beauty softly came from its speakers. Rhys was left paralysed, somehow unable to move to the sound of its perfect performance. No word or lyric overcame the simplicity of the rift, and so it was left alone to merely sing the world to sleep.

As it played, the room morphed around him. Instead of bright fields, he felt as if he'd been transported to the stars. Satellites and moons sprawled around him, drifting by freely. Space seemed so calm, so devoid of chaos. It lacked life, but maybe that was its secret. His legs trod through plains of stardust, with rings of far beyond planets paving his way forward. Trance. Pitiful, as did Farhawl's corruption appear. Life seemed smaller yet better from far away. One planet's destruction was another's birth: the cycle of the gods locating their perfect strain. But he didn't think too much about life, no, Rhys looked to purely wander the void as it flew past him, and the piano reverberated throughout every known nook and cranny the universe had to offer. It followed him once into the light and another time into the darkness. It didn't need the soft voice of an opera singer to carry it. The universe was built on simplicity, where life was plagued with complexity, he thought as it rocketed him into the far reaches space.

A spark came from within the radio, and the universe collapsed into a mist. Through the clouded vision, he found himself back in the blackened, shadowy shop he'd always been in. Life continued as it always had. Trucks pulled up outside and voices calling for the 54th replaced the piano. He turned back to the radio and saw it switched off.

He tried the switches and dials again to no avail. So, as he walked to the grim and colourless outside world, he wondered if the radio had ever turned on in the first place.

Act Two

Cone, Sweet Demise

Chapter 19

The Child

Was she, though? Had she ever been one? When starved of a life, are men and women dead or just hollow? Impurity had made filth of its deeds with outrageous and barbaric results. Sinful years in an imperfect world left but a shell of a girl, one stripped of a childhood. And without that childhood, was she even a child?

The devil's cold aegis, to her own personal world, had been disastrous and endless. A parentless life stuck within concrete walls to sing the same tunes before dinner and to sleep in the same defunct mattresses as she had done in infancy – all of it spindled her within a dreary box of memoirs. She would have never called it a bad childhood, per se. A bad childhood would've implied that something had happened throughout. Her truth was contrary. A forgotten town in a forgotten mountainside; under no guidance but that of a false idol, a carer who didn't care. She spoke only when spoken to in a household where their tongues were kept in glass jars. Life had been one art project, a progression through drawing on scraps of paper, carving little wooden chips with a rusting pen knife found out the back of the orphanage. That was her childhood.

When she awoke, she was still in the truck, clumped in the back with her head resting against Oslo's padded arms. At first, her view was colourful and dreamlike. Sunshine came through the canvas pitching surrounding the troop bay and a warmth flooded the compartment. Disappointment soon followed.

Instead, the sunlight was just a silent soldier accidentally turning on his personal torch and cursing beneath his breath. The warmth came from no natural source. A stream of heat blew from little exhausts around the truck and it left a lingering stench of burnt diesel.

She sighed and rubbed her eyes dry. Inside her head, she heard her own second voice reminding her beneath her steel cap.

"Don't forget tomorrow." Its gentle tone tried to erase the roughness of the exterior world. Her realm felt much more calming. In it, there wasn't any concept of pain, just happiness. But, of course, it was nigh impossible, lest she planned to exile herself from reality. And for her, nothing nice had happened since the day she was conceived and abandoned on that stone footstep.

A bright turn had come her way. In her twisted sense of purposelessness, the men in uniforms showed up. They took the older ones and gave them guns behind closed doors. So much joy came through those children. No…wait…were they children? They had guns. Children don't use guns.

It was the first time she'd ever seen his face. In the waves of inspectors, tightly headed between boy and girls sixteen and up, *he* was among them. He had a peculiar look of disturbance on his mug. She remembered the wrinkles of stress across his brow and jawline. A nearly clean-cut hairline and beard looked impossibly different to how he was in the present hour. He was captured in a neural photograph. Back then, Oslo was unbearably unrecognisable.

Her trail of thought was lost when the truck jolted back and forth, stirring many in their poorly made slumbers. Oslo mumbled something and snapped awake with great beady eyes stressed and strained.

He looked down to her and sighed with relief. Another nightmare, she guessed. They'd become more frequent. By observation alone, she'd tried to teach herself why the men and women she lived with had become the way they had.

She lived with them, not worked with them. It wasn't service for her. Service was a dutiful career, one where it came towards a goal beyond her own understanding of the world. Here, that explanation felt irrelevant. She'd done nothing to help the apparent need for soldiers without fully realising it. She wasn't even under their guidelines, restrictions and regulations. Judges of unknown injustices simply gave her the gavel to the brain and put Oslo in charge of her. Or did he put himself in command? Again, the questions never stopped. She hadn't even said a word.

Oslo's great hand coated her head, with his thumb rubbing across her scalp. Her hair felt soft, even if unclean and greased.

For a few seconds, he looked at Evelyn as if she were his own flesh and blood.

"Aye, you with fourth platoon?" The soldier opposite them, who'd mistakenly turned on his torch, asked with a heavy whisper. It was just enough to be heard over the truck but quiet enough to keep the peace.

"Yeah, we are." Oslo spoke for them both, as always. She was more comfortable with that.

"Man, when they said there was a little girl there, I could barely believe it myself."

"I can't understand it either."

Both trailed off. Oslo's voice felt pained. He was agonised by something in which he refused to talk about.

"So – she your daughter or something?" Evelyn's heart awoke for just a moment. She lifted her head from Oslo's arm and looked up to him. All she saw was his hesitation.

"No, I just take care of her." His words were hurtful, more so to him than her.

"Guess it's easier when they aren't your own." The soldier said, before he reached into his pocket. "Though I do always keep a picture of my little angel."

In his hand, a small photograph laced in black, white and grey faced back at them. Evelyn reached out and took it from him, where she spent a moment eyeballing the image: beams and eternalised happiness forever captured on a single photo card. It was a beautiful thought.

"Her name's Lucy. Wouldn't trade her for the world." His finger reached over the image and pointed out a woman for Evelyn. "That's my wife. Gorgeous, isn't she?"

"She's pretty." At long last, Evelyn opened her mouth. As Oslo yawned the soldier smirked to himself.

"Oh, so you do talk?"

"Why wouldn't I?"

"I didn't mean it like that-" He hesitated, giving out a nervous chuckle to himself. Evelyn's eyes narrowed with estranged intrigue.

"Are you sure you're good with children?"

Oslo hid his own smile well as he flicked her head. She let out a quiet yowl and scowled up at him, seeing that his intervention be met with frustration.

"Manners, Eve."

"Nah, she's not wrong, mate." The soldier laughed, stirring some of the passengers a bit. "It's hard to talk to another one's daughter when your life revolved around your own. It's a lot to get used to; takes a father too much to adjust after he's been in service. Know what I mean?"

Oslo paused. His eyes blinked a few times and he stared into the muddy canvas sheet that surrounded them. Evelyn smiled up at him but found it fading when he continued to say nothing. His hand drew away from her head and laced with his other. An exhausted sigh left his lips and he leaned forward, pointing his head down to the truck's floor for three long seconds – she counted. When he finally found the effort to speak, it was with a heavy weight tied to his legs, to which he was dragged him to a dark depth of his own memory.

"Yeah, I think I do."

The truck soldiered on, weathering on through broken roads and dirt paths between cluttered forests. Out of the rear hatch, Evelyn could see the green and natural world, caked in raindrops. How she'd missed it…

Days spent in a world of brown muck and black charred soil had taken her away the beauty she adored so dearly about the outside world. Autumn had been settling in for days, and the florescent green tone soon transitioned into an auburn and ginger palette the deeper into Mullackaye they went. The branches looked much more alive in the warless world. They didn't twitch or twine with jagged roots and edges, she observed. All of their curvature was smooth, born out of a helpful soft hand from mother nature's soothing stroke.

She sighed. To be held carefully by their parental figure, to be moulded into perfection, seemed like such an alienated concept. Her own life was jagged, belittled and battled by hopelessness, whilst those around her seemed to have that kind and caring carpentry to straighten its rough edges. It hurt to see so many people act so lively, even if dragged to the brink of death in the foul conflict. Either way, it wasn't like she realised much of it herself.

Oslo still seemed a little shifted, mentally speaking. He hadn't been as cheerful as he'd always been as he stuck himself closer to her in recent hours. He'd learnt through strict trial that she could no longer be shielded from brutality. She'd seen Ryan's death. She'd been in the derailment. She'd been there, at Haria. What innocence she carried under her wing had been undermined and mistreated. A cold shoulder from the world nudged her into place and she was forced to purse her lips shut, with a rusted needle and breaking thread.

What greed had taken the Queen's people into such a shameful state? Ripping children from their homes seemed absurd, incredulous and dishonest. Evelyn, though, was proof on the contrary. If she was there, then who knew how many underaged warriors had handed their virtuous selves to the crown. Neither mothers nor fathers guided them, but Generals, orders and magazine clips. Instructions told them to climb atypical hills that didn't have paths to the top. It hurt Oslo so much to realise that. Evelyn may have realised it too, but whether she understood it was an entirely different box to open.

Bumps and holes in the road knocked the crew about. Enraged drivers cursed loudly at the wheel and thumped it with their fist.

"Alright, everyone out." After many revs of the engine, he gave up. "Give us a push."

The tired lot sighed and groaned whilst obediently following their orders. Around twelve jumped out first, assessing the situation and the damage to the vehicle. Some sort of slick pothole drifted the truck off course and their rear end had dropped down off the side of the road, sticking to the mud. Evelyn got out, as if her frail and wafer-thin stature made any difference to the vehicle's weight.

"Ready? And...push!" The wheels span whilst the soldiers threw themselves against it, using all their might to break out of their lodged position. Oslo was the first into helping, using all manners of brawn and broadness to push the truck. In no time, it was let out.

Evelyn hadn't done a thing. She stood on the side lines; her hands held onto her rifle as if it were a stuffed toy. A groan expressed her tiredness. Unsure as to why she felt so disappointed in the moment, she clambered back in and retook her position next to her guardian.

Another hour passed. The sun went behind dark clouds again and the leaves continued to turn a bright, dishonest orange. The further inland they went, the less of a warzone it appeared.

Houses stood tall, becoming more populated as they widened their gap from Haria's frontline. The streets were occupied. Free men, women and children occasionally cheered as the trucks passed by.

"You're doing your best!"

"Up and at 'em, lads!"

"The Star's work, all of you!"

Oslo grumbled each time. He placed his machine gun against the truck floor and then prodded his eyes with his fingertips. Just like before, most of the passengers had fallen asleep as they ignored the praise sent their way.

"What's wrong?" Evelyn asked, rather sheepishly. She hated asking questions and probing for answers. Life was too complicated for that. She hated complexity.

"I don't think they understand it quite well." He spoke with a low tone, bordering a grumbled murmur.

"Understand what?"

"The war."

There it was again: the silence. The stigmata in his side and the thorns in his heels. Whenever he kept quiet, it gave his thoughts a platform to talk of bitter truths in his ear. A life once left behind had sewn itself into his skin. Evelyn had noticed them on occasion. The cuts and the bruises that seemed to never go away, scars of another world once forgotten; *his* world, lost.

She'd never questioned it. What was there to question? He was the man who'd set his individuality aside to carry her shield. For the longest of their time together, her mind told her that he deserved his mystery. Yet she'd begun to realise one thing in her time of servitude, that time was valuable. At any second, a stray bullet could have clipped her wings and thrown her to the underworld. The chances she had to pry into her guardian's identity was fleeting.

"Oslo?" She politely mumbled, prodding his arm with her finger.

"Yes?"

"Why are you the way you are?" His smile faded as her ever-the-blunter enquiry came forth. He looked away from her, to the distant void, and leaned back into his seat.

"How well do you remember it?"

"It was months ago, Oslo. I still clearly remember it." Instead of staring at the void, she looked to the top of the truck's canvas coat. Her thoughts crossed an ethereal plain of dark memory. The hallway in the orphanage, the one where they beat the disobedient and deprived them of growth – the perfect shells to be filled with soldiers' souls. And the heavy boots of the military police, searching for draftees. All the older ones had been loaded into the cars. Her name had been called, despite regulations. Quotas had to be filled. Better her than the younger ones, they told her. She'd ran back inside. She was hidden in the cupboard. They turned beds up, flashed lights into dark corners. Then he found her. Dressed correctly with a clean-shaven head, he looked at her with hollow intent.

Then it hit him. When he saw her eyes, both fragile and tearful, he paused. He didn't call out to the other officers. He simply let them pass. She never knew why he changed, or if he had been brought to life that day. Back then it didn't matter. He offered her a chance. Through buildings and gardens, he snuck her to the edges of the town and gave her one last opportunity to run. She didn't. They found her again, that time with Oslo stood between them. The punishment was delivered. All titles were stripped and the crown denounced his service. An empty life had been rekindled with purpose as they placed him in rags and sent him to the back of the car. From predator to prey, he'd become a conscript, like her. But he didn't seem bothered at first.

No, he appeared to be okay. He smiled and told her it'd all be fine, that he'd keep her safe if she wanted him to. She said yes. She couldn't have asked for anything more.

Time flew by. They were posted to Rhys' squad. Oslo kept his promise. He stood by her. And through all that they'd been through, there was something Evelyn still didn't know: why?

Why had he done anything to begin with? Why had he given up his life of wages and wealth for a decomposed husk, a girl that hadn't seen life since the day she was brought into it? Even if, both socially and politically, Evelyn had zero understanding of why she was in the place she was, she knew that she needed to hear him say why.

"There wasn't much choice for you."

"I know." Her voice went frail, quivering in her throat as the vivid memory projected onto the walls in one hallucinogenic showcase.

"And who wouldn't have for someone like you?"

"But you didn't know me."

"I felt as if I had once before, like I'd seen you somewhere during a time when things were a lot happier." His cryptic nonsense didn't satisfy her, but a tremble in his voice disturbed her progress. She heard a whimper from within his brutish mouth. And just like that, she stopped asking questions. "No, I didn't feel it. I'd lived it once."

Tiny trickles of rainfall pattered the canvas roof. The puddles they left behind showed reflections of the battle and the bombardment. All of the torment she'd been through, the things a child never should have gone through, stared right back at her. Usually, she would have cried and latched onto Oslo. That time she didn't. She just faced the watery mirrors and the rainfall with deafened attention. If it were just for an evening, she felt as if being numb to the pain then was better than being numb when she had the chaos surrounding her.

"Hey, Eve?" Oslo spoke, clearing his throat and pausing between his words. An awkwardness sat in the middle, pushing them apart metaphysically. "Don't forget tomorrow."

Her stare followed into the distant lands, her thoughts bringing up the calendar. Tomorrow was...

"Your birthday?" He grinned. The truck continued down its path to Fort Mullackaye.

Chapter 20

Replacement

Through the world-weary mist that coated across the farmlands, a towering grey silhouette crawled into view. She saw battlements lined with field cannons, machinegun emplacements and hooded soldiers bearing the brunt of the rainfall. She had been muted by its incredible presence. From the passenger's seat, all that she could hear were the pistons of their engine and the squeal of the breaks as they arrived at their first checkpoint.

There was a delay. A car sat before them, handing their papers and keeping up with the regular safety checks. It left an uncomfortable room for him to start talking to her.

"So, end of the road," he began, "you must be excited?"

Christa tugged at her collar as she freed her throat from the constriction of doubt. Had she come too far? To murder Lylith, and to give birth to Christa, had she stepped beyond her boundaries? It had been months since she'd committed to the exaltation. Reprogrammed, redesigned and reassembled, she had created her own artificial mind to stay beneath the radar of those who wished her well. But did they care about her? Maybe. In that moment, where Thomas asked about her excitement, she quivered at the thought that perhaps her mother truly did miss her, or that she believed Lylith was well and truly dead.

Out of anxiousness and concern, she played with her freshly trimmed short-cut. When she ran her fingers through her dirtied hair, there was something about it that just felt so artificial. A lump clogged her throat as she tried to speak. Her stammers took over her tongue.

"Well, I…I mean – I should-" Thomas looked at her and rolled his eyes.

"You can't be getting second ideas, now." His tone was spiteful, fuelled by a venomous fang obscured by his loyal mask.

"No, Sir." She mumbled.

"Good. Last thing we need is for you to turncoat back to the royals. We've put so much on the line for you, and lost more than we should have, just so you can fulfil this wish." His growl died down into a brooded hiss. Her rumination was a thorn in the progress they'd made. It had been the third time he'd lectured her that way and she'd grown sick of it.

"I know, Sir." Lightly, she exhaled and flushed her lungs anew. "But let's not call it the end of the road."

Thomas loosened his grip on the steering wheel before taking a deep breath of his own.

"Oh, yes. I guess we aren't there yet."

Her twisted fantasy couldn't quite compare to the reality she waltzed through. In the dreams of the consecrated associate of the royal family, heir to the Kingdom and successor to her great father, war savoured in holy light. Books that depicted wars of tragedy and heroism showed only of the flowers that bloomed on the battlefield, the men who stood on hills of their fallen comrades and those who gave their final epitaphs with recoil and burst. Yet outside of Sunar's graced lands, all she had seen was rain and thundered aftershocks.

And in turn, reality couldn't quite compare to the fantasy she drew in her muse. It was darker, scarier even. Fear ran amok and panic was the norm. A constant surveillance from unchallenged corruption made sure the people had their heads down in the mud. Human life had been lined up against the wall, with bayonets prodding their backs, and the war would be the final pull of the trigger to end it all. Civilisation would die with its inhabitants. For once in a while, Christa felt a part of Lylith speak from her polluted grave. She told her that maybe she should've been scared, like she should have been all those weeks ago. The field was no place for an aristocrat; the battle was no place for the spritely.

So they said, at least: the weak had no place there – they should be the ones at home, protected by the might of the gladiatorial defender – yet there they were in the hundreds of thousands, perhaps even millions. Conscripts and draftees were the half-snapped backbone bearing the weight of the nation's survival. The military served up rampant death and they were force-fed it. Disposable men in throwaway clothes stood in nonrefundable boots and they were all left on the side of the street, stood out in the rain to be shot. She couldn't bear it. And so, she reconciled her woes. This wasn't for her, it was for them, she said. Over. And over. And over. If nothing could be done, then she thought that in magnificence, she would suffer with them. As an equal, she had convinced herself, they would be as one community – as soldiers, a band of brothers and sisters.

"I'm sorry to have caused you all so much trouble." When she apologised, she didn't cower but instead sat up straight and fixed her ground with a strong stance. She took a long-lasting look at her reflection in the rear-view mirror. There, she saw a soldier in the making.

Thomas tapped the steering wheel impatiently as the checkpoint guards headed their way.

"Don't be. You'll make up for it soon." He left their conversation on a deafly note and rolled down his window, where he met the guard with a pulsing smile. "Good morning, Corporal."

Their conversation faded out when she walked back into her thoughts. Weeks of unending obedience all for the sake of enduring violence, to what end? Had she even questioned it in full?

For a short minute, she closed her eyes and leaned back into the passenger seat, her eyelids soon projected an illusion unique to her. Consternation struck her. All she could see was rain. Again, and again, the droplets that trickled across her forehead and down her cheeks kept up with her every move. It followed her. Drowned lands everywhere. She saw the abandoned settlement she'd trained at and the faces of the people she'd worked alongside. She could barely remember the comfortable life she'd left behind; days sat beside her mother as she attended a high court of justice had morphed into some dreamlike reverie. Her own mother, however, felt like an illicit fragment of a deathly nightmare.

So much rain. Just rain. Drop after drop, trickles that merged into one jagged path across her skin. A mumbling pitter-patter hit the steel on her head, soaking her clothes and numbing her body. Unless she opened her eyes, only the implantation of the soaked nation looked through her memory. For a dreamer, she hadn't quite grasped the brightness of it all.

A hand jabbed her shoulder. Her sharp revival left her befuddled for a second, turning back to Thomas's strong glare.

"Identification, Private." He ordered, enacting his authoritative persona just as he should've done. She hesitated and fumbled around with her pockets before she felt the chain of her false identity disk. "Thank you."

The officer glanced at it a few times before nodding and handing it back, then he waved them off to enter the fort. Thomas waited until the creaking of the ginormous steel gates silenced before he set off. And as the barriers moved, their gears and hydraulics blew steam and gas from tiny exhaust ports atop of the wall.

It gaped wider, opening the heart of the base through a small entrance ahead of them. The car in front turned its engine back on. Fumes of incinerated diesel and fuel came straight out of the gate. Christa spluttered as she quickly rolled the window back up. A potent storm of smog brushed against the glass and the sickly smell of exhaust fumes soured her senses.

"Get used to it. That's all these bloody bases smell of." Thomas laughed to himself as he placed his foot gently on the accelerator. The truck slithered forward.

Christa eyed the walls as they crawled past them and as they were swallowed by them into Mullackaye's great shielding, she took a breath of rotting air. During the transition between freedom and encapsulation, she saw the light in the sky eclipse under the roof of the wall's interior. The scene had changed. Her next act had begun.

She was granted a brief tour of her surroundings as Thomas followed the open runways and narrow roads between command posts, barracks, warehouses, hangers and armouries.

"So, how's this placement going to work?" She asked, a little too focused on the base around her to look Thomas in the eye. He, himself, was more attentive toward the road either way.

"I've got you a place within the 54th Defensive Regiment. They returned here about five days ago, or something. Straight from Haria."

"I see." Her quiet eyes continued to drift between the great mechanical beasts that sauntered by. She was left in awe at the show and prowess of machines roaming the land, piloted by the men and women in suits of doom. "Anything else?"

264

"Well, whilst I didn't get to choose your regiment, considering the demands for manpower replacements, I got to personally decide your assigned squad." He continued with a slight yawn. "4th Platoon of Bravo Company. A while back I met a quiet chap from there, some Staff Sergeant Hendricks, if I can remember."

"Luck of the draw?"

"Well, I at least knew they were a little battle-tested. They had a small tussle with the Ferusian Airborne and should now be back from Haria. He doesn't seem too pushy so you should be fine." Eventually, the little squeal of the truck's brakes brought her attention away from the motion-driven world beyond the window. She turned back to Thomas, who looked at her expectedly. "Well, let's get to it then. You've got friends to make."

His chipper tune returned and the discomforting smile grew on his face. For him, there wasn't so much trouble about lingering at Mullackaye. It let him make the calls he needed to and he assumed the Ferusian push would slither slowly, with enough time for him to get himself in check. His gloved fingers fiddled with his glasses before he turned, opening his door and getting out. He looked back inside and saw Christa still sat silently.

"You're not a princess, Private. You do have to open the door yourself."

Christa frowned at his festered witticism and left the truck, where she was blasted by the cold air that tickled her face. With their engine shut off, she took in the sounds of her new home. She attentively listened to the little details off in the distance: the gnawing of guns eating away at wooden targets on distant ranges, the fluttering of propeller-based aircraft rising in formation above, the jittering of tanks adjusting their steps along wide paths and the shouts of lieutenants disciplining their layabout soldiers.

She saw crowds clustered together across the road. Some of them looked surprisingly clean, easily distinguishable from the ones who'd returned from Haria in droves.

A typical obstruction lodged itself in her throat. The nervousness came back. What if she blew her identity? What if she was instantly recognised? She'd heard and read the papers, the early days where she had been reduced to a several month-long headline and a never-ending reference point in all media outlets. Radio broadcasts talked about it daily: ***The Missing***

Princess, the kidnapping that shook the nation amongst other worrisome headers. It saddened her to know such a great deal had been placed in finding her. Moments like those gave her ammunition to doubt herself over. Did her moral obligations outweigh her duty to the people? Maybe. But sometimes that was enough to ruin her day.

"Where are we going?" She pondered aloud, peering over the bonnet of the truck. Thomas stretched on the opposite side.

"To give your introduction."

"Already? But we just got here-"

"Better early than late."

~~~

"So, how'd it go?"

"They aren't having visitors. Not until she gets put in a recovery ward, at least."

"Ah. Sorry to hear about that."

Rhys perched himself atop of a few large wooden crates around the back of the building. A few splinters pricked him, but he paid little attention to them. Ella, with arms folded behind her back, loitered around with reddened eyes.

"It's okay. She needs her rest. Gwen too." Chained together by anxious reserve, they let the fleet of trucks and tanks chatter for them. Tremors convulsed the ground, with currents of motorised sprockets clattering through the area. Everywhere they moved, the whole world heard it. Such machines were built to be seen, to be heard and to be feared. As they moved, Rhys felt a disturbance strike his nerves with goosebumps forming all across his arms. Eventually, they passed, and Ella spoke again. "I still can't wrap my head around it."

"It's a lot to take on." Rhys looked to the passing tanks and sighed.

"She was just there, all nice and fine…"

"Then one second changes it all."

The rush of horrific memories clawed back into memory. One second. A single moment in time and space was enough to ruin a life or end it. In a sudden flurry of existentialism, he counted through those singular seconds.

266

First: an arrest that had begun it all for him. The conscription, the detainment from Galbraith and other dishonourable officers. To the frontline. Never to be seen again.

Second: a rigorous performance of gunfire. A crack of the skull. Ryan having his life emptied in an instant. No rest. No slow release. All ripped apart at the pull of a trigger.

Third: a certain derailment. Fire. Flame. Death all around. The miracles of survival or the curse of living. Tears and cries for help. Nothing anyone could do.

Fourth: a battleship floating above. Dreadnought's arsenal fired down without remorse. Fury ravished the lands. A hundred died. Another hundred came back traumatised. Sabrina became the victim. They all went home defeated.

A total of four individual seconds had changed the history of him. It had set men, no – victims, on paths they could not see the end of. It terrified him to no end to know that at any second his life would be over. Such mercilessness hounded his experience of war perfectly. If he thought of home and of peace for too long, he'd be open to a knife's stab or a gunshot. The tragedy of the soldier – blend into the repulsion around them or distract themselves long enough to be carried out of it in a body bag.

Ella let her hands slide into her pockets whilst she shivered a little. A bitterness in the air tipped their day with early signs of frost. Autumn felt short-lived with a coming storm of snow that snuck across the horizon. She looked back at Rhys and ignored the tanks as they were herded by.

"Do you think we'll be okay?"

Always the question with her, he thought, and the sting they provided was most uncouth – though it wasn't nearly the harshest thing he'd caught out there. She didn't seem to consider survivability anymore. It seemed irrelevant to make such promises. He couldn't bring himself to it. On the bygone days of rain, bruises and trudge, he'd told her she would survive, that she would see to the end of the conflict and live out the rest of her days in reconciliation. And now…?

It was an uphill battle to even get an answer out, truthful or not. The paradox of Ella was that to lie would prepare her for nothing, but to tell her the truth would rip any hope she still had out of her.

267

"I hope so." No answer could truly satisfy her lust for absolution. And even if it had, it hadn't satisfied himself. Everything was always unclear. Omniscience fell short of the Stars' capabilities and they lacked the omnipotence to do anything about it. Either they were cruel or useless. No idol could ever be perceived as benevolent for the human race ever again. But then again, the scriptures told the land that all that was wrong was the fault of mankind himself. What difference did that make in the hopelessness of Sunar's inability to save them?

The months they'd spent in service hadn't shown much promise. The uncertainty in his answer recognised how mystified their journey had become, with perplexing tributaries carrying them further off the beaten path. It wasn't a straight war. He felt disempowered to fight, but angry enough to continue.

Too much had been taken away. Jobs, sanities and lives, all into the firepit, all as hounds of hell to be let loose on their enemies that neutered them.

Kill. Be killed. Kill. Or be killed. Don't kill. Kill yourself. On repeat, the words waved across his mind in a creeping barrage. Every time Ella went silent, the ferment of his inner conflict poked out of its hole. He ignited fear in himself and it meant facing his reflection without zeal. He couldn't realise who he was and who he had once been anymore. And yet he still thought about it. Was he going to be okay? An innocent farmer's son. A descendant of irrelevance and triviality. He had been no one and he had liked it that way. The world's issues were neglected. Just a community of closely kept people ruled his decision making. Whether he had friends or not, life was a pattern that thrived on mediocrity. He took care of a disabled man and had security because of it.

He missed his father. To know how little he thought of home ached his heart. He could've told himself to pay attention to the light of his world, but the gunshots spoke louder than he did.

"You'll be fine." Ella's voice, as tender as it always was, brightened the dim and misty day. "Sabrina always said you would be, and I have no other reason to think you won't."

"How're you so sure?" He asked.

"I don't know."

Had the world been a nicer place, Sabrina would've been beside them, making a joke or two to have raised their spirits.

Sisterly love supported by emotions yet unconfirmed. Rhys left his eyes on Ella, imagining the day where she could leave the military for her own sake.

"Evelyn's craftwork is really nice." She observed, pointing towards his helmet. "So pristine. I watched her carve it."

"It's a great gift. And – I think it might just be the only reminder I have of home." He unclipped its straps and uncovered his scalp, where he held the helmet within a light grasp. He rubbed his thumb over the colourless rose. Such innocence at the tip of his nail, usually rested atop of his head; it all felt too surreal. A duality of meaning, a sense of direction and encouragement in life. The rose. Always the rose.

"What does it mean?"

For a minute, he sat and pondered. Had its meaning retained itself? The message of hope, beauty and taking the last laugh in death, the symbol of national pride and unquestionable honour in a destructive death.

'Pick me, for I will prick you.'

What were the thorns? Were they his guns and bullets, the bombs filled with small iron shrapnel? Had it been his will, weak and crumbled? Maybe it was his bite, the ridged teeth that waited to sink into the eyes and neck of the Syndicalist Reds? Vengeance was a powerful tool. He'd seen so much death that as each day passed he felt less sympathy for the man he'd killed. When he thought about the blood on the doorframe and the violence in the windmill, he asked himself if whether they deserved to die after all.

No. He couldn't let himself think like that, he internally concluded. He couldn't indulge the war, justify his actions and litter himself with vile illusions. All he could do was stay vigilant and keep his thoughts away from his past. As much as it would haunt him, he would fight it back with ignorance. Anything to get him out of the war, at the end of the day.

"I don't really know anymore." Rhys admitted with a pathetic sigh. Ella pouted and gazed off to the side. It looked as if she wanted him to say something encouraging again. "How was Evelyn's birthday?"

"Oh, it was nice. We didn't do much because we had sentry duties at ten, but Tyran showed her this lovely little drawing he'd been doing. She liked that."

"And when's your birthday?" He wondered aloud.

"It was a few weeks ago." She said.

"What was it?"

"My 23rd."

"And you didn't tell us?"

"I didn't think anyone would've cared that much. There wasn't much to celebrate either, with everything that had gone on." Opening Ella's mind gave him a blessing coated in razor blades. She spoke more which let Rhys know what her fragility was made of. With that came her crystalised hopelessness.

From across the courtyard, a call came forth. It spoke Rhys' name – and there was a man with his arm in the air, projecting it across to him. He looked over at the man and immediately caught glimpse of a long black coat decorated in medallions and achievements. A familiar polished black cap and Osakan grin could be read from a mile away. He'd seen it once and never forgot its slyness. On approach, the serpent's tail flickered and rattled with each step he took.

"Staff Sergeant Hendricks!" Mr Lee spoke with the same energy he had last time. Rhys could barely remember their last meeting in detail, only that the information they'd discussed and spread was false. "Alive and well, I see."

"I guess." He half-heartedly mumbled, pushing himself off of the box and saluting him as per standard. "Can I help you, sir?"

"Not me." At that point, Rhys noticed someone following closely behind his elusive visitor. The woman walked without much elegance, where she put only just enough effort to not drag her feet across the pavement. Her feather cut short hair looked as mildly groomed as any other soldier's. He'd never seen her before; for she was the moseying definition of bland incarnate. "Been ordered to give you a gift."

"A…" He stumbled on his words, confused on the man's illusive approach through the dying mist. "I'm sorry, Sir?"

"This is Private Lodvtz. She is now under your command." He pointed a sharp finger at him to order her to move. She nodded, just short of it being polite.

"Morning, Staff Sergeant." He couldn't get a reading from her personality, a blank slate of dullness with slight enthusiasm for her new placement toppled any immediate impressions. She seemed as enthusiastic to die as he was to get up in the morning.

"Right…? Good morning, Private-"

"Lodvtz." There was a short silence between them.

"Ah, right." Thomas stepped forward, and Rhys turned his attention toward him. "Sir, where did this come from? I wasn't aware we were getting new members?"

"I was passing by some of the commanders' offices and one of them asked me to bring her here. Fresh out of training. Just missed out on Haria, right?"

"Lucky." He paced over to Lodvtz and continued his struggle to gather his first impressions. She was like any other new recruit, disciplined and versed enough in the hierarchy to keep her mouth closed. And she showed respect for a man who barely respected himself. "Alright, I guess you're one of us then. Is there anything else I can help you with, Sir?"

Thomas shook his head, giving off a shrewd, devious grin to the group. And, rather ominously, he turned away with a silent wave and marched back into the daylight mist. He disappeared into the affinitive greyness as quickly as he had arrived. Left behind, the newly met Private stood silently; her eyes darted to her sides and she was unsure of what happened next.

"Up and leaves…great." Rhys grumbled. He wasn't too sure of what he had to do either. A child in a basket had been dumped on his doorstep. Her mind wasn't in infancy by age but by experience, and understanding of what she had to go through. "So, uh, fresh out of training?"

"That's right."

"Excited?" There was pained cynicism and bitterness to his words, one that even piqued Ella's notice. Suddenly, his voice became sharp and lacquered with an immediate distaste for the victim left by his heels.

"I'm excited to be doing my part, Staff Sergeant."

Nothing more had to be said. Rhys had fallen for the façade and deflated his mood. To him, she would be another Johan or Stephan, a proud serviceman who thought they were destined to be on a path to greatness, that the war held a moral absolution to it or that they were the right woman for the right hour. She was a woman, to him, who thought she could distinguish right from wrong. That was the first impression. It could've been wrong, but with boiling resentment for how doing his part had cost so much, it was no surprise that he'd reacted poorly.

He gestured with a finger and asked for her to follow him. As expected, she did so without hesitation. Ella begrudgingly tagged along.

"Where are you from?" Under the ambience of wartime activity, Rhys quizzed her with a slow and monotonous tone.

"Burno."

"Must've come a long way from the capital. Did they train you there, or something?"

"They did, Staff Sergeant."

"Stop calling me – sorry, just...don't call me by my rank, please." He whispered to himself. "And a late-comer?"

"Yeah."

"Why'd you join the militia and not the regulars?"

"Felt as if I belonged here more. Just normal people doing what's been shoved onto them." Christa slipped her hands into her pockets and eyed the passing shadows of parades and convoys. The fog then consumed them and all that was left was sound.

"That's...nice." He sighed.

Rhys' staunch pessimism created a low-hanging dark cloud over the trio. With every question asked they both sank in a pool of sadness. She felt patronised, though not by his words but by the man he seemed to be. Months of war had taken its toll on him.

No one seemed to mention the Queen, or the royalty, ever. Thomas barely spoke of her. On her tour of the base, no "queens" or "majesties" came about. Animosity had suppressed their right to criticise the high crown. That or they had become so sterilised by the conflict that they didn't have the time of day to blame someone else. It didn't change anything if they did. Whatever they said couldn't take them away to a heavenly field. Flowers didn't bloom when they verbally defecated onto those in power who held such responsibilities. It didn't matter anymore who failed them, just that they were failed and that it was unchangeable. She observed such powerlessness from the masses. They conformed as violent thugs that had been taken them from their homes and dressed them up to play soldier.

In the midst of it all, there wasn't a gram of honour. She could sense its absence. People looked around with deathly stares and dragged twenty cigarettes a day. They drank themselves dry, concentrating their blood with acrimonious flasks until they passively let themselves rot away. If she'd asked any why they'd taken their habits and addictions so far, she expected to hear of their displeasure for life.

Christa looked to her right where she saw Ella trailing not too far from the Staff Sergeant. When they eventually caught one another's eyes, she smiled kindly.

"Sorry, haven't properly introduced myself." Her formality died down as soon as she saw the lack of a rank slide. A private, nonetheless, just like her. With a flashy smile, she tried to prod back out some conversation. "I'm Christa."

"Oh…Ella." Timidly, she looked away from Christa and let her gaze drift ahead of them. "Sorry."

"It's…okay?" She didn't continue. Ella waned and lurked in her own mind as she moved a little closer to Rhys.

The day continued without much excitement. She was given the rest of her uniform and her equipment, then she was given an allotted time to accustom herself at the range.

Rhys had asked her about how she knew Thomas, and she regurgitated the same answer he'd instructed her to: that she had been awaiting reassignment and that he was told to deliver her. That was it. All as per her preparation.

She'd blended so well into the forces yet she immediately felt out of place. So many muffled gazes…

Numb eyes.

Cold fingers.

Pitiful hearts.

Even the ones who smiled looked cracked and crooked. She didn't question the rose carving she spotted on his helmet. Obviously, it intrigued her. Whoever Staff Sergeant Hendricks was, he had experienced things she couldn't quite imagine. She pitied him, all in all. When her mother, her majesty of cruelty, had given the order of universal conscription, he was the spitting

273

image of a layman most impacted by it. At last, she watched as he left her alone for the day.

She never got an introduction to the others, at least not straight away. She simply went to the range and hooked herself up with a rifle. From there, she sat down and watched the marching drills as they passed.

Christa was in no position to feel happy of where she was. All that self-pride she carried on her past life's back seemed to fizzle out, a thin vapour indicating of what was once alight. And whilst her determination to the people still stood, the eyesores of the suffering masses left her wondering if she could stomach the woes of the citizens. War had come a long way and onto their shores.

Remembrance of the courtly discussions made the conflict seem distant, foreign and far away. But they mattered not, for their beaches had gone from illustrious, glorious places of summer to battlegrounds of winter. And unless the combined armed forces of Kelan had the strength to break their enemy down, bone by bone, then the doomsday clock had surely begun ticking.

The fact she'd been a recognised as a replacement for empty boots truly showed how damned the days had become.

Chapter 21

In the wake of the tide

The hilltop horizons erupted with a volcanic magnitude. Stacks of smoke stretched up to the lunar sky and created a rising spire to heaven's gate. Schottenstein stood close to the valley's peak. Across the ridge, open-air defensive positions had been carefully placed to onlook the next hill ahead of them. The world appeared around him as a foreign battleground. Where they'd spent days bogged in watery corridors and reefs made of mire and gore, the land stretched for miles in juxtaposed greenery – where vegetation had still held its ground. Yet, he saw the grass beside the forests ablaze in the distance. Eight miles on his left, the trees burned and the flames roared. This was the land that many yearned to punish. For a lot of the soldiers, it didn't really matter how they did it; as long as it kept them alive, they couldn't care any less than they already did.

Twilight breezes touched his face with a chilled graze. He was awoken by the frosted vapour that caressed his cheeks and nose. The all-too familiar grumble of battle still droned on in the other valleys, though they sung in limited choirs. Finally, they had the room to breathe a little easier – as the fury dispersed across the wildlands: a conclusive reward for those who'd survived hell's first two layers.

It was but a breath of freshness after having exited the world of rottenness. It was beautiful, as he'd describe it himself.

In the dead of night, they held their acquired ground. A counterattack was, yet again, expected to arrive at a few minutes' notice. That time, however, the odds had been tipped in the favour of the machines. Exiting Haria's provincial mess had allowed for the deployment of armoured beasts, for the soft-soiled bog of the peninsula had been bypassed. And just beneath the ridgeline, three of his own walkers stood ready.

At the rear, ascending up the incline, Major Westra strode toward Schottenstein. In her hand was a burnt-out cigarette, the orange bud created a gingerly sunset on the tips of her fingers.

"So?" He weighed in on her. His eyes remained transfixed on the horizon of flame, the destruction of a God's countryside, and he hadn't turned to meet her – as if he could have smelled her arrival.

"High Command is going to place us with the South-Western Army once we're out of here." With a heavy cough, she looked ahead to the hilltop void they scanned over. "Doesn't look like we're going to the capital unless we clean it up quickly."

"There goes your chance, then."

The pair walked across the ridge and inspected the small detachment they commanded. Four machine gun nests sat tucked into the dirt, with five rifle squads spaced in between. Silenced walkers stood out of sight. At the cost of Haria's heavy toll, many mid-grade officers had their security shafted for frontline duty, all while waiting for the replacements due to arrive. All in all, he described, the disorder of the syndicalist forces gave their enemy all the chances to break them – which in several sectors, they had.

"Do you think any of this could've been avoided?" Schottenstein's mouth ran away from his mind and into a gulley most familiar to the silent hours of soldiery, where he pondered over the place where his life stood. Farhawl's isolated continental carnage drew that endless speculation. If, for instance, a small detail in the timeline had been changed, the butterfly's wings wouldn't have beaten up the hurricane. "Maybe if I'd eaten something different for lunch, we could've settled an armistice."

He laughed alone. Westra continued her stone-cold gaze into the night. The space between them grew quite naturally.

"Some things, Major, are unavoidable." She sat herself on the grass and relaxed, regardless of their pre-emptive status. "This is a war of victimhood, of vengeance. It was only inevitable if we are to bring order to injustice."

"Save the theatrics; and I wouldn't say that for everyone. You know damn well that the unions want to maintain their permanent revolution."

"Personally, I don't care." She scorned. "Let them use their bigger hooks to reel in the greater whales. A woman like myself, though, knows what's right."

"Ruining these fields is right for you, Emelia?" Hearing her name put her in a minute of silence. She pictured herself in the golden-red uniform she'd once worn, and the phantom feeling of its cotton body gave her goosebumps. Meanwhile, Schottenstein had still plastered his gaze on the fanatic flames and cursed beneath his breath. "Isn't it too much to ignite this land to a point of wreckage?"

"We can always plant more trees."

"There's enough destruction already – I'd say the lives and torn families are enough."

"When did you get philosophical?" She said as she eyed him form stoic face to his cold, curled toes, all to get a reading on him.

"I just think that maybe treating your enemy as you hope for them to treat you isn't so bad."

"Fuck that – what, do you expect them to hold the door to Kelan open for you? You gonna do that as well when they invade?" He finally lowered his gaze back down to the earth they stood on, and he turned to face her. "You're a well-and-proper idealist, and I fucking hate that."

When she finished, she gave him a somewhat courteous smile. It was – as much as it could've been – genuine. To him, it was a daunting sight.

He went back to the scorched lands off on the horizon and he was swarmed with the distilled and personal anger inside as the land showed its bruising. Maybe she was right, maybe she was wrong. He never had given the capacity to objectivise his own internal musings. And their setting gave no direct answer either. There was no war of honour nor political influence. They had entered a conflict of annihilation and, if one were to go so far, extermination. The syndicalists and its unions were curdled by the taste of monarchists' colourless blood.

Since the day he'd arrived, he hadn't felt morally superior on the murder plains of their warpath. The excursions of justice had their low points, but when no uplift resided by the beaten path then had it truly been a righteous voyage? Smiles came from the sadistic or for relief of burden. The bodies of fallen comrades, with enemies torn by their ligaments beside them, coated the soil in misery; for the syndicalists had worked with the Kelan monarchy to shower the world with blood over rain. Waterfalls and reservoirs could've been filled by the sheer guilt and sweat that perched onto his shoulder. Yet, he stood by his will of duty. What else could he do? And whatever he thought, he wouldn't dare press it against the unions for the sake of his family's safety.

"Did you hear about the other landings?" To vacate his distress, he struck up casual conversation with the Major.

"Which ones?"

"The ones that weren't a success, off on the Western seaboard. Eight thousand dead, supposedly. Harsher defences."

"That's just how things are." She lowered herself to the grass and brushed her fingers through the moistened blades.

Schottenstein stared at her. Her authority was shrouded by the regular's combat fatigues she still willingly wore. In an attempt to lift his own spirits, he prodded her with a little remark.

"You realise how unprofessional you really are?" He smirked.

"Is there a problem with it?"

"Not for me. And the soldiers seem to not mind. Just how come you're so laxed?"

"What's the point of being all uptight if I'm here to raze hell?"

He didn't press anymore into who or what she was. He'd barely learnt anything about her other than her drive to enact her own unholy crusade of barbarism against the woman in the high throne. Her grudge came lined with a disregard of the means. To her, the end was all that mattered, to which he had never questioned her of her ties to the place she so desired. It seemed to cut deeper than the false flags at their home shore, the suicide bombers and the terrorists with deep pockets.

He just couldn't unscramble her as a person, let alone if she were a monster. By what he'd seen, she was just an officer who took promise in joining the fray, but also one who had taught herself that her eternal victory came in a package of indiscriminate aggression to the end. Whilst off her hinges of battle, she almost looked pleasant. Almost.

"It feels good to finally return." A vixen's curl settled on her aged lips.

"Sir, I see a silhouette at 290. It's peaking." Squinting through the nightly gloom, a rifleman called in a baritone mumble toward Schottenstein. Westra slowly brought herself back to her feet.

"Alright, maintain assorted positions. Hold on my mark." Schottenstein tucked his hands into his pocket and pulled out a pair of gloves, encasing his cold fingers inside. He walked across the line and quickly checked over with those entrenched for the defence.

Patience was his virtue. He kept his body low to the ground and he casted a smaller shadow against the moonlit backdrop. The sky dimmed as the plumes of ash began to mask the moon's divine ray. Pious to the shade, the sounds of mechanical beings in motion gently sauntered through the wind. An amble of steel ignited its crescendo. The blisters on nature, the footprints of the walking guns, peered over the ridge. Their silhouette was faint to the unwary eye. They held their low profile but arrived only to oppose those who stood in their way. Apparitions of men clad in serviceman's clothing stretched across the opposing ridge. And with the whisk of a gloved palm, the skirmish struck the spark.

A hail of unsaintly sincerity let loose from the barrels of their machineguns. Green tracers scourged the gales and sped at their own admission. A few off-guard silhouettes were killed before their comrades had even realised, with their black outlines disappearing into the night. At a glance, they fought future ghosts clad in shadows.

To accompany their brothers in arms, the riflemen tossed their copper and lead into the pile. Casings littered the grass and the stream of spearing projectiles tore into the opposing hilltop. And whilst the machineguns continued their suppression, the riflemen reloaded and waited to pinpoint their shots for the kill. Then came the sound they waited for.

Across the pale horizon, a horse of processed mettle unveiled itself on the peak. It stood in the noise it barked and the great tank ascended to its upright posture to launch its first attack. The shell whistled through the air, even if for just half a second, and slammed into the hill. The damage was uncertain, and Schottenstein ducked behind the hilltop. Westra had spread herself further out to bring orders and encouragement of her own. She shouted and drew her own submachine gun, firing with short bursts alongside those who held the line.

The dust settled on the shell's impact zone and a second Kelan walker emerged from over the ridge. Two for one. When a shot from a nearby anti-tank rifleman scathed the thick armour, Schottenstein slid himself down a few metres, where he picked up his hands and waved to all three walkers out of sight. Their pilots closed themselves in the hatches and locked their bodies with the beasts, slowly edging up the ridge to the top. The tips of their smoking barrels emerged and they aligned themselves for the enemy's demise.

Marked by fury – written in an inelegant shade of crimson – the traced shells ripped through the dirt and pounded each side. The small arms fire diminished as they were weakened by the dominance of their mechanical overlords. Testaments to one another's inherent determination left an even playing field. Schottenstein flinched when he saw the twirling glimpse of a shell pierce through one of his own walkers. The echo of iron and steel being torn and concaved inward was a sound he'd never thought to have experienced.

A product of war had made its mark; the smoke and flame ignited from within the tank as the shell hit its munitions storage. The shockwave tossed Schottenstein aside. His back slid and landed against the dirt with a soft thud. He grunted as the pain felt ever so detached from Haria's cold numbness – with a stark sting to his spine and torso. His ears were slathered in a ringing squeal and his eardrums were pressed to their limits. He lifted his face from the dirt and looked back at the walker, laid crumbled and collapsed against the surface of the hill. An imperfect circle left an opening on the tank's front, whilst the rear had been completely blasted; the steel had been spread out like a firework's burst frozen in time.

The flames lit up their position and the warmth brought a bittersweet sense of unwelcomed touch to his body. As he stared the fire down with the wind taken out of his lungs, he noticed the nearby forest in flames. Yet he did not cower. No. He couldn't. Immediately, he crawled away from the blazing carcass of his walker and lurched back up the hill, where the flicker of dirt splashed against his face.

"Focus on their walkers! Keep them at bay!" He could barely hear his own voice over the sting in his ears. All words appeared muffled, his words in particular, and the dryness of his throat worsened the burn on his tongue. Yet he pressed on. Westra indoctrinated herself into the firefight with her guns red-hot. She'd lost her sense of superiority and joined as an equal to the men she commanded.

A walker of their own landed a perfect shot and in barrelled a crippling AP shell to an adversary's leg. The Kelan walker crumbled into the ground, and from its cockpit came an apparitional figure scrambling out of the main hatch. Schottenstein watched with burnt irises as one of his own machinegun nests locked on to his struggled escape and, in one quick burst, his body toppled back into the broken, smoked-out machine.

From there, the battle died down. The shooting grew less frequent but their attention remained as durable as ever before. The second Kelan walker retreated in haste and descended back down their side of the hill, only to disappear out of sight and mind for good. There was an attempt to reorganise what had been floundered by the bombardment of their guns. But as the second faint counter-offensive started, it was almost immediately seized by fifteen seconds of morale-ruining suppression. And when the guns fell silent, the grass had been cut afresh.

"Are we not going after them?" Westra ran over with an exhausted pant, still on her blissful adrenaline-fuelled high.

"Not now. We can't overextend our lines; they'll wait for us in the night, and we should follow suit." Her voice was muffled to him, as was his own. He looked at the tank as its flames fizzled out, short-lived, much alike its pilot. Two still remained well intact, though their paint and bodies were scratched up by the hellfire they'd withstood. "Tell them to keep their post, I need a fucking break."

He trudged down the hill, out of the line of sight, and sat down at its belly beside a tree. The chilled air caused him to shiver. Having felt the warmth of the flame, he almost missed the devastation it had caused.

And he hated that fact; he'd seen death as he always had, something to loathe to the end of time and to relish in its products and golden linings. The warmth it had created and the cackle of the furnaced horror – a hidden beauty, perhaps: a picturesque painting on the mantlepiece, to admire at and to smile upon. But that was insanity to him. He admitted that, for a partial second, he was comforted by the balm of heat, and that the elation of pain stiffly awoke him from the dream. It hurt. Such euphoria in the face of the end. If by chance, he thought as if Westra's condoning of Armageddon really was the natural process of a mind ruthlessly raped by battle. And yet he'd only experienced a small dose of its injection.

It didn't take much for a man to lose himself when death was involved. He just hoped it'd remain as an accidental injection of dopamine and adrenaline. The proviso he wrote for himself ordered him to take control of his mind. Falling down into the mausoleum of madness would have been worse than a clean execution at sunrise.

To embed his livelihood into the flames of a man's death had distracted him long enough to not see Westra approach.

"You okay, old man?" She prodded his relaxed body with her capped boots.

"We're the same age…" He spoke with a great exhalation. "And yes, I'm fine. Just overwhelmed."

"Try not to be. You're an officer, not a recruit." She looked behind her, seeing the smokestack from their destroyed tank barrel into the sky. Their hill made its ultimate contribution. All around them, the inclines and valleys each had their own towers of ash and fumes. Smouldering staircases to the tolerant topside of the world were at every mile. The grasslands had been transformed into industrial plains. Instead of coal or wood, it was the bodies of thousands, the homes and the orchards of decayed fruits all used as fuel. Their acts of vengeance were noticed even by the distant stars. The clouds, the storms and the endless sea of ash was visible from space. They charred the air and poisoned the waters with each step they took. She frowned at him, knowing full well that his realisation of their warpath wouldn't change a damn thing.

"Thanks for the *advice*, your grace." With gritted teeth and an ironic smirk, he mocked her. She kicked him again, that time slightly harder.

"Shut the fuck up, prick."

"You even talk the same as them, still."

"What of it?"

"You're a mixed bag, Emelia. A messy one too. From one side to the other." He pressed his skull against the trunk and gazed toward the hidden stars. Billows blackened the night sky further. The air began to smell of charcoal. "And to think you've got your own reasons to be here."

"Everyone does."

"Mostly for the Unions' wish to destabilise the oppressors down south, that they'd birthed themselves. Another exertion of influence. The other nations won't ignore this."

"What we do is no different to how Queen Tala handles conflict." She argued with a vile stiffness. She walked amongst a nation that held her dedication with iron cuffs. Then, she could've been the harbinger of their nightmares. "As she knows well herself, violence assumes the greatest form of authority. She controls her people like she controls her enemies: with lies and coverups."

The iron fist. A gauntlet of steel. The glove of diamond. Unbreakable, and unfixable. It cuts all those who wear it and cracks the will of the people it hammers down upon. A self-sacrifice. Tear up their tickets to heaven for the sake of order and control. It was when Westra's policy on life came through that he truly began to fear her.

She wasn't intimidating because she killed people, he would be a hypocrite if so.

No, she held her firm grip on him simply because she didn't care about the reasons. She saw opportunity. There was no path to a permanent revolution. No syndicate stood at her helm. Schottenstein wasn't even sure if she believed in it. What she did see, however, were her means to an end. A return of suffering and agony by her strike. If their citizens hadn't been safe, then Tala's own weren't exempt from such punishment. Their existence was a crime. Association was a plea for death. To her, there was only herself and those that were tools, murdered subjects to gnaw at Tala's mind. She wished to return a favour and a grudge long awaited. She had nothing to lose and so much to gain. Everything she'd once possessed she had willingly abandoned. Her job, her security and her beliefs. He never knew the exact details, but what he could only suspect by the fire in her eyes was that she would've done this at any point in her life. She was a vehicle without breaks.

"And if she exerts her fury on the innocent of my homeland, ideological or not, I can't stand for it." She lit a small cigarette and inhaled it like oxygen.

"So, this is just some crusade for you?"

"Maybe."

283

"Then what's your next step?" Curiosity had taken him by the collar and he was led to pursue answers best left covered.

"I'm switching assignments soon. Word is that you'll fall under a new colonel or general in the coming days. I'll be heading on to lead another company." Her throat coarsened at the drag of her roll-up whilst she exhaled a thin trail of ash. She followed the vapour and smiled wearily; destined for greatness, in her own eyes, she relished in her position of power.

So, it was true that she was no commissar of the people, neither that of a political officer that strove to spread only the government's faith. She was a fiend with her eyes on a singular prize. A dangerous combination for those with an eroded iron gaze. And what gas had sanctioned her spite? No, not the cleanliness and holiness of oxygen, but the poison of carbon monoxide. She knew her limits and stepped ahead of them. To her, it was personal, even if it shouldn't have been.

Schottenstein had no legitimate quarrel with her vengeance. Its reasoning appeared easily traceable to the conversant eye. However, he feared the damage that it would cause. Who knew what would get caught in between? Forests turned to plains of stumps and embers. Towns were crumbled by artillery bombardments and she, with the twinkle of anger in her iris, would go through whatever stood in her way to get to the monarch. He didn't need to know the outcome of her violent surge, but instead the journey to get there. And seeing her separate to her own specialised company left him powerless to stop anything.

And that was all he was. Powerless. Whether he liked it or not, there were guns trailed on the army's back. To lose would be a disaster. So many pledged that the monarchy must die, lest abolishment weren't enough. Blood had to be spilt. There was justification and there was reasoning. Stuck to the rails, he mumbled his curses and let himself sit in the darkness. There would be no grand conclusion to the skirmish.

Resting on the burning tank, the fire faded and the light gently drifted into nothingness.

Westra strode back up the hill and left Schottenstein to his own. The night went back to how it was before. A gentle murmur of artillery and grenades sounding off the evening blues, the aurora of flares sparkling high in the sky and the faint whistle of winds flowing between battles. He shared his depression with no one else. Beneath his legs, a carbine sat unused.

Over time, his eyes readjusted to the cloak of the dark hour. Forlorn trees paraded their beauty with drifting leaves. Some stood untouched by the destruction of war. He would've smiled if he had the soul to do so. Quietly, he rose from the bark he lay against and wandered toward the trees.

His fingers handled their coarseness whilst he felt the sensation of a quiet and peaceful world, one separated from the other engulfed in flames.

And at the left, he saw it; nowhere near a hundredth of an acre, a small allotment, surrounded by an ankle-high green picket fence, remained unscathed. His curiosity was trapped in seconds, and he circumnavigated it. Inside stood rows of small crimson flowers that hid a bedding of thorns underneath its beautiful sortie.

"Such luck, you have." He whispered to himself as he concluded his lap around its perimeter. Not a footstep in sight. Like barbed wire, the thorns kept any destructive boots and ankles away from its gorgeous exterior.

Along the edge closest to the hill, a small sign written in Kelan rhetoric left him only to speculate on its message. Perhaps it asked for trespassers to watch their step, or to proclaim its ownership to an old withering couple, smiling in the distance at their prized flowerbed. Gradual intrigue forced his hand toward the petals. He shone a light to a single rose and reached forward, plucking it with a vile tug. He didn't notice the sting at first, but when he lifted the rose from the earth and closer to his face, he saw a trickle of blood gradually coat both the stem and his fingers.

He watched as the warm liquid merged with the faded flower, dyeing it a bleaker shade than it already was. Within the crimson petals did the blood flow, arcing in vein-like swirls. Soon the sepals pointed towards the soil, weighed down by the pressure of a bleeding man.

Chapter 22

Within the white branches

Blight flew in on a clawed seat, clasped together with the talons of a thrush. A song wailed from its beak and it waved the world around his ethereal flight. It sounded like the wind.

Gravity let loose its constraints and forced Rhys into a glide through nowhere. The uncanny visions of debris and dust soared past him. He flew down a slim paved corridor, a crevice of civil destruction, and the songbird's gust wrangled with his hair. A rush of adrenaline and motion pushed against his clothing. Acceleration. Faster. No slowing down. On either of his sides, the street-side buildings sprang past him in perpetual movement. There was no sky. No clouds sat above him. Beyond the pale sand, the remains of a broken city, the lunarlike distance held nothing. Emptiness – the architects of cultivation had been triumphed by the draftsmen of demolitions. Crumbled stores, markets and homes all fell into one elongated strip.

The wind rode in from nowhere and, in a frosted tingle across his skin, he felt it all over. His body endlessly sailed down the street of wreckages and demolition in the songbird's jagged claws. Then, thick clouds of ash blocked his path. And yet despite this, the unearthly rush of his conscience stormed into the gas and scorched sediment at full speed. His throat was flooded with a raw anguish. A flame built up on his tongue. It burned.

Wherever his gaze followed, so did the direction he flew. Everywhere he looked seemed to be forward. The street turned as he did. He overtook cracked windows, broken bedrooms and buried mantlepieces. Through the dash of squalls, the scurry of sound against his ears, the wraithlike host he was in picked up a second sound. Footsteps? A clatter of iron against stone. And...cloven hooves? He closed his eyes again and reopened them to a new scene.

With his gravity still disconnected, his body drifted through a freshly formed white overworld. A blizzard spoke in nature's tongue as it demanded his attention. He gave it obediently. Soon, across the hissing wisp of the crystal snowstorm, came the sight of a million trees. The whiteout took shape. A forest in the middle of winter; why was he here? Where was he? He lost personal interest after just two questions and his attention went back to the voices over the silver estate.

His gaze came close to the tree trunks, narrowly avoiding their passing by a metre or less. And then he stopped mid-flight.

The perception of pursuit, or escape, halted. His body no longer flew through the willows. It hanged still, airborne in an empty forest. The trees had no tops, and only the trunks that towered up into the snowy sky made contact with the clouds. All sorts of greenery had been buried, and the reds, the yellows, the pinks and the blues of the petal kingdom had fallen beneath white seas. Tabula rasa. A blank slate of earth. Farhawl as a plain of oblivion and absence. He was in a forest where things came to fade away. He was in his place of limbo.

And as the world turned to deafness, gravity slowly lowered his feet to the ground, and his boots landed in the snow. He left no print as he found himself left wandering, blindly, through a vapid sanctuary.

He walked on for a while. Nothing really happened. There was no wind anymore. Just the sound of his boots crunching against lifeless snow lived rent-free in the surrounding solitude. There were no footprints nor any way to distinguish which direction he headed in.

And then it came again. The hooves. They pattered around him in circles and swirls. He saw a few prints in the snow, but no source. He twisted, turned, and found nothing. And when he looked back…

Behold! Before his eyes, an elongated face of fur stared him down. As shock overcame Rhys, he held his breath. He felt its exhales against his skin. Its fur was a coat of pure silver. Smooth, and silky, yet distinguishable from the snow it stood in by the iced glimmer it held. Rhys didn't say or do anything. He tried to circle his way around it, but its eyes and head traced his movements. When he narrowed his eyelids, the colourless elk's did the same.

"Who elected you to come here?" Its mouth didn't move as it pestered him with incoherent abstracts, but he heard its voice as clear as day. Rhys stared at the forest, and looked back only to see that the elk hadn't disappeared. "Or did you bring yourself?"

Its eeriness precluded Rhys' own ability to retort. The creature stepped closer and scrutinised his face with glassy judgements. When it spoke again, he could feel its voice echo between the trees and back down his spine.

"Have you spoken to father? Does mother know you're not coming home?"

"Am I going to die, then?" Rhys asked the beast, and heard the question reverberate again throughout the forest, then back into his earlobes.

"You may return as you are now, but not as you were. The son will die in the mind, not the body."

He froze. Even if the vision was beyond reality, he found that he couldn't speak out against it. The oracle of the conflict, the war…it looked down upon him with a frown. Well, it was difficult to tell if an elk could frown or not. Could it understand his emotional turmoil? Did such a beast get the intricacies of how a man felt dying over and over in a war over pamphlets and manifestos?

"Have you seen yourself?" Its stance lowered, and the great antlers upon its scalp contorted up into the sky like the trees around them. "Mirrors can be fogged by smoke. See yourself with clear gazes."

A tumorous thump assaulted his head. Without thinking, Rhys' body took control over itself. His hands scooped snow from the floor, which left no dent in the sea, and he placed its icy remains against his forehead. When he blinked, he opened his eyes to the sight of another's view. He saw himself, his hands, his dirty face, the facial hair stretched across his unshaven jaw and cheeks, the unkept ruffle of hair and the bags layered upon bags sat underneath his brooding eyes. What he saw was what the elk saw, what everyone else saw: a tattered human. He had become one husk, with all life sucked out by an aged pipeline. Fatigue. Tiredness. Those were the highlights of his reflection. There was no carefree farmer's boy anymore. He couldn't even see himself wearing dungarees, or with plaid shirts and strips of corn hanging from his dry lips. His build had perfectly moulded into the boots and shirts the militia had issued him.

"You've become attracted to purity, to innocence. Truly a changed man, wouldn't you say?"

He hated the voice of the elk. It sounded familiar, but not in a personal fashion. It was his demonic lovechild of every known voice mankind had to offer, the social pressures of a million tongues. It was a blend of all things individual and unique, into coagulum. And then, it fractured apart, and each question came in untimely barrages and flurries – all with a different tongue behind it.

"Who do you think you are?"

"What are you even looking for?"

"Do you love her?"

"Do you think you have the strength left to save yourself?"

"Do you get to choose if you die free or consumed by conflict?"

"Can I ask…?" Rhys interrupted, with his own dullness staring back at him. He saw his arms move, rubbing against the viewport he watched himself through. He observed his own movement cautiously. "Where will I be when the guns fall silent? Or when the bombs stop falling – the blades dull, and where the teardown concludes?"

"Does it end?" The elk asked back. When Rhys blinked, he was back in his own body and back in his own eyes. He stared at the elk with a terrified expression.

It walked backwards and inched toward the mist that formed around them.

"Instead, ask yourself whether you're going to make it stop or if you walk away liberated."

"And if it doesn't?"

Rhys desperately tried to keep up with the elk. His boots slotted into the hoofprints it left behind. The creature snorted and extended its antlers further into the sky, latching onto every tree around it. Moments before the creature vanished, it gave its last retort:

"Does mother know you're not coming home?"

~~~

He rose to no shine. A gasp left him struggling to breathe. He tried to control himself as he wearily wandered his stare around the office. Familiar. Dark. No colour, except the odd shade of the deep ocean abyss. His lamp had faded out. The bulb: dead. An annoyance to awaken to. He cursed its state and rubbed his eyes. A small issue, ever so small in fact, tediously flaked his attention away from real concern.

Let in by the crack beneath the door, a weak beam of light told him that it was still daytime. The hour didn't really matter.

Rhys stood up and let his blood return to its usual flow. Lightheaded, he waited in hush, holding a hand to his forehead. At first, he contemplated collapsing back into his chair and returning to his slumber, but the slack he'd made reflected poorly to his officers. Last thing he needed was another one telling him he was behind on schedule for another hundred paperwork forms.

To think that weeks before he'd been on the frontier of Kelan's fate. Trenches and bombs, guns and fire. The military had sent him to the end of the world and brought him back to sign papers, to commit to mundane office work and to join infants of war in defending a quiet, empty wall. The change in scenery had staggered the stark acclimatisation of his people.

Outside, it was strangely quiet. The usual interlude of gears grinding and aircraft raging past had been abnormally restrained. What had been the bane to his nights, the reminder of what life he was chained to, became something to miss. In hours of silence, his mind would be the speaker. And, lords forbid, the last thing he needed was another conversation with himself.

His hand went to firmly grasp the frozen brass doorknob and, with a slow turn, he looked back into the darkness that was his cubby office. It was still the backroom of an entire military complex, used to scrub up small documents and to write reports on training or whatever. He hated the room only because he hated writing those reports. Objectively describing his involvement in any conflict without a hint of emotion was toilsome, and it played with his frustration. He'd spend hours telling officers how awful it had been for Squad 2 without really telling them anything at all, for the formalities and procedures blocked his desire to get out and scream his woes. All that mattered was if they won or lost, and Rhys' group had lost more than just a battle.

Finally, he twisted the doorknob and let the light briefly fill up the hideaway. He shielded his eyes to the brightness. The greyness of the world had been cleansed with a new palette: white.

Parallel to his door stood a grubby dust-covered window, one that overlooked the nearby open road between his building and the next. And beyond its withered translucence was a new season, a new time and era. Winter. Snow. It drifted down from the sky in lightly spaced flakes, and little piles had begun to settle on the concrete undergrowth.

He'd never seen the end of that year's autumn. The leaves fell a long time before, and by then he'd not realised that they had retired for the year. And when they had withered and died on the floor, everyone had their attentions elsewhere to notice.

Was it any different? Snow replaced rain. It was all the same to him at first. The sky bled in a different colour, and that was all there was to it.

Any semblance of a blue sky had been lost to the change of seasons. A single cream blanket had spread from one end of the horizon to the other. Nature had lost its panoply, its spectrum of colours and life. Dullness prevailed. Rhys spectated it with dry eyes and sighed, as he always did. He then closed the office door behind him, walked into the corridor and then left the building, leaving behind a valueless state of mind.

Two days ago, another complication had hit the squad's morale. The news had spread like wildfire around Mullackaye. At four o'clock in the morning, through the deathly night, a man abandoned his post and waded hopelessly outside of the fort. He left his rifle behind and dropped his pack and was said to have let his arms hang helplessly by his side. There was no energy; only his desire to leave drove him. They said he had no expression on his face, and that he mumbled obscenities towards those who tried to bring him back. What escalated the situation to violence wasn't common knowledge. Some said it was a drawn handgun, or a blade being unsheathed to secure his freedom. Ten minutes into the crisis, a gunshot was heard through the twilight sky and the man was dead. He had been court-martialled for desertion. Many badmouthed both his intended cowardice and the men who swiftly put him down. If there was one positive, in the crown's understanding, his example made it clear that abandoning one's duty was intolerable.

Then it faded away. The story wasn't important by day two. No one cared or they just had something else to eat up. Empathy dried up. There was no burial ceremony, as the only closure came to the memory of his desecrated name. Even Rhys, with guilt on his sleeve, tried his hardest to just sit aside the conversations. It was just another report to write.

Rhys was never quite sure as to why Dynis deserted the army, at least during that week. Another able, and capable, body had been taken away by madness. And the thing that hurt Rhys the most was how indifferent he was to the tragedy, as if he initially never knew the man. The calamity came from not the man's death, but the fact he had to convince himself that something terrible had just happened.

Out of thought, he toured the outside. He'd left his helmet somewhere else, hiding that colourless rose from the storm of the winter's approach.

"Staff Sergeant!" Energy burst into the scene when two soft, hands clad in woollen gloves latched onto his left arm. Ella had stalked up on him without as much of a squeal.

"Hey, you okay?" He didn't want to think of himself. He ignored such self-reflection and felt a little pulsation in his chest as he saw her locked to his side.

As the sky had lost its colour, and that the world had surrendered itself to mediocrity and misery, Ella's aura outshone the misfortunes she'd bordered herself with. The warmth and tenderness of her sacramental figure, a blossom in a tree engulfed in flames, he simply felt calm by her sight alone. He began to assume that everything would be okay as long as they stared at one another.

"Sabrina is open to a visit!" Unrestful, her smile spread an infection of dopamine through her fragile superior. The ecstasy of her impatience disconnected him from the troubles of the modern day. It was a phenomenon, a feeling so enticing that Rhys began to understand why he looked to her with such awe. She was the gateway to a fantasy world of perfection. "Gwen came by the warehouse earlier and just told me they're willing to let see her someone once, but I asked her if you could come too."

"Wait, really?" He perked up blissfully. "I can't imagine…how lonely she'd have been."

"Well come on, then! Let's not keep her waiting!" She loosened her grip and turned, quickly making her way ahead toward the nearby medical station. Rhys watched as she gracefully moved with an innocent, energetic persistence.

Perhaps, he thought, there would be a day that enhanced itself with boundless memory. It took him back to the summer, where he and Sabrina had stood aside, together, and watched Ella observe the sunbathed fields. He didn't care if nothing happened that day. Its tranquillity had given him a temporary paradise. He yearned for something like that day, where there was no war to worry about, where death wasn't a concern, or when they could carry hearts in their hands, instead of guns. And to think, a woman so shaken and brutalised by the war as Sabrina had deserved that more than he did. She needed that bliss. Turmoil could finally take another rest.

A spurt of tempo highlighted the rhythm of gladness in his heart. He waltzed through the glen of sporadic joy. From what little they'd heard about her progress, sectioned off by one-line summaries of her condition, to then see her with their own eyes hit an itch left unscratched for weeks. A woman, flipping between consciousness, alone in a room full of the damaged.

The gates to the facility were open, presenting eerie corridors lit by flashing bulbs. Frost scathed the edges of its windows. Inside, each breath was infused with a cloud of condensation. As soon as Rhys had stepped within, the atmosphere thinned and the air became hardly breathable. That initial rush of pleasure had been poisoned when he felt the chill of the hallways, the distant and faint cries of the pained soldiers wronged by their enemies. Ella's smile shrivelled up once she saw how gloomy it was on the interior. She worried for her sister, yet the desire to see her still kept her head where she wanted it – high up.

Rhys sucked in the pessimism once his teeth began to chatter. He let his imagination run feral. Portraits of Sabrina rotting away her personality, livelihood and existence and dispersing her into carrion…

Mild. The air tasted flavourless. They stepped down the wide corridors, where medical staff traversed between rooms with needles and bandages in their clutches. The critical wards: where

293

those awaiting their trial by the gods sat in spring beds, yielding the judgement against them. Every door they passed held a different performance. Men cried at their hopelessness. Women jolted at the nightmarish replays of their final living hour. The environment of the building was drastically different to any other part of the base. And all that time, since the Battle for Haria, and bolstered by the recent defence of the Western Seaboard, Mullackaye handled the mortally wounded beneath fluorescent medical lamps. Rhys' inner sickness gradually came back. The ache in his forehead returned and the desire to curl back into his hideaway office stabbed into his chest. But Ella persisted forward, inconsiderate of the surroundings around her. All she cared about, at least in that minute, was facing her sister and hearing her words of care.

And there, they arrived. Ward 3:21. It was a quiet room. Through the door, only the clatter of vials murmured from within. Ella held her place outside, turning back to Rhys. He stood close to her, and he reached out and wrapped his fingers around her arm.

"Are you going to be okay?" Why did she ask him that? Did she ask him it, or did he imagine her saying that? He shook his head and rubbed his eyes, warming himself up to the reality that may have laid within. Sabrina *was* alive. She would be as soon as they walked in there. He needed to believe that and to embrace her brightness again. For the sake of his sanity, he told himself he needed her.

Ella went in first; Rhys tailed her with his hand still loosely on her arm. Both looked around the large and relatively empty ward. A few dividers between beds were left open. And at the end, near the fogged and mould-ridden windows, a figure lay hidden. Ella looked at Rhys, and he looked back at her. Their lungs were clasped shut. Something felt wrong. It was in the air. Maybe she didn't realise it, but Rhys surely did. Together, they inched toward where Sabrina was sat. Before his eyes fell upon the woman who'd carried his mind forward, his own voice mumbled in his head: she deserves the bliss he wanted.

A lot can happen in a few seconds. In but an instant, shocks between synapses can cross the bridges of the nervous system. Natural reactions can find issues around them at that instantaneous glance, and a realisation of something wrong can work upon instinct. It was an inborn reaction, a desire to keep oneself alive and well. When faced with the aftermath of a friend's horrific trauma, that very instinct had told him to immediately turn away, to keep his own mind pure of the corrupted bliss he had painted of her, because when his eyes fell upon Sabrina, he didn't see her. He saw someone else entirely.

A large glass container had been placed atop of her burning cheeriness, and the flame she warmed others with had deoxidised. No longer dressed in a military fatigue, she sat upright against the wall, the mattress holding her leg in place. He saw her emptiness. At first, she didn't even look up or realise they'd arrived. Her stare was fixated to what wasn't there.

Still clad in bandages and wraps, the injury Rhys had once seen was still there. Of course it would be – why wouldn't it be, he asked himself. There was no miraculous regrowth of lost limbs. And Sabrina couldn't keep her eyes off of it. Her hand was extended toward it, only to fall short of the stub she called her own leg.

Rhys soon noticed that there wasn't an emptiness to her. She wasn't like him, where the emotions were ripped from his soul and scattered across a heartless wasteland. No, she was filled with emotion, and only one. Sabrina was horrified; at what she had become, at what had happened to her, at where she was and at the spectral spike that infused pain into her body.

"Sabrina!" Ella lunged forward, just barely holding back from a full-on charge. She was instantly by her side with her arms lovingly wrapped around her. Again, Sabrina hadn't quite noticed straight away and she hesitated before looking up from her dishevelled state.

"E-...Ella?" And as if time had completed its medication, she spoke. Hearing her name caused the younger sibling to unleash a flood of tears and she buried her face into Sabrina's shoulder, whispering sweet innocence.

"I'm so sorry, they wouldn't let me in to see you. I've thought about you every day and I've been so worried and terrified! I'm just so happy to see you're okay-"

"Okay?" She responded with a dismal reach into the unknown depths of her fear. "That's...new..."

And as the words left her chiselled lips, the lights of the ward withered away. A cloud of ash encompassed Rhys as he continued to stare at the woman who laid without a hint of happiness in her soul. His heart sank. His lungs filled with the gas. His stomach twisted and downed mysterious toxins.

"Why are you here?" She couldn't speak beyond a croaked mumble, her voice damaged by hours of agonised screaming. Ella loosened her hug and tried to compose herself.

"To see you! I've missed you; we all have! I wouldn't go another day without having you if the world would let me." Her stream of tears continued, dampening both her cheeks and Sabrina's. "I was scared I'd lose you."

"Oh…"

Rhys stepped back. The noise of his boot caught her attention, and she slowly faced him. His lungs stopped working. He couldn't tell what her eyes were saying to him, as her words spoke nothing but of hopelessness. Meanwhile, he locked his gaze with hers and moved a little closer. The fog between them thickened. A constraint against his chest crushed his inadequate confidence.

"Hey…"

"Hi…"

Neither could read one another's lips. The two who depended on her light only saw a bleak shade. Like an old lighthouse, she had become derelict, and that her purpose had long surpassed its effectiveness. Times changed. Her guiding shimmer had died out, whilst Ella and Rhys' hopes had been shipwrecked.

Two strangers continued to embed their stares deep into one another's – all in an intense, yet horrified penetration of ones' souls. With machetes and torches, they scouted the lost jungles to their minds, to their beauties, and found nothing but cryptic emptiness. The worst thing Rhys realised was that they were then strangers.

"Can I talk to you two separately?" Her drones were slow. Rhys nodded, and he willingly dragged himself out the room first, leaving Ella to have her own privacy. Just beyond the doorway was a small wooden chair. He planted himself within it and buried his face into his hands.

For an hour, his throat remained clasped shut. There was a pain unlike any other, like he'd actually been shot in the thorax. It transcribed his agony into nervous anxiety. A lightness struck his skull and the nauseous spindle churned his body. He barely eavesdropped their conversation. He didn't want to hear it. He didn't want to hear her.

Why did he feel so sick seeing the woman he had cherished so much? Because of pity, or because of anger? Had it caused him to hate the Ferusians a little more? They were the ones that took her out of her body and replaced it with a dying husk. Surely, they were to blame.

However, it wasn't satisfactory to lay the faults on them. It was all too easy. Too obvious, even. A man who built his existence on hating himself would not suffice labelling the might of the suffering she endured as Ferusian. There were two parties in war, and both could be equally as guilty to him, or as innocent as the other. It was as war was, and there was no moralising the endless slaughter. She was in the wrong place at the wrong time, at the wrong minute. An instant, irreversible act had assassinated who she was without giving her the favour of killing the rest.

The sickness continued, and it plagued his body, whilst he waited for his chance to hear her talk. Intermittently, Ella bawled to herself, though her words remained indiscernible at their distance apart.

He was determined to take his focus elsewhere and he, regrettably, read his thoughts in silence. Rhys tried to think of home, yet the faces of his parents were blank. A nearby window continued to be showered in snow; he turned his eyes to the spectacle. The patters, much gentler than that of rain, were sweet, calming even. Shamefully, however, they were drowned out by the pained disconnection of two hearts. And whilst he informed himself that it was just an emotional reunion, Sabrina barely felt the same woman. It wasn't a reintegration. Instead, it was an introduction to an entirely different host. Birthed from pain, raised in agony and matured in dejection.

At the strike of the morning clock's chime, Ella emerged from the ward. Cheeks smothered in tears were still moist. She walked over to Rhys and gifted him a soft, yet shaky, smile. And as he stood up, to get ready to take his place beside Sabrina, Ella gave him a tightened hug. It wasn't anything like the last time they'd embraced one another. That time, there was weakness to her arms, a coarseness to her grip. The tenderness was shallow.

Wholeheartedly, Rhys welcomed the embrace regardless. She still gave him a comfort he couldn't replicate anywhere else, even when torn down by her own emotions. It wasn't exciting, or fantastical. The sad part, for him, was that it was just nice enough to make him feel something familiar.

Time's fleeting capacity swept by. They had to separate at some point. When they pulled apart, she wiped her eyes dry with her knuckles and sat down in the chair he'd left for her. Neither exchanged any briefs or greetings.

Rhys scrutinised the ward's entrance. A breeze slithered out and ungracefully slipped by his face. It brought a chill, and not one from the seasonal shift. He wasn't scared to face Sabrina – he told himself that. Seeing her had been a part of his wishes for weeks; what he feared was seeing the imposter in her place.

He returned and made his way to her bedside. Beside her, the aura that once flourished from her presence had been suppressed and even neutered. Polarised faces turned to one another and their eyes met yet again. Once upon a time, Rhys would fall into her stare willingly with love and attention, where his awe transported him to another world of blossoms and buds. Hidden within her black pupils was a light show, powered by a generator of intimacy. As an explorer, he'd lose himself in wherever her eyes took him. Though, as all lights and stars eventually do, she'd been extinguished. Her sate frittered away. Her duty had gambled her livelihood, her persona and her true form with excruciating stakes.

"Did she say anything?" Faint – that's how he described her. Her skin, her complexion and her voice, all disrupted in glimmer. Rhys shook his head. "That's fine then."

Sabrina looked away. He'd never seen her so quiet or irresponsive since...

Rewind. A dark hour. The night hung low. Clouds blocked out the light. The soil surrounded them. Everywhere he or she looked, it was all the same. A disfigured field. Craters everywhere. Bodies buried in both rain and mud. The greater the darkness, the better it was. Twilight hid away the corpses, the limbs that missed torsos, the remains of bones and muscle. Torn flesh painted the ground, just below her leg. And when he found her, she shivered and squirmed, shaking to escape the man who came to rescue her. A feathered lip, tattered by bombs and shells, trembled in fright.

"I can't forget it, Rhys," she droned, "It – it hurt me so much."

"I can only imagine…"

"Yeah, you can." Her eyes greeted the walls and the windows and they fogged up just as they had with the fickle and demonised snow. And the awkwardness of her expression, the uncertainty of their connected voices, stuck blistering razors between them. She sank into the bed to lose her barely straightened composure, whilst her leg disappeared beneath the blankets. "What have you been doing?"

"Whatever the brass has told me to do. Forms, patrols, sentry duties. I finally got the letters done."

"What letters?"

"The ones for the families." He paused. He'd focused on his twiddling thumbs upon his lap. Long nights. A hundred drafts. What went from a personalised message for the kin of the deceased soon transformed into a standardised set of tragic exposition. Condolences this and hero that. "Well, the ones I could. There was no one to write for Ryan's, I'm not allowed information on Christopher and-"

"Stop, please."

"Oh – sorry." He noticed that her eyes produced a weakened glare; from the surface to the core, her eyes dug through the world and stopped for nothing, until they had reached a thousand miles. An immobilised Sabrina pulled her hands towards her biceps and she hugged herself.

A certain jitter decreed her body as she leapt into the occasional ticks on her lips. She blinked sporadically to force her eyes open. Rhys knew that she was afraid to close them, lest the wilting visions of a blood-soaked yesterday consumed her.

"Which one of us is at fault?" Past the colourless glass, the mists of an impure winter cloaked the world. Alone in the ward, without a nurse or medical officer in sight, their capsule took them through a familiar blank world. Rhys heeded her words with regret. She spoke no differently to how he thought. A collapse into nihilism held dangerous paths for men and women who were armed. "Is it us?"

"At fault for what?" Rhys dared her with a feeble mutter, moving a hand toward her own. He didn't pry it from her self-embrace, so he just rested it atop, unwilling to dictate her.

"For everything. This and that, death and more death. Did we do something wrong?" She began, her eyes forever burying itself into the distant oblivion. "Is it the Queen? The monarchs? Or the Ferusians…are they like us?"

"We shouldn't dwell on it."

"Why not? You always did." The jab struck him with a piercing slash, paralysing him in place. Her tone, whilst embedded with sorrow, was sprinkled with spite. Disillusioned spite. Regretful anger. "Because we go through this every month, some tragedy happens and we just go on to the next one. Why the fuck do we deserve this?"

"We don't, Sabrina. *You* don't."

"Then why does it happen?"

"Because…I don't know. Sab', if I had the answers-"

"You'd be – you'd be dead, like me. Maybe…unwilling to live in a world like this? On your own accord…"

His heart dislocated from his chest and burst out into the wilds. An ache unlike any other ridiculed his weakness and it ferally shredded apart the timeless honesty she threw at him. In darkened hours, the thought of the act crossed paths with him when the nightmares grew fiendish, deceptive of the nihilistic authenticity of life's greatest absence – meaning.

Who would choose to live in a world where clubs were used to cave men's skulls in, for wages or duty, or where survival meant loading a bullet into a rifle and to line it up against another's head? Ideology tore apart every innocent aspect of life he'd once known. The world of adults, of older yet misguided individuals in positions of rulership, had been a direct enemy to the innocence of his childly irrelevance. And when the opposing forces, the beliefs of humanity's next plunge into evolution, came down to who had the greatest aim, or the strongest swinging arm, or even the best machine, then their beliefs meant nothing. Right was never right and wrong was never wrong. A world of grey blankets, all placed atop of one another, suffocated those who tempted themselves with its warmth.

Sabrina knew Rhys couldn't carry the confidence it took to be alive and well. And despite this, he was still there. He hadn't taken a knife to his neck or cleaned the barrel of his rifle with his mouth; no, he was still there. He was still kicking, regardless if he struggled. When the dreadnought bombarded the face of Farhawl, he ran and shielded himself. He spoke to people. He learned to admire and to adore. And most of all, he tried.

And why? The answer felt all the too obvious. Rhys, much alike all good men, was afraid. He was scared, petrified, but never paralysed with absolute fear. It stopped him from plummeting into death's fingers. It wouldn't be a release and he feared it. Life was all he had, even if it was fucked beyond all repair. Leaving it meant abandoning the people beside him. That alone was terrifying enough.

Fear alone had kept him alive. It wasn't that he agreed with it at all, but in that ward, before Sabrina's judgement, that was just how life was for him.

"If I didn't deserve this, then who did?" Her eyes began to moisten with the release of her pained rant. "Rhys, we've been fighting for people to go through what we do. If we don't deserve it, then who does? Do the people who did this to me deserve anything ten times worse?"

She uncloaked her leg and stared at it with all the loathe caught as a twinkle in her eye. Her ferocious tone forced Rhys to follow her to the stub, the missing piece to her whole. For her eternity, she had to live with that: a physical reminder that she had been ripped apart by the jaws of war.

"How can I protect Ella like this? How can I be there for anyone when I've had my fucking leg-"

"Sabrina, please-" Rhys tried to urge her back to her calmed acceptance, yet she charged forward with a hand reaching out and she grabbed onto his wrist. Her grip was extremely tight.

"I can't ignore this, Rhys. I can't ignore any of this. It's there, right in front of me, below my knee. Look at it! Why do I have to accept that this is will be my everything now?" Cast to a pot of incensed iron, her turmoil inflamed into a heavy wildfire. Her expression was erratic and her eyes were locked onto the stump. Her barbed fingers only tightened around Rhys' wrist like handcuffs. An intrinsic lust for a cooperative mind forced her to control him, to then keep him on her side. "How can I protect the people I need to? How can I tend to them at any moment? In what world can I be there for my own fucking sister when those monsters try to stab her, rape her or kill her? What the fuck am I going to do!?"

Rhys was utterly stunned. Her quiet fury fluctuated an emotional distaste throughout the ward. The flame from her lips castigated the silence of the room. She bellowed to melt the winter around them. Such anger – such tarnish.

"Maybe-"

"No. You don't get it, do you? You don't have any siblings. You don't have a promise to save them. Our fucking home – everything we had as – as children, was all burnt to the ground and she – right there – watched our parents go up in bloody flames. And the whole world just fucking walked past her, you know?" Every word became more enunciated as she preyed upon with the thistle of her tongue with her teeth. She'd nearly bitten it off. And yet, she spoke with a degree of control over her volume, as she knew full well Ella was just outside. "My own sister, my kin, a small barely adolescent child, sat on the pavement crying her eyes out…it – it hurt so fucking much. All the people, those who came to extinguish it all, just – ignored her tears. But I didn't. I never did. I told her I'd be there for her, in every step of her life. Do you even know what it's like to break your own promise?"

There were many ways in which Rhys could've responded. So many options, all the charm or spite in the world at the tip of his tongue; yet he said nothing.

Rhys was trapped back in limbo. Her words tore at him and pecked away at his skin as ravens had to corpses. His dishonesty, however, was with himself. Truth be told, he could have named several times that he'd promised himself to keep his squad – the innocents of tomorrow and criminals of today – alive. He remembered promising to Ella that he'd save Sabrina.

"Why did you save me?" She asked.

"I…" He hesitated, stumped by her aggressiveness.

"Why couldn't you have just left me out there? Why did Gwen have to tell you where I was when…when I told her to let me die?"

"Don't say that."

"I could've walked amongst the stars, and told my own parents how proud of Ella I was myself, as a clean woman with no hate to her name, and yet you dragged me back to this fucking nightmare…"

A gust of wind whistled through the small cracks in the walls. The temperature dropped and she curled back under the blanket. Her eyes were wet and red whilst her face was rinsed by a frozen paleness. Her weeps were more distinguished that time around. Not a word. She could barely form a sentence. She was a whimpered child, coiled up against the warmth of a fabric, just like Ella always had been. Truly, they were sisters: bound by the same tears from different eyes.

He felt as if there were no appropriate way to retort her cruel reality. Riddled by guilt, tormented with her venomous tongue, he sat with his eyes to her cheek. They followed the trails of tears that navigated across her face. Soon, his eye moistened, though no tear left his lid.

"Sabrina…" He stammered out her name. It proved hopeless. She stayed in her ball of emotions and left him to hold back his own sorrow. "Please understand me…I came for – I came for you, and Ella. She needed you. She still does. I do too."

Eventually, her hand macerated from his wrist and fell back under the covers. And she cried. Oh, did the siren wail. Rhys tried to, as well, but by the width of a hair he withstood his need to cry. He couldn't think of any other day that had hurt like that hour did. No vision of death, corpses or fire had challenged it. There wasn't a stagnant face, an emotionless suppression of his own fear; he wanted to cry because it was all too much. It raised a question, analysing what evil would suffice: the instant death of a friend or the drawn-out decline of his crippled, decaying mind.

Vindication to the court of human sacrifice held Sabrina accountable for nothing. Except the jury didn't need evidence. All it took was the soul of a single innocent to pledge allegiance to the ordeal of war. Names, faces, races, sexualities or virtue mattered not. Sabrina opened her mouth to cry, nothing else. A bilingual shift – she'd become fluent in the most universal language of all: suffering.

The pitiless stump placed beneath her knee only showed her pain's glacial peak, for below the solemn tides stretched torture unseen to the outsider's view. And it went down for miles, to the core of the planet, to linger forever. Infused with the molten prime of her home, the abode of brutality, it gradually liquified her hopes and dreams. Aspirations traded in for blood, ambitions for shrapnel wounds and desires for fatality: a market built for the soldier.

"Listen," Rhys drew his final breath with an affectionate whisper, "I *will* protect Ella for you. We'll figure something out. And she'll protect us. When the war ends, we can give you something – a life elsewhere. I don't know what, but we'll find it. Okay? Together…"

Regardless of if she smiled ever again, whether the sun shined or the snow piled up, he pledged to never see that promise go unfulfilled. But his tears never stopped begging to be released – for as she put it herself: "*Did he even know what it was like to break his own promise?*"

Chapter 23

The Foreigner

Alas, the winter barked its torturous tone. The enthralled eyes at the spectacle of snow turned to glares of fret, and the unease in the cold's bite nested in everyone's skin. Those stormy days were encored by blizzardy nights, only to be followed up by an immeasurable whiteout in the early hours. Whetstones of ice sharpened the air and her throat ached with its razor-like lesion whenever she inhaled. The freshness of the autumn downpour had been wiped clean by the daylight eraser – time.

All across Mullackaye – and the acres of land within its spanned walls – the crystal carpet brought the spectrum of summertime colouration to its knees. The remaining gamut of the white winter, the olive uniforms and the grey architecture beheld the dystopian old age, and it casted a shadow reminiscent of the medieval aeon. The end of the year had approached them and with it came the snarl of nature's lupus.

Christa faintly drifted through the hallways of the logistical den she'd hauled small crates to. On her way, she passed soldiers talking amongst their brothers and sisters or rivals and heroes in arms. Back outside, an inhumane stillness beset the world. Yet inside, where warmth was just a few degrees above sub-zero, she heard the many characters of the militia's men. She noticed the lacking presence of the regulars. Many of those professionals had been sent out to fight, professionally of course, in the distant fields, whilst the 54th Defensive Regiment served their original purpose – as a garrison force.

She heard the livelihood in their chinwags. The sickly jokes and the banters between them were in every corridor – for the comedy club was the only source of entertainment that the many misguided had. Their coarse words preceded hearty chuckles.

"You 'eard the difference between a '*Syndie*' and a roach?"

"Nah, mate?"

"Neither 'ave I!"

Albeit their creativity lacked, she thought, there was a sort of sickening joy to back-and-forth nature of their jives and jokes. She would've lied if she had denied the tasteless smirk of her own.

She, however, could not shake the sensation that she had; it was as if she had stepped into another realm, where she desperately attempted to imitate the community around her. The crown's people spoke with such looseness or vulgarity that it did quite charm her, yet she came across only as a braindead facsimile by comparison. Her past life's days in courtly orders and of starkened etiquette did mismatch the tiresome nature of the people.

"Bower's on the bottle again, as you'd expect." One said.

"Toss piece could drink our whole rations if he isn't careful." Another chuckled.

"Too right, too right." A third affirmed.

The voices came and went as she traversed through the narrow lanes of the warehouse. She wasn't quite sure of where she had to go. The day had been quite unkind to her, with six hours of a guardsman's duty on the perimeter, to which she, as expected, saw nothing but a frosted bleakness from sky to soil. And then she searched for someone. Not anyone in particular, but rather anyone that she recognised. Of course, she was lonesome in her efforts to remain unnoticed.

Eventually, she found herself in the main headquarters of the 54th, a large warehouse with walkers littering the central hall. She briskly wandered to the 4th Platoon's subsection on the building's side avenues, underneath her company's half of the building, and she closed the door behind her. And then, a deafly silence came.

She darted her eyes between the many rooms and labels above her. Her legs were still as she mindlessly waited for something to happen. And, as it turned out, just down the corridor did a head poke out. A scruffy man with barely any age left in his skin scanned either direction, eventually taking notice of the dumbstruck woman.

"You lookin' for something, love?" He wasted no time and immediately quizzed Christa – the flattery of his crooked tooth deflected from her at an instant.

"Are there any members of Squad 2 around?"

He then let out a vehement cough into his sleeve. She hadn't budged where he wanted her to go, and it took him a few seconds to get any answer out. As she waited, patiently, she eyed the sofas and seats by the windows. A man and a woman played cards with one another, but they only had half a deck between them.

"Yeah," he finally spluttered out, "just down the hall. Few of them are in. Door on the right." His mind trailed away for a second, when suddenly he pulled it back in with a sudden huff. "The door says *Squad 2*, just go in that one."

He then disappeared back into his room and shut the door behind him. So, left otherwise as a silent audience to the world's dullest game of blackjack, she began the journey down the short, slender hallway, all whilst her mind went off on its own expedition.

In all honesty, she wanted to be someone. A total covert life made her as inadequate as the forgotten names of days gone past. For all they knew, Princess Lylith Redgrine was either dead or captured, and she decided to use that as justification to open up and create a character of her own.

She still saw her dead-name in the newspapers that were scattered across the base. In all her life, she never expected to look at her once-self and to have felt pity. She wasn't *her* anymore. No, Christa told herself that she never was her. Still, she asked about Lylith a few times. What had her mother been doing? How was Lylith's family? How was Christa's family? To think that, by all technicalities, one Mr Lee could have registered as her father and mother – for he was the one who birthed the legal identity she donned.

Before she could have delved into her own identity crisis, the door bumped into her. Well, she walked into it actually, but that was besides the point. She readjusted herself and pressed her hands against its roughened, chipped body and carefully pushed it open. The doorknob wasn't even necessary as it hung just barely by its hinges.

Mutters were settled below at the bottom of the descent, adorned by a flicker of a fluorescent bulb. To not suck up her hesitance, she strode down the steps thoughtlessly and barely gave her attention to the heavy creaks of each stair.

Bottom step. Around the thin-wall corner of the staircase was the scarcely lit table, as were those sat around it. She first caught glimpse of a short man, glasses pressed against his nose, beside a great hulk of a soldier. On the latter's side, a smaller, far frailer girl seemed lost in her own thoughts. Once the bottom step let out its weary cry, bending underneath the weight of her kit, their eyes turned to her.

Mystical. A ghostly drift – she hovered inside the room and loitered at the bottom step. Quickly, she read the chamber and fixed her stance to better accommodate for its silent friction. Her gut tightened. Had they recognised her?

Their bequeathed gazes treated her like what she was: an outsider. A foreigner not by nation, but by class, experiences and understanding. Strangely enough, whilst they looked upon her body with friendliness at the tiller, they sailed on winds of social alienation.

"Can I help you?" The shorter man firs said, all whilst he remained in his hickory chair. She noticed that, on his shoulders, were the all-important rank slides of an NCO. From there, it was only a matter of eased deduction.

"Corporal Aviadro, I'm guessing?"

"Ooo, hear that, guys? I'm famous now, aren't I?" He plastered a shit-eating grin on his mug without so much of a care for professionalism. It wasn't what she expected but as far as things went in the militia, she wasn't sure what she expected at all. "Something wrong?"

"Oh, no." She meandered over carefully, stepping at a tortoise's pace. She then realised that he was still waiting for an answer, so she cleared her throat and stopped at the table's edge. "Uhm, I came to introduce myself. I haven't really gotten to meet any of you yet. Private Lodvtz."

Mateo brightened up a little, and he rose up to lean over with an extended hand. The two others kept quiet in their seats.

"Ah – thought we'd never get to meet you. Proper myth you were, mate." And as he smiled, she too felt the cheek of her character shed light on itself.

"I am something of a mystical person."

Their hands met in the middle and they locked together with a bountiful amount strength, seemingly from nowhere. Their delicacy wasn't the Corporal's way of approach. Though, she

308

could've easily picked up on that fact just by the scruffiness of his appearance.

The larger man, with arms folded across his chest, lifted a single hand to statically wave to her.

"Private Verdana." He stated with a strong, though quiet, brusqueness. With the same free hand, he pointed to the far younger girl by his side, someone who'd only just caught the eye of Christa. "And this is Private Evelyn."

"Nice to meet you both, too." She smiled when Evelyn lifted her colourful eyes from her paper sheet and she beamed back at her with a gentle nervousness.

"Take a seat. One of the guys just went out to get us some water."

And she did. Within seconds she had integrated herself into the party and she sat beside the Corporal. It took a small amount of effort to reignite the conversation she'd interrupted, but soon the minutes were flying by and the day seemed a little cosier than its predecessors had.

She mainly kept quiet and listened to what they had to say. It was menial stuff at first. Daily happenings and tripe only somewhat interesting to those who understood the base's archetypal culture. There was the complaining about lieutenant this and captain that. Like a gallop of hooves, the topics came in steady beats. They discussed the beginning of the winter like there were simple villagers; small talk seemed to be the best way to destabilise the worldly fixation on their larger-than-life conflict.

During their conversation, Christa found herself flashing glances at Evelyn time and time again. She barely chimed in or piped up, entranced and mesmerised in her personal sketches. Christa couldn't quite see them from her side of the table, but the colourless line art held no clear thematic style, at least as much as she could tell. Twirling pencil strokes and brutalist straight lines crossed over one another, making for sight of awe. She was experimenting with her graphite tool. Her vision was unclear and colourless, though Christa placed her bets on a lack of art resources for that.

"-and I'm not really sure, mate, if this snow will be any better than before." Mateo whined.

"Bold of you to hope at all that we'll get a Hail Sunar, of any kind, any minute soon." Oslo pressed his back into his chair and drifted his eyes to the decayed ceiling. "How'd Ferusia turn up a deal with nature like this?"

"Nah, it fucks with them too, so that's a bonus. At least we have a building with heating." Oslo turned and gave him a doubtful look. "Okay, a building with warmth." Still the questionable gaze. "Okay, a building."

"Whatever, mate."

Injured by hours of displaced sleep, he let out a terrific yawn. His expression of fatigue was interrupted by the door swinging back open and the flurry of rapid steps that descended down the stairs.

And in came another man; he was one as unrecognisable as the triage Christa had stumbled upon. Dangled before his face were several bottles of unmarked liquids.

"Sorry, friends. There were problems with the taps and stuff and I couldn't be bothered to walk to another part of the base." The Redussian strode forward and placed the bottles down at its centre. "Found these though so all's not lost."

Unlike some of her peers, Christa hadn't given much thought to his national origins. A faint memory from another time reminded her of many immigration situations between Kelan and Redus, and so the sight was barely a surprise for her compared to that of the real working-class soldier.

The bottles clattered against each other and chimed without rhythm. Mateo rushed for the first taste and snatched one, but failed to get past the bottle cap. Christa, still dressed in her patrol fatigues, reached for her belt and drew out a small blade for him to use.

"Cheers, m'dears." Despite her months out of the capital, the loose tones of the fighting men and women never failed to make her day. She smiled silently whilst Mateo took the knife and popped the bottle lid off, doing the same for the others. "Ooh~ smells strong."

Evelyn took her own bottle, before Oslo snatched it from her hands and took a whiff of its odourless contents. His face scrunched up as he took a quick sip. Suddenly, he gave a harsh snap at the third man.

"Tyran, this is liquor, isn't it?"

"Vodka, but we can pretend it is."

"Right. Well…cheers." He looked gently back at Evelyn, who in turn faced him. "Sorry, Eve'. Can't let you drink this."

"Ah, come on." Mateo started, already half a bottle in to his delight. "She's sixteen now, let the girl have a swig." The bitter scene of tasteless liquid sat on the edges of his lips as he called out with a mischievous grin.

"No."

"Come ooooon-"

"No." Oslo stood his ground, to which he reassured Evelyn with an honest smile. She seemed a little out of her comfort zone to comment on the situation, so she planted her eyes back into her drawing. "Not worth ending up on the beaten path of fools we're on."

Mateo didn't press on any further as he rolled his gaze back to Christa. His giddiness seemed natural, provocative of the constant torture that was their lives. And, whether it was unlike any other comrade he'd had, she found a strong admirability for his willingness to stay happy.

"Oh, yeah. This is Christa." Addressing the Redus man, he pointed out her rather alien accompaniment. "And this is Tyran."

"Out with the formality and ranks already?" Her smile brightened her dry and vapid taste in the liquid.

"I don't really care for that shit, and neither does Rhys."

"The Staff Sergeant, right?"

"Yep. Met him at all?"

"Only once or twice." She recalled Rhys' ominous cloud that hung over his head and the dreariness of his body as it dragged through fogged day. Along the path he took, stormy skies watched intently from grim overlooks. First impressions were everything, and all she took was that he was sour over the state of his existence. Whilst Mateo was the spice that improved the taste of a poor one's life, Rhys was its natural flavour.

"He's a great guy, don't get me wrong, but we haven't really seen him, casually, in weeks." Mateo began with a heartedly yawn. "Him and Ella, more specifically. But," he paused and grinned, "I know about them, mate."

"Well, they are concerned about Sabrina, more than any of us. And rightfully." Tyran took his seat at the table. In his eyes were the drawn lines of fatigue and the grime of a tankman's maintenance.

Finally, Christa had a small stake on the conversation. The elusive Staff Sergeant Hendricks, a man who was supposedly her valiant leader. Teachings from the court over military meritocracy felt contradictory to how Rhys looked and acted on their first encounter. The formation of the militia remained as enigmatic and stigmatised as she could ever have imagined.

"Is he a veteran, at all?" Out of the blue, Christa let her thoughts take flight through her lips.

"A veteran of farming, mate." Mateo laughed.

"Then why is he in charge of us? Shouldn't it be someone with a bit more – I don't know – bravado?"

"Calm down, missy, using the big words." Oslo backhanded his shoulder and corrected his manners for him. After a whispered back and forth, Mateo cleared his throat and answered it in earnest. "I guess because they were really desperate for people, I guess. We don't really know the reason why he was elected as a Staff Sergeant and, knowing him as a mate, I bet he doesn't either." Mateo's analysis did little to dispel the enigma. Rhys had the conundrum of power delegated to the oddly weaker man. "I really feel bad for him, y'know? Putting all that guilt on his shoulders."

She watched as he downed the rest of the bottle in two swigs. Times of misery beckoned for that unsavoury nourishment. Uncouth smells tickled her nostrils. It smelt of decay or vomit. She searched for a window, or any sort of ventilation, but found no such thing. They were more or less sat in a bunker, with one door to the outside world.

Secluded enough to be alone, the party let the silence of their drinks make way for the sultry presence of the winter's opening act.

Back at the group, however, the conversations soon started back up. Tyran muttered about mechanics and tanks for a short while, notifying it as his only time seeing Ella in the flesh. Mateo droned on the path of incomprehensible as he brought up existing stories that she'd missed the start of. And Oslo seemed lost in his bottle whilst he stared at the murky ceiling.

Christa got out of her seat and, by intrigue's drive, sauntered over to Evelyn, peering over her shoulder to study her artwork.

"Hey," she softly asked, "what're you sketching?"

"I don't know." Evelyn shrugged. She let her hand scout each corner of the page with the graphite touch. Indirect, yet fluent. Though unaware of where her pencil took her, they did so with an inherent confidence. "He told me to not prepare too much for future things – or I get disappointed."

Christa held her breath and lost her gaze to the hypnotic swirls of the pencil. She watched its withdrawn tenderness against the page. Seconds later, a hard-pressed line would break up the motions. It was architectural. She moved with purpose, despite her not knowing so. The foreigner couldn't quite explain why she enjoyed Evelyn's project so much. The innocence of her focus left her mindful of not the war but the normality of a life left behind. A time where flowers bloomed, instead of existing only on a sheet of paper.

It was a window to her mind, to the shallow naivety she'd rectified during her time of service. Christa didn't know her, but she felt as if she understood her through the language of sight. Every now and then, her hand twitched, or she'd lose the grip on her pencil, only to take a calm, and tranquil, breath and to start again.

"She was the one who carved Rhys' helmet with that rose." Oslo muttered. "Someone's gift to him."

"Were you at Haria?" Taking her chance, she inserted her query without much consideration for the conversation. Directed at Oslo, he gave her a stiff answer.

"Yeah, we were."

"How was it?" She knew the answer, she just wanted to hear him say the words.

"How was what?"

"The Battle? The fighting?"

"Have you not seen combat yet?"

"No?"

Oslo ran his fingers through his beard. He uncoiled its loops and scraggles, and then he turned back to Christa with a chained memory projected through his eyes – like flames reflected in a camera lens.

"How much do you want to know?" She stumbled at his first response. Then, she redefined her focus and mumbled.

"How much should I know?"

313

"Hell. It's no place for any man nor woman. I don't care if it's our nature, there just isn't something right about it." Oslo's demeanour poured out tributes to the cold reality he'd stemmed from. It was subtle. The change in his voice, expression and focus told her more than she'd bargained for. "It's best to talk about what it did to us, not how it was. Three of our squadmates are dead. Two transferred out of spite. One is missing. We have one in a stable yet life-changing condition and one cursed with the responsibility of bearing all the blame."

Unsure of what to say, Christa looked back to the table, to the standing four bottles perched aside one another. Had she never asked, the atmosphere would've remained as loose as ever. Though, in the pursuit of understanding those she came to fight alongside, she tempted the reality of war against her shining preconceptions. Her veil temporarily broke, and the kind, well-mannered voice peered its head.

"I'm…oh, my…I'm so sorry."

"Why?" Evelyn, rather unexpectedly, put her paper down to ask the obvious.

Why? Yeah…why? Why did she feel sorry? Was it for empathy, or was it for the responsibility she still held on that tight little collar around her neck? But it wasn't her responsibility, no. It was that of Lylith's. She was a relic, a deafened soul sent out to the endless void of memory. Yeah, that was it, she told herself internally. Christa felt as if it couldn't be her fault anymore. She was there with them, about to get into the thick of it and help save Kelan through trials and tribulations. The unsuitable optimism she had for the war kept her going. She saw an end where they obtained victory, where justice was given to her side. Ideology would not rule them and the accountability for the war would not be put on the innocents forced to take it while they were down. Thousands of voices cried for reparations to the violence that ensued. Across the nation people screamed and whimpered, with holes in their bodies and blood on their skin. Why did she feel sorry for them? It was because she was there to save them. Her complex had taken over. Under her breath, she cursed the Ferusian onslaught as barbaric. It was their fault to her, and she would put an end to it.

"It's just not fair to you or the fallen." Yeah…she decided to go with that one. It felt more honest, she thought.

314

How haunting it could be to lie to oneself. Was there shame in outcasting the truth of her character for hope and empathy?

In another world, discrete from the dreamland of handcrafted diamonds, Lylith looked at her and cried out for a bit of help.

They went back to their usual conversation. And though she barely noticed it, her mind unobtrusively left its final message to the people and honour she'd left behind.

"I'm sorry, mother. Forgive me tomorrow."

Chapter 24

Ad Victorium!

"*F*ight hard enough and you will taste defeat, even in victory. It's such a stupid phrase, that even I, as a Major, cannot take seriously, but I must.

I cannot lie to my men, nor to those who choose to raise their arms for causes of their own calibre. Standing before us are the brutes of troubled times. They are neither Kelan nor Ferusian. These sights of war have no nationality, ethnicity, gender, or any identifiable physiques. What we will lose is our confidence and ourselves – come the end of the day, our own goals will consume us in these violent settings. We will lose a lot of our own in these coming days. I know it. We have many young soldiers at our disposal and I hate writing letters to their families.

Family – a greater body and community that exhibits the state of the unions. We are a collective. We suffer at the same time, just as we prosper. In this war, we are to all take the hit for our brothers and sisters, mothers and sons, to spread the values of the working unions to the doorsteps of foreign people. I don't quite know if I like what we do anymore. I can't tell the men that, in case they tell a Commissar.

These pages are just ramblings, aren't they? I write as I speak, to myself or to someone else. No one will read this. But I like writing like it. It means that in the off-chance a soul finds my ramblings on my bullet-riddled corpse someday, I'd still seem to have a lick of human on my lips. Maybe, though, I just haven't fought hard enough to lose that part of me yet."

He was forced out of his literary world when another person's hands clipped onto his shoulder. He paused, folded the paper up

316

and then propped it back into his jacket. Behind him was the firm hand that latched to his shirt's epilates. Westra, again.

"I won't even ask, don't worry." She gave him what seemed like a friendly smile. She had a lost motherly blaze in her eyes, for whatever reason, that had been obstructed by a thousand miles of ash and smoke. The spirit of her morning smile, however, had been excelled by the critical countdown to her next step forward.

"What is it now?" Schottenstein wiped his face with his sleeve and took a short look around him. "Is it nearly time?"

"Yep." She nonchalantly whistled between her words and withdrew her hands, burying them into her pockets. All up and spirited, she continued her eagerness as it was. "19th Armoured Battalion is going to join us on this one. High Command granted us all manners of support. Planes, artillery, maybe a Sky Carrier if we're lucky."

"And that's what you came to tell me?"

"Always so combative, aren't you?" Her teasing manner fell flat against his crude judgement. "Was just striking up a conversation. Nothing wrong with that, is there?"

"Right…"

"And we've been doing exemplary work, I'll say. Fucked up so much and now look where we are! The road to Mullackaye! Ooh, how many history books do you think your name will be printed in?" As she stood, giddy and proud of her approach to exoneration, Schottenstein scrunched his detest for her unrivalled polarisation and relaxed his mind. Just then, the sky was littered with a fresh shower of ice and snow. "If we're swift enough, we'll catch the Burno siege in no time."

"Great…first rain, now snow. How the fuck are we supposed to work in conditions like these?" He hopelessly asked as he deflected her own ramblings.

"By fighting hard."

"Do you think I don't, Miss Westra?"

"*Major*. And no, but you always look like you're about to turn around to walk away." She prodded him with her usual stale, yet effective, provocation and he rolled his eyes away from her. In his hand was his tin flask, and he lifted the lid to his blue lips.

"Would that honestly be the worst thing I could do?" An iced stream of his day-old brew trickled down his throat. "Besides, you'd know about turncoating."

"You know, if you tried hard enough, you could be the littlest bit charming. Or does being a cunt pay up more?" Her fuse was short lived as Schottenstein let out a discrete titter.

"You're impossible to figure out."

"Do you find it amusing?"

"No, I find it intimidating."

With the acrimonious ails of the seasonal storm quivering the world as they spoke, Schottenstein stretched in his seat and took to his feet, only to wander back out into the snow. He'd wrapped a thin woollen headdress around his skull, leaving only his eyes, nose and mouth exposed to the elements. Outside, crowded gatherings of huddled soldiers waited in the cold for the order to move.

They'd left behind Haria as many of them had found it: a prototype of cultural, geographic and military extinction. And once the Haria line had been pierced, additional landing points were secured on unscathed terrain. Fleets of walkers, tanks and infantrymen had arrived by sea, and the occupation of at least 900,000 troops had soon filled up the main line of the South-Western Army, with a further million on either flanks.

Battles had erupted all across Kelan's northern regions. In Haria's collapse, forgotten towns became areas of strict contest. The bloodshed was beyond clean, though that went without saying and the results varied across the front. Victories and defeats came to either side en masse. Urban hotspots turned into vital warzones. Assaults that challenged the expectations of mobile, mass warfare had then blistered Farhawl's surface in a blaze of ash. The dreadnoughts and fighter planes intercepted one another in high-stake duels above the clouds. Walkers clashed on the horizons of morning sunrise whilst infantry squads engaged in brutal man-to-man showdowns. At the time that the snow had begun to fall, nearly 4,000,000 Ferusian soldiers had been deployed, with countless casualties across the board. The war machine had been kicked into overdrive, and an all-or-nothing attitude overcame either side's adrenaline reserves.

He waded on through the snow. Schottenstein knew that their next objective was to be another sluggish run through the grime. Fort Mullackaye. The march to the western plains had already proven itself as cumbersome and relentlessly tiresome.

318

Their trucks and motorised logistics had found themselves ambushed on the regular and walkers fended off small battalions on their own. Kelan blended its conventional fighting force with officially adopted doctrines of squad-autonomous guerrilla insertion strikes. Though the Major's company had been sparred much of the brunt, the burden had left several without winter clothing or appropriate ration supplies.

"Weather is surely shit." Westra caught up to him, with her hands still tucked into her bottomless sleeves. He wasn't sure why she persistently followed him.

"If there's really a god then he's definitely a Kelan troop." He began, then he faced her. "The other officer's not giving you the time of day?"

"Well Captain Claus called me a *whore of war* – can you believe that? Anyway, the others don't seem any better than you."

"Charmed." He shunted her off. "Now, what about moving out?"

"Colonel Strauss wanted to say something before we haul off." She tucked her hands into her pockets. Her firearm hung loose around her back by its sling.

"How far away are we?"

"Hundred or so miles, maybe?"

"A few days' journey, if the weather holds up."

A hundred thousand rows of teeth chattered against themselves with their hosts' faces buried into thin headscarves. The mobile force had been at a standstill on the edge of their last area of operation: a relatively quiet and empty village by the name of Charneston, left unturned by the two sides preserving its shelter. Whilst Schottenstein wandered through the obscured masses, he passed the final few Kelan soldiers being tossed into a crudely dug mass grave – it housed around fifty of the settlement's defiant defenders.

Their opponents hadn't been pushovers. Too many had placed themselves in dire circumstances to protect their homes and their families. Their uniforms differed from those encountered at Haria, though that mattered little to the men they fought. They were under the enemy's banner. That was all the reason to engage them in bloody trial.

Along the snow-covered road sat a stationary convoy that waited for its passengers to haul up.

But stood on the bonnet of a leading motorcar, a figure called out to the infantrymen that lurked around him. He dressed only to impress. A narrow-rimmed elegant cap, that exhibited the cross of the unions, peaked his red-rimmed, black uniform, decorated in an additional spectrum of medals and ribbons. At his belt, the laced scabbard of a steel blade clipped to the hilt. The head of the Union's forces adorned the commissar's wardrobe – he appeared as the people's aristocratic ruler, with a flashy grin in his assertive presence.

"Gather around, revered liberators!" The Colonel started with a hearty call to the soldiers swallowed in the snow. Some onlooked with respect and attention, whilst others sluggishly pushed their eyes toward his direction. "Today, we stand in the morn of our greatest challenge yet, comrades. To our South-West lies a vital asset to the hellish forces of this wretched nation: Mullackaye Fortress. Whilst our comrades assault the East, inflicting their might and the worker's mettle on strategic positions, we have our orders to push to on to the West. Our target bears arms of its own. An airbase, military fortress and a key link to the Kelan military railway complex – it is within our duty to the freedom of the working man to tear down the establishment that holds them headstrong and foolish. We expect to face the enemy along the way, and we-"

It was alike any other syndicalist grandiose speech, yet there was a sickened lodge in Schottenstein's throat. Some of the soldiers called it the "Liberal's Flu", a short-term illness to which the mind strayed from the pockets of the commanding Unions, egged on only by personal mental distress. And it had started to infect him too, for he was fuelled by an unheard orchestra's welcoming, with an emotive yet powerful choice of words that riled up the warriors under their command. And still, to Schottenstein, it felt almost sacramental under the cult of productive liberation. The moral high road had always been an easy path to take. Good against evil. Man versus beast. All so righteous. As soon as they blamed themselves, they fell under the flu's influence. That was why Schottenstein maintained himself so cautiously. The guilt and horror of the war could not shift him too far, lest he was to end up a broken man caught in the stocks. He had people waiting for his return, and to him that was all that mattered. It took an entire life's effort to ensure he returned no different than he'd left.

The Colonel concluded his speech with the raising of enamoured voices, and he announced their commitment to the people of, as quoted, both the oppressed and their families that had been left behind. Many cheered. The odd few concealed their dissent. The Major just looked on with a fiend by his side.

"Load up! Take your places. We leave when the last man gets on." A Lieutenant Colonel called from the front.

Schottenstein walked past his soldiers and exchanged short greetings, with handshakes and gifted smiles. Whilst they loaded into the trucks, he quietly picked a lightly crowded vehicle in the middle of the convoy and climbed his way inside.

The engines roared. Chronic coughs of smog exhausted from the chariots. The frozen aftermath of the incoming winter was admixed with the scent of overcooked fuels and the racket of deafening engines. He cared little of the orchestra's conductor. To him, the tunes that made up their swollen performance were forged in a breeding ground of lacklustre pride. He scanned the back of the truck and discovered the usual unrecognisable faces. All had their own lives, beliefs, desires and morals. Some were loyal, others were afraid. He knew that it had been the exact same for the Kelan warriors they challenged. All unique. All alive. All in the same violent rocking boat. He decided to not pay attention to his own men so as to ignore the humanity of his enemy for just a little while longer.

~~~

The National Charter – a decorative decree of romanticised orders, and a foul instruction given until the last man fell – had been drawn up several days before he had swung into action. For Thomas, it had been at the slow-burning end of his cloaked voyage. He told himself to force open the opportunity for the greater good's prosperity. And with the odds backed against him, he made it clear to his collaborators that he had a decisive, albeit desperate and fickle, last chance.

Diplomacy is a powerful weapon and a crux to the unwise. The speaker wants something, so he targets another with words. He sways them with promises and ensures to uphold most of them, so as to not break the trust. A pact is formed and the speaker gets what he wants. It takes a trade, to give something important to them and insignificant to the speaker.

"I have it." He muttered into the microphone. His finger left the PTT trigger and the foreign-made handheld radio let out a harsh static chime. When nothing came through, he pressed it again and reiterated his point. "You'll uphold your end of the exchange, correct?"

"We have our promises. You'll require some patience, though I will say. You've been careless and left it down to chance."

"It's hard to be flawless." Thomas looked back up to his secluded officer; to double check, he walked over to his door and ensured that it was double locked. Last thing he needed was another officer walking inside. "Not to mention the Haven Charter being drawn complicates my situation."

"A new order from the throne?"

"They've even black-inked most of it from me – hard to believe, ay?"

"What do you know about it?"

"That's not in our-"

"Tell me or I'll cut the deal." The modulated threat had him by the throat. The sweat formed on his brow and he dabbed it away with a handkerchief. "You said it complicates things. I want to know what it is."

"Look, all I know is that they're selecting key figures from the national register. High profile figures, I mean. Doctors, scientists, politicians, engineers, and all the works. They're shipping them off somewhere, as some contingency plan, whilst the public are now being ordered to take arms to the last inch of land."

Thomas eyed the walls as if there were cameras in them. He scanned every detail, every cranny and patch that looked uneven. He sauntered over and rubbed his fingers and hands, gently tapping them with his fingers in search for any hollowed points. All the while, the static speaker chastised his desperate attempt at maintaining his reassurances.

"And you expect us to have guaranteed delivery during a huge battle? Your gamble is insane." Knowing full well that his capabilities were simply flying by chance, Thomas didn't question the contact's strict inquiry. To submit his confidence

322

would've meant sacrificing the diplomatic position he'd created. "Your feats are held together by matchsticks!"

"Insanity has gotten me this far. If I could've been far more direct, I would have. We couldn't just get on a boat and ship them over. We've been too cautious and now we've got no choice but to act when our chances collide whilst retaining our covert nature. One slip up and they are discovered." He scrambled for some of his papers and lit them on a tableside candle. With clouded eyes he watched as they turned to blackened flakes. The fact that his task had slipped so far from his grasp, with continuous backend misjudgements on his behalf, had him in a state of disarray.

"Alright. Then I beg of you to keep the target alive until I can send someone over." The harshness of the radiophonic accent lessened as it was weakened by impartial acceptance. "Do you still have your little beacon?"

Thomas reached for his chest pocket and unclipped the tightly secured gadget inside. Barely the length of a used pencil or the diameter of a pocketknife, it sat nicely on his open palm. At one end, a small bulb lay defused and lifeless.

"I do, yes." He admired it with his free hand whilst he used the other to hold the microphone to his mouth. "Fascinating piece of work, isn't it?"

"It'll buzz when it's time. You understand Morse?"

"Don't insult me."

"Then follow the light's message. Whoever we send will tell you where they are." Before Thomas could bid his farewell, the voice drew its final warning. "And, must I remind you, to not mess this up. We've pulled many concessions for you to make this deliver regardless of an international conflict. If you fail, we won't make any attempt to halt this war – for the Unions will not concede an inch; that is considering this would even work against someone like her majesty."

And with its conclusive mocking tone, the signal cut out. The final ultimatum was set in stone and the writing faded onto his walls with a distorted ink splodge. Each day, he dwelled upon how legitimate his plan had become. He banked on human emotion in a time where it was easier to dissociate the opposition as one of mankind – and it hoped to stop something already in motion: total war.

Thomas sat down in the crooked seat behind his untidied desk. With two shivering fingers, he drew the glasses from his face and lambasted his inner sense of reason with an aloof hiss. Backing out meant nothing in the grand scheme. He had caught himself far too deep into the end of his principles, to stay consistent in his task than to plan effectively for the right move. Failure meant what had already occurred would only continue on to the bitter end. Those desperate times called for his desperate and, rather indecent, sacrifices. One eye for millions, he said, and a utilitarian ethos went on to be his only conceivable option. Those chances had run their course and he had missed opportunity to climb aboard. From the very beginning, he was frantic in his decision making, for he chewed whatever he couldn't swallow. And then, as the cards were being dealt in the final round, he had one chance to see negotiations and ransom play out exactly as he had orchestrated.

He didn't know her. All of it had just been chance and opportunities. And the fact it'd all came about so well meant that he had little to no regret of putting her in harm's way. The Haven Charter would go on, and if his name was on its list, then he vowed to himself to go AWOL if he were out of options. Little had he knew how hopeless his attempts truly were until he was to meet them in the field, dressed to deal with the devil.

~~~

Twelve days. It took the convoy twelve excruciating days to cross over the vast plains. Along the roads, the fractured remnants of a professional army waylaid and opened fire upon them with rancorous effectivity. There were bodies that had to be left behind. Only a few were spared the time to be buried, but the rest had the snow do it for them. By summer, their preserved bodies would rot for all to see.

Hell's frozen highway, he called it. At any minute, a bullet could have torn through the driver's skull and the roads would be transformed into a battleground. The forces tasked with seizing Mullackaye had been taught a harsh lesson that the defenders planned to take their brunt on their feet as more radical tactics laid on the road ahead. First were minefields that were intentionally mislabelled, and road signs were turned to face the incorrect directions. Then, hit and run squads launched bombs at the trucks, and some slapped satchel charges to the sides of their walkers. And in two instances, an officer and two soldiers were murdered by Kelan soldiers disguised as Ferusian riflemen. A swarm of distrust flew from head-to-head throughout the convoy. At one point, even a night patrol guard questioned Schottenstein on the intricacies of Ferusia's home culture to only reaffirm that he was, indeed, the real deal. By each mile was a presentation of esteem and dread, compiled into a dirtied mound at the back of every rifleman's mind. Several soldiers set off on their own accord in the dead of night, whittling their numbers down through the worsened nature of deserters. Commissars became far more erratic as they watched their troops with eyes pried open by clothes pegs.

Schottenstein found it increasingly difficult to stay silent on his discontent.

On the first day, he had changed his clothes to fit that of a regular soldier's: a steel helmet, a cosy – though equally as itchy – balaclava, a shortened battle dress, webbing and back-held equipment, as well as a primary firearm to accommodate his officer's handgun. His duty had always been to act as the highest authority for the frontline infantry. Previously, he wasn't to put his life in harm's way beside those who followed his orders, but the further into the iced apocalypse they went the surge demanded his dutiful compliance to the lesser men – not that the syndicate would've allowed such hierarchal language, it was just that Schottenstein knew where it was. He had no problem with such close encounters with the clashes in the fields for it was honourable to die beside a brother or sister.

The road ahead frittered away once the snow had dawned the early stages of a blizzard. Where their paths had disappeared beneath the white blanket, they simply turned to the fields and ploughed through the harsher terrain. Mobile bipedal walkers, encased pigeon-like striders armed with high calibre tank-destroying or anti-personnel cannons, took to the front and rear of the pack and acted as the first response to any immediate threats. And there were plenty for them to react to.

Like an overwhelming tide at dawn, they raced through the lands with a soul-crushing sluggishness and they pushed far deeper into the heart of the Kelan battleground. The closer they

325

came to the fortification, the worse the narrative became. Towns had been laid waste to by aerial bombardment, to which they loosened the defender's grip on the local areas but scattered the sheltered needs of the army. Many retreated before the expedition arrived on-scene. Small bands of daring legends fired from windows or appeared out of the snow where the majority went on to fight another day. Schottenstein respected their resolve as much as he had grown to fear it.

All for the sake of victory did it take the greatest sacrifice of all. Schottenstein continuously silenced his woes from his subordinates and he stitched his mouth shut.

"Five minutes until dismount! Check your gear, wake yourselves up and listen carefully." On the approaching strait of ice, Schottenstein awoke the few that had managed to slumber under such gruelling pressure.

The drivers pressed on their brakes and carefully turned the convoy into neat columns. The delicate dance of parking chain-wheeled trucks into formation kept their movement at a snail's pace. Shortly after, the trucks then unloaded their passengers and tents, followed by the quick instalment of tents, foxholes and sandbags that had soon changed the lonesome snowscape into a readied command post. Ten minutes later, the sea of walkers and towed artillery pieces caught up to the line and what ensued was a two hour long logistical nightmare.

Schottenstein oversaw their preparation from off to the side. The army spanned far and wide, and had spread their greyish mass throughout the valley's horizon. There were lines that were drawn in the snow and, as briefly drawn up by their generals, a formation of battle was soon set up. All the awaiting infantrymen prepared to advance across the fields to their target, and all the while a storm stalked toward them.

He gazed across the celestial lowlands with stinging disparity. He hadn't seen forecasts so rampant and carnivorous, even in the accustomed northern peaks of Ferusia. The mordant winds brought goosebumps to attention all across his body. In his onlook, he boxed away the idea of unfamiliarity and occupied his thoughts with one truth: that the day had been immortalised by its demoralised details. The overall preparation and the orderly fashion of speeches, briefings, digging and eating all came together to forge a melting pot of wearied winter warriors, all who clutched themselves tightly in the hopes they didn't freeze to death before the grand entanglement. Many chose their preliminary meals with great care, devouring sausages, recently toasted bread, warm soup and fried onions as per the finest of their cuisines. Never plentiful portions had been handed out, for the dangers of stomach cramps, whilst juvenile to any citizen back home, presented a genuine threat that could've disrupted and defeated the fighting spirit they needed to triumph.

In the preceding hours before the battle, Schottenstein found himself both tired and ultimately bored. He couldn't have imagined that the greatest battle of his life would have been preluded by such mediocrity. People rarely acknowledged their presence and job. A lot of the soldiers spoke with ingenuine happiness and forced ignorance. It was better for them to go down with a smile on their faces than to be swamped by the damning fixation on death. Unfortunately, the Major hadn't quite done the same. He respected his crowd to the fullest yet had no connection to his own subordinates other than the upmost respect. But even as a valued officer, he lurked in hushed professionalism. The only person he really knew of was-

"Want to come and take a look at it?" Westra asked, tapping her knuckles against his steel helmet. There it was again: the smile. It had the innocence of a wolf dressed sharply in a lamb's gown. His paranoia had gotten the best of him and he eyed her with disgraced uncertainty.

"Look at what?"

"The fort. You can see it from the top of the hill."

"Do we have the time to?"

"Well, we're waiting for the air force and sky navy to show up so I think we've got time." Her carefree nature perched itself on her expression.

Then, he saw the different woman – like she had peeled her obsessive skin and had unveiled the next layer down. Rosy cheeked, flushed by the nip of the day, pale faced and blue lipped, something more susceptible to the weather, like he was. But he looked away from her gleaming eyes and took the offer.

"I've nothing better to do."

Together, they slipped off along the way to the top. Their slope, at first, wasn't too kind to them, though in some sort of infantile turn it resembled a game. Straight to the peak did they clamber their way, as a competitive pair making the run without prompt. Like his own soldiers, Schottenstein felt a little like how it was to be ignorant of the ruthless carnage ahead of them. It was a tragic shame that the bliss became a posthumous memory.

And there it was. As soon as his line of sight had clawed its way over the sky-touching zenith, any idea of an insignificant and weakened adversary fell apart. Awestruck, he lost himself as he gawked at their grandiose target. For several miles, the walls towered along an unimaginably broad vista. It was no simple stronghold or castle – it was a citadel in its own right. What he witnessed was a city built exclusively for the military. Inside, the tops of towering concrete spires made their silhouettes visible through the decaying sunlight, where great batteries of embedded within its gargantuan infrastructure. But only minutes later had their view faded once the snowstorm had taken first flight.

"So that's it, then?" He asked, wrapping his arms around himself. "That's our target?"

"Sure is."

"Is our force-"

"Big enough? Strong enough? Once the remaining assets arrive, it might be." The hounds of winter yelped between them, and she was cut her off for a second. Their clothes flapped in the wind. "It'll be a great fight."

"I hate it when people say things like that."

"Don't find yourself jealous just because I have a greater grasp on-"

"On what?" He snarked.

"Justice." That enduring goal of hers refused to properly shed. She continued on a path that he had to stand by and watch. Something inside of him grew. Detest? Distrust? Maybe it was anger and fear. Neither were comforting. He worried for those in her wake.

"Do you intend on ending this war?"

The Major didn't utter a word. She instead kept her eyes fixated on the large grey blob covering their distant, translucent view. Meanwhile, he whispered to himself of his pessimistic woes on her seething radicalisation.

Westra continued to hold her tongue. Either way, it told him everything he needed to know.

"You can keep pretending it's justice." He spat, taking his leave back down the hill. She was left standing atop the peak, and it was as if she herself had become the greatest judge in the court of war as she left her verdicts to the approaching slaughter.

Time slipped by for a while after. More vehicles and infantrymen arrived in their drowsed droves. Thousands of them, even. The scale was still hard to believe. In Haria, they masses were confined to trenches which had shrouded the full extent of the battle. The reds crawled between one another like rats to sewers, yet it all still felt rather small until it was their turn to go over the top. Yet there, on the solstice prairies, the armies stood for as far as the world could stretch. Mullackaye had to be their true obstruction to the doctrines of war. Two great armies were to collide in siege, with one devastated and the other victorious. To most, this fit the old vision of a glorious war: honourable, grand and bold. Choirs were to sing songs of praise for their absolute victory, or catastrophic demise. They would be remembered and immortalised through melody, through music, and poetry – as the bards of the last age had done for their knights. They stood on the fringes of human history; at the edge of the world.

Consequently, the core of the planet quaked for their arrival. The soldiers, sat beside their preparations, felt glasses jitter and the wind drown out. It was a sound unlike anything else: a drone so haunting that the spirits of the dead hid away. And when they looked to the sky, a cluttered, shadowy cloud drifted above. The skies dimmed and the deafening roar of thunder started. A terrific display of the morning's divine aerial battle proclaimed the start of a brutal conflict. Schottenstein watched the cloud race from the horizon to over the hills. And then, the rain started. Atop of Fort Mullackaye, steel droplets, made from sixty percent amatol and forty percent trinitrotoluene, rapidly descending by the drive of their 300kg weight, let out a shriek comparable to the extinguished breath of a dying deity. The armada of bombers had arrived on scene.

The weather's payload carpeted the objective they were due to assault. It would be a single trip for most, layered by four immediate waves of explosive consignment, like a welcoming gift for the festivities of the encroaching entanglement and violence. He listened to the patter and rumble of the engines fade away after the squadron's prelude came to an end.

329

"Bomber Command has issued its strike! Artillery, commence fire mission, Grid 3642 on a wide sweeping effect. And – FIRE!" Seconds later, the cannons screamed their ferocious verbiage. Thumps of ignition were followed by the thuds of impact. The everlasting bombardment was upon their enemy. It was the most tremendous showcase of man's ability to overwhelm itself with fire. "First wave, get to your positions!"

Under the cloak of the blizzard, the soldiers waded toward the frontline. A line of white trees adjacent an open field of snow was their stating point; and the field, in its open and uneven ground, coated with many defilades, was one in which they'd have to cross. Schottenstein hadn't really taken in the full extent of their task. He linked up with the first crowd and saw them all clad heavily in their padded uniforms.

The heat of their boiled blood was enough to keep them warm. They stood in columns of two to three, lined behind an assortment of walkers. He followed his own directions and took a waltz to the frontier.

Majors of the past had been strict commanders, relying on the prowess of their men to get the job done. Ferusia's shortcomings had continued to disregard that fact. He was a fighting man, and a fighting man would always be so right up until he rose the ranks further beyond. Schottenstein felt no safer from death than the privates and corporals beside him. He nodded to them and patted their backs, though he was unable to shake the strangerhood of his presence.

"Keep your hearts empowered. Stay behind the walkers until we get close enough. Let them take the brunt!" He delivered the orders to the silent masses. They nodded and gave confirmation with a single:

"Yes, Comrade!"

He looked beyond the walkers and spied on through the snow to only see the disappointing obstruction of white mists. The distant silhouette of the walls had been obscured only further by the hour. The hammering of artillery guided them in the right direction; and the dead piper upheld its heading.

Follow the noise. Shoot if necessary. Stay alive. Keep the men and women alive. Holdfast and strike at the heart. Kill. Murder. They'll just do it to them. This is their land, for now. There is no compromise. Compromises were for the lost. The enemy knew

330

where it was. Schottenstein took a deep breath. He was scared. Terribly afraid, in fact. There was no other way to put it. The man was to march with the many other faceless warriors into a wall of gunfire, shielded only by the distinction of a semi-sentient metal canister. But what he did was understand that it was natural to be afraid. When he knew that, he made it his priority to suppress it.

He breathed. Breathing was all he could do. It was all any of them could do. They were all so utterly terrified. Sometimes even the bravest of soldiers feared death, not for what it did to them but for what they left behind: an incomplete war, or a missing victory, or perhaps a fractured family. People. They were all people, some more human than others.

To his left, another sortie spread itself asunder. At least twelve rows of tanks and soldiers stood, thinned out in uneven formations. And in the middle of them, bipedal walkers broke the arrangement up. Shells were loaded into the main cannons. Magazines were fitted into their rifles, submachine guns and handguns. An exposed gunner stood at the back of the tanks, holding a deployed machine gun of their own. Schottenstein kept breathing. He continued to breathe. There was nothing else. Savour the air that he can muster, he thought to himself, for if he were hit by a stray bullet, he'd have taken his time for granted.

"Thirty seconds before we move out!" Voices recalled the message one after another. He repeated it himself, telling those around him of what was to come. The squeal of shells overhead drowned out the crystal wonderland they'd strode through. A single field. One way. "We are the centre assault! Brace yourselves!"

Another wail seized the sky. A rush of wind barely clipped them as two fighters soared past. Some men cheered as they came ever so close to gunning down one which they pursued. Each second added an additional layer of white noise. Soon enough, they became deaf to the hostilities in their jacked-up adrenaline surge.

Severer winds violated those who waited. Faces were tucked into their shirts and bodies huddled against one another. Schottenstein stood at the front of his pack, right against the tank's steel body. He pressed his face against it and felt nothing but an iced shell.

"Ten seconds!"

It mattered not if there were no judicial conclusions in the world. There never had been any. He recalled what he said to Westra: he questioned whether or not he understood it himself. The war had been built on the meanings of revenge and of the begrudged. Diesel fuelled the war machines whilst hate drove their silos, refineries and the workers supplying their demand.

"Five seconds!"

He felt as if this was no different to any other soldier. Somewhere, across the front, a soldier on their side felt the same sensational fear. The countdown. It hurt everyone. Race, gender, sexuality or ideology mattered not. Draconic means harmed all. Countdowns were preluding to viciousness. It held no barriers, nor regarded any. It was the great equaliser, a disease of fear.

Intoxication: the injection of panic, dread and horror. The beginning of the end, rigidly knitted into one soiled package.

Demoralisation: the realisation of what they'd become. Monsters. Victims. Either side of the coin was a death sentence for humanity.

Acceptance: Either a man accepted the creature he'd become, knowing to not let the war consume him and to push through until he, himself, could return home in one piece, or he would die afraid and confused. To live scared was to die in fear.

Even if it was all unfair, he knew that of all things in the world, Konrad Schottenstein wanted nothing more than to return home, to see his family, his friends and village, regardless of the ideologies that drove them.

"Alright, comrades! Advance!" The skreiches of artillery shells were drowned out by the officers blowing into their own whistles. A high-pitched scream linked the dispersed army together, and the charge forward was ignited. There was no honourable war cry. A synchronised roar of engines ignited spoke in their place.

Immediately, the bodies pushed against Schottenstein's back. They packed themselves as sardines, tightly against the tank's rear end as it lunged forward, beginning the march ahead. His ears rang when they fired, sending shockwaves through the air. Overhead, aircraft circled and danced with their enemies, before disappearing into the mystical panorama.

And then came the most powerful ensemble ever to have been formed. Further than the eye could see, wave after wave of tracers and lights flashing at the speed of sound zipped past them. Triggers were pulled and guns taunted the passage. Those caught on the outskirts of the pack felt a sharp pain in their side before dropping to their knees.

He pressed himself against the walker harder, giving as much space to those following in its footsteps as he could. The man atop, blaring speeches of anger with a belt-fed machinegun, fell aside. He toppled from his position with an eye hanging loosely from its socket amongst other facial defamations.

"Stay behind the tank!" He shouted.

He thought not of home, or of no atheistic deity, but of the battle. It was done in a brash attempt to reconcile with the mission, not the end, to understand that their time was then to conquer new heights. Death had its bag full, however, and Schottenstein would not fit in a crowded sack. He held onto his heart and thought of his life and of the moment. He clenched his firearm, leaning around the tank and he took occasional blinded peeks at the defenders.

They couldn't see the wall. Wandered souls blindly marched toward the objective. Many couldn't run. The snow was too thick to sprint through. The further they travelled, the thinner it got. The cannons continued their barrage and the artillery would not relinquish its fierce hand.

Snow crumbled beneath their capped boots. An aurora of shells, bullets and flares fanned out across the hoary, silver cosmos. Accompanied by the piercing distortion of lead scraping against steel, the softness of the idyllic snowflakes was indistinguishable. So much aggression, anger and an incitement to kill, all rolled into a single minute. Another man clambered atop of the tank and mindlessly took the machine gun for himself, then he unleashed a daring wave of lead against their blinded targets. The fire became less concentrated. With every shot the tank made, a short interval of relief was set upon the soldiers.

He waited for the next shot, before rounding up those behind him. Through unity, they would have their success. A grey slab formed in the white mist. The wall was close. The gunfire no longer seemed coordinated down and their time was then. Two bipedal walkers on either side of them marched ahead and stormed ahead at a rapid pace. Guns blaring, unleashing merciless suppression, and with an affinity for speed, Schottenstein raised a fist and called out the order.

"Now, spread out! Take to the field. Let the armour cover our push. Get to the walls and outer defences. Seize them for yourselves!" He told them in confidence. They knew there was no choice, neither was there one for him. Continue the pressure, he thought, until the walls themselves would crack.

On command, they sprawled out. Some were immediately welcomed by twenty rounds piercing their chest, with their bodies falling unceremoniously, whilst others narrowly avoided being struck. Schottenstein saw a man take a bullet to the shoulder, only to get himself back onto his feet and ignoring the blood colouring the snow he stood on.

They just kept running. Shots were fired back at the walls. Schottenstein couldn't recall what happened in that field, on that day, in its entirety. He just ran. Occasionally, he'd lay down in the snow, or trip over a body or two. Regardless of his own life, he ran. They followed him. He thought he'd die that day, and on that minute and perhaps he was to, but not in that minute.

Miraculously, he found himself tumbling into a darkened dugout hidden under his boots.

Caught off guard, he helplessly dropped down five feet into the pit, bruised and battered. Yet, even through the blood-boiled shock of the fall, the instincts hammered in by gruesome hardships forced his hands to ready his weapon. Laid broken on his side with a sharp pain flooding his shoulders, he raised the barrel to a man dressed in dark military fatigues. He was irresponsive to the Major, scared even. Schottenstein, however, did not hesitate. He pulled the trigger and the man was shoved into the trench wall with blood on his belly.

He couldn't even hear his own gunfire through the noise of the battle. It didn't matter to him. Survival was the new objective: to clear out what looked like a small connection of tunnels and trenches, until the others flooded inside.

He hadn't seen any of his own comrades arrive. Even if they never turned up, he was fixed on making a mess of the defenders, for the next wave was filled with avoidable casualties if the good soldiers did their rightful job. And with his reasoning replaced with the human conscience to persist, thrive and conquer, he scrambled to his feet and kept his submachine gun at the ready. Blood stained the dugout walls. He barely batted an eye.

He never doubted himself or belittled his choices, and he abandoned any sense of moral duty to anyone but his own kind. Survival always came first. Why did it matter? This was a war. War didn't have a place for dissent in the heat of the moment, and you could not moralise the slaughter. The only thing a warrior could stay true to was victory.

His authoritarian roots had hammered in his duty. Death or dishonour didn't exist. Honour was a belittlement to will.

Let it be known that a man will always do anything it takes to see his family once more. The grand state of the unions and their control could not suppress his internal promise to see the ones he loved.

Schottenstein did not feel regret. His heart wretched at the sight of his kill, but his body and soul kept its course. Because the man knew there would be all the time in the world to regret his decision to fire upon the hesitant soldier – that was why he kept silent. If he panicked then, the cost of redemption would be his life.

He continued through the trench. About a hundred metres from the wall, he breathed well knowing the pit put him out of sight from the topside. So he pressed on, stock planted firmly in his shoulder. Muscle memory put it in just the right spot. Comfort was irrelevant. He didn't need to feel anything other than control over recoil. No emotions. Keep to the mission, he continued to think.

The first corner came to. Bodies were already scattered on the floor, mutilated by the first artillery barrage. Beneath a thin line of iron roofing, many had stood little to no chance. He pressed on. Ignoring them was a priority.

He turned another corner and saw two with their firearms at the ready. Hesitation caught the best of them whilst Schottenstein, in his primal instinct, peppered them dry until he had no more bullets to spare. Their corpses painted the town a deep crimson. He dared not describe their conditions. The bodies themselves became colder than the frosted air. It could not be any more nightmarish if it tried to. But then again, he was instead more concerned about getting the fresh magazine into his gun than he was about the state of the deceased husks.

And at last, he pushed toward the back of the trench. Down the avenues, both left and right, he saw soldiers clad in familiar attires arrive. The waves began to make it in at his side. Swarms of bodies flooded the defences, overwhelming them in seconds. Blasts from grenades, mines, mortars and all manners of ordinance shattered his sense of hearing. The tinnitus only numbed him. It was one less sense to worry about.

He spun around the last bend and discovered a pair of soldiers, alone and backed into the corner with nothing but a single handgun between them. How their misfortune had come about was of no concern. The split-second choice he had, however, differed from his carnivorous and predatory execution.

With the world seemingly collapsing all around him, he walked toward them, sights trailed on their cowardly wince. What compelled him to offer mercy was never discerned, it was just one of those choices the man had made in the heat of battle.

"Down!" He shouted. His own voice was a muffle to him whilst he uttered one of the few Kelan words he knew. The screams broke through the noise of battle. One raised their hands, moving his mouth to spout foreign clemency. It didn't take a linguist to know his pleas. The man who begged wanted life. But as he kindly stepped forward, there was a movement on his partner, armed with a 9$_{mm}$. "Down!"

Both squeezed the trigger, but only one of the two's shots connected. The Major watched as the second soldier's body fell limp, lacking any sort of glorious, slow and endearing demise. The other man screamed out, but immediately raised his hands with tears streaming down his face.

By the time he'd gotten him on his knees, a squad of his own arrived and pulled the last survivor back away from the frontline violence, back into the tunnels they'd first arrived in.

Men work in mysterious ways. Monsters act with consistency. To Schottenstein, whether the world thought of him mutually, that was his one gift to the world – a random chance of mercy. A little empathy in a grave encounter was more than anyone else could have given.

Absolution's path had been opened. A great pardon of those sanctioned through war was upon them. The end. The finale. Closing curtains; the show's final act came close. Where Schottenstein found himself was on the quiet splutter of humanity's last calm breath. It would not end in the tributary of war, the battles that ravaged the nation to ash, but instead it'd be found in its aftermath.

That was where he found himself. Decline began with a bang and was followed by the striking silence. The guns fell quiet, for once, shortly after for but a minute. Tanks stormed up with great leaps and bounds. Planes continued to dart above them. The artillery loaded itself for another volley, readjusting its aim for the next section to storm – over the wall and beyond. The maroon carpet had been laid out.

He sat breathless against the trench floor. Beside him were the corpses of the unknown. He reached into their collars and found small identity discs with generic names on them. Nothing stood out. Service numbers and surnames. A single letter represented who they had once been.

Who would remember them? History only remembered one in every million. Everyone else was expendable for some protagonist's rise to fame. Each individual who crafted the immortalised were tools to handmaking heroes and villains.

"How many history books do you think your name will be printed in?"

How many? None. Konrad Schottenstein was an irrelevant title to the next generations. He rested beside the dead. He had as any chance of being championed as the common corpse at his left, or the bleeding mess of a man to his right. Really, he didn't actually care that much. History wouldn't want to remember him. It'd glorify or demonise him. Every man and woman on the harsh front were cruel beasts with twin-twirled horns, all for one fact – they were the humans that the gods had given fire.

He dwelled over how, to the Kelan theology, mankind was the gods' manifestation of satanic short-sightedness. Their main theist agenda was that of self-loathing. Free will. A hunger for flesh and blood. Callous desires for power; these were their burdens.

The syndicalist's utopia had been a cynical fantasy right from the beginning. To deny it was to be a slave. To agree was to be a proclamation of injustice.

337

It was only a minute of silence. He thought that if it had been any longer, it'd have begun to hurt. And if it had been any shorter it'd have been meaningless. A single minute was enough. Sixty seconds to repent, before lunging back into the fray.

"Sir, are you okay?" A private approached him, carefully stepping over the dead. His voice was muffled by the cloth that covered his young face. "Sir?"

The Major looked up quickly, snapping out of his mindless trance. He nodded with a fake smile.

"I'm as alright as I can be, Private."

"You're not hurt?"

"Not at all. Are you, or the others?" He spoke as if he knew him.

"We can't quite tell. Pioneers are planting some explosives though. Sergeant told me to clear the area." Schottenstein broke into a heartily chuckle as he heard the young man's bitter professionalism.

"In the way? Send him my apologies. I was just taking a breather." He rose to his feet. The wall's tops above him appeared to be vacant, at least along the edge. The blitz had blessed their rapid advancement upon the keep. In truth, the dominant presence of temporary air superiority and fire support had won them the hour. But a strategist feared an easy victory for fear that he missed the trap that lured them in. And with that, Schottenstein shifted away from the line of sight of the wall's ridge.

He breathed easy knowing that the first part was done and that he was relatively unscathed. Ignoring his concerns, and by placing trust in his commander's wishes, he walked alongside the soldier who guided him out of the blast zone.

From the West, the gunfire kicked off again. The silence was short lived. Picturesque views of tracers soaring to the endless sky crafted an eccentric light show above.

"Wish we could take a picture." He pondered aloud. The private didn't respond. Not the conversationalist. At least Westra responded.

Feeling as if he didn't need to be around for the first blast, he took a step aside. Across the way, he saw grapples being fired up to the walls, with many preparing to make the first climb. And though he felt as if his duty warranted a break, he knew no such gift would be granted. But as he walked toward one of the gathering parties, he heard his name being called from behind.

"Major? Major Schottenstein?" He turned, seeing a lieutenant scavenge around helplessly. "Major Schottenstein?"

"Right here, Lieutenant." With a raised palm, he beckoned the officer to head his way. A thinly timed miracle, he believed. What luck.

"Colonel Strauss is asking for you to fall back to the reserve line."

"What for?"

A hundred feet off to the left, the snow was forcibly returned to the clouds by a fierce explosion. The Lieutenant ducked his head, holding his arms to his helmet.

"I don't know, but I think you should hurry for your own sake."

Back into the professional mind, no respite to his own thoughts. He called himself careless for drowning out his environs. The hinterlands of the great and promiscuous battleground were ever the more unforgiving. Lolling about just left him as another target, and he was surprised to have gotten the luck to rest in the first place.

Whatever duty he'd been called to, he hoped that it would've been easier than fending off the soldiers seeking his death. Sometimes, that idea of a desk job suited those dreams perfectly.

None of that mattered though. It didn't make a difference to who he was or where he'd been sent. As a Major to the Ferusian Expeditionary Force, the supposed liberating fleet of judicial and sacramental enforcement, it was his duty alone to do as instructed. Lives on his side depended on it. Lives of the future depended on it. Every little action he made rippled history. And every inaction did so tenfold. That was the soldier's decree.

Chapter 25

Iron Rain

In the end, there would be nothing left, as each atom would be scrubbed from reality. Particles of dust would float around in the empty plain of nothingness that appeared; where memories had to be gathered from their disjointed solitude, the collectors would search through an anguished existence. Unity and love would perish. Rhys returned to that thought several times over throughout his service – and the near-nihilistic premonition that the supreme hellfire would vanquish his being kept him clung to what little hope saved him from becoming the felo-de-se of tomorrow. And, whilst cosseted within Mullackaye's impenetrable walls, his thoughts of that dreaded aftermath brought about the bombardment that shattered the windows.

The barrages crept forward, taking each metre by immeasurable force. Frosted winds were warmed by the fury of their weaponised inferno. The clouds cracked asunder and the partition of the sky left open a gateway for bombs and shells to arrive through.

Abstained within the small dark office, the alarms were raised far too late. A shallow winter's morn with a crystal white sun kissing the infinite wonderland had been the prelude to the chaos. The news of an impending army fell short on deaf ears. Radio signals weakened and the general positioning for the Ferusian storm was based on their previously predictive movement; they usually had appeared in one town, gradually closer to Mullackaye than the last, only to have disappeared into the fog and raze another. Yet their hopes were flawed as twenty towns were skipped, and then came the arrival of a tremendous fighting force.

Seasons of peaceful loneliness waned. They marched through the heart of the homeland and took homes and shelters to house their fighters. Over the course of their march, any and all resistance had been quelled with steel boots, crushed under the weight of mechanical prowess. The terrifying performance of modern-day machinery was used to carve out their progress, through flesh and bone. And during their approach, where every day they announced how close they thought the Ferusians were, Rhys seemingly ignored it.

Beginning with the frostbitten wilds, the first assault came from the sky as the air turned to gall, to which it poisoned the wooden lungs of every poor soul on base. Many of them were forced to stay indoors to combat the declining temperature. Those trialled with defending the walls stood around metal fuel drums burning old documents, wooden knickknacks and incompatible flammable fluids. Word spread around the fortress of the ones who had died through hypothermia in the night. It was a horrible death. Slow. Painful. Agonising. Shivering. Alone. No warmth. It was too much to comprehend.

To die by the comfortless winds was certainly a paranoia that swelled up a storm through Mullackaye. Far too many took their off-patrol rotas as a chance to hide inside, where they could fleece their pale faces with faltering room temperatures. Rhys returned to that same dark office, just barely over sub-zero. Nothing happened. He passed papers and signed documents. Among them were the letters to homes that he wrote for – though he suspected that many of those addresses may not have even existed anymore.

And then, the alarm sounded. It was barely precautionary, unsure of what it had heard through the howls of the blizzard, and it arrived as a latecomer. A gunshot or five came before the siren. A small exchange between arms, lost to the unknown, and the confusion spread like wildfire. And then the bombs fell.

Beside his resting arm, Rhys had positioned a small glass of water. When the skies first rumbled, so did his beverage. Drones crescendoed until it joined the howls of the wind. Insect-like swarms appeared in the skies above the base. The blackened spots drifted in perfected avian formations. Anti-aircraft guns, scrambled by cold troops, fired into the air as they unleashed their returning payloads. The explosions were, at first, distant compared to where Rhys slumbered. That was until they crawled toward him with their claws in the soil. Dust first fell from his decaying ceiling as a preliminary, split-second warning, before the windows were smashed into oblivion.

He could not describe the horror with his own words, for he had instinctively buried his eyes into his sleeve. Terror from the unforgiving songs blasted through the sky. Each bomb contributed to the grander musical endeavour. They whistled their downward spiral, rapidly descending on the people below, and then they erupted the storm. The winds were their fretboard, and down the strings did they dive. Punctured ears felt the piercing ring of their approach, and they heard them grow louder and louder until the payloads were on top of them. And then: the impact. Asteroids of manmade proportions, diluting the land's lifeforms with fire, steel and detonation. He felt the planet tremble as it shook under his seat, all as the outlandish screams demonised the harsh winters to great avail. Overwhelmed by its sound, he dove to the floor, just in time to feel the nearest impact.

Beyond his door, the windows burst into a thousand daggered splinters. He heard each individual shard pepper his door like rain. Shouts bounced down the corridors as many barked orders of chaotic panic.

"Take cover!"

"Down, now!"

"Bombs! BOMBS!"

A persistence of harrowing savagery had bled his mind dry of safety. They were but men against themselves. There was no fighting back in that instant – and most importantly, there was no way they could see the enemy. And they just soared on by above, like doves without a care in the world. They didn't have to realise their own destructive power, they just had to keep doing it until it was time to refuel and rearm.

For Rhys wasn't on Farhawl, scraping by on the layer beneath heaven; he was sanctioned by the knowledge that his existence, his land and globe was but the third layer of hell's downward plummet.

The deluge massacred the wastes. The bombs dissolved into flames and ash. Smoke dispersed through the air and faded into the arctic winds as a toxic tinge. Sitting up, Rhys hesitantly looked around. He first saw his door hanging on by a single hinge. He clambered to his feet and staggered over toward the broken entryway where he was met by rubble. An opening to the frozen world stood bare in place of a window where the concrete wall opposite his office had been absolutely demolished. When he set foot out into the corridor, the crackle of the glass beneath his feet whetted the ambience.

The last bomb had finally dropped and the world was left barren for mere moments.

The first thing he heard when his eardrums reconstructed themselves was the ear-piercing screech of blaring alarms at full might. Men and women, emerging from side-lined rooms, ran out into the cold. Wrapped in woollen jackets and clutching guns by the trigger, those prepared to do so stormed out into the mists with confusion and a general panicked mindset. Rhys stood back, dazed by the defamed standings of unprepared men. A bloodbath had found its footing on his doorstep. By his toes was a forearm left severed from its origins. And near to his window was the burst open head of an unlucky soldier. In his sickening twist of trauma, Rhys nearly burst out laughing at the watermelon-burst of the man's fleshy membrane that sat in place of his face.

His eyes were frozen still, as was the wetness of his face. Any other bodies had been left buried by a mound of brick and debris. Except, off to his right, he blocked out the less dismembered, and far more human-appearing, dead just down the hall. The survivors, who had been in their rooms like he himself was, rushed to the sides of indistinguishable corpses. But unlike Haria, there was no stench – that was the first estranged thought that came to his mind. Everything in general, bar the horrific sights, was invisible to the senses. Bitten with the soulless paralysis of the icy gales, the he only accompanied his gazes with a beaten sense of direction. He trudged, or rather stumbled with trembling hands, back into his office to grab his headgear and rifle, though he did so without so much as a hint of enthusiasm. Then, he pieced together his webbing and ensured his magazines had ammunition inside. He tried to think little of what had happened, but his mind had been beaten into a pattern of responsibility, controlling his terrified body to gather his weapons for war.

The soil underneath them had erupted, yet he just instinctively pieced together his boots and coat, and then he prepared to walk over the scorched earth. Because he was alone, and for all things evil that scared him more, he wished only to find safety.

He was taken away as his body autopiloted through the broken window, and he avoiding the sharpened shards still stuck upward in the rubble. He banked left away from the impact zone, and then he veered to the right off into the mist. He ran through the snow, shielding his eyes as a distant sound of a bombardment picked up, that time from the guns and cannons beyond the walls. He didn't stop. An arch of burning vapour ripped through the atmosphere, and it prepared its descent back onto the base for another hour of devastation.

Just by the noise alone, he knew it was artillery that time. He'd heard it peppering the land in Haria. It was indistinguishable from the devil's tears, trickling onto the earth where it left no trace, other than a burrowed pit upon impact. The first blasts were further away, toward the northern-most walls. He didn't stop to check. His body kept its stride going, occasionally running past scrambled footmen meandering towards any vacant posts. All the while, the alarm continued to blare out its vile song. Rhys covered one ear, only then realising he couldn't hear anything with it. The nearby blast had beaten his left eardrum it to submission. No worries, he thought, it'd recover eventually, if he were to live long enough.

He soon realised where exactly he was leading himself toward and so he pressed onward to the armouries and maintenance warehousing, where he hoped to find not only a quiet mechanic working on her walker, but also several other squadmates who sought shelter.

He arrived to face a crumbling building, with steel contorted and bent out of shape. Gaped like a whale's mouth, the front iron door had been blasted open. The fragments of a detonated payload sat in the snow, buried in the standing walls and concrete. A direct hit, or as close to one as it could be. Worrying for those inside, he pushed through the thin crowd of stunned soldiers outside, all who huddled around several injured and shellshocked victims. They called for medics into the great wastes. Little hope stood for the limbless souls, who held their last moments in absolute agony. Rhys felt a pain in his stomach as he rushed over them, as if they weren't there. At the very least, he watched his step and tried his hardest not to jolt the unrestful. He instead noticed that he was skating over the pools of snow-soaked blood.

Inside lingered the foul smell of smouldered fumes. The first thirty meters of the interior had been rocked and upturned by the shockwave, with tools scattered across the floor and two destroyed walkers on either side of the entrance. One missed a leg. The other had a snapped barrel, broken like a twig in a child's hand. He persisted through, seeing the engineers and soldiers reaching inside for components, mechanical parts or, in one tank's case, the still body of a bloodied woman. He'd never seen the place so alive – contrarily, it was only to pluck the dead out from the wreckages.

A toxic thickness to the air clogged his airway. He scrambled through desperately, moving between fallen girders and iron cabinets. The deeper he went into the roofless warehouse, doused in a snowberry cascade, the greater his concern grew. Reformed squads nearby haphazardly checked over their machines for irreparable damage. Some loaded their pilots inside and sparked to life at the turning of their ignition keys.

"Staff Sergeant!" He heard a voice beckon him from the back of the hall. As attentive as a mutt, he frantically snapped his head toward it. He dashed and darted between the battered pileups until he spied his speaker. "Over here!"

Tyran waved, stood atop of their own walker. He felt a small rush of adrenaline as a familiar face guided him toward a clearer light. Surrounded by the blizzardly holler of the intruding elements, Rhys reeled himself closer to the vehicle.

"Thank the stars," he whispered to himself, before he raised his voice, "what's…what are we doing?"

"Compiling ourselves. I'm doing surprisingly okay, as is the tank." Tyran muttered under his sweaty brow. As they conversed, he unlocked the main pilot's hatch and clambered inside. He wiped his face with his sleeve and he gathered his breath. "We – uh – we couldn't find anything wrong with it."

Rhys heard the fumbling of gloved hands, turning dials and flicking switches, until an eruption of smog burst from its rear exhaust pipe. The engine roared and announced its surviving prowess, and it was enraged by its disturbed slumber. Beneath its steel shell, the hydraulic extension of shock absorbers brought it off the ground. Tyran gave a mixed blend of a chuckle and worried sigh to himself. It was *something*, alright, but it hadn't done much to temper the situation of fire he'd been subjected to.

345

"How's it looking out there?" He asked Rhys.

"I don't know." The SNCO took another hard glance around the warehouse and he reaped the scale of which the bombs had ravished the fort. "I've… – god, I don't know, mate."

"Ella will be back in a second, she was just grabbing her rifle I think." Hearing her name filled Rhys with a senseless and inexplicable nirvana – blessed be her angelic ways, for she brightened the path just a little in total darkness. That alone was enough. "Then we'll just see where we're needed."

"We'll…uhm…we'll find someone who knows-"

"Tyran! – they wanted us to head more toward the interior's reserve lines." A shaky voice joined the ranks as Ella darted out of an off-to-the-side storage room, brandishing a loaded rifle with its safety catch on. As she emerged, her trail of thought had soon been interrupted by the presence of Rhys.

Surprisingly, she ran toward him first, where she reached out and slathered him with a hug of pure gladness. It was all very sudden. Everything had been, but hers was in good faith.

"Oh, thank the stars, you're alright!"

She expressed her gratitude just beside his ear with a kind-hearted whisper. The sultry swing of her quietened lips and tongue garnered his full attention. Yet of course, it couldn't last. She separated rather hastily and stumbled around, fiddling with the straps of her gear as constantly as she could. "We were worried about where everyone was. Have…have you seen anyone else?"

"Not yet." A crescendo from the unending hammer of artillery shells gave him an uneased edge.

Where he visibly trembled, stirred by the blasts he'd once experienced, Ella reached out and grabbed his wrist to soothe his woes. He backed away toward the tank and, out of trauma, prepared to dive into cover if need be.

"We shouldn't linger around here, it's getting worse."

"Someone out there – they told us to…" Ella clambered atop of the tank, out of breath, and fiddled with obscure levers and contraptions build into the walker's hull. Her voice bounced between a frail and stoical mess of insecurity whilst she desperately tried to replicate the collectedness of a soldier. She'd fractured her words apart with a struggled lung pleading for release. "...some officer told me we're to hold the interior reserves."

"How close is that to-"

"The medical wards? Close enough." Tyran piped up, beginning to close his hatch. "She asked the same question earlier."

Interlocking systems encased the pilot within his walker, hiding what little flesh the beast had to offer. And it then was brought alive with a fully functional roar. Tyran guided it forward and loosened the locked-up gears in its ligaments. Ella scrambled off to the left as to not stand in its way. The hall emptied as the fleet of operational walkers marched through the blasted doorway, disappearing into the crystallised winds.

Like larvae, they scattered and painted themselves in the bleached overworld as they set out to strike a heavy steel hand to the invaders. Tyran marched the machine forward and tore through the warehouse's fallen debris as if they were toys in the living room. Rhys and Ella stood behind it, beside one other, and held onto their weapons tightly.

Out in the cold exterior storm, three predatory, flesh-eating sounds dominated the land.

The first was the artificial voice of a tamed monster that stomped wherever commanded. It circled behind the warehouse and made its trip towards the interior, hoping that the rest of the 54th's broken remnants were still in one piece after the terrific cannonade that had swept around them in a wide, sweeping storm.

The second – a rumble of gunfire and artillery that exorcised life along the perimeter – lurked unkindly as ambience. Raw power trumped their base's strength. The sound told them, in clear detail, that all men where equal when set against a thousand siege guns.

Lastly, the third circumjacent sound: the tormenting storms ahead. Rhys pictured them as every scream that drifted through the infinite cosmos, and all that twirled between broken windows and tree stumps to be gifted no response. When he would die, letting out his final scream, perhaps another man would hear his voice in the winds as he heard those that had perished before.

The bombardments came in strict, formalised intervals. Distant shells mumbled the terrible voices of the soldiers on the ground. Everywhere they turned, the undying terror spoke to them in rhythmic thuds. And when the shells stopped trouncing their everything, the gunfire rose up in its place. Guns. Bombs. Shells. Guns. Shells. Guns. Bombs. They all made the same thing for Rhys, with barely any variation. The identical absolutes in their presence were clear: Violence. Carnage. Death. Brutality. Infertility. Nothingness.

Rhys looked around to see all but the egg-white of the winter – the blank slate of a vapid nature. Charged coils of frost danced between the legs of the walker and brushed against his face. In their little whispers, he heard not the screams of those left behind, but something of a tune. From far ahead, blasted through the mists of Mullackaye's winter, came the polyphonic cradle of one's national anthem. It bled into the frame. Ella kept her head down and eyed the snow, as Rhys peered from behind the tank. Then came the meaningless accompaniment of pride-stricken voices.

> *"In the land of pride and progress,*
> *Taint all ye' who yearn to oppress.*
> *Stars protect us from the demons;*
> *From yonder shores, they hail.*
>
> *Mettle conquers might, courage in my blades.*
> *Fickle are their wills, the spades of their graves.*
> *To the people, the kingdom and the blood,*
> *To the world of woe, we prevail."*

As wayfaring strangers, they promenaded over to the sound. First, the two piles of sandbags, each with its own shivering machine gun crew, welcomed them. Between those frozen statues was a parted gap for the tank and, further down the avenue, they saw the likewise adornments of soldiers from the 54th. They occupied their idle last hours and dug pits, carried crates and materials, boarded up windows and generally set up a defensive perimeter around the sector.

Rhys recognised few faces, though all were not by name; their pale collusions with death were made clear by their colourless skin, and they were all dressed sharply for their last purpose.

348

Some waved to the walker. Others were truly glad to see something powerful on their side. Things had been so unkind to them that the first sight of a metal stallion brought them confidence. They were the 54th after all – the damned from Haria's frontier.

Tyran stopped the tank in its place, swung the hatch open and poked his head out to the left. Just off to the side of the crudely shovelled road, he saw a man conducting an invisible orchestra. Flick – went his wrists. He slow danced with the wind and pirouetted on his back heel. All the while he rotated around a small radio, he hauntingly sang the anthem just a semitone off key. Rhys found himself starstruck and locked in place as he watched the intoxicated ballet ensue, and he then found his gut displaced at the eerie sound of his hoarse croak.

"Excuse me, Sir?" Tyran called from the cockpit. The man turned though he did not respond. He continued to waltz on his own, with soldiers walking by uninterested, as if they were in the proximity of a sane man. "Sir? We're part of the 54th too, where do you want-"

"Shh, shh, shh! This is the best part..." He waved a long finger in the air as the instrumental picked up, echoing throughout the smothered land.

"Sir?" Tyran tried again, with patience tested to their absolute limit. His calm demeanour in a full-scale invasion of Mullackaye had the Redussian hanging by a thread with blood pumped straight to his head.

"But isn't it truly so fitting to die for one's country, as it sings to you its dainty tune?" No one answered him. Out of his mind, Rhys thumped the tank's shell to get them moving. Tyran didn't budge. "Oh, a Redus-man? Well maybe you can't relate."

"Sir, where do you want the walker to go?" He tried one last time and to his luck he managed to snap the officer from his entrancement.

"Take it more toward the centre. We have several waiting for positioning. The commanding officer will give you your placements." The dancing man was interrupted by another voice. On the opposite flank, a blackly-dressed long coat stood independent of the olive drabs of the commonfolk around him.

"Pay no attention to him, Staff Sergeant." His voice crept in. Slowly, he walked over to Rhys and wiped his glasses clean. "Unsettling circumstances tend to make men ecstatic."

"Sir." Rhys saluted. Thomas shrugged off the sign of respect with the wave of a gloved palm.

"Nice to see a good man's face." The adjective assigned to Rhys stuck out to him. He wasn't quite sure why, but it did. A liar's tongue, maybe; or the presumption of who he once was. "I have a few of your squadmates over here, if you'd be so kind to join them."

Listening to Thomas toyed with the turmoil of the day. Far away rumbles from the subsequent conflict gave his words a measly soundtrack. Each word was spoken as if it were made from caramelised camaraderie. A falsehood of unity, friendship even, could've been described as that of a business relationship; like that of a farmer exchanging tongues with a neighbouring cultivator.

Thomas placed his hands into his bottomless pockets and led the way with an empowered stride. Rhys looked to Ella, who looked to Tyran. The pilot nodded silently and he climbed back inside to take the vehicle to its new home. The remaining pair followed after the intelligence officer. At the least, they were hopeful to see the faces of their own tribe again.

On account of their departure, the dancing officer was left to himself. Faded songs began to haunt the air, creeping behind and following on Rhys' tail.

"You've done well to get this far, haven't you?" Rhys thought he heard Thomas say something, but his mouth didn't move. It was his voice, undoubtedly. Ella didn't take any notice either.

He had felt as if his mind had decayed and rotted away, as an abandoned carcass, for weeks on end. The mental strength of the weakened man resumed its deterioration. Reality became indistinguishable from his incomprehensible dreams. The phony world meshed with the truthful plain. He blinked a few times and returned to the present reality.

"Uh, sir…" He braced himself. "What's the strategy here?"

"On paper, a well-rounded defensive approach that incorporates doctored intelligence, asset control and ground supremacy within the grand battleplan." Thomas rubbed his hands together and then he scrubbed his glasses with the fabric of his gloves. To Ella, his words meant nothing.

"And in practice?" Rhys urged.

"Well, I suppose it's a last man standing type of ordeal." He didn't let out the usual smug chuckle or high-energy quip. There was no comfort in his truth. The preservation of it was critical to them at the cost of an unhappy, pessimistic death.

In war, the long-standing trend had always been that the first casualty of war was truth. For the soldiers on the frontier, however, that first death could've been anything else, for they didn't care about factual information. The truth of the matter, for them, was that they were going to die. Wolves were at their door, and they fearlessly lobbed explosives at the walls until they it all caved in on them. Above their heads, there were the swarms of insects, an armada of fighters and interceptors, that danced with in competition – the stakes being their lives, and supremacy for the skies. What's more, the snow had inflicted either side with frostbitten torment. The Ferusians boiled their blood to stay warm, meanwhile the Kelan troops sat in both demoralised and shaken states. The truth was the least of their concerns. Their first casualty was the innocence many had taken to their deathbeds.

He could see it in the eyes of the men and women who indolently passed by, with their lethargic strains were but colourless glints, and they all talked with dreadful misconduct. A few huddled together and cried to let their tears form as ice. Others simply watched over the winter rind. Hope laid in the outer defences. Once the Ferusians were inside, all men and women knew that the result would be an inevitable travesty.

"What's our contingency plan?" Rhys pressed on, scavenging for that little silver lining he yearned for.

"Wish I could say we have one. Queen's drawn up a few charters as of recent." The officer turned as he gave them a grim expression – then, he flamboyantly reiterated it in the monarch's own flowered words. "The war shall continue. In fields, streets and homes. Resist occupation; uphold our individual identity from their collective venom. Let them tread on no one. Victory will come."

"And that's it?"

"Well, she has other confidential plans. Can't spill them though."

Ella continued to not add anything in to their disheartened talk. She stepped closer to Rhys and held onto her rifle sling, wrapped with overbearing slack around her shoulder. She shivered at both the thought and harsh bitterness in the troubled air. What was to come was something she couldn't have ever prepared for, mentally or physically.

"So, we're to sit here and wait here until we get killed?"

"Until we have an opportunity to break out, or if the Central Army Group sends reinforcements."

Honestly, there was no real reason Rhys pressed onwards other than to reassure him that the foretold disaster would pass by harmlessly. Thomas hadn't written the script; he only rehearsed the parts he was given. At least, that was what Rhys imagined. Every man was an everyman, a little piece of someone else's bigger tale. And Rhys could've been anything to the world, yet all he seemed was immaterial. He did what others told him to do: he woke up, shot to kill and then he tried to forget the blood on his skin. If there had been more to him, Rhys had buried it at that point. He pretended to care. Still, he just wanted the news that – by some marvel – things were going to be okay.

They arrived at the adjacent building to the casualty ward Sabrina was stationed in. Security looked incredibly tight, to which most of its personnel were made up of the remnant 54th and another brow-beaten regiment absorbed into its ranks. They just manned the guns and positions until their time came to withstand hell, with brooding stares and shivered fingers.

The buildings themselves were spread out across the interior rather spaciously. In between each were mazes of roads and runways that had separated them. Littered in defensive pockets, snowed out foxholes and small concrete shacks, the soldiers rested for as long as they could. A glance from one alone told Rhys of the oncoming traffic – a queue had formed at hell's ajar gates. The men and women of the 54th stared down their winter foe with hopelessness, but with that came the fact they had nothing to lose. They were to give what they could take. And the lurking mutter of the battle beyond kept everyone on edge and just barely awake. It could've very well been the end of the world. In Haria, there was room to walk back on. For Mullackaye, however, it was like an airtight box that suffocated those inside as it gently compressed under its own pressure. Its boundaries were well-defined, its reaches: claustrophobic.

Those who looked on hopefully still held onto the responsibilities of warriors. They checked their guns and made sure they didn't freeze up. Some even urinated on their machine guns to clear the frost from their barrels.

No more than a year before, life had been so unrecognisably civilised, as far as the common man saw. People did business and went about their day, ignoring the common malpractices of peacetime. Rhys' life had been contained and stowed within a little camouflaged box. He'd contributed to society through his familial care.

But then, as he sauntered on lost in thought, he stumbled into the line of sight of a particular pair of spectacles.

"You son of a bitch-" Hearing Mateo's voice brought a great deal of relief to him. He could count on the Corporal to be tactlessly louder than the surrounding environment. The wished to indulge his nonchalant nature. "Absolute persistence, you have, mate. Did you ever get your rest?"

He meandered over, and the little man firmly held onto Rhys' shoulder as he pulled him in for a welcoming hug. He had the greatest smile on his face. It was so lifelike and animated. Infectious, even. Rhys smiled back at him, then to Ella.

"I'm about to collapse, mate. I'm 'this' close."

He unwound their embrace, letting Mateo see the distraught fatigue that defined his facial creases. Ella gave a little wave to Mateo and they exchanged a few less-enthusiastic greetings. When they were done, she snapped her gaze up to the Staff Sergeant and leaned closer.

"Can I go see her – please?" A pitiful eye met his attentive face. With Thomas' battleplan fresh in his mind, he knew that their time together was short. She needed to spend every minute with Sabrina. All he did was nod and like a dog off a leash she beelined for the medical ward. Only Mateo, Thomas and Rhys were left in their clutter.

"Where are the others?" Thomas eagerly broke the winds of silence, and he fiddled with his brass coat buttons rather keenly. Mateo pointed to the corner, silently making a hand gesture to signify going around it. "And is Christa there?"

"Uhm…yeah, sure she is."

Off the officer went – in a flash. He too saw his own target and homed in rapidly. Rhys and Mateo watched on with wordless interest, and there was a glint of worthless intrigue in their eyes.

"Funny man, he is." Mateo reignited their talks.

"Intelligence Office. He's been lurking around for quite some time." Rhys said. He patted Mateo on the back and the two shared a walk through the snow, savouring their brotherly conversation before it wouldn't have paid to have been ignorant to their situation. "He's the one who brought the Christa to us."

"All seems a bit strange, don't it, mate?"

"What does?"

"Him. And her. Calls her by first name and then runs after her. She once mentioned him too, I think – in one of *those* ways, y'know. The ones you just know that are – like – yeah, they know each other more than they lead on. And he came and brought her to us. All just a tad weird." The lack of hindsight left them partially stumped, and Mateo shrugged with a little grin. "I've given up on guessing. Whole place is a bit fucked in the head, mate."

"Yeah."

Rhys' empty response drifted through the air with the snowflakes around it. There was a minute-long silence, fuelled by the awkward loom of the impending tomorrow. So they stopped, just before they turned the corner to the rest of the squad. And in their followed transcript, neither dared shed a tear as they spoke with contented realisation.

"So," Mateo started, "guess this might be it, huh?"

"Yep."

Silence.

"You think there'll be a spot in heaven for us?" Rhys asked, lost in a sort of scanted thought process.

"Not for you." They quietly laughed at the same time. Mateo nudged him with his elbow. "Then again, do postmen get a seat by Sunar?"

"Mate, if soldiers get to, then so do we."

A persisted emptiness went on.

An apathetic rift held back their true fears.

"Rhys, if this does happen to be it, let's get one thing and one thing only straight, alright?"

"What is it?" He listened to his Corporal with piqued curiosity.

"You've been fantastic. And I mean it. We don't see you that much, but we all think you've been fantastic for what you've at least done for all of us." Rhys stopped walking. Frozen in time, he heard Mateo's words play out over and over again. One. Two. Three times. Four times. An eighth. Fifteenth. It kept repeating. He smiled. It was a smile he hadn't done before. All the edges and curls in his lips had been defined by their own damned memories, until then. And when he heard those words, despite telling himself that they weren't the slightest bit truthful, it was the thing that ended up he needing the most: a compliment in a time of hoarse hatred. Mateo didn't have the gall to even shoot him down. And it mattered not if it were a lie, or a layered by biases. He wasn't just a postman, a little civil servant with rounded glasses and a sarcastic temper; he was the friend Rhys needed when the world was burning.

"Thanks." He spoke timidly, but maintained his smile. Neither said anything after that, not until they turned the corner.

There, he saw the rest of his squad laid out in their own little clutter. Or rather, he saw what was left of them, plus one. Oslo sat in front of Evelyn, physically blockading the chilling winds from striking the girl. At the back, the long-forgotten face of Gwen seemed occupied in Christa's presence, whilst they casually conversed with one another to sing the blue in their skin away. Thomas lurked beside them, actively lurking over the squad's newest recruit. Mateo joined them and his voice rang out with the immediate crack of a joke.

"Nice to see you." Oslo's booming baritone voice welcomed Rhys with solemn despondency.

"Good to see you guys too." He returned the greeting.

Timidly, he peered behind the gunner to meet Evelyn. At a glance, he couldn't even tell that she'd grown at all. She still looked exactly as she did at fifteen – tiresome and worried of how little she could comprehend the severity of her numbered days. She had her face tucked into her collar, buried beneath a layer of sleeves and a steel helmet.

Rhys frowned and turned away. Such a horrific belated birthday gift: annihilation. At age sixteen, Rhys had just learnt to go to the nearest towns on his own and gathered resources for the farm. He wrote in papers, read books and spectated aircraft as they flew by. Exploration, maturity and an ease into the real world, they were golden years by some unfaltering comparisons to his present.

Evelyn's sixteenth anniversary had existed where such infantile innocence had no place. Loomed on her doorstep were bombs, guns and men who were willing to take her life if she were to commit the crime of self-defence. There was no worry of what future she'd come to, or where she'd go to educate herself, or if she would be able to afford a house in ten years, or in what dingy bar would she meet her future spouse. In the case of Evelyn, she had to worry if she'd be alive the next day or hour. Her demise could happen at any minute. And for what partisan politics did she fight for?

Similarly, Rhys wondered if his own death would even mean something to anyone, or anything. To what measure did his sacrifice give anything to Kelan, to the Queen or the people around him?

The poor girl uttered a disquieted perturbance, indirectly mutating the epidemic of the finite hope.

Hope. *Hope*. Hope this, hope that. All he'd thought about, all Ella and anyone else had trembled for was hope. Mythical, yet close enough to be nostalgic. It hid in tall grasses, doused in snow and trampled by passing boots. It came unnaturally. Rhys made his own insignificant hope by holding dear the cherished moments of conversation.

"How are you guys holding up?" He asked the pair.

"Good." Bringing a hand to his beard, Oslo ruffled out the snowflakes caught within its webbed net. Quite clearly, they all were the contrary. It was for the better that neither were honest with one another. "And you?"

"Good, good..." A searing blaze interrupted him, creating a towering shadow across the opaque horizon. First came the smoke, then the sound. Everyone flinched, waiting a few seconds before going back to their conversations. Their fingers were all inched a little closer to their triggers than before.

"Seems rough up there." The gunner muttered his obvious euphemisms, and he was quick to move Evelyn further to his rear, and she then hugged onto his back. "I'm sure we'll find a way out. We did before, didn't we?"

With a curled finger, he lifted Evelyn's helmet up, revealing her warm, moistened eyes. She'd been crying again. Oslo frowned. He shook his head and gave her a colourful smile of his own.

"Hey," he cupped her attention in his glistening care, "chin up, Eve. We've got days ahead of us, yet."

She felt obliged to his paternal influence and kindly reciprocated her glimmering blessedness. Rhys saw it from a distance. A smile. Albeit saddened – escorted by the tears of her incredible fear – but a smile, nonetheless. A consequential fire blazed among the squad. Through a heartless ocean stood a wholehearted soul – fractured – that beckoned for a return to form; to a time when knives weren't at necks, or when teeth weren't clamped down on their fellow man's arteries.

"Can you do me a favour though?"

"Sure." She spoke, hoarse at the throat and croaked like a little forest frog. Sitting upright, she emerged from her foetal position and rose up, blossoming.

"I need you to go inside, head to the little makeshift armoury. I need to do some weapon maintenance." She nodded. Oslo smiled. "I'll join you in a few, promise."

As she wandered off, disappearing into the facility, Oslo sighed to himself and rubbed his eyes. The tired giant's smile melted away.

"I can't imagine how you must feel." Rhys engaged first in conversation, where he walked over and leant against the wall building wall beside the gunner. To their left, Christa, Gwen and Mateo chuckled together at the latter's story. Thomas just kept standing there, painfully out of his place and usual crowd. For a short while, Rhys was left on his own with the man who desperately shielded his lifeblood. "I'm sure we'll get you guys out."

"Maybe." Oslo shrugged. He seemed to care little of their state, rather his mind was elsewhere.

"You two have a strong dynamic." Running his mouth, Rhys let out a pathetic little smile of his own. He would've patted the behemoth's back yet he did no such thing, fearing that he would have provoked an uncertain reaction from the eerily still, calm and collected soldier. "You make a great father figure."

"I don't think so." He mumbled – a solemn grin came to his face, but it did so to chastise his inner turmoil. Whatever he said, an exhaust of mixed emotions shrouded the man. His voice was unnerving, but his smile and face of comfort seemed accepting of it all. "Either way, the strongest links in the chain are the ones formed with a purpose. Mine is to ensure she gets the life she needed."

"And hers?"

"To give me a second chance – to try it all again." Towering in the distance, the bombardments picked back up again. Each one brought its own shockwave through the snow, just gentle enough to feel against their skin. The thumps granted the snow their doped ballroom dance, forcedly twirling them in fanatic spirals until they crashed in a heap on the mounds below. Behind each flake, a trail of white dust spun on the wind's axis. And, like their predecessors, they found themselves getting caught in Oslo's beard again. "But it's the little things you've got to be willing to die for, unless you want to see them perish first."

Rhys watched as he too stood up and brushed his body down to scrape off the stains of snow. Under his chin, the clips of his helmet hung loosely and swung from side to side as he adjusted himself. He finished fixing his dress and gave a last sweep through his beard.

"I see you're still wearing it." He pointed at Rhys' helmet, noticing the rose carving still decorating his steel skeletal shell. The two shared a little smile. "She told me she's happy that you do."

"Anything to be a crowd pleaser." Chuckling, Rhys took off his helmet and caught his own glimpse of the petaled drawing. His service had distracted him long enough to forget what it meant.

"Anything as a service to her is a service to me, tenfold." He approached Rhys and patted him on the shoulder. His great hands engulfed his blade in a single grasp. "Just don't get blown up, though. She'd hate that."

As the two shared the last titter, he went off around the corner, lugging his machine gun around with him.

They tried to ignore the distant gunfire as it rose and dove in acrobatic cyclicity. It was impossible to escape from, however. Like drums of war, their echoes ran faster than they did. The beats of their rhythmic syncopation overwhelmed the striking thrashes of thunder. Hell's maleficent choir chanted its of-key melodies. The lyrics were not of human tongue. Placeholders, such as bangs, crackles and zips, stood in the space of words. And as it was so distant, the finer details of ejected shells bouncing off of concrete, bolts cycling and the individual sound of screaming men was unheard of. Yet it was still grander than ever before.

In Haria, they could see the devastation around them. But in the snowy mists, where their view had been obstructed from about thirty metres onward, their only tease of battle's sensory experience came from the thunderous sound it created.

Whilst his eyes were fixated on the rose, he took what little time he knew they had to ask himself what he was doing. Ella went to spend their intermediate respite to pursue one last moment with Sabrina. Evelyn and Oslo retreated off beside one another to maintain their little tools together. And as a collective, Gwen and Mateo stood beside the dazed Christa, not used to the grand battle, with an indefinable figure stood beside them. Thomas watched a little pocket item. Maybe it was memorabilia, but in his expression, he seemed little worried for his safety. Either he'd accepted their closing hours or he knew he'd be fine as an Osakan dressed unlike any other.

Rhys, though, had been left to sit stand with no one. He looked at the helmet continuously. The rose. The painting back home. Home. He wasn't exactly sure how far away his home was anymore. It was out there, somewhere. Hopefully, it had been left untouched. There was nothing significant about it. He worried for his father. He worried for his mother, who hadn't even seen him be taken away. The day he had been conscripted, the neural connection to his memories and comfortable life had faded. It weakened. And as it did so, he felt weaker himself.

There was no home for Rhys anymore. When he looked to the helmet, and the colourless steel rose implanted on its temple, he heard a slight voice traverse the air. From the aether, twisted by the astral warp of its tone, the beast's tongue came through.

"Does mother know you're not coming home?"

Rhys thought he was getting closer to the answer. It gave him a headache to remotely ponder over his dreams. They were nonsensical at first. All imagery without substance or meaning. Absurd, if nothing less.

A man blinded by sorrow could not identify the warning signs of his predators. Perpetrators ranged from mere men to times of misfortune. Rhys understood perfectly that he was a victim to the war. Unfortunately, when everyone around him was also a victim, he felt no drive to fix himself. It was down to those around him, to the ones who looked at him with longing eyes and brotherly glints. Everyone needed fixing. To repair their minds would be to save them all, to let them roam free of the war and settle elsewhere, where violence was a backroom box left unopened.

Sadly, healing one another took time. Time was precious and fragile. And with the knights of hell then entering their keep, it was clear to Rhys that he would get no time at all.

Chapter 26

War

Dust settles when the storms cease to exist. Storms, however, stop under one conditional factor, yet the aforementioned dust is also what perpetuates its driving component: for unrest maintains its course. Explosions and eruptions, both natural and artificial, disrupts the peace and fuels the tempest economy. Ruptured shockwaves spread across the airwaves and keep the storms in motion. It has been millions, if not billions, of years since the dust had last been settled – and since then, a permanent hurricane has remained in an infinite current. So, to settle the dust and to put the world to rest, there was a single, conjectural aspect of reality that needed removal – as to replicate its absence before the first harsh winds. And that would be life. Everything. Existence.

When Ferusia detonates their bombs against the sickly will of its adversaries, it unfortunately continues to disrupt said peace, yet if it weren't to, it would succumb to the very storms it tried to stop. See, they are trapped in a loop and a paradox. To stop violence, they must combat violence, which means they themselves would need to be stopped. However, pacificism has been an irregular term that has adhered to one thing: allowing oneself to be exterminated.

Man cannot fight brutality by merely slumbering aside. He awakens, and he should take his knife and put an end to the beast at his door. The silence only persists for as long as the corpse takes to decay, where another beast will ignite the flames again. Dust settles only when the swirling gusts high above the clouds stopped their course. And how do they stop?

They don't.

Man has no control over violence. He has no control over those who seek to kill him, be they sentient or dormant, for they too have as much free will as he does. Existence has always worked on a mechanical level. Human free will has never been a fluid dynamic. All it includes is the ability to adhere to nature or to die by its striking hand. Life has been mechanical all along. Nature is specifically engineered against us. The winds don't stop blowing until the world stops spinning, and only then shall it melt into a fiery lair for the devils of hell, where the dust can settle once more.

And what does this discovery entail? What does it mean for man, for the mortal Ferusian of this perpetual revolution, and what does it change? Nothing. But by our strongest desires to conquer our living hell, for ourselves and for the workers around us, and in our struggle to uphold morals in which we hold true, the Covenant of Syndicalism, then we as the people must be eternally braced for war. Peace is a farce, for we will always have foes. This is why as men we must engage in the politics of war and why we should deliberate what it means to live in Farhawl, lest we were to die.

- Union of Peace: The Lecture of War

~~~

"Major."

"Colonel."

Strauss and Schottenstein nodded at one another, greeting with a salute instead of a handshake. Less than a mile away, the continuation of the thriving battle serenaded their high-and-mighty presence.

"I'm glad my levied man caught you alive." The Colonel tussled with his brass cufflinks as he ushered out the mappers still occupying their tent.

"Thank you – a minute later, and you'd have found it nigh impossible."

"Yes, comrade, yes." And at the wave of his colourless gloves, he silenced the Major. "I won't dwell on that, though. And I'll cut to the chase; I've got a job for you. An important one too."

362

As he was briefed, Schottenstein's eyes darted his around the vacant tent. It was empty, save for the unmanned mapping and radio equipment inside, and the heavy winds clouded their words with the flapping of their canvas shelter. He listened carefully to Strauss clearing his throat, pulling a pencil-thin iron rod from his pocket and beginning his little behind-closed-doors conversation.

"We've got a deal with an inside figure. The plan's all over the place, though. Falling apart at most turns, yet the Union of Intelligence and the contact are both adamant on persisting. Can't say I'm too fond of it."

"What's this deal?" Suddenly quite eager, the Major leaned closer and lowered his voice.

"Within the fortress is a high valued target. A Kelan VIP, if you will. They've been said to be crucial ransom material to barter, through psychological pressure, a surrender and a ceasefire. And we honestly could do with one ourselves – back in the fatherland, there's been rising concerns over the war's fatality rate – as well as the loss of life fracturing the non-industrial sectors of our infrastructure." Broodingly, a dark cloud crossed the sky and blocked out what little light the sun had shoved into the tent. It was like they were beside a wavering candle, flickering out as the clock struck the hour. "Yet the Unions agree that they do not want a status quo outcome. As things stand, we achieve victory through diplomatic prowess or through continued military action. And with Queen Tala stating her position of standing ready to the end, they say this is our little shot to prematurely force her to submission."

"Right…" He took a second to process the information. Then, to gain better clarity, Schottenstein "This all seems a bit…haphazard. But – what's my part of this?"

Colonel Strauss smiled at his quick shift to compliance. It appeared that his judgements were true, and that Schottenstein, though barely a famed figure, was quick to understand that something bigger than both of them was at stake.

"Well, bureaucracy be damned, their delegate linked to this grand scheme is already among our ranks, and I see her as less favourable. A certain Major Emelia Westra." The sheer weight and mention of her name turned the roar of the battle to a twofold volume. Schottenstein knew of his own concern regarding her ill-defined political ties. Additionally, knowing briefly of the intricacies of what she sought for in war, his chest conflated the sensation with sickness. "You two have been working aside one another, haven't you?"

"As far as professionals go."

"This conversation doesn't leave this tent."

"You have my word." Strauss took a second to peer outside, then nodded at his spoken promise.

"Well, within two hours she'll be setting off with a small escort to the contact's rendezvous point – they know she's in there, and we're scratching all the covert-operator shit for an immediate extraction. But I want you to join her, and to bring a few of your own too. She's a menace and a minx for evil's work, and her personal search for stupendous revenge is deep-seated and rooted in the pockets of the Union of Peace. And if this is the best chance we have at concluding this war, before the bloodshed excels tenfold, then the last thing we need is for it to be hijacked by the bitch."

He sauntered over to the unoccupied tables and unfolded one of the maps left crumbled on the desk. Schottenstein ambled over slowly, and he curiously overlooked all the information presented to him, from hastily drawn markers to lines of attack, all the way off to the most isolated section of the wall, adjacent to a thick grey blob that represented a forest.

"You want me to testify if she does something wrong?" He enquired assiduously.

"I want you to make sure, with the necessary interceptions, that she doesn't let her ego disrupt this operation. We'll say she trusts you more than anyone else; what is your relationship with her?" The returning question caught him by surprise and left him hanging with a stuttering hesitation.

"Well – we do talk, but... – it's never been nothing really beyond that. I think. She's friendlier to me than I've heard from the others, but we clashed many times."

Strauss knew that the officer was mutually different toward Westra. The battle between political assets and operational control over the military had plagued several of Ferusia's smaller external conflicts consistently. With higher stakes, it seemed as if neither were ready to let it happen again.

"I suspect they've made a grave error – or that they plan to perpetuate this war out of a misguided desire to tear down Kelan in its entirety." The dreaded voice of reason butted shoulders with the menacing extent of his task. "Many politicians back home suggest that this is the best chance we have and sharing their vision, and that if we were to abandon it now, we would lose the prime opportunity. I say, comrade, that we can't subject more of our own to demise on this scale anymore."

Pointing to the somewhat outdated map of the fortification, he circled his finger around to the bottom right. Specifically, he pointed to the outside region of the overall battlefield: the southern-eastern forest.

"Our contact says that you'll be meeting here, or at the least somewhere in that area. When walking with her, I want you to enact the will of virtue without her interference hindering the greater good. You'll head out later but know that your time is limited. The *USC-Ornament* has landed nearby and is bringing over a retrofitted engine to slice through the gates of this place."

"I'll do my best."

Schottenstein saluted him a second time and made his way toward the exit. He was stopped, however, when his departure was interrupted by a small addendum.

"And Major," they faced one another, "if she does something, you are authorised under my orders to relieve her of her duties, by lethal force. I'll see that it doesn't impede your career – and that you will be granted legal protection."

"Thank you."

Schottenstein left the tent with a seal in his throat. Moments before, he had been on the frontline delving in the consequences of all-out conflict, yet the appointment of a political nature took the centre stage. He'd read stories as a child of spies, masters of espionage, all that worked against one another when their wrists were connected by handcuffs. And whilst those tales and fantasies were thrilling to read, finding himself alongside the political violence and unsteadiness of Ferusia's war plan made him sick.

He stood outside and loitered for a while. There was no sign of Emelia. She'd been gathering her own small force, and had hyped her inner-psyche up as she prepared for the little expedition that she'd dreamt of. Whether she knew Schottenstein was to join her or not hadn't been unveiled. It didn't change anything. He knew that the cleanest victory option lay vulnerable to the itchy trigger finger of an entrusted crusader.

365

~~~

Information from the frontline continued to vary. Fluctuations in the truth were doubtable, but the sugar-coating of its disaster had been loose at best. The officers that visited the interior weren't strangers to defeat. Some spoke with respect for the men and women beside them, be they conscript or the last of the professional servicemen who hadn't made an escape. On the other hand, there were others who tried to pass the narrative that the front had not yet crumbled. And whilst Ferusia itself had not entered the fort beyond several platoons, the nation itself was at a complete and irreparable loss.

Precise artillery bombardments left an area of effective impassability between the reserves and frontline defenders. It became a particularly heavy-tolled bloodbath for those who underestimated its wrath and sent soldiers en masse to reinforce the main line.

Mullackaye had been transformed into yet another sinful place for the wicked to thrive, as were all lands the war had dined on. The sun no longer shone upon it. Great clouds of ash, from carnivorous bombs and smouldering diesel fumes, spread through the sky like a fungal infection, proliferating in thin veins until they combined into a larger mass. A new night had begun before the midday had even finished.

Rhys continued to listen to the aural dislocation of battle. It became less consistent in its intensity where it rose and fell in a dramatic performance. To one side, he heard the mentioning of a Sky-Dreadnought on-arrival to dominate conquest for the skies. Whether he heard its arrival hadn't been clear, for the bombs and guns had started to sound as one.

They'd waited several hours. No one had differed much with their activities. Mateo still gave his one-man comedy routine. Gwen stood by and warmed up to his little performances. The de facto father kept the young girl occupied with maintenance off in another building. All the little things kept going on as they had before, desperate to block out the eternal stain that had ruthlessly bestowed their land with greed and disease. Rhys kept off to the side as a fly on the wall. He didn't interfere. For once, each squadmate needed their own little coping method to go by without interruption. As it was the least he could do as a leader, Rhys granted them their time to themselves.

Lazily, he walked through the snowdrift and travelled between sentry posts. Quiet nods to the people stationed within them was about as far as their interactions went. Those who bowed their heads back didn't respect or know the man, but instead the rank that he wore. The arrowed insignias of his status weren't anything more than plastic crowns held together by wet tape and glue.

He found the gramophone again. It hummed – a pathetic auditory whine had been left alone, however. The officer who danced was nowhere to be seen. He'd withered into the frozen air. All such peculiar sights had Rhys questioning if his eyes were as honest as the light. The gaze of a madman never saw through a thinly cut spying glass, upon paradise or heaven. Instead, he presumed his lens had been dug out of the ground – a diamond, translucent eyepiece compressed beneath six feet of soil and stone. The sights of the wicked world around him had been so fanatically insane that a younger version of himself would write them off as fiction. Hell, even a man of whom was only an hour or so older, he struggled to comprehend whether the day itself was anything other than surreal imagination.

In tardy motion, Rhys clipped his helmet back around his skull. The colourless rose found itself half obscured by the snowflakes that settled on the cold steel.

"Hark! The winter's bellowed its last omen. The death of the flowers. Shrivel – life shall only shrivel." A sentry barked out to the winds. Rhys ignored his insanities and moved on,

Pulsating through his chest came the nerves of a worried mind. He sauntered around, confused and dazed as to where he could go for a reckoning or consolidation with his internal strife.

More men and women arrived in beaten collectives: wiped out squads, bullied platoons and disbanded companies. Some contended the lieutenants and sergeants that manned the interior's reserve line. Those who begged entry were sent back toward the battle. Only a few were permitted to pass: the critically, yet fixable, wounded and the highest of authorities.

By eavesdropping their futile requests, he was gifted the dismal impression of the situation that had unfolded. Small detachments of Ferusian infantrymen had scaled the walls with

367

ladders, ropes and grapples. A small pocket of around five buildings and three acres of land had been seized and heavily entrenched. No vehicles had been brought into the base and Kelan's mechanised deployments were giving their worst to the invaders. The details were little and didn't define who had won the dawn of the end, but Rhys was certain that the victor had already been decided for Mullackaye's fall.

The siege continued. Those able enough to trek to the interior were considered valuable fighters, returned by trucks and disappearing into the blizzard. Rhys looked away, spared only by the 54ths strict orders to build up the last line of defences.

Thus, hark again! The barbarism of an industrial demonic presence cried out in the peaceless day. The sudden mechanical roar of a single engine caught many attentive eyes staring into the white abyss. Screeching through the winds, the noise of metal being carved into created a haunting drone. One distressed soldier buried his fingers into his ears and cowered in his foxhole. He was unable to take the excruciating bellow that had dominated the hour.

The further Rhys had strayed from his allies, the more alien the battle and people from it appeared. The childlike anxiety of standing alone, without their parent, sank into his spine and heart. Of course, there were people around him. They weren't really his people though. They too were just shells of men from different corners of Kelan – like humanoid essences that had taken arms as brass automatons.

Rhys rushed aside and, with his mind set on escaping the carnage of noise, he barged through the double doors into the nearest facility. He wrapped his fingers around the wooden frame of his rifle and hugged it against his chest. He felt insecure. Even inside, the drone of the slicer haunted those hallways. Say grace, he told himself, or he'd find himself unprepared at rusted golden gates.

Finally, he found them. A connection of blood. Kinsmen in arms, silently hiding from the castigating artistry bleed into the valley. Just outside their room, a few smashed windows had been boarded up. Sabrina's ward, however, was as untouched as ever before. She'd been moved to a repurposed back room, where she lay as its only occupant. As she was right at the back of the casualty centre, she only heard the suffering of the other patients from down the halls.

"I…" Rhys cut himself short with a misunderstanding of what he wanted to say. In a sudden trance, he had gone from being there, out on the reserve line, to appearing by her side in but an instant. So, he just stood there, and gradually Ella fine-tuned her sight to him, where she let out a weary smile. Rhys asked, in desperation: "Are you two alright?"

"We're fine."

He had expected Sabrina to respond and was surprised to see the younger sibling give him the softened, though weakened, answer. He trekked over to her bedside void, where he saw the casualty staring emotionlessly to the walls. Ella held onto her petty fingers and fondled her palms with her thumbs. Sabrina's light had faded. Her only clear movement that he could see was the subtle rise of her chest when she inhaled.

"Is she…?"

"Sleepless. Exhausted, really. She was given anaesthetics not long ago, something about treating a pain which wasn't even there. Phantom limbs." Ella didn't break eye contact with Rhys. "I can't help but think that it's our parents pulling at her foot – the one that has gone to the other side."

He didn't know how to respond – she was talking in hysterics. Between the depressive nature of his idol's fizzling brightness and the spit of a retrofitted dreadnought engine that carved through the great iron doors of Mullackaye, there was no comment he could have ever been made to lighten the mood. To provide something, even if it had just been the littlest piece of comfort, he went over to Ella's side and stood close by. Their shoulders touched and he found the conviviality of one another's dwindling lives.

"So," Sabrina broke the minute-long rest and rolled her eyes toward him, "what have you been doing?"

"Oh…" He smiled a little, hearing her voice clearly in a seemingly normal conversation. "I've mostly been walking around our sector."

"She told me something big is coming. I heard them – the bombs; they woke me from my nightmare…"

"I'll be honest," he frowned, "I've been walking around mostly to look for a way out. I know there'll be one somewhere."

369

He avoided disclosing his lack of hope. She didn't need it. Neither did Ella. He wanted them to have something that he found unobtainable: a little edge in the game of life that would send them off free. Rhys convinced himself that by virtue and sacrifice he may not have the means to make it to the end with them. But to change truths, he'd concluded that he would use what little power hell had given him to grant them passage on. They deserved the decorated years whereas he barely deserved a day.

Then, at the least, one of them could surpass Armageddon and formulate their own futures.

It beset him rather ruthlessly when he looked upon her tender grace. Ella's hands cradled Sabrina's palm, whose skin had been epoxied in the cold-blooded stillness of the season. Hindered by her opioid injection, he traced an outline of a familiarly sluggish man in her suffering. A father, in fact. Rhys saw the seeds of his own precursor's agony through her missing limb. And as an equal, Rhys began to see himself in Ella's place. The careful handling of her hand and the devotion to the lost body of another; he saw his existence collide with hers. He empathised with her pains as it had been his childhood, an unforgettable day in which his father returned from war with an arm and a leg, fractured forever. He put his hand atop of hers and Sabrina's and linked them in a triad of silent, rose-coloured thought. Only Rhys smiled. He told himself that the moment to become the beacon was right then.

"We'll get out of this, together. You, me and whoever we can bring with us." Wishfully, he caressed his own mind with the whispers of proclaimed faith. All falsehood remained cloaked, for he clenched onto the seams of his fabricated destiny. Dying happily outshone the unsanitary crypts of decay that Kelan had become; for they were the fates of the sullied. He sought to escape the indefinite bereavement humanity faced. "Until then, have faith in me – please?"

Readied by his ignited flame, he threatened the bringers of his injustice with arson. A blaze that could not be contained then torched the air around him. He knew that in mere hours he would clash face to face with the Ferusians. No memory or recollection of his remorse had survived his temporary purge.

The man he killed at the beginning of the war had been morphed through fanatic dreams into something faceless again – he was a monster, and Rhys was king the king of his lovers' safety.

The memoriam vinyl was itself scratched and had been reprinted, remastered and recrafted by his hand. That Ferusian wore a mask now. And the blood that stained the windmill door frame was blue. The liquid was thinner, and the viscosity of its human properties were weaker than ever before. What he had killed was an aggressor, not a man with a family. A terrorist. An enemy. Even if he lied to himself, he knew it was for a cause of survival. Ignorance perversely kept him safe from realising how brutish he'd have been willing to go for the sake of so few. Then, however, he did not feel ignorant anymore.

"How long before they reach here?" Ella curled her fingers around Sabrina's and sat beneath the gradual warmth of Rhys' reddened palms.

Their audience had been themselves and the disparity of used hospital equipment. Stacks of vials and closely packed beakers lay worn out or cold. A nurse ran in only to leave shortly after grabbing her needed tools. She didn't even acknowledge their presence. When she left in such a furious hurry, Rhys continued.

"Soon. Hours, days maybe? It all-" He stammered, but recorrected his thoughts with a clear throat. "For as long as they hold, we'll be safe."

"Stars – this is…it's all so scary." Ella drifted off to her mind.

All their days together had thus far held their vile and sickly visions to her glassy eyes. Soon, he predicted, she would've been buried by its insufferable presence, more so if he didn't act in her favour.

Time ticked by. Bombs descended barbarically onto the distant battlefield. Artillery shells hammered the dirt with its eighteenth great volley. The planes in the sky were almost gone, for so many had plummeted back to the land.

He pictured their desolate holding ground. There were men that waited in warm coats with scantily clad weapons that begged to be used. Imagining the tyranny that occurred in the first waves had him stumped. Not once had Rhys found himself marching toward the enemy to take their land and their blood. There was his own country; a placated construction of knee-bending victims.

Whose will they bent to was neither satisfactory nor safe. The monarchy had them bleeding for security, and the syndicalists had them drained for obliteration.

And then, the sharp sound of slicing stopped. The tectonic rumble of the engine overheating gave them a brief amount of breathing room. He let out a dragged exhale and had let his eyes fall onto Ella beside him, faced away from the casualty. Sabrina lulled herself onto her side where she closed her eyes for just a minute's rest. He wondered if she still dreamt of sunlit days or if the nightmares of reality had stolen her escapist, ethereal world. Likewise, he asked himself if she ever thought of those glorious summer hours they'd been together for, where the warmth and the brightness of it all kept them the happiest they'd ever been. After the rain, where Rhys was found on the steps grieving, had she ever considered how bright she'd been, or to what extent she'd affected his world? The colour had all gone to waste though. Depleted to white overlays, a colourless requiem for the tortured lost days, the butterflies hung still in the freakish air. The soldiers were all nettles: ignored and feared until they were broken down and chewed upon. The poisonous glitter of their past year had guided them toward the edge of a steep cliff. At the bottom of the drop were stirred oceans that waited to consume their flesh like carnivores.

Ella turned to look at him, breaking herself free of her mind's distortion. She was hesitant to meet his own gaze. A radiographic wave bridged the gap between their black and blue lips. Along the peaks of the wave were the cries of equalised pains. Neither knew where they were headed. And Rhys, finally understanding Ella just that little bit more, saw no blissful ignorance inside her. Instead, she had been transformed into the knowing citizen, the conscientious scribe, that had the weight of her world gagged by thin-threaded string garrots.

Murder was on her mind. Though unlike her Staff Sergeant, she hadn't submitted to being an accomplice of its terror. She wanted to preserve her right to have clean hands. Doing nothing to help the flow of chaos, all she worked on was living in the fragments of paradise. And its final piece was presented before her on a hospital bed, missing a critical limb and pausing for the final closing curtain. If she had one duty to maintain, it was that for the angelic enveloper to conceal what little prettiness had not been covered in blood-infused resin. She let out a sigh.

"Best get back out there, shouldn't we?" Rhys could tell that her voice was dishonest.

"Do you want to go back out?"

"No." Shying away from his face, she exorcised her beauty for trauma. "I want to stay with her, forever."

He dipped his head gently. A nod was all he could give. As a staff sergeant, he had duties to keep his footmen in the fight. Yet he felt as if her presence would detriment everything, herself included. She did not want to kill and most likely couldn't have – and when that time came, that would have been where her life ended. He didn't doubt it one bit.

"Stay here – safe, but…keep yourself armed." He stood up, and checked over to make sure her rifle was nearby. It was just beside the bed, slumped and free. Steel blessed with reinforced oak, leant calmly alone. Its presence tried to rope her into using it, but for a while longer she resisted the urge to enact vengeance. "I'll be back if things go wrong."

"And what if you don't?" Her trembled cry left much to be desired: hospitality, confidence or even happiness overall. With daring hands, he pulled her to his body and embraced her in an adorned hug. His hands rested upon her shoulders whilst she left hers loose. Eventually, she reciprocated the gesture and tried to smile.

"I'll come back. If I don't, you either hide yourself or run. If you can no longer do any of those, surrender. Live on at the first chance you get." A finalised whisper swept her and he let go, then he strode to the exit. He left with a purpose. If he looked back again, it was to give her a short curl of his lips. He tightened his steel crown and scratched his growing facial hair, then he exited off for what seemed like a final trip outside. A horrifying stand in resilience and resistance awaited his participation. The gnarl of his conscience's voice told him that the battle would not play nice any longer. At no point had he gone to put his life on the line for his nation. Instead, he had looked to the individual that tried her hardest to focus his mind on flourishing. Tiny blossoms of snow carpeted his path outside and the effigy of someone special materialised in his senses. Conclusively, the last burst of determination he'd ever properly feel came to rest as he accepted his ill-fated future, the greatest lie of all.

Back in the ward, however, the linger of Rhys' pleasantries wafted on and died in the corridor. Ella lost her smile and she quickly went back to eyeing Sabrina. She lay still but did not sleep.

"Even now, he's trying to project himself on us." She grumbled shakily. Ella leaned forward, attentively paying attention. She still sought out the words she always spoke; ones of wisdom and understanding, sprinkled with maternity and topped with cream. "If you have no other choice, you should make a stand, Ella, not give up. We…can't escape."

"Sabrina?" Whispering to her sibling's doctrinal alternative, she felt a chill shrivel her nerves.

"I don't think they'd accept prisoners like us. And – god – I'd rather not give them the bloody chance to tell me." The eager machines outside let themselves be heard once again. The slicing of the final layers of metal called through the sky. The doors were nearly open for all demons to enter.

"What should I do then?"

"I can't protect you anymore. Not like this, never like this." Sheepish trembles forced her onto her back and she pushed herself into an upright position. Ella saw the pain in her expression and heard it in the self-harming of her hopeless words. "You're going to have to protect yourself. I don't want you to rely on me."

"Sabrina, what did you tell Rhys," Ella let her pleas drift into Sabrina's ears, "when you two first spoke in the ward?"

Her question came without warrant. The penultimate growl of the grizzling battle accelerated her heart. Ella could not bear the silent treatment. She knew she saw something sorrowful in Rhys eye the moment he had departed – the change of his tune was clear for her.

"I asked him why he didn't leave me to die out there…and that I wanted to be left to rot knowing I couldn't protect you anymore." She curled her fingers into her palms and tucked each of them underneath her arms. She pampered and coddled herself into a tight constriction, and she brought her eyes to her remaining knee. "I didn't want to come back to this nightmare. He brought me back. And – and now I've got to watch you die."

Ella sat there, stunned. Her eyes hosed out her sadness and she sobbed into her own hands. Both had buried themselves into their skin and they soaked their skeletons as they sowed their hearts to the cursed briny.

She didn't want to fight; she didn't want to die. Truly, she had never feared death as much as she had then, and to realise that it was within her own grasp and ability to produce it tremored her innocence.

The door was locked and the walls had started to close in on her. The air she breathed was tarnished with exhaust fumes. In her lonesome imagination, she pictured the spirit of her existence fleeing to puny avail. She feared it more than ever before. Death. And in order to stop Sabrina, or even herself, from being anchored to the ocean floor, the time to kill had dawned upon her.

In essence, Ella Mistral was the psychologist who suffered from depression – an immovable and cruel setting of confliction between occupation and the abstract liability of cursing oneself.

Sabrina's words stung as harsh as ever. Music boxes of illegitimate thoughts unlocked themselves at her vile submission to violence. Unsung verses of egregious pain played out to her ears. She had listened to the most heretical sin of all: losing hope. And for the woman who brought so much light to both Rhys and herself, the revelation of her deathly wishes struck a nerve so aggressively that it had snapped. She recoiled in her seat. Then, she let her cries fall to silent, pathetic whimpers.

Misusing her attention, she didn't quite notice the screaming of melting steel enter its diminuendo. A great explosion ruptured the land and shook the cabinets around her. Tiny vials clattered together and chimed under the pressure of the shockwave. Dust fell from the ceiling and tickled her forehead. The world crumbled around her. For, sadly, the time had arrived.

Upon the loose-minded men and women of the militia, the greatest army to ever challenge them had cracked their protective shell. Under no god's grace, the wall and gates to Mullackaye had been broken, and in came a wave of tanks and soldiers to swarm the inside. When the first iron beast stepped into the fort's grounds, the day froze beside the snow. War had caught them.

Chapter 27

Breach

Gifted by the will of their ideological crusade, the gateway had been scorched to molten steel. Red hot meres melted away the snow around them and it charred the grass and cracked roadwork underneath. The black-and-blue defenders had pulled themselves back a hundred yards, primarily to avoid the ungodly ignition of the retrofitted slicer. On return, they loaded their field guns and kicked their horses into retreat. A princely array of cannons spanned far across the flat concrete everglade. Their presence opened the way to tremendous violence. Blinded by the blizzards, both forces challenged one another with suppressive resistance.

As the smoke cleared, which had been flavoured a phosphorus sting throughout the surrounding area, bullets took flight. Bolts chambered fresh rounds and spent them imprecisely. A wall of fire forced the aggressors into measly wreckages for cover. Grenades flew and mags were dumped. Walkers marched to act and scrutinised the barren fields, where they swiftly crushed the first line of infantry with unimpeded strength. The primitive strategy of brute force had worked; whereas, in contrast to its completion, the ground was littered with men and women who screamed for mercy. So little was pieced together, and what little cohesion they could muster in the ferocious flood fell swiftly to machine guns and rifles. They were initially compressed into close proximity, and their shoulders barged against one another, blades readied.

Faces met cheeks as either side met skin to skin. When they clambered over sandbags, desperate Kelan soldiers dragged them into the snow and thrusted knives into their chests. In their rush forward, the shock and awe of the Ferusians' pace overwhelmed several small pockets with pitiless ease. They rapidly advanced in a whimsical blitz – thousands were coked up on adrenaline and mindlessness. The brutal matchup had been met. The uncherished plight of everlasting screams, torturous pleas for friends to save them, whilst they laid in pools of their own blood, and the final gut-wrenching howls of the silenced – the war had left its chains and was in full force. And with their deaths, for both for the Ferusians and Kelan soldiers, their voices were cradled by the blizzard's aggressive wind.

Individual voices travelled on for miles. The speed of sound threw their suffering into the air and let the interior lines know of their folly. Casualties rapidly rose in the hundreds. Tanks cut down advancing soldiers like scissors to paper and slaughtered those that came to replace them. Chameleonic ice recoloured itself to the crimson paintjob of human essence. Those who caught a whiff in the unrest were sickened.

Lined with broken windows, regular buildings were transformed into pillboxes. An arsenal's worth of automatic fire spiralled out the glowing sunset tones of their overheated barrels, and they were pierced through cracked walls, open window panes and the skin of their foes. Freshly warmed casings rattled against the walls and floors as spilt change would. Men sat on rooftops with anti-material launchers and threw explosive projectiles on unsuspected vehicles below. The Ferusians never ceased their advancement – their faces were pressed against raging guns and their backs were cattle prodded by the sybarite commissars of the union. For whilst they still had the momentum, it was paramount, for their chance at remaining within those walls, to seize as much land as humanly possible before the warriors lost their drive.

Things quickly became more static, however. Instead of throwing their lives away in the masses, the syndicalist forces paced themselves steadily, using whatever advantageous set piece they had available. Captured defensive positions protected them from tidal waves of fire. They swivelled anti-tank emplacements back around and turned them against their own creators, and many Kelan troops, prior to their retreat, scuttled the weapons they could not bring with them. Drowned by the sensory overload of sound and the touch of frost, few acknowledged the bodies scattered all around. The scourge had been primal, and in rearing its ghastly, repulsive head, the soldiers became animals.

And as reds pushed on, they heard their foreign tongues insult them, knowing full well that their last words should have been in defiance.

"To hell, syndie!"

"For Queen and Country!"

They inhaled the nauseatingly vile taste of the air one last time – they were preparing another call of aggression – however their enemy's bullets struck them down as they lodged into their chests, heads, stomachs and hearts, and they fell to the floor, many with their arms in the air. Their bloodied bodies stroked across the wall like paintbrushes to a grey canvas, until they whittled out their shock and dropped dead. Some hadn't died in the instant and were forced to live out an additional few seconds of pain before the shock swallowed them whole.

Tanks danced and swayed between buildings as they attempted to outmanoeuvre and outflank their opponents. Their cannons and shells tore straight through steel and concrete. The pilots inside micromanaged each and every calculated move they made, for only one of the duellists to slip up and face execution via the enemy's titan. Stacks of smoke towered from their burnt carcasses – jet streams of exhaust pipes spitting out flames made for the most spectacular demises ever recorded.

The spiked-up racket and powerful tremors through the ground told those waiting in the reserve line that an abolition of modern civility had descended on their keep. Rhys, among those who lay in fear, was cowered in a small trench, one barely large enough for him to stand up straight without exposing his head. A quite inhuman beast buried its steel toes into the snow, ten metres off to the rear, whilst its engine growled.

The fighting was still a way away, yet each second it gained its ground toward the interior. The bells tolled to the masses – their day of reckoning had come.

"Just hold on, let the others weaken their advance!" One lieutenant called with fidgeting hands.

Rhys looked around for his squadmates. Beside him, Oslo stood tall and bold in a gunner's post. His left hand was firmly wrapped around the trigger, with the right one stabilising the stock planted into his shoulder. He tightened the small metallic plating on his forearm, a scarcely adopted addition to ballistics protection, and he rubbed his biceps for warmth. The spiteful sting of the winter's air had numbed his thoughts for him, which manifested in a neutral, emotionless stare out into the distant mist.

Hours, however, dragged by. They waited. And waited. And waited some more, before finally waiting. The roar of the battle never quite stopped, yet the 54th were never ordered to abandon their posts, even to assist the dead and dying out yonder. A private equipped with a radio kit rested against the snowed-out walls of their position whilst another staff sergeant conversed with its recipient through a scratched-up microphone. Back and forth, Rhys listened to the one voice present and, through peculiar intrigue, he tried to piece together their conversation with his imagination:

"Our position is still secure. We don't have a visual on advancing hostiles yet. Could stay like this for a few hours. Maintain defence, over." That was where Rhys entered the eavesdrop. He could see and hear the exhaustion in the SNCOs presence – and he was desperate to alleviate the friends he knew out there. Yet he could do nothing to help those in the carve-up.

"Please help us, we're being slaughtered out here!" Rhys heard a false mouth speak from inside his head. Without prompt, he'd created his own tongue for the radio operator out in the field, the one who he couldn't hear.

"We're under orders still to hold. Captain Laskey informed us that they sent the 5th Sappers to back you up, over?"

"There aren't enough men in the world to help us. Why aren't you helping us?" The imagined speaker said, received not by through the radio but by Rhys' psyche.

"Eastern sector tells me they're pushing back their advance… Assess what assets are still under your control, over."

"Help us, please!"

"That's good news. As long as you keep them out, they can't chain up their string of attacks." He conversed, abandoning the fragile formality of it all.

"Rhys…"

"What is their armour count? Do you-" The staff sergeant's voice was then melted away by the ghostly talk.

"Rhys."

"How're the casualties doi-"

"Rhys!"

"I-"

"RHYS!"

Rhys opened his new eye. He sat up responsively, and he scanned around him to see that the rumble of the battle had dimmed, as had the sky. He had arrived to a wraithlike plain. There he was: still in the trench. No one else was; it was vacant, other than his presence inside. An abhorrent chill lingered in the air still. Everything appeared still as a shadowy and polar shade of purple – the invisible aurora of his nightmares brightened, then died quietly.

"Rhys. Are you there?"

Weightless, his body lifted up off the ground, tearing him from his cowered foetal sleep. He fluttered without wings. His feet barely touched the wooden boardwalk at the bottom of the trench; and soon, he was climbing upward to the sky. A desperate battle between gravity and a physics-defying inception pulled him up the golden parallax stairway. Scarcely visible illuminations pushed through the menacing black clouds above. The dream constrained him toward the cheerless nebula. As his skin contacted its smoky construct by touch, it flickered into a clear and transparent piece viewport. No light came through. It was less of a window and more a screen that projected an artificial light from outside his own realm. There, a hand moved forward through the obstructions of the misted sky and it touched the glass-like screen that faced him. Rhys recoiled gently, with his body hung high above the empty field of battle, frozen in a stillness unfamiliar to the soldier.

The other side looked wonderful. Embellished free winds swirled around the glory of the sun's ray. Angels cavorted and frolicked. The hand that touched the glass ceiling of the world kept its palm flat and Rhys placed his own against it.

"I know you're there, Rhys."

Suddenly, his collar was tugged at with unparalleled strength and he plummeted back into the soil. The light crumbled and the world was plunged back into darkness. He gagged as the collar constricted around his neck – his eyes turned puffy, pink and wet as he could no longer breathe. His arms flailed and he pulled at his shirt, but the force on his throat came ever the tighter.

"Look at me, Rhys. Look at me."

The force that buried him revealed itself. A skeletal hand slid from his collar to his shoulder. Its fingers laid tenderly against him; the coarse barbs of its wire-like bones carved into his skin. He saw his own blood in the corner of his eye.

He couldn't turn to face it. The dreamscape shattered and cracked. Oxygen within the imagined paradise was replaced by a poisoning carbon monoxide substance. He suffocated, though his eyes remained open.

"You can see me. I know you can." Theatrically, the skeletal hand pinched his chin and forcibly turned it toward the entity. His eyes were locked into a staring match with the glassy gaze of a gas mask. *"That's right. You see me, don't you?"*

It dawned on him that he was within lucifer's lucid cage. Control became a figment of imagination, or rather it had never been a part of it. A fearful glint twinkled in his deadened eyes. The noise of the wind corroded. All that remained was the voice of the beast before him.

He first recognised the mask. He felt as if it had haunted him once before. The plague of his nightmares, he thought, and then he remembered how it had replaced the faces of those in vivid memories. The perishing of other souls, the day their identities were lost, were clad in nothing more than gas masks and dusty filters, who died in their place. He shivered at the sight. On its hands, a glove grew and stretched across the skeletal hand like a fresh layer of skin.

He tried to close his eyes and wake up from his unending nightmare. He didn't want to dream anymore. But he was still chained down to the floor by the throat.

"Don't you love it? Don't you love me?" Like paper burning in a fire, its mask was smouldered to ashened particles. Horror laid before his eyes. Behind the cowl was the soothing face of Sabrina, glazed in blood. *"Don't you love her, too?"*

The apparition leaned forward and planted its blazing lips against his. Absented comfort doused him in lipstick toxins as the warmth of her adulterous embrace smeared his tongue. It seared his pain and cauterized his cuts. Her blood soaked into his skin. It ran down his veins, flooded his heart and corrupted his organs. The silked slime of her gums merged with his, and he tried to scream.

Its viral contamination had burst his blood cells and choked his organs of their fleshy colour. Linked by the connected lips, Rhys wriggled and resisted its pain. He closed his eyes and

381

gagged, still trying to plead for the mimic to stop. And then its scorched heat disappeared. In its place came the frozen temperature of a blue kiss.

Finally, their mouths parted. To his fright, the creature's face copied Sabrina's no longer. Its iced sting belonged to the shivering stain of Ella's blight. The transformation was seamless and had outpaced the blink of his asphyxiated eyes. Icicles draped from the tips of her unusually white hair. He pushed himself further into the dirt to escape her grasp.

"She completes you, criminal. She tastes of you." It taunted. Its speech layered itself with a thousand chorused voices, as had the elk of the white forest: a crowd unanimously talking, all out of sync from one another. *"They make you forget you're in hell."*

And what of it – he thought – why couldn't he escape reality? What stopped him from being like everyone else and seeking pleasures from the vapid beauties of the world, the empty corners in which skin collided and combined into one?

"Because your fantasies are like this: twisted and empty. It is no different from where your body resides." Whilst it read his thoughts and unspoken words, the mask regrew around Ella's face like weeds and vines. The particles reconnected and the voice returned to a singular strand. *"Love me. Love me enough to watch the world burn around us."*

The world flipped on its head around him. Along every axis, he twisted and spiralled out of control into a motion-sickening corkscrew. He lost sight of the ghost and tumbled underneath the soil. Brute force shattered his spine. It left him paralysed in the dirt. He blinked again and gasped for a poisonous cloud of gas. Ash swarmed across his body and swallowed him whole, and when he opened his eyes to the clearing smog he was greeted by an unrecognisable location.

Sands stretched farther than the eye could comprehend. Adjacent to its dipped sun-starved decline, a sprawling ocean replaced the horizon. Still, the waves gently curled toward the shore and carried the sand away. The corrosion sliced into Kelan's coast. Rhys was stuck to the shore, unable to move his flimsy limbs. He let out a muffled scream, silenced still by his inability to breathe. Meanwhile, he saw his limbs as phantoms when he looked to the floor. A piece of paper laid beside his empty knees. On them were three letters – M.I.A.

The crunch of sand beneath his anchored shoes caught his attention. He swivelled his eyes to the right and held onto his anxiety protectively. The creature had returned and it donned its signature, ghastly cowl again. It careened its head to the side and stretched out its emaciated palm toward him.

"You can't walk on absent feet. You can't hold them with fingerless hands." The curled ball of bone-fingers moved for its frayed jacket. Without unbuttoning itself, its hand faded through its chest and drew a handgun. Rhys' eyes widened and the panic realised itself instantly. He wriggled but remained unable to break free of his mortal coil. The creature cocked the gun's hammer and angled it toward Rhys's head. *"And they cannot hold a man who isn't one in the same – whose soul is so misguided that it's lost in the darkest forests of thought. Now wake up. Duty's calling."*

Compressing the trigger with its deathly finger, the gun flashed, and the eyes of the dreaming Rhys were blackened in an instant.

Rhys erected his consciousness and sprang from his tight sleeping space. He clutched his chest and checked if he were breathing, finally discerning that he had returned to some semblance of the real world. The beat of his heart pulsed in his ears as he scrutinised his vicinity. To his right, Oslo still stood in the same position. The bear turned his eyes over to his staff sergeant and gave him a weary smile.

"Nice sleep?" The joke fell a little short. Neither really laughed.

"No...I...how long was I-"

"About an hour. Not sure how you dozed off like that." Oslo's baritone voice drifted off and he turned back to face his post.

Alarmingly, Rhys jostled himself a little upright, and when he sprawled his gaze across his slumped body, he saw the thick blanket of snow that had moulded with his clothes. From head to toe, he had been slathered in a fresh coat of ice. When he lifted his fingers to brush it off, he noticed the severe trembling they suffered from. They were pale, almost enough to have turned blue, and his teeth chattered against one another. Lost warmth left him numb at each limb. If the winter had finally decided to cull his sanity, then it had already married his body off to the bachelorette corpses around him. A thump against his head worsened as the chill in his skin marred his senses. And it was as he focused on the frostbitten air that he noticed something eerie.

A tonal shift had come about the hour. The gathering firestorm had physically departed and it had only left remnants of its choking presence. He was able to clearly distinguish his own clattering teeth in the silent strangeness protruded by the distant chaos' breather. Isolation had settled in. The men and women in the thousand foxholes cautiously eyed the mist, for with indescribable silence came the notion that they had no idea what was go – with carnage, at least they could see their deaths arrive in a fleet of fire.

Rising up the trench's walls, he took a long look out across the blizzardly plain and, as expected, he was met with than the long-overstayed whiteout that obstructed the horizon. A few foxholes and sandbags were placed a metre or so in front of his own, angled off to the side to avoid having their heads clipped by Oslo's machine gun. But beyond their protection lay the colourless mist in its entirety.

Several gunshots whispered their savage sonnets, and to the untrained eyes and ears it would've appeared that the battle was over. Rhys unfortunately knew better, though. It hid amongst the snow and crawled its way towards his lap, where it would curl up and wait until it exploded – the beast of war, spreadeagled on four legs, that was on its paced approach.

A vast spread of singular echoed gunshots belted out to the dark skies. It all sounded so widespread when instead, in reality, it had constricted around their position.

"What's happening?" He asked Oslo, lowering himself to a quiet murmur.

"I," the gunner paused to think, "don't know. Mate, there's so much going on that I can't tell. The fighting sounds a lot more spread out and infrequent. No doubt about it that they'll be on their way."

"Did the frontline collapse?"

"Maybe." The chilling realisation that they were open to a beating then exposed him to the bitterness incarnate. His mind raced with unseen anxiety whilst he tried to maintain a steady expression.

A nod. He rattled his brain inside his skull and looked over the excommunicated horizon. Its lack of a bombastic presence had actually started to haunt the battlefield, and in a twist of fate, he thought to himself how he would've preferred to see, in full clear view, the savagery that awaited.

And when the view from his eye-height trenchline blended with the abhorrent calls of downscaled firefights, the difference between a metaphysical cognition or the bleak overload of reality became muddled – and he latched on to the reactions of those around him to confirm whether he truly heard battles afar.

Off to the far right, a commotion broke free of its cage. Their eyes turned to see it play out: that same staff sergeant, the one who was once on the radio, held the radioman by the shoulders as he snivelled and wept. The latter's face had become an ugly mess of snot and red puffy eyes. His hands were caught in a trembling fit whilst his body was propped up only by the grip of his commanding SNCO. His boots were worn thin and his clothes looked older than he did. However, no one intervened and instead chose to spectate the eventful spur.

"On your fucking feet, mate." He didn't yell. Already enough attention was planted on them. There wouldn't have been any need to attract any more. "What do you think you're doing?"

"I want to go home…I – I quit."

"This isn't some paper round; you can't just quit and leave it at that."

The young man refused to meet his superior's eyes. Hell, it was a stretch to even call him a man. He seemed just barely on the fine tightrope line between adolescence and maturity. Rhys speculated that he couldn't have been much older than Evelyn was.

"Now get up and stand on your own two-bloody-feet." He commanded of the boy's returning obedience.

"I'm not going to. I can't! It's all- "

"You want a place in heaven, mate?"

"What…?" Stunned, the boy broke rank and file, and he looked directly into his superior's eyes, with but tears clouding his view.

"Come on, do you want to get to heaven?"

"Y-yes, yes I do, Staff Sergeant."

"Then get up and stand ready. Don't beg for ascension and rule out dying – and they don't take cowards."

Things continued like that for a while. Those were the final words he paid much attention to. It hurt to see others break apart and fracture themselves by sheer pressure. Ideally, he felt such a way out of empathy and for a desire to see others thrive. Truthfully, on the contrary, Rhys felt like he was watching revisions of himself. Cowards, as they could call him. Fools. Wimps. Whiners. Selfish, self-assured bastards. Selective Samaritans – mendicants of his own good deeds. Thinkers, not actors. Philistines in denial. Cowards. These words, traits, names and actions had distorted his personality. He didn't seem to care about the one true good message anymore. Only for a select few people did he offer his condolences or his pledge of allegiance. Ella. Sabrina. Mateo. Oslo. Evelyn.

Squad 2 was truly no more. Then again, it hadn't ever been whole to begin with. Its positions were filled: an anti-tank rifleman, scouts, shocktroopers, a gunner, a marksman, a combat medic, an engineer too, and the grace of a walker pilot. They were a skeleton crew on a ship that sailed in the cascade of ice. Amidst their ghostly place in the 54th Defensive Regiment, the most fractured bone of them all had been told to be a leader. The band of brothers and sisters were divided by an inept coward. It lacked a frontrunner and so it could have never truly been complete.

He sighed. Of course he did. What else could he have done? Could he have ran up to the staff sergeant, the one who mirrored his rank and responsibility but outmatched him in presence and substance? Definitely not. He'd have been chewed out and publicly labelled as a quitter. Weaklings exposed themselves when their lives needed rehabilitation. Rhys' mouth was taped shut. He never wanted to see himself in such a vulnerable place. And to admit he needed help was like accepting defeat. He wanted to be the one who controlled his future.

Yet he'd depended on Sabrina before. It had broken him extensively when the time came for her to suffer a callous destiny. To preserve that sane beauty, he returned with the suicidal remains of her mind. And then, he'd turned to Ella for that cherry blossomed grace he lacked. Guilt fostered the destructive tendencies he partook in.

"Oh god," he whispered to himself, "what would happen to…"

"You say something, mate?" Oslo separated from the commotion when he noticed Rhys' troubled gaze. As expected though, the response classified his thoughts.

"Nothing. Just a bit dazed."

He looked to the right and saw the boy stood at his post, shielding his eyes with his sleeve. He wiped himself dry. And much like a coward, like how Rhys had for months upon months, he went back to standing in line. He was no conscientious objector; he was a soldier by proxy and commission of the crown, a name on a register and nothing else.

These soldiers, all of them, were all just that. Heroes didn't last. It was their names that did.

And, truth be told, their names were to be forgotten – all of them. In some utopian, idealist mirrorland, their identities would've all been plastered on great memorial structures or referenced in historical textbooks for generations to remember. Reality, though, dictated that they were unlucky numbers in a socio-political lottery machine.

And even if they were remembered through memoriam, then how? Would it be to tell the tale of their sacrifice and of their struggle to survive? Were they villains? Or would they be recalled as noble warriors who took up the mantle of royal determination to kick back the red menace? That was to say if they'd be given the time of day to begin with. As things went, the Ferusians were winning the war, and the victors were always right.

Everyone was back in line. Rhys wiggled his toes to keep his cold blood flowing. Additionally, it gave him something else to focus on. The little frozen tips of his feet were shielded by thick woollen socks that made him itch, so much so that it maintained at least some sensation in the bewitched cold.

His little offshoot of thought was cut short when the gunfire suddenly reared its ugly head again.

Eyes and ears turned to the left as the sound of a repeating machine gun, one of their own, let out a blazing bellow. Those sat down and slumped together for warmth scrambled to their feet and latched onto their firearms for security. Their voices lowered whilst the machine gun continued to rattle.

For six seconds it shot non-stop. No pauses. No mercy. And then, at the seventh, it came to a swift end.

Officers then began to call down the lines to figure out what was going on.

"What the fuck was th-"

Fire and the electric jolt – the heartbeat skip was incriminated with a breakneck shot.

Lightning struck their position; its thunderous shock took the shape of brass bullets. Rhys ducked back into their trough the second it started, only narrowly avoiding the initial wave of lead. The swarm of insect-like projectiles arrived in furious vulgarity, and it had done so without warning.

The snowy perimeter of their defences was punctured by a thousand lead drills, and it brought the dirt, sand and concrete with it. Chiselled materials were kicked around helplessly while the soldiers hugged the walls and stayed below the line of suppression. An unlucky few were cut down where they stood.

Some desperately held onto their helmets, worried that if just a millimetre of their skull was exposed then they'd be ripe for death's picking. They all cowered for their lives. It only took just one trigger compression to kill someone. The storm they faced made their deaths seem inevitable.

"Where are they?" Oslo called, unable to redeploy his machine gun. Rhys peered over the top of the trench for just a second.

"It's too foggy," he gasped and retreated into cover, "I...I can't see anything."

"Let's just hope they can't, either."

"Bring up the walker!" Cried a lieutenant. Scratched by the inconsiderate barrage it faced, the nearby mech blasted its engine on. Its ignition roared between the trenches and it began to sluggishly adjust its position. Tyran was inside, piloting the beast expertly. "Open fire!"

A basaltic release of carnivorous bullets spewed from its auxiliary anti-infantry armaments. Closeted fury stormed out of its casing. The belt fed bullet after bullet into the fold. A sunbeam of tracers illuminated the starless sky. Seconds later, the fire that came their way depressurised and loosened its grip on their necks. Oslo was the first to reveal himself to the open field, placing his bipod down against the floor and opening up into the mist without a proper sight on their enemy. One by one, the riflemen joined in, standing across the line and suppressing the living daylight out of the aggressors.

He inhaled and sucked up his hesitation. Rhys let out a panicked call to arms and rose to the occasion, rifle in hand. He took to the stage and pulled the trigger to add his blades to the grinder.

Each shot booted the rifle into his body with significant force. It pressed hard against the plating of his combat gear at each kick. He ignored the pressure and fired relentlessly into the fog. He was gifted with the fortune of being unable to see his target, to which he then switched his tune and thanked fate for its coverage.

There was no way to tell if he'd killed anyone. They were covered up by the lying curtain of the blizzard. And with the Kelan force releasing their strengthened defences, those that advanced toward them were met with a terrifying fate.

He scanned the hellhole with a sharp yet stunned eye. The overwhelming overture of guns killed the silence and slaughtered the momentary bittersweetness of the fight. As Rhys emptied his magazine, bullet by bullet, he paid no attention to the many questions he had. Round after round, his firearm ejected smoking casings to the side and onto the floor. They scattered across the trench bed and the brass tinted leftovers littered in mound. Piles formed in closely knitted pockets as they melted the snowdrops that landed upon them.

Three. The spiralling twirls of red-toned tracers introduced the finale of the world. He had achieved its greatest destruction.

Two. Second to last round. He checked the chamber and saw a bullet object to leaving the round. Its refusal left him exposed and undefended against the enemy. He unjammed the weapon with a several jagged tugs at the charging bolt. Pervasive hesitation reimbursed the sour hostilities of his nerves and worked in favour of the Ferusians.

One – the last bullet.

A glorified noise came from the gun's internal systems, clicking with a harsh, metallic and mechanical sound. Before, he'd have seen it as a satisfying end to shooting down a range or being granted the ability to step away from the depressing atmosphere of holding such a weapon. Locked into a trench, with bullets headed his way, there was no greater frustration than an empty magazine.

He reached into his webbing and fumbled around the pockets that grew deeper the minute he needed to find something in them. Ridges of a frozen metal box stroked against his quivering fingers. Bingo!

He pulled at it in an attempt to slide it out of the satchel, but it took far too many tries. Eventually, he yanked it out with such a force that he lost his grip and it tumbled to the bottom of the trench. It splashed against the casings and bounced aside as he chased after it.

"Fuck…"

He apprehended the runaway magazine. His heart raced as he clambered on to his side to shove the ammunition back into place. "Get in you…fucking…"

He forced the rounds back into the rifle with irrevocable force and primed the first round. He quickly shoved himself beside Oslo, who'd made an occupation out of placing bullet after bullet down onto the umbrage of the concrete promontory.

Terror arose when the *THUNK!* of a launcher made itself clear through the gunfire. He looked up to see little rounded canisters, propelled by the compressed blast of a rifle-mounted catapult. They span as they indiscriminately planted themselves into the ground. A few metres ahead, one landed before the pair and they pulled themselves back into the pit.

"Grenade!" Someone shouted, and a chain reaction of explosions ravished their eardrums. The assaulted and unlucky men to their right looked to their feet and saw a second land beside them. Rhys felt the shockwave funnel down the trench way. Shrapnel darted around only to be soaked up by the nearest bodies. The closest ones were thrown aside, splattered against the walls with devastating force.

Seconds after, the screaming returned in a massed wave.

Rhys lifted his head from the floor and turned to face the carnage. A lake of around fifteen soldiers laid in grimly stacked piles, either clutching on to their entry wounds in agony or motionlessly cleft away from their souls. Pleas for parents soaked the burst eardrums of those who remained. Medics were called, shots were exchanged and the return to the gothic form reignited itself. Aggressive defence dawned in chorus to the combative, euphoric ideologue in their garden, sowing seeds of arbitrary prejudice. He violently coughed when the vapour of torment inundated the atmosphere. Around him, grenades detonated and discarded stone, shrapnel and blood in their fiery blasts. Tyran's walker took several steps rearwards as it spaced itself away from the small-arms explosives.

Oslo grabbed Rhys' forearm with an iron grip. He forced him back onto his feet.

"What is that? Is that my...-" A net – constructed from human tissue – scooped up his attention as he heard the cries.

There, the cowardly boy waited with the bodies circled around his meagre collapse. His hands covered his stomach. He exposed it as his arm soaked in a sticky residue, and all eyes could then witness the tear straight across his torso, revealing his shrunken, sickly bowels spilt onto his groin. A torn-off gobbet of his stomach lay free in the snow. By the thread of tissue and the nerve, the forever stone gaze of his left eye lay dangled across his cheek – it had broken free of its socket. He opened his mouth to scream and cry. But for the betterment of his transitory decay, he passed out from the shock of it all, and the blood poured out like wine against a crystal-white carpet. Rhys had seen it with irresponsive terror, stunned but the aloof barbarism left unchecked, and it repulsed him to a state of shock.

The sounds of the battle faded with his hearing. He was collapsed against the trench wall, eyes still trapped on the soulless shell of the boy. All the while, the armed forces of Ferusia maintained their advance, and they kept up their feverish suppression to great effect.

Gunfire that poured from the trench had been weakened by the eternal stream that impaled their lungs. Their numbers dwindled.

Oslo disregarded the pain and stood his ground. He exposed his weapon, lined it up to the vista and held the trigger down without a hint of hesitation. His teeth were gritted together, grinding the bone gears in his jaw. Steaming lead returned the aggression they had flung at him. On his mind was the only greeting they deserved – welcome to Mullackaye. And there, in the concrete and snowed out trenches, a daughterless father shrugged off sight and sounds that encircled him.

Thenceforth, the wall of flesh stepped aside for the steel cavalry to march in.

The machines casted indistinct outlines in the anarchical climate. Imposed shock ran through the first wave survivors when they soon realised what was upon them. Their legs, brutal and endowed, carried unrivalled cannons. Before they'd even broken through the mist, some fired their shells. A trail of orange stardust exhausted behind the first short as it barrelled toward Rhys' position. It came at such a pace that he had no time to react. It soared mere metres over his skull and slammed against the leg of Tyran's walker. An incredible *clang* called out. By the luck of the sloped armour on its knee and angle of attack, the shell deflected skyward and joined its sibling stars in the sky, and the orange glisten faded out. A formidable mark had been left in its wake. It had left a vicious imprint on the walker's legs, and Tyran staggered his chariot sideways, returning fire with his own ferocity.

Rhys spectated as the nearby flock of walkers marched into action, blasting over the infantry, as they took little interest in their weaker, fleshy compatriots.

The battle bent to the tanks' conclusive will for mechanised dominance. Rhys pulled Oslo down with him when the shells started flying.

He took a second-long peak over the ridge and saw the red knights of the arctic descending upon them. They were incarcerated within woollen armour, and their ideological wardens processed their resolve and placed their faith in their rifles. A war cry unlike any other outpaced them.

The pair followed the gunner's example and Rhys whispered a fabled name. A hyper focused, chronic endurance stole his attention.

Eleven militaristic commandments set themselves in mossy limestone tablets and were embedded into the trench wall he faced.

I. *Fix his stance.*

II. *Ensure he was properly equipped.*

III. *Engage in judicious strategies.*

IV. *Don't let them outsmart him.*

V. *To no ends shalt they lay a finger on her.*

VI. *Have no sympathy.*

VII. *End all empathy.*

VIII. *Hollow their skulls.*

IX. *Accept submission, for her.*

X. *Take another life.*

XI. *End them.*

The feverish insanity allowed for him to steady his nerves. Gripping his rifle, loaded with a ripened magazine, he took aim and fired at the blackened shapes wandering along the panorama. With such an extent of fire forced upon the advancing figures, he took no recognition in those killed by his bullets. There was no reason to claim accountability. In the end, they would do the same to him. He forgot that they had emotions of their own. All he was exposed to were the clothed-up faces and balaclavas of the invading soldiers – such inhuman features of the modern soldier made it easier to call them monsters.

"Stand your ground!" A hasty figure wrapped in ribbons and medallions called to the castrated masses. He limped down the line with one hand hard-pressed against the open entry wound on his thigh whilst he left a trail of crimson liquid breadcrumbs wherever he went. His pale body drifted across the frontline. Spooked soldiers looked away from his ghostly face, rather facing the battle ahead than the deathlike phantasm that egged them on.

Defined uniforms ran straight at them underneath the tank's suppression. Oslo sprang from his position. A rusted belt of ammunition was chambered to his hulking weapon. He lugged it over the edge and hammered the trigger down as hard as ever before.

They dropped so easily, like wingless flies struck by lightning. Five of them. Ten. Fifteen. He knocked down the approaching crowd in an indiscriminate volley. A squad's worth of soldiers had been immediately purified by their venomous arms. Rhys winced toward their demise yet suppressed any desire to hold back. He emptied the remainder of his magazine and reloaded again, that time without the troubled fumble to burden him.

He remained dexterous. For several minutes, the battle reached its ultimate peak. The interior perimeter was challenged by the encompassing and overwhelming might of the Ferusian war machine. Doctrines that lacked mercy were enacted. Overcome and overpower the enemy, they would, as if it were the battle to end all wars. Rhys bled through his magazines. Bullets scraped by the sandbags and concrete battlements of the trench.

Minds were numb.

Fingers were cold.

Hearts were frozen.

Farhawl stood still. In came the brigade, escorted by its corps of killers. He thoughtlessly imagined that it was not by choice. Maybe it was. Maybe he had a duty to fulfil, and it was when the injustice came at its full extent, bearing all of its fangs and claws, that he realised there would be no other option but to become the butcher.

He was lost in the transition – the semblance of the panicked man, gone – and to a fabled warrior he became, a tale of mythological uprisals. He was, for some time, a warrior. The real Rhys looked back upon it and cried for remorse. But at that hour, nothing else but his life mattered, for better or worse. When the world he saw as true died in battle, the correct and deadened face of the dishevelled man prevailed.

That weapon inside of him had been left lurking within Rhys. It had seen the oasis inside of him and begged to take a sip from the pool. And when it finally reached it, taking the slightest sip of its sickly nourishment, it realised how much anger had revelled in enacting vengeance. Were he to ever describe it, on the rocking chairs before ignorant journalists, he would have said:

"My life, for what it was worth, mattered not for what I had to go back to, but for the anger in which I had to give."

All that the withered soul needed was to take all of his qualities aside. He had to ignore the pain. He had to pay no heed to that second voice in his head. He shouldn't have been mindful of caring, for his enemies or his allies. For as long as he held only the heart of that who he loved at the forefront of his fight, he didn't need other reason to put men down like mutts.

The forces made excruciating progress, and Rhys made sure they bled for every metre they gained. In his walker, Tyran fired off another shell. Rhys saw the accelerated mass jackhammer its way into the closest tank, ripping and tearing through the steel and flesh inside. A fiery blaze ignited from within as the engine and munitions combined into a single blast. The few men that took cover behind its legs were engrossed in the flames. Against his eyelids, he felt the heat from his cobbled hiding spot.

The tank's movement was calculated. Tyran's affinity for micromanaging his beast left a lasting impression on the soldiers around him.

Some paused and gawked in awe as he would pre-emptively move his shielded legs toward the next shot, deflecting them aside, as if the metal limbs were his own.

Each rebound left the steel screaming. However, its focus on the armoured opposition left the infantry free to push forward, until they were met with the militia's steadfast fighters.

With each shot Rhys took at the wandering infantry, a shell tumbled downward to the ground.

One down.

Two down.

Three down.

Fourth dead.

Fifth killed.

Sixth slaughtered.

A nightmarish spectacle of men dropping dead like insects disproved the safety in numbers, where a single man with the right tool could silence a thousand voices in an instant. Rhys didn't respond, however. He kept firing. His webbing grew lighter with each magazine he spent. Yet, he never felt any more buoyant. He ignored it, and still the weight of guilt deliberately balanced out his bulk. The fatigue of the fighting man got to him. He gasped for air again, as his levelled-self had poked through his jaded anguish, and he was breathless at the intense fury that he had provided.

Minutes passed. Guns fired. People died. Rinse and repeat. Second by bloody second, the gruelling grinder fed fear's inoculation. They became numb, and then number. Their hearts would beat out a slower rhythm. Figures emerged from the fog, slinging grenades at the 54th's place, and then slowly they made their way forward. Broken vehicles became sources of shelter and the snow concealed the cautious. Rhys knew that it was only a matter of time before they would've drawn too close.

On the left, he saw several Ferusians tumble over the ridge. They descended into the gutter and made work of draining its occupants. Rhys pushed past Oslo and brought his rifle to. He watched the men struggle, unsheathing their blades and thrusting them with repetitive shanks. He took a few steps forward. He cleared his vision. One by one, he trod over fallen bodies to get a good look at the next man he'd bleed dry. In the confusion, many of their allies hadn't noticed the breach, but he did. Rhys raised his weapon and lined it up to the unfamiliar parties breaking in, and he fired. Once. Twice. And for safe measure, thrice.

Two were put down by force. He ambled closer, the eyes of cowering men and women meeting his. Seeing the dead Ferusian in their trench launched a panic that rippled through the masses. Some turned, digging themselves deeper into the concrete for protection. Others hastily reorganised their squads to better prepare for another breach. Rhys wasn't sure how they could hear each other through the carnage. Throughout the blisk turned snowstorm, the product of sound administered their sanity. Noise, like the roar of million lions, bellowed in the loudest fashion. The evocative entourage of guns and grenades performed tunes prophetic of the nation's end.

"They're getting in close, brace yourselves!" The rampage disrupted their steady hold. Alike the medieval keeps before them, Mullackaye had been devastated by the assault. Their defences weakened mutually with the soldiers inside in the battle of attrition.

396

Rhys darted back to Oslo. A rush of blood came to his head. From above, several figures dropped down onto his position, and he was immediately tackled to the ground.

He felt the tight blades of the man's nails dig into his sleeves whilst he wrestled him to the floor, forcing Rhys to let go of his weapon. A Ferusian was atop of him. Caught off guard, he had been blindsided by the murderous beatdown. A clenched fist hammered into his chest and blew the wind out of his lungs.

He winced through the agony. The split-second glimpse he had of the ruthless aggressor revealed her face, for her mask slipped as she primitively caved in his body with her hands. The Ferusian slammed her fist across his cheek, a move which threw his situational orientation back into gear. She had the upper hand as she pinned him to the floor amidst an all-out brawl.

She reached for the dagger on her chest rig but she struggled to keep him pinned. Fight. He had to. There was no choice. The pain in her eyes, the momentary aggression caught in an adrenaline-fuelled drug, all told him that it was a duel of fates.

One of Rhys' knees was free from her weight. He pulled up to his chest and kicked against hers, shoving her off him. Whilst she staggered away, he rolled over and reunited himself with his weapon. He didn't aim, and he fired several times in her direction. The force in which he had displayed barely registered with him as he broke line of sight with the soldier.

There he was, breathless on the iced floor. He couldn't move. His muscles ached. His senses came back, and in that instant, he was terrified.

The tint of a blood-raged filter snapped away, and he saw the raw carnage that surrounded him. He lay still for some time. Any fighter could've taken him in that moment, but nothing came of it. He sat up slowly. Then, in his dazed confusion, he called out a name.

"Oslo!" He yelled in a coarse voice and he wheezed from the bruising on his skin. The gunner didn't turn, locked into a state of combat. He blocked all but one sound out: the oversaturated presence of his firearm's labour. It was a miracle that his situational awareness hadn't gotten him killed. "Hey!"

Rhys reeled himself over to the man and grabbed his bladed shoulder.

He caught a glimpse of Oslo's poignant stamina. He hadn't moved position, and around thirty bodies had toppled before they'd reached him. And there wasn't any sign of him stopping. The more he took to the graves, the less there were to harm his familial protectorate.

"Oslo, come on!" He yanked his shoulder again, finally withdrawing the man out of the gung-ho reverie he'd been bound to. Rhys turned away to look down the trench, spotting yet another three Ferusians entering their keep. He stepped away from Oslo and aimed, no longer out of a desire to kill but instead out of a knee-jerk reaction of fear. The tally was mystifying, and he inexplicably lost track of the lives he'd taken. He'd fed into the hate.

"Come where?!" Oslo yelled. His machine gun exhausting a sunflower-afterglow – it was a turbulent product to his staunch dedication.

"I…I don't fucking know-"

A seismic rupture interrupted his trail of thought. Tyran's armoured machine sprung back into the scene, strafing aside the anarchy. From the ejection port, a split golden casing was spat out of the walker. Vapour trailed out of its cracked tip. Inside, the cranks were pushed and pulled, and in he loaded the next round. When it fired, the snow around it was shaken aside. A rift in the winter, in time and in space was created. It climaxed in its impact, where the shot broke through another syndicalist tank.

"Get behind the walker, we can't stay in the trench."

"What-"

"Just follow me!" Rhys pulled up his weapon and, with words alone, forced the gunner to trail him. They navigated the turns and corners of the drain, stepping around the blood flow on the arctic seabed.

The nearest stairs to Tyran's tank were concealed by two corpses, collapsed on the first and third step – both had several wounds in their backs. Rhys peered over, still feeling the bullets soar overhead. If they waited, they would be swarmed. If they ran, they risked being gunned down. Rhys waved to the tank, but its autonomous actions remained unaltered.

"This way!"

Settling for the doctrine of unthinkable confidence, he clambered up the stairs and beelined toward the armoured hull.

Oslo hesitated at the sight of his selfless rush. Then, he too chased behind him eventually, and they dashed the twenty metres to their first stop.

That must've been what it was like to run through the fields of the afterlife. There were snowy clouds all around them, and the floor itself was like a spring skyscape underneath their rugged boots. The wind was rough yet it barely made a scratch. Their bodies were numb to the pain at the bite of the cold. If someone told them they'd been killed, then hell – it wouldn't have been half-easy to discern whether it was true or not. There wasn't a bird in sight. Those who had died were all that accompanied them. However, they weren't angels. They were still corpses, letting slip their essence until they were drier than their bones.

Rhys tripped and slid behind the walker, and was then soon joined by his accomplice. They pressed their bodies against opposing legs of the beast, giving them at least a full layer of protection.

"What is the plan here, then?" The gunner called. "Where are we going?"

"Just keep firing, give me a second!" Rhys leant out from his cover and searched the mists again. Kelan soldiers ran from their positions and retreated further into the interior. An allied tank nearby was crushed beneath the augmented force of impact. A shell carved right through the inches of steel armour as if it were oxygen. He waved for Tyran's attention, but he didn't notice they were there.

To the left, he saw the demons begin to advance yet again. Their blitz was irregular. In Haria, they'd learnt that sparing their aggression bogged them down. They held no second to rest, rotating into a full mass assault. Tyran's vehicle lugged to the left to silence their advance, gunning them down over and over.

"They're not slowing down!" He yelled, facing Oslo.

"I know!"

"The medical centre is that way." He pointed to where the men ran.

"Yeah, so keep firing!"

"Oslo, we have to go back! The others-" He was met with a stubbornness most uncouth.

"And they won't reach her if we stand here and kill them all. We can't keep running."

Like hell he was going to stand fast and watch as they were circumnavigated – lest they wished to remain helpless and absent from their friends' final moments.

"They're just walking around us, for fuck's sake." Taken aback by Rhys' imprudent panic, Oslo thumped the side of the tank. There was little chance that Tyran would've heard them, and the split decision between the armoured beast and the hospitalised, bed-ridden Sabrina wasn't a difficult choice at the time. And Rhys tempted his fate with one last aggressive persuasion. "Don't leave Evelyn alone!"

His eardrums were handed a heavy dose of tinnitus squeals when the tank fired again. The air itself was displaced and his bones jittered inside his body. Caught in the sadistic turmoil of fire and ice, the inability to read the battlefield had forced him to be self-sufficient. For him, the greater good was out of the picture.

If there were ever a time to die, it had been before everything went downhill. He could have ascended, thinking he'd done the right thing. As the tanks were destroyed and as they left behind charcoaled sculptures, contorted and twisted by their concussive end, the time of good will was over. It was a haunting sensation to realise that throughout a complete wasteland of crystal white snow, the only colour present had been the incensed towers of smoke plumes, the smouldered wreckages of vehicles and the constellation of bodies that filled up trenches and open-fields alike.

Invading Mullackaye had the Ferusians not only shooting at a concrete barrel, but also had them climbing inside the barrel to catch the fish themselves.

Rhys took notice of his nameless allies who had managed to escape the trench. They retreated as fast as they could, firing behind them wildly. He saw them hobble, stagger and bear through the pain of their bullet marks. Medics carried officers over their shoulders and soldiers dragged themselves through the charred snow.

"We're heading back; the defence is headed inland." Oslo accepted to never lie down and die; he told himself that he would fight until the air was vacuumed from his lungs. He agreed with Rhys' plan, albeit a little reluctantly. In death, it had to be for the right thing. Always the right thing. Never the wrong, the hopeless or the otiose.

Order had been bested by the final playing card of dismay. The shot, stemming from a rifled barrel, approached the walker's flank. It buried itself into the joints of the tank and ripped the components inside to shreds. Wires, electrical circuitry, pneumatic pressure valves and gears were exposed, hissing as they were consumed by the successful blast. Rhys pushed himself away from the incapacitated vehicle in shocked bereavement. Small arms fire still concentrated on its shell, peppering the front and the pilot's hatch. He watched as the vehicle tumbled to its top right where its leg had been severed off.

There was no sign of life, no movement or sound from within. Just another cold corpse in the icy desert. Oslo grabbed onto Rhys' arm and pulled him further away from the tank.

"Let's fucking go!" He eyed the tank whilst the gunner dragged him. Perhaps there were a sign of life inside. It was quite possible that the shot hadn't-

The ignition, seconds later, intervened. A furious combustion sparked from its hull. Another shell slammed into the walker's side and collided with its munitions chamber, detonating it from the inside. Rhys was helpless. He could only watch as their armoured wonder piece was caught in the fulmination. In a second, its pilot had been transported to the other side with barely a build up to his cremation. Squad 2 had lost its vehicle and Tyran went down with it.

Rhys ran with Oslo as fast as he could, dragged down by the horrific sight of another man's death. Behind him, the occupied trench flooded with Ferusian units. Their tanks slowly edged their way closer and they carved down the last remaining armoured assets that obstructed them. Bullets came by as the infantry committed to their next charge. Finally, it had become a race against time and the enemy.

Horror. That was what he'd been exposed to, time and time again, with the fractured insults of reality construing his persona. He'd side-lined his morality for the sake of survival. He'd watched another one of his own disintegrated in a furious ball of ash and smoke. The bruises were all across his body, blackened and blued to suit the winter's stain. He had actively murdered and taken more lives than the Stars had once permitted of him. From one life to a collection, he'd racked up a means to call himself a killer. That desire for survival had become unwelcomed. But in his ecstasy of the violence, he'd returned to the form he'd started at. Endless retreat. Running in regret. Combatting insanity.

"Come home, Rhys. Show me how much you love it."

Chapter 28

The Ticket to Elysium

The light had been exiled from the porous heart. Thump. Trickle. Thump. Trickle. Fine-tuned to an old crippled state, the effigy of prolonged pain, Sabrina's soul was incapable of separating itself from the excruciating trauma that had inflicted her. The harrowed hours had made silent way for the sombre rise to the recurrence of anguish. Across that soundless build-up, Ella had rarely left the room and she only did so to have a break or to fill their water flasks. Bless her, she thought, for having been the one to take up Sabrina's self-created mantle. However, she wished she hadn't deep down.

She felt so pathetic. A pitiful palpation, over many days, reminded her of the victimhood she had possessed. In time, perhaps there would have been a chance to grow above it all. But when the world around them crumbled and burned, to what point was resisting the hopelessness a valid and commendable act to her? She couldn't run. She couldn't walk. And without the help of an aid, she couldn't even stand.

She was a blizzard in summertime – and her out-of-place presence among the living trounced her sense of belonging beside the people she held dear. She was a shell of a former dame, and Sabrina, more than anything else, had wanted nothing more than to look after those that lived rent-free in her dreams. She had wanted to convince herself that she was robust or efficient in pathfinding the futures for the weak. Of all things, she had once known her reason of purpose better than anyone else had: to protect the frail, to solidify hope and to ensure that above all, Ella survived with a smile on her face. She wanted to rectify the betrayal of their parental abandonment and to extinguish the anger that she'd been cursed with when she saw them go out in a blaze of self-inflicted horror. And the rage had taken her to the highest peaks of that purpose. But the war, the Ferusians and the insufferable will to keep her alive had taken it all away, like a carrot on a stick before her broken body.

Take them back, she asked internally, to a better time. Life's cruel mistress was that of her fate. It had meddled with mortals and left her scarred. She looked at her surroundings to see its damage.

Once, she'd been atop of a wall with the sister she loved and the man that coronated himself as the king of isolation. The divine sunrays had tickled her cheeks and they blushed her rosy-red prettiness. The world had parted its grim clouds for a single day. It had been her day. Farhawl wanted to be gorgeous and by grace and glory it had made her an angel.

And then she had found herself broken. Purged. Discriminated. Burnt, then frozen. Plundered. The dampness to the air had turned to ice. Everyone and everything had plunged her into a greyscale river and left her to drown. Ella was the only buoy that kept her afloat. At the least, it kept her alive, but didn't stop her from drifting toward the waterfall rapids at the end of the stream.

Black canisters and red needles. Bandages wrapped around each other, emptied first aid kits and small vials of anaesthetics left untouched. Very few injured soldiers survived long enough to make it to the medical facility, and thus the ghostly atmosphere never disappeared. The temperature turned Sabrina a colourless tone. Filaments stood upright across her skin. As she grew colder, and the battle outside became wilder, Ella dressed her in spare military garbs. She didn't quite know who they had belonged to. They weren't around to do anything about it so it didn't matter. It was half a size too small for her.

Ella overtured a vague sweetness in the air when she began to hum. The soft squeeze of her voice cuddled Sabrina with fingertip strokes. Isometric levels of pain were numbed and the comforting tease of a wonderful life poked its head through her lips. Righteous commodities, like beauty and peace, were quick to disperse.

Her enlightenment was cut down. It started with the low rumble of machine gun fire, then the roar of rifles. Ella closed her eyes and hummed louder, trying her hardest to overpower its presence, yet it was a futile act. Try as she would, the show lights had been turned on and the last performance had started. The doors were locked and the audience could not leave their seats. Swords had been set in stone – the final fight delivered its operatic monologue.

"Where are the others?" Sabrina, filled with disgust, shifted in her bed. Her fingers fumbled with her buttons whilst she had to process her insecurity.

Ella had reached her limit. Wasted time had left them with holes in their chests. It was undesirable to navigate the perplexed nature of life's vindictive maze, and she wished to withdraw her responsibilities. But at that moment, she had realised that Sabrina could do nothing to cradle her like she had a hundred times before.

"Hey-" Torn by her conflated ambiguity, Sabrina mumbled with a slurred tongue. She was swiftly interrupted by Ella's whimper.

Her throat had been lined with thorns and prickles. Every word she spoke was met with agony.

"I don't know."

"Gwen's still here, isn't she? And Evelyn?" Sabrina spoke to herself. Deafened pride left her to converse alone. "And I heard that Christa never left for the frontline. If they're around..."

Her voice faded. It was as she noticed the way her sister's eyes met the concrete floor...

Unsure of what to do, she clenched a tight fist and slammed it down on her bed. Her eyes and ears explored the room, desperate to find a fleck of relief. There had to be something – anything other than Ella's printing train ticket to the afterlife. But all she could see was the drearier contours of their dishevelled ward. It was her waiting room to the last leg onward to the other side. And with the broken glass frames of cabinets, the splintered wooden shelves piled in the corner, she couldn't have asked for a more apt place to cease and disappear within.

The time to unify had seemingly passed. Squad 2 had been arrested by malicious circumstances. Some bathed in the bloodied pools and the rest waited, alone and scattered. It angered her. They used to have something, if nothing but a proof of concept of promise or a collective, one that stood the test of what was thrown at them. She used to own an electrical spark in a bottle with Rhys' name on it.

405

Had she not been the one to spiritually die, to wither and fizzle out, things could have been vastly different. So much so, she told herself. Life could have still held the modicum of perfection. She'd found herself strapped to the utopian lust that Rhys had shown her. Deny the present, she would, and legitimise the fantasies of her future; for the sake of a warmer winter, she wished to collapse and to wake up in paradise as if nothing had happened at all. Life had been a series of disappointments and aggressions that gnawed at her. When she fought back, it lashed out and taxed her a limb and a mind.

When she became latched onto Rhys' state of mind, that desire to only pursue the pure sustenance in a bottle of poison, it begged a horrid question: how slow would the final day be?

Thunder cried out the news: humankind creates its own vigorous storm. Where the rain and snow had governed their days, the sound of constant conflict strung them up and kept them on the railroaded path to the underworld. It had been their handler. Guns and cannons were never silent. A production of deconstruction, to tear down lives in droves, changed the soldiers like her permanently. Sabrina had been transformed. Ella had been ravished and disenfranchised. They'd witnessed beyond a scuffle on the front and had danced with the extinction event of yesterday. The sound of all that encompassed them had curated a state of panic and expectancy of atrocity.

She wanted a way out; not of the hospital nor the fort, but all of it. Everything. From the days she woke up to the nights she fell asleep, and all the hours between it. The noise made her teeth grind, her bones shudder and her skin crawl. All the horror that stemmed from their war tormented her.

"Go…go find them – you'll need them when you get the chance to leave." Contrary to Ella's belief, Sabrina had found herself at the yield of terror, not anger.

"I'm not leaving your side." Her whisper was colder than the air. "I won't let them take you."

"Ella-"

"And I won't let you leave me!" She yelled. Sabrina fell silent. "Please stop wanting to disappear! Do you know how much it hurts me when you wish for death? Even when I'm sitting here, next to you until the end of the world, you're still going to ask for it, aren't you?"

406

The air between them sharpened an icy dagger sheathed within their tongues. A confrontation brewed and Ella curled her fingers. She dug her nails into her own leg and kept her eyes fixed onto the floor, her voice grew hoarser by the minute.

"You don't get it…"

"No, I don't. But I know that right now you're not the same sister I love. Whatever you're becoming, I hate it."

Taken back by her venomous spit, Sabrina didn't even attempt to rebuttal her. Ella was right, regardless of her unsettled spout of anger. Breaking down, she sniffled into her sleeve.

"Please don't leave me. I don't want to be alone. I never want to be alone, ever. Please just… – just have a little bit of faith, because I really need it right now."

Her words crumbled and the droplets of her tears soaked into her clothes. Juvenile, weak and lost. By her bedside, she was beside all that her world lived for, losing itself before her very eyes.

The ground rumbled as hell unearthed itself and the lights flickered. The time had come.

~~~

Christa held her breath. She'd been wandering from room to room, helping the shorthanded medical staff wherever she could. The rush took her between wards and patients. Casualties bellowed out harrowed screams. The medical corps barred her from most of the rooms and left her to drift between delivery jobs in the hallway.

At least she was good at following orders. To an extent, it hadn't been too dissimilar to her life as a monarch. Someone else always led the pack and she'd resorted to being a pedestrian to the path laid for her. It had never been her duty to plant the paving stones for others, not until she would have been coronated herself. Yet, out in the militia, she felt as if the orders given to her went toward great things. Moving precious supplies, calming nervous individuals and standing guard with the sentries meant something to her. A life of meaningless materialism was incomparable to where she was. Because of it, she had been the only one with a smile on her face.

Patterned with floral pleasure, she walked that soldierly walk with a poster-child beam on her face. Everywhere she went, an irradiation followed. Medical officers and repurposed combat medics gave her a kindly nod as they passed.

Had she accomplished anything by being there, she asked herself. Well, she knew not of the answers, but her masters knew that she'd made the journey and defied the orders of the crown, something which few souls accomplished on the scale she had. Many considered a vulnerable Lylith to be in the hands of the Ferusians, criminals or whichever peddled conspiracy ran the story. Not only that, but Christa had also obtained the freedom to be owned by the militia.

It hadn't quite hit her. She remained blissfully unaware that, in truth, she'd fallen under her mother's crown again. If she were to die, it would be under the orders of Tala's dynasty. She was in the pockets of her Queen, her lifeblood, and she served her as a faceless ghoul.

But those little birds that were propped on her shoulders were silenced at the first catch of a waterlogged weep. Immediately, Christa inhaled the rotten miasma that came from inside the isolated ward. The voices snared her mid-motion and she halted outside, both curious and worried for what occurred inside.

A thirst for emotional injury had been quenched. Ella begged and pled for her sister's life. Christa's curled lips straightened, and were then dragged down by the gravity of her tousled diffidence. A decayed fragrance stemmed from her panic. The words she spoke brought with it the influence of the unsettled. Her mind, once staunch and accustomed to her desire of heroic victory, was flooded with a dirty truth: she didn't belong among the dying.

She rewound the previous minutes back. It hadn't occurred to her that none of the soldiers, officers or nurses smiled at her. When they nodded, it was with a grim, downtrodden, ghostly gaze, a glimpse into their soulless hosts. Every man felt like a monster; every woman pictured themselves as terrorists. Disorder had profiled them and taken advantage of their once spirited faces.

Winding further, she recalled those of her own squad, the ones she shared drinks and tongues with. Even in laughter, they had hollowed-out eyes, colourless and drab. Their smiles were never quite convincing anymore.

And then, there was the beginning. The thought that changed it all still haunted her. She was in a grand hall, filled with golden medals, purple ribbons and crystal wine glasses. Placed on a cushioned throne, she peddled her mother's will by allowing the conscription to pass. She only complained when it was all over, unable to handle the responsibility of her national desires and position of power. Her political stance became bedroom tears and a cause for a parental lecture.

The armed forces held no place for her. Christa's face was blank. Objections to her cause were introduced in pieces. Those gathered shards painted an incomplete piece: a portrait of Lylith.

She placed her palm against her forehead, where the tumorous irritation brewed. Curtailed from that name, and that memory, she barely contained her disdain for thinking so far back. Months had passed. Hell, a year may have too. Time was falling apart around her. She didn't even know what the date was or how many weeks were left of the battle. In it was Lylith. Her true self. A denied truth, or a falsified lie, though either were indiscernible for her.

Dysphoric, Christa battled that fallen identity with a shrivelled gaze plastered onto the floor.

"I'm not her anymore…" She whispered in solitude. Anything to do with that name was heinous, a crime even. She, Lylith, was a weak woman, a maiden with no backbone to challenge her flesh and blood. She was convinced that Christa was contrarily headstrong. The beast to the monarch's beauty was her obedience to inaction. Yet, Ella's words had set her down a self-tormenting cul-de-sac to a determined end.

When the soil and concrete shook, she felt her stomach sink. A sickness came to her throat, and she made her way toward the facility's stairs.

She took each drear step skyward with half a heart of effort. Her body trembled. A draft passed down the stairwell, let in from the door-left-ajar that led out to the snow-shelled rooftop.

Outside, the oxygen was stale. The acrimony in the wind repressed her animated radiation. A vibrant performance whistled around her. A clear and frightening display of unseen gunfire, explosions and turmoil harassed her ears. The sky was lit up by a thousand orange tracers, signifying to the ground teams where their shots were slated to land. To make things worse, it was closer than ever before. She guessed that she had barely an hour at the speed it approached, and that was if she were lucky.

She walked over to the rooftop railing and wrapped her fingers around the pale, iron pipes. For some time, she stood there alone. All she had were thoughts and questions, the bane of one's reflection. Had she gone too far, or had she not done enough – the arguments clashed in her mind. She prayed to the stars whilst she still could. Her pleas were for everything: a blessing, forgiveness and hope.

Her voice was tender yet pitiful when she spoke to the highest powers, as it had been weakened by the weather around her. She could barely think straight.

> *To the Great Stars in the sky,*
> *Lesser these evils, and intrude with your victory.*
> *Where we are trespassed upon, please value our lives.*
> *Our creators, I beg for grace-*

Five metres off, something whizzed toward the safety rail. It struck viciously against the iron tubing and deflected downward into the rooftop floor. Snow and dust kicked up from the impact. She was hesitant and eyed the sparked spot. Her eyes were in the right place in time to witness a second tracer fly overhead and she cowered down to the floor. It was a stray, but its screaming strike brought nothing short of instant anxiety.

The door behind her swung open and out came the Osakan storm. Her eyes were hooked and drawn over, to which she met the uncourteous arrival of Thomas.

Stress had been painted across his face. His hair appeared as if it had been showered in pig fat, no thanks to the lack of sanitation on hand. The vapour of the exhausted man's breath showed his speechlessness, fanaticised further by the emptiness of his fraught lungs. He adjusted his glasses and powerfully strode over to her. Christa tried to beckon for him to cower against the floor. A staunch resolve ignored her gestures and the occasional encroaching bullet cracked by, and in rapid motion he slithered closer.

"For the love of-…why are you-" Like an illegitimate guardian, he scolded her and locked his fingers around her wrist.

410

He'd arrived with such blitz that it caught her off guard. She struggled to maintain her balance when her cuffed limbs were dragged on in his trail. In Thomas' free hand, she noticed a small flashing light that blinked in an irregular pattern.

"What're you doing? Slow down!"

"I've spent a good twenty minutes looking for you, and we're on eggshells. Why is it so hard for you to just stay put?"

Christa was incompatible to the restlessness he exhumed. The calculated man, once selective with his words, sounded as if he couldn't formulate a mindful sentence without bursting his banks. He brought her inside, back to the top of the stairwell, where he stopped and let go of her arm to put his gloves on, all the while he shat bricks.

She glared at the blinking metal rod clenched tightly in his free hand. Its flashes were so sporadic that she fell into a trance, lost in its scarlet pattern:

Beep-Blip-Beep-Blip. Beep-Beep-Beep. Beep-Beep. Blip.

Thomas finished dressing his hands in woollen gauntlets and unbuttoned his trench coat. From within, he drew a revolver. Christa shouldn't have been surprised to have seen it, but the untimely arrival of the firearm hammered in the gravity of her situation.

Tightly, he held the noir hand cannon with an itchy trigger finger.

"Right…right…" He unlocked the weapon and spun the 8-cylinder chamber around, where his attention was engrossed into each click it made as it rotated. Sophistication and adornment brought personality to the revolver. Across its main body were the personal engravings of Osakan alphabetical decoration, pronouncing words and phrases foreign to her. Serpentine letters overlapped one other and gave his personalised tool of aggression an unsolicited amount of beauty and craftmanship to an otherwise rudimentary weapon.

With enough bullets in the chamber to put down a party, he saw no need to wait around any longer.

"Follow me."

"Wait, where are we going?" She protested yet allowed him to stumble ahead.

411

"Fucking hell, I don't mean stay put *now*, come on!" He returned to her side and grabbed her abrasively by the arm, tighter than before. His grip dug into her wrist and left cold imprints on her pale, tulip-dressed skin.

The two made their way to the bottom of the flight and they cautiously avoided the clusters of medics and soldiers that clogged up the hallway.

An abrupt sound of glass smashing in the neighbouring wards dispersed the crowds. "Bullets!", the people cried, and they cowered in anticipation for a second one to run through the window panes. Thomas kept his momentum and dragged his payload with him. One moment of reflection had been pushed aside for the dread colliding with Christa.

"Sir!" She exclaimed with frustration. No retort. He continued to lead her through the ground floor hallways, darting between rooms in search for an exit, bleating expletives at each empty outcome. Tracers glided outside and their infrequent glazes of crimson and emerald shades became clearer in the snow-plagued sky.

Peeled eyes took notice of their escape. Another officer stepped in front of them, about to interject and question their haste. He never uttered a word, however, as Thomas lifted a small identification document. The man backed down immediately.

Her struggle was suppressed by the motion of the hour. A few backroom turns later and the fleeing duo had found themselves in the vicinity of an unseen fire escape.

"Sir, please can you-"

"I'll tell you when we get there." Sparked Thomas, eager to shoot her request down. And, without hesitation, he braced his body, ran for the door and shoulder barged his way through.

~~~

As were the cinders that charred the surface of Farhawl, the stick of embers between his lips, was ignited by the industrial flames caught in their fingers. He had chained together two drags before, and he had bled through the boxes for no better reason than leaving them aside. The first and second were dry, lacklustre, but the third clutter put Mateo into a coughing fit. He spat at the snow and the bud dimmed. He paid little attention to the sounds of the conflict. With a little more time to spare, he thought he'd make the most of it stood outside a forgotten fire exit.

Gwen peered through the door with all the judgement and spite in her stare, but she hung close to his presence for the gods' gift of simply not caring enough.

"Fuck…" A seared smog clogged up his lungs and the heat dried his throat. He kicked his boots against the entryway and gestured for Gwen to join him outside. Her attention had waned a little, yet she intently listened from the other side and eventually gave in to his demands, where she propped the door open with a slow pry. "Y'know, these handouts are some of the lowest quality packs I've ever had. You couldn't get cancer if you tried."

"Mateo-"

"And, like, they barely stay lit up. Look, this is the third time I've had to light the little shit. Talk about service, mate." He was lost in endless thought, and it took the weight of the door against his back to push him out of his rant.

"Why aren't you coming inside?" She softly pled as she poked her head outside. His free adolescent attitude frustrated her. "Can't you hear it?"

"Yeah, I can." He spoke through gritted teeth, and the wind – coupled with the warzone – howled between his words. The sputter of sparks on his brass lighter fell silent. Temporarily, he looked as if he gave up, but then he played up his spirits with a smile. "I still have time."

"For what?"

"You think I'm gonna let the Red's have any smokes to find?" In dire straits, he pled his infantile act of martyrdom.

Then, it was back to the immobile occupation of the side entrance – he returned to striking the serrated sparkwheel of the lighter against the new cigarette in his hands, and he was lost the split-second flicker of the ignition whilst it reflected against his spectacles.

For evermore, as he wanted, there was comfort to owning a menial conversation, regardless of the tearaway riot against peace barely a kilometre out. The insignificant happenings of their daily lives were the among the most missed. Placed in a societal-alternating age, forced to live out the greatest shift in human politics since the collapse of old Feras monarchy, there seemed to be no space for localised, tedious behaviour; and it was the little

413

things that made them human – the jabs, cheers and jeers, the laughs and stains of boredom – which had been lost to the winds.

They couldn't complain about their breakfast, or how someone had been uptight to them in passing, as their worldview had been defiled. They had once taken each little frustration and spark of joy for granted. Each grain of sand, snowflake and raindrop, all which cradled a small memory, had gone off with the storm.

Gwen had loitered around the facility over the course of the day. She'd spent a few hours ensuring Evelyn wouldn't stray off to the frontline, treating her more as an infant than a juvenile. She saw in the girl's eyes that estranged unease and tension; the temptation to run and find Oslo must have been excruciatingly hard to suppress. Her fingers tapped against her lap and she had scrubbed her weapon for hours on end, belligerently, whilst her guardian was out sleeping in the fires. And in witnessing the squad's members transform, she had been led back to Mateo, a man hadn't changed a bit.

His borderline nihilistic words complimented his willingness to do as he was told. The jokes and baseless spouts of informality were just products of his acceptance.

"Are you going to come back inside?" She asked as she opened the door a fraction more.

"Yeah – yeah, give me a second, mum." Never had she wanted to hit a man as strongly as she did then. "Having me a last ciggy, mate."

But the lighter didn't cede to his demands. It had submitted its spark to the snow. And so, Mateo, in his frustration, tossed it into the fog. The glimmer of its half-rusted brass casing vanished in the pallid garden of ice. He couldn't hear it hit the ground, and it was as if he'd thrown it into space.

He eyed its vanishing act until the winter nebular obscured his vision completely. An ever-present drone of battle stalked his shoulders, and he shrugged it off with another chuckle.

Gwen withdrew her steadfast perseverance and, eventually, pulled herself out into the shivering winds to be at his side. The bite of the cold was instantaneous and she felt the teeth of mother nature, with its bone-like icicles, plant into her neck. Mateo appeared undaunted to its effects until she noticed the pallor of his skin.

She noted to herself that laid by his side were his weapons. A .30 carbine and the anti-tank launcher, tucked in a corner against the walls of the exit's concrete porch.

"Here," she said, unveiling a lighter from her webbing, "try mine."

"Such a darling…" He grinned, delighted by her charity. Even though he'd given up on his lighter, his fingers were unwilling to let the cigarette go unfinished. Blessed with her gift, he took the cleaner, unused lighter and they both clasped hands to cup the flame. A small victory was achieved when he managed to relight his little tabaco pastime.

A truly despicable nature was it to lend him only the warmth of a disgusting rod, packaged within a cardboard packet; that roughened taste that latched onto his throat, the burning ash that tickled his teeth and that devil-tongued lick on his empty lung, it was all so impure yet masochistically enjoyable, all the while the military couldn't provide him with a warm bed and bath.

"You going to be long?"

"Just a bit. I'll be ready in time for war, dear."

"You're such an arsehole…" The bitterness in her voice almost seemed genuine.

"Hey – what?" He faced her with the usual shit-consuming smile.

"I don't know, when you say stuff like that it makes my skin crawl."

She spied the snowflakes' dance and occupied herself with raw musings. Harmed in the restless sky, pirouetting to the tune of battles around them, the snow was pressed to its limits and broke apart in the restless wind. She'd lost sight of something beautiful. Her mind twirled and the wintery petals mislaid their tenderness.

"What's going to happen?" She mumbled lowly, speaking up when no answer came back. "Do we have a chance at going home?"

"Probably not." The passive blaze on the bud of his cigarette scorched his tongue. He was caught in a coughing fit, forcing him to bury his mouth into his sleeve and to reconfigure himself.

"Couldn't you say something nice for once."

A toadish croak troubled his voice when it slipped out his lips.

"I mean, maybe? I don't know, mate. Everyone keeps asking each other these questions and it's clear none of us have an answer."

"Peace of mind. It might lend you some genuine happiness, for once." Her jive led to Mateo's calm titter. He took off his glasses and battled against the condensation obscuring the lens with his sleeve. But when he rested them back onto his ice-caked nose, they were swiftly desaturated with a layer of fog.

"See? I can't do shit. I just make the best of it." In his last drag, his sigh filled the empty space between them. "We'd be better off if we stopped pretending that we can change everything."

"Some of us had dreams and careers-"

"-and there's your problem." With a quick shrug, he jabbed the glowing bud into the wall, where the ash swayed until it sank into the ground, and the embers were dead. Even the grey dust, infused with the quietest fire, vanished in the whiteout. Its temperature was worthless. "I like the tenacity, though. Sometimes I wish I was still like that."

Inside, from behind the closed door, the echo of frenzied voices crept toward them. Gwen listened out of necessity. And then, suddenly and without warning, the door was forced open by the heavy barge of a man's shoulder, making ease of Mateo's back rest.

He was thrown forward. The force tripped him over nothing and stumbled into the snow; rather luckily, his arms soaked up the brunt of the impact, but he was left dazed on the floor. Gwen stepped aside and shrieked out of surprise.

When he came to but a second later, Mateo plucked his glasses by the rim and pulled them out of the snow. He looked behind him and saw the hurried pair correcting their balance.

In the few seconds he had to register their identities, he saw the vague faces of two covert peers. Christa was restrained, as if the teeth of a viper had pierced her wrist, by the hushed Mr Lee. The ghoul had fastened the woman to his hand. Her eyes, both vapid and still, made her protest subtle. Mateo caught the slightest glimpse of her pain until the officer tugged at her arm.

"Step aside!" Mr Lee barked, out of breath and mind accordingly. Mateo crawled sideways to clear a route for them. And without another word, he towed Christa into the mist.

416

Excitement quickly took control of Mateo. He scrambled to his feet and grabbed his carbine. Gwen was astounded by his sudden surge ahead. The hawkish temptation to investigate them had taken him to a thrilling place of intrigue.

"Hey, what're you doing?" Gwen asked but did little to block his way.

"You see that, shit? Where the hell do you think they're going?"

"In the middle of all of this, you're-"

"-going to take a look? Yeah! More fun than waiting to die!" Struggled fumbles with her tongue created a noiseless response. She threw her hands into the air, then ducked them back down when the rattle of gunfire crescendoed. "I'll come back later, don't wait up."

And just like that, Mateo had bleached his body in snow, camouflaged into anonymity. She only hoped that he would come back.

~~~

What was the heavier burden? Had it been the weight of their lives strung up on the line, the mass of their worlds on their shoulders or the bulk of their equipment?

Oslo and Rhys placed their faith in their endurance – not about how they could withstand the predators on their tail, but rather the durable wish to keep on running.

Adrenaline pumped through their hearts at maximum velocity. Their lungs were tested to their excruciating limits. The hares, held helpless against the jaws of foxes, fled through the snowed concrete gorge, where structures were grey glaciers in the middle of the sea.

Iron toes ripped through the concealed runways and, though at first barely visible, a grey outline manifested. Rhys quickly looked back as the clamour of steel legs grew louder and louder.

And then his heart stopped. He saw it, on their tail. A nurtured beast, raised in the production lines of the reds, stood strong.

"Don't stop!" He shouted. The glimpse of a towering behemoth gaining traction clamped down on his security. Their vacillated bodies were sluggish at the submission to winter.

417

It couldn't have been much further, he thought, and he felt as if they'd been on the retreat for hours. It wasn't far, it couldn't have been.

The few more souls who'd retreated had been caught. Those segregated by a lack of energy were cut down by falcons. The chilling drone of gears shifting, diesel-exhausting and ammunition belts feeding into autocannons ultimately slaughtered the cattle. Whatever machine was on their rear, it wasn't alone and it hadn't shown any sign of slowing down.

Its guns blared at the volume of a pocket artillery piece yet fired at the rate of a machine gun. Its rounds, infused with explosive material, burst around the vulnerable soldiers caught in its sight. Fortunately, its shots were just loud enough to mercifully deafen their final cries.

Hearts pumped. Lungs tightened. Veins bulged. A pain in the chest, for the phantom bullet of anxiety had moulded to a serpent, a constrictor binding his prey hostage. And it was getting closer.

We can make it.

I can make it.

Where is the fucking building?

Why is it still coming after us?

Gods, help me!

Across the weeks of combat and the exposure to death and obliteration at every turn, whatever deities that loomed above must've imagined that he became a hardened, unshakeable body of frosted iron. To the contrary - and likely to their amusement - he was the opposite. Spineless. Fearful. Self-preservation had taken control. His morals - or, perhaps more accurately, the tattered scraps of their remnants - were meaningless. The face of the final act was then. Rhys refused to stop writing his finale. He added pages to the script, puffed out bitter blathering, like a baker adds sawdust to his famine-bread. There would be no glorious, storied epilogue nor closing statement until he decided there was. It didn't have to end. He wanted there to be compassion, with loved ones circling a mahogany desk littered with opulent dairies and ostentatious wine glasses. He begged for, instead of snowfall, confetti and blossoms to rain on the effusive opera.

The bipedal walker had taken full shape, and skyward it stood, tall and strong. It was impossible to detach himself from the fear of its spectral presence at each interval where he peered behind him. What was once a colourless blob had unveiled its details and, in turn, uncovered them.

He kept going. And going. And going. And going. There was nowhere else to go but forwards. He felt his lungs reach critical mass as they collapsed under the pressure. He nearly slowed down. His vision faded. It was going to catch him and, when it did, he would be torn by its cannons. But he never stopped. And by the skin of his teeth, was he glad to have done so.

The quill, clutched in nature's fingers, made cursive adjustments to his fate. Luck arrived at seven-hundred and ninety metres per second, capsuled within a seven-kilogram shell. It spiralled over the pair at such an accelerated pace that they didn't see it pass, and only felt the tremor in the air left by its sail.

Sparks and shards splintered in all directions. A collision most grand pierced through the armour, slicing deep into the pilots' capsule. A vile and haunting steel scream grabbed Rhys' attention, pulling him aside to spectate its termination. Eyes front, dried by the radiation, and with turbulent unease he watched as its internal mechanisms ignited in a flaming incandescence. An arduous bonfire crispened the armoured shell of the walker. The slow-burn blackened its painted skin, and it was far unlike Tyran's own demise. The instantaneous relief of his eruption was vacant, and the Ferusian crew before him were roasted at an excruciating deliberateness.

The walker toppled aside and buried itself into the snow whilst the fires raged on. A cackled flame barely let the panicked cries of the pilots leave their mortal casing.

In its burial, Rhys and Oslo took the opportunity to retreat unopposed – if only for a few seconds – and they arrived at the smoking barrel of an anti-tank emplacement.

A shivering crew greeted them with a hesitant shout. Dressed for a battle against the elements that froze their nerves, exhausted arms loaded in another armour-piercing shell. Brief moments of steaming vapour that leaked from the barrel and breach led to crowded hands snagging up the heat in crumbs. The pair approached them and walked by their great cannon with gratitude. Rhys opened his mouth to thank them but was interrupted by a second shot. The recoil of the machine tremored the snow and they went back to ignoring them. He took one last look behind him, and Rhys saw the burning debris of the walker that lay wasted and deceased. The second shot had finished off whatever pitied souls were left inside its carcass.

It was truly for the better, Rhys thought. The voice of his mind was thickened by gritted teeth and tissue. His stare was left on the charcoaled metal and, for a disturbing second, he was satisfied with the cannon's response.

Oslo was well-aware of how constrained their time was. He pulled on Rhys' shoulder and brought him back to his side of reality.

"They're still coming. Let's get to the others." An unmeasured desire to return to his holy relic was clear. And Rhys didn't dispute it. Together, they picked up the pace and journeyed the last leg into the interior. The cannon kept blasting until they could hear it fell at the hour's hand.

Another hundred metres ahead, their destination stood alone. The windows were left cracked, porous for the anesthetised weather. A wounded exterior made clear its vulnerability. Days before, the treatment of its safekeep had been sacramental. Brightened faces tried to reassure the weakened. Rhys remembered when Sabrina had been exactly that – a reassurance.

Against those pretences, the medical facility had become camouflaged. Its unrecognisable fissures, where bullets had chiselled its exterior, turned it into any other military asset, disregarding the comfort of its medicinal purposes. Whatever lurked inside mattered very little, for the kindness it had once blessed others with had disintegrated.

Guns poked out of the missing window frames. The carvings of stray bullets had told them their time was nigh. Imminent violence waited on the edge of the interior. On the rooftop, Rhys made out the faint silhouettes of marksmen and anti-tank riflemen, set up in anticipation for what came next.

The pair rushed inside and stumbled through the front door. Everywhere they looked they saw soldiers. Doctors and medics had been replaced with warriors, ordered to hold until they bled no more.

Rhys knew that the time of defiance had long passed. Mullackaye had fallen. Denial of such a fact spoke volumes of their determination. Gone were the rose-tinted views of Kelan's glory. War took no qualm toward itself. Soldiers were at the mercy of each other, nature, their leaders and whatever virtues they held to be true. And because of that, their time had come. In a literal sense:

Give them victory, or deliver them to death's doorstep.

Chapter 29

The Last Procession

Regression – the secession brought by misfortune. A shrivel, transformative remould shaped into something hollow, built on the foundations of its environmental struggles. Recuperation and recovery had been reconstructed into resistance. Tables were placed on their sides. Doors, closed off. Windows were turned into pillboxes. The medical facility had regressed parallel to ached bodies torn apart by their unrelenting surroundings. In greyscale, toned to fit purgatory, the soldiers sat in wait. The cracks in the walls had long been for show, but when the final hour dawned, they were as clear as dawn.

Oslo pulled ahead, reaching the main intersection in the hallway. To the right, a flight of stairs, bogged down with a huge crowd, led to Sabrina's ward, whereas the left headed to his stop.

"I'm going to grab Evelyn." He informed Rhys, speaking through the graveyard silence. Bootsteps and nail-drops chimed where voices wouldn't. The building's occupants all knew what came next and dared not to speak its name.

"Alright," Rhys nodded, "come to Sabrina's ward when you've got her. Know where that is?"

"Yeah."

"Good, I'll see you there then. Don't be long."

As the two parted ways, he couldn't shake how alone he felt amidst the crowd of fighters. A newfound determination clotted their hearts. Survival was but a backdrop to the honourable solution: to die a death worth more than submission. Not only had Mullackaye fallen hours before they'd reached the interior, but Kelan itself was on the verge of imminent collapse. Contrarily, Rhys knew that Kelan had already crumbled; the crown had not yet admitted it.

He trudged to the stairs and took each step slothfully as did a false prophet ascend to heaven. The golden escalator laced with diamonds that led to paradise was no more. A crowded monochrome staircase, dusty and fouled by the stench of sweat and blood, took him to where he desired the most.

Upstairs, he saw the common trend between the pale bodies. Their sleeves, chests and shoulders were covered in the all-too-familiar insignias of the 54th, bound then and forever by blood and death. There were only a hundred or so left at most. Maybe there were others scattered across the other interior facilities. It mattered not. The regiment was finished. There was the last stand of the platoons and companies; their grandiose finale of gore and suffering, seasoned by the drizzle of blood and liquid iron.

Rhys recollected himself when he was stood outside Sabrina's ward. He didn't enter at first. Something held him back. A shameful black cloud hung over his head, and it rained down acidic virulence, for he then entered the room as a crusader, a survivalist with blood on his shirt and someone else's heart on his sleeve.

He placed his hands on the wooden obstacle and pushed against it as gently as possible. The whine of its hinges announced his entrance and the eyes inside turned to face him.

Like a carbuncle on the squad's face, the allies inside saw the stain enter the room. Rhys, with staggered steps, walked inside. He blinked once, twice, and opened his eyes to see someone propelling toward him. He tensed up. A hand moved down to his hip, where his rifle had been left dangling from its sling. And though he thought he'd entered the devil's cave, the nostalgic embrace took him into submission.

"Rhys!" Ella spluttered out, tightening her grip around his body. "You're okay! Thank everything, I was – we were so worried!"

A stunned Rhys waited whilst he reconfigured his mind to accept the arousal of her human touch. His frozen hairs stood on their ends. His shaken expression told tales of traumatic activities. Ella pulled herself back a little and gazed into his empty stare.

So faint and colourless were his grim eyes, and as they landed upon her delicate face he saw – for what seemed like a split second – a mask on her face, with filters and goggles that

423

obscured her angelic beauty. Where she breathed, the disturbed sound of her muffled respiration deranged his attention.

He blinked, and the mask was no more. Her face had returned. A joyous shift left him to act on instinct. And without warning, or build up, Rhys leaned forward and placed his lips against hers.

The kiss blocked out the room around them; spiralled fireworks and a galactic supernova detonated outside, and there was colour for the first time in months. Yet a tragic realisation cut his sudden action short: the temperature of her skin.

The brevity of his action lured him to question why he had done such a thing where her lips were so frostbitten and violet. In a sense, he could taste the spite of the masked mimic, the apparition of his sleepless days and nights, and felt the fear return.

Before the third heartbeat had passed, he pulled away and turned his gaze elsewhere. Something so derelict as her chill had turned him scarlet – he harked little praise and shrivelled up his confidence.

"Where…are the others?" He asked in a hoarse croak. Confused from what had happened, Ella barely stammered out a response.

"I…I…uh-" Try as she did, the stutter maintained and she looked around with flourished cheeks accompanied by a trembled hand.

How unfair, Rhys thought, to have placed such conflicting emotions on her in time for crisis. Why had he kissed her? Because there was something in the moment he loved and feared, as it had commanded him to do so.

"Let's get Sabrina."

She was alone. In the coldest corner of the ward, her bed had been propped upright. She was dressed in the clothes that gave her no mercy: a singular shoulder plating, a zipped up windproof smock and plenty of empty pockets, all coloured in the same dark olive tone then synonymous with the fashion of war. She bore no armoured headdress and instead wore an issued beret given to her by a traditionalist officer, so much to at least identify her as one of their own through the confusion of battle.

On her left breast, a clementine ribbon dashed with two baby blue lines, asymmetrical of one another, added an unprecedented spruce to her ragged attire.

424

"Hey, Sab'." Rhys quietly stalked over to her. She was sat listed over to the side, though upright, and her leg hung off to the side of the bed, as if she were about to stand up. He confirmed that nothing about her had changed for the better, as her left leg was still sealed shut by a tied, trousered knot.

She carefully looked up to him, and nothing remarkable came of it. There was no traumatised, emotional distress, nor was there any sign of glee. All that was held in her glistening irises was her fatigue.

Tired of waiting. Tired of suffering. Tired of living past her due process from Sunar.

"You good?" She gave the most energy-deprived nod in response. "Where were you?"

"Out on the front. Interior's defensive ring. Maybe a kilometre out, or more…or less." Her silence led to his continued tongue. "I wasn't quite sure of how far out we were."

"How was it?"

"As good as it could be."

"So as awful as ever?" Usually, Rhys would've smiled, or chuckled even, at the remarks. She would have too. Their eagerness to halt such happiness told him everything he needed to know.

There was a slight pause as Ella came back over to them. He noticed her smiling slightly, both out of permanent distress and impure joy. Most probably at Sabrina openly talking more, but she did give him a quick glance and a hesitant curl of her lips. Couldn't have happened at a worse time, he thought. Any other day and he'd cherish her response to his inept act of affection. Or was it his cry for comfort? Rhys wasn't even sure how he felt anymore about anyone. If they were going to die, he couldn't admit that those memories and emotions mattered.

"Tyran's dead." The brevity of his announcement alongside the gloom of his tone silenced the trio. The bombshell had been dropped so suddenly upon them that no one really reacted at all. Unsure of how he felt, he just kept talking as if it were the only sanctity he could provide. "Went up in the tank. I think he took several of the reds down before they finally got to him."

"Oh, Rhys…I'm…"

"Sorry?" He filled in the blank. Ella nodded.

Grief would have struck him at any other day. Tyran was a good man, all thing's considered. He kept moderate, was a quiet soul and could pilot their war machine. It hadn't clocked until then that he had worked closely with Ella. And to seem so uncompassionate, it was truly a dreadful way to go about helping her.

"No – no. I should be. Sorry, I…– shouldn't have dropped that on you."

For a brief minute, Ella shed a tear to herself. Peculiarly, she had an uncontrolled smile as she cried, quite clearly for varying reasons. She desired only to feel better. She moved closer to where Rhys stood and slowly moved her fingers to his sleeve, holding it with a pinch just out of Sabrina's line of sight. He let it happen.

"So," he coldly shifted topics, "what's that for?"

He prodded her military ribbon, garnering a brief impression of its silky touch. No military award had the right to be so soft, he pondered. It felt a little unnatural.

"Distinguished valour and persistence." He heard the venom in her mocking tone. He knew not of its purpose. She had no family back home to see her prize, and were she to die in the battle it would've been as if she never achieved the award in the first place.

"It takes courage to live in a land like this." Rhys mumbled out, enabled by her relevant misanthropy.

"Then call me a coward."

Her grimdark attitude cauterised the conversation and sealed it shut. The desire to see her spirits ascend had grown ever-more with time. The decline had forced her hands to shackles. Rhys felt no different to her. Where he had originally wanted a release from the world, he was none the more willing to do it himself. It carried far too much responsibility for either to pity themselves.

She'd wrapped herself in lemon skin; soured, atrocious, bitter unpleasantries relinquished her charm for tart. Her words carried baggage comparable to Rhys' – she too knew that they weren't heroes, nor would they ever be.

But by the grace of fantasies yonder, he falsified an idea that one day, he could've been one, that a scatter of goldstone dust would brighten the cracks of his blackened prison cell. Yet to tell his tale and to spread the good word of the one that got away, he would've needed a legacy to make it out of his turmoiled battleground. Rhys caged the thought, but left the door open for it to return, because the only thing he conjured in his head was the prospect of getting out of Mullackaye for good.

To evacuate from their mortal turmoil required him to wade into the mists beyond. But the chaos of the situation had yet to give him the chance, and their circumstances seemed ever the more hopeless. If it were to happen, it would have to have been by his hand.

And by Sunar's fury, the ground was resuscitated as it shook at the force of a million bombs. The glass containers itched one another's bodies and chimed out a staccato chime. The beds creaked and the doors whined on their hinges. Rhys held on to Sabrina's cradle and Ella held on to his arm. Sabrina wasn't bothered enough to stabilise herself. A sonar pulse of tectonic power rattled the facility for ten seconds. After that, it fell silent and the world was a little less volatile.

"What the bloody hell was that?" He whispered.

Rhys unravelled his grip on the bed frame and took a step back toward the closest window, where he wiped it clear of condensation. A quick peer through the looking glass revealed nothing at first, and to no surprise over what he had expected to see in the great nothingness.

Something, however, came through. A mysterious entity occupied the swallowing fog.

It was made of flame, and exhaled a vapour of ash. It outshone the stars and, ignited as a golden ball on the horizon, it drowned the darkness of day. An orange glow overthrew the tenuous greyscale. A tremendous brightness, as prominent as the sun at dawn, glimmered and etherealised the external scape. Its initial burst was short-lived as it projectile vomited its dancing blazes to heaven, dissipating in mere seconds. He saw a nauseating illness in that blast and it sickened him, for the otherworldly ghosts that made up the mist were relit like candles, with their beady spirit-eyes enflamed.

And then it died down. No one else joined him at the window's side and he couldn't have been so sure if they'd seen it too. The ginger glow of the misplaced winter-spice refused to die out completely, though. It lurked as a faint, treacle radiance, rosier than the blood of their fallen brothers, just across the horizon's surface.

Suddenly, the door swung open. Three familiar faces ran inside, lugging their weapons close to their chests.

Gwen had pushed through first as she hurried the pair behind her. In her path came Oslo and Evelyn. And that was it. No one else followed them in.

"Hey, what was-"

"Good to see you're okay, Rhys." Gwen laid out a few ammunition pouches on a nearby desk, setting the vials and empty containers to one side to gather dust.

"What just happened?" He asked a second time, his mind on the edge of panic.

"Nothing, yet. Some emplacements outside temporarily stalled their advance but two of them just returned battered and bruised." She gritted her teeth and rubbed her arms together for heat. "Looks like they're on their final approach."

As she slid by his question, he thought nothing more of it. The eruption outside was left unanswered, and with the proximity of their enemy he thought it was best to pursue those answers only when they had the space to breathe. Or rather if they were granted such room.

A hurried Oslo placed Evelyn into the corner of the room, just out of sight from the windows. With all the blood-pumped, stress-induced bodies of the 54th gathered in Sabrina's quarters, the air was a little thinner. The stench of battle reeked from Rhys and Oslo's clothing. The horrors they'd escaped were upon them once more, as wolves stalked their prey from hidden immediacy.

"Stay clear of the windows. If they get us all-" Oslo stopped, breathed and looked Evelyn in her eye with a reassuring smile, though decrepit. Her desolate denial of the end's approach left her in a fit of sorrow. He looked to Rhys, then back to her, and gave her a warming hug, changing his tune from professionalism to fatherhood. "They won't get us, Eve. We'll retreat when things get too tough, alright?"

For many times had the orders told him that there was no way out, that he was doomed to die on the field of battle trapped beneath concrete rubble. He wanted to bail out of the window, but to where he was unsure. There hadn't been any sign of hope or relief. He trekked back to the window, where the blaze had seemingly vanished from view, and he looked out with skittish unease. Ella watched him with a troubled lump in her throat.

"Still looking for a way out?" Sabrina whispered to Ella. They faced each other with differing expressions: one was of a disheartened desire to flee – hopeful, if anything, to see the next sunrise bless an eventual spring – and the other was anaesthetised and sedated by her acceptance.

"We can just leave, can't we? What's stopping us?"

"There's nowhere to go."

"But what if there was?" Ella's eyes moistened once again. Her growing anxiety had been left unchecked.

"There isn't."

Her tongue had sailed off with the iced wind. The winter bite gnashed between her teeth, and the words she spoke were part of the frost. The eyes, a once colourful and beautiful tone, were crystalised as jaded diamonds. And yet Ella refused to believe Sabrina had fallen for good. The aroma of chance, of hope even, had never left her mind. But it wasn't pure optimism that kept Ella going – instead, it was the horror of the closing hour that dawned.

"Please smile for me…" She too turned bitter as she became eager to combat her sister's vulgarity. "Is it too much to ask for you to come back?"

A stalemate had been reached. The status quo had fallen on radicalised and opposing poles: the fleeting stability of the woman and the ruins of the subjugated casualty. Their whispers fell only on their own attention, and after her retort Sabrina reserved her chilled tongue. There were no winners.

But urgency arose. Beyond the dirt-stained glass, the grime of battle had seeped through the cracks in the window. A sound – so well accustomed to the squad's remnant – chose to announce its arrival. A rattle of submachine guns and rifles, grenades and exhausted diesel hollered them to attention. They stood still and watched the hallways.

Rhys was quick to move. He made headway for the door and opened it to dash back out to his commanders. Where he expected to see the soldiers gallantly finalising their defences, or to be encouraging one another with cadence, the truth outside was a poignant, melancholic still.

A gathering. Forty, maybe fifty, soldiers crowded in the middle of the room, forming a horseshoe formation. At the centre point stood a chaplain and a broken gramophone propped up by two choirmen. The legs of the machine were missing. Its splinters dug into one of the hands of its carriers, spilling its chariot's blood. The choirman paid no attention and committed to his duty.

The hallway had fallen into dead silence. A pin drop could have disturbed the congregation. Rhys looked back into the ward, and by an unknown driving force he closed the door behind him to investigate the session alone. He waltzed the grey path, through the glacial hallway, and approached the collective. There, he heard the sermon in motion.

"-for this is where we must close our eyes and look to our hearts and memories." The chaplain spoke with velvet consolidation. He requited the call for peace, and placed a valiant calmness to those around him. His fingers, wrinkled and scabbed, made clear that he too was in no place for someone of his wiry stance. "Take a minute to think of all the memories you have collected. They may be with the brothers and sisters around you, or the quietest secrets you shall never speak. Think of those places. Think of home. Think of you."

With incredible obedience, the crowd had their heads bowed and their eyes closed. Hands were clasped together, locked by the curl of their fingers. Some held hands and others stood alone. Their peace temporarily drowned out the rising storm.

Rhys buried his eyes into the floor but he refused to close them. He was just a few short meters off to the rim of the party, but he was still well within earshot. And under the guidance of the chaplain, he made the minutes count as he thought of the happiness that he'd left behind.

The farm. The family dinners. Collecting resources and travelling between towns. The rare times his mother came home, money in hand, and when she gave him a hug. The summer nights and winter mornings. A breath of fresh air. The light breezes of springtime. The faces of the beautiful. Sabrina. Ella. Their time on the wall. That one blistering day. Her shining face. The dreams of a kiss. Clutched hands. Brilliant smiles. Banterous talks. They were proud of him. He was gleeful. Being called fantastic; a lie so beautiful that he chose to believe it then and there.

The time came for the silence to end. It arrived absent of a shout; it creeped in slowly, borne on the honeyed voice of the chaplain.

"Our time may be hard-pressed, but I implore for a few moments of your peace. It matters greatly for our resolutions to come into fruition, lest we arrive to Sunar with chips on our shoulders."

Time dared to dance with the sermon's limitations. An evanesced moment was all that was to spare. The rumbles, guns and sirens of battle had set foot into their garden. They breathed in and all let out a slow exhale. Rhys heard the tremolo breaths and the unsteady beats of their timid hearts. Coming to terms with death was a great trial of courage and appreciation for the life they'd lived. Not many could say that the militia had granted them so much value to do so.

"To the benevolent Sunar, and any other voices amongst the twilight sky that wishes to hear us," the chaplain said stalwartly, "it is without debility to say the fight will soon be over. We face fate and we smile. Our lives – your creation – is a vessel for which we carry your praise. And in the afterlife, may you accept us for what we have done, who we are and forgive us for the things we have become. From whence we came, we will peacefully return. Your light…"

He huffed, and the smoke that drifted from his lips clouded the air. Rhys made clear the motions of his hands, where he unveiled a small vinyl disc from a folder and placed it on the gramophone.

"You'll have to forgive me, brothers and sisters. We usually have an organ for this." The gentle and melancholic chuckle stammered from the audience's throats. Rhys tried to smile at it, but the sticky sound of the war approaching put him off. "Now, please join me in hymn. The second verse is for you all."

A flicked switch sent the record spinning. The fragile fingertips of the chaplain pinched the needle and he stabbed it into the vinyl. Like a tame bonfire, it crackled out the speaker to start with, and then the tune began. A symphony, spoken through the artificial playback, all too recognisable. Rhys knew of its organic sound, realised from a brass mouth. His father had sung it a few times before he went off himself to fight in a foreign land.

431

And there it was again, right at the end of the line. If anything, it taunted Rhys passively.

Though their arms were burdened by the weight of the machine, the choirmen's lungs and vocal cords were empowered tenfold by the piece. The final prelude chord struck and they sang their mark on history.

> *At lasteth, he doth lie, in gradual rest,*
> *And feast on clandestine rye.*
> *In time, we pray, ev'rm're*
> *On thy plains, unto sky.*
> *Keep us, hold us, nev'r-ev'r fault us;*
> *Safekeep thy love.*

The hymn paused, and those around him closed their eyes for the last time. They tilted their brows to the ceiling, though their hidden gazes clearly saw the sky beyond. A celestial peace had infiltrated the regiment. A calm, glorious community before the world came crashing down had emerged. And in unison, they all sang together. Rhys exempted himself.

> *In skies, she doth fly, 'longside thy light*
> *And see to the holy call.*
> *In time, we pray, ev'rm're*
> *On thy grace, until we fall.*
> *Love us, hold us, nev'r-ev'r leave us;*
> *Deliver us.*

A closing accompaniment of hums in tune to the gramophone's whispers ended the piece. A silence held for a few more seconds, and then it all came back to reality. The noise of battle flooded the halls as a quiet murmur. Crumbling footsteps of soldiers on approach, moving with rapidity and blitz, escalated from their stillness. The chaplain nodded.

"Peace be with us. May we be blessed with luck and grace henceforth."

It all changed. In the blink of an eye, Rhys saw them spread out in their ranks, never near or beside their fellow countrymen. They had their rifles unslung and they had let their voices sail down the hallways in desperation. Tables were turned over and crudely constructed sandbag chokepoints were manned. He couldn't react with confidence over what he had seen, and so Rhys returned to Sabrina's ward, where the rest of the squad waited restlessly.

He floated back inside and left the door open behind him – not before he made one last look at where the precession had been seen. Inside the ward, a bed had been turned over as a small makeshift barrier. Oslo's machine gun sat primed atop of the aluminium frame, where its bipod held it up. Evelyn hadn't left her corner. Sabrina and Ella were several metres apart. The latter held her rifle with a shaken grip whilst Sabrina was slumped against a wall, unable to stand on her own foot. Gwen slugged around an anti-tank launcher. He was unsure where she'd found such a thing, yet it helped trigger an all-important question that he'd forgotten.

He looked around one more time to confirm his confusion, and then went to Gwen for answers.

"Where's Mateo?" With that realisation, a quick follow-up enquiry forced its way out as he tallied off the absentees. "And where's Christa?"

"Christa was pulled away by Thomas, they were headed to the internal command centre – I think." The medic answered in a huff, plagued with the exhaustion of her additional baggage.

"Thomas? Wait – what for?"

"No clue. He just…- I don't know, he just stormed past us with her at his heels." She stopped what she was doing and tried to relax her shoulders, but the upsurge of wartime ambience left her incapable of doing so. "Mateo just ran after them. Just like that – stupid fuck. He left his launcher too, but he at least took his gun – said he was going to take a look and that he'd be back."

"Did they desert?"

"I don't bloody know!" They looked around quite helplessly. Then, they'd found their mutters overwhelmed by the gunfire headed toward their building. It was only by luck that their room faced the rear end of the compound, freeing them of focused fire against their windows.

"It can't be, not with someone like Thomas." Rhys muttered.

"Fuck 'em," Oslo chimed in, "we don't know anything. No Thomas, no Christopher. Fuck it all and pay attention."

"Next time," Gwen coughed, "make *Corporal Aviadro* realise that."

The outside hellscape rampaged through rapid motion. Soldiers, scattered in other parts of the hospital, had opened up with hateful retaliation. Their gunshots resonated down the hallway, and the purge was in play.

A boon, so righteous in death's tongue, let out a steady growl. It was the warning call to the few left. Their time was up. In came the hounds, and with them were the snarling bites of their steel teeth, launched from bloodied rifles.

Ella forgave her distances and immediately latched back on to Sabrina's body, and she assisted her limp off to the corner, where Evelyn waited impatiently for the little miracle she had hoped for. On death's approach, Rhys' heart stuttered and his dysfunctional lungs broke beneath the weight of his pressure. He stormed over to Gwen and wasted no time in pressing for any answers.

"The command centre, right?" The doglike exhaustion in every pant did nothing to quell the tension.

"Yeah, that's where they were headed."

"Anything of value there? Something Thomas needs?"

"Fuck knows…" Gwen thought a second, before drawing up assumptions. "Better defences? A bunker, maybe?"

The odds of such protection were low, yet incredibly tempting. With the sounds of battle just beyond the patio, the dreary acceptance to lay down arms and die had disformed into denial. He wanted to survive. All of them did, truly, from the bottom of their hearts. The truth of the matter was that they had nowhere else to go, lest they chanced the mad dash for survival. And with Mateo's disappearance, Rhys permitted the willingness to prolong the collapse of everything around him.

To him, the shame came from failure when the chance to escape was still alive, even if on life-support. And as long as there was still one option left on the planet, he was willing to do anything to go through with it.

"Hold the door!" A shout came whilst the voices of the militia's dread shuddered its hinges.

Shells ejecting from their magazines rained down on the concrete floor. Each penny-weighted chime sang its tone-deaf tune, plastering an artificial songbird's call, like a music box with rusted components. Windows on the lower floor were smashed

434

and cracked. The echoed cry of a man realising his end came to light.

"Grenade!" He called, and the powdered mist engulfed the bottom flight.

The lights flickered, turned off and plunged the facility into an ashen crepuscule. The death strokes of paint came clear, the rooms were slathered in a scenic horror whilst the snowstorm outside intensified and the natural light dissipated. The clearest beacons down the hallway were the muzzle flashes. They were directed outside for a small while longer. Rhys peered further down the darkness and saw a man already collapsed against the wall, a wound to the neck, his life quenched beside the intense fire.

The dust didn't let up. A second explosion went off and the teeth of its shrapnel scarred the walls. Markings akin to the nail-scratchings of a desperate man stained the parapets at the top of the stairwell. He threw himself back into the ward. They were practically on top of them.

The front door to the facility had been kicked in. Shocktroopers – armed with submachine guns – swept the rooms. The ambience of a brutal engagement, where hands clashed before the gunshots could, echoed the futile struggle. A flash of a painted memory, where knives went into chests and bullets lodged themselves into foreheads, put Rhys' distress at the front of his mind. He panicked and scrambled to the back of the room.

"No, we can't stay here. They're inside!" He lurched out his words. His remnant squad looked between him and the door with disjointed comprehension. "Keep watching the door, we're leaving."

He pressed his face against the window, and tried to follow it down the side of the building. The drop couldn't have been more than a floor. It wouldn't have been a problem for himself, but the injured and weak may have-

"Where are you going?" Gwen demanded. Her eyes were still plastered on the open door.

"We'll…" With his soul barely composed, he thought for a split second for their limited options. "We'll jump. Out the window. Which way is it to the command centre?"

"Rhys, we-"

"We're leaving. Now."

435

"There's nowhere else to run! Stop-" Gwen's accent had turned into a haunting, spiritual taunt. He wasn't sure if it was her speaking to him, but he still answered aloud.

"If you want to stay, you can." To excuse his cowardice, he pleaded with the others. "Maybe…we'll be fine there. We're not dying, today. You're not dying today!"

His aroma of panic latched on to Evelyn, who covered her ears and begged for sanctuary. Her foetal position caught Oslo's eye, and he acted on impulse. He left his machine gun beside Gwen and held the girl tightly.

"Fuck it, I want out!"

The mounting tide of violence crept up the stairs like a four-legged beast. Soldiers willing to take the aggressors on without regret were slaughtered on those very steps, letting their blood flow as rivers did down mountains. On Oslo's agreement, Rhys stepped back and raised his rifle by the stock. He swung it once against the window and cracked its shell. A follow up swing smashed it, and the frostbitten air swarmed the room. He dropped the weapon by Gwen's side and took a step back, eyes covered.

The edacious gust tethered their resolve to the end goal – escape. Oslo was the first to clamber against the sill, and he dove down into the snow. There was no noise as he fell. It was as if the winter had swallowed him whole. But the waving of a dirty hand beckoned for them to drop Evelyn into his arms. Rhys acted without hesitation. He grabbed her and carried her to the edge, giving an unheard warning call.

"Catch her!" He loosened his grip and watched her fall into the whiteout. It looked as if she'd hit the target. "Go on! We'll be right behind you!"

"Are we doing this?" Ella clenched on to Rhys' arm again. He nodded silently and ordered her to step forward.

"I'll toss Sabrina down to you. Go, now!" The thump of his heart minced his ribcage. A morning cusp of sinister reality taunted him, it defiled him. He was the war's whore. He wanted to run far away, through mist and murder, and to see the dew of a summer's morn.

As he forcibly steered Ella toward the window, he peered below the drop. There was no sign of Evelyn nor Oslo, and he could only have hoped that they'd made their daring dash to safety. Then, he was in thought again, at the time where the seconds counted the most. Everyone knew the general direction they had to take, but a few degrees off course could've been-

"Move back. Move. Back!" At the top of the stairwell, the militiamen retreated behind their final defensive line: scavenged sandbags laced with books and trinkets all stood in front of turned-over tables, hospital beds and cabinets. Bipods were deployed, fingers itched on triggers and eyes were locked to the entrance. The foreign voices of Ferusian shocktroopers swept through the halls. And, with weapons primed, they ascended the stairs to the top floor.

Gwen raised her weapon and watched the door, begging for Rhys to speed up the process.

Without grace, Ella was hoisted onto the sill, and she plunged herself into the whiteout. He watched over the ledge in search for a sign of life. Soon enough, her bleak figure was seen.

"Keep your eyes on the door, I'll-"

His voice was cut short by the opening of hell's safekeep. When its iron hinges and locks were cut through, the carnage of violence had returned. The walls were endlessly disfigured by the indiscriminate swarm of bullets. Machineguns carved into the bodies of the first few to catch their sights. Muzzles flashed like supernovas in eruption. Lights, lit and silenced in the blink of an eye, torched the darkness.

Severed hearts were trampled on by the ongoing wave. Each ballistic tore through muscle and bone, teeth and tongue, until its wretched entrance had annihilated their victims. Pleading cries added another disturbing ambience, of gargled screams drowning in their blood, of ached hearts beating their last thud, and of the furious war-cry: to the end! There were those that begged for help, the cries for a medic that never existed, and those who besought execution for their misery. Gwen wanted to go back out to help them, but a sealed fate awaited those who stood their ground. Death's instigation had expressed its true power.

Her eyes were locked on to the hallway, hands trembled and breath uneasy. The iron sights of her firearm could barely hold still in the quaking of her palms. Rhys acted on instinct. He grabbed the crippled icon of his sins and held her tightly. Sabrina, overwhelmed by the noise, held him back. He looked over the edge and called out to her sister.

"She's coming down now!" A second before he let go, he whispered his condolences into her white-tulip cheeks. "I'm sorry."

The disparaged second was suspended as his fingers unravelled her chariot. Like petals from a late-autumn floret, she was plucked out of the sky by the wind and tumbled freely to the ground. A thick pile of snow awaited her landing, with Ella's arms to soften the fall. In the slowness of the trice, Rhys saw Sabrina's face during her downfall. It was blank. Cold, sedated and emotionless, even. The seams of a golden strata, the veins of the most beautiful soul he'd once known, were gone, and the coal irises that replaced her trashed the goddess-like picture.

Had the woman preserved her past self, a tear would have rolled down Rhys' bloodshot eye. Yet those tears were nothing more than a thought – like a hope lost when the brain gave in – and he stared at her vanishing into the mist, and into Ella's weakened arms.

Much to the same protocol, he shouted down to them with a croaky, battered tongue.

"Run! We'll meet you there, I promise!"

As he turned, he saw Gwen take aim at a figure. He rushed over to her side to grab his weapon and when she fired, a soul staggered to the floor. The figure landed with an inaudible thud and they pressed against the wall. A few seconds of life tried to prop itself back upward, but their strength left them and they collapsed in a bleeding heap, streaking their blood against the wall. Gwen stood still, unable to comprehend what she had done.

Rhys held on to his weapon as if it were his safety rope and rushed for the window. He tried to drag the medic with him, but her hesitation left her blindsided to the opportunity.

And a second after, a small compact shell clattered and bounced into the room.

Each cast iron clunk sang in a wind chime's mimicking tone, lacking all the serenity and kindness however. He caught a glimpse of the ridged shell, and that the top striker was missing. Its fuse had been lit, and the countdown was on its last leg. Rhys let go of the stillborn medic and ran for the window. There was no hope for the hesitant.

Two seconds to go.

438

He placed a hand down onto the broken glass all across the window frame and it pierced the shard straight through his palm. The skin and tissue tore and yet the pain hadn't registered at first. Adrenaline pushed him forward. His breath – it was the stillness of it that told him he was about to die.

Then, the rupture came.

A pocket-sized bomb detonated in the ward. The force barely pushed him forward but a sharp prick caught his shoulder. He fell forward, tumbling out of the window, and the plume of smoke and shrapnel consumed the room behind him.

The air brushed against his body. In limbo, the fall took him down the chimney of a demon's dark abode. It kept going; more, and for forever, he was sure he'd never reach the bottom. Funnelled pain lay dormant in his body as he twirled in freefall. The world had been completely consumed by the ever-parched arctic. And just as it all felt endless, the bludgeoning force of the ground pummelled his body and halted him, and his world, in an instant.

A most uncomfortable silence tuned the performance of battle to an astral absence. There was a ring in his ears and it spoke over his surroundings with such priority and importance. It shielded him from the noise, the screams and the bursts of endless arson. Rhys wasn't sure if he preferred the terror or the pathetic, mind-raping squeal of tinnitus. It was all or nothing at all.

There he lay, crumbled against the snow. A concrete layer had been hidden beneath the hills of white. He barely shifted in his place; the sheer force of his brutish exit had briefly paralysed him. His eyes rolled in their sockets, looking left, right and below him.

Gwen: no body, no weapon, no footprint. Had she perished in the grenade's detonation, he first hoped that it would have been instantaneous. Yet, alike his recent fallen colleagues, he shunned out their memory as quickly as he'd created it. Their ghostly evaporations shafted a mental turbulence he wished to only avoid. So a clean slate was wiped, and a new ink seeped into its porous materials – his blood.

He held a hand to his shoulder to reach the pain and found the unrecognisable substance of his own construction. It stained his jacket and seeped through the threads, onto his fingers. The crimson tributaries trickled along his knuckles, down to his wrist, where they disappeared into his sleeve. It was the warmest thing he'd touched in months. No fire nor flame compared to the malaise of his boiled blood.

Psychogenic tremors polluted his impure hands. They trembled and the shock slowly settled in. There was no pain, not in the wintertide gulch that numbed him. A chasm of disturbance, with the ordeal of fear, pained him more than the injury.

The squeal in his ears hadn't let up. He moved his bloodied palm to his head and felt his frosted hair. A quick scan of his flanks revealed his helmet, sat alone in the snow. He forced himself to roll onto his side and he reached for its metal shielding. The stained, moistened hand made first contact.

He brought the shrill skull-shell to his heart. His pulse drew fresh ink for the steel canvas. The blood on his hands and jacket smeared the rose carving with a sable, unbearable shade of paint.

All the gaps, cracks and scars that Evelyn had created were filled in. The flow of his bristled brush – the tips of his fingers – sprawled the blood with pristine precision, all purpose driven across the guidelines of his rose. It had soaked outside of the flower's outline and made patches where his fingers stroked, but the one thing that was certain was the completion of the art piece: the rose had been varnished. It was, at once, finally whole.

Rhys lifted it from his chest and looked at his mishandled creation.

Above him, the sounds of gunfire inside the building continued on. He slowly brought himself to an upright seat, putting his sullied helmet back on and he planted his palm against the shrapnel and shattered glass stab wounds. He flinched; the pain smeared itself across his body.

With gritted teeth he sank his chin into his chest. He inhaled and exhaled slowly, controlling his respiration through the unregistered panic that was sure to set in. He placed one hand against the snow and, with as much might and mettle as he could muster, he pushed against the ground and lifted himself up to his boots. He staggered when he stepped forward. Everywhere he looked, he saw an absence of life. There were shadows of bodies that rushed through the blizzardly mist. Some had guns, others seemed to float as spectres.

The cruel punch of his wounds barrelled down his leg and he panicked. Blood continued to flow between the fabrics of his clothing and across the ridges of his roughened skin, and all the while he was peppered with the products of the unceremonious winter.

And the defaced mutt dared to drive on through the concrete wilderness. Each stagger was fastened down by the wolves that sauntered around him. His vision became blurred.

Behind him, where he dared to never look again, another blast flattened the east wing of the hospital. A shockwave pushed the snow ahead of him, and Rhys took the opportunity to follow through its cracks. He went into a sequence with weakened legs. His posture staggered, he whimpered and whined but kept going.

Only the next objective took the forefront of his muse. He had to survive. There was no negotiating about it.

Chapter 30

Stand to…

~~…feel sorrowful?~~

Like the occultists and necromancers of death's eve, the ripples of battle scorned and plucked the pain from the corpses of the murdered, ice capped environment around them, and they resurrected suffering to send upon the dying few on their knees, still. Machine guns serenaded the mood of the battlefield and the rifles reciprocated their barbed kisses all around them. An irrevocable ring, propped up in the lowest chasm of the underworld, encircled them with savagery. Oslo cusped Evelyn's shoulders within his hands and shielded her body with his towering figure. There was no telling how far they'd gone, or how much further there was left to go. Where they ran, there were repetitions that made it seem as if they'd ran in a constant loop.

All the heaped rubble piles from the decommissioned facilities began to look the same. There were no landmarks nor signposts that indicated where they had to run, or if they'd fallen off course. The tightrope path got thinner by the second, and they were left traversing down Phlegethon's tight strait to nowhere. Mullackaye was irrevocably unrecognisable. The site may as well have been scrubbed from all maps and globes, for the site of evisceration had been made.

As they ran, Oslo whispered empty promises to Evelyn. His voice was but a rumble in the quakes of chaos that surrounded them.

His field of view had been quashed by the blizzard's climax. He was carried by luck, running blind through the fading world. Wherever he turned, there were the wraiths of grey materials passing by, oblivious to their presence. Yet as invisible as they felt, the contrarian truth rushed to disprove their safety.

Shoulders collided in heavy contest. A brute force of incautious travellers met in the middle of nowhere and sent both parties into a plunging tumble. Oslo lost his grip over Evelyn during his crash. Temporarily, he was buried beneath the snow and the arm of their new confidant.

The younger soldier fell forward by herself, and she threw her arms out in front of her. Her palms were scraped by the concrete beneath its winter blanket. Evelyn winced and scurried across the floor. Her skin went from the blue of the arctic seas to a gushing pink. She brought her hands to her chest and sat up on one knee, pleading to herself over all the stinging aches that encompassed her palms.

However, when she turned around to be recovered by her guardian, she bore witness to the inception of a standoff.

For the man that had unintentionally rammed into them wore a uniform unlike her own. His face was exposed as his scarf loosened and the pale, fresh appearance of a young Ferusian man stared back at Oslo. The latter turned and raised his hand forward, gesturing for him to yield before the trial.

"Stop! Stop, wait!" For what felt like the first time, Evelyn heard fear in her guardian's voice. She sat, dumbstruck at the taut encounter. But in his hesitation, the Ferusian didn't gun him down with his submachine gun, and he instead stared at him with toiled eyes.

She saw the hours of wear and tear placed upon his shoulders. The journey into battle, the encrusted sheet of ice on the tip of his tongue, where he had travelled for miles in conditions unimaginable. Battle, weather and fear had taken its toll. He held back and stepped away slightly, visibly trembling at the sight of Oslo. She watched as his hands wrapped around his firearm tighter.

Unending screams from the conflict surrounded them like a gladiatorial audience in wait.

Evelyn hyperventilated. She watched as two titans, one of flesh and another of steel, stood weakly in the face of one another. Oslo didn't move and continued to hold his hands in the air as if to tame a vile beast. And the Ferusian soldier clung onto his weapon knowing well that his life could meet is end. The turmoil of his internal debate was kept within his glassy eyes, and

443

it put the man at the helm of a hair-trigger as did the judicial judgement of the reaper.

The temperament of mercy was dead. Oslo shook his head as the man's hands shifted toward the handguards of his weapon and he raised it forward.

Suddenly, Oslo lunged with all the force he had, arm extended, and he went straight for the gun. He struck its iron barrel with a flat palm and forced it aside when the barrel blared its seared flash of fire. The men were locked in an intense struggle over control for the weapon, wheezing as he'd found himself at the bite of the attack. They tussled madly over the tool, spinning in dance as they put all their might into seizing the arms. Oslo had quickly buried his back into the soldier's front and wrapped one arm around the shooter's trigger hand. Desperately, he used his free grip to direct the barrel into the snow.

But the girl – the silent spectator – had paused as she saw the formation of a red stain in his torso, for the first bullet had not missed its target. A soggy, scarlet dye coloured in his stomach dress – yet her guardian continued as if unfazed. His struggle manifested a single tear, pushed out through his troubled stress.

Evelyn tried rising to her feet when the gun blared out its song, masking the air in a furious whistle as each round was ejected into the snow a mere metre away from where she sat.

Then the gun *CLICKED*, and its magazine was empty. At the first opportunity, Oslo made his strike. A free elbow jabbed rearwards into the Ferusian's chest and he thumped him once, twice and thrice until he let go of the submachine gun, stumbling rearwards as their bodies departed. The gunner lumbered toward the girl, and in his pain-fuelled shock he discarded the empty weapon.

"We leave…now-"

It came at an instant – there was a terrible, horrendous sight to behold, and her world froze. Evelyn, whose eyes were fixed on the man who'd sworn to protect her, hadn't noticed the still very alive adversary reaching for a holster on his hip.

An applause made from five raucous gunshots encored the intense struggle. For the first shot, there was near to no reaction from Oslo other than a jolt of the spine. The second and third ripped into his skin and stopped him dead in his tracks. The final two were but nails in the lid of his casket, the shovel at his burial ground and the ignition switch for his cremation. His expression was forever frozen still and chest turned scarlet. He collapsed, still and silent.

The piercing ring of the firings' presence was then ensued by the surrounding battle's radical lawlessness. Evelyn sat empty handed. Her palms were buried in the skin-numbing, blood-freezing snow, whilst her eyes were fixated on the crestfallen body laid half a metre from her boots.

She pulled herself up and crawled her way over to him. When she collapsed by his side, she expected – no, begged – for him to get up and to do something, to move and heroically fend off the monster that had bested him – but he did no such thing. He continued to lay there. For ten seconds. For twenty. Thirty. A minute. Two minutes.

Past the third interval, Evelyn's hands fell loose from his body. She shook him no more and eyed his still body with five tears in his back. Her vision became blurred. Tears welled up and she spluttered a short intake of breath.

The killer rose to his own two feet, where he looked down upon the scene with an unreadable expression. Was it fear? Regret? Satisfaction? Maybe there was a hint of relief, or a cunning masquerade of guilt in place of his cruel endeavour. It mattered not. Evelyn looked at him and saw only the beast with the four curled horns. The soldier let his steaming handgun slip from his hand and fall into the snow, unsure of how to collect himself. He too was in shock. A first kill, perhaps, or the trial of his own misdeeds laid out before him.

His face was blurred out of reality. The shiver of the cold left a sting on her tears and she couldn't see anything for a while. The howling winds worked with the excruciating blare of battle to drown out her sorrow, to pretend that it wasn't there. Isolated, she looked at Oslo again.

Then, nothing else mattered. The one she wanted to call for her father, her guardian spirit among an army of devils, but he was nothing short of a dead man. It was quick. It had happened too quick to properly register in the girl's head. She pled beneath her breath and cried out his name.

And then, she became truant to her past goal. Only her grief persisted. All her pain signified the final space around her: a solemn snowfall where everything faded into a colourless, empty space. The soldier grabbed his submachine gun, put in a new magazine, stared at her with a debate on his lips, and he stumbled away, leaving his handgun behind to bury the evidence of what he'd done.

She pressed her face into Oslo's back. Her skin merged with the blood that had left his twisted helix of anguish. It painted her soul; it traced her features with his essence. She let it happen. The land distorted around her too. Mountains formed out of nothing; their peaks were constructed from the jagged dagger-rocks found in the underworld. A hundred of them lifted sky-high and disappeared into the clouds. At the base of those mountains were skulls and bones, beaten and cracked. A million of them. Maybe more.

Her cries became silent. She knew that, there and then, she had lost everything. She'd convinced herself that there was no way for her to carry on unguided, alone and unprepared. An abyss stared at her blood-coated face, and she stared back into it. All she saw was snow and the machinations of her violent illusions.

They were virtuous souls, those hallucinations, with their tribulations and pains drifting through a river of sorrow. Their trial was incomplete, yet she felt fractured as a result. There was no road ahead of her – and she let out a final tear.

Where all things were unreal illusions, there were but three staunch realities: Oslo's body – raped by conflict and the swift, indiscriminate harvest of the war –, herself and the leftover handgun, three bullets left in its magazine, to which her eyes landed upon it. She watched it become buried over the hour, counting the snowflakes as they hid the history of Oslo Verdana.

~...lament for passion?~

Ella had never considered herself much of a theist and had only attended congregations across her lifetime when it best suited her solitary interests. It had been what many religious neighbours referred to as false idolisation, a reluctance to place faith in the stars and final solutions of their divine ways. And she agreed.

446

She never saw the stars as holy bodies, relics of a bygone era of pious prosperity and eternal peace; her faith had been allotted only to the angelic protection of her sibling.

Yet in the demonic battle for Fort Mullackaye, she'd noticed that her principles had been flipped on their heels. Where she hated the dancing flames of the incendiary war, she had hoped that the whiteout would shield her from the trauma that taunted her. Nevertheless, the contrary came forth: she felt uncomfortable, isolated and in a constant paranoia regardless of where she looked to. The sheet of ice and snow instead preserved her scars. And her faith was…

What even was her faith anymore, she asked once, twice for surety, but she drew blanks again.

As she hoisted Sabrina through the valley of crystals, her undying faith had reached its mortality. It became one with reality. She flashed fast gazes at her sister throughout their escape, and there was only emptiness and pain in her expression each time she looked.

How does one hold themselves stout as their guardian seraph's convictions are torn piece from piece?

And the valley she walked through refused to open up to the light. There were devastated buildings, ransacked and pillaged through modernised, mechanised warfare, and they were left in near copy-and-paste states. Broken glass, dusty pools of ash lingering from concrete debris, and several scattered bodies. Like many before her, she felt on loop – and she was left in an uncaring cycle until something came to claim her dwelling. Purgatory had begun its lesson. And Ella – dazed and confused as to where she should go – let herself wander ahead with her prize wrapped around her neck.

"Ella…" Sabrina's chilling tone left her lips, but the noise encompassed all around her, as if she weren't the speaker. "Where…are we?"

Ignorance was her best bet. She tried to suck in her emotions and take charge of the situation. It was under Rhys' orders that they'd reach the command station. Death would not do them part. It tried to before, and Sabrina too had given the end her blessing – but Ella refused to give death an inch.

Lamentation suddenly struck her chest and eyes with piercing force, and without reason she collapsed down onto her knee and started to weep. A howling whimper showered down their embankment – she sank in the snow and lay around the reeds of nothing. She had broken down after a mile of responsibility had beaten her to a pulp.

Sabrina lay beside her, having fallen without her sister's support. The abraded body was immobile and her eyes were open, with her breaths still visible through the fog her exhalation created. And in her terrible little puddle of sorrow, she believed she was being drowned in the bitter cold.

I can't stop crying, she told herself in thought, *and there's nothing I can do to stop it.*

The snow before them was laid like a white river, but as the sun was blocked out by the great fog around them it turned itself an otherworldly shade of black, like the waters to the deepest oceans.

Where they were, in Mullackaye, was on the fringe of everything – the battles, the war and the gateway to heaven. It was a gloomy landscape where gods watched others sail by. They were left on the sickly path to the command station – their docking port – with their sails at low mast.

Ella casted her teary eyes upon the sea she sank into. Through the mist, only the crumbled buildings, corpses and occasional shadows of hell's army charging past them livened the decomposed scene.

A ruse had spat in her eye: there was no perfect outcome. The war had torn her apart, crippled her limbs and injected her mind with grievances. She was infringed by terror, indoctrinated with fear, and had been sacrificed without hope; she broke at her final trial – a body of frozen water, a canal to the ends she'd asked for.

"Ella," Sabrina's haunted words swirled in the wind's current, "are you still there?"

"Yes…?" She retorted, weakly.

"Ella, I can't see…I can't see anything."

She looked over at Sabrina and, through watered glances, she helplessly saw her final thread snaping. Sabrina's eyes became blacker than the hollow cosmos; she looked around with their frightening absence. Another tear trickled down Ella's cheek as her mind fractured and disfigured her sister's image. The illusion of horror, and the pictures of unsettling dysphoria, tormented her – all whilst the sound of gunfire persisted.

448

"Your…eyes?" She questioned Sabrina, and reached out with polar palms. She discarded her rifle off to their side.

Her words staggered and neither said anything else for a drawn-out minute. Soon after, Ella's reach collapsed into the snow when her arm fell loose. She was motionless; her arm not quite extended enough to touch Sabrina's face.

Through her moistened irises she witnessed the hallucinogenic scene gnaw at her figure. She teared up at the sight that frequented her fears and backed away weakly. The blackened eyes peeled her anxiety's blanket away and it exposed her nerves for the world to see.

"Stop…please…"

The silence of their conversation was surreal. Her phobia had left Ella at a dangerous impasse. How she proceeded was beyond her control, understanding and authority. She was hopeless, and useless.

She told herself that over and over in her mind: "*Useless. Useless. Useless.*"

Sabrina had lost all of her will, her way of words and happiness. Something unseen had been uncovered by the war's filthy grip. And it was ugly, desecrating on her past self. It was all unbelievable. She still hoped through all the hurt and pain that it was all a cruel nightmare.

And she waited, with a primed request held back until they were alone, until everything around them had collapsed in a ball of flames, until the stars themselves were to explode, and until the fabric of reality had been toyed with to paralyse her obstructor. Ella couldn't protest what she didn't know – and Sabrina continued to glare at her sibling, then her rifle, then back to the horrified face.

Visibly disturbed, Ella recoiled away from the dreadful shell of her sister. Like the weeks before, she became something else. Her blooming hyacinth appearance, of colour and unmatched beauty, had wilted at the turning of season. Her leg had been the trampling of her flowery self, and the shells of the bombardment had been the boots in which she was crushed. And since then, her petals fell off one by one. Go on, or give up. Go on. Give up. On. Up. Yes. No. Should she? Shouldn't she?

She hadn't realised that Sabrina's last petal was on its final strand. The corolla had vanished.

Like a stillborn, Ella left herself curled up in a flaccid foetal position, knees to her chest and eyes buried into her sleeves. Her wailing was muffled by her arms. Her fear had completed a rowboat's journey – a cold, unseen river had been crossed. Abstained with inaction – she'd paid her pittance in stillness whilst the sailor for the world's chaos accepted her transaction.

A heavy overcast descended upon them. And when the mist settled, there was an inaudible voice speaking to her. Its words were drowned out by the echoes of the world's end. And she wished she had heard it, as the following sound forever silenced her road to Elysium.

~~...resist the scalds?~~

He'd done it. He'd left the building and had taken the loosely known path to the command centre. To him, there was little time to pay reverence to the battle that surrounded him. The shadows of the greyed-out masses flew by. He did wonder if any of them flowed down the same stream he did, yet not once did he raise his voice to ask. Simple desires had him narrowed on a few things:

> *Find the building.*
> *Find his allies.*
> *Don't die.*

He found the last one amusing. In his wounded palm sat the rear handguard of his rifle. The free, uncut hand was tightly pressed against his shrapnel wound in his shoulder. He held it tightly, pressing against it and gritting his teeth to bear the agony.

Each step forward was with overclocked power. He pushed his limits and staggered ahead regardless of the fragility of his mortal shell. In the end, he wanted nothing else but to see past the violent days. Hot on his heels were the cavalries and chariots of hades, where in place of valiant of steeds there were blood-thirsty hounds waiting to claim his soul for the night's banquet.

Rhys had never been so determined in his life. Nothing was to stop his push for victory. To him, that didn't mean triumphing in the field of battle – never again. It meant running, hiding and escaping the madness of the world. But along the vile river he so drifted down, in ice and polar sheet, something changed.

The sounds of battle diminished over a sudden second. First the wind broke through the diminuendo and then came the trailing of voices. He didn't slow down. He told him it was just a trick of the ear, of the mind and of the devil. Yet where he trekked, the silence became more apparent.

Soon he was alone once more; not just by the solitude of his body, but by the absence of sound altogether. There was nothing. Even the wind had crawled to its crib. The snow drifted mutely and the mist remained unclear. He felt his body grow colder. Then, he thought it was time as his skin hit sub-zero. Perhaps he'd lost too much blood. The pain had grown numb in his shoulder and the shock had persisted. Fortunately, he was still alive. He could feel things, and he could taste the disease in the atmosphere. Yet all his relief changed when the glow poked through the fog.

He'd seen it before. Back at the hospital, that roaring distant fire. A glow so vibrant in the colourless lethargy around it. An ocean's span of a horizon of a blistering blaze stood ahead of him, before he stumbled into its parted way.

He blinked, and at either side of him were the banks made from torched light. A crackle, familiar and unwelcomed, flooded his ears. And he stopped walking, finally, for he found himself in a corridor of incendiarism.

The snow beneath his boots seemed unaffected by their heat yet he felt their burning aggression against his skin. It warmed him in a way that he couldn't bear. He wanted comfort, not burns.

Auroras of inferno flared the beaten, plutonic pathway before him. Weary hesitation stuttered his drive. A plume of ash eradicated the glacial mist and occupied its vacant space. And the tips of the flames danced as they were forever repetitious, yet always various. He saw no further than a metre ahead of him, and the white palette became a viscous, glutinous grey. Snowflakes were infused with the light of a withering star – the red embers reigned and danced as aristocrats in a ballroom. A sting came to his eyes and he shielded them with a flat, bloody palm. His blood bubbled and boiled whilst he was placed in the cauldron of Mullackaye's disintegration.

Wherever he looked, he saw faint signs of life being scorched in the banks of his river, where they squandered and flailed in and amongst the reeds constructed from red-hot iron brands. Tributaries ablaze flowed into the main path he sailed through. Come around him, he asked, as in came the flesh of his imps.

Rhys' showed no fear in his eyes because he was too tired, too fatigued by battles and wounds. There came a point where the broken man, crushed and remoulded by the makers of his destruction, turned to incoherence and confusion at the peak of his trial. A desperate Rhys waded through the sea of flames and tried to pay little regard for his firestorm.

The flames tickled his skin at the tips of their orange flickers. Sensations of a deathly frostbite merged with his skin. He was forever frozen in death-valley, even if he were being burned alive.

He knew that, from behind, he was being stalked. A figure, masked and without a fresh filter, breathed asthmatically. It placed its boots in the exact same footprints Rhys had left and they fitted perfectly. Rhys didn't dare look behind him and kept his eyes forward, to the place he wanted to go. His trial couldn't last any longer, not if he knew there was nothing left for him to sacrifice then and there.

In the end, the open sea of flames became confined. A metal box appeared around him by the time he'd blinked, and in every direction were cabins and corpses. He was inside a train, a carriage most familiar with indiscriminate incineration. From the barricaded doorways, arms stretched out and flailed wildly, their skin made of charcoal and soot. Rhys pushed past them and their fingers frittered to dust.

The steel casing of his railed chariot began to bend under the scorching temperature. Molten tears flowed down the corridor. They followed Rhys – his liquid, magma-like disciples. The smoke thickened and the screaming was dampened. With a final push, he broke through a door at the end of the carriage's walkway and fell for a hundred metres at minimal speed. He blinked again, and his hands were planted deep into the snow. He looked around him, and the flames were fanned.

The peaks of the towering fires curled and arched over him, blocking out the sky and creating a tunnelway laid out just for him to pass through. Rhys immediately pulled himself back up and onto his feet, and continued to stagger on through.

A twinge most painful grew in his shoulder. His teeth clenched and he bit into his own tongue whilst he forever pushed through the storm. He was encompassed by a confined fireplace, and he soon covered his eyes from the embers and reached forward.

"Let…" He wheezed, spluttering out his only request. His hands, stretched far ahead of him, were met was an ashen fabric. Instinctively, he tightened his grip and clutched onto the tattered jacket with his bleeding palm. There, he looked up, and faced the figure with the mask, still breathing slowly. "Me…go…"

Glass stare contested his own strained eyes. He saw himself in the reflection of the black, opaque lens. Illusively observant, it analysed the pain – and the fatigue – in Rhys' expression and mind. Despite its haunting presence, it granted him one unspoken answer.

Fingers of bone and charred tissue raised with its right hand and pointed further into the tunnel of flames. Rhys followed its direction and, just several meters off, a door had manifested. It was made of iron, had no windows and was bolted shut by a large pitchfork crank. Steam flowed from the door's undercuts. There was no frame nor walls to prop up the gateway, and it stood alone in the tunnel's most furious blazes.

Rhys returned to the figure's mask. He was hesitant, unsure of where to go. Would it take him to the end, to face a three-headed hound of hell, the forks of Ferusia's revolutionary storm? Or, could he have faced freedom, like that which he pled for?

Without any other options, except to remain in his canal of anguish for eternity, he took the only option presented for him. He unfurled his fingers from the figure's fabrics and stumbled toward the door, hesitant and slow. When he reached the obstruction, he placed his hands on the crank. The sensation was difficult for him to describe. He saw the searing of his flesh, the burns given to him by its unsurmountable temperature, yet he couldn't say he felt the burn. He persisted until it would move no more, and the door sluggishly opened with an industrial shriek. A gust of wind blasted through tunnel. Rhys turned and watched as the violent storm pushed the flames aside and scattered their embers into the air, leaving behind no traces of a scorched world. The figure was gone. The fire was extinguished. And when he looked back at the door, it too had vanished.

He was still in the mist, standing in the midst of his expedition. About thirty metres ahead of him, the silhouette of a building stood tall and silent. The command centre, without as much of a sound coming from within. He stepped a little closer and saw the blacked-out windows. At the front, only one of the double doors was left open, and under the wind's lift papers were blown around the land. Documents, folders with burn marks on them, and a few bullet casings. There wasn't a sign of life from within the crypt.

And then, the shuffle of boots. A scuffed sound came from his left. Rhys let go of his wound and held his rifle upward, raising its sights to the noise. But before he could say anything, the shadowed person came closer and into a clearer view. He froze and was stunned to stillness. Ella hauled a cargo most unsettling – a bloodied corpse named Sabrina.

Chapter 31

Tartarus

Through what badlands did the mind wander, when it had spied the deformation of the fragile and the beautiful: the sullied bodies of crestfallen archangels. Ella hadn't noticed him, with his rifle raised, as she pled to the heavens with tears of ice. Endured trauma had demonstrated with one horror-induced picture – a crying woman, stripped of her family, who was left to wade through the blizzard with her kin dead in her arms. An inoculation of shock sent the sensation through his veins. Rhys' mouth dropped, as did his firearm, and he gradually plucked out the gruesome details of her passing.

Her trousers were egregiously filthy, saturated with snow, and the knot that closed off her missing limb's phantom space had been undone. It hung insecurely behind her. There was blood all over her spine, and there were patches of it that had carried over to Ella's hands to her own chest. And at her head...

With a defeated glare, Rhys faced the discomfiture and the filth that had been made of her. Her parietal bone was cracked open by the force contained within teeth-bearing bullets. The abuses to her caved skull blared the loudest with an austere drape made from the strands of her rear lobe. A thinned stream of blood painted the snow in a salivating deluge. And as she was brought closer, the bloodied whites of her eyes were still, whilst an unblinking stare forever scrutinised the sky, though her left glare had rolled back into her shattered skull. Ella's rifle was blemished with her sister's essence, and she was imprisoned behind her sister's dirtied back, of whom she'd slung over at a crooked angle.

"Fuck..." Of all the death, the destruction and the violence that stalked him, the crude markings of Sabrina's murder hit him in a way he could not comprehend. Hours, days, weeks and months of bloodshed had all but prepared him for a moment like that, and he failed at first sight of her fallen figure. A panicked breath stammered out his doubt. "No, no, no- oh fuck, no…"

His disbelief turned to denial and he blinked, time and time again to see if his eyelids could wipe whatever horror before him away. The impeding stampede of his collapsed world had struck him with an iron gauntlet, deep into his chest, and had ripped his lungs out as the pulsed uncontrollably.

He couldn't breathe. Her body, her ruptured skull, her inhumane looks, it-

He couldn't think straight. His heart raced on the kaleidoscopic downward spiral. It hurt as a piece of his heart was taken from him.

"Sabrina…" He staggered forward toward Ella, who'd tripped and had fallen onto her back. She cared not for the blood and grey matter that stroked her chest or face.

"Get up! Don't leave me…" Her pitiful cry fell only onto one pair of ears – Rhys heeded her plight and stooped down to her side, reuniting the pair in profane matrimony.

Pleas were but pleas, and they were strangers to the undoing of the necrotic. They remained indifferent to the vile nature of death. For every tear she shed for Sabrina's life, a tear was wasted.

Ella changed her tune and cried as if she were mute. She shielded her face from everything around her and buried it in her sleeves. There, she sobbed imperceptibly to herself, taken over by her uncontrollable quiver. The throbbing ache in Rhys' shoulder appeared inconsequential compared to the desecration of his holy archousa. A single feat had stripped Sabrina of all enlightened kindness. It created the polarity between sister and sibling, carer and patient. And, at the end of it all, the pressure had cracked her skull and brutalised her to oblivion.

Unsure of how to respond, Rhys kept his arms by his side and maintained a sluggish knee beside her. Careful hands cuffed Ella's wrists and drew them away from the body. She didn't resist. Gently, she was pulled aside, half a metre away, and both of them sat together in the snow to the tune of rattling machine guns several hundred metres off. He pulled her closer and embraced her one more time. She broke down into tears again as loud as ever before, and he did nothing to stop it. He was powerless, all in all. There, he positioned himself in such a way that she faced away from the corpse, whilst he took in the unbelievable sight to confirm whether it was real.

His fortune, in war, had been a myth. Conflict could not bear baskets of fruit. The myths about honour, or glory, were just perpetuations of monarchs and masterminds, and those who undermined the weak were shielded from the darkness of the dead.

He looked at Sabrina the same way he had once looked at Alexander: with the utmost swarm of fear. The good men and women never lasted out there. Festering in his mind and soul was the broken stance on their inhumane crusade, the burning mechanical fumes and the countless sacrifices that amounted to nothing, and everything that had made up his servitude to his nation was plastered as an act of victory where only defeat lurked. Alexander had set free the serf, but in his death, as had Sabrina, he had left a cold, confused and lone body to wander the realm without purpose.

Everything that the war had offered Rhys came on rusted iron platters; and the dust-covered porcelain dishes were stacked with decayed meat, churned through grinders, chewed by wolf-like teeth and spat back out to be served again. Not even the heroes saw a positive light. Alexander had been a man of necessity, not morality. Rhys' duty had been for survival, an obligation for the society and people that had raised him, and yet they were losing and cut down in droves by an unending storm of Ferusian bodies and bullets.

And he looked at Sabrina's caved skull with only defeatist questions on his mind: what did he even fight for? For men and women, like Sabrina, like Ryan or Tyran, to get carved up in the peasantry's banquet, or to see the fearful and defeated be executed for treason, such as with Dynis? In what world would have Rhys fought for such a place, a nation that was yet to reward him with anything other than misery? His world, of course, as he always had done.

But his world had taken away Sabrina, the goddess to Ella's life, and had left Rhys with something fragile – an infantile soldier who struggled to accept her fallen family.

Yet he did not cast pity for himself, for he had fought for such a place to be preserved without any great attempt to stop it. He never looked away from Sabrina's resting body, or from the entrails of her brain frittered against the cracks of her skull. He blamed himself for it and for what she had done.

Though, a faint part of her still lived on in Ella, even if but a memory, or an illusion to the madman's desire. He told himself that he would love whatever flicker of her spirit remained.

"Ella…?" He whispered underneath the putrefied gunfire.

The quivering soldier brought her arms up and around Rhys. Her voice was faint whilst her incoherent string of fumbled, teary-eyed words saturated her hysteria. There was very little he could say or do to alleviate her torture.

"Ella, we have to go."

An anchor rusting with guilt and regret latched on to his heart, and to the depths of blame it sank. Her lack of response only soured the taste of the liquidised pain he drowned in.

"Please? We can't…stay here. We should go." Rhys flinched as the nearby sprawl of a firefight accompanied the blizzardly wind. As such, and as it always had been from the start, time was of the essence. "It's what she would want, right? For us to go and to live on? Ella, come on, say something."

"I'm not even sure what she'd want anymore." Her bawls grew louder, and her grip became tighter. There was little choice left. He shuffled on with her still locked in his embrace, and moved them both away from Sabrina. He couldn't bear to see her like that anymore.

The blood, the bone and the lifeless stare in her wide-open eyes, and the torturous spread of her lips apart, to see her shattered teeth and disfigured throat, there the bullet had entered.

"Then come with me, we'll go someplace else."

Helpless and confused, she walked the path Rhys took her across. Toward the steps to the command centre they went, and they dared to never look behind them. There was no need for a ceremonial burial. The snow had taken responsibility as her undertaker, and had soon buried Sabrina in a casket of ice.

To leave just like that was the strangest decision Rhys felt he'd ever made. He made no attempt to stick around, to say goodbye or mourn his fallen ally, regardless of the anguish in his heart. But he'd set aside everything he wanted to do for Ella to move a little closer to home. He'd been possessed by the spirit of a guardian, a flowery summer-lady that had done the same for the broken man and the crying woman. He did what was best for everyone: he left.

Sabrina – her name, voice and agony lingered in his head as they ascended the lonesome stairwell to the front door. The deterioration that had torn her down was almost unbelievable. He denied, for a second, the pain that she had gone through, and her loss of hope at the will of her trauma. From the woman waltzing freely amongst the clouds, to the injured, shivering rat in the mud of no man's land, she'd been toyed with under the order of war. And to think, Rhys thought, that she'd done it – she became a true soldier of Kelan: broken, disorientated, hopeless and dead. Yet she was no martyr, not for anyone. She was but a name that would live for only as long as he and Ella did. And to that end, he guided Ella to the building in the hopes of finally leaving Mullackaye behind.

Abandoned papers twirled around them as they fled the door unattended; they disappeared into the snow the moment they broke free. One landed against his shoulder, and the numb stain of his own frozen wound shot a painful flare in his arm. He said nothing and he conquered the stairs with Ella linked hand-to-hand to him.

They lurched through the open door unopposed. Inside, a furious blink from withering mercury echoed the erratic beat of their hearts. A ghastly breath of the war's ill-wind blew away flakes of their livelihood, and quenched its own vile appetite. The resonance of battle roamed the hallways, with each passing shockwave filling the rooms with a tremored dust, so much that a faint muffle clouded its voice. Several pieces of broken furniture lay toppled, and the few cabinets left bolted onto the walls had been ransacked of the handguns that once occupied their shelves.

Ella's trembled breath had been watered down by her tears. It had taken up arms and occupied the vacancy of noise. But she held her breath when she looked back at Rhys and saw the murky patch of ooze upon his shoulder.

Her shock resisted her urge to speak. For a quick minute, she crept into control and pulled Rhys toward one of the over-turned chairs deposed by its previous owners. A little effort returned the seat to its former form – the crude, oak throne of a helot – and through teary eyes and choked out voice cracks she beckoned for Rhys to take a seat.

He fulfilled her wish without reluctance. The chair creaked beneath the weight of his gear.

Rhys reached into his webbing and fumbled around in its pockets and pouches until he retrieved a small piece of packaging. When unravelled, a field dressing, weaved around a central absorbent padding, gained its freedom to heal. Ella guided the wrap around his shoulder, yet it felt far too little too late. A lack of anaesthetic complicated the relief process. The first spurt of agony had passed yet the process of concealing the wound was ever the more teeth-gritting. He keened for his shoulder as the cloth met his torn skin.

Neither had any sort of legitimate medical treatment or training to use. Yet, he was blessed by a caring twirl of cloth and hand. He winced as her fingers danced around the wound with delicacy and an unforeseen sense of proficiency. On occasion, she slipped up and brushed the small punctures, causing him to jolt. She withdrew her hands each time and apologised inaudibly. Once one wound was addressed, she moved to the glass stab on his hand, something both had neglected for the longest while. A sudden, albeit weak, persistence kept his bindings together, with her beside the chair, until his lesions were finally clothed in helical dressing.

"Thank you." His words left his lips and touched her heart. Perhaps the sincerest gift of gratitude came with the fewest words, and Ella briefly smiled through her troubled expression.

Two drafts clashed in the middle of the corridor. One, from his right, came from the front door left untouched. The other originated from the corridor down to his left. There was no clear bridge to the outside world. The ever-present feeling of frost had finally gotten to the pair and the terror behind its enigmatic omens of death came at the turning of the season – the end days for the world they'd grown to suffer within was neigh.

She sat beside him on the floor. They looked at each other and shared a weary smile. They took turns to make a noise, as if they were to say something, but each time they quickly retracted it. But then, the blossom withered.

Swept up by grief, she cowered in her place, and Rhys watched Ella as she broke down into tears once more. Unsure of what to say, he remained idle. He wanted to take his numb, trembling fingers and place them against her cheek or forehead, where she could rest on the balance of his fingertips. Yet he kept to himself whilst she navigated her sorrow with ultimate failure.

A pejorative scorn left him restless and troubled. In the hour, he'd done little for her, or anyone, and that slither of hopelessness drove him closer to the edge. A fatigued ambition brought him up to his feet, slowly, and he curled his shoulder in a test for his dressing's integrity. There, he walked from left to right. The taint to his lungs was disinterred by its trembled motion. By the stars, he hated everything. He hated it all. A dark cloud that hung above his head as he scolded his direction, concocting a downpour so imperious it made him go under.

He then checked his rifle whilst the minute passed. Magazine in, then out, assess the bullets. It wasn't his original service rifle, but it had done its job back on the frontline. Eight rounds, maybe. He held the magazine with shaky hand. Four witness holes patterned down the casing proved his estimation wrong and revealed only three rounds left, where each viewport would show the bottom half of one bullet and the top half of its successive round. He'd barely kept a track of how much he'd fired during his escape and trial in the trenches. The euphoria of pulling that trigger, sending the inescapable ecstasy of recoil doing his shoulder, was quite intoxicating, so much so that he'd forgotten the times he'd pulled it on a Ferusian.

He scanned his chest rig and noticed that he still had several magazines to his name. Four full ones, and his fifth on the verge of being spent. The sounds of him exchanging his magazine for a fresh one couldn't drown out Ella's tearful howling.

Still unsure how to proceed, he walked over to Ella and stripped her of her own rifle. The smaller carbine, also tuned to hold .30 rimless cartridges, and its magazine configuration was more in tune for a higher capacity of weaker rounds, all of which were encased in thin stick magazines rather than his box counterparts. Rhys found that, within the details of a small nit-pick, that there was such an unremarkable amount of polish to it. Forever upkept but never used. He wondered even if she'd tended to the weapon so much so that it was in a better condition than when factory new. But in truth, there wasn't anything extraordinary about the fact her gun only had twelve bullets, with only one having already been spent. Yet his desire to occupy his mind with anything other than the horror that had haunted him

461

then outweighed anything else. He took any food-for-thought that would distract him.

He'd never seen Ella fire a weapon outside of their early training exercises. Not at the windmill, nor at Haria. And in Fort Mullackaye, she'd managed to steer clear of frontline service as she tended to her sister's fleeting existence. But, as Rhys had realised even before he'd taken her weapon, it was all for the hope of recomposing himself.

"Hey, I'm going to check out the hallway, see if anyone is-" He paused, seeing Ella too lost in her tears to notice him talking. "I'll see if anyone's around. I'll stay near, don't worry."

He set her rifle down by the side of the chair, then helped Ella to sit in the seat herself.

The few blinking lights strapped to the ceiling made him feel nauseous as he wandered further into the building, where a long straight corridor met his path. He roamed deeper into the dim corridors of the building's interior, hallways spanning a hundred metres into pure, almost translucent darkness. Just beneath his concern for Ella, his mind was riddled with questions regarding the whereabouts of the centre's occupants. Not a sign of life presented itself, and as he wandered through the hallway, his boots kicked two bullet casings on the floor. He looked down at them and spied four more; small calibre, likely of that to a snub-nosed handgun.

A pool of blood was between Rhys and the casings, and it tainted the brutalist, concrete hallway he trod through with a splash of colour. Curious, he turned around and saw nothing else of the sort, for the blood was alone. He gathered that it was a single confrontation maybe, but there were no signs that the Ferusians had stormed the building, or if they still occupied it if they had. He walked further along the trail, but regularly looked behind him to ensure Ella hadn't moved.

And there, he saw the blood trail again. Some of it was dry, others still flowed semi-freshly from a side room. Rhys prepared his rifle. He quickly checked that it was all loaded and ready, and then put one boot ahead of the other; he swung around the frame of the doorway the blood led into. Until then, he was assertive in his movements. But he froze the moment he turned that corner.

An instant rush of confusion caught him and strung him up. Indecent mysteries came forth, for he saw the fallen body of another soldier. Four, maybe six, holes were in his jacket, torn by the piercing of a handgun's rally. He lay flat on his back; by the looks of it, he had dragged himself to the room where he exhaled for the last time. Sat lopsided upon his nose, with a cracked frame and two broken lenses, a pair of small, circular spectacles lay cold. Rhys staggered, lowered his rifle and held his breath.

The strike of fate's hand slapped against his chest. He rushed a few steps forward and brought himself to the dusty floor beside the meagre figure. Rhys was left dumbstruck, such as sailors were like when cursed to see their crew thrash and struggle as they sank to the ocean floor. The man, Mateo, was already dead. He'd joined the pile of bones by the ocean's bedding to add another name to the expansive headstone in Squad 2's name.

At the will of the devils that dawned in war, Mateo had been slain by methods left only to the imagination. Gunshots to the chest, a thin blood trail along his path, and the collapse on the floor; all signs pointed to a fast yet painful agony to end on. His own carbine was just to his side, not a round spent.

Beside the body was an uncovered pit that descended down into a nightly dwelling.

Rhys quietly asked himself what had happened, as to why his body had been laid beside a gaping abyss, with bullet holes littered across both torso and chest. He shook him by the shoulders and, unsurprisingly, got no response in return. Mateo was as dead as a deer.

The struck match, ignited by the murder of Sabrina, had fizzled out the moment he reached the postman's corpse, but the ongoing smell of sulphur lingered around him. To him, it was all acquitted pain, set free by the powers that be above and around him. It came at him so suddenly, and so fast, that there was barely a moment to register Mateo's fate. He was dead. Gone forever, never to wake up and shake his hand, or to quip something provocative just to get a kick out the suffering around him. And for a little while longer, Rhys was convinced that he'd meet him later, alive and well, and that what he saw before him was a crude, cruel illusion given to him. But when he touched Mateo's shoulder, and shook his body for a response, he felt the cold rush through his fingers.

463

His body was real. Maybe two litres of blood either trickled into the corner of the room, or flowed to the right toward the hole he'd deliberately ignored.

Rhys sat still for a few minutes, and each chime on the clocktower was like a year's passing. Rhys had been inflicted with a misconstrued emotional baggage, where upon seeing the death of a man he respected greatly – of whom he'd taken advice from and learned the vindictive presence of all that surrounded him – and he didn't shed a tear, even if he wanted to. He wanted to cry, and yet he just couldn't. He sat there with sucked up fear and he left his emotions to fester and feast upon the heart-shaped box he had locked it within. Something compelled him to a vow of silence and he was polarised from his true self.

Whilst he considered his service to the crown to be illegitimate, buried within the hopelessness and falsehoods of his very existence was a commitment to the ones he loved. It was all he had left to sustain himself – a final thread at the end of the yarn.

Beside Mateo's corpse was something of an enigma. A taciturn burrow built into the floor, unveiled by the wide-open one-by-one metre trapdoor, stared at him with an intense darkness. The light above him showed a floor, covered in swirls of dust and the second pool of blood. A light breeze brushed against his brow whilst his eyes met the darkness with horrified intrigue. He looked back at Mateo and was unsure of what he'd uncovered, and how it related to his condemnation.

"What were you doing, mate?" He asked the body.

His headspace was nowhere near in the right place for deductive reasoning. He had one goal in his mind, and it meant leaving Mullackaye behind to rot and burn, as all things in the war had.

Time had fled before he was ready. Not a single officer was in sight, and the opening of a crypt beneath their feet had left him rather dumbfounded. Yet it almost aligned with what he had hoped for. An hour before everything had shattered apart, he'd demanded for a place of refuge, for a place to persist and elongate the road to death, to continue life out of fear for what came after. And there it was before him. A tunnel. A hiding place, or a route to escape. Mateo's life had stonewashed barely half a metre before he'd descended into the dwelling.

He looked around and made his way back outside the office, making headway for where Ella sat still. On approach, he caught the crescendo of her weeps until he was by her side. Hesitantly, he placed a hand on her shoulder.

"Ella?"

Novel incoherence took her tongue and whispered out slurs of uncertainty. She looked up slightly, but paid little courtesy to his words.

"We can go. Back there…" Where his finger followed, he knew Mateo's body still laid, and it pained him to know she'd need to face it. "There's a sort of – a basement place. I was thinking we could look there, and see if it takes us someplace safe. But-"

A pause broke his sentence up again, and he fumbled with his thumbs whilst his hesitation silenced him.

"I found Mateo." He said, a seething sting pricking his spine as the news finally crept out. "He's in the room where I found the basement. I…think he was shot – several times."

"Rhys…" Through waterfall-drenched lips, Ella's voice broke free on trembled supports. "I-…I'm so-

"No, please… don't say anything. Not until I need it."

"But-"

"Ella," he spoke without delay, "come with me. Please. We-…we can leave now, leave all of this shit behind. I can't spend another minute here, and you can't either."

"No, you're right. I can't." Her thin voice barely disturbed the haunting ambience around them. She looked him in the eyes once more. "But I don't know what to do or where to go. From here, or anywhere, it's…all gone."

"We aren't. But it's either we stay here and get killed or we just leave. We're not made for this. None of us were. And we finally have the choice to go." He clasped his shivering hands around hers and brought them to his chest. "We…don't have to die."

A familiar pause hung between the pair for several seconds before she drew away her drowned irises. She shook her head with a weakened counterfeit curl of her lips. She stood up, hands still cusped in his, and looked back at him with tears abseiling her cheeks.

"What's the point, Rhys?"

465

"To survive! Go someplace else. Leave the military. Let the war tear itself apart, for all we care. And we can find a place to stay and-"

"But why?!" An unseen aggression slipped between them and she broke her hands free. She quickly grappled onto his jacket and clenched on tight, and she shook him. "My sister is dead, Rhys. My sister is fucking dead. What part about that don't you understand? The last person in my fucking family is outside covered in snow and all we're supposed think of is what's next?"

"Ella, please-"

"No, Rhys. I can't." Her hostility turned to tears, and her words trembled as her anger churned with her sorrow. "I can't go anywhere. She's not here, and I don't even fucking know what to do about it. Is there even anything I can do?"

"Yes, there is. We can go."

"Where?"

"Anywhere but here."

"Why?"

"Because what would Sabrina want you to do?" Her grip tightened around his jacket. Rhys, dazed by her anger, pressed forward with an unsteady voice. "She wanted to protect you, and that didn't mean waiting for the end to sweep you away, did it? It meant going, running. Elsewhere. Anywhere. To stay alive, and to keep her alive. Because otherwise we're just going to rot away here, and…I don't want that."

"But I'm-"

"I'm scared shitless too, but I can't let you go. I don't want that for you, and neither did she." Stood between them, once more, was that everlasting silence. It halted time itself and let them linger in an eternal stasis of pain, trauma and grief. He felt her unsteady breath against his face as they held each other. And, at the end of their standoff, she succumbed to the weight of her tears and collapsed against his support.

Rhys didn't say much at first. He just watched her cry into his gear, dazed and confused by their encounter. She mirrored what he felt himself, but that anger and fear inside her compelled him to keep trying something. She was the last thing keeping him together, and, in the name of his life, he wanted to return that feeling.

"You don't have to see him. I could move him if you-"

"Please, let's just…go." She spoke in puny bursts, and he accepted her wish with a distempered heart. They grabbed their rifles with moistened eyes and left the seat behind.

They took the journey through the walkway. The plastic shine of the bulbs evinced their last leg to an unpromised escape. Their boots crossed over the cylindrical brass bullet casings and broke through the dried-up border of bloodstains on the concrete. And then, the final showcase came forth, the epilogue before their encore trek to elysian fields.

His encoder rested at the bottom of Mullackaye's catacombs. Wherever it led, he hoped it would transfer his spirit to another land within which he could finally prosper.

Eventually, they turned the corner and faced the entryway to salvation. Sprawled in the same place Rhys had found him, Mateo's emotionless stare toward the ceiling greeted their passing. Ella stopped for a second, hand still tightly entwined with Rhys', and she stared at Mateo's deafened body with mortification. He too was degraded by bullets and forever left on the cusp of escape, mere centimetres from the open pit Rhys led her toward.

An arachnid sting pricked her self-confidence again. She buried her face into Rhys' unbandaged shoulder and whispered sweet nothings to no one. The constant presence of death at every turn, alley and room left her in an unending cycle of suffering over inhumane sights.

However, she noticed that Rhys had stopped in his tracks. His attention was given to the office room door. There, inscribed in a clear typeface, the possessor of the boxed resting place proclaimed itself:

Intelligence Office – Thomas W. Lee

Fourteen characters of the Osakan script sat underneath the localised translation, likely retelling his name in his native tongue. Rhys watched the words merge into one as his head began to spin.

There were no answers, not there or anywhere. Everything had an answer hidden just outside of plain sight and Rhys told himself that he'd be unwilling to uncover a conspiracy.

467

The draft that came from its depths let out a little chime, and a whistle gave its most foul out-of-tune lullaby. Its discordant arrhythmic voice signalled their closed decision. Desertion, it would be.

He looked at his hand, then locked with Ella's, and hoped for one last chance to have his finale.

Chapter 32

The Tunnel

"Where are the others?" Ella's question delayed their descent, and the pair were left stuck in place. He hadn't considered that. The sting of their names, like needles and nettles, sent a shooting pain through his body.

She was still latched onto the present, not the future that he was increasingly reliant on. Where no fury matched the hour's scorn, he looked to tomorrow to ease thenceforth.

But when Rhys didn't answer, her concern slowly crept back into view. That passive insecurity returned and, with her terrible skill to stay alert and pragmatic, the reluctance to follow him to the escapist's world cursed her.

"Rhys, where is Oslo? And Evelyn? And-"

"Gone, I think." Put bluntly, Ella's queries stopped and the pair were dumped in silence for a boiling minute. She looked to the floor, where Mateo laid, and her hand constricted Rhys'. She was fearful of the answer, but through hesitation she perservered a little bit further

"How – how do you know that?"

"I don't."

"Maybe they're just-"

"Gwen was still in the ward when they gave us a bomb." But in saying that, Rhys couldn't quite paint the clear image of those sporadic moments. "We're alone, and we should head on."

The adrenaline had blurred everything of her untimely end, so much that it almost became a fever dream. All he remembered was the haze, the grenade, the instinct, a flight towards safety and nothing else.

"But what about Oslo and Evelyn? We haven't seen them; they could be waiting outside…for us." She jadedly asserted her compassion for a final hurrah.

"If they make it, they'll make it." With a cold tongue, he left it with a sigh. "Come on. The same can't happen to you if we stay."

There was a façade of a good soldier and an officer that battled with some personal selfishness. It had unmasked itself the moment they'd understood that those other people, the men and women, boys and girls, who'd been through hell with them had been but stepping stones to a final obsession. Then, they revealed all that they were: an unwillingness to hold dear any reminder of the war, even at the expense of their own brothers and sisters in arms.

Rhys was blighted by such a persona. All he cared for was Ella. And Sabrina. To him, they'd been everything the war wasn't. He wanted to be with them for as long as the violence continued, to help him escape the realities around him. Whether through lamentation, loathing, or familial integration, he wanted the grace he saw in them until it transported him to another world: their world – of both beauty and pride.

He had lost himself in an almost perfect goddess that never crossed off reality from his temptations – a much needed kindness exasperated and indulged, and had temporarily released him as his ecstasy. So, what of Oslo and Evelyn? They'd be a blinded duo of circumstance, ripped from their cores at the sake of a potentially unheroic sacrifice, and that was just how things had been. He couldn't change that. A land he found himself so powerless within had made his mind well and proper, and he knew that to traverse to another plateau of consciousness was the only step forward he had to count on. It wasn't that he didn't care for them anymore. Instead, he'd accepted that what had happened was definite, and that doing what little he could to garner a better tomorrow was all but wise. Any connected links between him and the war was just going to cause more pain.

And after seeing Thomas' name, the links to Mateo's corpse, the abandonment and mystery behind the lack of command, he thought nothing of it but the emptiness where the oasis had ran dry. Conducting investigations dug deeper graves for the uninvested, and whilst the rich yield was almost too tempting to

470

ignore, he tried to stay out of the shadows. He wasn't a man who could, or would, change anything other than where in the world he suffered. He surrendered his moral compass, the duty to friend and nation, and he turned away from the door. The pretences were clear: it was no longer his problem. Only Ella was.

The cold hand entwined with his and she squeezed his palm. It was a request to just move forward – although not out of determination. She'd temporarily surrendered to his pessimistic woes and accepted a purpose unknown to herself. Both refugees descended down each step into the trapdoor. Around them, the gainsboro-tinted scheme of the command centre transitioned to an infinite rose-wine bleakness. There, a darkness cradled their descent and softened the fall.

The soles of his boots landed in Mateo's blood. A steady hand guided Ella around and away from the ooze.

With a readied rifle, Rhys became the pointman and a pathfinder amid a steel-lined crypt. He looked to his left, and saw a desolate ruby-hue avenue with blinking, bloodied lights. They gently came and went yet made no siren's call. Their soothing pattern, however, let Rhys fall into the comfort of their slow, methodical evolution. Slowly on. Slowly off. Slowly on…

The other way wasn't so welcoming. A fortified door had been bound shut by a haphazardly, half-arsed work of welding which removed the choice of where to wander.

Rhys thought nothing of it. If the journey was to be linear for just a little while longer, then so it would be. The dainty lights beckoned his attention and he followed without question. He let go of Ella's hand to prime his weapon should the threats have arisen. Immediately, she pressed herself against his back and unslung her own firearm.

There was a bizarre hum that escorted their first steps into the austere shadows. Partnered with the echoes of their boots and the arctic moistness of the air, the lights nonchalantly murmured beside their orderly beacons.

Their clothes drank the tan of the tunnel, tinting themselves in crimson complexion. It was only then that Ella noticed the bloodied paint on Rhys' helmet. Under the red light, the shading was anomalous to the contrived order, like a spotlight in a broad, summer's daylight. Its unnatural coat had been dyed in a sickly splatter. They continued down the railroad to where they hoped

471

salvation lay, and traveling all the way with them was the squad's mural, doused in liquid disorder. She juddered at the thought of its tasteless completion – a dead girl's art, filled in by sacrificial paint, as if by uncanny reason she were still kept alive through his own blood.

The rose on his steel-crown equated to the death of a time once cherished, where even with the constant threat of a looming defeat had flourishment between friends, lovers and rivals blossomed into fruition.

"I just want things to go back."

In prayer, she fretfully whispered, and her voice fell upon the usual deaf audiences. Rhys was fixated on the corridor ahead where he focused more on keeping a steady breath well-paced.

Back when the realities of war hadn't poked their greased scalps over the horizons, her troubles were focused, confined to humanitarian woes. She recalled it; they had been a band of misfits, rich and poor, all clamped together for one daring struggle. There was almost a romantic fable to be found. And she fulfilled her role, as a coward who could do no harm, except in the machines she maintained.

She was the tinkerer finally gifted a job, to purpose the pleasures of her peacetime talents with wartime prosperity. But hell's banquet had given her very little time to even think of what she'd become. She couldn't remember the last time she had actually fixed something, rather than scramble to retrofit pieces of wire to sacrifice functionalities for the overall machine. All of her memories had been consumed by fear.

She then thought of a place with promise: a camp, traditional squad story as far gone as a breeze in a typhoon, to which she first imagined she'd fall into. A once cheerful dame, with all the love she could've ever known, had morphed into an eternalised corpse left with a deformed skull, and gone was the veil of the romantic's war. The prosperous became the poor and the glowing hearts hardened into shadowed stones. And all the horrors she'd seen there, the death, the abuse and the trauma, somehow felt like a dream compared to where she had arrived at long last.

It was the calamity of the last man standing: to live another day was promising, but to share that day with no living man was true punishment.

Rhys had been there with her for some time, but she asked herself of what he too had become. She knew nothing of his life, his struggles and aspirations before the war had brought them together, and even then, their early days had been met with distance and anxiety. Whatever he once was, it had spiralled out of control, and out came the confused product of an inconsistent man. A shrivelled mind, broken and battered by depression and insanity, yet a clear-cut desire to reject death in the pursuit of heaven.

Rattling away in his hands were the pins and pieces of his rifle, caught in his dreadful shiver. He pressed onward with his left foot ahead of the right whilst he blocked out what they had departed from.

"We're nearly there." His promise was brought upon feral respirations and through gritted teeth. "Each step is one closer to better pastures."

Oh, the meadows he imagined. The green vistas and floral prairies. He could smell it: Home, where the winds were free-spirited, instead of confined to the moistures of a vapid tunnelway. Trees that spanned miles greater than the eye could see, and roses, fertilised by the blood he'd sacrificed in his trials, they too coated his ideal canvas. He clenched his left hand around his gun's handguard tighter than before, and the all-too real fantastical image planted in his mind gave him a nauseous drive.

He saw Ella there, roaming in those fields, clad in a daisy-chain dress. Every petal interlinked and morphed into a single fabric, covering all of her skin. She was glorified by the god-rays that shone down on her, and by God was she beautiful to him. The wind itself twirled around her as it dared not to hush the solstice serenata she conducted. The clouds spelled out Sabrina's name and the panoramic prospect rose with further dales and fallows. On a hilltop sat an abode of his dreams: a white, ankle-high trident fence surrounding a bungalow cottage that overlooked the many valleys afar. Each stake in the soil had a carved-out name in its wooden body. They said things of encouragement, matched with their identities.

They read: Mateo - it wasn't your fault, Rhys. Oslo - it wasn't your fault Rhys. Evelyn...

Each picket emboldened the wrong path of reassurance. It was anyone's guess as to who carved out the words, but he couldn't

473

care any less. It was his wish for that beautiful, sweetened release of bile from his namesake. He wanted to be free of responsibility; and that dream of ultimate freedom had him drooling at the mouth, craving its blessed nutrition. He forgot about the demons that haunted him, and those that broke down Ella, for they were headed to a land of light where hell was but a fairy tale.

Then he blinked, and the sun itself had burned out. He was back in the tunnel, a kilometre through the dingy subways and not a metre closer to home. The walls were still the same shade of red, then black, then red, and the sky had been reduced to a two-metre-tall ceiling swathed in ice and moisture. His eyes were strained as he searched vigorously for the way out. Every corner he turned led him to another dead end, or another welded shut entryway. He walked for what felt like miles. Ella kept herself adjacent to him whilst Sabrina's soul was tugged behind them on an iron leash.

Two eternities passed as the redline was reached. A scream of colours broke through his eyes and infected his mind. No matter where he looked, there was a crimson confinement or the perpetual path to somewhere inconceivable. The ceiling quivered as they burrowed beneath the remnants of battle. Filth and ire, in stagnant water droplets, trickled to the floor, their impact echoed throughout the darkness. Those trickles fell en masse, creating a brutal rainfall locked within the enclosed habitat.

Bliss! The ripples through the soil diminished, and at the turning of a corner, Rhys was met with a blush on the rose canvas. A change had been found: a glorious white that seeped through a slightly ajar doorframe. He respired in knowing their liberation was within reach.

The winds that guided them broke through into the tunnel with a terrific bitterness. Their raw wintry bite challenged them, yet Rhys deflected its deterrence. They pressed onward, rifles in hand, and he reached for the handle. He pulled it; the haunted screech of its hinges beckoned the outside world to see them. A heave and a half pulled back with all of the door's weight. The tingle of the frosted air tempted him a yard too far, and he brought all his might together to open up their path.

Eventually, the screeching steel ceased, and the crystal-white shine of the snowed-out world blinded them. It was the most holy of spectacles. However, a grey serpent had hidden itself in the brightness, and where he'd expected a lonely road to victory…

"Halt!" They ordered, with their sights trailed on his heart.

Chapter 33

A Greater Purpose

"Hands! Up!" A hysterical, lone and commanding voice took control of the flurried callouts given by the many, and their foreign tongue barely mended the simple demand he made. A heartbeat of hesitation held Rhys motionless. Eight loaded rifles trailed every millimetre of movement he made.

Ella was quick to submit as she dumped her weapon to the ground, and she froze up when she looked upon his reluctance. He could feel his heart in his neck – a maniacal constrictor squeezed his blood to his head and crushed his ribs. The anxiety tore into him. He shook; a trembled hand was unsteady against the trigger, and the fingers were but a hair's thread from defiance.

"Gun! Down! Put it down!"

Rhys' lungs were at their highest pressure, and he was so close to acting upon resistant instinct.

Fight or flight. Live or die. So much time spent in combat and in ruin, to survive and to break free, for then it all came down to that moment: a tumbling instant, where freedom was left on a second's decision. He moved his index finger mere millimetres closer to the trigger and their voices faded away as he was drowned in internal strife.

Their mouths still made the outlines of words and displayed their commands with expressive aggression, yet they were noiseless. He'd barred them out of his head. In his self-made silence he scanned over those who dared to oppose his one chance at release.

Eight. Helmets. Uniforms. Patches in Ferusian. Mostly rifles. Two submachine guns. One had a grenade on his belt. Most wore balaclavas. It concealed them from the winds. His choice simple. Live as a prisoner, or die a free man. The choice was-

"Rhys!"

Ella seized his arm and rifle a measly second before he made his choice. She held his bicep firmly enough to grab his attention, but gentle enough to not provoke him, and the with her other hand, she used all of her dwindled strength to lower his gun. Her voice rekindled the soundscape around him.

The Ferusian's themselves were paused in wait and they allowed for Ella to hold him in place. His heart ached, though. When he turned to greet her, where the grim eyes tugged against his one chance to be free, he came close to weeping.

"Don't, please…" She said as she echoed the thoughts of all around them, both Kelan and Ferusian.

Two words. That was all it took, from a tongue he knew and loved. He froze. Correcting his hesitation, his fear of death and fascination with a free life, she coaxed him into conceding for the betterment of their survival. He accepted their defeat without a word, and he rose his hands in compliance to their demands, and during the whole event, he trembled as if it were his last hour.

The soldiers grabbed their shirts and shoved them into the door they'd exited from. The pain of pressing against the cold burning stone of the door frame had him in agony. Otherwise, he had a short flash of thoughts during his arrest.

"This is it…?"

With an unheard voice, he questioned his wrought mind and wondered if there were any spirits that listened to his internal monologues. The demons that had previously followed him and that led him down potholed roads, however, had also decided that, for once, they'd leave him be to swallow his pride.

"What did I do wrong? How can I fix this?"

Not one delusion spoke back to him. He kept quiet as they bound his hands with paracords. The friction corroded his skin. Gritted teeth, watered eyes and a groan in pain spoke for him. He desperately returned to his muse and begged for those apparitions to take his hand.

"Is this what I get? Is this a punishment for something I can't change?" His pleas to the astral audience continued to be unnoticed. *"I just did what everyone else told me to do. I killed because I had to. But I hated it! Does that not make me different?"*

477

His face was pushed deeper into the iced concrete walls that surrounded the door. One man held him in place, who tightened the rope binding, whilst another unstrapped the webbing from his body. He was left in just his combat fatigues and nothing else.

A hidden thud trotted beside them, and, as per his volition, the sound of ghostly hooves inched through the crystalised domain.

"Tell me I'm different. All of this couldn't have been for nothing! Please, tell me I'm different. I'm not a killer. I'm..."

Like a shackled felon, his convictions were realised by all but himself. The hooves of the elk trod around the perimeter, out of sight and unnoticed by everyone else. It judged him; he could feel its arctic eyes pierce the back of his skull like an ice pick.

His struggles, internalised within his wooden heart, had materialised into shame, denial and self-loathed brutality. All that he wanted had frittered away to ashes, lost to the winds, and in their place had been left a blundered soul in the wastes.

Yet, he barely resisted his trial. He felt the tips of his captors' gun barrel prod his skull and spine. He kept as still as he could, and moved only when they wanted to puppet him. Finally, he was in utter defeat. The strength to fight had been routed. A spectre's chuckle taunted him again.

He heard Ella's sobs beneath the Ferusian voices and under the illusions that haunted his end. A tear from her eyes became a needle in his heart – and the tragedy of it all was his lack of response. Anything he wanted to say couldn't save her.

In time, the soldiers had finished their pat-down search and he was yanked away from the wall like a doll. Rhys saw his own blood splattered onto the concrete, and the taste of it was on his tongue. It was hot – as the warmest beverage on the battlefield – and it tasted like salt. Or ice, maybe, the difference wasn't all too clear.

A gush from his nostrils trickled down to his lips. A single stream reached his chin and fell into the snow, which left a crimson breadcrumb trail back to the tunnel door.

A shot rang out in the dark overworld. It brought him out of his state and fish hooked his eyes to his surroundings as he first searched for the gunfire.

He readjusted his focus to the forests. His breath was sliced short as he saw it. With trunks that receded into the misted sky, spiralling and twisting in illogical ways, and branches that dominated one another, he was in the woods of his premonition. Those unforgettable twines of bark, wearing coats of snow around their shoulders, all stood in an endless formation. The uniformity of chaos – filed by rank, but all vying for the architecture of insanity. Not one tree was suited for a bird nest. And as they walked in an unknown direction, the elk's hooves followed closely by as it was clandestine to the witnesses.

The soldiers talked amongst themselves. He couldn't understand their tongues, but even if he could he wouldn't notice their verbatim callousness. They then had their teeth and tongues contort and fuzz into incoherence. Their conversations were just ritualistic chants in his head. Ella's cries acted as their rhythmic pacer, and Rhys felt his stomach churn.

No matter where he looked, the branches remained. Even behind him, the tunnel door had faded into obscurity, shielded by timber and hoarfrost.

A sudden jab at the silence came at the second gunshot's ring. A three-round burst in clean succession. It ended as quickly as it had begun. A gut-wrenching punch buried its fist into Rhys' lack of hope, for they were headed towards the sound of the execution.

But for once, Rhys felt glad to be separated from his own rifle. Its piercing output harmed either end of the weapon. For its victim, the bullet to slaughter a god, and for its user, the soul-killer that turned them into men like Rhys: empty shells and husks enslaved by incredulous destinies.

His throat had clotted with all the swallowed blood he'd indulged and he stopped for a minute to heave the then tasteless drink. The Ferusians gave him only a few seconds, before the prod of a rifle's barrel in his spine reminded him to keep moving as instructed. He left his mark in the snow as vomit, bile and blood; it was ugly as he felt.

The turn of the hour came in a flash. Five minutes through the dreary boulevards of lumber soon killed the sky. The clouds and the mist merged into one beast – an omen of the end times. Hidden within its body was a harbinger of death, laced within a contract between two souls, and the deadened horizon was reborn as a monster.

To Rhys' left, what he sought in the moment revealed itself. The elk. Of all of the Stars' creations, he thought, and it was the horned mammal. The beast only watched and it refused to hold his hand. It spoke to itself, but he couldn't hear its words. Everything was still a haze.

"Forward!" The steel-clad tongue of the Ferusian pushed his attention to his frontal face.

There, the fragments of a camp site formed in the mist. Mounds of snow were piled to mimic a temporary defensive trench. Behind each one was a pair of riflemen who eyed the party as they crossed their border. Rhys's eyes dashed around in fitful panic as his inner tumult bubbled and boiled. Wherever he had found himself, it belonged to a band of brothers opposing his nation.

Further down the trail – where the familiar imprints of boots marked the way – two tents had been pitched with minimal success. One was tattered, torn by the winds, and the other collapsed moments after it came into view.

And through the miasma was a voice. The words were faint, but if there was one distinction that captured his attention it was its language. Stress obscured his attention and he hyper-focused onto it. Not a second later, the figures came into view.

"-as per agreement! What you're doing is-…its treason to your people, and to the good men of today!"

The venue faded in. It all arrived in creeping motion. First to sprout through the fog was a corpse. A uniformed man, highly-esteemed according to his choice of attire. His uniform was soaked in red across the stomach. Next to his hand was a handgun, cold and unspent.

Up next was a small crowd of soldiers who blocked the path to whatever voices battled one another.

Three people. One was knelt down on the floor, with their back to the imprisoned latecomers, and two more were stood before them at the stern of the debate. The first was another officer, faced away from her opponent as they fiddled with their winter coat. And the other…

"I've done my part, Major! And it's time you do yours too, for the sake of everyone here." There was a great unease between those present. The riflemen that watched had readied arms, but some looked between one another to contemplate the arguments presented. None dared to speak up as the fresh reminder of their other officer still lay near as a recent reminder.

And to his shock, the man who led the argument was a trickster. He was an enigmatic figure who dressed like no other. His shoe and cap polish he'd grown to relate to him had faded. He walked around with erratic insecurity, a never seen emotion to the elusive figure: one Intelligence Officer – Thomas Lee.

"I come here for a deal; we have a chance to end this bloodshed with one fell swoop and you want to crush all that was set up?"

Rhys couldn't quite believe what he saw. An underground tale had been dug up by mere coincidences. Whatever it was, it had happened underneath his, and the nation's, nose. But as he dwelled upon the confusion of it all, he looked to the third figure and his heart wretched for the absurdity.

Bound with the same cords that held him in place, there was Christa – she was in her own shackles. She snivelled and sobbed aloud. Her tears were leased to the snow. Rhys' head span and he felt the sickness return in full force. A sharp pain knocked against his ribs and he staggered, only to be held in place by those that persecuted him.

It was then that Rhys noticed that the ambience of battle was near-enough silent. Light adorned itself with a familiar colourlessness, but the winds carried words, not gunshots. A shame, however, came from those tongues that spat with comparable intensity.

He stared at Christa with a basket of concern. He barely knew her, yet they were together, tied by bindings and kept on the banks of a poisonous stream toward fate. Teething queries chewed him out. A lot was happening around him, and he had the slightest clue as to what it was and why. The stress took a chunk out of his lung. A panicked state overcame him, and he fell to his knees.

Overloaded, his senses scrambled in his skull and a dizziness struck out. His vision was painted with an uncertain filter. Two hands reached beneath his arms and pulled him back on to his feet, forcing him to stand and to wait his turn.

Thomas strode between Christa and the empty space that led toward the Major. In order to focus on the confrontation, Rhys ignored the pried eyes of the elk at the corner of the camp. A wave of shadows encircled the Major, and her silent tone painted her with a graphite brush; her clothes misshaped and moulded to her skin like a viper's scales. He gawked without blinking; he feared that if he looked away once more, she'd transform into a serpent with a thousand bladed fangs.

"Will you say something? We're talking about a hundred thousand more lives, maybe a million more!" Thomas walked toward the Major, and the spectators aimed their guns at him. "Fucking…spineless bitch! You'll take this idiocy to your grave when this sun sets, I warn you! Everything, all the planning and the-

Rhys leapt in his skin at the gun's abrupt cut-off. A spectacle of revulsion was summarily revered by appropriate horror. Spurts of blood fountained out of Thomas' forehead whilst his body fell to the floor like a sack of grain. He had dropped the moment it had entered his skull, where it had lodged deep inside his cranium. His eyes were locked opened with a stare colder than the ice in the air. Flickers of blood settled on the shoes of the Major. Her face was in view, revealed behind a smoking handgun barrel.

And then, there was silence. Thomas didn't even twitch. It had been a flawless summary execution. No splatters of brains, no cracking of skulls – just a clean, quick wipe of life at the pull of a single trigger. One entry hole. No exit.

A fully viewed Major stood without a waft of amusement on her face. The venomous exterior Rhys had painted in her name bared its forked tongue. She kept her handgun in her hand but removed her finger from the trigger. There, she let out a huff.

"Throw him next to Konrad." Two soldiers rushed in to fulfil her word. They lifted the fallen Osakan – one at the feet and the other at the shoulders – and dumped him beside the first body they'd seen.

Christa's shrieks were as loud as ever. She pled with herself, uttering silent self-appointed blessings. Whoever she begged to hadn't listened. The soldiers around her took no pleasure in her pain, yet a strong aura of peer-written justice pressed them on.

The Major looked beyond Christa, toward the crowd that had brought Rhys and Ella to her doorstep.

"And what's this? Who're they?"

"Unsure," answered the spearhead of the group, "they emerged from the tunnel just now."

In a fit of panic, Christa swivelled on her knees, and a stone dropped into her gut as she made out the clear distinctions of her surviving squadmates. They saw her eyes, stained so red that not a speck of white surrounded her irises. Washed out, bloodshot and agonised, Rhys didn't believe that he'd seen such an emotionally destroyed face – not since Sabrina.

Her blue lips trembled out of fear and snot oozed from her nose. She mouthed something, but her cries blocked any semblance of clarity. Their eyes met somewhere in the middle. Where she pled for her life and safety, Rhys returned a cold, expressionless glare, iced with streaks of blood from his nose. She didn't recognise the harshness in his emotion.

She broke back down into incoherence as her prettied worldview was shattered. She searched for comfort as she stared at the teary-eyed Ella.

"Were they with him?"

"Not sure. They arrived too late, if so. And alone."

"Right," the Major raised her voice, "send Bermann to weld it up – and get him to bring Effler, just in case."

Rhys noticed the sky darken and a fume of black soot leak from her nostrils whenever she exhaled. Her hair was caught in the wind and it twisted and entwined with visions of ever-growing branches. And when he saw a scorpion emerge from her threads, and through the creativity of his insane imagery, he saw it slowly enter her mouth as she spoke and he felt his heart stop right there. She walked a little closer. Her industrial breath blasted what little courage he held on to. Piece by piece, Rhys' organs boiled inside his furnace of dread. The trees marched closer with her and it trapped him in a wooden cage with the Major.

"Are you here for her?" She interrogated him first.

Fazing through the tree trunk walls, the Elk poked its horned head into Rhys' view. He cut away from the Major's eyes and looked upon the beast. Its fur was torn, patchy from the withers of an eternal fire. He eyed the forest it stalked through, and the orange glow of tempered firestorms on the horizon put him on edge. His respiration was short, sporadic and sore. The Major snapped her fingers in front of him, and the fire was put out.

"Hey, eyes front! I asked you a question."

"I…"

"This woman," she pointed to Christa, edging in her desire to talk of her victory, "do you know who she is?"

"I'm not sure if…" Rhys' head slumped toward the ground, and he slurred in his speech. "…my mother love me if I came home…like this?"

"What?" Her stare wasn't quite of pity, or hilarity, but rather a study into his head. Something meticulous had crossed her mind. "Ah, I see…"

Despite his sanctions, his surprise came with insurmountable uncertainty. She backed away, and she walked toward Ella with prowess and presence. Rhys struggled for the first time and he tugged at his roped hands, only to feel a rifle-stock whack against his hip. He yowled out in tired pain as he collapsed for a third time, and he was quickly pulled back onto his feet, as he was not allowed to rest.

"And you? Do you know this woman?" The Major pointed at Christa again, who still bawled aloud to herself, as she addressed the other young woman.

"C-…Christa?" Ella stammered out. Her tears were nothing like her previous howls – she wasn't grieving a lost soul, or fearful of the future. No, she was petrified of dying. One wrong word and perhaps…

"Is that what she's been calling herself?"

"I-"

"You don't know, do you?"

"I don't know what's happening…" A blotted temper, smeared with her impassioned squall, did little to correct the woman. The eyes of the predator rested on her fragile, incapable state. Of all the fear and dread, her shudders were amplified. A fit of terror – the shock almost had her in a permanent seizure.

The Major looked down upon her. All in all, the two brought before her were weak in the soul and body. They bled onto her soil and sullied the scene with insecurity. She backed away and gave them the space to breathe. Her attention was still on Ella, but her eyes faced Christa.

They all pitied the outsider in different ways. The bruising beneath her eye, the little stream of blood that blended with her rivers of tears, the audible wail she gave out, that patch of Christa's hair, torn out by hand, and the abuse done to her clothing – remorse came cheap, but her punishments had been penniless.

484

"This, right here, is a creature – a monster of ideological terror." The Major introduced Christa again whilst she prodded the bounded soldier with her pistol. "She woke up one morning and thought she was one of the good ones. But no, reality caught up to her, as did the wills of her broken, disenfranchised victims. What you look at here is the woman of the hour – the priceless Princess, Lylith Redgrine. She's the chief playing the soldier."

In a time where he cared, Rhys might have gasped, or spat out his own blood in shock. There could have been a unanimous slap of the cheek, an expression of bewilderment at the all too true revelation that had been beneath his nose. But when faced down with the truth, there wasn't a lick of bother.

"Why does..." Rhys coughed, dribbling his last bit of swallowed blood into the snow. The Major looked at him, seemingly interested in what he had to say, and she darted over to take a knee by his side. With a dreary pace, he continued: "Why does it...matter?"

If any light had found refuge in the Princess' eyes then it had been sucked out by those the last quartet of words. His callous tone was brindled, a sawtooth sentence that carved out a chunk of her hope. Her eyes pled to him. She begged aloud with her own tears. Somewhere, on some other page, there would be a fantastical trick, where the hero would then have unsheathed his blade, flapped his cape and duelled with the Major, winning the battle and hearts of the Ferusians by honour and skill alone. Yet Rhys' eyes led to a heartless soul, and it watched her with a certain hatred.

"That's a good question, Sergeant." The Major paused and whispered to him with flexible curiosity. "Is it Sergeant? Can't tell by the insig-"

"Why...am I here?"

A little chortle left the Major's lips. Her disorientating charisma came from her candour. Rhys could tell that whatever had happened, she had been victorious, and she was relishing every theatrical moment of it.

"Don't you see, militiaman? Look, take a peep." She jabbed his side with her finger, and then she cupped his chin with her other hand. Her skin was colder than the air. And there, she directed his eyes wherever she pleased. "There we go. Have a nice, long stare. She's one of them, you know? The Monarchs.

The Redgrines. The ones who rounded you all up and told you to die like good little subjects. How does that make you feel?"

He answered with a hushed inhale, exhale and sigh. A scorn had infested his thoughts and he gave her no words to work with. But she knew the crude thoughts that enlightened him. A pike stole his stare and impaled his attention. The invisible catcher was in Lylith's image. The Major's fingers separated from his chin. However, her authority lingered, for he stared at Lylith with disdain as the Major had wanted.

"You know what? Fuck it. This isn't about ideology. Forget Syndicalism. Forget Monarchism. We aren't preachers, Sergeant. This woman has the blood on her hands. And look, she's been stained with it for so long that she thought a soldier's uniform could mask it. Guilt. She knew what she had done, yet did nothing of value to stop it. She had the power, the *influence,* to abdicate the wicked. But she was compliant. And now she's here, trying to make up for her-"

"Shut up! Shut up, shut up, shut up!" Lylith broke her silence and screamed at the top of her lungs. "You know nothing about me. You're a violent thug! A turncoat who whores herself out to a regime that couldn't give a damn about what you believe in!"

Lylith's fuse was lit like a firework, and she blasted through croaks and cries to belittle anything that wasn't herself.

Yet her opponent went on unharmed, and in fact she snarled back as quickly as she had been interjected.

"She didn't even stop the crown court. And all the violence, it's on account of her mother. Yet this woman, if she had any of the responsibility to be one, thought that going through all the trouble just to land here, in her own shit, was worth it." The Major sneered with a provocative grin. To her, the sweetness came in a foil package, and she had every intent to relish the words that one in a billion got the chance to say. "Any sane person if her position of power should have stayed at home and denounced it aloud. Or was a stunt like this really worth it? The people don't even care about you."

"Shut up!"

"Militiaman, do you know anyone who'd even shed a tear when the headlines read: Kidnapping in the Devil's Mansion!"

"Shut up! Shut up!" She repeated again and again.

486

Rhys again abstained from handing over an answer, and the silence told them all what it would've been. He wasn't even sure if he had cared much himself. For some time, interred in the concrete that boxed in his soul, he'd grown to hate the very lords that owned him.

"They hate you, Lyls. You're not important anymore. Fuck, even Mr Utilitarian over there," she paused to point at Thomas' still body, "even he thought your worth was that of a gambling chip. And do you know why?"

"Shut-"

"-Because you're a fucking dictator! Just like you're mother. You're someone who thought they could inspire people to deal with the problem, cause instead of fixing it, you were too caught up in looking pretty for the cameras, like all of this is some sort of end-all fable. It's disgusting. And people like the militiaman know-…somewhere…you…carnage…"

Edicts of trauma set their hand back onto the deck, and they drew a card of drowsiness – a move that broke down the Major's words and forced silence upon the bound man. Rhys lost his sense of direction, even though he was held still in place. The trial for Lylith Redgrine was a pale ember in the flames of his personal war. Insignificance left her as a blur, for his insatiable fixation on his last residence blocked her out. He looked to where Ella was, and saw her as clear as daylight.

The Elk kept its distance. The circulation of the trees, dancing in and out of the camp, softened their motions and allowed the creature to saunter through. He strode across the campfires and tents. And it found its way to his side, unnoticed by the camp's guards. It trotted between Rhys and Ella, and scoffed at him. He'd never seen such a creature do that.

And when he looked away, the beast vanished once and for all. It was tired of seeing him wither away. It had all the answers it needed, and his fate was decided. Rhys stumbled in his dizziness, and the Major's voice flooded his ears.

"Make a choice, militiaman." Back in reality, the Major was stood before him. Her coats of feathers, plumes of smog that seeped from her lips, and her dishevelled devil-like features had all vanished. All that Rhys had extremified had boiled down to an imposing woman, armed with a pistol in her hand and the control over everything that happened next. He held his breath in response. "She lives in a fantasy. You've got two ways to disprove her."

The unmistakable sound of a five-inch blade being drawn from its sheath sank the anchor in his stomach. A glimmering, stainless piece of steel, serrated to inflict such unbearable agonies, landed in the corner of his eye. A gloved hand wielded its hilt. His heart was suspended in time – he pictured it being raised against his throat. To make a martyr, a symbol of failure, it required a brutal example.

Imperfect as was the flow of the hour, a change came over the horizon. A surprise, in fact, took the reigns and led the chariot elsewhere. The blade went down to his hands to carve away at the bindings, which freed his hands.

The two soldiers who had stripped him down returned to his side, his webbing and rifle shared between them, though his firearm itself was unloaded. Despite being free, he barely moved, and he stood there with grave futility. It was as if everything worked against the simplest answer: to kill him and be done with it, lest they weren't done with torturing him some more.

But it was the Major's words that next surprised him the most.

"You can go. Leave her behind and let the day have its way with her, or you can be her fool and make the ends be as quick as a bullet." Her eccentric wisdom was all too much of an illusion to Rhys. She laid out two choices with only one answer.

All around him were the eyes of the armed, the dangerous and the prepared. Thirty guns trailed his every blink, exhale and shiver. Invisible spotlights shone upon them. He looked to Lylith, who struggled and shook. Her breath was unsteady. Blood rushed to her head and her ribcage clutched her lungs firmly. Tears spewed from her eyes as her words came out as sordid bile.

"Don't go! Please, they-…they'll kill me! Just help me, I'm begging you!"

Her face waved through a fish-eyed view that came as Rhys' heart sank. The choice itself had been the easiest he'd made all day but the agony that came with it wasn't any less potent. His providence struck gold when he came to realise the honest truth. The Major didn't pity him. Her choice of life and death was built on false kindness. Instead, she weaponised him; she turned him into a tool of torture to leave one last sweltering iron-brand on Lylith's tormented skin. His life didn't matter, as either way he was the paper in which a message was delivered to the crown: Reluctance. Disloyalty. Betrayed wrath. Karma.

His head span.

His heart shrunk.

His hands tingled.

His mouth dried up.

His eyes watered.

His chest tightened.

The anger settled.

The pain numbed.

The world twirled.

The mists blackened.

He had his answer.

"I'm…" Unable to apologise, for there was no reason to, he accepted the gifts of the Major. Life – his weapons and gear – he loosely cradled them in his arms. He watched as Ella was gifted hers too, but her lifeless, unbound hands held onto them as insecurely as possible. If the madman had truly been given a choice, he would've felt something; remorse perhaps, but the damage had been dealt. Something inside him fluttered as he saw Ella approach him as silent as a spirit. She didn't belittle him, or question the choice he made. She too realised that it was the only option they had. At that second, he fell in love with the compliance.

He left his apology to hang unfinished forevermore. His stark realisation was that he felt the crown was owed no apology. He didn't know Lylith. He knew of a Christa, a mysterious woman who had faded in and out of existence as invisible ink dried on a canvas. Her unceremonious arrival, and death through reality, had brought absolutely nothing to Rhys.

And in the motions of his thoughts, Rhys had decided that those who bore the crown weren't his responsibility. What happened to them happened to them, and he could leave their tribulations to fade into taboo. He was a farmer, a soldier, and history had never been for him to write.

Silently, Rhys and Ella walked away. A certain freshness of unchained freedom was spoiled by the cries and screams of Lylith behind them. Neither looked back at her, for they believed that their time was forever in another land.

A corridor guided them out of the camp. Two parallel lines of Ferusian soldiers, eyes and guns watching their movement cautiously, led them through the snow. If they had looked behind them, they wouldn't have seen the warden of the forest or her shackled prize.

The Major had stuck to her word, and they found themselves at the end of the road. The soldiers' line concluded, and an open forest granted them their gift – the escapade of the twin survivors. He finally looked back and saw the last remaining soldiers in sight stare at them with emotionless glares. Their eyes had been poured from glass, and their breaths were pumped by gears. Like machines, they watched them take their final steps out of the forest and into their own future.

They walked for a mile ahead, and the mouth of the world unlocked its jaw and showed them what laid outside Mullackaye. The trees were gone and a vast plain of hills and meadows painted in snow were left to be crossed. Rhys had forgotten that there was a world untouched by battles and brutality, where the remnants of a pre-war Kelan were counted as blessings.

He watched glacial wintery fields of tall-standing grass fly in the winds. Even if their vision had still been choked by the blizzard, he felt infinitely less claustrophobic than he had in Mullackaye. Gone were the prohibitive steel-reinforced walls that housed the filled graves. Away went the soaring of planes, bellows of moving mechanics and orchestra of guns. Just then, there was just the wind and the woman by his side. Elysium had arrived, he first mistakably thought, and he took a step forward into the wilds, with a rifle in one arm and Ella in the other.

Neither said a word, as they didn't want to interrupt the gunshot in the woods.

Act Three

The Twig that Snapped

Chapter 34

Inversion

A coronation for cold pastures had laid out a dazzling blanket as far as the horizon spanned. Hilltops were dressed with a blinding crystalised tone; its undying persistence of white blended the sky with the ice, where the empty canvas of monochrome lands disorientated him the further, he went. The dales were an incomplete image, lacking their greenery and emerald tides of flora and fauna. Wreaths in grass graveyards were uncovered when his boots dragged through the shards of ice, snow and soil – and beneath them were also the wilted petals found disconnected from their motherly stalks.

Sanctioned spirits left their marks on the world by disarming logical constructs of reality; up was down, and down was up, and the chill in the air burned. The wind blew from beneath them and, wherever Rhys looked, the strangest of sensations gathered around him.

Across the ailing countryside, the snow fell in reverse. It rose up into the sky, lifting the flakes to the heavens, yet it never ridded the wastelands it had settled and occupied. They were cradled toward the clouded sun, as if the snow itself had been abducted by the highest power. Rhys didn't join them. The rapture hadn't chosen him and he wept for the reality of it all. So, he walked, and did so for a long time, through a valley in which the blizzardly flurries were inverted and travelled to the stars.

And the days had gone. They walked for miles on end, wading between old farmhouses and washed-out homesteads left standing in ruin. Aftermaths of battles long-gone had borne baskets of plentiful lifelessness, so much nothing that he couldn't comprehend how much 'nothing' there really was around him.

Among the first he passed came a small shed, with one of its four walls broken and shattered. They found bullet holes across the standing corners of the building, and a foul scent lurked within. They didn't investigate. Then there was a cabin. The night had begun to settle in and Rhys couldn't waste his hours being picky over their accommodation. Both he and Ella settled there when the sun had disappeared beneath the clouded dew skyline. What was left inside the cabin were old photographs of greyish figures all smiling and posing in tidy uniforms. Two mounted fox heads were plastered onto the walls of the main room, and the bedroom was ransacked for anything of value. The window to the bedroom quarters had been smashed and a violent stream of snow had made its way inside, so they barricaded the bedroom shut and slumbered in the living room on stiffened wooden seats.

Rhys specifically remembered how Ella had slept much more comfortably than he'd anticipated. At first, she cried, maybe once or twice, by a candlelit ration pack she hadn't finished, then she tearfully sang a psalm to herself before she slipped away into a dream – at least he thought of it as a dream, as she had barely stirred. Contrarily, he comforted himself in picturing what it was she dreamt of. And in those self-curated predictions, the dreams she had mirrored his own visions: the flourishing fallows and prairies spanning for miles, doused in a rose-gold treacle of poppies and marigolds, with a glimmer of the stars brightening the world around it. As long as they were together in what little hope they had, he was able to rest – but the pain did not permit his own slumber that eve.

Dawn came with a boisterous wind. Ella was awoken by the sound of the barricaded bedroom door bashing as gusts pressurised the cornered chamber. There wasn't much of a sunrise, just a transition from bleak mist-covered twilight to tawdry greys.

Another cold ration pack filled their stomachs and accompanied their crude reawakening. Ella kept quiet whilst Rhys grumbled to himself with black bags beneath his eyes. In his pack, he scooped out stale bread and the remains of the last night's cold soup. The morning had seen the room upturned, looted for small things that could assist in their wayward wanders.

The soup was supposed to be entwined with the flavours of chicken, not that there was a lick of the bird inside it, but the breakfast bile tasted like sawdust and chippings melted down and served as a liquid. Rhys' discontent, his fatigue and his frustration

494

all seemed to combine into a visible distress. Ella had picked up on it and she shifted across the hardwood floor to his side. A gentle hand rested on his arm whilst her head nested into his shoulder.

However, they couldn't stay like that forever. Rations were thin and the loneliness was ever the more dangerous in the wastes of Kelan's winter. So, they got back onto their feet, scavenged through the main room's drawers and grabbed one or two dishcloths. It wasn't much, but it made do as a little extra scarfing for the journey ahead. Soon after, they set out for the next day.

Reality ran rampant outside. Wherever Rhys eyeballed in the dead of day, there was a strange contusion to the fabrics of truth around him. The hills rose and fell with respiratory motion – each turn slower than the last. Eventually, they stopped, and the world was dead. The snow no longer rained upwards. A chaotic mess of snowflakes drifted in all directions, and it bemused him, causing him to stumble with nausea a few times. Ella never really caught on to the anarchic bedlam the world had shown. Acres of it, all warped and wicked, as far as the eye could see, yet she turned the blind eye, as he thought. Rhys planted his gaze to the ground and walked onward, with Ella latched on to his left arm.

He wondered what would freeze up first: his hope or his blood. The drop in temperature had been gradual, but the lasting effects in the crest of winter's occupation laid out its final test. The two weathered through the whites of Kelan. Old and broken homes, bombed out foxholes and an abandoned ranger camp. Nothing of value came from any of them, just dirt and bones.

Not a lot happened. He pried the shape of a trench-coated figure in the austere bleaks but chose to ignore it. The past was exactly that – and he planned to leave it all behind, even the trauma. No ordeal slowed him down. Whenever Ella grew weak, he gifted her his strength. And when his arms grew tired, she cradled his gear to relieve the weight.

He couldn't have asked for a better confidant in the end. All of which he had lost had been through barbarism that paled when compared to his guidance to emancipation. Ella – the woman who, through sacrifice and suffering, had given him the strength to seek liberty. She had taken the mantle and carried the torch of which she wasn't aware of; for Sabrina, she would continue what she had indirectly started. Rhys was sure of it.

Contrariwise, the man could only go as far as his memories would allow him. He could have walked as far as Kelan's shores would've let him, but the red stains on his skin couldn't be washed off.

That evening, the pair had found themselves in a hamlet at the edge of a small lake. The thrashings of the storm had also turned each hovel into a graveyard. Rhys found a few rifles laid scattered around the settlement's centre, abandoned near a frozen firepit. Someone had been and gone days before them, and they had been ransacked by the snow's inflicted quandary.

Arguably, their luck had given them a single gift – the scholarship of solitude. No sign of life gathered in any of the huts. Rhys searched them all, one by one, whilst Ella tagged along to avoid him straying too far from her.

It was first on that night where Rhys had realised how much of a blur his days became. A numbed mind misplaced recent the memories of blank-sheet landscapes and brutalised homes in favour for the sleepless nights, in which he sat there and watched Ella get her rest like a guardian owl.

What was it? The third day or the second? The fifth or the fifteenth? It was a case of waking up, travelling for miles in an unknown direction, and then resting in any house they could find, all the while the fog casted an opaque lens ahead of them. They relied on scanty chance and a sense that something better awaited them tomorrow. And when the sun set each night, that summer's hope dwindled.

Rhys asked himself the following morning about what had happened to him. His memory had waned. The homes all around had been torn from their stems. Embers had long settled underneath the seasonal madness. Charred planks of wood creaked and cried as the winds threatened to topple them over. Two stood unrattled by their former perpetrators.

He remembered Ella had specifically opted out of splitting off between homes for privacy, and that they had spent another night in one cold shack in the middle of who-knew-where.

And then – something of a blur. Another cold meal of stale carbs and a small ounce of fibre, and while he sat on the same wooden bench with her, he fell asleep in her arms as she twirled his unwashed hair. But he remembered that they had talked before he fell asleep and had broken their glass ceiling, for better or for worse.

"I miss her." She started, dry-eyed. Rhys found the dying breath of a bedside lamp, with two matches left. He lit it, and saw her in the faint yellow glow. "I just...miss her so much. And...I'll never see her again, will I?"

He'd grown to hate questions like those. The pain laced between her teeth, firmly rooted from her tongue, spread into the air like toxic fumes. The words had drunk from the chalice of carbon monoxide, and the bilious smell made him feel sick. The forefront of it all had been that her vocabulary had done nothing but retell what he wished to unhear and what had always caught up to them.

"It's just...again and again, in the blink of an eye, she was gone. And..."

"I know. I miss her too." He whispered his piece.

He'd held his empty meal packet with his bandaged hand for quite some time. Anything to occupy his frozen fingers was welcomed, and in those quiet moments he let go of the paper bag and gradually moved them to her palm. He knotted their fingers together. She didn't protest.

Something was on her mind. He could tell by the strain in her eyes, and the air stirred like the dawn of a storm. Grief stole her soul and held it for ransom. It was on the tip of her tongue.

"Ella," he intervened in the brooding feel of the boxed atmosphere, "what do you want to do when we find our haven?"

"What?" He'd caught her a little off-guard.

"Well we're-...I mean we're not soldiers, not anymore. Is there any – I don't know...profession, maybe, that you'd like to return to?"

His stall came to a near impasse. Her face told him that she gave only a half thought to it. And his efforts to talk brighter than the flickering lamp beside them were faintly met with a struggled response.

"I guess I'd do engineering again. Or mechanics. In the cities," she murmured, "if they're still standing."

Another minute slogged by. It had been the longest minute that had ever passed – the kind of dreaded sensation that came with walking across needles and knives, right before a pitfall into punji sticks, all while his legs were held down by an anchor of what fleeting happiness was left. Something had been brooding on her tongue.

Their pain was chained to the walls around them and slowly immersed them in a poisonous gulf. The vacuum exchanged places with the false truth of Rhys' cheerful, and hopeful, future endeavours. The flame inside the glass lamp was dampened. And then, when the sixtieth second finally arrived on its rusty carriage, Ella looked at Rhys with a stare that pierced his very state of being. The movement of her lips were engraved into his mind, forever and ever.

"She shot herself."

The pin hit the ground. The dance of the flame warped the light around him. An eventide mace struck at his head, and the black agony that ensued left him with a stare that carried on to the edge of the universe. He wanted to call a claim to the judges of truth, to hail a declaration of absurdity in use to harass him, and for justice to intervene in her wicked lies; he wanted them to give him a release from the weaponised impishness that falsehoods had haunted him with. He desired the status quo of it all not being true.

A rejection of what was real came to him in a flash. His flesh seared at the sight of the radical truth. Alternate realities plagued his desires and he shook his head. The free hand of his trembled and the conjoined grip with Ella's tightened.

But when he expected to have misheard her, she kept talking and, deep down, he wished she never had opened her mouth at all.

"I…I just…I gave up for a moment." Hauntingly, Ella didn't cry as she spoke, and she talked in a defeatist's tone. She eyed at Rhys with damaged torment. "And I dropped my rifle to curl up and cry – and I did, until she just…took it."

"Why…?" He trailed on from her words.

"I'm sorry I…you deserved to know."

"I didn't deserve this."

"Neither did I-…but she did it, Rhys. She did it. And I miss her so much, but I…I hate her for it. Rhys, I hate her. Everything about it. She…she just…why, Rhys? Why do people do this? Why does anyone do this? Why can't-"

Her sentences shattered as her sanity slipped down the dark well. The longer she spoke for, the more contorted it became. It dropped five pitches and raised at a million decibels. The

haunting twist of her tongue began to beat against Rhys' head.
And then, she became muffled, like her voice was obscured by a
mask – he felt the room gyrate. The whirl revolted him. The
furniture laughed at him. The snow outside repeated her words,
each snowflake retorting the cursed phrase.

"She shot herself."

"She shot herself."

"She shot herself."

Unseen alarms wailed and a siren for insanity set the room
ablaze. The flame in the lamp became a bonfire. The roar of its
cackling spit, with the cinders that scorched his skin, mocked him
profoundly. It hurt. It hurt so much. The walls had eyes, and they
beheld him with pronged two-fork tongues slipping out of their
pupils. Then, each and every inanimate object grew a pair of
elliptic spectacles, all of shades of brown, red, black and white.
The screams in his head became so much more feral. Until-

The lamp extinguished.

For a while, everything was still.

Ella's soft breath came through.

Her hand took his and placed it to her breast.

She held it tightly.

And then, in the pitch-black underworld they hid within, she
pressed her lips to his.

Rhys' mind muddied the springs of those cherished memories.
Something of an unimaginable embrace took control of them
both. The darkness enveloped them and gave birth to the beast of
two spines, flexed inward to better connect their skin. They were
wedlocked in passion yet it did nothing to numb the agony he felt.
They lost control in one another's softened palms, clasped
together like shackles as the night was built on stubborn desire
and passion.

Yet the night concluded with a realisation that their ketamine
regression wore off with inconclusive depression. She told him
she loved him, and he said it back just as slowly. Had it been
truthful was forever unknown to the man, and he held his tongue
and stared at the ceiling. Soon after, she opened the aqueducts in
her eyes and rehydrated her skin with tears. She welted again, and
curled into a ball beneath their scavenged blanket. She said her
name again. Sabrina. Oh, by the Stars existence, did the sting
pierce deeper. Rhys sat up, alone, and faced the wall, hands to his

knees and eyes locked on to absolute nothingness. He thought to himself: *"You're a marvel, Ella."* And she was, no less but a miracle that led to nowhere. He looked at her with compassionate intent but was barred from entry by the inescapable horrors that haunted him

Ella eventually drifted to sleep, Rhys' palm still pressed against her cold breast, and he was left to bare the night once more alone.

Perhaps he remembered more than he'd thought, or more than he'd have liked to. Something clung on to his throat. The floorboards creaked before dawn and he'd turned to face it, catching the eye of an infernal beholder.

There it was. He could just barely see it, a transparent figure that prowled the gloomiest corner. From the waist down, there was nothing. It blended into the darkness and had commenced a stalking glare. The gas-masked shadow tilted its head as Rhys did too. And when the lover held his breath, so did the apparition. The wind's overbearing clamour unhurriedly turned to white noise. His ears were inflicted with a fetid irritation. He blinked, and the figure began its transformation.

From its hovering torso, two more arms sprouted like stalks, limp and lifeless. He heard the relocation of bones beneath the ghost's skin: *click, snap, crack.* A kick suddenly revitalised its nerves, and the arms were in motion, planting sticky, ectoplasm palms on the ceiling and walls. They grew longer, and longer, and made their way toward his naked body. The glass-eye face remained as still as ever, mimicking Rhys' uncontrolled respiration in perfect synchronisation. Its bones then snapped again. Rhys scouted out Ella, who was still sound asleep, though when he faced the creature again, its eyes were mere millimetres from his.

The rapid expulsion of his breath returned from the gas mask's filter, then scoured and battered. A toxic fume flooded his nostrils and he was locked in place. The screams of white noise grew ever the louder, intruding his only moment of unsteady tranquillity. Its hands moved up to his cheeks and caressed them in a way Ella had done.

"Stop…" His whispers were met with sharper breaths, heavier plumes of a toxic aroma and a taste of his own impurity. "Please…"

Such pleas were silenced. The hand of bones placed itself upon his lips and lowered him to the floor. It had him pinned with the utmost strength. No struggle could challenge its grip. And it influenced Rhys with its third arm, taking his own hands and pushing them against his throat. He began to choke. The paralysis of the night held him in place and he could do as little as watch his own death.

Suddenly, the entrails of the poltergeist spilled as its stomach split and exploded open. Blood – of which he couldn't feel – slathered his skin, flowing between his lips and down his throat. His eyes were of an intense bloodshot frenzy and the goggles of his creature only reflected his face. So therefore, as his lungs were flooded to the brim, the strongest scent of ash filled his nostrils.

The mask burned away. It withered and peeled back by an unprovoked spark. He fearfully whispered his final oaths as it frittered to dust, unveiling the most agonising of sights: unleashed were the devil's aspects, for he faced Rhys with a smile and a jeer.

~~~

What hailed the following morning was the nauseating spiral of grief. He opened his eyes to the mixture of greys and browns on the lifeless walls. Everything was still. Rhys looked around with overwrought eyes made with a strain so rich he felt as if they'd been gouged out. He put his fingers to his lips and noticed they were as dry as ever, though the sweetened taste of Ella's skin was still on the tip of his tongue.

When he panicked and glimpsed at her body, he saw the still maiden in her deepest slumber and he sighed with relief. Forty winks into the morning, her cosied soul kept as quiet as the shallow winds outside. Her season turned as she did – she rolled onto her left shoulder and faced Rhys with squeezed shut eyes, frizzled hair and a softened snore. She was as magical as any dreamlike flesh from a fairy tale. Her pure excellence calmed Rhys' initial tension, but only that. Whilst she slept, he looked back to the walls with keen, anxious blinks between long stares.

A stillness had thankfully returned to his reality. It became sensible, reserved in its twisted mannerisms toward Rhys. His perception of all that encompassed him was free from being struck down. If the final blow had been dealt to him the night before, then he breathed easy knowing that perhaps the worst was over.

Warm, like the swinging breezes of spring, was the music in the air. The storm had passed and in its place was a monophonic melodious shanty, an alteration between the softest of winds to the easiest of currents. Rhys walked to the nearest window, still undressed, and wiped off the icy condensation. There, he saw the clearest of snowscapes, a brindled world of absolute white and pure grey. The pianissimo patter of snow tumbling against the glass drew its last breath. For the first time in days, there was tranquillity.

Yet the equanimity brought no smile to Rhys' face. He watched, through tired eyes, out to the cleared world. The fog had passed and there sat a scene.

It was the among the most egregious of pictures. The full extent of the Ferusian military decorum. The nearest town was but a mere two hundred metres from the lakeside hamlet. Or rather, what was left of it.

He stared at the debris with scrambled emotions. For he saw the war's end, it had seemed, and the finale held no restraint. Life and all forms of civilisation had been pressed into the soil, flattened for the ages to come, only to be rebuilt when restoration sought its lost obscurity. He didn't see any loss of life from the looking glass but he didn't doubt its presence at all. He then frowned. He told himself that it didn't matter what he thought anymore. It wasn't like he could've reversed the suffering caused.

And that crucial detail is what had left him. He didn't want to apply any of that to himself. If anything, it was utter defeatism, and to have laid in submission to the end of times meant he had given up the last drive of good will in his heart.

A stir kicked at the back of the room as Ella returned to the land of the living. She rose up leisurely, swathed in their flimsy blanket. The improper place she found herself in barely shifted her. She stretched and shivered, then slipped on her dirty militia button shirt. Only then did she notice Rhys by the window whilst he watched the world rest in peace.

"Hey, are you okay?"

"I will be." He paused. Every second he spent eyeballing the freshened landscape the worse he felt.

The climate latecomer had done nothing but hinder the week with misery. The dead remained dead and the lost were never found. And all that he wished for was the butterfly's wings to have flapped a day earlier, to have had fate change the fabrics of time and history to an appealing alternative. Maybe then the others would've been there with them.

He didn't like to trouble himself over the idea of destiny until it concerned him. There, however, he felt as if it had all been set in stone to beat the deadened legs of the crippled man. He watched things remain still and quiet. The apocalypse, he thought, had lifted its coating and had unveiled its grand physique.

"You sure?" Her words were but deafened placebos. He couldn't feel the sweetened anaesthetic effects they usually had in them. "…it's…"

Her hands parted to either side of his hips and met as his stomach, where they caught one another and locked him in her embrace. Her new form, a dilettante of comfort for his soul, cushioned his emotions for a quick minute. A softened cheek pressed against his back. He loosened her grip to turn and face her, and they shared a morning brushing their tongues together. He put on a smile. She didn't, though, and she turned away.

The two didn't talk much as they got dressed. Neither really spoke of the previous night and Rhys most definitely didn't mention the haze at the twilight's peak. If anything, it was a nightmare. Nothing more. Nothing less. To conquer his trauma, he told himself that he needed to reject its impurity, to start anew as a strong, courageous figure that lived through hell to meet his new life. What happened had happened. The lost remained as such, and he was to be the manifestation of a recovering heart.

Such idealism was a false truth, however. Rhys wasn't sure if he'd ever recover. The demons that stalked him from the shadows, the devil in the corner of his eye and the screams, shouts, pleas and memories all forged a terrorising pigment on his dismembered persona. In fireplaces, he still saw the flash of a rifle's barrel. He still saw the detonation of a satchel charge, or the eruption of artillery shells bombarding the surface of the planet. He still saw wildfires inside carriages, burnt wreckages of tanks, of planes, of ships and of bodies, crisped and charcoaled through incineration. And in the chandeliers, he no longer saw them as lamps and lightbulbs but as illumination flares that brightened the darkest of battlefields. Houses had become bunkers and windows were pillboxes. Cars were logistics trucks and roads were ambush points. Windmills were battlegrounds and fields were places where men weren't meant to trek. Each walk to work would be a patrol and each day felt as if it would be his last.

Frankly, he couldn't bear it anymore. But when Ella's lips had pressed against his, his obsessive passion for reconciliation entered overdrive. He pictured her as a saint. His existence was to hold her to him, and to secure their fates as two; for her, if anything. For everything she'd done and was yet to do. Each day, he dreamed of her purity entering his veins, to which she could cleanse his demons. He didn't want her – he needed her. And as he came to believe that, the hours and days, even weeks, went by, and he had started to lose himself.

Chapter 35

On this Hill, he shall

Day…something? The very concept of dates and calendars had left him, but he knew that the sun had risen and sunken countless times too many. And when it did, he barely registered the inadequate progress they'd made.

Morning – he'd wake up from whatever hovel they chose for the night, maybe after a night of heated passion to quell the tears, then they packed their belongings and edged along a silent path. After that, up came Sunar's radiance, yet with the infinite horizons of acidic, lifeless clouds it was quite the insipid gift as they only received a scratch of sunlight. The expedition took them through hills, forests and fields of crops, though most of them had been forcefully burned to the ground by the scourge of armies.

Afternoon – he'd search for shelter. When the sky turned from grey to black, their task shifted from conquering the wastes to shielding themselves from its starved appetite. The hand of hope dragged them through towns that had been swallowed by nature. A rare sight, it was, to stumble across a building that had been left standing. And the tides of war had swept through such areas, so much so that the unique fortune of temporary havens were numbed. They all had the same greyed out, faded wallpaper. The discoloured, stripped down decorations, and the faded antiques of furniture, were almost always broken. The cupboards had been raided and the cutlery was scattered on the floorboards, some by the doors and some by the stoves. The repetition was constant. Over, and over, the conditions of their refuge were a stagnant familiarity. Each brick was identical, with the same placement, barely varied, and the assumptions of hell moved them in circles that spiralled downward. It didn't matter if the next town looked any different – for the room they stayed in was always the same either way.

Night – so much the same from nothing. Ella cried. Rhys recollected on the things that haunted him. Sometimes they fucked, sometimes they didn't. He once said he loved her, but she didn't say it back. Maybe she was caught in the passion, or just didn't hear it. He said that to help him sleep, even if the shadowy figure still stood in the corner to watch him. By the stars, he loved her. He loved her so much, more than he knew.

And then…day…whatever it was…-but it didn't matter. Whenever it was, that's for sure. The days weren't progressing toward anything, so he cared even less about their numbers and forms. They were on a motionless cycle: Wake up. Walk. Fail. Fuck. Repeat. That once crystal-clear photograph of a blossomed land, with flourished tills in the morn and starstruck glimmers in the eve, had started to distort and crease in his fist. From jade meadows to white departures, endless seas built on the backs of gravestones – no land offered his desired comfort. And so, he put all his faith in Ella. Where she had grown distant and quiet over the vast hours spent walking, he sat beside her and he'd take her hand, where he talked to her about the things he was grateful for. Her. The promise. The memory.

Over time, though, the days alternated their positions. In the first, she sat next to him and used her grief to place her soul beside his. She followed him without as much of a second thought. As the days went on, and the world stayed exactly the same, she made less of a ruckus, and the quieter she became the worse she felt, until she spoke no more. So, he reversed his role.

"You good?" He asked.

"Yeah. Fine." She paused.

It mattered very little in what he said. Her tone grew weaker and her eyes were drawn further from his. And during the nights, when she croaked and choked on her own sorrow, she moved further away from where Rhys laid. Her heart didn't intertwine with his – even when her body did. Something overcame her: a bitter understanding of what little she'd done to pursue her victories.

The days mounted up a thousand hours for him to think to himself. Rhys's loudest compatriot was that of his thoughts. It affirmed his beliefs and reintroduced that cycle of belief – for he had his faith in the woman beside him, and she would do everything to make it worthwhile. He started to feel those thoughts take a paramount centre-stage position in his thoughts. And, with the quieter she became, and the less challenge there was, he had let it become his ruling sail for the waves.

"You'll make me right – I know it – and she knew it too. An angel without wings…" He looked at the dingy ceiling with a confident smile of his own internal wisdom. "It's out there, that little fenced area, and we'll get there…I know you know it. I know it so very well. Green places. Lots of them. Maybe some wheat, and some nature trails. I think it'll be lovely. Very lovely…have you ever seen the summers in Western Kelan? They're beautiful. I haven't ever seen anything like them. I'm sure the next summer would be fantastic. Very much so. And you'll be there. It'll be prettier that way."

He'd whisper to her, hands unlocked. To himself, he spoke of optimistic futures. Her eyes faced the floor, not his, but he was fine with that. She was just tired out. Too much walking did that to anyone, he'd say.

But on the inside, she was strung up in limbo – the hours of heart ache, of the stress that consumed her, and the pain of Sabrina's vacancy grew a sourness in her throat. The gall and poison of misdirection, of treating herself with sex and unsure love, created a wedge in her chest that pried her heart from her breast. Each day, Rhys' optimism grew as they became more entangled, yet she felt none the happier. Anaesthetics numbed agonies and they didn't fix them up with pretty little bows of pink and blue.

The further they marched through Kelan, the broader the single-colour spectrum became. Each mile was all the same. The promises she'd also conditioned herself to dream of – in the safety on a summer's hill that Rhys wanted – seemed all the less obtainable by the metre. The white yard yielded no sanctum for the lost, and when she crossed the twelfth at each interval, her stare mimicked the one that Rhys had learnt masked.

That night, unlike any before, the eventide obscurity came in like the curtains of the stage: the hulking mass of velvet tatters that slowly blocked what they came to see. And behind the curtain, serendipitous words left the actors mouths.

"Rhys-" Suddenly, she broke her asserted silence. A palm wiped her eye, and she sat up straight, a few feet further away than she had been the other night. "Where are we going?"

"What do you – hey, you know where we're going."

"I never have." Her dejection worked through Rhys' guts like a bayonet, all whilst her eyes teared up at her outspoken pressure. It caught him off guard. No, she just needed reassurance. That was it. He needed to treat her as they had treated him.

"Look, we're going home, Ella. It'll be a better place – for you and me." She gave the floorboards an unsure look. He was quick to interject when he shifted himself closer by an inch. "I didn't think it was possible, not at first, but this…we've left. And I – I feel more hopeful than ever."

"Are you?"

The flatline of her courage went straight through his chest. An agonising pain, constructed out of paper-thin optimism, tore with his heart.

It felt like a challenge, or perchance a press to reaffirm his confidence; Sabrina would have done that. And Ella would too, so long as he painted it that way. So, he nodded to her and tried to put on a smile that she would believe. After all, she made him feel safe, and the littlest bit closer to paradise, so of course he wanted her to trust his notion.

"I am, truly. We're nearly there."

"Where?"

"Anywhere. The old life. A village or town, a quiet place to sit and let things happen. Don't have to be a part of this war anymore."

"What old life, Rhys?" Her scorn crept out from under the rug, and she placed it on her head like a crown to behold. The voice she had found wasn't fiery or infused with explosive misunderstanding, it was laced with the reality she had found. "We go places and find the same thing: nothing. Nothing at all. I'm – I'm just starting to think that-"

"Ella, no-" Yet her voice overpowered his again.

"-to think that you're taking me nowhere. There *is* no old life. I'm with you, not Sabrina. That's not old. And it doesn't feel much better when it's spent watching everything wither – I don't want to keep going this way."

"And I don't want to…" He thought about his words carefully, but stumbled over his caution. "I can't think about all that has happened anymore. I have to run, Ella, forever. We can go for miles, upon miles, to another world if we have to, just to leave this all behind."

Soon, a desperation slipped through the wounds on his body. He shook his head to deny the chance of something being wrong. He wasn't drunk on optimism – he was terrified of losing the one thing he felt in control over. But she had kissed him other days, and he had pledged to have his way, to have her clear his palette and to have focused him on one beautiful thing at a time.

He was intoxicated off of the love that wasn't quite there, and he held out his hopes for her to fall into place, to treat him as Sabrina had once done. He yearned for it, as if it were the last thing he had left to look for.

"Where are we running to, though? Do you even know where we're going?"

"I already-...I already said that I did."

"Where even is *'anywhere'*, Rhys? We've gone there and you just keep going. I keep breaking down and... you keep – you just scream in the night, you plead at names you say you don't remember, and then claim you're escaping it all – that it's all just *fine*."

"Why are you like this? What's happened?" Sour judgements came from his tongue, and he stared at a stranger he never knew.

A confused barrier had been placed between them. He waited, unsure if the gates would lift. Her eyes were flooded with tears and she crawled her knees up to her chest. Her outburst had taken him back a few months to see the same woman, ripped apart by fear for what awaited them in the coming days. He was sure of it, that she'd been there, happy with him, and that she had always been. Yet she mirrored the defiance of Sabrina when she'd thrown all the flowery sunshine out the window when Rhys needed it the most.

Life's greater intention, to pin the savagery of misfortune against Rhys, had placated his thankful tenderness, and with the drug of adrenaline he felt his chest beat like an ensemble of war drums. A thousand strokes per minute ridiculed his ribcage, and he became short of breath.

"Ella, for fuck's sake, what are you on about?"

"I want to know why I'm still here. What am I even doing anymore?"

509

"You're being a saint! That's what you're doing, and that's what you've always done!" An attempt to get closer was repelled by her equalling the distance away from him. "Ella, please, not now – not whilst we're so close."

"We don't even know where we are-"

"But we're together, and that matters, right? You, Sabrina and I."

"Sabrina's dead, Rhys! Stop saying that my fucking sister is alive and well. She's dead!" Her mouth ran dry of sweet nourishment, and the scorches of a furious breath erupted with volcanic energy. "She killed herself. And she told me, over and over again, that you had brought her back – and I didn't believe it at first, but you did! You brought her back from-…from the dead, to prolong her suffering – and she did it. She finished the job herself where you fucked it all up."

"Ella-"

"And then you…I don't know what you do. You crawl to me and pretend that everything is going to be okay. And it makes me want to think that too, but you're taking me to a place that doesn't even exist, Rhys. I'm running circles around nothing!"

Speechless, the moribund soul he cradled let out its final whimper, and Rhys was sanctioned into silence. His right arm was left suspended in the air, locked in the half-hearted motion of reaching out for her. Her cheeks were doused in a thousand litres of tears, where they convulsed into many tributaries before they converged on the tip of her chin. Nothing of what she said was with confidence and that alone had broken down his with minimal effort.

He wasn't sure if he wanted to feel infuriated by the accusations or disheartened by all she had to say. But he defended his place and his future. It was the last thing he had to protect. It had to be left unharmed, or else he would cease to have purpose.

"Whatever… – whatever's made you think this way, I'll stop it. Please, I promise." His voice lay on a crooked tongue, and he barely believed the things he said. "-please, I just need you to be here, with me."

"Why?"

"Because you have what I need. You have the sweetness…and the-"

510

"Is that it?" She looked at him with a stern expression, before she hesitantly shook her head. The tears had opened up a fresh dam for her to drown herself in. "Oh no, I see. I see it. You...you still love Sabrina. You think I'll be her just for you, don't you?"

"That's not-"

"It is. And...and everyone's expected me to be that for you. They have, haven't they?" His lack of response broke her into the most uncomfortable smile she'd ever made. Her heart sank, yet what did it matter when Rhys' was anchored to the seabed.

The sardonic glimpse of reality settled in; neither loved one another. Her physique angled as she screamed at the ground, kicking herself with a bottled anger unlike any he'd seen. The tears soiled the wooden floor. She stumbled to the furthest corner of the room to – from what Rhys could see – stand beside the masked figure.

It was there. Breathing. Again. He widened his glare as she entered its body. She walked through the apparition, unfazed by its presence. The mask perfectly fit her jawline, and her hair matched the tendrils of smoke that seeped from its corpselike body.

"You're a fucking lunatic."

"Ella-"

"I wanted you to be happy, and you kept on using her memory to make yourself feel better. Do you have any idea how awful that makes me feel?"

He felt he had no option but to respond with a reserved, silent voice. The judges were watching him with curled lips and joyous laughter. What other entertainment could top the man being faced with the final knockout? The jeers, smears and smiles played in his head. Above her shoulder, the gas mask spirit drifted against gravity's will.

And what was most amusing was that he never properly took his stance, he let her rebel and he pretended that, internally, it would all go back, that it was just a bump in the road.

"And I'll tell you what I want: I want to go home – okay? I want to go to bed and cry, but not here. If you're going to drag me with you, just to put yourself on some little pedestal, then I know I don't belong here anymore." She wailed; the burn of her tears carved across her face. Upon her cheeks, they resembled the antiques of a cracked ceramic mask. Every time she smiled it was with utter virulence.

She saw his eyes as those of a malice mutt, kicked about for so long that it bit the wrong people. His teeth had been in her neck, mumbling Sabrina – forever, her name was trapped between his lips.

"You can stay here. Keep walking, for all I care. I'm not Sabrina. I shouldn't even matter to you."

"Ella," he choked on his own anxieties, "please, I love you!"

"Leave me alone. Leave her alone." Rhys wasn't even sure if he imagined it, but as her body merged with that of the trench-coated nightmare, he could've sworn he saw her lips twirl at the spite of her tongue. "I was wrong to think you saved her."

With a swift swipe, she gathered her belongings – all except her rifle, which she had knocked to the floor – and she beelined for the door. Handle turn. Wind rushed in. He shivered, but the fire in her heart kept her warm enough to press on. And as it slammed, all fell silent. Ella had left the building.

Rhys was left alone with his thoughts. He looked to the corner, and the spectre was absent. All sound was cut.

He gradually lowered himself onto the floorboards, convening his mind with his knees to his ribs and back to the wall. Kept musings wandered between the seconds that passed. The brief blast of the cold caused him to shudder a few more times. It hurt like all hell. What it was couldn't be deciphered. He sat. Silently, he waited.

She would come back, he thought to himself, there was no reason to leave. He wasn't wrong. He needed her. She was the fabric that held him over the gorge, preventing him from toppling to his end. Sorrow drained through him rather than gliding across his skin. Each cell in his body, each microlitre of blood, was abruptly infected by the pain. Yet the freshness was what osmosed out of him, and all that was left behind was grime and gall. Every lesion on his skin was reopened.

The sun set, then it almost instantly rose again. It sank. And rose. Down. Up. Ascend. Decline. Brighten. Fade. His. No one's.

The wall caught his eyes and taped them together. Plasticine hopes melted at the heat of the fury, then froze in the chill of the night as a collapsed mess. Time morphed to second-long intervals of dusk and dawn. Waves of rot scourged the building he hunkered in, bringing not only the grey tide, but a drain of warmth and light – and all of it added to death's reap. The scythe cut at the door when the wind did, and Rhys locked his legs with his arms.

Not a tear left his eye. He stared with the driest of deserts that had a lens of pure reluctance. He saw clearly yet couldn't make out what had happened. She was there, for what felt like all of his time, then, she had vanished.

Scattered on the floor, two rifles lay side by side – his and Ella's. Both had their barrels faced him and each had their magazines ejected, stored in his combat webbing. And for a second, the fact such suicidal ideations occupied his mind was enough for him. He should've been sickened. But he shook his head. She would come back. She had to. He knew he was at fault but the brutality excused him. He was clean. His hopes were banked on his passive morality.

Abominable creatures arrived from beneath the floorboards and furniture. Roaches and rats scaled the walls with ease and gnawed through the paper, tearing away wood chippings to fall to the ground.

The urgency of the day-night cycle created an epileptic show. Flickering strobes unsteadied his pried open eyes, burning his retinas with disordered assaults of passing hours. It hypnotised him and held him at its mercy. Everlasting sights of tearing walls and anarchistic spotlights murdered all cohesion. He was lost in the whims of his disturbance, and a ghostly cornucopia basketed his lost settlement before his eyes.

Wood-chippings rained onto his scalp and the splinters planted themselves into his shoulders. In an instant, the world melted with the walls of his crypt. The frittering oak fragments snapped and glided in the wind, all until the silence was broken. The creaking of walls came, and a few bootsteps arrived at his side.

Eye contact wasn't necessary. Fingers of bone curled around his back and beneath his legs, hauling him from the floor he'd waited at. The sound of its used-up filter parodied his choked defeat. Communal discomfort banished their souls to the wind when the corners collapsed.

All in one motion, the walls malformed under their own weakened foundations. They fell outward and uncloaked a black

513

abyss. The floor then floated through empty space, and the chill of the sunless sky froze the rats and roaches. Cradled in their arms, he was lifted toward the only remaining door by the spirit. Just beyond its obstruction was the howl of the nightly wind. Time had chosen when to set itself. Under the influences of his puppeteer, he was stood up and dressed to survive the outer wilds of the winter.

Yet he wanted to remain indoors. Ella would show up, he just knew it. Or perhaps she was still outside, waiting by the door to clear her head. Something…like…that.

It had to be. The journey could not be without fulfilment. The stars, with all the scriptures that had been written to uplift the damned, were there to promise light at the end for the deserving, hearty men that endured. Such a craving authorised his reach forward as he twisted the door handle.

Never had the ice of the lost polar caps been as cold as the brass-knuckle he shook hands with. His skin turned a deep sapphire whilst the hairs on his arm were frozen mid-climb to goosebumps: curled and trapped in halted motion. The skeletal hands crawled up his arms with the same sensual pacing of Ella but all the comfort of razors. They encompassed his knuckles with its palms and pushed him toward the final click – and the door was open.

A blast of voracious storms poured through. The gateway back to his reality was open, and a vibrant tussle of snow and land welcomed him. Two snowflakes darted into his eyes and he blinked madly until he could see once more. He looked back into the room to see the furniture be tugged across the floor, into cabinets and dressers, before falling off the edge of existence and into the blackened space beyond. Eager to not join them, he was forced to push through the gateway and to return to the outside world.

The tyrants of nature were having their way, frivolous amongst each other's deathly presence. Order seemed forever gone with all the dreams they had crushed. But when Rhys stepped forth into the light, and when his boot first crushed the snow and pressed into the frozen soil, everything just stopped.

In an instant. That was it. The snowflakes were stranded in an anti-gravitational stasis. Talks between gales were hushed as tape was plastered over the winter's voice. Stillness, like nothing else, left time to rest, and the spectacle of suspended snow glimmered an unequal spray of colour. Light refracted through their glassy miniatures, sprawling an array of blues and reds in every direction. The sky and land were soon merged into one rainbow palette, yet their disorder did little to ease its damnation. Rhys walked forward with his hand to his gut – a sickness arose from his stomach – for as long as he could keep himself sane. He then broke down to his knees and hurled yesteryear's food.

When he looked back up, the hypnotic trance of colour was gone, and the blackened sky retained its heavy occupation. Nothing else had moved, just the removal of all equity in light. The sound was isolated around him and only his movements could be heard. They were condensed, lacking presence or reverberance to showcase the scale of the realm.

With an empty stomach, he staggered back to his feet and wiped the grime from his mouth with his sleeve. It had no scent nor taste.

A garish pool of acrid lumps formed at his fingertips whilst bitter visions of a scrambled psyche disorientated him further. Moments after landing on his soles, he was met with the apathetic abyss staring into his heart. The paused progression of the night and storm persisted, and he gathered himself to withstand the search.

"Ella!" He called through the hollow expanses and received no response, even from his own echo. "Ella, come back inside!"

He trod forward. His skin and shirt plucked immobilised snowflakes, depraved of their gravity, from their limbo as he barged into them. Their chill was barely noticeable. In fact, he was given the temperate mediocrity of an empty, uninhabitable room, much alike the inside of an upside-down cup placed atop a lambent candle. His gleam pushed him away from the house. He searched behind it, on top of it and then to its distant reaches. The vast plains of snow blistered him with an eyesore of vapid plains where nothing else existed.

He walked ahead with his eyes set for where the moon hardly shone: atop of a nearby glacial hill. There wasn't a hint or clue as to where he should've gone. Nature covered her trail and banished all need for an alibi – she had strayed from his bricked path.

The unsettled mind took course. Strange whisps of failure rushed through his body. The adrenaline of anxiety and panic set in motion the last leg of his falsely emboldened journey.

He arrived at the base of the hill and noticed a jagged silhouette waving to him at its peak. It was of no hesitation that he started to climb, exhausting the last of his withered energy to conquer the final step in his quest. He was sure he'd find her up there. Something told him, a feeling so deeply infused that it manifested its own voice.

"He shall, he shall…" Enticed by its vapid promises, he dug his fingers into the snow and clawed his way further up the mound. To the throat of his world, he watched as the peak was stretched through reality, elongating tenfold until tears in the universe damaged its fabric.

This was it, he pondered with a cracked smile on his face, and there was nothing that would stop him. The journey had halted just before the cliff face – and sheer destruction was an obstruction he'd avoid by mere millimetres. He'd heard the tales. The Generals, Captains and Privates of history, all bound by heroism and rebellion against dark fates. This was his moment. It may not have been told to the future ears of bedlam minds, restless children or uninspired troopers, but it was a story he could be thankful for.

Poetic prose was his future, with the damned misfortunes being what created the better being, asserting triumph over Kelan's pandemonium. And as the hill turned into an insolent mountain, he exerted his limits until there, along a silver ray that traced the nightfall, he had flown all the way to the moon, where he hoped to kiss the platinum dust beneath his feet.

There was a birch tree sat alone in the glimmer of the night. Its arctic tiger-stripe skin waved like water and breathed in rhythm to his lungs. The terrestrial flora had been sprained by serrated branches that went in whatever direction they desired. Leafless, bare and naked, it had nothing to hide the phantom misery that awarded his soulless determination.

Rhys arrived on his scabbed knees and stayed there when his eyes met it. Vines of ice, wrapped around the strongest branch, anchored toward the core of the planet. Held in its neck-tight loophole was a woman.

This woman was utterly lifeless. Her neck bled a blue sea; the frosted vines carved in with needle-thin sharpness. All four limbs lethargically drooped whilst her unconscious body swayed in the sudden return of a magnanimous breeze. Her stomach bred wildlife as a burrow had been carved out of her womb. The pelt of a hollow fox comforted itself in her torso, surrounded by a thousand mites that chewed her rotten innards. The bleak glass eyes of the beast mocked him without giving as much of a blink. A shiver erupted from her chest and launched the foulest of frostbitten feelings into Rhys' system. He was assaulted by the sight, the sound and smell. Anguish, dear soldier, anguish.

Murder, manic murder; his heart was crushed beneath his entwined tendons. Neural agony tremored his heartbeat and the pacing of his breaths shrunk to indefinite hush. A single tear broke the barriers to his agony and unleashed the full stream. He planted his face into the snow and screamed. Bloody murder! He cried upon the absence of an encroaching daylight, and the carbon dioxide flood extinguished the flame in the cup.

The silent war was over. Bellows of a year's holdup unleashed at the snapping of the final straw. Battles anew bombarded his head, bruising and cratering every spark of life left in it. The drains in his eyes awoke the loudest cry of the night. He forced his head out of the snow, and plundered his heart with the blurred visions of the tree. Beside the woman appeared an additional twenty bodies. He knew their names. They had known his. And throughout the night, he fell into a turbulent hour with nothing left to hold him up. So, he stayed there, for as long as the world would let him, and he cried, and cried, and cried-

Thank you for taking the time to read my first novel. I'd love to hear what you thought of it, even it's a review or you just contact me. Again, thanks for sticking with it to the end, whether you enjoyed it or you didn't. – Lots of love, Ed

Printed in Great Britain
by Amazon